COLLECTED
S·T·O·R·I·E·S
OF WALLACE STEGNER

ALSO BY WALLACE STEGNER

FICTION

Remembering Laughter (1937)

The Potter's House (1938)

On a Darkling Plain (1940)

Fire and Ice (1941)

The Big Rock Candy Mountain (1943)

Second Growth (1947)

The Women on the Wall
  (short stories, 1950)

The Preacher and the Slave (1950:
  reprinted as *Joe Hill:*
  A Biographical Novel, 1969)

The City of the Living
  (short stories, 1956)

A Shooting Star (1961)

All the Little Live Things (1967)

Angle of Repose (1971)

The Spectator Bird (1976)

Recapitulation (1979)

Crossing to Safety (1987)

NONFICTION

Mormon Country (1942)

One Nation (with the editors
  of *Look*, 1945)

Beyond the Hundredth Meridian:
John Wesley Powell and the Second
  Opening of the West (1954)

Wolf Willow: A History, a Story,
  and a Memory of the Last Plains
  Frontier (1962)

The Gathering of Zion: The Story of the
  Mormon Trail (1964)

The Sound of Mountain Water
  (essays, 1969)

The Uneasy Chair: A Biography of Bernard
  DeVoto (1974)

The Letters of Bernard DeVoto
  (editor, 1975)

American Places (with Page Stegner and
  Eliot Porter, 1981)

One Way to Spell Man (essays, 1982)

The American West as Living Space (1987)

COLLECTED
S·T·O·R·I·E·S
OF WALLACE STEGNER

COLLECTED S·T·O·R·I·E·S

OF WALLACE STEGNER

WINGS BOOKS
NEW YORK • AVENEL, NEW JERSEY

This 1994 edition is published by Wings Books,
distributed by Random House Value Publishing, Inc.,
40 Engelhard Avenue, Avenel, New Jersey 07001,
by arrangement with Random House.

Random House
New York • Toronto • London • Sydney • Auckland

Printed and bound in the United States of America

All the stories in this work originally appeared in the following publications: *The Atlantic Monthly, Contact Magazine, Cosmopolitan, Esquire, Harper's Magazine, Mademoiselle, Rocky Mountain Review, Southern Review, The Virginia Quarterly,* and *Woman's Day.*

Library of Congress Cataloging-in-Publication Data
Stegner, Wallace Earle, 1909–
[Short stories]
Collected stories of Wallace Stegner.
p.   cm.
ISBN 0-517-12188-3
I. Title.
[PS3537.T316A6   1994]
813'.52—dc20   94-6607
                                                   CIP

8   7   6   5   4   3   2   1

For Mary, in gratitude for
fifty-three years of close
collaboration, and for
patience beyond the call of duty

FOREWORD

It would not be accurate to say that these stories gathered up near the end of a lifetime of writing constitute an autobiography, even a fragmentary one. I have tried autobiography and found that I am not to be trusted with it. I hate the restrictiveness of facts; I can't control my impulse to rearrange, suppress, add, heighten, invent, and improve. Accuracy means less to me than suggestiveness; my memory is as much an inventor as a recorder, and when it has operated in these stories it has operated almost as freely as if no personal history were involved.

Nevertheless the thirty-one stories in this volume do make a sort of personal record. I lived them, either as participant or spectator or auditor, before I made fictions of them. Because I have a tyrannous sense of place, they are laid in places that I know well—many of them in Saskatchewan, where I spent my childhood, and in Salt Lake City, where I misspent my youth, and in California, where I have lived for forty-five years, and in Vermont, where I have spent at least part of the last fifty summers. I have written about the kind of people I know, in the places where I have known them. If art is a by-product of living, and I believe it is, then I want my own efforts to stay as close to earth and human experience as possible—and the only earth I know is the one I have lived on, the only human experience I am at all sure of is my own.

Any reasonably long life, looked back upon, irresistibly suggests a journey. I see these stories, inventions on a base of experience, as rest stops, pauses while I tried to understand something or digest some action or clarify some response. As a journey, my life has covered a good part of the twentieth century, and it has been quintessentially American, though it could not now be reproduced: childhood on a belated and benighted frontier, youth in a provincial capital, maturity with the whole confused world to run in. And along with the expansion of my physical universe, a corresponding social and intellectual expansion; for as a child I knew little beyond the atomic, migrant western family that pursued an American dream already over for almost everyone else, and pursued it sometimes beyond the boundaries of the law. I had a long way to go, and the faster I traveled, the faster the world rolled under me and the further I got from the primitive, deprived, barren, lawless, and sometimes idyllic condition from which I started.

But few lives take the shortest distance between two points. Certainly mine did not. It backed and filled and lost the way and found it and lost it again. The traveler, moreover, has been largely created by the conditions of his beginning, and retains the tastes, prejudices, and responses that the early stages have bred into him. That is why I have made no attempt to arrange these stories so that they make a nice progression from simplicity to complexity, past to present, primitive to civilized, sensuous to intellectual. They lie as they fell, perhaps because I don't believe there is any clear progression to illustrate, or that this journey has any clear destination.

Because the individual stories were written over a span of many years, and because many of them, especially the Saskatchewan stories, look back twenty years or more from the time when they were written, and because the world and I were changing at an ever-accelerating rate, some stories reflect events, social attitudes, and even diction that now seem dated. (For instance, the boy Johnny Bane in "Pop Goes the Alley Cat," written just after World War II, is referred to as a Negro, not a Black, because Negro is what he was when I wrote the story.) I could have written that sort of thing out of the stories, and changed social and sexual attitudes, and altered dialogue, only at the cost of a fabric that had been carefully woven in another time.

I have not written a short story for many years. It seems to me a young writer's form, made for discoveries and nuances and epiphanies and superbly adapted for trial syntheses. Increasingly, in my own writing, the novel has tended to swallow and absorb potential stories. (Bernice Baumgarten, my first agent, who handled all my early stories, used to say that a short-story writer lives on his principal, using up beginnings and endings.) Whether because of a shortage of beginnings and endings or for other reasons, I found fairly early that even stories begun without the intention of being anything but independent tended to cluster, wanting to be part of something longer. That is why several stories written and first published as stories were later cannibalized and used as chapters in *The Big Rock Candy Mountain* and *Recapitulation* and *Wolf*

Willow. I have juggled these back to their original state and let them fall as randomly into this collection as they fell into *Harper's* or *Atlantic* or some other magazine in the 1930s and 1940s and 1950s. In their independent form, they actually mark the traveler's route better than they do as segments of longer books.

WALLACE STEGNER
Greensboro, Vermont
September 7, 1989

CONTENTS

COLLECTED
S·T·O·R·I·E·S
OF WALLACE STEGNER

THE TRAVELER

He was rolling in the first early dark down a snowy road, his headlights pinched between dark walls of trees, when the engine coughed, recovered, coughed again, and died. Down a slight hill he coasted in compression, working the choke, but at the bottom he had to pull over against the three-foot wall of plowed snow. Snow creaked under the tires as the car eased to a stop. The heater fan unwound with a final tinny sigh.

Here in its middle age this hitherto dependable mechanism had betrayed him, but he refused to admit immediately that he was betrayed. Some speck of dirt or bubble of water in the gas line, some momentary short circuit, some splash of snow on distributor points or plug connections—something that would cure itself before long. But turning off the lights and pressing on the starter brought no result; he held the choke out for several seconds, and got only the hopeful stink of gasoline; he waited and let the flooded carburetor rest and tried again, and nothing. Eventually he opened the door and stepped out onto the packed snow of the road.

It was so cold that his first breath turned to iron in his throat, the hairs in his nostrils webbed into instant ice, his eyes stung and watered. In the faint starlight and the bluish luminescence of the snow everything beyond a few yards away swam deceptive and without depth, glimmering with things half seen or imagined. Beside the dead car he stood with his head bent, listening, and there was not a sound. Everything on the planet might have died in the cold.

Indecisively seeking help, he walked to the top of the next rise, but the faintly darker furrow of the road blurred and disappeared in the murk, the shadows pressed inward, there was no sign of a light. Back at the car he made the efforts that the morality of self-reliance demanded: trying to see by the backward diffusion of the headlamps, he groped over the motor, feeling for broken wires or loose connections, until he had satisfied himself that he was helpless. He had known all along that he was.

His hands were already stung with cold, and around his ankles between low shoes and trouser cuffs he felt the chill like leg irons. When he had last stopped, twenty miles back, it had been below zero. It could be ten or fifteen below now. So what did he do, stranded in mid-journey fifty miles or more from his destination? He could hardly go in for help, leaving the sample cases, because the right rear door didn't lock properly. A little jiggling swung it open. And all those drugs, some of them designed to cure anything—wonder drugs, sulfas, streptomycin, Aureomycin, penicillin, pills and anti-toxins and unguents—represented not only a value but a danger. They should not be left around loose. Someone might think they really *would* cure anything.

Not quite everything, he told the blue darkness. Not a fouled-up distributor or a cranky coil box. Absurdly, there came into his mind a fragment of an ancient hymn to mechanical transport:

> *If she runs out of dope, just fill her up with soap*
> *And the little Ford will ramble right along.*

He saw himself pouring a bottle of penicillin into the gas tank and driving off with the exhaust blowing happy smoke rings. A mock-heroic montage of scientific discovery unreeled itself—white-coated scientists peering into microscopes, adjusting gauges, pipetting precious liquids, weighing grains of powder on minuscule scales. Messenger boys sped with telegrams to the desks of busy executives. A group of observers stood beside an assembly line while the first tests were made. They broke a car's axle with sledges, gave it a drink of the wonder compound, and drove it off. They demolished the carburetor and cured it with one application. They yanked loose all the wires and watched the same magic set the motor purring.

But here he stood in light overcoat and thin leather gloves, without overshoes, and his car all but blocked the road, and the door could not be locked, and there was not a possibility that he could carry the heavy cases with him to the next farm or village. He switched on the headlights again and studied the roadside they revealed, and saw a rail fence, with cedars and spruces behind it. When more complex gadgets and more complex cures failed, there was always the lucifer match.

Ten minutes later he was sitting with the auto robe over his head and shoulders and his back against the plowed snowbank, digging the half-melted snow from inside his shoes and gloating over the growing light and warmth of the fire. He had a supply of fence rails good for an hour. In that time, someone would come along and he could get a push or two. In this country, in winter, no one ever passed up a stranded motorist.

In the stillness the flames went straight upward; the heat was wonderfully pleasant on icy hands and numb ankles and stiffened face. He looked across the road, stained by horses, broken by wheel and runner tracks, and saw how the roadside acquired definition and sharp angles and shadows in the firelight. He saw too how he would look to anyone coming along: like a calendar picture.

But no one came along. Fifteen minutes stretched into a half hour, he had only two broken pieces of rail left, the fire sizzled, half floating in the puddle of its melting. Restlessly he rose with the blanket around him and walked back up the road a hundred steps. Eastward, above jagged trees, he saw the sky where it lightened to moonrise, but here there was still only the blue glimmer of starlight on the snow. Something long buried and forgotten tugged in him, and a shiver not entirely from cold prickled his whole body with gooseflesh. There had been times in his childhood when he had walked home alone and been temporarily lost in nights like this. In many years he could not remember being out alone under such a sky. He felt spooked, his feet were chilled lumps, his nose leaked. Down the hill, car and snow swam deceptively together; the red wink of the fire seemed inexpressibly far off.

Abruptly he did not want to wait in that lonely snow-banked ditch any longer. The sample cases could look after themselves, any motorist who passed could take his own chances. He would walk ahead to the nearest help, and if he found himself getting too cold on the way, he could always build another fire. The thought of action cheered him; he admitted to himself that he was all but terrified at the silence and the iron cold.

Closing the car doors, he dropped his key case, and panic stopped his pulse as he bent and frantically, with bare hand, brushed away the snow until he found it. The powdery snow ached and burned at his fingertips. He held them a last moment to the fire, and then, bundled like a squaw, with the blanket held across nose and mouth to ease the harshness of the cold in his lungs, he started up the road that looked as smooth as a tablecloth, but was deceptively rough and broken. He thought of what he had had every right to expect for this evening. By now, eight o'clock or so, he should have had a smoking supper, the luxury of a hot bath, the pleasure of a brandy in a comradely bar. By now he should be in pajamas making out sales reports by the bedlight, in a room where steam knocked comfortingly in the radiators and the help of a hundred hands was available to him at a word into the telephone. For all of this to be torn away suddenly, for him to be stumbling up a deserted road in danger of freezing to death, just because some simple mechanical part that had functioned for thirty thousand miles refused to function any longer, this was outrage, and he hated it. He thought of garage men and service station attendants he could blame. Ignoring the evidence of the flooded carburetor, he brooded about watered gas that could make ice in the gas line. A man was dependent on too many people; he was at everybody's mercy.

And then, on top of the second long rise, he met the moon.

Instantly the character of the night changed. The uncertain starlight was replaced at a step by an even flood of blue-white radiance. He looked across a snow meadow and saw how a rail fence had every stake and rider doubled in solid shadow, and how the edge of woods beyond was blackest India ink. The road ahead was drawn with a ruler, one bank smoothed by the flood of light, the other deeply shadowed. As he looked into the eye of the moon he saw the air shiver and glint with falling particles of frost.

In this White Christmas night, this Good King Wenceslas night, he went warily, not to be caught in sentimentality, and to an invisible audience he deprecated it profanely as a night in which no one would believe. Yet here it was, and he in it. With the coming of the moon the night even seemed to warm; he found that he could drop the blanket from across his face and drink the still air.

Along the roadside as he passed the meadow and entered woods again the moon showed him things. In moonlit openings he saw the snow stitched with tiny perfect tracks, mouse or weasel or the three-toed crowding tracks of partridge. These too, an indigenous part of the night, came back to him as things once known and long forgotten. In his boyhood he had trapped and hunted the animals that made such tracks as these; it was as if his mind were a snowfield where the marks of their secret little feet had been printed long ago. With a queer tightening of the throat, with an odd pride, he read the trail of a fox that had wallowed through the soft snow from the woods, angling into the packed road and along it for a little way and out again, still angling, across the plowed bank, and then left a purposeful trail of cleanly punched tracks, the hind feet in line with the front, across the clean snow and into the opposite woods, from shadow across moonlight and into shadow again.

Turning with the road, he passed through the stretch of woods and came into the open to see the moon-white, shadow-black buildings of a farm, and the weak bloom of light in a window.

His feet whined on the snow, dry as metal powder, as he turned in the loop of drive the county plow had cleared. But as he approached the house doubt touched him. In spite of the light, the place looked unused, somehow. No dog welcomed him. The sound of his feet in the snow was alien, the hammer of his knuckles on the door an intrusion. Looking upward for some trace of telephone wires, he saw none, and he could not tell whether the quivering of the air that he thought he saw above the chimney was heat or smoke or the phantasmal falling frost.

"Hello?" he said, and knocked again. "Anybody home?" No sound answered him. He saw the moon glint on the great icicles along the eaves. His numb hand ached with the pain of knocking; he pounded with the soft edge of his fist.

Answer finally came, not from the door before which he stood, but from the barn, down at the end of a staggered string of attached sheds. A door creaked open against a snowbank and a figure with a lantern appeared, stood for a moment, and came running. The traveler wondered at the way it came, lurching and stumbling in the uneven snow, until it arrived at the porch and he saw that it was a boy of eleven or twelve. The boy set his lantern on the porch; between the upturned collar of his mackinaw and the down-pulled stocking cap his face was a pinched whiteness, his eyes enormous. He stared at the traveler until the traveler became aware of the blanket he still held over head and shoulders, and began to laugh.

"My car stopped on me, a mile or so up the road," he said. "I was just hunting a telephone or some place where I could get help."

The boy swallowed, wiped the back of his mitt across his nose. "Grandpa's sick!" he blurted, and opened the door. Warmth rushed in their faces, cold rushed in at their backs, warm and cold mingled in an eddy of air as the door closed. The traveler saw a cot bed pulled close to the kitchen range, and on the cot an old man covered with a quilt, who breathed heavily and whose closed eyes did not open when the two came near. The gray-whiskered cheeks were sunken, the mouth open to expose toothless gums in a parody look of ancient mischief.

"He must've had a shock," the boy said. "I came in from chores and he was on the floor." He stared at the mummy under the quilt, and he swallowed.

"Has he come to at all?"

"No."

"Only the two of you live here?"

"Yes."

"No telephone?"

"No."

"How long ago did you find him?"

"Chore time. About six."

"Why didn't you go for help?"

The boy looked down, ashamed. "It's near two miles. I was afraid he'd . . ."

"But you left him. You were out in the barn."

"I was hitching up to go," the boy said. "I'd made up my mind."

The traveler backed away from the stove, his face smarting with the heat, his fingers and feet beginning to ache. He looked at the old man and knew that here, as at the car, he was helpless. The boy's thin anxious face told him how thoroughly his own emergency had been swallowed up in this other one. He had been altered from a man in need of help to one who must give it. Salesman of wonder cures, he must now produce something to calm this over-worried boy, restore a dying man.

Rebelliously, victimized by circumstances, he said, "Where were you going for help?"

"The Hill place. They've got a phone."

"How far are they from a town?"

"About five miles."

"Doctor there?"

"Yes."

"If I took your horse and—what is it, sleigh?—could someone at the Hills' bring them back, do you think?"

"Cutter. One of the Hill boys could, I should say."

"Or would you rather go, while I look after your grandpa?"

"He don't know you," the boy said directly. "If he should wake up he might . . . wonder . . . it might . . ."

The traveler grudgingly gave up the prospect of staying in the warm kitchen while the boy did the work. And he granted that it was extraordinarily sensitive of the boy to know how it might disturb a man to wake from sickness in his own house and stare into the face of an utter stranger. "Yes," he said. "Well, I could call the doctor from the Hills'. Two miles, did you say?"

"About." The boy had pulled the stocking cap off so that his hair stood on end above his white forehead. He had odd eyes, very large and dark and intelligent, with an expectancy in them.

The traveler, watching him with interest, said, "How long have you lived with your grandfather?"

"Two years."

"Parents living?"

"No, sir, that's why."

"Go to school?"

He got a queer sidling look. "Have to till you're sixteen."

"Is that the only reason you go?"

What he was trying to force out of the boy came out indirectly, with a shrugging of the shoulders. "Grandpa would take me out if he could."

"Would you be glad?"

"No, sir," the boy said, but would not look at him. "I like school."

The traveler consciously corked his flow of questions. Once he himself had been an orphan living with his grandparents on a back farm; he wondered if this boy went as he had gone, knocking in imagination at all of life's closed doors.

The old man's harsh breathing filled the overwarm room. "Well," the traveler said, "maybe you'd better go finish hitching up. It's been thirty years since I harnessed a horse. I'll keep an eye on your grandpa."

Pulling the stocking cap over his disheveled hair, the boy slid out of the door. The traveler unbuttoned his overcoat and sat down beside the old man, felt the spurting weak pulse, raised one eyelid with his thumb and looked without comprehension at the uprolled eye. He knew it was like feeling over a chilling motor for loose wires, and after two or three abortive motions he gave it up and sat contemplating the gray, sunken face, the unfamiliar face of an old man who would die, and thinking that the face was the only unfamiliar thing about the whole night. The kitchen smells, coffee and peanut butter and the moldy, barky smell of wood from the woodbox, and the smell of the hot range and of paint baking in the heat, those were as familiar as light or dark. The spectacular night outside, the snowfields and the moon and the mysterious woods, the tracks venturing out across the snow from the protective eaves of firs and skunk spruce, the speculative, imagining expression of the boy's eyes, were just as familiar. He sat bemused, touching some brink as a man will walk along a cutbank trying to knock loose the crumbling overhang with an outstretched foot. The ways a man fitted in with himself and with other human beings were curious and complex.

And when he heard the jingle and creak outside, and buttoned himself into the overcoat again and wrapped his shoulders in the blanket and stepped out into the yard, there was a moment when the boy passed him the lines and they stood facing each other in the broken snow.

It was a moment like farewell, like a poignant parting. Touched by his pressing sense of familiarity and by a sort of compassion, the traveler reached out and laid his hand on the boy's shoulder. "Don't worry," he said. "I'll have someone back here right away. Your grandfather will be all right. Just keep him warm and don't worry."

He climbed into the cutter and pulled over his lap the balding buffalo robe he found there; the scallop of its felt edges was like a key that fitted a door. The horses breathed jets of steam in the moonlight, restlessly moving, jingling their harness bells, as the moment lengthened itself. The traveler saw how the boy, now that his anxiety was somewhat quieted, now that he had been able to unload part of his burden, watched him with a thousand questions in his face, and he remembered how he himself, thirty years ago, had searched the faces of passing strangers for something he could not name, how he had listened to their steps and seen their shadows lengthen ahead of them down roads that led to unimaginable places, and how he had ached with the desire to know them, who they were. But none of them had looked back at him as he tried now to look at this boy.

He was glad that no names had been spoken and no personal histories exchanged to obscure this meeting, for sitting in the sleigh above the boy's white upturned serious face, he felt that some profound contact had unintentionally, almost casually, been made.

For half a breath he was utterly bewitched, frozen at the heart of some icy dream. Abruptly he slapped the reins across the backs of the horses; the cutter jerked and then slid smoothly out towards the road. The traveler looked back once, to fix forever the picture of himself standing silently watching himself go. As he slid into the road the horses broke into a trot. The icy flow of air locked his throat and made him let go the reins with one hand to pull the hairy, wool-smelling edge of the blanket all but shut across his face.

Along a road he had never driven he went swiftly towards an unknown farm and an unknown town, to distribute according to some wise law part of the burden of the boy's emergency and his own; but he bore in his mind, bright as moonlight over snow, a vivid wonder, almost an awe. For from the most chronic and incurable of ills, identity, he had looked outward and for one unmistakable instant recognized himself.

BUGLESONG

There had been a wind during the night, and all the loneliness of the world had swept up out of the southwest. The boy had heard it wailing through the screens of the sleeping porch where he lay, and he had heard the washtub bang loose from the outside wall and roll down toward the coulee, and the slam of the screen doors, and his mother's padding feet after she rose to fasten things down. Through one half-open eye he had peered up from his pillow to see the moon skimming windily in a luminous sky; in his mind he had seen the prairie outside with its woolly grass and cactus white under the moon, and the wind, whining across that endless oceanic land, sang in the screens, and sang him back to sleep.

Now, after breakfast, when he set out through the west pasture on the morning round of his gopher traps, there was no more wind, but the air smelled somehow recently swept and dusted, as the house in town sometimes smelled after his mother's whirlwind cleaning. The sun was gently warm on the bony shoulder blades of the boy, and he whistled, and whistling turned to see if the Bearpaws were in sight to the south.

There they were, a ghostly tenuous outline of white just breaking over the bulge of the world: the Mountains of the Moon, the place of running streams and timber and cool heights that he had never seen—only dreamed of on days when the baked clay of the farmyard cracked in the heat and the sun brought cedar smells from fence posts long since split and dry and odorless, when he lay dreaming on the bed in the sleeping porch with a Sears, Roebuck catalogue open before him, picking out the presents he would buy for his mother and his father and his friends next Christmas, or the Christmas after that. On those days he looked often and long at the snowy mountains to the south, while the dreams rose in him like heat waves, blurring the reality of the unfinished shack that was his summer home.

The Bearpaws were there now, and he watched them a moment, walking, his feet dodging cactus clumps automatically, before he turned his attention again to the traps before him, their locations marked by a zigzag line of stakes. He ran the line at a half-trot, whistling.

At the first stake the chain was stretched tightly into the hole. The pull on its lower end had dug a little channel in the soft earth of the mound. Gently, so as not to break the gopher's leg off, the boy eased the trap out of the burrow, held the chain in his left hand, and loosened the stake with his right. The gopher lunged against the heavy trap, but it did not squeal. They squealed, the boy had noticed, only when at a distance, or when the weasel had them. Otherwise they kept still.

For a moment the boy debated whether to keep this one alive for the weasel or to wait till the last trap so that he wouldn't have to carry the live one around. Deciding to wait, he held the chain out, measured the rodent for a moment, and swung. The knobbed end of the stake crushed the animal's skull, and the eyes popped out of the head, round and blue. A trickle of blood started from nose and ears.

Releasing the gopher, the boy lifted it by the tail and snapped its tail-fur off with a dexterous flip. Then he stowed the trophy carefully in the breast pocket of his overalls. For the last two years he had won the grand prize offered by the province of Saskatchewan to the school child who destroyed the most gophers. On the mantel in town were two silver loving cups, and in a shoe box under his bed in the farmhouse there were already eight hundred and forty tails, the catch of three weeks. His whole life on the farm was devoted to the destruction of the rodents. In the wheat fields he distributed poison, but in the pasture, where stock might get the tainted grain, he trapped, snared, or shot them. Any method he preferred to poisoning: that offered no excitement, and he seldom got the tails because the gophers crawled down their holes to die.

Picking up trap and stake, the boy kicked the dead animal down its burrow and scraped dirt over it with his foot. They stunk up the pasture if they weren't buried, and the bugs got into them. Frequently he had stood to windward of a dead and swollen gopher, watching the body shift and move with the movements of the beetles and crawling things working through it. If such an infested corpse were turned over, the beetles would roar out of it, great orange-colored, hard-shelled, scavenging things that made his blood curdle at the thought of their touching him, and after they were gone and he looked again he would see the little black ones, undisturbed, seething through the rotten flesh. So he always buried his dead, now.

Through the gardens of red and yellow cactus blooms he went whistling, half trotting, setting the traps anew whenever a gopher shot upright, squeaked, and ducked down its burrow at his approach. All but two of the first seventeen traps held gophers, and he came to the eighteenth confidently, expecting to take this one alive. But this gopher had gone into the trap head first, and the boy put back into his pocket the salt sack he had brought along as a game bag. He would have to snare or trap one down by the dam.

On the way back he stopped with bent head while he counted his day's catch of tails, mentally adding this lot of sixteen to the eight hundred and forty he already had, trying to remember how many he had had at this time last year. As he finished his mathematics his whistle broke out again, and he galloped down through the pasture, running for very abundance of life, until he came to the chicken house just within the plowed fireguard.

Under the eaves of the chicken house, so close that the hens were constantly pecking up to its very door and then almost losing their wits with fright, was the made-over beer case that contained the weasel. Screen had been tacked tightly under the wooden lid, which latched, and in the screen was cut a tiny wire door. In the front, along the bottom, a single board had been removed and replaced with screen.

The boy lifted the hinged top and looked down into the cage.

"Hello," he said. "Hungry?"

The weasel crouched, its long snaky body humped, its head thrust forward and its malevolent eyes staring with lidless savagery into the boy's.

"Tough, ain't you?" said the boy. "Just wait, you bloodthirsty old stinker, you. Wait'll you turn into an ermine. Won't I skin you quick, hah?"

There was no dislike or emotion in his tone. He took the weasel's malignant ferocity with the same indifference he displayed in his gopher killing. Weasels, if you could keep them long enough, were valuable. He would catch a lot, keep them until they turned white, and sell their hides as ermine. Maybe he could breed them and have an ermine farm. He was the best gopher trapper in Saskatchewan. Once he had even caught a badger. Why not weasels? The trap broke their leg, but nothing could really hurt a weasel permanently. This one, though virtually three-legged, was as savage and lively as ever. Every morning he had a live gopher for his breakfast, in spite of the protests of the boy's mother that it was cruel. But nothing, she had said, was cruel to the boy.

When she argued that the gopher had no chance when thrown into the cage, the boy retorted that he didn't have a chance when the weasel came down the hole after him either. If she said that the real job he should devote himself to was exterminating the weasels, he replied that then the gophers would get so thick they would eat the fields down to stubble. At last she gave up, and the weasel continued to have his warm meals.

For some time the boy stood watching his captive, and then he turned and went into the house, where he opened the oat box in the kitchen and took out a chunk of dried beef. From this he cut a thick slice with the butcher knife, and went munching into the sleeping porch where his mother was making beds.

"Where's that little double naught?" he asked.

"That what?"

"That little wee trap. The one I use for catching live ones for the weasel."

"Hanging out by the laundry bench, I think. Are you going out trapping again now?"

"Lucifer hasn't had his breakfast yet."

"How about your reading?"

"I'n take the book along and read while I wait," the boy said. "I'm just goin' down to the coulee at the edge of the dam."

"I *can*, not 'Ine,' son."

"I can," the boy said. "I am most delighted to comply with your request."

He grinned at his mother. He could always floor her with a quotation from a letter or the Sears, Roebuck catalogue.

With the trap swinging from his hand, and under his arm the book—*Narrative and Lyric Poems*, edited by Somebody-or-other—which his mother kept him reading during the summer "so that next year he could be at the head of his class again," the boy walked out into the growing heat.

From the northwest the coulee angled down through the pasture, a shallow swale dammed just above the house to catch the spring run-off of snow water. In the moist dirt of the dam grew ten-foot willows planted as slips by the boy's father. They were the only things resembling trees in sixty miles. Below the dam, watered by the slow seepage from above, the coulee bottom was a parterre of flowers, buttercups in broad sheets, wild sweet pea, and "stinkweed." On the slopes were evening primroses, pale pink and white and delicately fragrant, and on the flats above the yellow and red burgeoning of the cactuses.

Just under the slope of the coulee a female gopher and three half-grown puppies basked on their warm mound. The boy chased them squeaking down their hole and set the trap carefully, embedding it partially in the soft earth. Then he retired back up the shoulder of the swale, where he lay full length on his stomach, opened the book, shifted so that the glare of the sun across the pages was blocked by the shadow of his head and shoulders, and began to read.

From time to time he stopped reading to roll on his side and stare out across the coulee, across the barren plains pimpled with gopher mounds and bitten with fire and haired with dusty woolly grass. Apparently as flat as a table, the land sloped imperceptibly to the south, so that nothing interfered with his view of the ghostly line of mountains, now more plainly visible as the heat increased. Between the boy's eyes and that smoky outline sixty miles away the heat waves rose writhing like fine wavy hair. He knew that in an hour Pankhurst's farm would lift above the swelling knoll to the west. Many times he had seen that phenomenon—had seen his friend Jason Pankhurst playing in the yard or watering horses when he knew that the whole farm was out of sight. It was the heat waves that did it, his father said.

The gophers below had been thoroughly scared, and for a long time nothing happened. Idly the boy read through his poetry lesson, dreamfully conscious of the hard ground under him, feeling the gouge of a rock under his stomach without making any effort to remove it. The sun was a hot caress between his shoulder blades, and on the bare flesh where his overalls pulled above his sneakers it bit like a burning glass. Still he was comfortable, supremely relaxed and peaceful, lulled into a half-trance by the heat and the steamy flower smells and the mist of yellow in the buttercup coulee below.

And beyond the coulee was the dim profile of the Bearpaws, the Mountains of the Moon.

The boy's eyes, pulled out of focus by his tranced state, fixed on the page before him. Here was a poem he knew . . . but it wasn't a poem, it was a song. His mother sang it often, working at the sewing machine in winter.

It struck him as odd that a poem should also be a song, and because he found it hard to read without bringing in the tune, he lay quietly in the full glare of the sun, singing the page softly to himself. As he sang the trance grew on him again; he lost himself entirely. The bright hard dividing lines between individual senses blurred, and buttercups, smell of primrose, feel of hard gravel under body and elbows, sight of the ghosts of mountains haunting the southern horizon, were one intensely felt experience focused by the song the book had evoked.

And the song was the loveliest thing he had ever known. He felt the words, tasted them, breathed upon them with all the ardor of his captivated senses.

> *The splendor falls on castle walls*
> *And snowy summits old in story. . . .*

The current of his imagination flowed southward over the strong gentle shoulder of the world to the ghostly outline of the Mountains of the Moon, haunting the heat-distorted horizon.

> *O, hark, O hear! How thin and clear,*
> *And thinner, clearer, farther going!*
> *O, sweet and far, from cliff and scar. . . .*

In the enchanted forests of his mind the horns of elfland blew, and his breath was held in the slow-falling cadence of their dying. The weight of the sun had been lifted from his back. The empty prairie of his home was castled and pillared with the magnificence of his imagining, and the sound of horns died thinly in the direction of the Mountains of the Moon.

From the coulee below came the sudden metallic clash of the trap, and an explosion of frantic squeals smothered almost immediately in the burrow. The boy leaped up, thrusting the book into the wide pocket of his overalls, and ran down to the mound. The chain, stretched down the hole, jerked convulsively, and when the boy took hold of it he felt the terrified life at the end of it strain to escape. Tugging gently, he forced loose the gopher's digging claws, and hauled the squirming captive from the hole.

On the way up to the chicken house the dangling gopher with a tremendous muscular effort convulsed itself upward from the broken and imprisoned leg, and bit with a sharp rasp of teeth on the iron. Its eyes, the boy noticed impersonally, were shining black, like the head of a hatpin. He thought it odd that when they popped out of the head after a blow they were blue.

At the cage by the chicken house he lifted the cover and peered through the screen. The weasel, scenting the blood of the gopher's leg, backed against the far wall of the box, yellow body tense as a spring, teeth showing in a tiny soundless snarl.

Undoing the wire door with his left hand, the boy held the trap over the hole. Then he bore down with all his strength on the spring, releasing the gopher, which dropped on the straw-littered floor and scurried into the corner opposite its enemy.

The weasel's three good feet gathered under it and it circled, very slowly, around the wall, its lips still lifted to expose the soundless snarl. The abject gopher crowded against the boards, turned once and tried to scramble up the side, fell back on its broken leg, and whirled like lightning to face its executioner again. The weasel moved carefully, circling.

Then the gopher screamed, a wild, agonized, despairing squeal that made the watching boy swallow and wet his lips. Another scream, wilder and louder than before, and before the sound had ended the weasel struck. There was a fierce flurry in the straw of the cage before the killer got its hold just back of the gopher's right ear, and its teeth began tearing ravenously at the still-quivering body. In a few minutes, the boy knew, the gopher's carcass would be as limp as an empty skin, with all its blood sucked out and a hole as big as the ends of his two thumbs where the weasel had dined.

Still the boy remained staring through the screen top of the cage, face rapt and body completely lost. And after a few minutes he went into the sleeping porch, stretched out on the bed, opened the Sears, Roebuck catalogue, and dived so deeply into its fascinating pictures and legends that his mother had to shake him to make him hear her call to lunch.

BEYOND THE GLASS MOUNTAIN

∎   ∎   ∎

Someone had left a funny paper in the booth, and while he waited with his ear intent on the regular buzzing rings, Mark let his eye follow the pictured squares. I know somebody that likes your new hat, Emmy, Kayo's balloon said, and Emmy's pleased balloon said, Well, for thirty-nine-fifty they ought to, who is he? and Kayo's balloon said It's Beefy McGuire, he'd like it for his bird's nest collection, and on the fourth ring the line clicked and Mel's inquiring voice said, "Hello?"

The voice was as familiar as yesterday, a voice whose wire-filtered flatness Mark had heard over telephones ten thousand times. The rising hairs prickled on the back of his neck; he felt as he might have felt if a door had opened and the face of someone long dead had looked casually out.

And he noted instantly, in refutation of his fears, that the voice was sober. He found himself leaning forward, grinning into the mouthpiece.

"Hello, you poop-out," he said. "This is Canby."

The old password came naturally, as if he were back seventeen years. In their college crowd everybody had called everybody else Canby, for no reason except that someone, probably Mel, had begun it and everyone else had followed suit. There had been a real Canby, a sort of goof. Now he was a CPA in Denver, and the usurpers of his name were scattered from coast to coast.

"Well, Canby!" the filtered voice said heartily. "How's the boy?"

There was a pause. Then Mel's voice, more distorted now, beginning to be his clowning voice, said suspiciously, "What was that name again?"

"Canby," Mark said. "Cornelius C. Canby." He raised his head, grinning and waiting for the real recognition.

"Cornelius C. Canby?" Mel's thickening, burbling voice said. "I didn't get the name."

"It's a hell of a note," Mark said. "Your old friend Canby was here, and you didn't even get the name."

Mel's voice was thick as glue now, like something mired down, except that on occasional syllables it fluttered upward like a mud-heavy bird. It was a maudlin, wandering, caressing voice, very convincing to strangers and drunks, and it always made any drunk his instant pal. "*Canby?*" it said. "D'you say *Canby*? Cornelius Canby? Well my God. Wonnersnev-ercease. *Canby*, after all these years! Come on over here and shake my hand. Where are you? Hire a car. Wait a minute, I'll come and get you myself."

"Don't bother," Mark said. "I can walk over in five minutes." He grinned again into the mouthpiece. "Are you at home or out at some bar?"

"Just down at the corner pub having little drink," Mel said. "But I'll be home in minute, home quick as you are. Not far away." There was another pause. "What was z'name?"

Mark was beginning to feel a shade uncomfortable. The clowning was routine, but there was a point where it should have stopped. It left things uncertain. "You stinker," he said, "this is Aker. Remember me?"

The drunken voice was an amazed buzz in the earpiece. Out of the buzz words formed. "You mean Belly Aker, the basketball player, erst-while holder of the Big Ten scoring record?"

"The same."

"Not Mark Aker, the eminent penicillinologist?"

"It is he."

"Well my God," Mel said. "I remember you. Seen your name in the Alumni Magazine."

The words degenerated into a buzz, then became articulate again.

"You old spore-picker. How's boy?" Then in a moment the earphone bellowed, "What the hell you standing around there for?"

"Hold it," Mark said. "I'm on my way."

He hung up and stepped out of the booth self-consciously, looking around to see if anyone had been close enough to hear the nonsense he had been talking. As he walked through the drugstore and out into the street he found himself explaining as if to some critical stranger. Just to listen to Cottam, you'd think he was a maudlin sot, but that's just a manner he wears. He puts it on for the same reason some people put on dark glasses. . . .

He found himself at the corner of College and Dubuque Streets in Iowa City, at a little past ten on a Sunday morning in May, and as he stopped on the corner to let a car pass, the utter and passionate familiarity of everything smote him like a wind. Mel's voice on the wire had prepared him for nostalgia. Now the past moved up on him in a wave; it was as if he had never left here, or had just awakened from a long confused dream and found the solid and reassuring edge of reality again.

The brick street ran warm and empty down across the powerhouse bridge and up the other side, curving under big elms and hickories. On the crown of the hill across the river the Quadrangle's squat ivied towers barely topped the trees, and over on the other hill to the right the stone lace of the hospital tower rose above the massive rectangularity of the medical buildings. The lawns below Old Capitol were almost deserted, and the locusts were shrilling in the streetside trees.

Odd compulsions moved him. He found himself reciting the names of all the main university buildings. Crossing the river, he ran his hand along the cool cement rail as if establishing a contact, and halfway across he looked back to see how the union and the reserve library strung out along the riverbank, and the footbridge arched across to the experimental theater. The banks of the river had been landscaped since his time, but otherwise he saw no change. The highway traffic west poured across the Iowa Avenue bridge, and the law commons clung to the limestone bluffs. Mark looked curiously at the few students he met, wondering if they felt as he felt the charm and warmth that lay in the brick streets and the sleepy river and the sun-warmed brick and stone of the university. Probably no one appreciated things like that until they were gone and lost and irretrievable.

On his left as he stepped off the bridge he saw the little eating shack where he and Mel had had long johns and coffee practically every morning for four years. The mere look of its outside, patched with Coke signs and Baby Ruth signs and Chesterfield signs, filled his nostrils with the peculiar and unique odors of the place: coffee and smoke and slightly rancid fat, oily-sweet doughnuts and baked paint and the reek of the bug-spray they used on the cockroaches, and under all the watery, tarry, wet-mud smells of the river.

The metal rasping of the seventeen-year-locusts rose loud as a cre- scendo in a symphonic poem as he climbed the hill, and it struck him as amusing that he too should return here at the end of exactly seventeen years. He couldn't quite imagine where those years had gone; it did not seem that either he or the town had changed a particle. The tennis courts he passed reflected hundreds of remembered mornings like this, and in the field house beyond them were whole lifetimes of recollection.

He would have liked to go in under the big round roof just to soak himself in the sensations he remembered: smell of lockers opened on stale gym clothes and stiff sweated socks; steam and thumping radiators and liquid soap smell; sweat and medicated foot baths and the chlorine smell and the jiggly reflecting chemical blue of the pool; splat of naked feet on concrete, pink of bare flesh, lean bellies and tiptoe bunching calves, the bulging triceps of the gymnastics team working out on the horses. Most of all, the barnlike cold of the basketball floor, and the tiny brittle feeling of coming out before a game to warm up in front of that crowd-faced emptiness, and the clubbing roar of crowd-sound as you drove in for a set-up. It was the same roar whether you made it or missed it.

All of it was still there—unimaginably varied smells and sounds and sights that together made up the way he had once lived, the thing he had once been, perhaps the thing he still was. He was in all of it, and Mel with him. It came to him like a pang that never since the days when he and Mel used to fool around after lunch in the Quad cafeteria, throwing rolled-up paper napkins at water tumblers, had he had a completely relaxed and comfortable ability to enjoy himself. They had made games out of everything; whole Sunday mornings they had spent throwing curves with pot covers in Mel's mother's kitchen. In those Damon-and-Pythias days there had been a sharp and tingling sense of identity and one intense and constant comradeship, and those were the best days of his life. Passing the field house, he passed himself and Mel as they had used to be, and the feeling that he had not merely lived it but was somehow contained in it was as pervasive as the mild spring morning, as insistent as the skirring of the locusts. It was like sky-writing on the big warm sky.

The light over the whole hill was pure, pale, of an exaggerated clarity, as if all the good days of his youth had been distilled down into this one day, and the whole coltish ascendant time when he was eighteen, nineteen, twenty, had been handed back to him briefly, intact and precious. That was the time when there had been more hours in the day, and every hour precious enough so that it could be fooled away. By the time a man got into the high thirties the hours became more frantic and less precious, more needed and more carefully hoarded and more fully used, but less loved and less enjoyed.

Then he was pushing the doorbell button, bracing himself obscurely for something—for joy? for recognition? for a renewed flood of this potent and unexpected nostalgia?—and the door opened. Mel stood there in his shirt sleeves, a little mussy as usual, still deceptively round-armed and round-faced, with his beaked nose and his tender child's mouth.

He was either drunk or playing drunk. He smirked, and his eyes blinked in owlish amazement. "Let me shake your hand!" he said, and hauled Mark inside.

Tamsen got up off the couch where she had been sitting with a highball in her hand. As she came forward, smiling, transferring the glass to her left hand, Mark noted how she adjusted her face for greeting. She was probably prettier than she had ever been, her hair in a long bob with sun-bleached streaks in it, her face smoothly tanned, her eyes candid, her smile white and frank. Presumably the two of them had been drinking together, but where Mel was frowsy and blinking, with red-streaked eyeballs, she was smooth and sober and impeccable.

"Of all the unexpected people!" she said, and gave him a firm hand. She left him in no doubt who was in command in this familiar house, who had established dominance.

Mel's hand pulled him around. "Canby, you old snake in the grass, where you been? I've tried to call you up every night for ten years."

"You did," Mark said. "Twice. Once in New Haven and once in New York. Both times at two in the morning."

Tamsen laughed. "Old Melly," she said, almost as if affectionately. "Every time he gets tight he wants to call somebody up. The further away they are, the more he wants to call."

Mel was standing spraddling, a little flickering smile on his mouth.

One hand was on Mark's shoulder. With the other he captured Mark's right hand again and shook it slowly. His breath was heavy with whiskey, and Mark felt dismayed and half sick. He had been so sure at first that the thickening voice had been put on as part of the old clowning act. Now he was bothered precisely as he had been bothered by those telephone calls. Even while he laughed at the ponderous solemnity, the incoherent, bumbling, repetitive nonsense, the marvelously accurate imitation of a soggy drunk, Mark backed away, because he couldn't be quite sure that the act was conscious any more. The act had become the man, and he went around living and acting out a grotesque parody of himself; or if it hadn't become the man, then it had been put on defensively so much that communication was no longer possible. Nothing had come of those telephone calls except a mumble of doubletalk and affectionate profanity, and yet Mark felt that there had been in each instance a need, a loneliness, a reaching out. He felt that there was the same thing now, if Mel would let it show. The old comradeship was there; this drunken parody was embarrassment as much as anything, the defense of a thin-skinned organism.

"Been peeking down those microscopes," Mel said solemnly, pumping Mark's hand. "You biological old pot-licker. D'you invent penicillin?"

"I'm a modest man," Mark said. "Two or three other people helped."

He got his hand free, and as his eyes crossed Mel's there was almost communication between them, a flash of perfectly sober understanding and warmth. Mel's delicate, bruised-looking lips pursed, but then the look slipped and was gone, and he was pawing for Mark's hand again, saying, "Canby, you old Rhodes Scholar, slip me the grip."

Tamsen was amused. "You should charge him. Remember when he paid a barfly a dollar an hour to shake his hand down at Frank's?"

"Kept me poor," Mel said, with a sweet imbecilic grin. "Lose all your friends, got to buy more." He smiled into Mark's face, hanging to hand and shoulder, and Mark looked deep behind that idiot alcoholic smile trying to compel expression of what he knew was there: the recognition and the pain. Mel beamed at him.

Tamsen too was staring, tipping her head sideways. "I can't get over how much you've changed," she said. "You used to be such a string bean."

"Cheer up," Mark said. "I'm still a string bean at heart."

"No fooling," Mel said. He plucked the cloth of Mark's sleeve, sniffed his fingers. "Where'd you get that jacket?"

"Montreal," Mark said, and immediately felt an obscure guilty shame, as if he had been betrayed into boasting, rubbing in the fact that he had gone up and out in the world and Mel had been marooned behind. "I was up there a couple weeks ago at a genetics conference," he said lamely, in extenuation.

For an instant he was furious at Mel, so furious he shook. In college it had been Mel who had everything—money enough, and clothes, and a car, and a home where starveling students could come like grateful sidling dogs off the street. And he had been brought up well, he had good parents, his home was full of music and books and a certain sense of social grace and personal responsibility. Mel had taught the whole unlicked lot of them something, how to win and how to lose, how to live with people and like them and forgive them. He had never owned a dime's worth of anything that he wasn't glad to share. Now the shoe was on the other foot. Now Mark had gone higher and farther than any of them had ever aimed, and it embarrassed and enraged him to know that he could give lessons to Mel. And it was unjust that having shared everything for four years in college, they couldn't share this trouble that Mel was in now.

Tamsen's level blue eyes were inspecting him, and it struck him that here at least was something they had never shared. He had always known more about Tamsen than Mel had. When he stood up as Mel's best man he could have told the bridegroom the names of four people who had slept with the bride. He wished now that he had; he had wished it a hundred times. And catching Tamsen's eyes, twinkling with a little spark of malice, he knew she understood precisely what he was thinking. She had always been shrewd, and she had been all her life one of the world's most accomplished and convincing liars. When she went after Mel she had fooled even the people who knew her best, made them believe she was infatuated. . . .

"I tell you for sure," she said, "if you'd been as good looking then as you are now I'd never have let old Melly take me in to church."

"Maybe there's still time," Mark said.

Mel's tugging hand hauled him around. "You've *changed*, you know that, you damn Yale professor?"

"So have you," Mark said, but his attempt to hold Mel's eye was unsuccessful, and he added, "I stay in nights, now. Once I got free of your influence I steadied right down."

"That's fact," Mel said. "Terrible influence. Half stiff ten-thirty Sunday morning. Blame that boy of mine. Got his old man out playing baseball with a hangover before breakfast. You ever meet that boy?"

"Never did."

"Where is he, Tam?"

"He's around," Tamsen said. "How about me getting you two a drink?"

Mark let her go. It was a way of getting Mel alone. It seemed to him that some of the drunken pose fell away from Mel as soon as his wife left the room. He looked into the streaked eyes and shook his head and grinned. "How are things going, anyway?"

The eyes were round and innocent. "Things going wonderful. I run the business now, since my dad died. My dad was a good business man, you know that, Canby?"

"I know that," Mark said. "It wasn't business I was thinking about." With a quick estimate that he might have only two minutes more before Tamsen returned, he opened his mouth to say what he had come to say, and found that his tongue wouldn't go around it. In that instant it was clear that you did not come in on an old friend and say, "I hear your wife's been playing around with a golf pro. I could have warned you about her that way. Probably I should have. But I hear you found out all right, and were all set to get a divorce. Bailey told me that much, a year ago. Then I heard that instead of getting a divorce you went down to St. Louis, you and Tamsen and the boy, and stayed six months, and came back home and no more said about any divorce. Get rid of her. She'll cheat on you all her life, and break you in the process. If she's pulled some lie out of the bag and convinced you that you were mistaken, don't believe it, she could lie her way out of hell. For the love of God, get that divorce, for the sake of the boy and for your own sake. She'll suck you dry like an old orange skin. You're already so far gone I could cry—soggy with alcohol and with that comedy-routine front on all the time. Come and stay with me, I'll line you up with Alcoholics Anonymous if you want. Give me a chance to pay some of what I owe you."

You simply did not say things like that. Even thinking about them made them sound self-righteous and prying. Instead, you looked uneasily at your oldest and closest friend, trying to surprise in his eyes the things you knew were there, pain and shame and bitterness and defeat. But there was too thick an insulating layer between. Seventeen years were too many. Mel was like the elk in Jim Bridger's Yellowstone story. He grazed on the other side of the glass mountain, clear and undistorted, looking only a hundred yards away. The hunter's gun went off, and the elk didn't even raise his head, didn't even hear the report. He just went on grazing, with blankness like a membrane over his eyeballs and an unpierceable transparent wall between him and the world.

Mel's lips twitched. He lurched forward, looking puzzled and solicitous. "Whazza name?" he said, besotted and polite, and turned his ear sideward like a deaf man.

Mark pushed him away angrily just as Tamsen came in with glasses. Mel took two and handed one to Mark with a crooked grin. "Here, rinse your mouth," he said.

Tamsen raised her glass. "Here's to the local boy who made good." They clicked glasses elaborately all around. Irritated, baffled, frustrated, gnawed by that odd obscure shame, Mark drank with them to himself.

"I was thinking about you the other day," Tamsen was saying. "We were down watching the spring canoe race and two kids went over the falls by the power plant just the way you and Mel did once."

"I hope they didn't swallow as much water as I did," Mark said.

"Yeah, but this the other day was an accident," Mel said. "You, you pot-licker, you put us over there just to duck me."

"I was along," Mark said. "I went over too. Remember?"

Tamsen shook her head. "You were a pair," she said. "I guess I'd forgotten what a pair you were."

They sat nursing their drinks, the door open upon the street and the locust noise, and groped carefully backward for the things to remember and laugh about, gleaning the safe nostalgic past. But it was not the canoes over waterfalls, the times Jay Straup tried to climb Old Capitol steps in his old Model T, the picnics on Signal Hill when all the farmer kids used to creep up and spy on the college kids necking, that Mark wanted to remember. People who recalled such things and shook their heads over them bored him. He kept looking at Mel in search of that spark of understanding, and he kept wanting to say—

Remember the times we used to go out on dates and come in late in your old Ford, and stop down along one of the river joints for a pork tenderloin and a ginger beer, two or three o'clock in the morning, only a truck driver or two on the stools? How good sandwiches tasted at that hour, and how late the moon would be over the bluffs when we came out yawning and started up to your house? Remember the mornings we woke up in this house, this very house seventeen or eighteen or twenty years ago, and found the sun scrambled in the bedclothes, and had a shower and breakfast and went out onto the sidewalk, not for anything especially, but just to be outdoors, and walked under those trees out there up to the corner and back again, loafing, alive to the fingertips, talking about anything, nothing, girls, games, profundities? Remember? It isn't what we did, but what we were, that I remember, and I know that what we were is still here, if we'd peel off the defenses and the gag-lines and the doubletalk routines and the Montreal jackets.

The porch thudded with feet and a chubby boy of twelve came in with a bat in his hand. He stood forward gravely when Mel introduced him, shook hands with polite indifference, coasted into the kitchen and came back gnawing on a cookie.

"Canby, my friend," Mel said to him, "you'll be as fat as your old man."

The child was a curious blend of his parents, with Tamsen's deceptively clear eyes and Mel's twisting delicate mouth. He looked at his father over the cookie, grinning.

"Stay away from pappy," Tamsen said. "Pappy started out to cure a hangover and behold he's swizzled again."

A grunt that sounded almost like an angry outburst escaped Mel. He lunged for the boy. "Come here!" he said, as the boy eluded him. "Come here and I'll knock your two heads together."

Still grinning, the boy banged out onto the porch. "How about another drink for the two old grads?" Tamsen said.

"Why not?" Mel said, but Mark rose.

"I've got to catch a train at twelve-thirty."

"You don't have to go," Mel said. "You just came, Canby."

Mark put out his hand to Tamsen. "Good-bye," he said. "If you ever come east don't forget me."

He was trying to decide whether the look in her clear eyes had been triumphant, or whether there had actually been any look at all, as he and Mel went out the sidewalk and down to the corner. They did not speak on the way down, but on the corner, under the warm shade, their voices almost lost in the incessant shrilling of the locusts, they shook hands again. Mark knew there was no use in trying to say any of what it had been in his mind to say. But even so he gripped Mel's hand and held his eyes.

"I wish you the best, you bum," he said, and his throat tightened up as it sometimes tightened at an emotional crisis in a play. "If you're not so stiff you can't listen straight, listen to this. I wish you the best, and if there's ever a time I can . . ."

He stopped. Mel was looking at him without any of the sodden fuzziness that had marked him for the past hour. His eyes were pained, intent, sad. On his delicate bruised lips there was a flicker of derision.

THE
BERRY
PATCH

That day the sun came down in a vertical fall of heat, but the wind came under it, flat out of the gap beyond Mansfield, and cooled a sweating forehead as fast as the sun could heat it. In the washed ruts of the trail there were no tracks.

"Lord," Perley Hill said. "It's a day for seeing things, right enough."

He jerked off his tie and unbuttoned his shirt, rolled up his sleeves and set his right arm gingerly on the hot door, and as Alma steered the Plymouth up the long slope of Stannard he looked back across the valley to where the asbestos mine on Belvidere blew up its perpetual white plume, and on down south across the hills folding back in layers of blue to Mansfield and Elmore and the shark-fin spine of Camel's Hump. Just across the valley the lake was like a mirror leaned on edge against the hills, with the white houses of the village propped against its lower edge to keep it from sliding down into the river valley.

"It's pretty on a clear day," Alma said, without looking.

Perley continued to look down. "Things show up," he said. "There's Donald Swain's place."

" 'Twon't be his much longer," Alma said.

Perley glanced at her. She was watching the road with rigid concentration. "Having trouble?" he said.

"I thought I told you. He's in hospital in St. Johnsbury. Stomach trouble or something. With Henry and George in the navy, Allen can't run it alone. Donald's had him put it up for sale."

"I guess you did tell me," he said. "I forgot."

"Already sold half his cows," Alma said.

They passed an abandoned farm, with a long meadow that flowed downhill between tight walls of spruce. "Looks like a feller could've made that pay," Perley said. "How long's it been since Gardner left here?"

"I remember coming up here to pick apples when I was about fifteen," Alma said. "Must be ten-twelve years since anybody's worked this place."

Perley drummed on the door, grinning a little to himself at the way Alma never took her eyes off the road when she talked. She faced it as if it were a touchy bull-critter. "Kind of proud of yourself since you learned to drive, ain't you?" he said. "Be putting Sam Boyce out of business, taxiing people around."

She took her foot off the accelerator. "Why, you can drive," she said. "I didn't mean—"

"Go ahead," Perley said. "Any OPA agents around, you can do the explaining about the pleasure driving."

" 'Tisn't pleasure driving," Alma said. "Berrying's all right to do."

Perley watched the roadside, the chokecherry bushes getting heavy with green clusters already, the daisies and paintbrush just going out, but still lush in the shaded places, the fireweed and green goldenrod flowing back into every little bay in the brush.

Just as Alma shifted and crawled out onto a level before an abandoned schoolhouse, a partridge swarmed out of a beech, and Perley bent to look upward. "See them two little ones hugging the branch?" he said. "They'd sit there and never move till you knocked them off with a stick."

Alma pulled off the road into the long grass. An old skid road wormed up the hill through heavy timber, and the air was rich with the faint, warm, moist smell of woods after rain. Perley stretched till his muscles cracked, yawned, stepped out to look across the broken stone wall that disappeared into deep brush.

"Makes a feller just want to lay down in the cool," he said. "If I lay down will you braid my hair full of daisies?"

The berry pails in her hands, Alma looked at him seriously. "Well, if you'd rather just lay down," she said. "We don't have to—"

"I guess I can stay up a mite longer," Perley said.

"But if you'd rather," she said, and looked at him as if she didn't quite know what he'd like to do, but was willing to agree to anything he said. She'd been that way ever since he came home. If he yawned, she wondered if he didn't want to go to bed. If he sat down, she brought a pillow or a magazine as if he might be going to stay there all day.

He reached in and got the big granite kettle and set it over her head like a helmet, and then fended her off with one hand while he got the blanket, the lunch box, the Mason jar of water. "Think the army had wrapped me up in cellophane too pretty to touch," he said.

"Well," she said, "I just wanted to be sure." She looked at his face and added, "You big lummox."

He nested the pails, hooked his arm through the basket, slung the blanket across his shoulder, picked up the water jar. "If I just had me a wife would do for me," he said, "I'd lay down and get my strength back. With the wife I got, I s'pose I got to work."

"Here," Alma said mildly. "Give me some of them things. You'll get so toggled up I'll have to cut you out with the pliers."

All the way up the skid road under the deep shade their feet made trails in the wet grass. Perley jerked his head at them. "Nobody been in since yesterday anyway," he said.

"Wa'n't any tracks on the road."

"Thought somebody might've walked," Perley said. "Haven't, though."

"Be nice if we had the patch all to our lonesomes," she said.

They came out of the woods into a meadow. A house that had once stood at the edge was a ruined foundation overgrown with fireweed, and the hurricane of 1938 had scooped a path two hundred yards long and fifty wide out of the maples behind. Root tables lay up on edge, trunks were crisscrossed, flat, leaning, dead and half-dead. Perley went over and looked into the tangle. "Plenty raspberries," he said.

"I've got my face fixed for blueberries," Alma said. "We can get some of those too, though. They're about gone down below."

Perley was already inspecting the ruined cellar. "Ha!" he said. "Gooseberries, too. A mess of 'em."

"It's blueberries I'm interested in," she said.

"Well, I'll find you some blueberries then." He tightroped the foundation and jumped clear of the gooseberry bushes. Fifty feet down the meadow he went into a point with lifted foot, the pails dangling in one hand. "Hey!" he said. "Hey!"

When she got to his side he was standing among knee-high bushes, and all down the falling meadow, which opened on the west into a clear view of the valley, the village, the lake, the hills beyond hills and the final peaks, the dwarf bushes were so laden that the berries gleamed through the covering leaves like clusters of tiny flowers.

"Thunderation," Perley said. "I never saw a patch like that in fifteen years."

Before she could say anything he had stripped off the army shirt and the white undershirt and hung them on a bush, and was raking the berries into a pail with his spread fingers.

By the time two buckets were full the wind had shifted so that the trees cut it off, and it was hot in the meadow. They went back into the shade by the old foundation and ate lunch and drank from the spring. Then they lay down on the blanket and looked up at the sky. The wind came in whiffs along the edge of the blowdown, and the sweet smell of the raspberry patch drifted across them. Away down along the view that this house had had once, the lake looked more than ever like a mirror tipped against the hills. Below the village Donald Swain's white house and round red barn were strung on a white thread of road.

Perley rolled over on his side and looked at his wife. "I guess I never asked you," he said, "how you were getting along."

"I get along all right."

"You don't want me to sell any cows?"

"You know you wouldn't want to do that. You were just getting the herd built up."

"A herd's no good if you can't get help."

"People are good about helping," she said.

"What'll you do when there ain't any more people around? Seems like half the place has gone down country or into the army already."

"It's been going since the Civil War," Alma said, "and still there always seems to be somebody around to neighbor with."

He rolled onto his back again and plucked a spear of grass. "We should be haying," he said, "right now."

"Sunday," she said.

"Sunday or no Sunday. There's still those two top meadows. Those city kids you got can't get all that hay in."

"All they need is somebody to keep 'em from raring back in the breeching," Alma said. "I'll be behind with a pitchfork if I have to."

"I can see you."

She did not stir from her comfortable sprawl, but her voice went up crisply. "You thought we ought to sell when you got called up," she said. "Well, you've been gone going on a year, and hasn't anything gone wrong, has there? Got seven new calves, an't you? Milk checks have got bigger, an't they? Learned to drive the tractor and the car, didn't I? Got ten run of wood coming from DeSerres for the loan of the team, an't we, and saved the price of feed all that time last winter."

"Allen Swain can't make it go," Perley said.

"His farm don't lay as good as ours, and he's got a mortgage," she said. "Mortgage," the way she said it, sounded like an incurable disease. She half rose on her elbow to look at him. "And I ain't Allen Swain, either."

"So you want to be a farmer."

"I am," she said.

Perley picked another stem of grass and grinned up into the tops of the maples. They had been growing densely before the hurricane, and the going down of trees on every side had left them standing tall and spindly. The wind went through their leaves high up, a good stiff wind that bent and threshed their tops, but only a creeping breath disturbed the grass below. It was like lying deep down in a soft, warm, sweet-smelling nest.

"Laying here, you wouldn't think anything could ever touch you," he said. "Wind could blow up there like all get-out, and you'd never feel it." Alma's hand fell across his chest, and he captured it. "Unless you stuck your head out," he said.

For a while he lay feeling the pulse in her wrist.

"Smell them raspberries?" he said once, and squirmed his shoulders more comfortable against the ground. "There ain't anything smells sweeter, even flowers." Alma said nothing.

"Funny about a berry patch," he said. "Nobody ever plowed it, or

planted it, or cultivated it, or fertilized it, or limed it, but there it is.
You couldn't grub it out if you tried. More you plow it up, the more
berries there is next year. Burn it over, it's up again before anything
else. Blow everything down, that's just what it likes."

He filled his lungs with the ripe berry odor and let the breath bubble
out between his lips. "Don't seem as if you'd ever have to move," he
said. "Just lay here and reach up and pick a mouthful and then lay some
more and let the wind blow over way up there and you never even feel
it."

"It's nice," Alma said. "I didn't hardly think the blueberries would
be ripe yet, it's been so rainy."

"Makes you think the world's all right," Perley said, "the way they
come along every year, rain or shine."

Alma stirred. "We better get busy," she said. "Some gooseberries,
too, if you'd like some."

"Might use a pie," he said. He sat up and stretched for the pails.
There were only the granite kettle and the two-quart milk pail left.
"You lay still," he said. "I'll get some."

" 'Tisn't as if I needed a rest," she said. "Here I've been just having
fun all day."

"Well, take the kettle then. It's easier to pick into." He picked up
the milk pail.

"Perley," Alma said.

"Uh?"

"This is what you want to do, isn't it? I mean, you wouldn't rather
go see somebody?"

He watched her steadily. "Why?"

"Well, it's only two more days. I just—"

"I already saw everybody I want to see," he said. "I was saving the
last couple days."

"Well, all right," she said, and went into the blowdown with the
kettle.

He picked very fast, wanting to surprise her with how many he had,
and when after a half-hour he worked back toward the side where she
was picking he had the pail filled and overflowing, mounded an inch
above the brim. He liked the smell of his hand when he scratched his
nose free of a tickling cobweb. For a moment he stood, turning his face
upward to watch the unfelt upper-air wind thresh through the tops of
the maples, and then he came up softly behind Alma where she bent

far in against a root table to reach a loaded vine. He bent in after her and kissed the back of her neck.

"How're you doing?" she said, and worked her way out. Her shirt was unbuttoned halfway down, her throat was brown even in the hollow above where her collarbones joined, and her eyes sought his with that anxiety to know that he was content, that he was doing what he wanted to do, which she had shown all the time of his furlough. "I got quite a mess," she said, and showed the berries in her pail. "How about you?"

"All I want," Perley said. He was watching the sun dapple the brown skin of her throat as the wind bent the thin tops of the maples. "I wouldn't want any more," he said.

THE
WOMEN
ON THE
WALL

The corner window of the study overlooked a lawn, and beyond that a sunken lane between high pines, and beyond the lane a point of land with the old beach club buildings at one end and a stone wall around its tip. Beyond the point, through the cypresses and eucalyptuses, Mr. Palmer could see the Pacific, misty blue, belted between shore and horizon with a band of brown kelp.

Writing every morning in his study, making over his old notebooks into a coherent account of his years on the Galápagos, Mr. Palmer could glance up from his careful longhand and catch occasional glimpses, as a traveler might glance out of the window of a moving train. And in spite of the rather special atmosphere of the point, caused by the fact that until the past year it had been a club, there was something homey and neighborly and pleasant about the place that Mr. Palmer liked. There were children, for one thing, and dogs drifting up and down, and the occasional skirr of an automobile starting in the quiet, the diminishing sound of tires on asphalt, the distant racket of a boy being a machine-gun with his mouth.

Mr. Palmer had been away from the States a long time; he found the noises on the point familiar and nostalgic and reassuring in this time of war, and felt as if he had come home. Though California differed considerably from his old home in Ohio, he fell naturally and gratefully into its procession of morning and afternoon, its neighborhood routines, the pleasant breathing of its tides. When anything outside broke in upon his writing, it was generally a commonplace and familiar thing; Mr. Palmer looked up and took pleasure in the interruption.

One thing he could be sure of seeing, every morning but Sunday. The section was outside the city limits, and mail was delivered to a battery of mailboxes where the sunken lane joined the street. The mail arrived at about eleven; about ten-thirty the women from the beach club apartments began to gather on the stone wall. Below the wall was the beach, where the tides leaned in all the way from Iwo and Okinawa. Above it was the row of boxes where as regularly as the tide the mail carrier came in a gray car and deposited postmarked flotsam from half a world away.

Sometimes Mr. Palmer used to pause in his writing and speculate on what these women thought of when they looked out across the gumdrop-blue water and the brown kelp and remembered that across this un-interrupted ocean their husbands fought and perhaps bled and possibly died, that in those far islands it was already tomorrow, that the green water breaking against the white foot of the beach might hold in sus-pension minute quantities of the blood shed into it thousands of miles away, that the Japan Current, swinging in a great circle up under the Aleutians and back down the American coast, might as easily bear the mingled blood or the floating relics of a loved one lost as it could bear the glass balls of Japanese net-floats that it sometimes washed ashore.

Watching the women, with their dogs and children, waiting patiently on the stone wall for that most urgent of all the gods, that Mercury in the gray uniform, Mr. Palmer thought a good deal about Penelope on the rocky isle of Ithaca above the wine-dark sea. He got a little senti-mental about these women. Sometimes he was almost frightened by the air of patient, withdrawn seriousness they wore as they waited, and the unsmiling alacrity with which they rose and crowded around the mailman when he came. And when the mail was late, and one or two of them sat out on the wall until eleven-thirty, twelve, sometimes twelve-thirty, Mr. Palmer could hardly bear it at all.

Waiting, Mr. Palmer reflected, must cause a person to remove to a separate and private world. Like sleep or insanity, waiting must have the faculty of making the real unreal and remote. It seemed to Mr. Palmer pathetic and somehow thrilling that these women should have followed their men to the very brink of the West, and should remain here now with their eyes still westward, patiently and faithfully suspending their own normal lives until the return of their husbands. Without knowing any of the women, Mr. Palmer respected and admired them. They did not invite his pity. Penelope was as competent for her waiting as Ulysses was for his wars and wiles.

Mr. Palmer had been working in his new house hardly a week before he found himself putting on his jacket about eleven and going out to join the women.

He knew them all by sight just from looking out the window. The red-haired woman with the little boy was sitting on the wall nearest him. Next was the thin girl who always wore a bathing suit and went barefooted. Next was the dark-haired one, five or six months pregnant. And next to her was the florid, quick, wrenlike woman with the little girl of about five. Their faces all turned as Mr. Palmer came up.

"Good morning," he said.

The red-haired woman's plain, serious, freckled face acknowledged him, and she murmured good morning. The girl in the bathing suit had turned to look off over the ocean, and Mr. Palmer felt that she had not made any reply. The pregnant girl and the woman with the little girl both nodded.

The old man put his hands on his knees, rounded his mouth and eyes, and bent to look at the little boy hanging to the red-haired woman's hand. "Well!" he said. "Hi, young fella!"

The child stared at him, crowding against his mother's legs. The mother said nothing, and rather than push first acquaintance too far, Mr. Palmer walked on along the wall. As he glanced at the thin girl, he met her eyes, so full of cold hostility that for a moment he was shocked. He had intended to sit down in the middle of the wall, but her look sent him on further, to sit between the pregnant girl and the wrenlike woman.

"These beautiful mornings!" Mr. Palmer said, sitting down with a sigh.

The wrenlike woman nodded; the pregnant one regarded him with quiet ox-eyes.

"This is quite a ritual, waiting for the mail," Mr. Palmer said. He pointed to the gable of his house across the lane. "I see you from my window over there, congregating on the wall here every morning."

The wrenlike woman looked at him rather oddly, then leaped to prevent her daughter from putting out the eyes of the long-suffering setter she was mauling. The pregnant girl smiled a slow, soft smile. Over her shoulder Mr. Palmer saw the thin girl hitch herself up and sit on her hands. The expression on her face said that she knew very well why Mr. Palmer had come down and butted in, and why he watched from his window.

"The sun's so warm out here," the pregnant girl said. "It's a way of killing part of the morning, sitting out here."

"A very good way," Mr. Palmer said. He smoothed the creases in his trousers, finding speech a little difficult. From the shelter of his mother's legs the two-year-old boy down the wall stared at him solemnly. Then the wrenlike woman hopped off the wall and dusted her skirt.

"Here he is!" she said.

They all started across the mouth of the lane, and for some reason, as they waited for the mailman to sort and deliver, Mr. Palmer felt that his first introduction hadn't taken him very far. In a way, as he thought it over, he respected the women for that, too. They were living without their husbands, and had to be careful. After all, Penelope had many suitors. But he could not quite get over wanting to spank the thin girl on her almost-exposed backside, and he couldn't quite shake the sensation of having wandered by mistake into the ladies' rest room.

After that, without feeling that he knew them at all, he respected them and respected their right to privacy. Waiting, after all, put you in an exclusive club. No outsider had any more right on that wall than he had in the company of a bomber crew. But Mr. Palmer felt that he could at least watch from his window, and at the mailboxes he could, almost by osmosis, pick up a little more information.

The red-haired woman's name was Kendall. Her husband was an Army captain, a doctor. The thin girl, Mrs. Fisher, got regular letters bearing a Marine Corps return. The husband of Mrs. Corson, the wrenlike woman, commanded a flotilla of minesweepers in the western Pacific. Of the pregnant girl, Mrs. Vaughn, Mr. Palmer learned little. She got few letters and none with any postmarks that told anything.

From his study window Mr. Palmer went on observing them benignly and making additions to his notes on the profession of waiting. Though the women differed sharply one from another, they seemed to Mr. Palmer to have one thing in common: they were all quiet, peaceful, faithful to the times and seasons of their vigil, almost like convalescents in a hospital. They made no protests or outcries; they merely lived at a reduced tempo, as if pulse rate and respiration rate and metabolic rate and blood pressure were all turned down. Mr. Palmer had a notion how it might be. Sometimes when he awoke very quietly in the night he could feel how quietly and slowly and regularly his heart was pumping, how slow and regular his breathing was, how he lay there mute and cool and inert with everything turned down to idling speed, his old body taking care of itself. And when he woke that way he had a curious feeling that he was waiting for something.

Every morning at ten-thirty, as regular as sun and tide, Mrs. Kendall came out of the beach club apartments and walked across the point, leading her little boy by the hand. She had the child turned down, too, apparently. He never, to Mr. Palmer's knowledge, ran or yelled or cried or made a fuss, but walked quietly beside his mother, and sat with her on the big stump until five minutes to eleven, and then walked with her across to the end of the stone wall. About that time the other women began to gather, until all four of them were there in a quiet, uncommunicative row.

Through the whole spring the tides leaned inward with the same slow inevitability, the gray car came around and stopped by the battery of mailboxes, the women gathered on the wall as crows gather to a rookery at dusk.

Only once in all that drowsy spring was there any breaking of the pattern. That was one Monday after Mr. Palmer had been away for the weekend. When he strolled out at mailtime he found the women not sitting on the wall, but standing in a nervous conversational group. They opened to let him in, for once accepting him silently among them, and he found that the thin girl had moved out suddenly the day before: the Saturday mail had brought word that her husband had gone down in flames over the Marianas.

The news depressed Mr. Palmer in curious ways. It depressed him to see the women shaken from their phlegmatic routine, because the moment they were so shaken they revealed the raw fear under their quiet. And it depressed him that the thin girl's husband had been killed. That tragedy should come to a woman he personally felt to be a snob, a fool, a vain and inconsequent chit, seemed to him sad and incongruous and even exasperating. As long as she was one of the company of Penelopes, Mr. Palmer had refused to dislike her. The moment she made demands upon his pity he disliked her very much.

After that sudden blow, as if a hawk had struck among the quiet birds on the wall, Mr. Palmer found it less pleasant to watch the slow, heavy-bodied walking of Mrs. Kendall, her child always tight by the hand, from apartment to stump to wall. Unless spoken to, she never spoke. She wore gingham dresses that were utterly out of place in the white sun above the white beach. She was plain, unattractive, patient, the most remote, the most tuned-down, the quietest and saddest and most patient and most exasperating of the Penelopes. She too began to make wry demands on Mr. Palmer's pity, and he found himself almost disliking her. He was guilty of a little prayer that Mrs. Kendall's husband would be spared, so that his pity would not have to go any farther than it did.

Then one morning Mr. Palmer became aware of another kind of interruption on the point. Somebody there had apparently bought a new dog. Whoever had acquired it must have fed it, though Mr. Palmer never saw anyone do so, and must have exercised it, though he never saw that either. All he saw was that the dog, a half-grown cocker, was tied to the end of a rose trellis in the clubhouse yard. And all he heard, for two solid days, was the uproar the dog made.

It did not like being tied up. It barked, and after a while its voice would break into a kind of hysterical howling mixed with shuddering diminuendo groans. Nobody ever came and told it to be still, or took care of it, or let it loose. It stayed there and yanked on its rope and chewed at the trellis post and barked and howled and groaned until Mr. Palmer's teeth were on edge and he was tempted to call the Humane Society.

Actually he didn't, because on the third morning the noise had stopped, and as he came into his study to begin working he saw that the dog was gone. Mrs. Corson was sitting in a lawn chair under one of the cypresses, and her daughter was digging in the sandpile. There was no sign either of Mrs. Kendall or Mrs. Vaughn. The owner of the house was raking leaves on the lawn above the seawall.

Mr. Palmer looked at his watch. It was nine-thirty. On an impulse he slipped on a jacket and went down and out across the lawn and down across the lane and up the other side past the trellis. Where the dog had lain the ground was strewn with chewed green splinters.

Mrs. Corson looked up from her chair. Her cheeks were painted with a hatchwork of tiny ruddy veins, and her eyes looked as if she hadn't slept. They had a stary blankness like blind eyes, and Mr. Palmer noticed that the pupils were dilated, even in the bright light. She took a towel and a pack of cigarettes and a bar of coco-butter off the chair next to her.

"Good morning," she said in her husky voice. "Sit down."

"Thank you," Mr. Palmer said. He let himself down into the steeply slanting wooden chair and adjusted the knees of his slacks. "It *is* a good morning," he said slyly. "So quiet."

Mrs. Corson's thin neck jerked upward and backward in a curious gesture. Her throaty laughter was loud and unrestrained, and the eyes she turned on Mr. Palmer were red with mirth.

"That damned dog," she said. "Wasn't that something?"

"I thought I'd go crazy," Mr. Palmer said. "Whose dog was it, anyway?"

Mrs. Corson's rather withered, red-nailed hand, with a big diamond and a wedding ring on the fourth finger, reached down and picked up the cigarettes. The hand trembled as it held the pack out.

"No, thank you," he said.

Mrs. Corson took one. "It was Mrs. Kendall's dog," she said. "She took it back."

"Thank God!" said Mr. Palmer.

Her hands nervous with the matchbox in her lap, Mrs. Corson sat and smoked. Mr. Palmer saw that her lips, under the lipstick, were chapped, and that there was a dried, almost leathery look to her tanned and freckled skin.

He slid deeper into the chair and looked out over the water, calm as a lake, the long light swells breaking below him with a quiet, lulling swish. Up the coast heavier surf was breaking farther out. Its noise came like a pulsating tremble on the air, hardly a sound at all. Everything tuned down, Mr. Palmer was thinking. Even the lowest frequency of waves on the beach. Even the ocean waited.

"I should think you'd bless your stars, having a place like this to wait in," he said.

One of Mrs. Corson's eyebrows bent. She shot him a sideward look.

"Think of the women who are waiting in boardinghouse rooms," Mr.

Palmer said, a little irritated at her manner. "Think of the ones who are working and leaving their children in nurseries."

"Oh, sure," Mrs. Corson said. "It's fine for Anne, with the beach and yard."

Mr. Palmer leaned on the arm of the chair and looked at her quizzically. He wished any of these women would ever put away their reticence and talk about their waiting, because that was where their life lay, that was where they had authority. "How long has your husband been gone?" he asked.

"Little over two years."

"That's a long time," Mr. Palmer said, thinking of Penelope and her wait. Ten years while the war went on at Troy, ten more years while Ulysses wandered through every peril in the Mediterranean, past Scylla and Charybdis and Circe and the Cyclops and the iron terrors of Hades and the soft temptations of Nausicaa. But that was poetry. Twenty years was too much. Two, in all conscience, was enough.

"I shouldn't kick," the woman said. "Mrs. Kendall's husband has been gone for over three."

"I've noticed her," Mr. Palmer said. "She seems rather sad and repressed."

For a moment Mrs. Corson's eyes, slightly bloodshot, the pupils dilated darkly, were fixed questioningly on Mr. Palmer's. Then the woman shook herself almost as a dog does. "I guess," she said. She rose with a nervous snap and glanced at her watch. From the sandpile the little girl called, "Is it time, Mommy?"

"I guess so," Mrs. Corson said. She laid the back of her hand across her eyes and made a face.

"I'll be getting along," Mr. Palmer said.

"I was just taking Anne down for her pony ride. Why don't you ride down with us?"

"Well . . ."

"Come on," Mrs. Corson said. "We'll be back in less than an hour."

The child ran ahead of them and opened the car doors, down in the widened part of the lane. As Mr. Palmer helped Mrs. Corson in she turned her face a little, and he smelled the stale alcohol on her breath. Obviously Mrs. Corson had been drinking the night before, and obviously she was a little hung over.

But my Lord, why not? he said to himself. Two years of waiting, nothing to do but sit and watch and do nothing and be patient. He didn't like Mrs. Corson any less for occasional drinking. She was higher-strung than either Mrs. Vaughn or Mrs. Kendall. You could almost lift up the cover board and pluck her nerves like the strings of a piano. Even so, she played the game well. He liked her.

At the pony track Anne raced down the fenced runway at a pink fluttering gallop, and Mr. Palmer and Mrs. Corson, following more slowly, found her debating between a black and a pinto pony.

"Okay," the man in charge said. "Which'll it be today, young lady?"

"I don't know," the girl said. Her forehead wrinkled. "Mommy, which do you think?"

"I don't care, hon," her mother said. "Either one is nice."

Pretty, her blonde braids hanging in front and framing her odd pre-Raphaelite face, Anne stood indecisive. She turned her eyes up to Mr. Palmer speculatively. "The black one's nice," she said, "but so's the . . ."

"Oh, Anne," her mother said. "For heaven's sake make up your mind."

"Well . . . the black one, then," Anne said. She reached out a hand and touched the pony's nose, pulling her fingers back sharply and looking up at her mother with a smile that Mr. Palmer found himself almost yearning over.

"You're a nitwit," her mother said. "Hop on, so we can get back for the mailman."

The attendant swung her up, but with one leg over the saddle Anne kicked and screamed to get down. "I've changed my mind," she said. "Not this one, the pinto one."

The attendant put her up on the pinto and Mrs. Corson, her chapped lips trembling, said, "Another outburst like that and you won't get on any, you little . . . !"

The pony started, led by the attendant who rocked on one thick-soled shoe. For a moment Mrs. Corson and Mr. Palmer stood in the sun under the sign that said "Pony Rides, 10 Cents, 12 for $1.00." They were, Mr. Palmer noticed, in the Mexican part of town. Small houses, some of them almost shacks, with geraniums climbing all over them, strung out along the street. Down on the corner beyond the car was a tavern with a dusty tin sign. Mrs. Corson unsnapped her purse and fished out a wadded bill and held it vaguely in her hand, looking off up the street past the track and the pinto pony and the pink little huddle on its back and the attendant rocking along ahead on his one thick shoe.

"I wonder," she said. "Would you do me a favor?"

"Anything."

"Would you stay here five minutes while I go to the store? Just keep an eye on her?"

"Of course," he said. "I'd be glad to go to the store for you, if you'd like."

"No," she said. "No, I'd better get it." She put the crumpled bill into his hand. "Let her have all the rides she wants. I'll be back in a few minutes."

Mr. Palmer settled himself on a chair against the stable wall and waited. When Anne and the attendant got back he waved the bill at them. "Want another ride?"

"Yes!" Anne said. Her hands were clenched tightly in the pony's mane, and her eyes danced and her mouth was a little open. The attendant turned and started down the track again. "Run!" Anne cried to him. "Make him run!"

The crippled hostler broke into a clumsy hop-skip-and-jump for a few yards, pulling the pony into a trot. The girl screamed with delight. Mr. Palmer yawned, tapped his mouth, smiled a little as he smelled the powder-and-perfume smell on the dollar bill, yawned again. Say what you would, it was decent of the woman to come out with a hangover and take her child to the pony track. She must feel pretty rocky, if her eyes were any criterion.

He waited for some time. Anne finished a second ride, took a third, finished that, and had a fourth. The attendant was sweating a little. From the fence along the sidewalk two Negro children and a handful of little Mexicans watched. "How about it?" Mr. Palmer said. "Want another?"

She nodded, shaken with giggles and sudden shyness when she looked around and found her mother gone.

"Sure you're not getting sore?" Mr. Palmer patted his haunch suggestively.

She shook her head.

"Okay," the hostler said. "Here we go again, then."

At the end of the fifth ride Anne let herself be lifted off. The hostler went inside and sat down, the pony joined its companion at the rail, cocked its hip and tipped its right hoof and closed its eyes. Anne climbed up into Mr. Palmer's lap.

"Where's Mommy?"

"She went to buy something."

"Darn her," Anne said. "She does that all the time. She better hurry up, it's getting mailtime."

"Don't you like to miss the mail?"

"Sometimes there's packages and things from Daddy," Anne said. "I got a grass skirt once."

Mr. Palmer rounded his mouth and eyes. "You must like your daddy."

"I do. Mommy doesn't, though."

"What?"

"Mommy gets mad," Anne said. "She thinks Daddy could have had shore duty a long time ago, he's had so much combat, but she says he likes the Navy better than home. He's a commander."

"Yes, I know," Mr. Palmer said. He looked up the street, beginning to be fretful. The fact that the woman spent her whole life waiting shouldn't make her quite so callous to how long she kept other people waiting. "We *are* going to miss the mailman if your mommy doesn't hurry," he said.

Anne jumped off his lap and puckered her lips like her mother. "And today's a package!"

Mr. Palmer raised his eyebrows. "How do you know?"

"The fortune teller told Mommy."

"I see," the old man said. "Does your mother go to fortune tellers often?"

"Every Saturday," Anne said. "I went with her once. You know what she said? And it came true, too."

Mr. Palmer saw the girl's mother coming down the sidewalk, and stood up. "Here comes Mommy," he said. "We'd better meet her at the car."

"She said we'd get good news, and right away Daddy was promoted," Anne said. "And she said we'd get a package, and that week we got *three*!"

Mrs. Corson was out of breath. In the bright sun her eyes burned with a curious sightless brilliance. The smell of alcohol on her was fresher and stronger.

"I'm sorry," she said as she got in. "I met a friend, and it was so hot we stopped for a beer."

On the open highway, going back home, she stepped down hard on the throttle, and her fingers kept clasping and unclasping the wheel. Her body seemed possessed of electric energy. She radiated something, she gave off sparks. Her eyes, with the immense dark pupils and suffused whites, were almost scary.

When they pulled up and parked in front of Mr. Palmer's gate, opposite the mailboxes, the little red flags on some of the boxes were still up. On the stone wall sat Mrs. Kendall, her son, Tommy, and the pregnant girl, Mrs. Vaughn. "Late again," Mrs. Corson said. "Damn that man."

"Can I play, Mommy?" Anne said.

"Okay." As the child climbed out, the mother said, "Don't get into any fixes with Tommy. Remember what I told you."

"I will," Anne said. Her setter came up and she stooped to pull its ears.

Her mother's face went pinched and mean. "And stop abusing that dog!" she said.

Mr. Palmer hesitated. He was beginning to feel uncomfortable, and he thought of the pages he might have filled that morning, and the hour that still remained before noon. But Mrs. Corson was leaning back with the back of her hand across her eyes. Through the windshield Mr. Palmer could see the two women and the child on the wall, like a multiple Patience on a monument. When he looked back at Mrs. Corson he saw that she too was watching them between her fingers. Quite suddenly she began to laugh.

She laughed for a good minute, not loudly but with curious violence, her whole body shaking. She dabbed her eyes and caught her breath and shook her head and tried to speak. Mr. Palmer attended uneasily, wanting to be gone.

"Lord," Mrs. Corson said finally. "Look at 'em. Vultures on a limb. Me too. Three mama vultures and one baby vulture."

"You're a little hard on yourself," Mr. Palmer said, smiling. "And Anne, I'd hardly call her a vulture."

"I didn't include her," Mrs. Corson said. She turned her hot red eyes on him. "She's got sense enough to run and play, and I hope I've got sense enough to let her."

"Well, but little Tommy . . ."

"Hasn't had his hand out of mamma's since they came here," Mrs. Corson said. "Did you ever see him play with anybody?"

Mr. Palmer confessed that he hadn't, now that he thought of it.

"Because if you ever do," Mrs. Corson said, "call out all the preachers. It'll be Christ come the second time. Honest to God, sometimes that woman . . ."

Bending forward, Mr. Palmer could see Mrs. Kendall smoothing the blue sweater around her son's waist. "I've wondered about her," he said, and stopped. Mrs. Corson had started to laugh again.

When she had finished her spasm of tight, violent mirth, she said, "It isn't her child, you know."

"No?" he said, surprised. "She takes such care of it."

"You're not kidding," Mrs. Corson said. "She won't let him play with Anne. Anne's too dirty. She digs in the ground and stuff. Seven months we've lived in the same house, and those kids haven't played together once. Can you imagine that?"

"No," Mr. Palmer confessed. "I can't."

"She adopted it when it was six months old," Mrs. Corson said. "She tells us all it's a love-child." Her laugh began again, a continuous, hiccoughy chuckle. "Never lets go its hand," she said. "Won't let him play with anybody. Wipes him off like an heirloom. And brags around he's a love-child. My God!"

With her thin, freckled arm along the door and her lips puckered, she fell silent. "Love-child!" she said at last. "Did you ever look at her flat face? It's the last place love would ever settle on."

"Perhaps that explains," Mr. Palmer said uncomfortably. "She's childless, she's unattractive. She pours all that frustrated affection out on this child."

Mrs. Corson twisted to look almost incredulously into his face. "Of course," she said. Her alcoholic breath puffed at him. "Of course. But why toot it up as a love-child?" she said harshly. "What does she think my child is, for God's sake? How does she think babies are made?"

"Well, but there's that old superstition," Mr. Palmer said. He moved his hand sideward. "Children born of passion, you know—they're supposed to be more beautiful . . ."

"And doesn't that tell you anything about her?" Mrs. Corson said. "Doesn't that show you that she never thought of passion in the same world with her husband? She has to go outside herself for any passion, there's none in her."

"Yes," Mr. Palmer said. "Well, of course one can speculate, but one hardly knows . . ."

"And that damned dog," Mrs. Corson said. "Tommy can't play with other kids. They're too dirty. So she gets a dog. Dogs are cleaner than Anne, see? So she buys her child this nice germless dog, and then ties him up and won't let him loose. So the dog howls his head off, and we all go nuts. Finally we told her we couldn't stand it, why didn't she let it loose and let it run. But she said it might run away, and Tommy loved it so she didn't want to take a chance on losing the pup. So I finally called the Society for the Prevention of Cruelty to Animals, and they told her either to give it regular running and exercise or take it back. She took it back last night, and now she hates me."

As she talked, saliva had gathered in the corner of her mouth. She sucked it in and turned her head away, looking out on the street. "Lord God," she said. "So it goes, so it goes."

Through the windshield Mr. Palmer watched the quiet women on the wall, the quiet, well-behaved child. Anne was romping with the setter around the big stump, twenty feet beyond, and the little boy was watching her. It was a peaceful, windless morning steeped in sun. The mingled smell of pines and low tide drifted across the street, and was replaced by the pervading faint fragrance of ceanothus, blooming in shades of blue and white along Mr. Palmer's walk.

"I'm amazed," he said. "She seems so quiet and relaxed and plain."

"That's another thing," Mrs. Corson said. "She's a cover-yourself-up girl, too. Remember Margy Fisher, whose husband was killed a few weeks ago? You know why she never wore anything but a bathing suit? Because this old biddy was always after her about showing herself."

"Well, it's certainly a revelation," Mr. Palmer said. "I see you all from my window, you know, and it seems like a kind of symphony of waiting, all quiet and harmonious. The pregnant girl, too—going on with the slow inevitable business of life while her husband's gone, the rhythm of the generations unchanged. I've enjoyed the whole thing, like a pageant, you know."

"Your window isn't a very good peek-hole," Mrs. Corson said drily.

"Mm?"

"Hope's husband was killed at Dieppe," said Mrs. Corson.

For a moment Mr. Palmer did not catch on. At first he felt only a flash of pity as he remembered the girl's big steady brown eyes, her still, rather sad face, her air of pliant gentleness. Then the words Mrs. Corson had spoken began to take effect. Dieppe—almost three years ago. And the girl six months pregnant.

He wished Mrs. Corson would quit drumming her red nails on the car door. She was really in a state this morning, nervous as a cat. But that poor girl, sitting over there with all that bottled up inside of her, the fear and uncertainty growing as fast as the child in her womb grew . . .

"Some naval lieutenant," Mrs. Corson said. "He's right in the middle of the fighting, gunnery officer on a destroyer. You ought to hear Hope when she gets scared he'll never come back and make a decent woman of her."

"I'd not like to," Mr. Palmer said, and shook his head. Across the lane the placid scene had not changed, except that Mrs. Kendall had let Tommy toddle fifteen feet out from the wall, where he was picking up clusters of dry pine needles and throwing them into the air.

The figures were very clean, sharp-edged in the clear air against the blue backdrop of sea. An Attic grace informed all of them: the girl stooping above the long-eared red setter, the child with his hands in the air, tossing brown needles in a shower, the curving seated forms of the women on the wall. To Mr. Palmer's momentarily tranced eyes they seemed to freeze in attitudes of flowing motion like figures on a vase, cameo-clear in the clear air under the noble trees, with the quiet ocean of their watchfulness stretching blue to the misty edge. Like figures on a Grecian urn they curved in high relief above the white molding of the wall, and a drift of indescribable melancholy washed across the point and pricked goose-pimples on Mr. Palmer's arms. "It's sad," he said, opening the door and stepping down. "The whole thing is very sad."

With the intention of leaving he put his hand on the door and pushed it shut, thinking that he did not want to stay longer and hear Mrs. Corson's bitter tongue and watch the women on the wall. Their waiting now, with the momentary trance broken and the momentary lovely group dispersed in motion, seemed to him a monstrous aberration, their patience a deathly apathy, their hope an obscene self-delusion.

He was filled with a sense of the loveliness of the white paper and the cleanly sharpened pencils, the notebooks and the quiet and the sense of purpose that waited in his study. Most of all the sense of purpose, the thing to be done that would have an ending and a result.

"It's been very pleasant," he said automatically. At that moment there came a yowl from the point.

He turned. Apparently Anne, romping with the dog, had bumped Tommy and knocked him down. He sat among the pine needles in his blue play-suit and squalled, and Mrs. Kendall came swiftly out from the wall and took Anne by the arm, shaking her.

"You careless child!" she said. "Watch what you're doing!"

Instantly Mrs. Corson was out of the car. Mr. Palmer saw her start for the point, her lips puckered, and was reminded of some mechanical toy tightly wound and tearing erratically around a room giving off sparks of ratchety noise. When she was twenty feet from Mrs. Kendall she shouted hoarsely, "Let go of that child!"

Mrs. Kendall's heavy gingham body turned. Her plain face, the mouth stiff with anger, confronted Mrs. Corson. Her hand still held Anne's arm. "It's possible to train children . . ." she said..

"Yes, and it's possible to mistreat them," Mrs. Corson said. "Let go of her."

For a moment neither moved. Then Mrs. Corson's hands darted down, caught Mrs. Kendall's wrist, and tore her hold from Anne's arm. Even across the lane, fifty feet away, Mr. Palmer could see the white fury in their faces as they confronted each other.

"If I had the bringing up of that child . . . !" Mrs. Kendall said. "I'd . . ."

"You'd tie her to your apron strings like you've tied your own," Mrs. Corson said. "Like you tie up a dog and expect it to get used to three feet of space. My God, a child's a little animal. He's got to run!"

"And knock other children down, I suppose."

"Oh, my God!" Mrs. Corson said, and turned her thin face skyward as if to ask God to witness. She was shaking all over; Mr. Palmer could see the trembling of her dress. "Listen!" she said, "I don't know what's the matter with you, and why you can't stand nakedness, and why you think a bastard child is something holier than a legitimate one, and why you hang on to that child as if he was worth his weight in diamonds. But you keep your claws off mine, and if your little bastard can't get out of the way, you can just . . ."

Mrs. Kendall's face was convulsed. She raised both hands above her head, stuttering for words. From the side the pregnant girl slipped in quietly, and Mr. Palmer, rooted uneasily across the lane, heard her quiet voice. "You're beginning to draw a crowd," she said. "For the love of Mike, turn it down."

Mrs. Corson swung on her. Her trembling had become an ecstasy. When she spoke she chewed loudly on her words, mangling them almost beyond recognition. "You keep out of this, you pregnant bitch," she said. "Any time I want advice on how to raise love-children, I'll come to you too, but right now I haven't got any love-children, and I'm raising what I've got my own way."

A window had gone up in the house next to Mr. Palmer's, and three boys were drifting curiously down the street, their pants sagging with the weight of armament they carried. Without hesitating more than a moment, Mr. Palmer crossed the street and cut them off. "I think you'd better beat it," he said, and pushed his hands in the air as if shooing chickens. The boys stopped and eyed him suspiciously, then began edging around the side. It was clear that in any contest of speed, agility, endurance, or anything else Mr. Palmer was no match for them. He put his hand in his pocket and pulled out some change. The boys stopped. Behind him Mr. Palmer heard the saw-edged voice of Mrs. Corson. "I'm not the kind of person that'll stand it, by God! If you want to . . ."

"Here," Mr. Palmer said. "Here's a quarter apiece if you light out and forget anything you saw."

"Okay!" they said, and stepped up one by one and got their quarters and retreated, their heads together and their armed hips clanking together and their faces turning once, together, to stare back at the arguing women on the point. Up the street Mr. Palmer saw a woman and three small children standing in the road craning. Mrs. Corson's voice carried for half a mile.

In the hope that his own presence would bring her to reason, Mr. Palmer walked across the lane. Mrs. Corson's puckered, furious face was thrust into Mrs. Kendall's, and she was saying, "Just tell me to my face I don't raise my child right! Go on, tell me so. Tell me what you told Margy, that Anne's too dirty for your bastard to play with. Tell me, I dare you, and I'll tear your tongue out!"

Mr. Palmer found himself standing next to Mrs. Vaughn. He glanced at her once and shook his head and cleared his throat. Mrs. Corson continued to glare into the pale flat face before her. When Mrs. Kendall turned heavily and walked toward the wall, the wrenlike woman skipped nimbly around her and confronted her from the other side. "You've got a lot of things to criticize in me!" she said. Her voice, suddenly, was so hoarse it was hardly more than a whisper. "Let's hear you say them to my face. I've heard them behind my back too long. Let's hear you say them!"

"Couldn't we get her into the house?" Mr. Palmer said to the pregnant girl. "She'll raise the whole neighborhood."

"Let her disgrace herself," Mrs. Vaughn said, and shrugged.

"But you don't understand," Mr. Palmer said. "She had a beer or so downtown, and I think that, that and the heat . . ."

The girl looked at him with wide brown eyes in which doubt and contempt and something like mirth moved like shadows on water. "I guess *you* don't understand," she said. "She isn't drunk. She's hopped."

"Hopped?"

"I thought you went downtown with her."

"I did."

"Did she leave you at the pony track?"

"Yes, for a few minutes."

"She goes to a joint down there," Mrs. Vaughn said. "Fortune telling in the front, goofballs and reefers in the rear. She's a sucker for all three."

"Goofballs?" Mr. Palmer said. "Reefers?"

"Phenobarb," Mrs. Vaughn said. "Marijuana. Anything. She doesn't care, long as she gets high. She's high as a kite now. Didn't you notice her eyes?"

Mrs. Kendall had got her boy by the hand. She was heavily ignoring Mrs. Corson. Now she lifted the child in her arms and turned sideways, like a cow ducking to the side to slip around a herder, and headed for the stone wall. Mrs. Corson whipped around her flanks, first on one side, then on the other, her hoarse whisper a continuing horror in Mr. Palmer's ears.

"What I ought to do," Mrs. Corson said, "is forbid Anne to even speak to that bastard of yours."

Mrs. Kendall bent and put the child on the ground and stood up. "Don't you call him that!" she shouted. "Oh, you vulgar, vicious, drunken, depraved woman! Leave me alone! Leave me alone, can't you?"

She burst into passionate tears. For a moment Mr. Palmer was terrified that they would come to blows and have to be pulled apart. He started forward, intending to take Mrs. Corson by the arm and lead her, forcefully if necessary, to the house. This disgraceful exhibition had gone on long enough. But the pregnant girl was ahead of him.

She walked past the glaring women and said over her shoulder, carelessly, "Mail's here."

Mr. Palmer caught his cue. He put out his hand to Anne, and walked her down across the mouth of the lane. He did not look back, but his ears were sharp for a renewal of the cat-fight. None came. By the time the man in gray had distributed the papers and magazines to all the battery of boxes, and was unstrapping the pack of letters, Mr. Palmer was aware without turning that both Mrs. Corson and Mrs. Kendall were in the background by the gray car, waiting quietly.

BALANCE
HIS,
SWING
YOURS

■   ■   ■

The ping of tennis rackets was a warm, summer-afternoon sound in the air as Mr. Hart came up through the hedge. He stopped to survey the grounds, the red roof of the hotel, the fans of coco palms graceful beyond the white wall. Past the wall the coral rock broke off in ledges to the beach, and beyond the sand was the incredible peacock water of the Gulf.

February. It was hard to imagine, with that sun, the brown skins of the bathers between the palms, the ping of rackets. The whole place, to Mr. Hart's Colorado eyes, was fantastic—hibiscus and bougainvillea and night-blooming jasmine. He squirmed his shoulders against the itching warmth of his first sunburn, caught the previous afternoon, and ruminated on the hardly believable thought that to many people this summer-in-February paradise was a commonplace thing.

The sound of tennis led him past the shuffleboard courts and around a backstop cascading with scarlet bougainvillea. A girl was playing with the pro, and beyond the court, in lawn chairs, lay two of the three people Mr. Hart had so far met. His reaction was immediate. Good.

Good it was the two boys, not the impossible Englishman who had descended on him at breakfast. He cut across the lawn toward them.

The young men in the chairs, one very blond, one dark and impressively profiled, did not stir. They lay in their swimming trunks, inert and sprawling, and when Mr. Hart asked, "Were you saving these other chairs?" they looked up indolently, two loafing demigods with mahogany hides. The blond one lifted his towel out of a chair, and Mr. Hart sat down with a sigh.

"What a place!" he said.

The blond one—Thomas, Mr. Hart remembered—turned his head. He seemed a pleasant sort of boy. "Like it?" he said.

Mr. Hart lifted his hands. "It's incredible. I had no idea—I've never been down before. Even the fishing boats coming in in the evening are a nice institution. Have you tried the fishing?"

"Once or twice," Thomas said. He slumped further down in his chair. Mr. Hart found a pack of cigarettes, stretched to pass them over Thomas' body. He got a shake of the head, no thanks, from the dark one, Tenney, but Thomas took one.

"I've been thinking I might hook up with a party," Mr. Hart said. "This water fascinates me. The water and these silly little mangrove islands. I've read about mangroves all my life—never saw one. Now I find they're not islands at all, not a spoonful of dirt in them, just clumps of ocean-going shrubs."

"Yeah," Thomas said. He lay with the cigarette between his lips, his eyes lidded like a lizard's against the sun. Tenney seemed to sleep.

"I guess I interrupted your siesta," Hart said. "I just can't get over this place. I'll keep quiet now."

"Not at all," Thomas said, but Mr. Hart leaned back and watched the tennis. He had no desire to intrude on people. And it was good tennis to watch, he admitted. But Eastern tennis, the rhythmical and somehow mechanical tennis of people who learned the game as a social accomplishment. In an obscure way he felt superior to it. He had learned in a different school, municipal hard courts, worn balls. Still, he felt he could lick three out of four of these mechanical marvels.

His eye was caught by Tenney's feet, big naked feet, arched like the feet of a statued Mercury and brown as stained wood, the leather thongs of the sandals coming up between great and second toes. They struck him as arrogant feet. The boy had a lordly air, sure enough. There was something really admirable in the way he and his companion lolled. This was their birthright, and their arrogance was simply acceptance of something perfectly natural and right.

The blond youth turned, and Mr. Hart nodded toward the court. "The girl has nice shots."

"One of these tennis drunkards," Thomas said. "Lives tennis twenty-four hours a day."

"I like to see that," Mr. Hart said. "I like to see people simply dissolve themselves in the thing that interests them. I can remember when I was that way about tennis myself."

"Oh," Thomas said. "You're a tennis player."

Mr. Hart shrugged deprecatingly. "Used to be, in a way. Haven't done much with it since college, just a game now and then."

"What college?"

"I grew up in the West," Mr. Hart said. "Went to the local cow college."

Tenney leaned toward them. "I hate to interrupt," he said, "but look what's bearing down on us."

He jerked a thumb. The impossible little Englishman, in his pink polo shirt, was walking springily on the balls of his feet down the path from the cocktail garden. "Oh, my God," Hart said.

The two were both looking at him. "Has he got to you, too?" Tenney said. His look of distaste had dissolved into cynical amusement.

"For an hour at breakfast," Hart said. "Why can't people like that go to Miami, where they belong? Maybe we ought to run."

They smiled their relaxed, indolent smiles. "Lie and take it," Thomas said. "That's the least painful way."

Mr. Hart slid down in his chair and prepared his muscles for the relaxed indifference with which this interloper would have to be met. "But what a blowhard!" he said. "Did you know he was being bombarded from all sides to write a play for Cornell? My God."

He shut up abruptly. In a moment the British voice—vulgar British voice, Mr. Hart thought—was right above him. "Ah," it said. "Taking a little sun?"

"Hello," Thomas said, pleasantly enough. Tenney looked up and nodded. So did Mr. Hart. It was a cool reception, but it wasn't cool enough, Mr. Hart thought, for this rhinoceros to feel it.

"Topping day for it," the Englishman said. He sat down and took out his pipe, watching the tennis game while he filled and lighted. His fingers, holding the blown-out match, waved gently back and forth.

"She's not bad, you know," he said conversationally. "Pity she doesn't have a sounder backhand."

Mr. Hart regarded him coldly. "What's wrong with her backhand?" he said.

"Not enough follow-through," the Englishman said. "And she's hitting it too much on the rise."

Tenney said, grunting from his slumped chest. "She ought to be told."

The Englishman took his pipe from his mouth. "Eh?"

"You ought to put her right," said Mr. Hart.

All he got was a grin and wag of the head. "Not in front of these pros, you know. The beggars think they know it all."

Mr. Hart impatiently recrossed his neatly creased legs. "You sound as if you were an expert," he said, with just the suggestion of a slur. It was exactly the right tone, ambiguous without being insulting. Sooner or later anybody, confronted by that tone, would begin to wonder if he were wanted.

"Know a bit about it," the Englishman said. He waved his pipe at the court, talking too loud. "Watch her forehand, too. She's cocking her racket up too much at right angles with her wrist." His head moved back and forth, following a fast rally. "So's the pro," he cackled. "So's the pro, swelp me. Look at 'im!"

"The ball," said Mr. Hart, "seems to be going back and forth pretty fast."

"Ping-Pong," the Englishman said. "Anybody who hit it instead of slapping it that way would have put it away by now."

Tenney was lying back staring at the sky, where a man-o'-war hawk alternately soared and sped on dark, bent wings. Tenney was like a hawk himself, Mr. Hart thought. Dark and built for speed. The Mercury foot, and the arrogance to go with it. He was built to run down little web-footed gulls like this Englishman and take their fish away from them. But all he did was stare at the sky and wag one foot over the footrest. Thomas, ordinarily more talkative, now seemed to be asleep. Mr. Hart simmered. It had been very pleasant, very quiet, very friendly, till this terrier with the big yap butted in.

". . . thing I miss in America," the Englishman was saying. "Never can get up a good game. Any public-school boy in England plays a good game as a matter of course. Here nobody seems to."

The idea came gently to Mr. Hart's door, and he opened to it. It might boomerang, but he thought not. His mind went scornful. Pestered to write a play for Cornell. Like hell. Bothered to do articles for the *Britannica*. My Aunt Annica. Aldington wanting him to come in on an anthology. In a pig's physiology. British public school likewise. Tennis as well.

"It *is* hard to get a game, sometimes," he said. "If I wasn't afraid of getting out of my class I'd suggest we play."

"Yes," the Englishman said cordially. "Have to do that."

"How about this afternoon, now?"

Tenney started to whistle lightly. The whistle was encouraging to Mr. Hart. It said, Go ahead, pin his ears down.

"This weather might not last, even here," Hart said. "Little exercise'd do us good. That is, if you'd step down to my level."

"Oh, step down!" the Englishman said. "Not at all!"

"Let's have a set then. The court'll be empty in a minute."

The Englishman knocked out his pipe, looked back toward the empty cocktail garden, puckered his lips. He had a pulpy nose and prominent teeth. "I didn't bring a racket," he said. "Perhaps . . ."

"The pro'll have some."

The Englishman rose. "Very well," he said. "I'll go pop into my things." He went toward the hotel, walking springily, a preposterous, lumpy little blowhard, and Mr. Hart dropped a look of grim anticipation at the two lazy, amused youths.

"The International Matches," Tenney said. "Shall I cry 'Well struck, Cow College!' now and again?"

"Don't encourage me," said Mr. Hart. "I might start shooting for the little stinker's belt buckle."

The Englishman looked even more preposterous in shorts than he had in polo shirt and slacks. His muscles were knobbly; his bones stuck out like the elbows of characters in comic strips. Mr. Hart, leading the way onto the court, was aware of the young men watching from their somnolent chairs. It was as if he had made them a promise. Opening the can of balls he made another to himself. He was going to play every shot as if dollars depended on it.

"Here we go," he said cheerily, and wafted a warm-up ball across the net. From the very awkwardness of the Englishman's run he knew his plan was not going to boomerang. The goof looked as if he'd never been on a court before. This, he told himself happily, was murder.

It was a murder that he enjoyed thoroughly. For three quarters of an hour he ran the Englishman's tongue out, tricked him with soft chops that died in the clay, outran him with topped drives into the corners, aced him with flat services, left him going full steam in the wrong direction for an occasional American twist. He was playing carefully himself, not hitting anything too hard until he got a kill, and then plastering it with everything he had. He blessed the high altitude and worn balls of his youth which had made him learn to murder a high ball. The Englishman's game, when there was any, gave him little to hit except soft high bouncers, big as a basketball and begging to be swatted.

As he went about his methodical mayhem his amazement grew. The Englishman didn't have a thing. Then why in the world would he have the consummate gall to talk the way he had? Mr. Hart could not imagine; but he saw the two watchers in their chairs, and his unspoken compact with them kept him at the butchery. The Englishman got six points the first set, and his face was a little strained as they changed courts. You bloody upstart, Mr. Hart thought. This is where you learn to be humble. He stepped up to the service line prepared to skunk the Englishman completely, never give him a point.

In the middle of the set the two young men rose and stretched and picked up their towels. They lifted their hands and walked off toward the bath-houses, and Mr. Hart, a little disappointed at the loss of his audience, went on finishing the thing off. The Englishman was feeling his shoulder between shots now. Obviously, thought Mr. Hart, he has pulled a muscle. Obviously.

At five-love the Englishman walked up to the net. "I say, do you mind? I seem to have done something to my shoulder here. Can't seem to take a decent swing."

Mr. Hart picked up the ball can and his sweater. Without really wanting to, he let the alibi establish itself. "No use to play with a bad arm," he said. And looking at the grimace pretending to be pain on the little man's face, he said, almost kindly and to his own astonishment, "It was spoiling your game. I could see you weren't up to scratch."

"Makes me damned mad," the Englishman said. "Here I've mucked up your whole afternoon. Couldn't hit a thing after the first game or two."

"Too bad," said Mr. Hart. And so, condoling one another, they went back to the hotel. It was funny. It was, Mr. Hart decided while he was dressing, so damned funny he ought to be rolling on the bed stuffing covers in his mouth. That he was not, he laid to the complete incorrigibility of that dreadful little man. People like that would never see themselves straight. No innuendo, no humiliation, would ever teach them anything. Hopelessly inadequate, they must constantly be butting into situations and places where they didn't belong. Mr. Hart shrugged. Let him live. The hell with him. If he couldn't be overlooked, he could be avoided.

He brushed off his white shoes, felt his tie, and looked in the mirror. Nose and forehead pretty red. For an instant of irritation he wished he wouldn't always burn and peel before he tanned. There was some system—tannic acid, was it?—but he always forgot till too late. The regulars around here, he was sure, never peeled.

In the dining room there were flowers bright against the stiff linen on every table, and the ladderlike shadow of a palm frond fell across the floor from the west windows. Mr. Hart answered the headwaiter's bow and stepped down into the cocktail lounge. There was no one there except two waiters, the bartender, and some stuffed fish. Outside, however, several tables were occupied. At one of them sat Thomas and Tenney, and as Mr. Hart started over he noticed that they still wore sandals and no socks. Their arrogant feet seemed at home and unembarrassed. He wondered if they wore socks to dinner, and it crossed his mind that he might be overdressing. White jacket might look like ostentation. He didn't want that.

"Well!" said Mr. Hart, and sat down. "What's a good drink here?"

Tenney shrugged. His amber, remote, hawklike eyes were away off down the garden, then briefly on Mr. Hart. "Rum collins?"

Mr. Hart signaled a waiter. The three sat quietly while people came in twos and threes into the garden. The young men did not speak of the tennis match. Neither did Mr. Hart. And he did not remember, until a small party came pushing a blue wheelbarrow with a sailfish in it, that he had meant to go down and watch the boats come in.

There were a gray-haired man and a blonde older woman and a wind-blown, pretty girl in the party. They came through the garden in triumph, calling to people to witness. Everybody seemed to know them. Everyone got up and crowded around and admired. Thomas and Tenney went over with their glasses in their hands, and Mr. Hart rose, but did not want to push in. "Fifty-nine pounds," the girl said. "And *I* caught it. Little me." The tempo of the garden had picked up; the lazy afternoon was already accelerating into cocktail hour, dinner hour, the evening dance. Mr. Hart, standing at the edge of the crowd, thought what really pleasant fun it would be to spend a day that way. The fishing party seemed pleasant, agreeable people. And it would be fun to catch a thing like that sailfish. Lovely to see him break the peacock water.

"Come on," the girl said. "I'm buying the drinks on this one." She hooked arms with Tenney and Thomas, the gray-haired man picked up the handles of the wheelbarrow, and they went up the garden to a table under the hedge.

Mr. Hart stood a moment alone. Then he sat down. The chatter, the bright afternoon sounds, went over him, and he heard the fishing girl's brittle tinkle of laughter. The long light of evening lay over the palms and the flowering trees and the golf-green lawn. Waiters tipped the umbrellas sideways and lifted the steel butts from the holes and stacked the canvas against the hedge. Mr. Hart watched them; his eyes went beyond them to the party at the hedge table, Tenney and Thomas leaning forward, no languor about them now, their talk animated.

Beside his own table he saw his immaculate buck foot. It irritated him, somehow, and he put it out of sight. The bronze feet of Tenney and Thomas, he noticed, were in plain view as they tipped their chairs forward to talk to the fishermen. The dead fish's fin stuck up from the blue wheelbarrow like a black-violet lacquered fan. It was while he watched them that the cold finger touched Mr. Hart, and he knew what it was.

The garden was full of people now, brown-faced, casual. They were necessary, Mr. Hart thought, to complete the picture. The whole garden, tipped with light through the palms, was like a Seurat. And he sat alone, outside the picture. There were two rings of moisture on the enameled table, left by the glasses of Tenney and Thomas. Very carefully Mr. Hart squeegeed them off with his thumb and finger and wiped his hands on his handkerchief. When he looked up he saw the Englishman, fantastically white and sluglike in this garden of brown demigods, standing in the doorway of the lounge in white jacket and ascot tie, looking around the tables.

For an instant Mr. Hart hesitated. He heard the brittle chatter and laughter from the other tables. His elbows felt the tug of hands, heard the voices saying, "Come on, let's have a drink on it," his bronze face felt the sun as he went with the others across to a corner table. . . .

His fingers went around the cold glass, raised it. With his other hand he signaled the Englishman standing in the doorway.

SAW
GANG

■   ■   ■

The sun had not yet risen above the woods when Ernie started, and the grass on the little road up through the hemlocks was crisp with frost. As he topped the stiff climb and came out onto Thurson's meadow, above the town reservoir, the first flat rays hit him in the face.

He put his double-bitted axe through the fence, climbed through after it, crossed the meadow, and jumped the swamp from hummock to hummock until he entered the cedars. Cattle had been among the low growth; their split tracks were sucked deep into the ground and half frozen there.

On the other side of the rail fence belting the cedars he came again into open meadow, still green after a late mowing, and saw the long hill ahead of him, winter-black spruce scattered through the dying color of the maples. October was a very taste in the air of smoke and frost and dried seed pods, and he filled his lungs with it, walking rapidly up toward Pembrook's farm and the crown of woods behind it where George Pembrook was cutting wood.

He did not trouble to stop in the Pembrooks' yard, but ducked under the last fence and went on up the skid road George had worn hauling limb wood down to his circle saw. As he climbed, the sun climbed with him, but the air still had its winy sparkle, and there was a smell from grass and weeds as the frost thawed.

Just where the skid road turned left up a little draw toward the sugarbush, he saw Will Livesy and Donald Swain coming across from the other side, both with axes. Their greetings were brief.

"Hi, kid," Donald said.

"Hi, boy," said Will.

They walked along together, not talking. Ernie, matching his behavior to theirs, walked steadily, watching the woods. Only when Donald Swain breathed his lungs full of air, shifted his axe to the other shoulder, and said, "Good workin' weather," the boy looked at him and they grinned. It was what he had wanted to say himself.

Ahead of them, back in the woods, the saw engine started, and a minute later they heard the blade rip across the first log. Will Livesy took out a turnip watch, turned it for the others to see. It was seven-thirty. "Ain't wastin' no time," Will said.

The saw was set up in a clearing at the bottom of a slope. Behind it was a skidway piled ten feet high with logs. George Pembrook was there, and his brother Howard, and John LaPere, the sawyer. George, dogging a log forward under the upraised saw, spat sideways on the ground, unsmiling.

"Up late last night?"

" 'y God," Will Livesy said, "I was up all night. Got any wood to chop to keep me awake?"

George looked at the mountainous skidway behind him. "Just a mite," he said.

Ernie stood his axe against a tree and jumped to roll a chunk, solid and squat as a meat block, from under the saw. Donald and Will squared away. Donald spat on his hands, swung: the blade bounded from the hard wood. A second later Will's axe came down on the other side, in the mathematical center of the chunk, and got a bite. Donald swung again, his blade biting into the crack his first blow had made, a quarter of an inch from Will's axe, and the chunk fell cleanly in two.

Everybody found a job and went at it. Howard Pembrook rolled logs down onto the track, George dogged them through and braced them,

LaPere dropped the saw onto them and whacked them into stove lengths, Ernie cleared them away, Donald and Will split. In the leaf-and-chip-strewn clearing, under the thinning maples, the pulse of the saw went up like the panting of a man.

Every hour or two, without talking about it, they changed off jobs, all except LaPere and Donald Swain. The work went on without pause while the sun climbed higher above the hill and the air warmed. Once in a while, seeing the lower part of the skidway bare, Ernie left his job and helped roll a new supply of logs down the skids with cant hooks. Nobody said anything.

About eleven, as Will was poking a six-inch pole under the saw, LaPere raised his denim cap and looked down his nose at the thing. Most of the logs they had been sawing were birch and beech and maple anywhere from eighteen to thirty inches through.

"Call that a log?" he said.

Will grinned. "George lost his fishpole."

A few minutes later, as Ernie rolled a big twisted knotty rot-sided maple log onto the tracks and Will dogged it forward, LaPere let the saw down experimentally and raked it across the crumbling bark. "Kind of gone by, ain't it?"

"Best George could find," Will said. He dropped the bracing lever across the log and threw his weight on it. LaPere bore down on the clutch and the jerking blade came down. Halfway through the pulpy log it hit a hard knot, the blade bent almost double, the log kicked sideways off the track as Will's lever slipped on the rotten bark and flipped upward like a swung bat. By the time LaPere could raise the saw the blade had jumped free and hung quivering, shaking shredded pulp from its two-inch teeth. Will was standing with his head down, feeling his jaw.

"Thunderation!" George Pembrook said. "That was a whack."

"Lever kicked up," Donald Swain said, watching Will. He said it for nobody in particular; they had all looked up instantly at the warning howl of the saw. "Took him right under the chin," Donald said.

Will felt his jaw tenderly. His hat had fallen off, and his thin red hair stuck up on end. Looking down from the platform, LaPere chuckled.

"Lose any teeth, Will?"

Will shook his head to clear it, felt his chin again, and cackled with sudden laughter. " 'y God, I didn't have 'em in!" he said. He rolled the log back with a hook, and they were working again so abruptly that Ernie had to jump to get the chunk from under the saw.

At noon, without comment, LaPere cut the switch and the engine stopped with three lunging coughs. Donald and George sank their axes in the chunk they had been splitting, they all collected their frocks from the trees where they had hung them, and within three minutes they were strung out along the trail on their way to the farmhouse.

Ernie did not push himself up with the others. Though he had known them all his life, he knew better at fifteen than to take it for granted he was one of them. In silence he followed the silent file until they came into the open opposite George's sugarhouse. There John LaPere, walking with George Pembrook, stopped and stared, and the rest piled up behind him.

"Great God, George!" LaPere said.

A little clump of spruces had been chopped down by the side of the road, and Ernie, coming up behind the clot of men, saw that the trees had been whittled and chewed and mangled with a dull axe and finally broken off instead of being chopped off clean.

"That city kid I had this summer," George said. "I think he used his teeth."

One by one, as they started again, the men looked at the mangled butts, then at each other. They whistled, grinning a little, and walked on. Will Livesy, a black smear of blood like a beard under his chin, turned and shook his head at Ernie, calling his attention to the stumps.

The table was set at the Pembrooks'. George changed from gum boots to slippers and turned on the radio while the men went one by one to the sink to wash. Ernie went last. By the time he sat down, the governor from Montpelier was discussing with the state the provisions he was making for coal supplies, and they listened to him in silence for twenty minutes, steadily consuming two plates apiece of Mrs. Pembrook's meat loaf, baked potatoes, hot biscuits, string beans, carrots, and sweet pickle.

They finished neck and neck with the governor, loitered briefly outside in the sun while George got back into gum boots, and then went silently back up the skid road past the sugarhouse and the gnawed spruce stumps and into the woods. Before LaPere had his engine started Howard Pembrook and Donald Swain were swinging splitting hammers on the tough and knotty chunks that they had rolled aside earlier.

In midafternoon George's hound wandered up muddy-footed from chasing through a swamp. It went around to each man, and each stopped for a second to scratch its ears, until it came to LaPere, up on the shaking platform. Then the hound sat down. "Hi, Sport," LaPere said.

About three-thirty, with the saw halfway through a big yellow birch log, the engine died. LaPere looked surprised. " 'Nuts,' said McGinty," he said. He opened the gas cap, stuck a twig down, raised his eyebrows, and reached for the gas can. Ernie, straightening up to ease his aching back, saw that none of the others was stopping. Howard and Will were rolling down a new supply of logs, Donald and George stacking stove-wood against the spreading pile to keep it from engulfing the splitting space. Ernie got the shovel and cleaned the sawdust out from under the track.

Through the whole afternoon, while the sun rolled down the long slope of the western hills and the hound got bored and wandered away and the stack of split wood got head high, and more than head high, they worked steadily and in silence. Ernie, his back and his belly sore from leaning and lifting, kept his mouth shut and worked with them. He knew they would never have worked like this for any employer, that they kept up the pace only because they all owed George help and would give nothing but their best day's work in exchange. Still, he kept listening, half hopeful that the engine would die again. The great pile of logs had receded twenty feet up the skidway, and sawdust was ankle deep all around the saw.

About four George began jacking the logs thirty inches forward instead of fifteen. "Got about enough stovewood," he said.

The erratic, tearing rhythm of the saw, the panting of the engine, went on, punctuated by the solid, wet *chunk* of the splitters' axes. Behind the splitters another pile began to grow, furnace chunks this time. The hound came back, found no one to scratch its ears, and disappeared again. The logs came faster off the skids now; George's hand on the dogging lever was almost as regular as a hand on a pump handle.

The sun was shining through the maples, almost flat over the hill, when LaPere cut the switch. This time the men did not immediately drop what they were doing. Ernie, looking around gratefully in the expectation that the day was finally over, saw Donald and Howard finishing up a dozen blocks. Donald, who had been splitting steadily, without change or rest, since seven-thirty, was cleaning up all the gnarled and knotty chunks that had resisted him before. LaPere was gassing and oiling the engine and taking out the blade for sharpening. Will was shoveling out sawdust. Unwillingly, because he couldn't help it, Ernie went and helped George roll down logs from the skids for the next day.

It was fifteen minutes before they all picked up their frocks. For a while George Pembrook stood looking at the two mighty heaps of sawed and split wood. "I'm obliged to you, boys," he said. "Way I felt when I was skiddin' them up, I thought there was a week's sawing there."

LaPere worked his eyebrows. "Can't be more'n about thirty run."

"If there ain't fifty already split I'll eat all the bark and sawdust," George said.

Winking at Donald Swain, LaPere drew his mouth down sorrowfully. "Never make fifty in a day, not without better help'n we had."

"Guess the help got to it fast as you could saw it," Donald said.

LaPere looked at the remaining pile of logs. "Only another half-day," he said. "You'll have about enough to last you till mud time, George."

They shouldered into their coats, grinning a little among themselves. Ernie, following their lead, looked at the piles of wood and knew that they had done a day's work that amounted to something. George already had enough wood there to last him two years.

His back ached as if a log had dropped across it, and a hard sore spot had developed under his left shoulder blade, but he followed them out of the woods feeling good, feeling tired and full of October smell and the smell of fresh-sawed wood and hot oil. As they left the woods he jumped for a limb and shook down a patter of beechnuts around him and Will Livesy. They stopped and gathered their hands full before following the others out.

Ernie, peeling a beechnut and popping it in his mouth, looked at Will, small, skinny, his chin still clotted with dried blood, and it was respect as much as anything else that made him say, "How's your jaw feel, Will?"

"Feels all right," Will said. " 'T ain't as bad as last time I got kicked. Wa'n't any horseshoe on it this time."

In the dusk they strung out into the open above the sugarhouse. Ernie, looking ahead, saw John LaPere stop momentarily beside the chewed and whittled spruce butts, turn his head, and stare. His voice boomed in the quiet, tired twilight, loud with wonder and laughter and disbelief.

"Great God!" he said, and walked on, shaking his head and laughing.

GOIN' TO TOWN

After the night's rain the yard was spongy and soft under the boy's bare feet. He stood at the edge of the packed dooryard in the flat thrust of sunrise, looking at the ground washed clean and smooth and trackless, feeling the cool firm mud under his toes. Experimentally he lifted his right foot and put it down in a new place, pressed, picked it up again to look at the neat imprint of straight edge and curving instep and the five round dots of toes. The air was so fresh that he sniffed at it as he would have sniffed at the smell of cinnamon.

Lifting his head backward, he saw how the prairie beyond the fireguard looked darker than in dry times, healthier with green-brown tints, smaller and more intimate somehow than it did when the heat waves crawled over scorched grass and carried the horizons backward into dim and unseeable distances. And standing in the yard above his one clean sharp footprint, feeling his own verticality in all that spread of horizontal land, he sensed how the prairie shrank on this morning and how he himself grew. He was immense. A little jump would crack his head on the sky; a few strides would take him to any horizon.

His eyes turned south, into the low south sky, cloudless, almost colorless in the strong light. Just above the brown line of the horizon, faint as a watermark on pale blue paper, was the wavering tracery of the mountains, tenuous and far off, but today accessible for the first time. His mind had played among those ghostly summits for uncountable lost hours; today, in a few strides, they were his. And more: under the shadow of those peaks, under those Bearpaws that he and his mother privately called the Mountains of the Moon, was Chinook; and in Chinook, on this Fourth of July, were the band, the lemonade stands, the crowds, the parade, the ball game, the fireworks that his mind had hungered toward in anticipation for three weeks.

His shepherd pup lay watching, belly down on the damp ground. In a gleeful spasm the boy stooped down to flap the pup's ears, then bent and spun like an Indian in a war dance while the wide-mouthed dog raced around him. And when his father came to the door in his undershirt, yawning, running a hand up the back of his head and through his hair, peering out from gummed eyes to see how the weather looked, the boy watched him, and his voice was one deep breathing relief from yesterday's rainy fear.

"It's clear as a bell," he said.

His father yawned again, clopped his jaws, rubbed his eyes, mumbled something from a mouth furry with sleep. He stood on the doorstep scratching himself comfortably, looking down at the boy and the dog.

"Gonna be hot," he said slyly. "Might be too hot to drive."

"Aw, Pa!"

"Gonna be a scorcher. Melt you right down to axle grease riding in that car."

The boy regarded him doubtfully, saw the lurking sly droop of his mouth. "Aw, we are too going!"

At his father's laugh he burst from his immobility like a sprinter starting, raced one complete circle of the house with the dog after him. When he flew around past his father again his voice trailed out behind him at the corner of the house. "Gonna feed the hens," he said. His father looked after him, scratched himself, laughed suddenly, and went back indoors.

Through chores and breakfast the boy moved with the dream of a day's rapture haunting his eyes, but that did not keep him from swift and agile helpfulness. He didn't even wait for commands. He scrubbed himself twice, slicked down his hair, hunted up clean clothes, wiped the mud from his shoes with a wet rag and put them on. While his mother packed the shoe box of lunch he stood at her elbows proffering aid. He flew to stow things in the topless old Ford. He got a cloth and polished the brass radiator. Once or twice, jumping around to help, he looked up to catch his parents watching him, or looking at each other with the knowing, smiling expression in the eyes that said they were calling each other's attention to him.

"Just like a race horse," his father said once, and the boy felt foolish, swaggered, twisted his mouth down in a leer, said "Awww!" But in a moment he was hustling them again. They ought to get going, with fifty miles to drive. And long before they were ready he was standing beside the Ford, licked and immaculate and so excited that his feet jumped him up and down without his volition or knowledge.

It was eight o'clock before his father came out, lifted off the front seat, poked the flat stick down into the gas tank, and pulled it out again dripping. "Pretty near full," he said. "If we're gonna drive up to the mountains we better take a can along, though. Fill that two-gallon one with the spout."

The boy ran, dug the can out of the shed, filled it from the spigot of the sixty-gallon drum that stood on a plank support to the north of the farmhouse. When he came back, his left arm stuck straight out and the can knocking against his legs, his mother was settling herself into the back seat among the parcels and water bags.

"Goodness!" she said. "This is the first time I've been the first ready since I don't know when. I should think you'd have got all this done last night."

"Plenty time." The father stood looking down at the boy, grinning. "All right, race horse. You want to go to this shindig, you better hop in."

The boy was up into the front seat like a squirrel. His father walked around in front of the car. "Okay," he said. "You look sharp now. When she kicks over, switch her onto magneto and pull the spark down."

The boy said nothing. He looked upon the car, as his father did, with respect and a little awe. They didn't use it much, and starting it was a ritual like a fire drill. The father unscrewed the four-eared brass plug, looked down into the radiator, screwed the cap back on, and bent to take hold of the crank. "Watch it now," he said.

The boy felt the gentle heave of the springs, up and down, as his father wound the crank. He heard the gentle hiss in the bowels of the engine as the choke wire was pulled out, and his nostrils filled with the strong, volatile odor of gasoline. Over the slope of the radiator his father's brown strained face lifted up. "Is she turned on all right?"

"Yup. She's on battery."

"Must of flooded her. Have to let her rest a minute."

They waited—and then after a few minutes the wavelike heaving of the springs again, the rise and fall of the blue shirt and bent head over the radiator, the sighing swish of the choke, a stronger smell of gasoline. The motor had not even coughed.

The two voices came simultaneously from the car. "What's the matter with it?"

His brow puckered in an intent and serious scowl, the father stood blowing mighty breaths. "Son of a gun," he said. Coming around, he pulled at the switch to make sure it was clear over, adjusted the spark and gas levers. A fine mist of sweat made his face shine like oiled leather in the sun.

"There isn't anything really wrong with it, is there?" the mother said, and her voice wavered uncertainly on the edge of fear.

"I don't see how there could be," he said. "She's always started right off, and she was running all right when I drove her in here."

The boy looked at his mother where she sat erect among the things in the seat. She looked all dressed up, a flowered dress, a hat with hard red varnished cherries on it pinned to her red hair. For a moment she sat, stiff and nervous. "What'll you have to do?" she said.

"I don't know. Look into the motor."

"Well, I guess I'll get in out of the sun while you do it," she said, and, opening the door, she fumbled her way out of the clutter.

The boy felt her exodus like a surrender, a betrayal. If they didn't hurry up they'd miss the parade. In one motion he bounced out of the car. "Gee whiz!" he said. "Let's do something. We got to get started."

"Keep your shirt on," his father grunted. Lifting the hood, he bent his head inside, studying the engine. His hand went out to test wires, wiggle spark-plug connections, make tentative pulls at the choke. The weakly hinged hood slipped and came down across his wrist, and he swore, pushing it back. "Get me the pliers," he said.

For ten minutes he probed and monkeyed. "Might be the spark plugs," he said. "She don't seem to be getting any fire through her."

The mother, sitting on a box in the shade, smoothed her flowered voile dress nervously. "Will it take long?"

"Half-hour."

"Any day but this!" she said. "I don't see why you didn't make sure last night."

He breathed through his nose and bent over the engine again. "Don't go laying on any blame," he said. "It was raining last night."

One by one the plugs came out, were squinted at, scraped with a knife blade, the gap tested with a thin dime. The boy stood on one foot, then on the other, time pouring like a flood of uncatchable silver dollars through his hands. He kept looking at the sun, estimating how much time there was left. If they got it started right away they might still make it for the parade, but it would be close. Maybe they'd drive right up the street while the parade was on, and be part of it. . . .

"Is she ready?" he said.

"Pretty quick."

He wandered over by his mother, and she reached out and put an arm around his shoulders, hugging him quickly. "Well, anyway we'll get there for the band and the ball game and the fireworks," he said. "If she doesn't start till noon we c'n make it for those."

"Sure," she said. "Pa'll get it going in a minute. We won't miss anything, hardly."

"You ever seen skyrockets, Ma?"

"Once."

"Are they fun?"

"Wonderful," she said. "Just like a million stars, all colors, exploding all at once."

His feet took him back to his father, who straightened up with a belligerent grunt. "Now!" he said. "If the sucker doesn't start now . . ."

And once more the heaving of the springs, the groaning of the turning engine, the hiss of choke. He tried short, sharp half-turns, as if to catch the motor off guard. Then he went back to the stubborn laboring spin. The back of his blue shirt was stained darkly, the curving dikes of muscle along the spine's hollow showing cleanly where the cloth stuck. Over and over, heaving, stubborn at first, then furious, until he staggered back panting.

"God damn!" he said. "What you suppose is the matter with the damn thing?"

"She didn't even cough once," the boy said, and, staring up at his father's face full of angry bafflement, he felt the cold fear touch him. What if it didn't start at all? What if they never got to any of it? What if, all ready to go, they had to turn around and unload the Ford and not even get out of the yard? His mother came over and they stood close together, looking at the Ford and avoiding each other's eyes.

"Maybe something got wet last night," she said.

"Well, it's had plenty time to dry out," said his father.

"Isn't there anything else you could try?"

"We can jack up the hind wheel, I guess. But there's no damn reason we ought to have to."

"Well, if you have to, you'll have to," she said briskly. "After planning it for three weeks we can't just get stuck like this. Can we, son?"

His answer was mechanical, his eyes steady on his father. "Sure not," he said.

The father opened his mouth to say something, saw the boy's lugubrious face, and shut his lips again. Without a word he pulled off the seat and got out the jack.

The sun climbed steadily while they jacked up one hind wheel and blocked the car carefully so that it wouldn't run over anybody when it started. The boy helped, and when they were ready again he sat in the front seat so full of hope and fear that his whole body was one taut concentration. His father stooped, his cheek pressed against the radiator as a milker's cheek touches the flank of a cow. His shoulder dropped, jerked up. Nothing. Another jerk. Nothing. Then he was rolling in a furious spasm of energy, the wet dark back of his shirt rising and falling. And inside the motor only the futile swish of the choke and the half sound, half feel of cavernous motion as the crankshaft turned over. The Ford bounced on its springs as if the front wheels were coming off the ground on every upstroke. Then it stopped, and the boy's father was hanging on the radiator, breathless, dripping wet, swearing: "Son of a dirty, lousy, stinking, corrupted . . ."

The boy, his eyes dark, stared from his father's angry wet face to his mother's, pinched with worry. The pup lay down in the shade and put his head on his paws. "Gee whiz," the boy said. "Gee whiz!" He looked at the sky, and the morning was half gone.

His shoulders jerking with anger, the father threw the crank halfway across the yard and took a step or two toward the house. "The hell with the damn thing!"

"Harry, you can't!"

He stopped, glared at her, took an oblique look at the boy, bared his teeth in an irresolute, silent swearword. "Well, God, if it won't go!"

"Maybe if you hitched the horses to it," she said.

His laugh was short and choppy. "That'd be fine!" he said. "Why don't we just hitch up and let the team haul this damned old boat into Chinook?"

"But we've got to get it started! Why wouldn't it be all right to let them pull it around? You push it sometimes on a hill and it starts."

He looked at the boy again, jerked his eyes away with an exasperated gesture, as if he held the boy somehow accountable. The boy stared, mournful, defeated, ready to cry, and his father's head swung back unwillingly. Then abruptly he winked, mopped his head and neck, and grinned. "Think you want to go, uh?"

The boy nodded. "All right!" his father's voice snapped crisply. "Fly up in the pasture and get the team. Hustle!"

On the high lope the boy was off up the coulee bank. Just down under the lip of the swale, a quarter-mile west, the bay backs of the horses and the black dot of the colt showed. Usually he ran circumspectly across that pasture, because of the cactus, but now he flew. With shoes it was all right, and even without shoes he would have run—across burnouts, over stretches so undermined with gopher holes that sometimes he broke through to the ankle, staggering. Skimming over patches of cactus, soaring over a badger hole, plunging down into the coulee and up the other side, he ran as if bears were after him. The black colt, spotting him, hoisted his tail and took off in a spectacular, stiff-legged sprint across the flats, but the bays merely lifted their heads to watch him. He slowed, came up walking, laid a hand on the mare's neck and untied the looped halter rope. She stood for him while he scrambled and wriggled and kicked his way to her back, and then they were off, the mare in an easy lope, the gelding trotting after, the colt stopping his wild showoff career and wobbling hastily and ignominiously after his departing mother.

They pulled up before the Ford, the boy sliding off to throw the halter rope to his father. "Shall I get the harness?" he said, and before anyone could answer he was off running, to come back lugging one heavy harness, tugs trailing little furrows in the damp bare earth. He dropped it, turned to run again, his breath laboring in his lungs. "I'll get the other'n," he said.

With a short, almost incredulous laugh his father looked at his mother and shook his head before he threw the harness on the mare. When the second one came he laid it over the gelding, pushed against the heavy shoulder to get the horse into place. The gelding resisted, pranced a little, got a curse and a crack with the rope across his nose, jerked back and trembled and lifted his feet nervously, and set one shod hoof on his owner's instep. The father, unstrung by the hurry and the heat and the labor and the exasperation of a morning when nothing went right, kicked the horse savagely in the belly. "Get in there, you damned big blundering ox! Back! Back, you bastard! Whoa! Whoa, now!"

With a heavy rope for a towline he hitched the now-skittish team to the axle. Without a word he stooped and lifted the boy to the mare's back. "All right," he said, and his face relaxed in a quick grin. "This is where we start her. Ride 'em around in a circle, not too fast."

Then he climbed into the Ford, turned on the switch to magneto, fussed with the levers. "Let her go!" he said.

The boy kicked the mare ahead, twisting as he rode to watch the Ford heave forward as a tired, heavy man heaves to his feet, begin rolling after him, lurching on the uneven ground, jerking and kicking and making growling noises when his father let the emergency brake off and put it in gear. The horses settled as the added pull came on them, flattened into their collars, swung in a circle, bumped each other, skittered. The mare reared, and the boy shut his eyes and clung. When he came down, her leg was entangled in the towline and his father was climbing cursing out of the Ford to straighten it out. His father was mad again, and yelled at him, "Keep 'em apart! There ain't any tongue. You got to keep Dick kicked over on his own side."

And again the start, the flattening into the collars, the snapping tight of the tugs under his legs. This time it went smoothly, the Ford galloped after the team in lumbering, plunging jerks. The mare's eyes rolled white, and she broke into a trot, pulling the gelding after her. Desperately the boy clung to the knotted and shortened reins, his ears alert for the grumble of the Ford starting behind him. The pup ran beside the team yapping in a high, falsetto, idiot monotone, crazy with excitement.

They made three complete circles of the back yard between house and chicken coop before the boy looked back again. "Won't she start?" he shouted. He saw his father rigid behind the wheel, heard his ripping burst of swearwords, saw him bend and glare down into the mysterious innards of the engine through the pulled-up floorboards. Guiding the car with one hand, he fumbled down below, one glaring eye just visible over the cowl.

"Shall I stop?" the boy shouted. Excitement and near-despair made his voice a tearful scream.

But his father's wild arm waved him on. "Go on, go on! Gallop 'em! Pull the guts out of this thing. Run 'em, run 'em!"

And the galloping—the furious, mud-flinging, rolling-eyed galloping around the circle already rutted like a road, the Ford, now in savagely held low, growling and surging and plowing behind; the mad yapping of the dog, the erratic scared bursts of runaway from the colt, the mother in sight briefly for a quarter of each circle, her hands to her mouth and her eyes hurt, and behind him in the Ford his father in a strangling rage, yelling him on, his lips back over his teeth and his face purple.

Until finally they stopped, the horses blown, the boy white and tearful and still, the father dangerous with unexpended wrath. The boy slipped off, his lip bitten between his teeth, not crying now but ready to at any moment, the corners of his eyes prickling with it, and his teeth tight on his misery. His father climbed over the side of the car and stood looking as if he wanted to tear the thing apart with his bare hands.

Shoulders sagging, tears trembling to fall, his jaw aching with the need to cry, the boy started toward his mother. As he came near his father he looked up, their eyes met, and he saw his father's blank with impotent rage. Dull hopelessness swallowed him. Not any of it, his mind said. Not even any of it—no parade, no ball game, no band, no fireworks. No lemonade or ice cream or paper horns or firecrackers. No close sight of the mountains that throughout every summer called like a legend from his horizons. No trip, no adventure—none of it, nothing.

Everything he was feeling was in that one still look. In spite of him his lip trembled, and he choked off a sob, his eyes on his father's face, on the brows pulling down and the eyes narrowing.

"Well, don't blubber!" his father shouted at him. "Don't stand there looking at me as if it was me that was keeping you from your picnic!"

"I can't—help it," the boy said, and with a kind of terror he felt the grief swelling up, overwhelming him, driving the voice out of him in a wail. Through the blur of his crying he saw the convulsive tightening of his father's face, and then all the fury of a maddening morning concentrated itself in a swift backhand blow that knocked the boy staggering.

He bawled aloud, from pain, from surprise, from outrage, from pure desolation, and ran to bury his face in his mother's skirts. From that muffled sanctuary he heard her angry voice. "No," she said. "It won't do any good to try to make up to him now. Go on away somewhere till he gets over it."

She rocked him against her, but the voice she had for his father was bitter with anger. "As if he wasn't hurt enough already!" she said.

He heard the heavy, quick footsteps going away, and for a long time he lay crying into the voile flowers. And when he had cried himself out, and had listened apathetically to his mother's soothing promises that they would go in the first chance they got, go to the mountains, have a picnic under some waterfall, maybe be able to find a ball game going on in town, some Saturday—when he had listened and become quiet, wanting to believe it but not believing it at all, he went inside to take off his good clothes and his shoes and put on his old overalls again.

It was almost noon when he came out to stand in the front yard looking southward toward the impossible land where the Mountains of the Moon lifted above the plains, and where, in the town at the foot of the peaks, crowds would now be eating picnic lunches, drinking pop, getting ready to go out to the ball field and watch heroes in real uniforms play ball. The band would be braying now from a bunting-wrapped stand, kids would be tossing firecrackers, playing in a cool grove. . . .

In the still heat his face went sorrowful and defeated, and his eyes searched the horizon for the telltale watermark. But there was nothing but waves of heat crawling and lifting like invisible flames; the horizon was a blurred and writhing flatness where earth and sky met in an indistinct band of haze. This morning two strides would have taken him there; now it was gone.

Looking down, he saw at his feet the clean footprint that he had made in the early morning. Aimlessly he put his right foot down and pressed. The mud was drying, but in a low place he found a spot that would still take an imprint. Very carefully, as if he were performing some ritual for his life, he went around, stepping and leaning, stepping and leaning, until he had a circle six feet in diameter of delicately exact footprints, straight edge and curving instep and the five round dots of toes.

THE VIEW
FROM THE
BALCONY

■   ■   ■

The fraternity house where they lived that summer was a good deal like a barracks, with its dormitory cut up into eight little plywood cells each with one dormer window, and its two shower rooms divided between the men and the women. They communized their cooking in the one big kitchen and ate together at a refectory table forty feet long. But the men were all young, all veterans, all serious students, and most of the wives worked part time in the university, so that their home life was a thing that constantly disintegrated and re-formed, and they got along with a minimum of friction.

The lounge, as big as a basketball court, they hardly used. What they did use, daytime and nighttime, the thing that converted the austere barracks life into something sumptuous and country-clubbish, was the rooftop deck that stretched out from the lounge over the ten-car garage.

Directly under the bluff to which the house clung ran the transcontinental highway, but the deck was hidden and protected above it. At night the air was murmurous with insects, and sitting there, they would be bumped by blundering June bugs and feel the velvet kiss of moths.

By standing up they could see the centerline of the highway palely emergent in the glow of the street lamp at the end of the drive. Beyond the highway, flowing with it in the same smooth curve, low-banked and smooth and dark and touched only with sparks and glimmers of light, was the Wawasee River.

More than a mile of the far shore was kept wild as a city park, and across those deep woods on insect-haunted nights, when traffic noise died for a moment and the night hung still around them, they could hear the lions roar.

The lions were in the zoo at the other side of the park. At first it was a shock to the students in the fraternity house to hear that heavy-chested, coughing, snarling roar, a more dangerous and ominous sound than should be heard in any American night, and for a moment any of them could have believed that the midland heat of the night was tropical heat and that real and wild lions of an ancient incorrigible ferocity roamed the black woods beyond the river. But after a week or two the nightly roaring had become as commonplace as the sound of traffic along the highway, and they rarely noticed it.

Altogether the fraternity house was a good place, in spite of the tasteless ostentation of the big echoing lounge and the Turkish-bath heat of the sleeping cubicles. They were lucky to be in it. They felt how lucky they were, and people who came out to drink beer on weekends kept telling them how lucky they were. So many less lucky ones were crammed into backstairs rooms or regimented into converted barracks. Out here there was a fine spaciousness, a view, a freedom. They were terribly lucky.

Deep in a sun-struck daydream, drowning in light and heat, the sun like a weight on her back and her body slippery with perspiration and her mouth pushed wetly out of shape against her wrist, Lucy Graham lay alone on the deck in the sultry paralysis of afternoon. Her eyes looked into an empty red darkness; in her mind the vague voluptuous uncoiling of memory and fantasy was slowed almost to a stop, stunned almost to sleep.

All around her the afternoon was thick, humid, stirring with the slow fecundities of Midwestern summer—locust-shrill and bird-cheep and fly-buzz, child-shout and the distant chime of four o'clock from the university's clock tower. Cars on the highway grew from hum to buzz-saw whine and slapped past and diminished, coning away to a point of sound, a humming speck. Deep inside the house a door banged, and she heard the scratch of her own eyelashes against her wrist as she blinked, thinking groggily that it was time to get up and shower. Everyone would be coming home soon; Tommy Probst would be through with his exams by four-thirty, and tonight there would be a celebration and a keg of beer.

For a while longer she lay thinking of Tommy, wishing Charley were as far along as that, with his thesis done and nothing but the formalities left. Then it struck her as odd, the life they all lived: this sheltered, protected present tipping ever so slightly toward the assured future. After what they had been, navigator and bombardier, Signal Corps major, artillery captain, Navy lieutenant and yeoman and signalman first class, herself a WAAF and two or three of the other wives WACS or WAVES—after being these things it was almost comic of them to be so seriously and deeply involved in becoming psychologists, professors, pharmacists, historians.

She sat up, her head swimming and the whole world a sheeted glare. Lifting the hair from her neck, she let the cooling air in and shook her head at the absurdity of lying in the sun until her brains were addled and her eyes almost fried from her head. But in England there had never been the time, rarely the place, seldom the sun. She was piggy about the sun as she had been at first about the food. From here England seemed very scrawny and very dear, but very far away. Looking at her arm, she could not believe the pagan color of her own skin.

Quick steps came across the terrazzo floor of the lounge, and Phyllis Probst stepped out, hesitating in the door. "Have you seen anything of Tommy?"

"No," Lucy said. "Is he through his exams already?"

An extraordinarily complex look came over Phyllis' face. She looked hot, her hair was stringy, she seemed half out of breath. Her brows frowned and her mouth smiled a quick weak smile and her eyes jumped from Lucy out across the highway and back again.

Lucy stood up. "Is something wrong?"

"No," Phyllis said. "No, it's just . . . You haven't seen him at all?"

"Nobody's been home. I did hear a door bang just a minute ago, though."

"That was me," Phyllis said. "I thought he might have come home and gone to bed."

"Phyllis, is he sick?" Lucy said, and took Phyllis' arm. She felt the arm tremble. Still with the terrified, anxious, distressed expression on her face, Phyllis began to cry.

"I've got to find him," she said, and tried to pull away.

"We'll find him," Lucy said. "What happened? Tell me."

"He . . . I don't know. Helen Fast called me from the Graduate School office about two. I don't know whether he got sick, or whether the questions were too hard, or what. Helen said he came out once and asked for a typewriter, because he's left-handed and he smudges so when he writes, and she gave him a portable. But in a few minutes he came out again and put the portable on her desk and gave her a queer desperate look and walked out."

"Oh, what a shame," Lucy said, and with her arm around Phyllis sought for something else to say.

"But where *is* he?" Phyllis asked. "I called the police and the hospital and I went to every beer joint in town."

"Don't worry," Lucy said, and pushed her gently inside. "You come and take a cool shower and relax. We'll send the boys hunting when they come."

They came, half a household of them, before the two girls were halfway up the stairs, and they brought Tommy with them. He walked through the door like a prisoner among deputies, quietly, his dark smooth head bent a little as if in thought. Lucy saw his eyes lift and meet his wife's in an indescribable look. "Thanks for the lift," Tommy said to Charley Graham, and went up the stairs and took his wife's arm, and together they went down the corridor.

Lucy came back down to where her husband stood. "What on earth happened?"

He pursed up his lips, lifted his shoulders delicately, looked at the others, who were dispersing toward dormitory and shower room. "We cruised the park on a hunch and found him over there tossing sticks in the river," Charley said.

"Why didn't he take the exams?"

Her husband lifted his shoulders again.

"But it's so absurd!" she said. "He could have written the Lord's Prayer backward and they would have passed him. It was just a ritual, like an initiation. Everyone said so."

"Of course," he said. "It was a cinch." He put an arm across her shoulders, made a face as if disgusted by the coco-butter gooiness, and kissed her from a great distance. "Kind of dampens the party."

"We'd better not have it."

"Why not? I'm going to ask Richards and Latour to come over. They can straighten Tommy out."

"Will they give him another chance, do you think?"

"*Give* him?" Charley said. "They'll force it on him."

In the lounge after dinner the atmosphere was weighted and awkward. Lucy had a feeling that somehow, without in any way agreeing on it, the whole lot of them had arrived at a policy of elaborately ignoring what had happened to Tommy. Faced with the uncomfortable alternatives of ignoring it or of slapping him on the back, encouraging him, they had chosen the passive way. It was still too hot on the deck for sitting; in the lounge they were too aware of each other. Some hunted up corners and dove into books. The others lounged and waited. Watching them, Lucy saw how the eyes strayed to Tommy when his back was turned, judging him. She saw that look even in Charley's face, the contempt that narrowed the eyes and fluttered the nostrils. As if geared up to play a part, Tommy stayed, looking self-consciously tragic. His wife was around him like an anxious hen.

Donna Earp stood up suddenly into a silence. "Lord, it's sultry," she said. "I wish it would rain."

She went out on the deck, and Lucy and Charley followed her. The sun was dazzling and immense behind the maple tree that overhung the corner. Shadows stretched almost across the quiet river. The roof was warm through Lucy's shoes, and the railing was hot to her hand.

"Has anyone talked to him at all?" she said.

Charley shook his head, shrugged in that Frenchy little way he had.

"Won't it look queer?"

"Richards and Latour are coming. They'll talk to him."

"What about getting the beer, then? It's like a funeral in there."

"Funeral!" Charley said, and snorted. "That's another thing that happened today. Quite a day." He looked at the sun, disintegrating behind the trees.

"Whose funeral?"

"Kay Cedarquist's."

"Who's she?"

"She's a girl," he said. "Maybe I'd better get the beer, I'll tell you later about the funeral. It's a howl."

"Sounds like a peculiar funeral."

"Peculiar is a small word for it," he said. In the doorway he met Art Morris, and haled him along to get the beer.

After the glare, the shade of the tree was wonderful. Lucy sat on the railing looking over the river, and a car pulled into the drive and parked with its nose against the bluff. Paul Latour, the psychology professor, and Clark Richards, head of the department of social science, got out and held assisting hands for Myra, Richards' young wife. For several seconds the three stood looking up, smiling. They seemed struck by something; none of them spoke until Professor Richards with his hand in his bosom took a stance and said:

> O! she doth teach the torches to burn bright.
> It seems she hangs upon the cheek of night
> Like a rich jewel in an Ethiop's ear. . . .

He was a rather chesty man, neat in a white suit; in the violet shadow of the court his close-clipped mustache smudged his mouth. Latour's grim and difficult smile was upturned beside him, Myra Richards' school-girl face swam below there like a lily on a pond. "Hi, lucky people," Myra said. "What repulsively romantic surroundings!"

"Come up," Lucy said. "It's cooler at this altitude."

They made her feel pretty, they took away the gloom that Tommy Probst's failure had dropped upon them all. When you were all working through the assured present to the assured future, it was more than a personal matter when someone failed. Ever since dinner they had been acting as if the foundations were shaken, and she knew why. She was glad Richards and Latour were here, outsiders, older, with better perspective.

As she sat waiting for them the lion roared, harsh and heavy across the twilight river. "Down, Bruno!" Henry Earp said automatically, and there was a laugh. The door banged open, and Charley and Art staggered the keg through, to set it up on a table. The talk lifted suddenly in tempo. The guests stepped out onto the deck in a chorus of greeting; the lounge emptied itself, lugubrious Probsts and all, into the open air. Gloom dissolved in the promise of festivity. Charley drew the first soapy glasses from the keg. Far across several wooded bends the university's clock tower, lacy and soaring, was pinned suddenly against the sky by the floodlights.

* * *

She saw them working on Tommy during the evening. Within the first half-hour, Clark Richards took him over in the corner, and Lucy saw them talking there, an attractive picture of *magister* and *studens*, Tommy with his dark head bent and his face smoothed perfectly expressionless, Richards solid and confident and reassuring. She saw him leave Tommy with a clap on the shoulder, and saw Tommy's smile that was like spoken thanks, and then Phyllis came slipping over to where Tommy stood, wanting to be told of the second chance. Some time later, when the whole party had been loosened by beer and a carful of other students had arrived, and the twilight was so far gone into dusk that the river was only a faint metallic shine along the foot of the woods, Paul Latour hooked his arm into Tommy's and unsmiling, looking glum as a detective, led him inside. By that time the party was loud.

Lucy stayed on the fringes of it, alert to her duties as hostess, knowing that the other girls forgot any such responsibilities as soon as they had a couple of drinks. She rescued glasses for people who set them down, kept edging through the crowd around the keg to get glasses filled, talked with new arrivals; circulated quietly, seeing that no bashful student got shoved off into a corner, making sure that Myra Richards didn't get stranded anywhere. But after a half-hour she quit worrying about Myra; Myra was drinking a good deal and having a fine gay time.

It did not cool off much with the dark. The deck was breathless and sticky, and they drank their beer fast because it warmed so rapidly in the glass. Inside, as she paused by the keg, Lucy saw Latour and Tommy still talking head to head in the lighted lounge. Cocking her head a little, she listened to the sound of the party, appraising it. She heard Myra's laugh and a series of groans and hoots from the boys, apparently at someone's joke.

She moved away from the brittle concentration of noise and out toward the rail, and as she passed through the crowd she heard Art Morris say, ". . . got the Westminster Choir and a full symphony orchestra to do singing commercials. That's what Hollywood is, one big assembled empty Technique. They hunt mosquitoes with .155's."

No one was constrained any more; everything was loose and bibulous. As she leaned on the rail a voice spoke at her shoulder, and she turned to see Professor Richards with a glass of beer in his hand and his coat off. But he still looked dignified because he had kept his tie on and his sleeves rolled down. Most of the boys were down to T-shirts, and a girl who had come with the carload of students was in a halter that was hardly more than a bra. She was out in an open space now, twirling, showing the full ballerina skirt she had made out of an India print bedspread.

"Find any breeze?" Richards said.

"No, just looking at the river."

"It's very peaceful," he said. "You're lucky to have this place."

"I know." She brushed an insect from her sticky cheek. It was pleasant to her to be near this man, with his confidence and his rich resonant voice, and a privilege that they could all know him on such informal terms. Until six months ago he had been something big and important in the American Military Government in Germany.

He was saying, "How do you like it by now? It's a good bit different from England."

"I'm liking it wonderfully," she said. "People have been lovely."

"Thoroughly acclimated?"

"Not quite to this heat."

"This just makes the corn grow," he said, and she heard in his voice, with forgiving amusement that it should be there in the voice of this so-distinguished man, the thing she had heard in so many American voices—the confidence they had that everything American was bigger and better and taller and colder and hotter and wider and deeper than anything else. "I've seen it a hundred degrees at two in the morning," Richards said. "Inside a house, of course."

"It must be frightful."

He shrugged, smiling with his smudged mouth in the semidarkness. "Myra and I slept three nights on the golf course last time we had that kind of weather."

"We've already slept out here a night or two," Lucy said. She looked across the shadowy, crowded, noisy deck. "Where is Myra? I haven't had a chance to talk to her at all."

"A while ago she was arguing Zionism with a bunch of the boys," Richards said. He chuckled with his full-chested laugh, indulgent and avuncular. "She knows nothing whatever about Zionism."

Lucy had a brief moment of wondering how a professor really looked upon his students. Could he feel completely at ease among men and women of so much less experience and learning, or did he always have a bit of the paternal in his attitude? And when he married a girl out of one of his classes, as Professor Richards had, did he ever—and did *she* ever—get over feeling that he was God omnipotent?

"I imagine you must feel a little as I did when I got back from Germany," he was saying. "After living under such a cloud of fear and shortages and loss, suddenly to come out into the sun."

"Yes," she said. "I've felt it. I take the sun like medicine."

"It's too bad we can't sweep that cloud away for the whole world," Richards said. He looked out over the river, and she thought his voice had a stern, austere ring. "England particularly. England looked straight in the face of disaster and recognized it for what it was and fought on. It's a pity the cloud is still there. They've earned something better."

"Yes," she said again, for some reason vaguely embarrassed. Talk about England's grit always bothered her. You didn't talk about it when you were in any of it. Why should it be talked about outside? To dispel the slight pompous silence she said, "I saw you talking to Tommy Probst."

Richards laughed. "Momentary funk," he said. "It's preposterous. He's one of the best students we've had in years. He'll come up and take it again tomorrow and pass it like a shot."

He touched her shoulder with a pat that was almost fatherly, almost courtly, and lifted his empty glass in explanation and drifted away.

In the corner by the beer keg, people were jammed in a tight group. A yell of laughter went up, hoots, wolf calls. As the lounge door let a brief beam of light across the deck Lucy saw Myra in the middle of the crowd. Her blond hair glinted silver white, her eyes had a sparkle, her mouth laughed. A vivid face. No wonder Professor Richards had picked her out of a whole class.

Charley broke out of the crowd, shaking his head and grinning, bony-shouldered in the T-shirt. He put a damp arm around her and held his glass for her to sip. "How's my Limey bride?"

"Steamed like a pudding," she said. "It sounds like a good party over here."

He gave her a sidelong down-mouthed look. "Doak was just telling the saga of the funeral."

Laughter broke out again, and Myra's voice said, "Doak, I think that's the most awful thing I've ever . . ."

"Tell me," Lucy said, "what's so screamingly funny about a girl's funeral?"

"Didn't you ever hear about Kay Cedarquist?"

"No."

"She was an institution. Schoenkampf's lab assistant, over in Biology. She had cancer. That's what she died of, day before yesterday."

Lucy waited. "Is it just that I'm British?"

Wiping beer from his lips with his knuckles, Charley grinned at her in the shadow. "Nothing is so funny to Americans as a corpse," he said. "Unless it's a decaying corpse, or one that falls out of the coffin. Read Faulkner, read Caldwell. Kay sort of fell out of the coffin."

"Oh, my God," Lucy said, appalled.

"Oh, not really. See, she was Schoenkampf's mistress as well as his assistant. He's got a wife and four kids and they're all nudists. I'll tell you about them too some time. But Schoenkampf also had Kay, and he set her up in an apartment."

He drank again, raised a long admonishing finger. "*But*," he said. "When Schoenkampf was home with Mrs. Schoenkampf and the four nudist children, Kay had a painter from Terre Haute. He spent a lot of time in our town and painted murals all over Kay's walls . . . haven't I ever told you about those murals?"

"No."

"Gentle Wawasee River scenes," Charley said. "Happy farm children in wood lot and pasture, quiet creeks, steepled towns. Kay told Schoenkampf she had it done because art rested her nerves. She had this double feature going right up to the time she died, practically."

"You're making this all up," Lucy said.

He put his hands around her waist and lifted her to the rail. "Sit up here." Confidential and grinning, he leaned over her, letting her in on the inside. It was a pose she had loved in him when they walked all over Salisbury talking and talking and talking, when they were both in uniform.

"But if she had cancer," she said, "wasn't she ill, in bed?"

"Not till the last month." He knocked the bottom of his glass lightly against the stone and seemed to brood, half amused. "She was a good deal of a mess," he said. "Also, she had dozens of short subjects besides her double feature. Graduate students, married or single, she wasn't fussy. Nobody took her cancer very seriously. Then all of a sudden she up and died."

Lucy stirred almost angrily, moving her arm away from his sticky bare skin. "I don't think all that's funny, Charley."

"Maybe not. But Kay had no relatives at all, so Schoenkampf had to arrange the funeral. To keep himself out of it as much as possible, he got a bunch of students to act as pallbearers. Every one of them had passed his qualifying exams. That was what got the snickers."

"Graduate students?" Lucy said. "What have their qualifying exams to do . . . ?" Then she saw, and giggled involuntarily, and was angry at herself for giggling. Over the heads of the crowd she saw the group of students still clustered in the corner. They had linked arms in a circle and were singing "I Wanted Wings." Myra was still among them, between Doak and the girl in the bra and the India print bedspread.

"Who?" she said. "Doak and Jackson and that crowd?"

"They led the parade," Charley said, and snorted like a horse into his glass. "I guess there were three or four unfortunates who couldn't find an empty handle on the coffin."

Sitting quietly, the stone still faintly warm through her dress, she felt as if a greasy film had spread over her mind. It was such a nasty little sordid story from beginning to end, sneaking and betrayal and double betrayal and fear and that awful waiting, and finally death and heartless grins. "Well," Charley said, "I see you don't like my tale."

She turned toward him, vaguely and impulsively wanting reassurance. "Charley, was she pretty?"

"No," he said. "Not pretty at all, just easy."

What she wanted, the understanding, wasn't there. "I think it's wry," she said. "Just wry and awful."

"It ought to be," he said, "but somehow it isn't. Not if you knew Kay. You didn't."

With a kind of dismay she heard herself say, not knowing until she said it that there was that much distress and that much venom in her, the thing that leaped abruptly and unfairly to her mind. "Did *you?*"

He stared at her, frowned, looked amazed, and then grinned, and the moment he grinned it was all right again, she could laugh and they were together and not apart. But when he waved his glass and suggested that they go see how the beer was holding out she shook her head and stayed behind on the railing. As he worked his way tall through the jam of shadowy people she had an impulse to jump down and follow him so that not even twenty feet of separation could come desperately between, but the bray of talk and laughter from the deck was like a current that pinned her back against the faintly warm stone, threatening to push her off, and she looked behind her once into the dark pit of the court and tightened her hands on the railing.

* * *

She disliked everyone there for being strangers, aliens to her and to her ways of feeling, unable from their vast plateau of security to see or understand the desperation and fear down below. And even while she hated them for it, she felt a pang of black and bitter envy of that untroubled assurance they all had, that way of shrugging off trouble because no trouble that could not be cured had ever come within their experience. Even the war—a temporary unpleasantness. *Their* homes hadn't leaped into unquenchable flame or shaken down in rubble and dust. *They* had known no families in Coventry. Fighting the war, they could still feel not desperate but magnanimous, like good friends who reached out to help an acquaintance in a scuffle.

She hated them, and as she saw Paul Latour approaching her and knew she could not get away, she hated him worst of all. His face was like the face of a predatory bird, beaked, grim-lipped; because of some eye trouble he always wore dark glasses, and his prying, intent, hidden stare was an agony to encounter. His mouth was hooked back in a constant sardonic smile. He not merely undressed her with his eyes; he dissected her most intimate organs, and she knew he was a cruel man, no matter how consistently and amazingly kind he had been to Charley, almost like a father, all the way through school. Charley said he had a mind like a fine watch. But she wished he would not come over, and she trembled, unaccountably emotional, feeling trapped.

Then he was in front of her, big-shouldered for his height, not burly but somehow giving the impression of great strength, and his face like the cold face of a great bird thrust toward her and the hidden stare stabbed into her and the thin smile tightened. "Nobody to play with?" he asked. There was every unpleasant and cutting suggestion in the remark. A wallflower. Maybe halitosis. Perhaps B.O.

She came back quickly enough. "Too hot to play." To steer the talk away from her she said, "You've been conferring with Tommy."

"Yes," he said, and a spasm of what seemed almost contempt twisted across his mouth. "I've been conferring with Tommy."

"Is he all right now?"

"What do you mean, all right?"

"Is he over his . . . trouble?"

"He is if he can make up his mind to grow up."

Now it was her turn. "What do you mean?"

The dark circles of his glasses stared at her blankly, and then she realized that Latour was laughing. "I thought you were an intelligent woman."

"I'm not," she said half bitterly. "I'm stupid."

His laugh was still there, an almost soundless chuckle. Beyond him the circle of singers had widened to include almost everyone on the deck, and thirty people were bellowing, "We were sailing a-lo-o-o-ng, on Moonlight Bay . . ."

Latour came closer, to be heard. "You mean to tell me you haven't even yet got wise to Tommy?"

"I don't know what you mean. He's a very good student—"

"Oh, student!" Latour said. "Sure, he's a student. There's nothing wrong with his brains. He's just a child, that's all, he never grew up."

A counterattraction to the singing had started in the lounge. A few of the energetic had turned on the radio and were dancing on the smooth terrazzo floor. Lucy saw figures float by the lighted door: Donna and Henry Earp, the Kinseys, Doak and Myra Richards, Tommy and Phyllis. The radio cut quick and active across the dragging tempo of the singing.

"But he was in the air force three years," she said. "He's a grown man, he's been through a lot. I never saw anything childish in him."

He turned his head; his profile was cruel and iron against the light. "You're disgustingly obtuse," his mocking voice said. "What did *you* make of that show he put on today?"

"I don't know," she said, hesitating. "That he was afraid, I suppose."

"Afraid of what?"

"Of what? That he'd fail, that he wouldn't make it after all."

"Go to the foot of the class."

"Pardon?"

"Go to the foot of the class," Latour said. "Look at the record. Only child, doting mother. I knew him as an undergraduate, and he's been trying for five or six years to break loose. Or he thought he was. If it hadn't been for the war he'd have found out sooner that he wasn't. The war came just as he graduated, just right so he could hide in it. He could even make a show like a hero, like a flyboy. But not as a pilot, notice. He busted out in pilot training. Somebody else would have the real responsibility. After the war, back to school where he's still safe, with GI benefits and no real decisions to make. And then all of a sudden he wakes up and he's pretty near through. In about three hours he'll be out in the bright light all by himself with a Ph.D. in his hand and a career to make and no mother, no Army, no university, to cuddle him. He wasn't afraid of that exam, he was afraid of passing it."

Lucy was silent. She believed him completely, the pattern matched at every edge, but she rebelled at the triumph and contempt in his voice. Suppose he was completely right: Tommy Probst was still his student and presumably his friend, somebody to like and help, not someone to triumph over. Sticky with the slow ooze of perspiration, feeling the hot night dense and smothering around her, she moved restlessly on the rail. Latour reached into the pocket of his seersucker jacket and brought out a pint bottle.

"Drink? I've been avoiding the bellywash everyone else is drinking."

"No, thank you," Lucy said. "Couldn't I get you a glass and some ice?"

"I like it warm," he said. "Keeps me reminded that it's poison."

She saw then what she had not seen before, that he was quite drunk, but out of her vague rebelliousness she said, "Mr. Latour, all the boys are in Tommy's position almost exactly, aren't they? They're right at that edge where they have to be fully responsible adults. They all work much too hard. Any of them could crack just the way Tommy did. Charley could do it. It isn't a disgrace."

Latour's head went back, the bottle to his lips, and for a moment he was a bird drinking, his iron beak in the air, at once terrible and ridiculous. "You needn't worry about Charley," he said when he had brought the bottle down. "Charley's another breed of rat. He's the kind that wants to wear the old man's breeches even before they're off the old man's legs. Tommy's never got over calling me 'Sir.' Charley'd eat me tomorrow if he thought he could get away with it."

"Who'd do what?" Charley said. He had appeared behind Latour with two glasses in his hands. He passed one to Lucy with a quick lift of the eyebrows and she loved him again for having seen that she was trapped.

"You, you ungrateful whelp," Latour said. He dropped the bottle in his pocket; his blank stare and forward-thrusting face seemed to challenge Charley. "I'll tell you what you think. You think you're younger than I am. That's right. You think you're better-looking than I am. Maybe that's right too. You think you could put me down. That's a foolish mistake. You think you're as smart as I am, and that's even more foolish." His thumb jerked up under Charley's wishbone like a disemboweling knife, and Charley grunted. "Given half a chance," Latour said, "you'd open your wolfish jaws and swallow me. You're like the cannibals who think it gives them virtue to eat their enemy's heart. You'd eat mine."

"He's distraught," Charley said to Lucy. "Maybe we should get him into a tepid bath."

"You and who else?" Latour said, like a belligerent kid. His sardonic fixed grin turned on Lucy. "You can see how it goes in his mind. I develop a lot of apparatus for testing perception, and I fight the whole damn university till I get a lab equipped with sound equipment and Phonelescopes and oscillographs and electronic microscopes, and then punks like this one come along and pick my brains and think they know as much as the old man. I give them the equipment and provide them with ideas and supervise their work and let them add their names to mine on scholarly articles, and they think they're all ready to put on the old man's breeches."

"Why, Paul," Charley said, "you've got an absolute anxiety neurosis. You should see a psychiatrist. You'll brood yourself into paranoia and begin to have persecution complexes. You've got one now. Here I've been holding you up all year, and you think I'm secretly plotting to eat you. You really should talk to a good psychologist."

"Like who?" Latour said, grinning. "Some punk like you whose soft spot hasn't hardened yet?"

"There are one or two others almost as good," Charley said, "but Graham is the best."

Latour took the bottle from his pocket and drank again and screwed on the cap and dropped the bottle back in the pocket. His stare never left Charley's face; his soundless chuckle broke out into a snort.

"A punk," he said. "A callow juvenile, a pubescent boy, a beardless youth. You're still in the spanking stage."

Winking at Lucy, Charley said, "Takes a good man."

"Oh, not so good," Latour said. "Any *man* could do it."

His hand shot out for Charley's wrist, and Charley jerked back, slopping his beer. It seemed to Lucy that something bright and alert had leaped up in both of them, and she wanted to tell them to drop it, but the noise of singing and the moan of dance music from the lounge made such a current of noise that she didn't trust her voice against it. But Latour's edged foolery bothered her; she didn't think he was entirely joking, and she didn't think Charley thought so either. She watched them scuffle and shove each other, assuming exaggeratedly the starting pose for a wrestling match. Latour reached in his pocket and handed her the almost empty whisky bottle; he removed his glasses and passed them to her, and she saw his eyes like dark holes with a glint of light at the bottom.

"For heaven's sake," she said, "you're not going to . . ."

Latour exploded into violent movement, reached and leaned and jerked in a flash, and suddenly Charley's length was across his shoulder, held by crotch and neck, and Latour with braced legs was staggering forward. He was headed directly for the rail. Charley's legs kicked frantically, his arm whipped around Latour's neck in a headlock, but Latour was brutally strong. Face twisted under Charley's arm, he staggered ahead.

Lucy screamed, certain for a moment that Latour was going to throw Charley over. But her husband's legs kicked free, and he swung sideward to get his feet on the floor. Latour let go his neck hold, and his palms slapped against Charley's body as he shifted. Charley was clinging to his headlock, twisting the blockier Latour into a crouch. Then somehow Latour dove under him, and they crashed.

The whole crowd was around them, shutting off the light from the lounge so that the contestants grunted and struggled in almost total darkness. Lucy bent over them, screaming at Charley to quit it, let go. Someone moved in the crowd, and in a brief streak of light she saw Latour's hands, iron strong, tearing Charley's locked fingers apart, and the veins ridged on Charley's neck as he clung to his hold.

"Stop it!" she screamed at them. "You'll get all dirty, you'll get hurt, stop it, please, Charley!"

Latour broke free and spun Charley like a straw man, trying to get a hold for a slam. But as they went to the floor again Charley's legs caught him in a head scissors and bent him harshly back.

"Great God," Henry Earp said beside Lucy. "What is this, fun or fight?"

"I don't know," she said. "Fun. But make them stop." She grabbed the arm of Clark Richards. "Make them stop, please!"

Richards bent over the wrestlers, quiet now, Latour's head forced back and Charley lying still, just keeping the pressure on. "Come on," Richards said. He slapped them both on the back. "Bout's a draw. Let go, Charley."

Latour's body arched with a convulsive spring, but Charley's legs clenched tighter and crushed him down again.

"Okay with me," Charley said. "You satisfied with a draw, Paul?"

Latour said nothing. "All right," Richards said. "Let's call it off, Paul. Someone might get hurt."

As Charley unlocked his legs and rolled free, Latour was up and after him like a wolf, but Richards and Henry and several others held him back. He put a hand to his neck and stood panting. "That was a dirty hold, Graham."

"Not so dirty as getting dumped twenty feet into a courtyard," Charley said. His T-shirt was ripped half off him. He grinned fixedly at Latour. Sick and fluttery at what had happened, Lucy took his hand, knowing that it was over now, the support was gone, the rest of the way was against difficulties all the way. "You foolish people," she said. "You'll spoil a good party."

Somehow, by the time she had got herself together after her scare, the party had disintegrated. The unmarried graduate students who had been noisily there all evening had vanished, several of the house couples had gone quietly to bed. The keg was empty, and a half-bottle of whisky stood unwanted on the table. A whole carful of people had gone out the Terre Haute road for sandwiches, taking Paul Latour with them. The court below the rail was empty except for Charley's jeep and Clark Richards' sedan, and the deck was almost deserted, when Richards stepped out of the lounge with his white coat on, ready to go home.

He came from light into darkness, so that for a moment he stood turning his head, peering. "Myra?" he said. "We should be getting on."

"She isn't out here," Lucy said, and jumped down from the railing where she had been sitting talking to Charley. "Isn't she in the lounge?"

"I just looked," Richards said. "Maybe she's gone up to the ladies' room."

He came out to lean against the rail near them, looking out across the darkness to the floodlighted clock tower floating in the sky. "It's a little like the spire of Salisbury Cathedral, isn't it?" he said. "Salisbury Cathedral across the Avon." He turned his face toward Lucy. "Isn't that where you're from, Salisbury?"

"Yes," she said, "it is rather like."

Then an odd thing happened. The southwest horizon leaped up suddenly, black and jagged, hill and tree and floating tower, with the green glow of heat lightning behind it, and when the lightning winked out, the tower went with it, leaving only the unbroken dark. "Wasn't that queer?" she said. "They must have turned off the floodlights just at that instant. It was almost as if the lightning wiped it out."

They were all tired, yawning, languid with the late hour and the beer and the unremitting, oozing heat. Richards looked at his watch, holding it so that light from the lounge fell on it. "Where can Myra be?" he said. "It's one o'clock."

Slowly Charley slid off the rail, groaning. "Could she be sick? Did she have too much, you think?"

"I don't know," Richards said. His voice was faintly snappish, irritated. "I don't think so, but she could have, I suppose."

"Let me just look up in the shower room," Lucy said, and slipped away from them, through the immense hot lounge. Art Morris was asleep on the big sofa, looking greasy with sweat under the bluish light. Down the long wide hall she felt like a tiny lost figure in a nightmare and thought what a really queer place this was to live in, after all. So big it forgot about you. She pushed the door, felt for the switch. Light leaped on the water-beaded tile, the silence opened to the lonely drip of a tap. No one was in the shower room, no shoes showed under the row of toilet doors.

When she got back to the deck, someone had turned on the powerful light above the door, and the party lay in wreckage there, a surly shambles of slopped beer and glasses and wadded napkins and trampled cigarette butts. In that light the Earps and Charley and Richards were looking at each other abashed.

"It's almost a cinch she went with the others out to the Casino," Charley was saying. "There was a whole swarm of them went together."

"You'd think she would have said something," Richards said. His voice was so harsh that Lucy looked at him in surprise and saw his mouth tight and thin, his face drawn with inordinate anxiety. "She wasn't upstairs?"

Lucy shook her head. For an instant Richards stood with his hands opening and closing at his sides. Abruptly he strode to the rail and looked over it, following it around to the corner and peering over into the tangle of weeds and rubbish at the side. He spun around as if he feared guns were pointed at his back. "Who saw her last? What was she doing? Who was she with?"

No one spoke for a moment, until Henry Earp said cautiously, "She was dancing a while ago, a whole bunch of us were. But that was a half-hour ago, at least."

"Who with?" Richards said, and then slapped at the air with his hand and said, "No, that wouldn't tell us anything. She must have gone for a sandwich."

"We can go see," Charley said. "Matter of fact, I'd like a sandwich myself. Why don't we run up the road and see if she's at the Casino? She probably didn't notice what time it was."

"No," Richards said grimly. Lucy found it hard to look at him, she was so troubled with sympathy and embarrassment. "Probably she didn't." He looked at Charley almost vaguely, and sweat was up on his forehead. "Would you mind?" he said. "Perhaps I ought to stay here, in case she . . ."

"I'll stay here," Lucy said. The distraught vague eyes touched her.

"You'll want something to eat too. You go along."

"No," she said. "I'd rather stay. I would anyway." To Charley she said, "Why don't you and Henry and Donna go? You could look in at the Casino and the Tavern and all those places along there."

With his arm around her he walked her to the lounge door, and everything that had passed that evening was in their look just before he kissed her. When she turned around Richards was watching. In the bald light, swarming with insects that crawled and leaped and fluttered toward the globe above the doors, his eyes seemed to glare. Lucy clicked off the light and dropped them back into darkness.

"Should you like a drink?" she said into the black.

After a moment he answered, "No, thank you."

Gradually his white-suited figure emerged again as her eyes adjusted. He was on the rail looking out across the river and woods. Heat lightning flared fitfully again along the staring black horizon. The jeep started down below them; the lights jumped against the bluff, turned twisting the shadows, and were gone with the diminishing motor.

"Don't worry," Lucy said. "I'm sure she just forgot about the time and went for something to eat. We should have had something here, but somehow with so many to plan things, nothing ever gets planned."

"I don't like that river," Richards said. "It's so absolutely black down there . . ." He swung around at her. "Have you got a flashlight?"

"I think so," she said, "but don't you suppose—"

"Could I borrow it, please?" he said. "I'm going down along the bank to look. If you'd stay here—if she should come back . . ."

She slipped in and past the still-sleeping Art Morris and found a flashlight in the kitchen drawer, and now suddenly it was as if she were five years back in time, the cool tube in her hand, the intense blackout darkness around, the sense of oppression, the waiting, the search. That sense was even stronger a few minutes later as she sat on the rail and saw the thin slash of the light down along the riverbank, moving slowly, cutting on and off, eventually disappearing in the trees.

It was very still. Perched on the rail, she looked out from the deck they were so lucky to have, over the night-obliterated view that gave them such a sense of freedom and space, and in all the dark there was no sound louder than the brush of a moth's wings or the tick of an armored bug against the driveway light. Then far up the highway a point of sound bored into the silence and grew and rounded, boring through layers of dark and soundless air, until it was a rush and a threat and a roar, and headlights burst violently around the corner of the bluff and reached across the shine of water and picked out, casual and instantaneous, a canoe with a couple in it.

It was there, starkly white, for only a split instant, and then the road swung, the curtain came down. She found it hard to believe that it had been there at all; she even felt a little knife-prick of terror that it could have been there—so silent, so secret, so swallowed in the black, as unseen and unfelt and unsuspected as a crocodile at a jungle ford.

The heat lightning flared again like the flare of distant explosions or the light of burning towns. Instinctively, out of a habit long outgrown, and even while her eyes remained fixed on the place where the canoe had been, she waited for the sound of the blast, but nothing came; she found herself waiting almost ridiculously, with held breath, and that was the time when the lion chose to roar again.

That challenge, coming immediately after the shock of seeing the silent and somehow stealthy canoe, brought a thought that stopped her pulse: "What if he should be loose?" She felt the adrenaline pump into her blood as she might have felt an electric shock. Her heart pounded and her breath came fast through her open mouth. What if he should be loose?

What if, in these Indiana woods by this quiet river where all of them lived and worked for a future full of casual expectation, far from the jungles and the velds where lions could be expected and where darkness was full of danger, what if here too fear prowled on quiet pads and made its snarling noise in the night? This fraternity house where they lived amicably was ringed with dark water and darker woods where the threat lay in wait. This elevated balcony which she could flood with light at the flip of a finger, this fellowship of youth and study and common experience and common hopes, this common belief in the future, were as friable as walls of cane, as vulnerable as grass huts, and she did not need the things that had happened that evening, or the sight of Clark Richards' tiny light flicking and darting back toward her along the riverbank, to know that what she had lived through for six years was not over and would perhaps never be over for any of them, that in their hearts they were alone, terrified, and at bay, each with his ears attuned to some roar across the woods, some ripple of the water, some whisper of a footstep in the dark.

VOLCANO

Once they had turned off the asphalt onto the rough graded road the driver nursed the car along carefully, creeping across bridges and through arroyos and along rocky stretches. While lighting a cigarette he explained to his American passenger.

"It is a car which cost seven thousand pesos," he said. "One does not treat it as if it were a burro."

"Truly," the American said.

"Partly it is the tires," the driver said. "Tires one cannot buy without paying too much to those who sell them illegally. But partly it is the engine. In the dust an engine suffers."

"I believe it," the American said politely. He was watching out the closed window, seeing how the ash had deepened in the last mile or two, how the bridge rails now were mounded with it, and how the pines, growing thickly on the sides of the countless little volcanic hills, rose listless and gray out of a gray blanket as smooth as new snow and as light under the wind as feathers. Across the west the cloud of smoke was blacker and angrier, funneling down so that its compact lower plume was hidden behind the hills. The sun, at the upper edge of the cloud, was an immense golden orange.

A horn blatted behind them, and the driver pulled half off the road. A car went by them fast, pouring back a choking, impenetrable fog of dust. The driver stopped philosophically to let it blow away before he started again. "Loco," he said. "That one has no respect either for his passengers or his engine."

The American did not answer. He was leaning back in the seat watching the blasted country outside. Occasionally they crept past adobe huts half buried in the ash, their corrals drifted deep, their roofs weighted down, the fields which had once grown corn and beans stretching away on both sides without a track to break their even, slaty gray. He thought of the little animals that had lived in these woods, and whether they had got out before the ash became deep, or had quietly smothered in their holes. A wildcat might make headway through it, perhaps, but not the smaller things, the mice and rabbits and lizards, and it was the small things that one thought of.

"What has become of the people from here?" he asked.

The driver half turned. Some, he said, had gone, many to the United States, being taken away in buses and trains to work as *braceros* in the fields of Arizona and California.

"Where they may be cheated and abused," the American said. "What of those who stay?"

"I will show you one," the driver said. A little further on he pointed to a gray hut under the ash-laden shelter of the pines, a few yards off the road. Peering, the American saw a woman standing in the door, her *rebozo* wrapped across her face, and back of her the cavelike interior and the gleam of a charcoal fire.

"Some, like that one, will not leave," the driver said. "The governor's men have been here and urged them, but they are foolish. It is where they were born; they do not want to leave."

"But what do they live on? They can't grow anything here."

"There are those who cut wood," the driver said. "Though the trees are dying, they are a thing that can be saved. Others, in San Juan, rent horses and burros for the trip to the *boca*. That one, she has nothing. She will die."

The road turned, and the American lost sight of the hut and the still woman in the doorway. Somehow, though the windows were tight shut

and the motor and the punished springs filled the car with sound, he
had an impression of great silence.

They curved left along a ridge and dropped into a valley, and the
volcano was directly ahead of them, not more than two miles away.
From its vent monstrous puffs of black smoke mushroomed upward,
were whipped ragged by the wind, belched up again. The side of the
cone, looking as straight at that distance as if drawn with a ruler, ran
down into a curving lava stream that stopped in a broken wall two
hundred yards short of the road. The west side of the cone was lost in
smoke.

The driver stopped and pointed. Under the lava, he said, was the
village of Paricutín. It was not possible to walk across the lava yet,
because it had not cooled completely and there were poisonous fumes,
but this was a good place to watch from, with the wind the way it was.

"In San Juan it will be dirty," he said. "One will not be able to see
much for the smoke."

"The horses leave from San Juan?"

"At about this time every afternoon."

"And there are people in San Juan still?"

"*Sí.*"

"*Vamanos,*" the American said. "If we wish we can come back here
later."

He sat forward in the seat, watching the volcano throw up its gobbets
of smoke. Through and behind the smoke, like distant flying specks, he
could see the rocks and boulders that were thrown up and fell swiftly
again.

"This trip by horse," he said. "What is it like?"

"It is something to be remembered," the driver said. "One goes up
in daylight, but on the return it is very dark, so dark that one cannot
see the horse's ears. And behind, as one comes down this black trail
that one knew a year ago as a cornfield, are always this noise and this
glare on the sky as if hell were open." He took his hand off the wheel
and raised it over his head. "There is always this feeling of something
behind," he said. "It is like fleeing the end of the world."

"You could wait for me if I went up?"

"Why not?" the driver said. "It is an experience."

They passed a corral, a hut, a clutter of sheds, another corral, its
gates hanging open under a gray drift. Then the houses closed in suddenly

and they were in a street. In the perpetual twilight of this town of San Juan men and women, wrapped to the eyes in *rebozos* and *serapes*, their bare feet gray and silent in the ashes, walked along under the overhang of thatch, and children leaned against the walls, only their eyes showing under the sombrero rims, and watched the car pass.

In the plaza three buses and a half-dozen cars were parked. Only when the motor was cut did the American realize that the silence he had been constantly aware of outside had given place to a thin, gritty patter on the roof. The driver gestured upward. "Here it rains cinders," he said. "It is necessary to keep the head well covered, and something over the mouth and nose." He tied a bandanna across his face and climbed out. "I shall see about these horses," he said.

The American waited. On the far side of the plaza a group of Americans, men and women, were already mounting. In odd mismatched clothes, suit trousers and leather jackets and sombreros and bandannas, the women in riding breeches or Levi's, all of them with their faces muffled, they looked like members of a comic-opera outlaw gang. The driver was having a conference with two Mexicans who were adjusting stirrups for the women. After five minutes he came back.

"It is a pity," he said. "This crowd which is to go immediately has taken all the horses available."

"It is not important," the American said. "Actually I am not so interested in the insides of this volcano."

He tied his handkerchief across his nose, pulled down his hat, and stepped out into the feathery ash. The air was thick with smoke, and cinders pattered on his hat and shoulders. He slitted his eyes against the gritty rain.

"If you would like me to show you around——" the driver said.

"It is not necessary," the American said. He went poking off up a street that opened on the plaza, his nose filled with the odor that he realized he had been smelling for some time, a sour, acrid, vinegarish odor like fresh-sawn oak. He saw many people, shrouded and silent, but they did not break the stillness in which the falling cinders whispered dryly. Even the handkerchief-muffled calls of the Americans riding off toward the crater, and the tooting of the bus horns in farewell, came through the air as through a thick pillow, and he did not hear his own footsteps in the dust.

Once, as he walked past a doorway into which a trail led through the deep ash, the accumulated ashes on a roof let go and avalanched behind him. He turned to see the last runnels trickling from the thatch, and two little Indian girls, each with a small baby hung over her back in the looped *rebozo*, came out of the doorway and waded experimentally in the knee-deep powder.

The end of the street trailed off into ashen fields, and for a moment the American stood in the unnatural gray dusk looking across toward the cone of Paricutín under its lowering cloud of smoke. At intervals of about a minute there was a grumble like far-off blasting, but because of the smoke which blew directly over the town he could not see the rocks flying up. The cinders were an insistent, sibilant rain on his head and shoulders, and his mouth was bitter with the vinegarish taste.

It was not a place he liked. The village of Paricutín, on the other side, had been buried completely under the lava. That was death both definite and sudden. But this slow death that fell like light rain, this gradual smothering that drooped the pines and covered the holes of the little animals and mounded the roofs and choked the streets, this dying village through which ghosts went in silence, was something else. It was a thing Mexicans had always known, in one form or another, else there would not be in so many of their paintings the figure of the robed skeleton, the walking Death. They were patient under it, they accepted it—but the American did not like to remember how alive the eyes of the Indian girls had been as they waded through the ashes with their little sisters on their backs.

On the way back to the plaza he met a pig that wandered in from a side street. The pig looked at him, wrinkling its snout. Its bristly back was floured with gray ash, and its eyes were red. It grunted softly, querulously, and put its snout to the ground, rooted without hope in the foot-deep powder, walked a few steps with its nose plowing the dry and unprofitable dust.

The American left it and went back to the car. In a moment the driver came from the bus where he had been gossiping. "Let's go," the American said. "Perhaps where we stopped first it is clearer."

They went back through the choked streets, leaving the silent Indians who moved softly as shadows through the dead town and the hog which rooted without hope in the ashes, and pulled off the road in deep ash at the end of the valley. For a few minutes they sat, talking desultorily in polite Spanish and watching the irregular spouting of the cone, opening the windows so that they could hear the ominous low grumble and the faint clatter of falling rocks. The cone was blue-black now, and the lava bed across the foreground was a somber, smoking cliff. It was a landscape without shadows, submerged in gray twilight.

"I have conceived a great hatred for this thing," the American said finally. "It is a thing I have always known and always hated. It is something which kills."

"Truly," the driver said. "I have felt it, as those who are in the war must feel the war."

"Yes," the American said.

"You have friends in the war?"

"Sons," the American said. "One is now a prisoner in Germany."

"*Ai,*" the driver said, with sympathy. He hesitated a minute, as if hunting for the correct thing to say to one whose sons were captives of the enemy. "You hear from him?" he said. "How does he endure his captivity?"

"How does one endure anything?" the American said. "I suppose he hates it and endures it, that is all." He looked out the window, raised his shoulders. "I have heard once only," he said for politeness' sake.

They looked across the gray waste that had once been a *milpa*, toward the smoking front of the lava bed. The light had changed. It was darker, more threatening, like the last ominous moments before a thunderstorm. The west was almost as black as night, but across the field spread a steely dusk that rendered every object sharp-edged and distinct. The American raised his head and looked at the ceiling of the car. The stealthy, light fingering had begun there.

"You see?" he said. "That is what I mean. It is something which follows. It is like a doom."

The driver made a deprecating gesture. "The wind has shifted," he said.

"It always shifts," the American said.

He stepped out of the car and stood shin-deep in the gray death, listening to the stealthy whisper and the silence that lay over and under and around. The crater rumbled far off, and boulders fell back with a distant clatter, but the silence still hung like something tangible over the valley.

As he watched, the heavy dusk lightened, and he looked up. By a freak of wind the smoke had been blown high, and though no sign of the setting sun came through the obscured west, a pale, pinkish wash of light came through under the cloud and let an unearthly illumination over the field of ash and the smoking cliff of lava.

Into that lurid dusk an Indian in white pajamas, with a bundle of wood on his back and an axe across his shoulder, came out of the pines at the upper edge of the lava and walked along the clifflike front. Little puffs of dust rose from under his feet. After him, fifteen yards behind, came another, and after him another.

The three strung out across the field, walking as silently in the rosy, metallic light as dream figures. The ones behind did not try to close the gap and walk companionably with the one ahead; the one ahead did not wait for them. They walked in single file, fifteen yards apart, each with his burden of wood on his back, and the little puffs of dust rose under their feet and the punched-hole tracks lengthened behind them across the field.

The American watched them, feeling the silence that weighed on these little figures more heavily than the loads upon their backs, and as he watched he heard the man ahead whistle a brief snatch of tune, drop it, start something else. He went whistling, a ghost in a dead land, toward some hut half buried in ash where a charcoal fire would be burning, and his wife would have ready for him tortillas and beans, with cinders in them, perhaps, like everything else, but still tortillas and beans that would fill a man's belly against the work that must be done tomorrow.

The American watched the three until they were out of sight around the shoulder of the hill. When he climbed into the car and motioned for the driver to start back he was not thinking of the steady smothering fall of the cinders or the death that lay over the streets and cornfields of San Juan. He was thinking of the eyes of the little Indian girls, which were so very alive above the muffling *rebozos*.

"It is a strange thing," he said. "This whistling."

The driver, reaching to turn the ignition key, shrugged, and smiled. "Why not?" he said. "The mouth is not made merely to spit with or curse with. At times it may be used for whistling, or even for kissing, *verdad?*"

TWO
RIVERS

∎   ∎   ∎

His father's voice awakened him. Stretching his back, arching against the mattress, he looked over at his parents' end of the sleeping porch. His mother was up too, though he could tell from the flatness of the light outside that it was still early. He lay on his back quietly, letting complete wakefulness come on, watching a spider that dangled on a golden, shining thread from the rolled canvas of the blinds. The spider came down in tiny jerks, his legs wriggling, then went up again in the beam of sun. From the other room the father's voice rose loud and cheerful:

Oh I'd give every man in the army a quarter
If they'd all take a shot at my mother-in-law.

The boy slid his legs out of bed and yanked the nightshirt over his head. He didn't want his father's face poking around the door, saying, "I plough deep while sluggards sleep!" He didn't want to be joked with. Yesterday was too sore a spot in his mind. He had been avoiding his father ever since the morning before, and he was not yet ready to accept any joking or attempts to make up. Nobody had a right hitting a person for nothing, and you bet they weren't going to be friends. Let him whistle and sing out there, pretending nothing was the matter. The whole business yesterday was the matter, the Ford that wouldn't start was the matter, the whole lost Fourth of July was the matter, the missed parade, the missed fireworks, the missed ball game in Chinook were the matter. The cuff on the ear his father had given him when he got so mad at the Ford he had to have something to hit was the matter.

In the other room, as he pulled on his overalls, the bacon was snapping in the pan, and he smelled its good morning smell. His father whistled, sang:

> In the town of O'Geary lived Paddy O'Flannagan,
> Battered away till he hadn't a pound,
> His father he died and he made him a man again,
> Left him a farm of tin acres o' ground. . . .

The boy pulled the overall straps over his shoulders and went into the main room. His father stopped singing and looked at him. "Hello, Cheerful," he said. "You look like you'd bit into a wormy apple."

The boy mumbled something and went outside to wash at the bench. It wasn't any fun waking up today. You kept thinking about yesterday, and how much fun it had been waking up then, when you were going to do something special and exciting, drive fifty miles to Chinook and spend the whole day just having fun. Now there wasn't anything but the same old thing to do you did every day. Run the trap line, put out some poison for the gophers, read the Sears, Roebuck catalogue.

At breakfast he was glum, and his father joked with him. Even his mother smiled, as if she had forgotten already how much wrong had been done the day before. "You look as if you'd been sent for and couldn't come," she said. "Cheer up."

"I don't want to cheer up."

They just smiled at each other, and he hated them both.

After breakfast his father said, "You help your ma with the dishes, now. See how useful you can make yourself around here."

Unwillingly, wanting to get out of the house and away from them, he got the towel and swabbed off the plates. He was rubbing a glass when he heard the Ford sputter and race and roar and then calm down into a steady mutter. His mouth opened, and he looked at his mother. Her eyes were crinkled up with smiling.

"It goes!" he said.

"Sure it goes." She pulled both his ears, rocking his head. "Know what we're going to do?"

"What?"

"We're going to the mountains anyway. Not to Chinook—there wouldn't be anything doing today. But to the mountains, for a picnic. Pa got the car going yesterday afternoon, when you were down in the field, so we decided to go today. If you want to, of course."

"Yay!" he said. "Shall I dress up?"

"Put on your shoes, you'd better. We might climb a mountain."

The boy was out into the porch in three steps. With one shoe on and the other in his hand he hopped to the door. "When?" he said.

"Soon as you can get ready."

He was trying to run and tie his shoelaces at the same time as he went out of the house. There in the Ford, smoking his pipe, with one leg over the door and his weight on the back of his neck, his father sat. "What detained you?" he said. "I've been waiting a half-hour. You must not want to go very bad."

"Aw!" the boy said. He looked inside the Ford. There was the lunch all packed, the fat wet canvas waterbag, even Spot with his tongue out and his ears up. Looking at his father, all his sullenness gone now, the boy said, "When did you get all this ready?"

His father grinned. "While you slept like a sluggard we worked like a buggard," he said. Then the boy knew that everything was perfect, nothing could go wrong. When his father started rhyming things he was in his very best mood, and not even breakdowns and flat tires could make him do more than puff and blow and play-act.

He clambered into the front seat and felt the motor shaking under the floorboards. "Hey, Ma!" he yelled. "Hurry up! We're all ready to go!"

Their own road was a barely marked trail that wriggled out over the burnouts along the east side of the wheat field. At the line it ran into another coming down from the homesteads to the east, and at Cree, a mile inside the Montana boundary, they hit the straight section-line road to Chinook. On that road they passed a trotting team pulling an empty wagon, and the boy waved and yelled, feeling superior, feeling as if he were charioted on pure speed and all the rest of the world were earth-footed.

"Let's see how fast this old boat will go," the father said. He nursed it down through a coulee and onto the flat. His fingers pulled the gas lever down, and the motor roared. Looking back with the wind-stung tears in his eyes, the boy saw his mother hanging on to her hat, and the artificial cherries on the hat bouncing. The Ford leaped and bucked, the picnic box tipped over, the dog leaned out and the wind blew his eyes shut and his ears straight back. Turning around, the boy saw the blue sparks leaping from the magneto box and heard his father wahoo. He hung on to the side and leaned out to let the wind tear at him, tried to count the fence posts going by, but they were ahead of him before he got to ten.

The road roughened, and they slowed down. "Good land!" his mother said from the back seat. "We want to get to the Bearpaws, not wind up in a ditch."

"How fast were we going, Pa?"

"Forty or so, I guess. If we'd been going any faster you'd have hollered 'nuff. You were looking pretty peaked."

"I was not."

"Looked pretty scared to me. I guess Ma was hopping around back there like corn in a popper. How'd you like it, Ma?"

"I liked it all right," she said, "but don't do it again."

They passed a farm, and the boy waved at three openmouthed kids in the yard. It was pretty good to be going somewhere, all right. The mountains were plainer now in the south. He could see dark canyons cutting into the slopes and there was snow on the upper peaks.

"How soon'll we get there, Pa?"

His father tapped the pipe out and put it away and laughed. Without bothering to answer, he began to sing:

> Oh, I dug Snoqualmie River,
> And Lake Samamish too,
> And paddled down to Kirkland
> In a little birch canoe.
>
> I built the Rocky Mountains,
> And placed them where they are,

Sold whiskey to the Ind-i-ans
From behind a little bar.

It was then, with the empty flat country wheeling by like a great turntable, the wheat fields and the fences and the far red peaks of barns rotating slowly as if in a dignified dance, wheeling and slipping behind and gone, and his father singing, that the strangeness first came over the boy. Somewhere, sometime . . . and there were mountains in it, and a stream, and a swing that he had fallen out of and cried, and he had mashed ripe blackberries in his hand and his mother had wiped him off, straightening his stiff fingers and wiping hard. . . . His mind caught on that memory from a time before there was any memory, he rubbed his finger tips against his palm and slid a little down in the seat.

His father tramped on both pedals hard and leaned out of the car, looking. He swung to stare at the boy as a startled idiot might have looked, and in a voice heavy with German gutturals he said, "Vot it iss in de crass?"

"What?"

"Iss in de crass somedings. *Besser* you *bleiben* right here."

He climbed out, and the boy climbed out after him. The dog jumped over the side and rushed, and in the grass by the side of the road the boy saw the biggest snake he had ever seen, long and fat and sleepy. When it pulled itself in and faced the stiff-legged dog he saw that the hind legs and tail of a gopher stuck out of the stretched mouth.

"Jiminy!" the boy said. "He eats gophers whole."

His father stopped with hands on knees to stare at the snake, looked at the boy, and wagged his head. "*Himmel*," he said. "Dot iss a *schlange* vot iss a *schlange!*"

"What is it?" the mother said from the car and the boy yelled back, "A snake, a great big snake, and he's got a whole gopher in his mouth!"

The father chased the pup away, found a rock, and with one careful throw crushed the big flat head. The body, as big around as the boy's ankle, tightened into a ridged convulsion of muscles, and the tail whipped back and forth. Stooping, the father pulled on the gopher's tail. There was a wet, slupping noise, and the gopher slid out, coated with slime and twice as long as he ought to have been.

"Head first," the father said. "That's a hell of a way to die."

He lifted the snake by the tail and held it up. "Look," he said. "He's longer than I am." But the mother made a face and turned her head while he fastened it in the forked top of a fence post. It trailed almost two feet on the ground. The tail still twitched.

"He'll twitch till the sun goes down," the father said. "First guy that comes along here drunk is going to think he's got D.T.'s." He climbed into the car again, and the boy followed.

"What was it, Pa?"

"Milk snake. They come into barns sometimes and milk the cows dry. You saw what he did to that gopher. Milk a cow dry as powder in ten minutes."

"Gee," the boy said. He sat back and thought about how long and slick the gopher had been, and how the snake's mouth was all stretched, and it was a good feeling to have been along and to have shared something like that with his father. It was a trophy, a thing you would remember all your life, and you could tell about it. And while he was thinking that already, even before they got to the mountains at all, he had something to remember about the trip, he remembered that just before they saw the snake he had been remembering something else, and he puckered his eyes in the sun, thinking. He had been right on the edge of it, it was right on the tip of his tongue, and then his father had tramped on the pedals. But it was something a long time ago, and there was a strangeness about it, something bothersome and a little scary, and it hurt his head the way it hurt his head sometimes to do arithmetical sums without pencil and paper. When you did them in your head something went round and round, and you had to keep looking inside to make sure you didn't lose sight of the figures that were pasted up there somewhere, and if you did it very long at a time you got a sick headache out of it. It was something like that when he had almost remembered just a while ago, only he hadn't quite been able to see what he knew was there. . . .

By ten o'clock they had left the graded road and were chugging up a winding trail with toothed rocks embedded in the ruts. Ahead of them the mountains looked low and disappointing, treeless, brown. The trail ducked into a narrow gulch and the sides rose up around them, reddish gravel covered with bunch grass and sage.

"Gee whiz," the boy said. "These don't look like mountains."

"What'd you expect?" his father said. "Expect to step out onto a glacier or something?"

"But there aren't any trees," the boy said. "Gee whiz, there isn't even any water."

He stood up to look ahead. His father's foot went down on the low pedal, and the Ford growled at the grade. "Come on, Lena," his father said. He hitched himself back and forward in the seat, helping the car over the hill, and then, as they barely pulled over the hump and the sides of the gully fell away, there were the real mountains, high as heaven, the high slopes spiked and tufted with trees, and directly ahead of them a magnificent V-shaped door with the sun touching gray cliffs far back in, and a straight-edged violet shadow streaming down from the eastern peak clear to the canyon floor.

"Well?" the father's voice said. "I guess if you don't like it we can drop you off here and pick you up on the way back."

The boy turned to his mother. She was sitting far forward on the edge of the seat. "I guess we want to come along, all right," she said, and laughed as if she might cry. "Anything as beautiful as that! Don't we, sonny?"

"You bet," he said. He remained standing all the way up over the gentle slope of the alluvial fan that aproned out from the canyon's mouth, and when they passed under the violet shadow, not violet any more but cool gray, he tipped his head back and looked up miles and miles to the broken rock above.

The road got rougher. "Sit down," his father said. "First thing you know you'll fall out on your head and sprain both your ankles."

He was in his very best mood. He said funny things to the car, coaxing it over steep pitches. He talked to it like a horse, patted it on the dashboard, promised it an apple when they got there. Above them the canyon walls opened out and back, went up steeply high and high and high, beyond the first walls that the boy had thought so terrific, away beyond those, piling peak on peak, and the sun touched and missed and touched again.

The trail steepened. A jet of steam burst from the brass radiator cap, the car throbbed and labored, they all sat forward and urged it on. But it slowed, shook, stopped and stood there steaming and shaking, and the motor died with a last, lunging gasp.

"Is this as far as we can get?" the boy said. The thought that they might be broken down, right here on the threshold of wonder, put him in a panic. He looked around. They were in a bare rocky gorge. Not even any trees yet, though a stream tumbled down a bouldered channel on the left. But to get to trees and the real mountains they had to go further, much further. "Can't we get any further?" he said.

His father grunted. "Skin down to the creek and get a bucket of water." The boy ran, came stumbling and staggering back with the pail. His mother had already climbed out and put a rock under the back wheel, and they stood close together while the father with a rag made quick, stabbing turns at the radiator cap. The cap blew off and steam went up for six feet and they all jumped back. There was a sullen subterranean boiling deep under the hood.

"Now!" the father said. He poured a little water in, stepped back. In a minute the water came bubbling out again. He poured again, and the motor spit it out again. "Can't seem to keep anything on her stomach," the father said, and winked at the boy. He didn't seem worried.

The fourth dose stayed down. They filled up the radiator till it ran over, screwed the plug in, and threw the pail in the back end. "You two stay out," the father said. "I'll see if she'll go over unloaded."

She wouldn't. She moved two feet, strangled, and died. The boy watched with his jaw hanging, remembering yesterday, remembering when something like this had happened and the whole day had gone wrong. But his father wasn't the same today. He just got out of the car and didn't swear at all, but winked at the boy again, and made a closing motion with his hand under his chin. "Better shut that mouth," he said. "Some bird'll fly in there and build a nest."

To the mother he said, "Can you kick that rock out from under the wheel?"

"Sure," she said. "But do you think . . . Maybe we could walk from here."

"Hell with it," he said cheerfully. "I'll get her up if I have to lug her on my back."

She kicked the stone away and he rolled backward down the hill, craning, steering with one hand. At the bottom he cramped the wheels, got out and cranked the motor, got in again, and turned around in the narrow road, taking three or four angled tries before he made it. Then his hand waved, and there was the Ford coming up the hill backward, kicking gravel down from under its straining hind wheels, angling across the road and back and up, and the motor roaring like a threshing engine, until it went by them and on up to the crest and turned around with one quick expert ducking motion, and they got in and were off again.

"Well!" said the mother in relief. "Who'd have thought of going up backward?"

"Got more power in reverse," the father said. "Can't make it one way, try another."

"Yay!" the boy said. He was standing up, watching the deep insides of the earth appear behind the angled rock, and his mind was soaring again, up into the heights where a hawk or eagle circled like a toy bird on a string.

"How do you like it?" his mother shouted at him. He turned around and nodded his head, and she smiled at him, wrinkling her eyes. She looked excited herself. Her face had color in it and the varnished cherries bouncing on her hat gave her a reckless, girlish look.

"Hi, Ma," he said, and grinned.

"Hi yourself," she said, and grinned right back. He lifted his face and yelled for the very pressure of happiness inside him.

They lay on a ledge high upon the sunny east slope and looked out to the north through the notch cut as sharply as a wedge out of a pie. Far below them the golden plain spread level, golden-tawny grass and golden-green wheat checkerboarded in a pattern as wide as the world. Back of them the spring they had followed up the slope welled out of the ledge, spread out in a small swampy spot, and trickled off down the hill. There were trees, a thick cluster of spruce against the bulge of the wall above them, a clump of twinkling, sunny aspen down the slope, and in the canyon bottom below them a dense forest of soft maple. The mother had a bouquet of leaves in her hand, a little bunch of pine cones on the ground beside her. The three lay quietly, looking down over the steeply dropping wall to the V-shaped door, and beyond that to the interminable plain.

The boy wriggled his back against the rock, put his hand down to shift himself, brought it up again prickled with broken spruce needles. He picked them off, still staring out over the canyon gateway. They were far above the world he knew. The air was cleaner, thinner. There was cold water running from the rock, and all around there were trees. And over the whole canyon, like a haze in the clear air, was that other thing, that memory or ghost of a memory, a swing he had fallen out of, a feel of his hands sticky with crushed blackberries, his skin drinking cool shade, and his father's anger—the reflection of ecstasy and the shadow of tears.

"I never knew till this minute," his mother said, "how much I've missed the trees."

Nobody answered. They were all stuffed with lunch, pleasantly tired after the climb. The father lay staring off down the canyon, and the sour smell of his pipe, in that air, was pleasant and clean. The boy saw his mother put the stem of a maple leaf in her mouth and make a half-pleased face at the bitter taste.

The father rose and dug a tin cup from the picnic box, walked to the spring, and dipped himself a drink. He made a breathy sound of satisfaction. "So cold it hurts your teeth," he said. He brought the mother a cup, and she drank.

"Brucie?" she said, motioning with the cup.

He started to get up, but his father filled the cup and brought it, making believe he was going to pour it on him. The boy ducked and reached for the cup. With his eyes on his father over the cup's rim, he drank, testing the icy water to see if it really did hurt the teeth. The water was cold and silvery in his mouth, and when he swallowed he felt it cold clear down to his stomach.

"It doesn't either hurt your teeth," he said. He poured a little of it on his arm, and something jumped in his skin. It was his skin that remembered. Something numbingly cold, and then warm. He felt it now, the way you waded in it.

"Mom," he said.

"What?"

"Was it in Washington we went on a picnic like this and picked blackberries and I fell out of a swing and there were big trees, and we found a river that was half cold and half warm?"

His father was relighting his pipe. "What do you know about Washington?" he said. "You were only knee-high to a grasshopper when we lived there."

"Well, I remember," the boy said. "I've been remembering it all day long, ever since you sang that song about building the Rocky Mountains. You sang it that day, too. Don't you remember, Mom?"

"I don't know," she said doubtfully. "We went on picnics in Washington."

"What's this about a river with hot and cold running water?" his father said. "You must remember some time you had a bath in a bathtub."

"I do not!" the boy said. "I got blackberries mashed all over my hands and Mom scrubbed me off, and then we found that river and we waded in it and half was hot and half was cold."

"Oh-h-h," his mother said. "I believe I do. . . . Harry, you remember once up in the Cascades, when we went out with the Curtises? And little Bill Curtis fell off the dock into the lake." She turned to the boy. "Was there a summer cottage there, a brown shingled house?"

"I don't know," the boy said. "I don't remember any Curtises. But I remember blackberries and that river and a swing."

"Your head is full of blackberries," his father said. "If it was the time we went out with the Curtises there weren't any blackberries. That was in the spring."

"No," the mother said. "It was in the fall. It was just before we moved to Redmond. And I think there was a place where one river from the mountains ran into another one from the valley, and they ran alongside each other in the same channel. The mountain one was a lot colder. Don't you remember that trip with the Curtises, Harry?"

"Sure I remember it," the father said. "We hired a buckboard and saw a black bear and I won six bits from Joe Curtis pitching horseshoes."

"That's right," the mother said. "You remember the bear, Brucie."

The boy shook his head. There wasn't any bear in what he remembered. Just feelings, and things that made his skin prickle.

His mother was looking at him, a little puzzled wrinkle between her eyes. "It's funny you should remember such different things than we remember," she said. "Everything means something different to everybody, I guess." She laughed, and the boy thought her eyes looked very odd and bright. "It makes me feel as if I didn't know you at all," she said. She brushed her face with the handful of leaves and looked at the father, gathering up odds and ends and putting them in the picnic box. "I wonder what each of us will remember about today?"

"I wouldn't worry about it," the father said. "You can depend on Bub here to remember a lot of things that didn't happen."

"I don't think he does," she said. "He's got a good memory."

The father picked up the box. "It takes a good memory to remember things that never happened," he said. "I remember once a garter snake crawled into my cradle and I used it for a belt to keep my breechclout on. They took it away from me and I bawled the crib so full of tears I had to swim for shore. I drifted in three days later on a checkerboard raft with a didie for a sail."

The boy stood up and brushed off his pants. "You do too remember that river," he said.

His father grinned at him. "Sure. Only it wasn't quite as hot and cold as you make it out."

It was evening in the canyon, but when they reached the mouth again they emerged into full afternoon, with two hours of sun left them. The father stopped the car before they dipped into the gravelly wash between the foothills, and they all looked back at the steep thrust of the mountains, purpling in the shadows, the rock glowing golden-red far back on the faces of the inner peaks. The mother still held her bouquet of maple leaves in her hand.

"Well, there go the Mountains of the Moon," she said. The moment was almost solemn. In the front seat the boy stood looking back. He felt the sun strong against the side of his face, and the mountains shearing up before him were very real. In a little while, as they went north, they would begin to melt together, and the patches of snow would appear far up on the northern slopes. His eyes went curiously out of focus, and he saw the mountains as they would appear from the homestead on a hot day, a ghostly line on the horizon.

He felt his father twist to look at him, but the trance was so strong on him that he didn't look down for a minute. When he did he caught his mother and father looking at each other, the look they had sometimes when he had pleased them and made them proud of him.

"Okay," his father said, and stabbed him in the ribs with a hard thumb. "Wipe the black bears out of your eyes."

He started the car again, and as they bounced down the rocky trail toward the road he sang at the top of his voice, bellowing into the still, hot afternoon:

> I had a kid and his name was Brucie,
> Squeezed black bears and found them juicy,
> Washed them off in a hot-cold river,
> Now you boil and now you shiver,
> Caught his pants so full of trout
> He couldn't sit down till he got them out.

Trout were boiled from the hot-side river,
Trout from the cold side raw as liver.
Ate the boiled ones, ate the raw,
And then went howling home to Maw.

The boy looked up at his father, his laughter bubbling up, everything wonderful, the day a swell day, his mother clapping hands in time to his father's fool singing.

"Aw, for gosh sakes," he said, and ducked when his father pretended he was going to swat him one.

HOSTAGE

He was looking at the Foxy Grandpa book that Mr. Richie had given him when he heard the lock click. Instantly he shoved the book under him and crowded back against the wall, his feet just sticking over the edge of the cot, his arms hugged tight around his body. In his terror his body felt small and insufficient, hardly enough to hang on to.

They came in just the way they had come in every day since they brought him here, Mr. Richie first, then the insurance detective from Montpelier, Mr. Richie's sharp little face poked forward, smiling, his eyebrows moving up and down, and the detective behind him tall and solemn, red-nosed, with his handkerchief in his hand. The detective had hay fever and his eyes always looked red-rimmed, like a hound's. Feeling the rough plaster wall through his shirt, and the bulge of the overall straps up his spine, the boy watched them come in and shut the door.

Mr. Richie sat down and thumped his knees. "Well, Bub," he said cheerfully. The detective also sat down, blowing his nose. It was all the same as it had been before. In a minute they would start asking him, and prodding him, and sticking their faces out at him, and trying to twist what he said into something he hadn't said at all.

"Treating you all right?" Mr. Richie said. His little fox face was grinning, and he twinkled under white eyebrows. He looked, the boy thought with surprise, a good deal like the pictures in the Foxy Grandpa book.

The boy nodded.

"You like being in jail, uh?" the detective said.

The boy shook his head.

"Now looky here, Bub," Mr. Richie said. "We ain't trying to be mean to you. You just tell us the truth about how that fire started and you'll be out of here in a minute."

"I already told you," the boy squeaked.

"You told us something," the detective said. "How about telling us the truth?"

Without taking his sharp, blue, twinkling eyes off the boy's, Mr. Richie dug into his coat pocket, got a cigar, bit off the end and spit it out, found a match, lighted it on his thumb nail, puffed, and said through the smoke, "Still an accident, was it?"

The boy nodded.

"You just went down with a candle to the barn and the swallows flapped around the light and scared you and you dropped the candle and run and that set the barn on fire."

The boy nodded, swallowing.

"You lived on a farm all your life," the detective said heavily, "and you don't know better'n to go into a haymow with a candle. You don't know swallows'll fly at a light. You don't know enough to make sure a light's out before you go."

The boy said nothing.

"Why'd they send you down there with a candle?" the detective said harshly, and stuck his face forward.

"There wasn't any coal oil for the lantern."

" 'Tisn't as if Branch Willard was any kin of yours," Mr. Richie said mildly. "He ain't but your stepfather. You don't have to protect him. He never treated you very good anyway, did he?"

The boy did not answer.

"*Did he?*" the detective said.

The boy jumped, but said nothing.

"Why hadn't Willard put any hay in that barn yet?" the detective said.

"He had."

" 'Bout five load," the detective said. "You think we're silly, boy? Everybody's got his hay all in, and there's Willard with a thirty-acre meadow he ain't touched."

"I guess he was busy," the boy said, and drew his knees up under his chin, crowding against the wall. "He was trying to sell the calves."

"And you know why," the detective said. He blew his nose, wrenching the end harshly. "He wanted 'em out of that barn when he burned it down. He wanted his insurance but he didn't want to lose his stock."

The boy hiccoughed. A nerve in his cheek twitched, and he put his hand over the side of his face. He looked at Mr. Richie for help, but Mr. Richie was rolling the cigar in his lips and looking out the window.

"He's a slick one," the detective said. "I never seen any slicker trick. Sending a kid down to the mow with a candle and then saying the swallows scared him. He sent you, didn't he?"

The boy kept still.

"Didn't he?"

"Yes, but . . ."

"What for?"

"The pitchforks."

"What'd he want of them after dark?"

"I don't know."

"Saving his pitchforks too," the detective said. He leaned back and reached for his handkerchief.

Mr. Richie blew half a dozen rings and said, " 'Tisn't as open and shut as all that, Rufe. How in thunder would he know the swallows'd fly down and scare the kid? How'd he know the kid'd drop the candle and run?"

"There's a fifty-fifty chance of a fire whenever you send a kid into a mow with a candle," the detective said.

The boy was looking gratefully at Mr. Richie. Mr. Richie lived in the village, and even if he did sell insurance and even if he had been with the detective when they came to take him to jail, he was somebody familiar, at least. And he wasn't as rough as the detective, and he smiled all the time.

"Just the same," Mr. Richie said, standing up and pointing the cigar at him, "we know Branch Willard burned that barn down a-purpose. You might as well tell us."

"I told you already," the boy said. "Honest, Mr. Richie . . ."

"We might's well go," Mr. Richie said, and put the cigar back in his mouth.

The detective rose, grumbling. "Three days," he said. "Three days already in this damn place where every meadow looks like it'd been planted to goldenrod. You'll never get anything out of this kid."

"Never did expect to," Mr. Richie said cheerfully.

"Then what are we keeping him for?"

"Got a right to hold him," Mr. Richie said. "Long as he says it was him burned down the barn we got a right to hold him."

"What good will that do?"

"Trouble with you," Mr. Richie said, holding the door open and twinkling past the detective at the boy, as if they shared a joke, "you ain't got enough imagination to bait a hook." The door closed behind him, the lock snapped, and the boy heard Mr. Richie's voice going down the hall. "What would you do, if you was Martha Mount, and you'd married a good-for-nothing like Branch, and he had an insurance fire, and they come and stuck your boy in jail for it? You'd stand it a day or so, maybe, depending on how much . . ."

The voice dwindled and went away, and the boy relaxed a little away from the wall. He pulled the Foxy Grandpa book from under him and looked at it stupidly. What if Branch *had* wanted the barn burned down? But he couldn't have. It was just like he'd told them. Big with terror as that night was, he went over it, trying to remember. He went out with the candle after Branch shook the kerosene can and found it empty, and he went creeping through the blackness that blanketed sky and ground, holding his hand around the candle flame to shield it from the wind that wandered down off the hill toward the swamp. He went in the cow stable and through the milk room and up the ladder to the high drive, and just as he stuck the candle on the beam the Things came, beating at the light, at his head, with fluttering, squeaking noises, and he screamed and ran through the black mow, banging into the double doors, ripping his fingernail trying to get the bars up. Then he ran across the back lot toward the lighted kitchen window, and slammed into a fence post in the dark, knocking his wind out, and the next he remembered was Mumma picking him up off the back stoop and carrying him inside. He was still crying a little, and his chest was still sore, when

Branch came in the back door and said the barn was afire, his candle must have dropped off the beam into the hay.

So it had been an accident, plain as that. How was he to know the fluttering things were swallows? The memory of the terrible black loom of the mow above the dim candle-glow, and the squeaking, beating things that swooped down, contracted his whole body in a shiver. He flapped the pages of the Foxy Grandpa book.

He wondered if the detective would put him in jail for a long time. Mr. Richie wouldn't let him. Mr. Richie was too jolly to let a boy get put in jail for an accident. He remembered the way the men in the store at the village had laughed one day when Mr. Richie was telling them a joke he played on a city man. The city man had bought a cow and brought it to Mr. Richie to make sure he hadn't got stung. And Mr. Richie had looked the cow over, opened its mouth and looked in, and said, "My gosh, man, this cow ain't got any teeth in her upper jaw. She'll starve to death in a week." So he ended up by buying a hundred-and-thirty-dollar cow for forty dollars, to make beef out of, and when the city man found out how he'd been fooled, he was so ashamed he sold his camp and moved somewhere else.

Mr. Richie, he assured himself, wouldn't let him get put in jail. Maybe Mumma would come down and get him out. That was what Mr. Richie seemed to expect. Only why should he just wait down here? Mumma was up at the farm. He could go see her if he wanted to. The memory of Mumma hanging on to him and crying and looking around in every direction as if she expected help to come from somewhere, when the detective and Mr. Richie came and took him away, made the boy swallow. He shut his eyes tight to squeeze the two big tears that oozed into his eyes.

Lying down on the cot, he craned under to look at the rusty springs, put his hand tentatively around the iron leg. Then he sat up, listening. Somebody was coming again.

The door opened, and it was Mumma. "Andy!" she said. "Little Andy boy!" She grabbed him in her arms and hugged him, and he smelled the store smell of her shirtwaist. "Have they scared you?" she said. "Have they been mean to you?"

"They keep trying to make me say Branch burned down the barn a-purpose," he said.

Her arms tightened around him; she kissed the top of his head and then held him away to look at him. There were tear streaks in the flour she had used to powder her face. "Did they feed you?" she said. "Have you had enough to eat? You look thin."

"Oh yuh," he said vaguely. He looked at the faces of Mr. Richie and the detective in the doorway. Mr. Richie winked at him.

"Do you mind staying here a little while longer?" Mumma said. "I want to talk to Mr. Richie."

"Can't I go?"

"I'd rather you stayed here," she said. He saw her lips pucker over her upper plate as if they had a drawstring in them.

"Mumma!" he said. "Don't you tell them anything just to get me out. They tried to make me say it wasn't an accident, but it was."

"Don't you worry," Mumma said. Her eyes blinked rapidly and she turned away. "I'll be back in a minute, Andy." She turned back, took him and shook his shoulders gently. "You won't mind, just for a minute, will you?"

They were a long time coming back, and when they came in he saw that she had been crying again. The boy stood up slowly. His mother came across the room very fast and hugged him tight again. Her voice sounded choked. "You'll hate your mumma," she said. "That's what I can't stand, you'll hate your mumma."

He clung to her, trying to look in her face, but she kept her face turned. Mr. Richie had lighted another cigar.

"They're going to put Mumma in jail," she said.

Andy's eyes went from his mother's averted, twisted face to Mr. Richie's. "You don't have to pretend any more, Bub," Mr. Richie said. "Your mumma's told us all about it."

"But it was the Things!" Andy said. "The swallows, they came down and knocked the candle out of my hand . . ."

"And it went out," the detective said. "Branch went down there afterwards and stuck a match in the hay, like he'd been planning all the time and then planning to lay it on you for being careless."

Andy's hands clenched in his mother's coat. "Mumma, he didn't, did he?"

She nodded.

"But why are they going to put you in jail?" he said. "You never did it. It was Branch."

"I helped him," she said. "You'll never forgive me, Andy, but I was even going to help him lay it on you, because I thought if it was an accident, and we didn't blame you for it, you wouldn't feel too bad.

But if there'd been any other way we could see . . . We were awful hard up, Andy."

The boy wet his lips. "Why don't they put Branch in jail?"

"He's left. I don't know where. They'll put him in too if they can catch him."

He stood very still, letting the detective's long face and hound-eyes, Mr. Richie's lips with the cigar between them, his mother's pale flour-streaked face twisted with crying, go round him in a confused blur. It was all a part, a continuation, of the terror that had first come on him when he went out into the pitch-darkness with his candle, that had sent him blind and screaming across the high drive under the black loft full of nameless fluttering Things, that had left him throat-dry and frozen when he looked out the door and saw the flames licking high from the open doors of the barn and knew he had done it, that had been with him for three days in the jail while the detective's face and Mr. Richie's face poked out at him, sharp-lipped, saying sharp words.

"I'm ashamed, Andy," his mother said. "I'm so ashamed I could die."

He swallowed, only half hearing her, and a thought came beating down like the terrifying wings from the dark mow. "What'll I do?" he said. "Where'll I go, Mumma?" He looked from her to Mr. Richie, and Mr. Richie smiled and winked.

"Your mumma and I talked it over," Mr. Richie said. "You're coming to live with me. I ain't so mean I can see a boy thrown out in the world like that. You'll go to school in the village. Think you can make yourself useful enough to earn your keep?" He smiled more widely, and winked again, his fox face full of good humor and friendliness, as if to say, "Sure you can, we'll get along fine."

Andy tugged at his mother's coat, still looking at Mr. Richie. "Mumma?"

"Mr. Richie's very kind to offer it," his mother said. "He'll take good care of you, and you'll be a good boy. Won't you?"

Andy looked at Mr. Richie's lips. Mr. Richie's hand came up and took the cigar out of them, and the lips smiled. Andy stared at him, hardly seeing him at all, seeing only the smiling lips. There was a mist over everything else. He smelled the store smell of his mother's clothes.

"Yes," he said. He laid his face against the store smell, and his fingers dragged at the coat. With his eyes shut tight he screamed into the muffling cloth, "But I'll hate him! I'll hate him as long as I live!"

IN THE TWILIGHT

The boy always felt October as a twilight month. Its whole function was the preparation for winter, a getting ready, a drawing-in of the sun like a snail into its shell, a shortening and tightening against the long cold. And that year, after his father bought the sow up on the north bench and brought her in to be fattened up in the corral behind the barn, he felt obscurely the difference between the two kinds of preparation going on. The footbridge came out, was piled up in sections and planks in the loft of the barn. That would go in again next spring, as soon as the danger of the ice and floodwater was over. But the sow was not going to be back next spring. Her preparation was of a more final kind.

He had the job of carrying the swill bucket to the corral every morning, carrying a sharpened stick to poke the frantic beast away from the trough while he poured the sloppy mess of potato peelings and apple peelings and bacon rinds and sour milk and bread crusts. The sow fascinated him, though he disliked her intensely. He hated the smell of the swill, he hated the pig's lumbering, greedy rush when he appeared with the pail, he hated her pig eyes sunk in fat, he hated the rubber snout and the caked filth on her bristly hide. Still, he used to stand and watch her gobbling in the trough, and sometimes he scratched her back with the stick and felt her vast, bestial pleasure in the hunching of her spine and the deep, smacking grunts that rumbled out of her.

In a sense she was his personal enemy. She was responsible for the nasty job he had every day. She was responsible for the stink that offended him when he passed the corral. She was dirty and greedy and monstrous. But she was fascinating all the same, perhaps because all her greed worked against her, and what she ate so ravenously served death, not life. The day she broke loose, and children and dogs and women with flapping aprons headed her off from the river brush and shooed her back toward the corral, the boy and his brother, Chet, stood at the bars panting with the chase and promised her how soon she'd get hers. In just about a week now she wouldn't be causing any trouble. Chet took aim with an imaginary rifle and shot her just behind the left foreleg, and then Bruce took aim and shot her between the eyes, and they went away satisfied and somehow reconciled to the old sow, ugly and smelly and greedy and troublesome as she was, because she was as good as dead already.

In the big double bed Bruce stirred, yawned, stretched his feet down and pulled them back again quick when they touched a cold spot, opened his eyes, and looked up. The mottled ceiling above him, stained by firemen's chemicals when they had the attic fire, was a forest. He could see a bird with a big, hooked bill sitting on a tree. He yawned again, squinting his eyes, and twisted his head, and from the different angle, it was not a bird at all, but an automobile with its top down and smoke coming out behind. His eyes moved over the whole ceiling, picking out the shapes he and Chet had settled on definitely: the wildcat with one white, glaring eye; the man waving a flag; the woman with big feet and a bundle on her back. He lay picking them out, letting sleep go away from him slowly.

Downstairs he heard sounds, bumpings, the clank of a pan, and his head turned so that he could look out of the window. It was still early; the sun was barely tipping the barn roof. The folks didn't usually . . .

Then he stabbed Chet with an elbow. "Hey! Get up. This morning for the pig."

Chet flailed with his arms, grumbled, and half sat up. His hair was frowsy, and he was mad. "Don't go sticking your darn elbow into me," he said. "What's the matter?"

"The pig," Bruce said. "Pa's butchering the pig this morning."

"Heck with the old dirty pig," Chet said, but Bruce had barely got his long black stockings on before Chet was on the edge of the bed, dressing, too. Bruce beat him downstairs by about a minute.

The kitchen was warm. The washtub and the copper boiler were on the stove, and already sent up wisps of steam. Both boys, out of habit, huddled their bottoms close to the open oven door, watching their father finish his coffee.

He seemed in high spirits, and winked at Chet. "What are you up so early for?"

"Gonna help butcher the pig."

Their mother, standing by the washstand with a couple of mush bowls in her hands, looked at them. "You just forget about the pig. Sit down and eat your breakfast. Are you washed?"

"No'm," they said. "But we want to watch."

She waved them to the washstand and set the table for them. While they ate, their father sat sharpening the butcher knife on the edge of a crock, and they watched him.

"How you gonna do it?" Bruce said. "Cut her throat?"

"Bruce!" his mother said.

"Well, is he?" Chet said. He added, "I bet it bleeds like anything," and stared at the glittering edge of the knife.

"You boys better go play in the brush, or go up to the sandhills," their mother said. "You don't want to watch a nasty, bloody mess like this is going to be. I should think you'd feel sorry for the poor old pig."

They jeered. Bruce got the vision of the throat-cutting out of his mind and punched Chet on the shoulder. "No more old slop to carry," he said.

Chet punched him back and said, "No more old ugly sow snuffing around in the manure."

"Sausages for breakfast," Bruce said.

"Pork chops for dinner," said Chet.

They giggled, and their father looked them over, laughing. "Couple of cannibals," he said. He reached out and yanked a hair from Chet's head, held it between thumb and forefinger, and sliced it neatly in two with the knife. Chet watched him with one hand on his violated skull.

"Well, I don't think they should see things like that," the mother said helplessly. "Heaven knows they kill a lot of gophers and things on the farm, but this is worse."

The father stood up. "Oh, rats," he said. "I always watched butcherings when I was a kid. You want to make them so sissy they can't chop the head off a rooster?"

"I still don't think it's right," she said. "When I was little, I had to go out with a bowl and catch the blood for blood pudding. It gave me nightmares for a month after. . . ."

She stopped and turned to the stove, and Bruce saw her shoulders move as if she had had a chill. He imagined her stooping with a bowl under the pig's red, gaping throat, and the thought made him swallow twice at the mouthful he had. But a minute later his father went into the cellarway and got Chet's .22, and they crowded on his heels as he picked up the knife and went out.

"Brucie," his mother said, "don't you go!"

"Aw, heck," he said, and deliberately disobeyed her.

The morning was crisp, sunny, the air tangy with late autumn. In the far corner of the corral the sow heaved to her feet, her hindquarters still sagging loosely on the ground, and stared at them. She did not come near, and Bruce wondered why. Maybe because they didn't have a pail with them. Chet leaned on the corral bars and jeered at her.

"All right for you, old sow. This is where you get yours."

Excitement prickled in Bruce's legs. He couldn't stand still. With his hands on the top bar he jumped up and down and yelled at the ugly beast, and all his hatred of her ugliness and her vast pig appetites came out of him in shrill cries. The sow got clear up, and the father spoke sharply. "Shut up. You'll get her all excited. If you want to help, all right, but if you can't keep quiet you can go back in the house."

They fell quiet while he loaded the single-shot Remington. The sow came forward a few steps, snout wrinkling. She stopped at the edge of the manure pile, under the hole through which it was pitched from the barn, and fronted them suspiciously.

"Where you gonna shoot her?" Chet whispered.

"Head," his father whispered back. "Don't want any holes in her meat."

He leaned the gun over the rail and took aim for what seemed minutes. Then the sow moved, and he took his finger outside the trigger guard and eased up. Bruce let his breath out in a long, wispy plume, thinking: if she hadn't moved just then she'd be dead now, she'd be lying there like a chicken with its head cut off. On a day like this, with the sun just coming up and everything so bright, she'd be dead. He swallowed.

His father reached down and picked up the butcher knife, sticking it into the top bar where it would be handy. "All right now," he said. He seemed excited himself. His breath came short through his nose.

He laid the barrel over the bar again, and his cheek dropped against the stock. The sow lowered her head and snuffed at the manure, and in the instant when she was frozen there, perfectly still except for the little red, upward-peering eyes, the rifle cracked thinly, dryly, like a stick breaking.

The sow leaped straight into the air, her open mouth bursting with sound, came down still squealing to stand for a moment stiff-legged, swinging her head. Then she was running around and around the corral, faster than Bruce had ever believed she could move, around and around, ponderous, galloping, terrified, a sudden and living pain. The constant high shriek of agony, sustained at an unsustainable pitch, cut the nerves like a knife.

The boy stood stiffly with his hands on the bar, watching her. He heard the click of the bolt as his father threw the shell and the snip of metal as he reloaded. Then his father was running, almost as heavily as the sow, but more terribly because he was the killer and she the killed. The boy saw his red face, his open mouth, as he pursued the sow around the corral, trying to stop and corner her for another shot.

The squeal went on, an intolerable sound of death, and the sow charged blindly around the pen. A trickle of red ran down over her snout from between her eyes, and she went on, staggering, a death that did not want to die, a vast, greedy life hurt and dying and shrilling its pain. Even through his own terror Bruce could not miss the way she scrambled to avoid the man with the gun. She plunged up on the manure pile, was cornered there, raced down and around the bars again, and then in one magnificent running leap went clear up over the manure, through the hole, and into the barn.

"God Almighty!" the father yelled. "Head her off. *Run!*"

The two boys arrived at the barn door together, slammed the lower half shut, and peered over. The pig's wild screaming came from the cow stable, empty now. The horses in the front stalls were trembling and white-eyed, and, as Chet pushed the upper door, the nervous mare lashed out with both hind feet, and splinters flew from the board ceiling.

Their father was beside them now, looking in, the gun in his right hand. His face was so violently red that Bruce shrank away.

"Get on out behind again," the father said. "If she comes out through the hole, yell and keep her inside the fence."

He went inside, and the boys fled around behind, their eyes glued to the manure hole, their ears full of the muffled and unceasing shrilling of the wounded sow. They heard her squealing sharpen, heard the new fear in it, heard their father shouting, and then she arched through the window again, jumping like a horse at a fence, front feet tucked up and hind legs sailing. Her feet hit the edge, and she fell rolling, but the squealing did not stop. She was up in a moment, head swinging desperately from side to side, and in that moment the father, coming around the corner, took quick aim and fired again.

The sow stood still. Her squeal went up and up and up to a cracking pitch. Her whole fat, mud-caked body quivered and began to settle, her legs spraddled as if to keep it from going down. Then the squeal trailed off to a thin whimper, the front legs buckled, the sow's snout plowed into the manure, and the father was over the fence with the knife in his hand. The stoop, the jerk of the shoulder, the rush of bright blood . . .

"Jeez!" Chet said.

Bruce, strangling, tried to look, tried to say something to show that it had been wonderful and exciting, that it served the dirty old sow right, but he couldn't speak. His eyes, turned away from the corral, were still full of the picture of his father standing over the dead sow, towering, triumphant, the bloody knife in his hand, his back huge and broad and monstrous with power. He gulped and swallowed as a rush of salty liquid filled his mouth.

"My gosh," Chet said. "Did you see her run? Right between the eyes, and it only made her squeal and run."

Bruce turned his head further and clung to the bar. He heard Chet's voice, going away, getting dimmer. "What's the matter? You're white as a sheet."

"I am . . . not," Bruce said. He straightened his shoulders and lifted his head, but a moment later he was hanging on the corral vomiting, heaving, clinging for dear life to keep the black dots in his brain from becoming solid.

And after a minute his father's voice, still breathless and jerky with exertion. "Couldn't stand it, uh? You all right, Chet?"

Chet said he felt fine, swell. Bruce clung to the voices, hung onto them desperately, because as long as he could hear them the terror wasn't total, the black dots weren't solid. "You better get on into the house," his father said, and then raised his voice and called, "Sis!"

His mother came and held him with one arm and led him back to the house and, still frantically clinging to voices, to meanings, he heard her say, "You never should have watched it, it's horrible, I knew all the time. . . ."

There was a while when he lay on the sofa in the parlor with his eyes closed. His mother came in once to see how he felt, but the duties in the kitchen and yard were demanding, and she stayed only a minute. Listening out of his still struggle with nausea, he heard the thumpings in the kitchen, the quick footsteps, the words, and as his nausea ebbed, he wondered what was going on now. Once, when the outside door was opened, he heard the voices of boys out by the barn.

Shame made him turn over and lie face down. What he had done was sissy. Chet hadn't got sick, and the other kids out there watching now weren't sick, or they wouldn't be yelling that way. But they hadn't seen the old sow run, or heard her squeal, or seen his father stooping with the knife. . . .

His mother was out there, though, helping to get it done, and she had said from the start that she hated it. Everybody was helping but him, and he lay inside like a baby because he couldn't stand the sight of blood. What if he'd been told to catch the blood, like Ma? The thought sickened him, and he lay still.

After a while he sat up tentatively, put his feet over the edge of the sofa. He didn't seem dizzy. And he had to go out there and show them that he was as capable of watching a butchering as any of them.

He felt a queer, violent hatred for the old sow. It served her right to be shot and have her throat cut, have her insides ripped out. He would go out and get hold of her insides and pull, and everything would come out in a bundle like the insides of a fish.

He stood up. The dizziness had gone completely. Listening, he heard no sounds in the kitchen. Everybody was outside. Taking three deep breaths, the way he always did before going off the high diving board the first time in the spring, he went out to the back door.

Four boys stood in a ring around his father, who was squatting on the ground. The pig was nowhere in sight, but Bruce saw his mother bending over one of the washtubs, and he saw the rope that went up over a pulley at the corner of the barn and trailed near his father's feet. Then his father took hold of the rope and pulled, and the boys took hold and pulled too, stepping all over each other, and the sow came in sight. But not a sow any longer, not an animal, not the mud-caked, bristly-hided old brute that he had carried slop to all fall. The thing that rose up toward the pulley was clean and pink and hairless, like the carcasses in Heimie Gross's shop, and, as it swung gently on the rope that bound its hind feet, he saw the flapping, opened belly and the clean red meat inside. She hung there, turning gently half around and back again, so innocent and harmless that the boy was no longer sickened or afraid.

His father saw him come out and grinned at him, wiping his red hands on a rag. "Snapped out of it, uh? I thought you were a tough guy."

"Brucie got sick," Chet said. "When Pa cut her throat, Brucie threw up all over the corral."

"Oh, I did not!" Bruce said. He clenched his fists.

"You big liar," Chet said. "I can show you the puddle."

Not daring to look at the other boys, Bruce went over to where his mother was washing a long, whitish mess of stuff in the tubful of bloody water. She held her face to one side, out of the steam that rose from the tub, and worked at arm's length. "Feeling better now?" she said.

He nodded. Conscious of the boys behind him, knowing they must be laughing at him, shaming him, snickering, he pointed to the stuff in the tub. "What's that?"

"Intestines," she said. "They have to be cleaned to stuff sausage in." With a disgusted grimace she went back to working the long, rubbery gut through her fingers.

Bruce stood watching a minute. So sausage was stuffed into intestines. He had always loved sausage, but he could never eat it again, not ever. He couldn't eat any of the old sow. Looking over at the pink, harmless thing swinging gently by its heels, he found it hard to imagine that this was the sow. The eyes were closed, the jowly face was hairless and mild, almost comical. There was nothing to remind anyone of that violence behind the barn, until you looked right between her eyes and saw the two dark dots there, not more than a half inch apart. There were the death wounds, there was the difference. He went up and pushed the stiff front foot, and the carcass swayed. It was funny those two little dots could make all that difference. A half hour ago the old sow had got up full of life, and now she hung like a bag of grain.

"How'd they get her so clean?" he asked Chet.

"Scalded her," Chet said. "You shouldn't've got sick. You'd've seen something."

"What'd her insides look like?"

"Go look yourself," Chet said. He waved at the tub standing against the barn wall.

Slowly Bruce went closer until he could see. The bloody mess appalled him, but he had to see those insides, had to look at them carefully to keep himself reminded that it was really the old sow hanging there. If he didn't keep remembering that, if he forgot the sow and remembered only the clean, butcher-shop carcass, he might forget sometime and eat some of her, and he knew if he ever ate any of her he would die.

His father came up past him, moved him aside. "One side there," he said heartily. "One side for the working men."

He put red hands down into the tub, sorted out the liver and heart. Grinning, he made as if to throw the great, wobbly, purple liver at Bruce, and Bruce felt his stomach go weak.

"What's the matter?" his father said. "Here I thought you were a tough guy, and you go around looking peaked as a ghost."

"I *am* a tough guy!" Bruce said, but looking across at Chet, he saw the superior smile, the hands in the pockets and the shoulders insolent. "I'm not getting sick," he said, and made his white face turn fixedly toward the tub of entrails. "I'm not sick at all!" he said, and laughed.

His father looked at him queerly. "You'd better go off and sit down a while," he said finally. "You're not quite in shape yet."

"I am too in shape!" the boy screamed. He wanted to run up and plunge his hands into that red tub of guts, just to show them, but he didn't quite dare. But he stood where he was, and as he stood, the little black dots came back before his eyes, and he stood still and stared through them, fighting them down in hysterical silence. Then his father, still watching him, pulled a flat flap of insides from the tub.

"Show you something," he said to the boys. "This's one that'll surprise you."

He dipped the flap in a clean bucket of water and washed it thoroughly. Bruce, fighting off the black spots, struggling to keep the slaughterhouse smell of blood and scalded hair from turning his stomach inside out, watched with the others. When it came out of the water clean, the thing looked like a flattened bag with a tube the size of a pencil sticking out one side.

"What is it?" Chet said. "Is it her stomach?"

The father laughed. "You've seen that old sow eat, haven't you? Think she could put all that in this little bag?" He flapped it, shaking the water from the end of the tube, and then put the tube to his lips.

At the sight of his father's mouth touching the raw insides of the sow Bruce felt the blood drain from him, and the black dots streamed thicker. He shook his head violently, but they stayed. Through their thickening darkness he saw his father blow into the tube, saw the bladder swell and tighten and grow round, big as a soccer ball. The father pinched the tube, found a piece of string and tied around it, and tossed the bladder out on the ground. It bounced lightly, one side patched with adhesive dust.

His lips tight on his nausea, the blackness almost covering his sight, Bruce stared at the wavering bladder on the ground before him, the tube poking out to one side. The insides of the old sow, the red, dirty insides of the old sow he had hated and seen die . . .

The vomit was in his very throat. He had to heave, but he couldn't. He wouldn't, with those boys around, his father there, Chet standing around with his superior hands in his pockets. The whole group of boys was staring, momentarily a little stupid, at the bladder the father had tossed out. Without thinking, in a wild leap to save himself and his nausea, Bruce sprang forward and kicked as hard as he could. It soared, and immediately all of them were after it, yelling, booting it down into the vacant lot.

Bruce broke into the running crowd again, got a chance, kicked the bladder hard and far, chased it, missed, chased again as Preacher-Kid Morrison booted it across the lot. His nausea was gone, his whole mind centered on that ritual act of kicking the sow's insides around, dirtying them in the dust of the field, taking out on them his own shame and his own fear and hatred and disbelief. And when they finally broke the bladder, far down the coulee toward school, he stood over it panting, triumphant, so full of life that he could have jumped the barn or carried the woodshed on his back.

BUTCHER
BIRD

■   ■   ■

That summer the boy was alone on the farm except for his parents.
His brother was working at Orullian's Grocery in town, and
there was no one to run the trap line with or swim with in the
dark, weed-smelling reservoir where garter snakes made straight rapid
lines in the water and the skaters rowed close to shore. So every excursion
was an adventure, even if it was only a trip across the three miles of
prairie to Larsen's to get mail or groceries. He was excited at the visit
to Garfield's as he was excited by everything unusual. The hot midsum-
mer afternoon was still and breathless, the air harder to breathe than
usual. He knew there was a change in weather coming because the
gingersnaps in their tall cardboard box were soft and bendable when
he snitched two to stick in his pocket. He could tell too by his father's
grumpiness accumulated through two weeks of drought, his habit of
looking off into the southwest, from which either rain or hot winds
might come, that something was brewing. If it was rain everything would
be fine, his father would hum under his breath getting breakfast, maybe
let him drive the stoneboat or ride the mare down to Larsen's for mail.

If it was hot wind they'd have to walk soft and speak softer, and it wouldn't be any fun.

They didn't know the Garfields, who had moved in only the fall before; but people said they had a good big house and a bigger barn and that Mr. Garfield was an Englishman and a little funny talking about scientific farming and making the desert blossom like the rose. The boy's father hadn't wanted to go, but his mother thought it was unneighborly not to call at least once in a whole year when people lived only four miles away. She was, the boy knew, as anxious for a change, as eager to get out of that atmosphere of waiting to see what the weather would do—that tense and teeth-gritting expectancy—as he was.

He found more than he looked for at Garfield's. Mr. Garfield was tall and bald with a big nose, and talked very softly and politely. The boy's father was determined not to like him right from the start.

When Mr. Garfield said, "Dear, I think we might have a glass of lemonade, don't you?" the boy saw his parents look at each other, saw the beginning of a contemptuous smile on his father's face, saw his mother purse her lips and shake her head ever so little. And when Mrs. Garfield, prim and spectacled, with a habit of tucking her head back and to one side while she listened to anyone talk, brought in the lemonade, the boy saw his father taste his and make a little face behind the glass. He hated any summer drink without ice in it, and had spent two whole weeks digging a dugout icehouse just so that he could have ice water and cold beer when the hot weather came.

But Mr. and Mrs. Garfield were nice people. They sat down in their new parlor and showed the boy's mother the rug and the gramophone. When the boy came up curiously to inspect the little box with the petunia-shaped horn and the little china dog with "His Master's Voice" on it, and the Garfields found that he had never seen or heard a gramophone, they put on a cylinder like a big spool of tightly wound black thread and lowered a needle on it, and out came a man's voice singing in Scotch brogue, and his mother smiled and nodded and said, "My land, Harry Lauder! I heard him once a long time ago. Isn't it wonderful, Sonny?"

It was wonderful all right. He inspected it, reached out his fingers to touch things, wiggled the big horn to see if it was loose or screwed in. His father warned him sharply to keep his hands off, but then Mr. Garfield smiled and said, "Oh, he can't hurt it. Let's play something else," and found a record about the saucy little bird on Nelly's hat that had them all laughing. They let him wind the machine and play the record over again, all by himself, and he was very careful. It was a fine machine. He wished he had one.

About the time he had finished playing his sixth or seventh record, and George M. Cohan was singing "She's a grand old rag, she's a high-flying flag, and forever in peace may she wave," he glanced at his father and discovered that he was grouchy about something. He wasn't taking any part in the conversation but was sitting with his chin in his hand staring out of the window. Mr. Garfield was looking at him a little helplessly. His eyes met the boy's and he motioned him over.

"What do you find to do all summer? Only child, are you?"

"No, sir. My brother's in Whitemud. He's twelve. He's got a job."

"So you come out on the farm to help," said Mr. Garfield. He had his hand on the boy's shoulder and his voice was so kind that the boy lost his shyness and felt no embarrassment at all in being out there in the middle of the parlor with all of them watching.

"I don't help much," he said. "I'm too little to do anything but drive the stoneboat, Pa says. When I'm twelve he's going to get me a gun and then I can go hunting."

"Hunting?" Mr. Garfield said. "What do you hunt?"

"Oh, gophers and weasels. I got a pet weasel. His name's Lucifer."

"Well," said Mr. Garfield. "You seem to be a pretty manly little chap. What do you feed your weasel?"

"Gophers." The boy thought it best not to say that the gophers were live ones he threw into the weasel's cage. He thought probably Mr. Garfield would be a little shocked at that.

Mr. Garfield straightened up and looked round at the grown folks. "Isn't it a shame," he said, "that there are so many predatory animals and pests in this country that we have to spend our time destroying them? I hate killing things."

"I hate weasels," the boy said. "I'm just saving this one till he turns into an ermine, and then I'm going to skin him. Once I speared a weasel with the pitchfork in the chicken coop and he dropped right off the tine and ran up my leg and bit me after he was speared clean through."

He finished breathlessly, and his mother smiled at him, motioning him not to talk so much. But Mr. Garfield was still looking at him kindly. "So you want to make war on the cruel things, the weasels and the hawks," he said.

"Yes, sir," the boy said. He looked at his mother and it was all right. He hadn't spoiled anything by telling about the weasels.

"Now that reminds me," Mr. Garfield said, rising. "Maybe I've got something you'd find useful."

He went into another room and came back with a .22 in his hand. "Could you use this?"

"I . . . yes, *sir!*" the boy said. He had almost, in his excitement, said "I hope to whisk in your piskers," because that was what his father always said when he meant anything real hard.

"If your parents want you to have it," Mr. Garfield said and raised his eyebrows at the boy's mother. He didn't look at the father, but the boy did.

"Can I, Pa?"

"I guess so," his father said. "Sure."

"Thank Mr. Garfield nicely," said his mother.

"Gee," the boy breathed. "Thanks, Mr. Garfield, ever so much."

"There's a promise goes with it," Mr. Garfield said. "I'd like you to promise never to shoot anything with it but the bloodthirsty animals—the cruel ones like weasels and hawks. Never anything like birds or prairie dogs."

"How about butcher birds?"

"Butcher birds?" Mr. Garfield said.

"Shrikes," said the boy's mother. "We've got some over by our place. They kill all sorts of things, snakes and gophers and other birds. They're worse than the hawks because they just kill for the fun of it."

"By all means," said Mr. Garfield. "Shoot all the shrikes you see. A thing that kills for the fun of it . . ." He shook his head and his voice got solemn, almost like the voice of Mr. McGregor, the Sunday School Superintendent in town, when he was asking the benediction. "There's something about the way the war drags on, or maybe just this country," he said, "that makes me hate killing. I just can't bear to shoot anything any more, even a weasel."

The boy's father turned cold eyes away from Mr. Garfield and looked out of the window. One big brown hand, a little dirty from the wheel of the car, rubbed against the day-old bristles on his jaws. Then he stood up and stretched. "Well, we got to be going," he said.

"Oh, stay a little while," Mr. Garfield said. "You just came. I wanted to show you my trees."

The boy's mother stared at him. "Trees?"

He smiled. "Sounds a bit odd out here, doesn't it? But I think trees will grow. I've made some plantings down below."

"I'd love to see them," she said. "Sometimes I'd give almost anything to get into a good deep shady woods. Just to smell it, and feel how cool . . ."

"There's a little story connected with these," Mr. Garfield said. He spoke to the mother alone, warmly. "When we first decided to come out here I said to Martha that if trees wouldn't grow we shouldn't stick it. That's just what I said, 'If trees won't grow we shan't stick it.' Trees are almost the breath of life to me."

The boy's father was shaken by a sudden spell of coughing, and the mother shot a quick look at him and looked back at Mr. Garfield with a light flush on her cheekbones. "I'd love to see them," she said. "I was raised in Minnesota, and I never will get used to a place as barren as this."

"When I think of the beeches back home in England," Mr. Garfield said, and shook his head with a puckering smile round his eyes.

The father lifted himself heavily out of his chair and followed the rest of them out to the coulee edge. Below them willows grew profusely along the almost-dry creek, and farther back from the water there was a grove of perhaps twenty trees about a dozen feet high.

"I'm trying cottonwoods first because they can stand dry weather," Mr. Garfield said.

The mother was looking down with all her longings suddenly plain and naked in her eyes. "It's wonderful," she said. "I'd give almost anything to have some on our place."

"I found the willows close by here," said Mr. Garfield. "Just at the south end of the hills they call Old-Man-on-His-Back, where the stream comes down."

"Stream?" the boy's father said. "You mean that trickle?"

"It's not much of a stream," Mr. Garfield said apologetically. "But . . ."

"Are there any more there?" the mother said.

"Oh, yes. You could get some. Cut them diagonally and push them into any damp ground. They'll grow."

"They'll grow about six feet high," the father said.

"Yes," said Mr. Garfield. "They're not, properly speaking, trees. Still . . ."

"It's getting pretty smothery," the father said rather loudly. "We better be getting on."

This time Mr. Garfield didn't object, and they went back to the car exchanging promises of visits. The father jerked the crank and climbed into the Ford, where the boy was sighting along his gun. "Put that down," his father said. "Don't you know any better than to point a gun around people?"

"It isn't loaded."

"They never are," his father said. "Put it down now."

The Garfields were standing with their arms round each other's waists, waiting to wave good-bye. Mr. Garfield reached over and picked something from his wife's dress.

"What was it, Alfred?" she said, peering.

"Nothing. Just a bit of fluff."

The boy's father coughed violently and the car started with a jerk. With his head down almost to the wheel, still coughing, he waved, and the mother and the boy waved as they went down along the badly set cedar posts of the pasture fence. They were almost a quarter of a mile away before the boy, with a last wave of the gun, turned round again and saw that his father was purple with laughter. He rocked the car with his joy, and when his wife said, "Oh, Harry, you big fool," he pointed helplessly to his shoulder. "Would you mind," he said. "Would you mind brushing that bit o' fluff off me showldah?" He roared again, pounding the wheel. "I shawn't stick it," he said. "I bloody well shawn't stick it, you knaow!"

"It isn't fair to laugh at him," she said. "He can't help being English."

"He can't help being a sanctimonious old mudhen either, braying about his luv-ly luv-ly trees. They'll freeze out the first winter."

"How do you know? Maybe it's like he says—if they get a start they'll grow here as well as anywhere."

"Maybe there's a gold mine in our back yard too, but I'm not gonna dig to see. I couldn't stick it."

"Oh, you're just being stubborn," she said. "Just because you didn't like Mr. Garfield . . ."

He turned on her in heavy amazement. "Well, my God! Did you?"

"I thought he was very nice," she said, and sat straighter in the back seat, speaking loudly above the creak of the springs and cough of the motor. "They're trying to make a home, not just a wheat crop. I liked them."

"Uh huh." He was not laughing any more now. Sitting beside him, the boy could see that his face had hardened and the cold look had come into his eye again. "So I should start talking like I had a mouthful of bran and planting trees around the house that'll look like clothesline poles in two months."

"I didn't say that."

"You thought it though." He looked irritably at the sky, misted with the same delusive film of cloud that had fooled him for three days, and spat at the roadside. "You thought it all the time we were there. 'Why aren't you more like Mr. Garfield, he's such a nice man.' " With mincing savagery he swung round and mocked her. "Shall I make it a walnut grove? Or a big maple sugar bush? Or maybe you'd like an orange orchard."

The boy was looking down at his gun, trying not to hear them quarrel, but he knew what his mother's face would be like—hurt and a little flushed, her chin trembling into stubbornness. "I don't suppose you could bear to have a rug on the floor, or a gramophone?" she said.

He smacked the wheel hard. "Of course I could bear it if we could afford it. But I sure as hell would rather do without than be like that old sandhill crane."

"I don't suppose you'd like to take me over to the Old-Man-on-His-Back some day to get some willow slips either."

"What for?"

"To plant down in the coulee, by the dam."

"That dam dries up every August. Your willows wouldn't live till snow flies."

"Well, would it do any harm to try?"

"Oh, shut up!" he said. "Just thinking about that guy and his fluff and his trees gives me the pleefer."

The topless Ford lurched, one wheel at a time, through the deep burnout by their pasture corner, and the boy clambered out with his gun in his hand to slip the loop from the three-strand gate. It was then that he saw the snake, a striped limp ribbon, dangling on the fence, and a moment later the sparrow, neatly butchered and hung by the throat from the barbed wire. He pointed the gun at them. "Lookit!" he said. "Lookit what the butcher bird's been doing."

His father's violent hand waved at him from the seat. "Come on! Get the wire out of the way!"

The boy dragged the gate through the dust, and the Ford went through and up behind the house, perched on the bare edge of the coulee in the midst of its baked yard and framed by the dark fireguard overgrown with Russian thistle. Walking across that yard a few minutes later, the boy felt its hard heat under his sneakers. There was hardly a spear of grass within the fireguard. It was one of his father's prides that the dooryard should be like cement. "Pour your wash water out long enough," he said, "and you'll have a surface so hard it won't even make mud." Religiously he threw his water out three times a day, carrying it sometimes a dozen steps to dump it on a dusty or grassy spot.

The mother had objected at first, asking why they had to live in the middle of an alkali flat, and why they couldn't let grass grow up to the door. But he snorted her down. Everything round the house ought to be bare as a bone. Get a good prairie fire going and it'd jump that guard like nothing, and if they had grass to the door where'd they be? She said why not plow a wider fireguard then, one a fire couldn't jump, but he said he had other things to do besides plowing fifty-foot fireguards.

They were arguing inside when the boy came up on the step to sit down and aim his empty .22 at a fence post. Apparently his mother had been persistent, and persistence when he was not in a mood for it angered the father worse than anything else. Their talk came vaguely through his concentration, but he shut his ears on it. If that spot on the fence post was a coyote now, and he held the sight steady, right on it, and pulled the trigger, that old coyote would jump about eighty feet in the air and come down dead as a mackerel, and he could tack his hide on the barn the way Mr. Larsen had once, only the dogs had jumped and torn the tail and hind legs off Mr. Larsen's pelt, and he wouldn't get more than the three-dollar bounty out of it. But then Mr. Larsen had shot his with a shotgun anyway, and the hide wasn't worth much even before the dogs tore it. . . .

"I can't for the life of me see why not," his mother said inside. "We could do it now. We're not doing anything else."

"I tell you they wouldn't grow!" said his father with emphasis on every word. "Why should we run our tongues out doing everything that mealy-mouthed fool does?"

"I don't want anything but the willows. They're easy."

He made his special sound of contempt, half snort, half grunt. After a silence she tried again. "They might even have pussies on them in the spring. Mr. Garfield thinks they'd grow, and he used to work in a greenhouse, his wife told me."

"This isn't a greenhouse, for Chrissake."

"Oh, let it go," she said. "I've stood it this long without any green things around. I guess I can stand it some more."

The boy, aiming now toward the gate where the butcher bird, coming back to his prey, would in just a minute fly right into Deadeye's unerring bullet, heard his father stand up suddenly.

"Abused, aren't you?" he said.

The mother's voice rose. "No, I'm not abused! Only I can't see why it would be so awful to get some willows. Just because Mr. Garfield gave me the idea, and you didn't like him . . ."

"You're right I didn't like Mr. Garfield," the father said. "He gave me a pain right under the crupper."

"Because," the mother's voice said bitterly, "he calls his wife 'dear' and puts his arm around her and likes trees. It wouldn't occur to you to put your arm around your wife, would it?"

The boy aimed and held his breath. His mother ought to keep still, because if she didn't she'd get him real mad and then they'd both have to tiptoe around the rest of the day. He heard his father's breath whistle through his teeth, and his voice, mincing, nasty. "Would you like me to kiss you now, *dear*?"

"I wouldn't let you touch me with a ten-foot pole," his mother said. She sounded just as mad as he did, and it wasn't often she let herself get that way. The boy squirmed over when he heard the quick hard steps come up behind him and pause. Then his father's big hand, brown and meaty and felted with fine black hair, reached down over his shoulder and took the .22.

"Let's see this cannon old Scissor-bill gave you," he said.

It was a single-shot, bolt-action Savage, a little rusty on the barrel, the bolt sticky with hardened grease when the father removed it. Sighting up through the barrel, he grunted. "Takes care of a gun like he takes care of his farm. Probably used it to cultivate his luv-ly trees."

He went out into the sleeping porch, and after a minute came back with a rag and a can of machine oil. Hunching the boy over on the step, he sat down and began rubbing the bolt with the oil-soaked rag.

"I just can't bear to shoot anything any more," he said, and laughed suddenly. "I just cawn't stick it, little man." He leered at the boy, who grinned back uncertainly. Squinting through the barrel again, the father breathed through his nose and clamped his lips together, shaking his head.

The sun lay heavy on the baked yard. Out over the corner of the pasture a soaring hawk caught wind and sun at the same time, so that his light breast feathers flashed as he banked and rose. Just wait, the boy thought. Wait till I get my gun working and I'll fix you, you hen-robber. He thought of the three chicks a hawk had struck earlier in the summer, the three balls of yellow with the barred mature plumage just coming through. Two of them dead when he got there and chased the hawk away, the other gasping with its crop slashed wide open and the wheat spilling from it on the ground. His mother had sewed up the crop, and the chicken had lived, but it always looked droopy, like a plant in drought time, and sometimes it would stand and work its bill as if it were choking.

By golly, he thought, I'll shoot every hawk and butcher bird in twenty miles. I'll . . .

"Rustle around and find me a piece of baling wire," his father said. "This barrel looks like a henroost."

Behind the house he found a piece of rusty wire, brought it back and watched his father straighten it, wind a bit of rag round the end, ram it up and down through the barrel, and peer through again. "He's leaded her so you can hardly see the grooves," he said. "But maybe she'll shoot. We'll fill her with vinegar and cork her up tonight."

The mother was behind them, leaning against the jamb and watching. She reached down and rumpled the father's black hair. "The minute you get a gun in your hand you start feeling better," she said. "It's just a shame you weren't born fifty years sooner."

"A gun's a good tool," he said. "It hadn't ought to be misused. Gun like this is enough to make a guy cry."

"Well, you've got to admit it was nice of Mr. Garfield to give it to Sonny," she said. It was the wrong thing to say. The boy had a feeling somehow that she knew it was the wrong thing to say, that she said it just to have one tiny triumph over him. He knew it would make him boiling mad again, even before he heard his father's answer.

"Oh, sure, Mr. Garfield's a fine man. He can preach a better sermon than any homesteader in Saskatchewan. God Almighty! everything he does is better than what I do. All right. All right, *all right!* Why the hell don't you move over there if you like it so well?"

"If you weren't so blind . . . !"

He rose with the .22 in his hand and pushed past her into the house. "I'm not so blind," he said heavily in passing. "You've been throwing that bastard up to me for two hours. It don't take very good eyes to see what that means."

His mother started to say, "All because I want a few little . . ." but the boy cut in on her, anxious to help the situation somehow. "Will it shoot now?" he said.

His father said nothing. His mother looked down at him, shrugged, sighed, smiled bleakly with a tight mouth. She moved aside when the father came back with a box of cartridges in his hand. He ignored his wife, speaking to the boy alone in the particular half-jocular tone he always used with him or the dog when he wasn't mad or exasperated.

"Thought I had these around," he said. "Now we'll see what this smoke-pole will do."

He slipped a cartridge in and locked the bolt, looking round for something to shoot at. Behind him the mother's feet moved on the floor, and her voice came purposefully. "I can't see why you have to act this way," she said. "I'm going over and get some slips myself."

There was a long silence. The angled shade lay sharp as a knife across the baked front yard. The father's cheek was pressed against the stock of the gun, his arms and hands as steady as stone.

"How'll you get there?" he said, whispering down the barrel.

"I'll walk."

"Five miles and back."

"Yes, five miles and back. Or fifty miles and back. If there was any earthly reason why you should mind . . ."

"I don't mind," he said, and his voice was soft as silk. "Go ahead."

Close to his mother's long skirts in the doorway, the boy felt her stiffen as if she had been slapped. He squirmed anxiously, but his desperation could find only the question he had asked before. His voice squeaked on it: "Will it shoot now?"

"See that sparrow out there?" his father said, still whispering. "Right out by that cactus?"

"Harry!" the mother said. "If you shoot that harmless little bird!"

Fascinated, the boy watched his father's dark face against the rifle stock, the locked, immovable left arm, the thick finger crooked inside the trigger guard almost too small to hold it. He saw the sparrow, gray, white-breasted, hopping obliviously in search of bugs, fifty feet out on the gray earth. "I just . . . can't . . . bear . . . to . . . shoot . . . anything," the father said, his face like dark stone, his lips hardly moving. "I just . . . can't . . . stick it!"

"Harry!" his wife screamed.

The boy's mouth opened, a dark wash of terror shadowed his vision of the baked yard cut by its sharp angle of shade.

"Don't, Pa!"

The rocklike figure of his father never moved. The thick finger squeezed slowly down on the trigger, there was a thin, sharp report, and the sparrow jerked and collapsed into a shapeless wad on the ground. It was as if, in the instant of the shot, all its clean outlines vanished. Head, feet, the white breast, the perceptible outlines of the folded wings, disappeared all at once, were crumpled together and lost, and the boy sat beside his father on the step with the echo of the shot still in his ears.

He did not look at either of his parents. He looked only at the crumpled sparrow. Step by step, unable to keep away, he went to it, stooped, and picked it up. Blood stained his fingers, and he held the bird by the tail while he wiped the smeared hand on his overalls. He heard the click as the bolt was shot and the empty cartridge ejected, and he saw his mother come swiftly out of the house past his father, who sat still on the step. Her hands were clenched, and she walked with her head down, as if fighting tears.

"Ma!" the boy said dully. "Ma, what'll I do with it?"

She stopped and turned, and for a moment they faced each other. He saw the dead pallor of her face, the burning eyes, the not-quite-controllable quiver of her lips. But her words, when they came, were flat and level, almost casual.

"Leave it right there," she said. "After a while your father will want to hang it on the barbed wire."

THE
DOUBLE
CORNER

■ ■ ■

The summer sun was fierce and white on the pavement, the station, the tracks, the stucco walls of buildings, but the pepper tree made a domed and curtained cave of shade where they waited— the twins languidly playing catch with a tennis ball, Tom and Janet on the iron bench. Sitting with her head back, looking up into the green dome, Janet saw the swarming flies up among the branches, hanging like smoke against the ceiling of a room. They made a sleepy sound like humming wires.

"I wish I thought you knew what you're doing," Tom said.

She looked at him. He was leaning forward, his hat pushed back, and with his toe he was keeping a frantic ant from going where it wanted to with a crumb. He had worked on cattle ranches as a young man, and she had always said he had cowpuncher's eyes, squinty and faded, the color of much-washed jeans.

"She's your mother," she reminded him.

"I know."

"If I'm glad to have her, I should think you'd be."

The boys were throwing the tennis ball up into the branches, bringing down showers of leaves and twigs. "Hey, kids, cut it out," Tom said. To Janet he said, "We've been all through it. Let it ride."

"But you had some reason," she persisted.

"Reason?" he said, and picked his calloused palm. "She'd be better off in an institution."

That made Janet sit up stiffly and try to hold his eyes. "That's what I can't understand, why you'd be willing to send your mother to an asylum." He was squinting, moving his head slowly back and forth, but he would not look up.

"I wish I could understand you," Janet said, watching the dark cheek, the long jaw, the leathery sunburned neck, the tipped-back rancher's hat that showed the graying temple. "Suppose you died, and I got old and needed care. Would you expect the boys to send me off to an asylum, or would you expect they'd have enough love and gratitude to give me a room in their house?"

"You're not out of your mind," Tom said.

"I would be, if they treated me the way she's been treated. Four or five months with Albert, and then he palmed her off on Margaret; and Margaret kept her a little while and sent her to George; and George keeps her two months and wants to ship her to an institution—would have if we hadn't telephoned."

Tom removed a leaf from a twig. "It isn't that she's not wanted. She just hasn't got all her buttons any more. She can't be fitted into a family."

"Well, I tell you one thing," Janet said. "In our family she's going to feel wanted! She's like a child, Tom. She's got to feel that she has a place."

"Okay," he said. He leaned forward and spit on the ant he had been herding. The boys had given up their ball and were sitting on the edge of the rocked-in well from which the pepper's trunk rose.

Janet watched her husband a minute. She did not like him when his face went wooden and impenetrable. "Tom," she said, "will having her around bother you? Will it make you feel bad?"

His faded blue eyes turned on her, almost amused. "Relax," he said.

The train whistled for the crossing at Santa Clara, and Janet swung around to the boys. "Remember?" she said. "We're all going to be extra nice to Grandma. We're not going to laugh, or pester, or tease. We're going to be as polite and kind as we know how to be. Oliver, can you remember that? Jack, can you?"

The twins stared back at her, identical in T-shirts and jeans, with identical straight brown hair and identical expressions of hypocritical piety. Unsure of what their expressions meant, she waved them out through the curtain of branches, and they stood on the blazing platform in the ovenlike heat until the train rolled in and the Pullmans came abreast of them and the train stopped.

Janet felt above her the cool air-conditioned stares of passengers; she saw porters swing out, down the long train. A redcap pushed a truckload of baggage against the steps of a car. Then, down toward the rear of the train, a man in a blue slack suit stepped down and waited with his hand stretched upward. In a moment he climbed up again and came down leading an old lady by the arm. Janet hurried down the platform.

The man in blue, a fattish man with bare hairy arms, clung to Grandma's elbow and smiled a sickly smile as Janet came up. He had sweated through the armpits of his shirt. Grandma Waldron leaned away from him, her little brown eyes darting constantly, her lips trembling on a soundless stream of talk. She looked agitated, and her arms were folded hard across the breast of her heavy coat as if she were protecting something precious. She wore black shoes and a black hat, and she looked intolerably hot. In her unsuitable clothes amid the white heat and the pastel stucco of a California town, she tugged at Janet's sympathy like a lost and unhappy child.

"Hello, Mom," Tom said, and came forward to kiss her, but she twisted away with her arms still clenched across her breast. She appeared to wrestle with something; her face was strained, and drops of perspiration beaded her upper lip. Then the head of a cat thrust violently up above the lapels of the coat, a panting cat, ears back, pink mouth snarling. Under Grandma's clutching arms its body struggled, but it could not work free. It yowled, strangling.

Grandma ducked around Tom and the man in blue and came up to Janet. Her soundless talking became audible as a stream of words so unaccented that Janet wondered if she heard them herself, if she knew when she was speaking aloud and when only thinking with her lips. Paying no attention to the cat writhing weakly under the old lady's coat, she put out her hands and made her voice warm. "Grandma, it's awfully nice to have you here!"

Grandma's voice rode over the greetings, and she did not relax her clutch around the cat to touch the welcoming hands. ". . . never get rid of that man," she said. "Came up before I even got settled in my seat and stuck like a burr all the way I know what he wanted, he wanted into my bag so he could steal my picture of Tom's family, said he wanted to see what they looked like if there'd been a policeman there I'd have had him arrested trying to get into my suitcase I've had to watch every minute."

Her brown, prying eyes lighted on Janet, then on the staring twins; darted up the platform, swung suspiciously to the man in blue, who was talking quietly to Tom. Janet saw Tom's face, expressionless, and all in an instant she wanted to shout at him, "Don't you think that! She's strange and scared, that's all. This is what shunting her all around has done to her. George should have known better than to send her all the way from Los Angeles with a stranger."

But she could not say this. She barely had time to think it before the long warning cry went up along the train, the porters swung aboard, the train jerked and began to roll. The cat was struggling again in Grandma's arms. The man in blue jumped clumsily and got aboard, waving to them from the steps. Above them the bands of windows with the air-conditioned faces and the stares of strangers moved smoothly past, and then emptiness and a hot wind closed around the last Pullman.

"Well, here we are," Janet said gently. "You remember the twins. Jack and Oliver."

Grandma's eyes darted over the boys. Her talk had gone underground, but her lips still moved. After almost a minute of absolutely soundless vehement talking, the words came to the surface again. ". . . torturing the cat, chasing it through the house. Broke the wandering Jew right off."

One of her hands let go long enough to cram the cat's head down again. "Kept wanting my cat," she said. "That man did. Kept all the time wanting my cat away from me like those other things he took, all my money and my picture and my best mittens. That man took them."

Tom came up and stood smiling into his mother's face. "Don't you know me, Ma?"

Her head shaking slightly, Grandma looked at him. "Always was wild. Running away to the North Pole. I told my husband all about him, you bet. My husband's the constable." She looked around sharply. "Is that man gone? If we had any proper laws he'd been in jail long ago he got my mittens and my money and he tried to get my cat."

"Come on," Janet said, and took Grandma's elbow with the gentlest of fingers. "Let's get home out of this sun."

After a moment of resistance, Grandma came along. At the car, while Tom was running down the windows to let out the accumulated heat, he caught Janet's eye. The corners of his mouth went down soberly, and she felt that she had been challenged. "Grandma," she said, "don't you think you should let the poor cat out so it can breathe? That man's gone now."

The old lady jerked her shoulders and looked around her hard, but did not relax her arms. Janet helped her into the back seat, climbed in after her, sat down scrupulously on her own side. "Please," she said, and smiled into Grandma's strained face. "It can't get away in the car."

For just a moment, holding the brown intent eyes, she felt that she was being probed and tested. Then Grandma's clenched arms loosened slightly, and the cat shot up under her chin in a convulsive squirming effort, twisted and clawed its way loose, and sprang to the floor, where it crouched with tail flicking. Grandma started half to her feet as if to grab it up again, shot a sidelong look at Janet, and settled back. Outside the car the boys were watching. Jack shoved Oliver, and Oliver returned the shove. "Meowwwrrrr!" Jack said. Their eyes glistened, and they giggled.

"Get in," Janet said harshly. The two climbed in beside Tom, and in a bleak admonitory silence they turned into the street. When they had gone a few blocks Jack leaned over the seat to look at the crouching cat.

"Boy, that sure is a beat-up old cat," he said. Oliver turned to look too, and then they huddled down in the front seat. Janet heard their smothered mirth, and catching Tom's eye in the rear-view mirror, she thought she saw laughter there too.

For a moment she relaxed, almost ready to laugh herself. But when she turned to Grandma, sitting stiffly with her watchful eyes on the cat, she saw Grandma's open coat. Under it the black dress was plucked and snagged, and the white neck was bloody with scratches.

But what a commentary! Janet thought. What a revelation of the old lady's fear and suspicion, when she would think it necessary to cram her cat into her bosom and cling to it in protection though it clawed her heart out.

She reached out and patted Grandma's arm. The old lady looked at her, and it seemed to Janet that there was no longer suspicion in her eyes, but only inquiry. "It's nice to have you with us," Janet said.

Words flowed over the old lady's lips, but none of them made any sound.

They topped the hill and came into their own valley, the slope falling away below them in orchard and hay meadow, rising again on the far side to the dark chaparral of the coast hills. Little ranches, squares of apricot and almond and pear trees, angular lines of pasture and corral, patterned the valley and the sides of the hills, and the sight of that sheltered country beauty made Janet turn to Grandma to see if she felt it too. But Grandma was soundlessly telling herself something. Of course she couldn't see it. Not yet. Grandma's mind was a terrified little animal trembling in a dark hole while danger walked outside.

"There's our place," Janet said. "The one with the white water tower."

Grandma's eyes darted, but Janet could not be sure whether they really looked or whether they only cunningly pretended to. Then the car turned into the driveway and stopped under the holly oak with the yellow climbing roses incredibly hanging forty feet up among its branches. The fuchsias drooped ripe purple on both sides of the front door; the hill went up behind in a regimented jungle of orchards. The air was hot, heady, full of brandied fruit smell and the intoxication of tarweed. Down at the stable, under the old pear tree by the fence, the two horses stood with their heads companionably over each other's backs, making a two-tailed machine against the flies.

"Isn't it lovely!" Janet said. "Isn't it perfectly lovely!" Very carefully and tenderly she picked up the cat, stroked its fur smooth; and watching Grandma, half expecting the old lady to snatch the cat away, she took it as a small triumph that nothing of the sort happened. Grandma got out, and Janet got out after her. "You'll love it here," she said, and smiled.

Through the whole ritual of arrival she kept that tone. Every gesture was a calculated reassurance; every word soothed. When she led Grandma down into the bedroom wing she threw open the door confidently, feeling that this room, like the valley and the fruit-scented ranch, ought to strike even a sick mind as sheltered and secure. The bed had a blue and white ship quilt for a spread; the cotton rugs were fresh from the laundry; the roses she had put on the bed table that morning breathed sweetly in the room; the curtains moved coolly, secretly at the north windows.

She still had the cat in her arms. It had relaxed there, its eyes half closed. "This is your room," she said to Grandma, and smiled again into the strained brown eyes. She opened the bathroom door and showed the white tile, the towels neat on the racks, the new oval of green soap. Her own quick glance pleased her: it was a room and bath she would have liked to be brought into herself.

"Boys," she said, "I think the kitty would like some milk. Maybe you could bring a dish in here."

They brought it in a minute, their manners still quelled, their eyes speculative. Jack set the dish by the bed and Oliver poured it full. Janet, stooping to set the cat on the floor, glanced up to catch on Grandma's face a look not of suspicion and unfriendliness, but a softened expression that almost erased the hard crease between her eyes. She looked for a moment like anybody's grandmother, soft-faced and gentle.

The cat's feet found the floor, and it crouched, looking up at the people above it. With his toe Oliver moved the dish of milk closer, and the cat fled under the bed. Grandma started forward, the wrinkle hard between her eyes again, her mouth beginning to go, and Janet stopped her with a hand on her arm.

"It's still scared," she said softly to the boys. "It'll be all right after it's got used to us. We'll leave it with Grandma now so they can both take a rest."

As she was herding the twins up the hall Oliver said, "Boy, that cat needs a rest."

"So does Grandma," Tom said from the dining room. "You guys can rest by getting some hay up into the mow."

"Can we ride Peppermint after?"

"She's got a saddlesore."

"We'll ride her bareback."

"All right."

They went out, and Tom looked at Janet with a peculiar sidelong expression. "The eminent psychiatrist," he said.

"It's working, isn't it?" Janet said. "She let me take her cat, and she's already starting to relax a little."

"I hope it's working," he said.

"Tom, don't you want her to be better?"

"Of course. I'd give an arm."

"She's just like her poor cat," Janet said. "She's been so pushed down and crammed under that she—"

They both began to laugh.

"Probably we shouldn't," Janet said. But she added, "At least it's human to laugh! At least she's part of the family. Isn't that better than some old inhuman institution where she'd just be a number and a case history? They wouldn't laugh at her in a place like that. They wouldn't have the humanity to."

Next morning Grandma came with them to the orchard. She was quite calm, and for five minutes at a time her lips, instead of trembling on a stream of soundless words, were quiet, a little puckered; her eyes followed the preparation for picking with what seemed to Janet interest. Tom set up the ladders and laid out a string of lugs in the shade, and Grandma watched the four of them climb into the foliage among the bright globes of fruit.

Oliver picked a ripe apricot and stood on the ladder ready to toss it. "Here, Grandma," he said, "have an apricot."

He held it out, but the old lady made no move to come near and get it. "Just help yourself off the trees anywhere, Grandma," Janet said, and gave Oliver a sign to go on picking. When they were all up on ladders and busy, Grandma stooped quickly and snatched up a windfall apricot from the ground.

"No, Grandma," Janet said. "From the trees. Pick all you want. Those on the ground may be spoiled."

Grandma dropped the windfall and wiped her fingers on her dress. After a moment she started at her hurrying, shoulder-forward walk down the orchard toward the lower fence.

"Do you want her taking off across country?" Tom said.

"Who do you think you are, a jailer?" Janet said. "Let her feel free for once."

"I haven't got time to go out every half hour and round her up."

"You won't have to. She'll come back."

"Sure?"

"Absolutely sure," Janet said. "Wait and see."

Thrust up among leaves and branches, they looked down to where Grandma's figure had stopped at the fence. The old lady looked around furtively, then stooped, picked up something from the ground and popped it into her mouth.

"You've got a ways to go," Tom said, and his voice from the other tree was so impersonal and dry that she was angry with him.

"Give her a little time!" she said. "Give her a chance!"

She was confident, yet when Grandma had not returned at eleven her faith began to waver. She did not want Tom to catch her anxiously looking down the orchard, but every time she dumped a pail in the lug she snatched quick looks all around, and she was almost at the point of sending the boys out searching when she saw the gingham figure marching homeward along the upper fence.

She threw an apricot into the tree where Tom,was picking. "See?" she said. "What did I tell you?"

Every morning thereafter, Grandma took a walk through the orchards and along the lanes. Every afternoon she settled down in the wicker rocker on the porch, and rocked and talked and told herself things. Janet, working around the house, heard the steady voice going, and sometimes she heard what it said. It said that Simms, the drayman, had his eye on Grandma's house and was trying to get her moved out so that he could move his daughter and her husband in. It said that the minister was angry at her, ever since she sided with the evangelicals, and wanted the Ladies' Aid to leave her out of things. It said that George's wife was trying everything to get George to send Grandma away. Just the other day Grandma had overheard George's wife talking to the cleaning woman, plotting to leave Grandma's room dirty and then blame her in front of George. These were things Grandma knew, and she proved them with great vehemence and circumstantiality.

Sometimes Janet came and sat beside Grandma. When she did, the talk went underground; the lips moved, sometimes fervidly, and the little brown eyes snapped, but there was no conversation between them. Janet might comment on how the air cooled down when fog rolled over the crest of the coast hills, or might point out a hummingbird working the flower beds, but she did not expect replies. She took it as a hopeful sign that her presence did not drive Grandma away or stop her enthusiastic rocking, and sometimes it seemed to her that the rhythmic motion erased the strain from the old lady's face and smoothed the wrinkle between her eyes.

Then one afternoon Janet came quietly on the porch and found Grandma rocking like a child in the big chair, pushing with her toes, lifting off the floor, rocking back down to push with her toes again.

She was not talking at all, but was humming a tuneless little song to herself.

It was early August, and dense heat lay over the valley. The apricots were long gone; in the upper orchard the prunes were purple among the leaves, the limbs of the trees propped against the weight of fruit. The unirrigated pasture was split by cracks three inches wide, and even in the shade one felt the dry panting of the earth for the rain that would not come for another three months. Looking out over the heat-hazed valley, Grandma pushed with her toes, rocking and humming. Her face was mild and soft, and Janet slipped into the next chair, almost holding her breath for fear of breaking the moment. It was so easy to make a mistake. Weeks of improvement could be canceled by one false move that the sick mind could seize on as it had seized on a harmless conversation between George's wife and her cleaning woman.

It was Grandma herself who spoke first. She looked over at Janet brightly and said, "Tom's a handsome man."

"Yes," Janet said.

"He's filled out," Grandma said. "He was a skinny boy."

She went back to her humming. For ten more minutes Janet sat still, wishing that Tom were there to see his mother as she had once been, speculating on how the moment might be stretched, wondering if possibly this was a turning point, if Grandma had come out of the twilight where she lived and would from now on shake off the suspicions and the fears. The vines over the porch moved sluggishly and were still again.

Janet stood up. "It's hot," she said. "Shall we get ourselves a lemonade, Grandma?"

She appraised the quick look, the interrupted humming, the break in the even rocking, and knew that everything was all right, she hadn't broken any spell. Grandma started to rise but Janet said, "Don't get up. I'll bring it out."

"I'll come along," the old lady said. In the kitchen she stood behind Janet and watched the lemons squeezed, the sugar added, the ice cubes pushed from the rubber tray.

"I like it better with fizz water, don't you?" Janet said. Grandma appeared not to understand, but she watched carefully as Janet filled the glasses. "Now a cherry," Janet said. "We might as well be festive." She looked at Grandma and laughed, surprising a tremble of a smile. Out on the porch she heard steps, and in the hope that Tom might have come in, and that she could demonstrate this miracle to him, she hugged the old lady around the shoulders and walked her through the French doors.

The steps had not been Tom's. Oliver was sprawled in the wicker rocker, his legs clear across the porch, his face sweaty. He looked up limply, brightened at sight of the glasses of lemonade.

"Hey! Can I have one?"

"If you want to fix it yourself. Grandma and I are having a party."

"Aw corn," Oliver said. "I haven't got the strength." He lay out even flatter in the chair, egg-eyed, his tongue hanging out. "This is the way they look when Popeye hits them," he said.

"Weak as you are, you'll have to move," Janet said. "You're in Grandma's chair."

He opened one eye. "Grandma's chair? How come?"

"Oliver!" his mother said. "Haven't you mislaid your manners?"

He rose promptly enough, a little surprised, and Janet ruffled his hair as he went by. But she couldn't miss the way Grandma's mouth had tightened and trembled, and how when she sat down again she sat on the front of the chair, unrelaxed, the mild look that had been briefly on her face replaced by a look of petulance and injury.

Three days later, when they were just beginning to pick the prune crop, Grandma moved.

Janet was preparing lunch when Tom and the boys came in from the orchard and started for the bathroom to clean up. Within a minute Oliver was back. "She's in our room! Mom, she's moved into our room with all her stuff!"

In Oliver's footsteps Janet went down the hall. Grandma sat stiffly on the boy's bed. The end of her suitcase showed under the bed, and the dresser was heaped with her clothing. From across the hall Tom appeared, scrubbing with a towel. Janet, stepping softly, went into the room and said, "Why, Grandma, don't you like your own room?"

The old lady's finger leaped out to point at Jack, who ducked as if the finger were a gun. The finger shifted smartly over to Oliver. "He told me to move. That boy of yours. He didn't want me to have the nice room with the bath when he only had this little one. He told me to get out."

Oliver's brow wrinkled, and his mouth opened. Tom took a step forward, but Janet stopped him with a look and squeezed hard on

Oliver's shoulder. "There's just been a mistake," she said. "If either of the boys said that, he didn't mean it. The nice room with the bath is yours."

"He told me."

"If he did he didn't mean it. Did you, Oliver?"

"I never said anything of the kind. I was out in the orchard all morning."

"If you said it you didn't mean it, did you?"

"I never . . . No, I didn't mean it."

"Now let's get Grandma moved back before lunch," Janet said brightly, and motioned Jack to take some clothes from the dresser. When he moved to lift them off, Grandma took them from him with a hard look; he stood back and let her carry her own things to her room.

Back in the kitchen, Oliver said, "Boy, she's crazy as a bedbug. I never said a word to her. Where does she get it I made her move? She's nutty."

"Say she gets notions," Janet said. "I shouldn't have to tell you again. She's had a hard life. If we humor her and treat her nicely maybe she'll get well."

Oliver thoughtfully ate a prune off the work table. "How'd she get that way, fall downstairs or something?"

"I don't know," Janet said. "It just grew on her, I guess."

That was on Friday. On Sunday afternoon, when the prune orchard was dotted with people from the city who had come down to pick their own fruit, and Tom and the boys were out distributing ladders and pails and weighing up baskets and keeping the unpracticed pickers from breaking down limbs, Janet took a cool limeade in to Grandma and found her gone. Her closet was empty; her bureau drawers cleaned out.

Janet went out through the porch, across a road's-width of passionate sun, and under the shade of the oaks, where Tom had his scales. She waited while he weighed two baskets of prunes and carried them to a car. "Grandma's gone," she said when he came back.

She saw his patience bend and crack, and she stood guiltily, granting him the right to blame her but at the same time not admitting that she was in any way wrong. After a moment Tom said, "How long?"

"I don't know. I just took a drink in, and she was gone, with all her stuff. Sometime since dinner. Maybe an hour."

"We'd have seen her if she'd come out through here," he said. He looked across into the orchard, where three different parties were picking. "I just about have to stay here till these folks clear out. Can you and the kids look?"

She called the boys and they came at once, intent, sun-blackened, interested like setters being called up for a walk, and she thought as they came under the bronze shade: My nice boys! She thought it with a rush of affection, irrelevantly, grateful to them for their clear eyes and their health.

Trying to forestall in them the impatience that had jumped into Tom's face, she put on a crooked and rueful smile. "Grandma's abandoned us," she said, making it a joke between them.

They groaned, but more to acknowledge the joke than for any other reason, and wobbled their knees and crossed their eyes in dismay. Jack ran up the ladder of the tree house built in the oak and stood like a sailor on the crosstrees, peering into the empty shanty with a hand cupped over his eyes. Oliver sniffed the foot of the tree, followed an imaginary trail into the garage, through the car, around the woodshed, and back to the driveway. "Hey!" they said. "No Grandma. Man overboard. Fireman, save my child."

The three of them went across the brittle oat stubble, stopped to search the pump house, glanced into the chicken house and disturbed some matronly hens. They went through the stable and tackroom, and Janet stayed below while the boys climbed up into the mow. A drift of straw and dust fell from the trapdoor and filled the slant sunbeams with constellations.

The boys came down again. "No Grandma," they said. "Call the St. Bernards; she must be lost in the snow."

They went to the stable door and looked down across the lower orchard and the dry creek bed toward Hillstrom's. There was a breeze coming around the corner, a cool, horsy breath. They stood in it, searching the neighboring orchard and pastures, looking along the quarter-mile of white road that showed on the ridge above Kuhn's.

"She couldn't have gone far, with the suitcase," Janet said. "Did you look carefully in the garage, Oliver?"

"She wasn't there. I looked all over."

At a slight sound behind her, Janet turned. Grandma's cat came out of one of the horse stalls, balancing his tail, blinking slit-eyed in the bright doorway, rubbing against her legs.

"Now where'd you come from, kitty?" Janet said. "Where's your mistress?"

"He comes down here to catch mice," Jack said. "I saw him with one the other day."

"But where's your boss?" Janet said, and stooped to let the lifting furry back pass under her hand.

There were footsteps in the tackroom, and Tom came in. "Find her?"

"Not a sign."

Tom stood with his hands in his back pockets, chewing his upper lip. "Oh, damn!" he said, without real anger.

Jack picked up the cat and stood petting it, watching his parents, and the noise of the cat's purring was loud in the stable until the noise of a car ground over it and drowned it out, and a green sedan came around the corner and stopped in the barnyard. "Is this where you can pick your own prunes?" the driver said. A woman and three children were crowding to look through the rear window.

"Up above," Tom said. "If you'll drive back up to the house I'll be with you in a minute." He looked at Janet. "You want me to go hunting, or handle the pickers, or what?"

"The boys and I can cruise around."

Then their voices filled the stable. "Mom! Here she is. Here she is, Mom!"

The sedan started to turn around. Back in against the manger of the second stall there was a threshing and rustling, and as Janet squinted into the shadows she saw Grandma sitting up in the manger. She reared up and scolded the boys, ". . . never get a minute's peace somebody always prying around spying on a person go away you boys or I'll tell your father he sent me down here now you leave me be go 'way."

"For the love of God, Ma, come out of there," Tom said. He went in and half lifted her over the front of the manger. Rigid with anger, muttering, she jerked away and came at a half run out into the doorway. The sedan was just leaving; Janet saw the faces staring, and then she grabbed Grandma and held her until Tom pulled her back inside. Grandma's clothes were slivered with hay, gray with dust. There were oat hulls caught on her lip.

"Oliver," Janet said. "Jump on that man's running board and show him where to go."

"Aw, Ma!"

"Please!" she said. "Get those people out of here!"

Tom hung on to Grandma's arm till the sound of the car had died. "I don't suppose it will do any good to ask you what you thought you were doing down here," he said.

Grandma sniffed. "I know I don't count for anything here," she said. "When I had my own home it was different, before Henry died, but around here I only do as I'm told. If you tell me to live in the stable and eat with the horses that's all right with me. I know I'm on charity, I don't complain."

Abruptly Tom let go of her arm. "You handle this," he said to Janet, and went out into the hot light that lay like a sea around the warm dark island of the stable.

"You must trust us, Grandma," Janet said softly. Without really watching him, she was aware how Jack stared with the cat purring in his arms, and she reached out to pull him against her, knowing how Grandma's queerness must trouble his understanding. "You must let us love you and take care of you," she said. "Don't feel that any of us are against you. We all love you. You don't have to move out of your room, or eat out of the horse's box . . ."

Before she could move Grandma had lunged forward and snatched the sleepy tomcat out of Jack's arms. She clenched it against her fiercely, fighting its clawing desperate feet, and turned half around to shield it from their sight. The cat yowled, a frantic squashed sound, as Grandma retreated into the stall from which she had just come.

Janet shook her head at Jack and whispered, "You'd better run up and help Dad and Oliver." She steered him to the edge of the hard sunlight, whispering, "We'll just let her alone a few minutes. She's so excited she shouldn't be pushed around. I'll bring her up in a little while."

"What if she—"

"Run along. She'll be all right."

Her own nerves were on edge; she was trembling. Back in the shadow the cat squalled again, and then the sounds were muffled, as if Grandma had got the animal under her sweater. After a minute or two they stopped entirely. Either the old lady had got over her fright and stopped squeezing the cat, or it had escaped.

Janet waited another five minutes. It was perfectly quiet; she heard the slightest tick of falling straw. She did not like to think of Grandma back there in the shadow, her mouth going on some vehement silent tirade, her mind full of suspicion and crazy notions.

She went to the front of the stall and said casually, "Shall we go back to the house, Grandma?"

Grandma jerked around. She had been bending over the manger, and now she pulled out the brown suitcase, the arm or leg of a suit of winter underwear trailing out of its corner. Janet smiled. "Did the cat get away? Never mind, he likes it here. He'll be back."

"That boy tried to steal it," Grandma said.

She came out quietly enough, but when Janet offered to carry the suitcase she swung it far over on one side, guarding it jealously, and Janet sighed. It was so easy to make a mistake. The slightest gesture of kindness was likely to rouse suspicion. You had to be as soft and smooth and easy as cottonwool, or you did harm instead of good. She watched Grandma marching ahead of her; as the old lady turned the sun was golden on the oat husks caught on her lip. Janet smiled, following her up to the house and into the cool porch, and, still smiling, followed her down the hall to her room.

It was not until two hours later, after she had calmed the old lady and talked her into taking a tepid bath, and had then started to unpack and put away Grandma's clothes, that she discovered about the cat. It was jammed into the suitcase, tangled among long drawers and petticoats and damask napkins. And it was desperately and resistantly dead. Its eyes were half open, its mouth wide so that the needle teeth showed in a grin. Its front legs were stiffened straight out, as if it had died pushing against the smothering lid.

That evening after dinner Janet sat on the porch looking across the little valley and feeling how the heat left the earth as the night came on. The boys were playing checkers in the living room behind her; she felt their presence in the lamplight that yellowed the windows. Tom was hammering at something down in the pump house. Grandma was in her room.

Over the ridge of the stable the pasture knoll beyond the Wilson place shone a lovely fawn color in the last flat sun. But all around, in the valley itself, the earth was already going gray and shadowy. In a little while the light would lift off the last knoll; the clouds would change and darken back of the coast hills; the ranches would begin to melt back into the trees; lights would wink on; the clean sky would be pricked with stars.

It was a most peaceful place and a peaceful life. Half irritably, she thought that Grandma should find healing in every hour of it. But she knew she would have to talk to Tom about Grandma later; for now she put the whole problem away, sitting with her hands turned palm upward in her lap and listening to the lulling rise of the night noises, crickets and tree frogs and the far musical cry of a train down toward San Jose. When it was all but dark she leaned near one of the open lighted windows and said, "Time for bed, boys."

"Just till we finish this game," Oliver said, and looking in, she saw them hunched head to head over the card table. There was a rhythm in that too, the same rhythm through which she herself swung, moving evenly through the warm, temperate, repetitive events of a life that was not going anywhere because it was already there; it lived at the center.

She heard Tom coming through the dusk, his steps soft in the disked ground as he crossed a strip of orchard, then grating in the gravel drive, and he came up on the porch and sat down heavily in the wicker chair beside her.

"Boy, I've got you cornered now!" Oliver said from inside. "You give up?"

"Like heck," Jack said. "Not as long as I'm in a double corner."

"Time they were in bed?" Tom said.

"They're just finishing a game."

They sat on without speaking in the dark. Out over the main valley, moving smoothly among the orderly stars, the running lights on the wing tips of an air liner winked on and off. Sometimes, when clouds bridged the main valley trough, the motors of a plane like that could fill their little hollow with sound, but now in the clear night the noise was only a remote and diminishing hum. The lights winked unfailingly far down toward the south until the hills rose and cut them off.

Inside, the boys broke up their game and snapped off the light. For a minute or two they stood together at the French doors looking out on the porch. "Well, I guess we'll go to bed now," one of them said, and Janet was amused that in the dark she really couldn't tell which one had spoken.

"I'll look in on you later," she said. "It's so nice out I think I'll sit awhile."

When they had gone, she and Tom sat on. The wicker chair squeaked; she knew he had turned his head.

"Well?" he said.

"Well?" She did not want to make it hard for him to begin; she even wanted with an odd sense of urgency to try again to tell him how she felt, how she knew that even a thing badly done, if it was done with love, was better than a thing done efficiently but without love. But she was in a defensive position, like Jack in his double corner. Tom had to move first. . . . "You realize she has to be sent away," Tom said.

"Why?" She would not move until he absolutely forced her.

"My God!" he said. "Why?"

She heard his chair squeak again. Another plane was coming up the valley, its motors a distant even drone. "I'll tell you why," he said. "Just because she breaks everything up. She can't live with sane people. She'll bust the whole pattern of our lives."

"By pattern you mean comfort," Janet said, and heard her own voice, stiff and resistant, and the irritation that jumped in Tom's voice when he answered.

"No, I don't mean comfort! I mean the way we live, the way the kids grow up. Do you think it does them any good, seeing her batting at empty air?"

Janet had thought of the boys herself, plenty of times. But they were steady and well-balanced. It might even teach them forbearance and kindliness to have the old lady around. It wasn't fair of Tom to bring them into it now.

"I wonder how the boys would like to be responsible for condemning Grandma to prison for life, just to protect their own routine?" she said.

"That's better than letting her break up other people's lives."

"Oh, break up our lives!" Janet said. "The little trouble we've had . . ." She leaned forward, trying to reach the vague shadow of her husband with her eyes and voice. "Don't you realize what it would mean if we sent her away? We'd be treating her exactly as strangers might treat her, as if we had no feeling for her at all. We'd be washing our hands of her, just so we could be more comfortable." She sat back, suddenly so angry and hurt that her hands shook. "I'm surprised you don't . . ."

"Don't what?" Tom's voice said.

"Nothing."

"Nazi methods?" Tom said. "That's what you were going to say, isn't it? You're surprised I don't want to cyanide her."

"You know I didn't—"

"Sometimes you have to do a thing you don't want to do," Tom said. "You can do it kindly, even when it's something hard."

"But that's just what I wish you could see!" Janet cried. "There's no chance of any kindness in an institution, and it's kindness she needs."

There was a pause. "So you don't want to send her away," Tom said. "Not even after that cat business."

"I couldn't forgive myself if we did," she said. "It would be throwing her out when she was crying for help and not knowing how to say the words. That cat was the one thing she had left to love. Remember how afraid she was that the man on the train was going to steal it? That cat was half her life."

"And she killed it."

"Out of fear! We haven't got her over her fear, that's all. She was getting along fine, till this last spell. I've got enough confidence in the way we live to think we can change her pattern instead of her changing ours."

"Then you're crazier than she is."

Janet stood up. Her knees were trembling a little, and the thought crossed her mind that now, without the cat, Grandma was going to be harder than ever to win over. Maybe she would even get the notion that someone in the family had killed it. But that was not the question. The question was whether they could feel right about giving her over to some cold-blooded aseptic hospital that would surely drive her deeper into her persecuted dream.

"I don't see how we could respect ourselves," she said. "It's at least worth a better try than we've given it."

For a time the little night noises were still. Then a cricket started up again, a tinny fiddling under the porch. Tom's face was lost in the dark, but finally he spoke. "Okay. You're the doctor."

"Just the thought of giving up after less than two months."

"Okay, okay."

"I wish you could see it, Tom."

"I see it," he said. "I just don't believe it."

She hesitated. Then she went past him, walking quietly as if he were sleeping and she did not want to disturb him, and opened the screen and let it close softly behind her. The house was still. The padded living-room rug muffled her steps, and she had a feeling that it was very late at night, though she knew it couldn't be past ten. There was a light burning in the hall, and by the diffused glow she made her way to the hall leading down the bedroom wing.

As if a hand had closed around her heart she stopped dead still at the entrance. Halfway down the hall Grandma was standing, looking into the open door of the boys' room. Her head was sunk between her shoulders with the intensity of her stare, and her mouth moved on some secret malevolence. She made no move to enter, but only stood there staring, stooping forward a little. Then she heard Janet and whirled, and all the light that filtered into the hall flashed in her eyeballs, and she scuttled down the hall and into her own room.

Janet fought her breath free, but the cold paralysis of fear was still in her legs. She took four quick steps to the children's door, listened. Their breathing came quiet and steady in the dark, and she sagged against the door in relief. From down the hall there was a muffled click, and she saw the shadowy crack along Grandma's door widen. When she stepped full into the hall again the crack softly closed.

Janet put her hand down, felt the skeleton key in the lock of the boys' door. That key would work in any of the bedroom doors. She slipped it out and started down the hall, and the stealthy crack which had opened along Grandma's door closed again as she came. Janet stood a moment at the door, listening. There was not a sound. With a quick movement she inserted the skeleton key into the lock and turned it. She leaned against the door with the key in her hand and said, "Oh, Grandma, I'm sorry, I'm so terribly sorry!"

All through the darkened house there was not a sound. Up the hall her boys slept undisturbed, and out on the porch her husband sat in the dark, looking down over the even pattern of his orchards. She thought of the windows that Grandma could climb out of, the screens that should be nailed tight shut, and though the key in her hand was still a rigid reproach, she hurried. She hurried with fear driving her, and she was crying, not entirely from fear, when she called to Tom through the open French doors.

THE
COLT

I t was the swift coming of spring that let things happen. It was spring, and the opening of the roads, that took his father out of town. It was spring that clogged the river with floodwater and ice pans, sent the dogs racing in wild aimless packs, ripped the railroad bridge out and scattered it down the river for exuberant townspeople to fish out piecemeal. It was spring that drove the whole town to the riverbank with pikepoles and coffeepots and boxes of sandwiches for an impromptu picnic, lifting their sober responsibilities out of them and making them whoop blessings on the Canadian Pacific Railway for a winter's firewood. Nothing might have gone wrong except for the coming of spring. Some of the neighbors might have noticed and let them know; Bruce might not have forgotten; his mother might have remembered and sent him out again after dark.

But the spring came, and the ice went out, and that night Bruce went to bed drunk and exhausted with excitement. In the restless sleep just before waking he dreamed of wolves and wild hunts, but when he awoke finally he realized that he had not been dreaming the noise. The window, wide open for the first time in months, let in a shivery draught of fresh, damp air, and he heard the faint yelping far down in the bend of the river.

He dressed and went downstairs, crowding his bottom into the warm oven, not because he was cold but because it had been a ritual for so long that not even the sight of the sun outside could convince him it wasn't necessary. The dogs were still yapping; he heard them through the open door.

"What's the matter with all the pooches?" he said. "Where's Spot?"

"He's out with them," his mother said. "They've probably got a porcupine treed. Dogs go crazy in the spring."

"It's dog days they go crazy."

"They go crazy in the spring, too." She hummed a little as she set the table. "You'd better go feed the horses. Breakfast won't be for ten minutes. And see if Daisy is all right."

Bruce stood perfectly still in the middle of the kitchen. "Oh my gosh!" he said. "I left Daisy picketed out all night!"

His mother's head jerked around. "Where?"

"Down in the bend."

"Where those dogs are?"

"Yes," he said, sick and afraid. "Maybe she's had her colt."

"She shouldn't for two or three days," his mother said. But just looking at her, he knew that it might be bad, that there was something to be afraid of. In another moment they were out the door, running.

But it couldn't be Daisy they were barking at, he thought as he raced around Chance's barn. He'd picketed her higher up, not clear down in the U where the dogs were. His eyes swept the brown, wet, close-cropped meadow, the edge of the brush where the river ran close under the north bench. The mare wasn't there! He opened his mouth and half turned, running, to shout at his mother coming behind him, and then sprinted for the deep curve of the bend.

As soon as he rounded the little clump of brush that fringed the cutbank behind Chance's he saw them. The mare stood planted, a bay spot against the gray brush, and in front of her, on the ground, was another smaller spot. Six or eight dogs were leaping around, barking, sitting. Even at that distance he recognized Spot and the Chapmans' Airedale.

He shouted and pumped on. At a gravelly patch he stooped and clawed and straightened, still running, with a handful of pebbles. In one pausing, straddling, aiming motion he let fly a rock at the distant pack. It fell far short, but they turned their heads, sat on their haunches, and let out defiant short barks. Their tongues lolled as if they had run far.

Bruce yelled and threw again, one eye on the dogs and the other on the chestnut colt in front of the mare's feet. The mare's ears were back, and as he ran Bruce saw the colt's head bob up and down. It was all right then. The colt was alive. He slowed and came up quietly. Never move fast or speak loud around an animal, Pa said.

The colt struggled again, raised its head with white eyeballs rolling, spraddled its white-stockinged legs and tried to stand. "Easy, boy," Bruce said. "Take it easy, old fella." His mother arrived, getting her breath, her hair half down, and he turned to her gleefully. "It's all right, Ma. They didn't hurt anything. Isn't he a beauty, Ma?"

He stroked Daisy's nose. She was heaving, her ears pricking forward and back; her flanks were lathered, and she trembled. Patting her gently, he watched the colt, sitting now like a dog on its haunches, and his happiness that nothing had really been hurt bubbled out of him. "Lookit, Ma," he said. "He's got four white socks. Can I call him Socks, Ma? He sure is a nice colt, isn't he? Aren't you, Socks, old boy?" He reached down to touch the chestnut's forelock, and the colt struggled, pulling away.

Then Bruce saw his mother's face. It was quiet, too quiet. She hadn't answered a word to all his jabber. Instead she knelt down, about ten feet from the squatting colt, and stared at it. The boy's eyes followed hers. There was something funny about . . .

"Ma!" he said. "What's the matter with its front feet?"

He left Daisy's head and came around, staring. The colt's pasterns looked bent—*were* bent, so that they flattened clear to the ground under its weight. Frightened by Bruce's movement, the chestnut flopped and floundered to its feet, pressing close to its mother. And it walked, Bruce saw, flat on its fetlocks, its hooves sticking out in front like a movie comedian's too-large shoes.

Bruce's mother pressed her lips together, shaking her head. She moved so gently that she got her hand on the colt's poll, and he bobbed against the pleasant scratching. "You poor broken-legged thing," she said with tears in her eyes. "You poor little friendly ruined thing!"

Still quietly, she turned toward the dogs, and for the first time in his life Bruce heard her curse. Quietly, almost in a whisper, she cursed them as they sat with hanging tongues just out of reach. "God damn you," she said. "God damn your wild hearts, chasing a mother and a poor little colt."

To Bruce, standing with trembling lip, she said, "Go get Jim Enich. Tell him to bring a wagon. And don't cry. It's not your fault."

His mouth tightened, a sob jerked in his chest. He bit his lip and drew his face down tight to keep from crying, but his eyes filled and ran over.

"It is too my fault!" he said, and turned and ran.

Later, as they came in the wagon up along the cutbank, the colt tied down in the wagon box with his head sometimes lifting, sometimes bumping on the boards, the mare trotting after with chuckling vibrations of solicitude in her throat, Bruce leaned far over and tried to touch the colt's haunch. "Gee whiz!" he said. "Poor old Socks."

His mother's arm was around him, keeping him from leaning over too far. He didn't watch where they were until he heard his mother say in surprise and relief, "Why, there's Pa!"

Instantly he was terrified. He had forgotten and left Daisy staked out all night. It was his fault, the whole thing. He slid back into the seat and crouched between Enich and his mother, watching from that narrow space like a gopher from its hole. He saw the Ford against the barn and his father's big body leaning into it, pulling out gunny sacks and straw. There was mud all over the car, mud on his father's pants. He crouched deeper into his crevice and watched his father's face while his mother was telling what had happened.

Then Pa and Jim Enich lifted and slid the colt down to the ground, and Pa stooped to feel its fetlocks. His face was still, red from windburn, and his big square hands were muddy. After a long examination he straightened up.

"Would've been a nice colt," he said. "Damn a pack of mangy mongrels, anyway." He brushed his pants and looked at Bruce's mother. "How come Daisy was out?"

"I told Bruce to take her out. The barn seems so cramped for her, and I thought it would do her good to stretch her legs. And then the ice went out, and the bridge with it, and there was a lot of excitement. . . ." She spoke very fast, and in her voice Bruce heard the echo of his own fear and guilt. She was trying to protect him, but in his mind he knew he was to blame.

"I didn't mean to leave her out, Pa," he said. His voice squeaked, and he swallowed. "I was going to bring her in before supper, only when the bridge . . ."

His father's somber eyes rested on him, and he stopped. But his father didn't fly into a rage. He just seemed tired. He looked at the colt and then at Enich. "Total loss?" he said.

Enich had a leathery, withered face, with two deep creases from beside his nose to the corner of his mouth. A brown mole hid in the left one, and it emerged and disappeared as he chewed a dry grass stem. "Hide," he said.

Bruce closed his dry mouth, swallowed. "Pa!" he said. "It won't have to be shot, will it?"

"What else can you do with it?" his father said. "A crippled horse is no good. It's just plain mercy to shoot it."

"Give it to me, Pa. I'll keep it lying down and heal it up."

"Yeah," his father said, without sarcasm and without mirth. "You could keep it lying down about one hour."

Bruce's mother came up next to him, as if the two of them were standing against the others. "Jim," she said quickly, "isn't there some kind of brace you could put on it? I remember my dad had a horse once that broke a leg below the knee, and he saved it that way."

"Not much chance," Enich said. "Both legs, like that." He plucked a weed and stripped the dry branches from the stalk. "You can't make a horse understand he has to keep still."

"But wouldn't it be worth trying?" she said. "Children's bones heal so fast, I should think a colt's would too."

"I don't know. There's an outside chance, maybe."

"Bo," she said to her husband, "why don't we try it? It seems such a shame, a lovely colt like that."

"I know it's a shame!" he said. "I don't like shooting colts any better than you do. But I never saw a broken-legged colt get well. It'd just be a lot of worry and trouble, and then you'd have to shoot it finally anyway."

"Please," she said. She nodded at him slightly, and then the eyes of both were on Bruce. He felt the tears coming up again, and turned to grope for the colt's ears. It tried to struggle to its feet, and Enich put his foot on its neck. The mare chuckled anxiously.

"How much this hobble brace kind of thing cost?" the father said finally. Bruce turned again, his mouth open with hope.

"Two-three dollars, is all," Enich said.

"You think it's got a chance?"

"One in a thousand, maybe."

"All right. Let's go see MacDonald."

"Oh, good!" Bruce's mother said, and put her arm around him tight.

"I don't know whether it's good or not," the father said. "We might wish we never did it." To Bruce he said, "It's your responsibility. You got to take complete care of it."

"I will!" Bruce said. He took his hand out of his pocket and rubbed below his eye with his knuckles. "I'll take care of it every day."

Big with contrition and shame and gratitude and the sudden sense of immense responsibility, he watched his father and Enich start for the house to get a tape measure. When they were thirty feet away he said loudly, "Thanks, Pa. Thanks an awful lot."

His father half turned, said something to Enich. Bruce stooped to stroke the colt, looked at his mother, started to laugh, and felt it turn horribly into a sob. When he turned away so that his mother wouldn't notice he saw his dog Spot looking inquiringly around the corner of the barn. Spot took three or four tentative steps and paused, wagging his tail. Very slowly (never speak loud or move fast around an animal) the boy bent and found a good-sized stone. He straightened casually, brought his arm back, and threw with all his might. The rock caught Spot squarely in the ribs. He yiped, tucked his tail, and scuttled around the barn, and Bruce chased him, throwing clods and stones and gravel, yelling, "Get out! Go on, get out of here or I'll kick you apart. Get out! Go on!"

So all that spring, while the world dried in the sun and the willows emerged from the floodwater and the mud left by the freshet hardened and caked among their roots, and the grass of the meadow greened and the river brush grew misty with tiny leaves and the dandelions spread yellow among the flats, Bruce tended his colt. While the other boys roamed the bench hills with .22's looking for gophers or rabbits or sage hens, he anxiously superintended the colt's nursing and watched it learn to nibble the grass. While his gang built a darkly secret hide-out in the deep brush beyond Hazard's, he was currying and brushing and trimming the chestnut mane. When packs of boys ran hare and hounds through the town and around the river's slow bends, he perched on the front porch with his slingshot and a can full of small round stones, waiting for stray dogs to appear. He waged a holy war on the dogs until they learned to detour widely around his house, and he never did completely forgive his own dog, Spot. His whole life was wrapped up in the hobbled, leg-ironed chestnut colt with the slow-motion lunging walk and the affectionate nibbling lips.

Every week or so Enich, who was now working out of town at the Half Diamond Bar, rode in and stopped. Always, with that expressionless quiet that was terrible to the boy, he stood and looked the colt over, bent to feel pastern and fetlock, stood back to watch the plunging walk when the boy held out a handful of grass. His expression said nothing; whatever he thought was hidden back of his leathery face as the dark mole was hidden in the crease beside his mouth. Bruce found himself watching that mole sometimes, as if revelation might lie there. But when he pressed Enich to tell him, when he said, "He's getting better, isn't he? He walks better, doesn't he, Mr. Enich? His ankles don't bend so much, do they?" the wrangler gave him little encouragement.

"Let him be awhile. He's growin', sure enough. Maybe give him another month."

May passed. The river was slow and clear again, and some of the boys were already swimming. School was almost over. And still Bruce paid attention to nothing but Socks. He willed so strongly that the colt should get well that he grew furious even at Daisy when she sometimes wouldn't let the colt suck as much as he wanted. He took a butcher knife and cut the long tender grass in the fence corners, where Socks could not reach, and fed it to his pet by the handful. He trained him to nuzzle for sugar-lumps in his pockets. And back in his mind was a fear: in the middle of June they would be going out to the homestead again, and if Socks weren't well by that time he might not be able to go.

"Pa," he said, a week before they planned to leave. "How much of a load are we going to have, going out to the homestead?"

"I don't know, wagonful, I suppose. Why?"

"I just wondered." He ran his fingers in a walking motion along the round edge of the dining table, and strayed into the other room. If they had a wagon load, then there was no way Socks could be loaded in and taken along. And he couldn't walk fifty miles. He'd get left behind before they got up on the bench, hobbling along like the little crippled boy in the Pied Piper, and they'd look back and see him trying to run, trying to keep up.

That picture was so painful that he cried over it in bed that night. But in the morning he dared to ask his father if they couldn't take Socks along to the farm. His father turned on him eyes as sober as Jim Enich's, and when he spoke it was with a kind of tired impatience. "How can he go? He couldn't walk it."

"But I want him to go, Pa!"

"Brucie," his mother said, "don't get your hopes up. You know we'd do it if we could, if it was possible."

"But, Ma . . ."

His father said, "What you want us to do, haul a broken-legged colt fifty miles?"

"He'd be well by the end of the summer, and he could walk back."

"Look," his father said. "Why can't you make up your mind to it? He isn't getting well. He isn't going to get well."

"He is too getting well!" Bruce shouted. He half stood up at the table, and his father looked at his mother and shrugged.

"Please, Bo," she said.

"Well, he's got to make up his mind to it sometime," he said.

Jim Enich's wagon pulled up on Saturday morning, and Bruce was out the door before his father could rise from his chair. "Hi, Mr. Enich," he said.

"Hello, Bub. How's your pony?"

"He's fine," Bruce said. "I think he's got a lot better since you saw him last."

"Uh-huh." Enich wrapped the lines around the whipstock and climbed down. "Tell me you're leaving next week."

"Yes," Bruce said. "Socks is in the back."

When they got into the back yard Bruce's father was there with his hands behind his back, studying the colt as it hobbled around. He looked at Enich. "What do you think?" he said. "The kid here thinks his colt can walk out to the homestead."

"Uh-huh," Enich said. "Well, I wouldn't say that." He inspected the chestnut, scratched between his ears. Socks bobbed, and snuffled at his pockets. "Kid's made quite a pet of him."

Bruce's father grunted. "That's just the damned trouble."

"I didn't think he could walk out," Bruce said. "I thought we could take him in the wagon, and then he'd be well enough to walk back in the fall."

"Uh," Enich said. "Let's take his braces off for a minute."

He unbuckled the triple straps on each leg, pulled the braces off, and stood back. The colt stood almost as flat on his fetlocks as he had the morning he was born. Even Bruce, watching with his whole mind tight and apprehensive, could see that. Enich shook his head.

"You see, Bruce?" his father said. "It's too bad, but he isn't getting better. You'll have to make up your mind. . . ."

"He will get better, though!" Bruce said. "It just takes a long time, is all." He looked at his father's face, at Enich's, and neither one had any hope in it. But when Bruce opened his mouth to say something else his father's eyebrows drew down in sudden, unaccountable anger, and his hand made an impatient sawing motion in the air.

"We shouldn't have tried this in the first place," he said. "It just tangles everything up." He patted his coat pockets, felt in his vest. "Run in and get me a couple cigars."

Bruce hesitated, his eyes on Enich. "Run!" his father said harshly.

Reluctantly he released the colt's halter rope and started for the house. At the door he looked back, and his father and Enich were talking together, so low that their words didn't carry to where he stood. He saw his father shake his head, and Enich bend to pluck a grass stem. They were both against him, they both were sure Socks would never get well. Well, he would! There was some way.

He found the cigars, came out, watched them both light up. Disappointment was a sickness in him, and mixed with the disappointment was a question. When he could stand their silence no more he burst out with it. "But what are we going to *do*? He's got to have some place to stay."

"Look, kiddo." His father sat down on a sawhorse and took him by the arm. His face was serious and his voice gentle. "We can't take him out there. He isn't well enough to walk, and we can't haul him. So Jim here has offered to buy him. He'll give you three dollars for him, and when you come back, if you want, you might be able to buy him back. That is, if he's well. It'll be better to leave him with Jim."

"Well . . ." Bruce studied the mole on Enich's cheek. "Can you get him better by fall, Mr. Enich?"

"I wouldn't expect it," Enich said. "He ain't got much of a show."

"If anybody can get him better, Jim can," his father said. "How's that deal sound to you?"

"Maybe when I come back he'll be all off his braces and running around like a house afire," Bruce said. "Maybe next time I see him I can ride him." The mole disappeared as Enich tongued his cigar.

"Well, all right then," Bruce said, bothered by their stony-eyed silence. "But I sure hate to leave you behind, Socks, old boy."

"It's the best way all around," his father said. He talked fast, as if he were in a hurry. "Can you take him along now?"

"Oh, gee!" Bruce said. "Today?"

"Come on," his father said. "Let's get it over with."

Bruce stood by while they trussed the colt and hoisted him into the wagon box, and when Jim climbed in he cried out, "Hey, we forgot to put his hobbles back on." Jim and his father looked at each other.

His father shrugged. "All right," he said, and started putting the braces back on the trussed front legs.

"He might hurt himself if they weren't on," Bruce said. He leaned over the endgate stroking the white blazed face, and as the wagon pulled away he stood with tears in his eyes and the three dollars in his hand, watching the terrified straining of the colt's neck, the bony head raised above the endgate and one white eye rolling.

Five days later, in the sun-slanting, dew-wet spring morning, they stood for the last time that summer on the front porch, the loaded wagon against the front fence. The father tossed the key in his hand and kicked the doorjamb. "Well, good-bye, Old Paint," he said. "See you in the fall."

As they went to the wagon Bruce sang loudly,

> Good-bye, Old Paint, I'm leavin' Cheyenne,
> I'm leavin' Cheyenne, I'm goin' to Montana,
> Good-bye, Old Paint, I'm leavin' Cheyenne.

"Turn it off," his father said. "You want to wake up the whole town?" He boosted Bruce into the back end, where he squirmed and wiggled his way neck-deep into the luggage. His mother, turning to see how he was settled, laughed at him. "You look like a baby owl in a nest," she said.

His father turned and winked at him. "Open your mouth and I'll drop in a mouse."

It was good to be leaving; the thought of the homestead was exciting. If he could have taken Socks along it would have been perfect, but he had to admit, looking around at the jammed wagon box, that there sure wasn't any room for him. He continued to sing softly as they rocked out into the road and turned east toward MacKenna's house, where they were leaving the keys.

At the low, sloughlike spot that had become the town's dump ground the road split, leaving the dump like an island in the middle. The boy sniffed at the old familiar smells of rust and tar-paper and ashes and refuse. He had collected a lot of old iron and tea lead and bottles and broken machinery and clocks, and once a perfectly good amberheaded cane, in that old dumpground. His father turned up the right fork, and as they passed the central part of the dump the wind, coming in from the northeast, brought a rotten, unbearable stench across them.

"Pee-you!" his mother said, and held her nose.

Bruce echoed her. "Pee-you! Pee-you-willy!" He clamped his nose shut and pretended to fall dead.

"Guess I better get to windward of that coming back," said his father.

They woke MacKenna up and left the key and started back. The things they passed were very sharp and clear to the boy. He was seeing them for the last time all summer. He noticed things he had never noticed so clearly before: how the hills came down into the river from the north like three folds in a blanket, how the stovepipe on the Chinaman's shack east of town had a little conical hat on it. He chanted at the things he saw. "Good-bye, old Chinaman. Good-bye, old French-man River. Good-bye, old Dumpground, good-bye."

"Hold your noses," his father said. He eased the wagon into the other fork around the dump. "Somebody sure dumped something rotten."

He stared ahead, bending a little, and Bruce heard him swear. He slapped the reins on the team till they trotted. "What?" the mother said. Bruce, half rising to see what caused the speed, saw her lips go flat over her teeth, and a look on her face like the woman he had seen in the traveling dentist's chair, when the dentist dug a living nerve out of her tooth and then got down on his knees to hunt for it, and she sat there half raised in her seat, her face lifted.

"For gosh sakes," he said. And then he saw.

He screamed at them. "Ma, it's Socks! Stop, Pa! It's Socks!"

His father drove grimly ahead, not turning, not speaking, and his mother shook her head without looking around. He screamed again, but neither of them turned. And when he dug down into the load, burrowing in and shaking with long smothered sobs, they still said nothing.

So they left town, and as they wound up the dugway to the south bench there was not a word among them except his father's low, "For Christ sakes, I thought he was going to take it out of town." None of them looked back at the view they had always admired, the flat river bottom green with spring, its village snuggled in the loops of river. Bruce's eyes, pressed against the coats and blankets under him until his sight was a red haze, could still see through it the bloated, skinned body of the colt, the chestnut hair left a little way above the hooves, the iron braces still on the broken front legs.

THE
CHINK

■   ■   ■

It is an odd trick of memory that after almost a quarter of a century I still remember Mah Li better than I can remember anyone else in that town. The people I grew up among, many of the children I played with every day, are vague names without faces, or faces without names. Maybe I remember him well because he was so ambiguous a figure in the town's life. He and his brother, Mah Jim, who ran the restaurant, were the only Chinese in town, and though Mah Li did our laundry, worked for us, delivered our vegetables punctually at seven in the morning three days a week, he was as much outside human society as an animal would have been. Sometimes I catch myself remembering him in the same way I remember the chestnut colt my father gave me when I was nine. I loved Mah Li as I loved the colt, but neither was part of the life that seemed meaningful at the time.

He called me O-Fi', because O-5, our laundry mark, was easier for him to say than Lederer. Every Monday morning he appeared at the back door with his basket, got the laundry, grinned and bobbed so that his pigtail twitched like a limber black snake, and said, "Velly good,

O-Fi'. Leddy Fliday." I have a picture of him in my mind, shuffling up the worn path along the irrigation ditch, dogtrotting in his hurry as if daylight were going out on him while he still had a lot to do, and his black baggy pants and loose blouse blowing against his body.

I have other pictures, too. Whenever I think of him a swarm of things come up: Mah Li and Mah Jim sitting in the bare kitchen of the restaurant, a candle between them on the table with its flame as straight as a blade, playing fan-tan in intent, serious, interminable silence. Somehow that picture seems sad now, like a symbol of their homelessness. They had no women, no friends, no intercourse with the townspeople except when men kidded them along in the way they kid half-wits, condescendingly, with an edge of malice in their jokes.

I remember Mah Li meeting someone on the street in winter, the white man stopping him to say hello, rubbing his stomach and saying, "Belly cold today," and Mah Li beaming his wide smile, jabbering, and the white man saying, "Put your shirt inside your pants and your belly won't be cold," and slapping Mah Li on the back and guffawing. Old jokes like that, always the same ones. And the kids who hung around Mah Jim's restaurant jerking the Chinks' pigtails and asking them if it was true that they kneaded their bread in big tubs with their bare feet, or if they really spit in the soup of people they didn't like.

The town accepted them, worked them like slaves for little pay, I suppose even liked them after a fashion, but it never adopted them, just as Mah Jim and Mah Li never adopted white man's clothes, but always wore their black baggy pants and blouses. They never got the white man's habit of loafing, either. Mah Li, for instance, when he worked for us in summers down at the potato field, tended his own garden from daylight till about seven, worked our potatoes till almost dark, and then came into town to wash and iron till midnight on the laundry Mah Jim had taken in for him during the day. Maybe they liked to work that hard; maybe it helped them against their loneliness. My father always said that a Chinaman would outwork a white man two to one, and do it on a cupful of rice a day.

It is around the potato field and the garden that most of my recollections of the Chink center. The second year he worked for us he asked my father if he could rent a little piece of land to put in vegetables, and Father let him have the ground free. Mah Li never thanked him— I don't think he ever knew what the word for thanks was. He just looked at him a minute with impassive slant eyes, bobbed his pigtail, and went dogtrotting down to go to work. But in July of that summer he appeared at our back door one morning just after I'd brought the milk in from the barn. He had a basket over his arm.

"Nice day, O-Fi'," he said. "Velly fine day!"

"It's a swell day," I said, "but you've got your dates mixed. It isn't laundry day."

"No laundly," he said, grinning, and passed me the basket. It was full of leaf lettuce and carrots and string beans and green peas, with two bunches of white icicle radishes sticking up in it like bouquets.

After that he came three times a week, regular as sunrise, with vegetables that were the envy of every gardener in town. And when Mother tried to pay him for them he beamed and bobbed and shook his head. I remember her saying finally, in a kind of despair, that she wouldn't take his baskets free any more, but he always came, and we always took them. It would have hurt his feelings if we hadn't.

It was Mother who suggested that I give the Chinese the suckers I caught in the river. We never ate them, because suckers are full of little needle-bones and don't taste very good. I just fished for the fun of it. So one afternoon I went down to the potato field in the river bottom, near the flume, with four big suckers on a willow crotch. Mah Li was moving down the field with a hoe, loosening the ground around the vines. When I gave him the fish he looked surprised, beamed, nodded, trotted down to the riverbank and packed them in grass, and rolled them up in a big handkerchief.

"Nice, O-Fi'," he said. I guess that was the way he said thanks.

That afternoon I hung around and helped him a little in the field, and went over with him to see his own garden. I remember him stooping among his tomato vines feeling the fruit till he found a big, red, firm one, and rubbing it off on his blouse and handing it to me. And I remember how heavy and sun-warmed that tomato was, and how I had to jump backward and stick out my face because the juice spurted and ran down my chin when I bit into it. We stood in the plant-smelling garden, under the yellow summer hills, with the sun heavy and hot on our heads, and laughed at each other, and I think that's where I first found out that Mah Li was human.

After that I was around the field a good deal. Whenever I didn't have anything else to do I'd go down and help him, or sit on the riverbank and fish while he worked. Just to watch him in a garden made you know he loved it. I used to watch him to see how long he'd swing the hoe without taking a rest, and sometimes I'd fish for two hours before he'd pause. Then he'd sit down on his heels, the way I've seen Chinese squat on the rails when they work on a section gang, and stay perfectly still for about ten minutes. He was so quiet then that bumblebees would blunder into him and crawl around and fly away again, and butterflies would light on his face. He let them sit there with their wings breathing in and out, and never made so much as the flicker of an eyelash that would disturb them. When he was ready to go to work again his hand would come up slowly, to pick them off so gently that they never knew he touched them.

His yellow hands were very gentle with everything they touched, even with the potato bugs we picked into tin cans and burned. Many afternoons in August I worked down the rows with him while he went bent-kneed along, his face placid and contented and his eyes sharp for bugs. He could do it three times as fast as I could, and cleaner too. We'd meet at the ends of rows every now and again, and dump the striped bugs out into piles, and Mah Li would pour kerosene over them and touch a match to it. Then we'd go down the rows again while the stinking smudge went up behind.

And then there was the magpie that I ran across in the brush one day when I was coming up from fishing. It was a young one, with a hurt wing so that it couldn't fly, but it ran like a pheasant with that one wing trailing, and I had a chase before I caught it. It was still pecking at my fingers and flapping to get away when I brought it up to show Mah Li.

The Chink's face looked as if a lamp had gone on behind it. He chirped with his lips, quietly, and put out a dry hand to stroke the feathers on the bird's head. After a minute he lifted it out of my hands and held its body cradled in his palm, stroking its head, chirping at it. And it lay in his hand quietly as if it were on a nest; it made no attempt to peck him or to get away.

"He likes you," I said.

Mah Li's shaved head nodded very slowly, his lips going in a singsong lullaby and his finger moving gently on the magpie's head.

"Think his wing is broken?"

He nodded again; his pigtail crawled up his back with the bend of his head, and then crawled down.

"You better keep him," I said. "Maybe you can fix his wing."

Mah Li fixed his narrow black eyes on me. I was always being surprised by his eyes, because just talking to him, working with him, I thought of him as another person, like anybody else. Then every once in a while I'd see those eyes, flat on his face, with scarcely any sockets for them to sink back into, and so narrow that it looked as if the skin had grown over and almost covered them.

"Slicee tongue," Mah Li said. "Talkee."

That night he carried the magpie home. A month later, when I saw it perched on the back of a chair in Mah Jim's kitchen, glossy and full of life, it opened its mouth and made squawking noises that sounded almost like words. By the middle of October he had it so tame that it rode around on his shoulder, balancing with its tail and squawking if he moved too fast and disturbed its footing, and whenever he chirped at it, it squawked and jabbered. I laughed like anything when I heard what it said. It said "O-Fi'! O-Fi'! Nice, O-Fi'!"

So that's the way we were, friends—very good friends, in a way—even though Mah Li touched my life only on one of its outside edges. He was like a book I went back to read when there was nothing else doing. And I suppose it was that quality of unreality about our friendship, the strange and foreign things about him—pigtail and singsong and slant eyes—that made me think of him always in a special way, and forced me into the wrong loyalty that night at the end of October in 1918.

I came downtown that night about eight o'clock to join the gang and pull off some Hallowe'en tricks. You were everybody's enemy on Hallowe'en. You hauled your own father's buggy up on somebody's barn, and pushed over your own outhouse along with everybody else's. I say that to explain, in a way, how I came to be lined up against the Chinks that night. Things like that were automatic on Hallowe'en.

We had planned to meet at Mah Jim's, but I found the crowd gathered a block up the street. They were all sore. I didn't understand very clearly then, but I gathered that they'd been fooling in the restaurant and Tad McGovern had hooked a handful of bars from the candy counter. Mah Jim saw him, and raised a fuss, but Tad wouldn't give them back. He challenged Mah Jim to wrestle for them. The Chink got excited, and jabbered, and the kids all ragged him, and finally Mah Jim got really mad. I never saw him that way, but he must have been, because he jumped on Tad and took the bars away from him, and when three or four other kids took hold of him to put him down he shook them off and grabbed up the poker from the stove and ran the whole crowd out.

So now they were just on the verge of getting even. They were going to tip over the Chinks' privy first, and then put the hospital sign on their front door, and then pour water down their chimney and put their fire out, and some other things.

I joined in and we went sneaking back through the alley toward Mah Jim's. It was a cold night, with a light snow that didn't quite cover the ground. In the dark it was just possible to see the pale patches where the snow lay. We crept up behind the laundry, just a couple of rods from the outhouse. Mah Jim must have closed up his restaurant after the ruckus with the gang, because there wasn't a light. The privy was just a vague blob of shadow in the dark.

We gathered behind Tad, waiting for the signal. Sometimes people stood guard on their privies, and we had developed a raiding technique that didn't give them a chance to do anything. When Tad whistled we rushed out pell-mell, about a dozen of us. Our hands found the front of the privy and we heaved hard, all in one hard running push. There was a startled yelp from inside, a yelp almost like a dog's, as the privy lifted and tottered and went over with a crash.

Tad let out a whoop. "Gee, the Chink's in there!"

"Let's lock him in!" somebody said, and a half-dozen boys dived for the door to hold it down. Someone found a nail, and they hammered it in with a rock.

I stood back, because I didn't quite like the idea of the Chink's being locked in there in the cold, and because I was a little scared at the silence from inside. After that one yelp there hadn't been a sound. Even when Tad put his face down close to the boards and said, "Hey there, you Chink Mah Jim!" there was no answer. Tad laughed right out loud. "Gee, he's so mad he can't speak," he said. He put his face down again. "When you get tired you can come out the hole," he said.

Then one of the scouts stationed at the back of the laundry jiggered us and we scattered. I ducked behind a shed in the back lot and listened. Someone was calling from the side of the restaurant. "Boys!" he said. "Boys, come out. I want to talk to you."

In the dark somebody made a spluttering noise with his mouth. "Try and catch us," he said.

But the voice went right on. I recognized it as belonging to Mr. Menefee, the principal of the school. "I don't want to catch you. I want to talk to you."

"What do you want to talk about?" I yelled, and felt big and brave for coming right back at Mr. Menefee that way.

But Tad McGovern, over behind the hardware store, shouted at me: "Shut up! It's a trick."

"No, it isn't a trick," Mr. Menefee said. "Word of honor, boys. I just want to speak to you a minute."

There was such an anxious, worried tone in his voice that I stepped out from behind the shed and into the open. I could hear others coming too, cautiously, ready to break and run, but Mr. Menefee didn't make a move, and soon we were all around him where he stood in the faint light from the street with his overcoat up around his ears and his hands in his pockets.

"I just wanted to tell you," he said, "that it wouldn't be quite decent to pull any pranks tonight. Three people are down sick and Doctor Carroll says it's the flu."

His voice was so solemn, and the thought of the flu was so awful, that we stood there shuffling our feet without being able to say anything. We'd heard plenty about the flu. It killed you off in twenty-four hours, and you died in delirium, and after you were dead you turned black and shriveled. I felt it then like a great shadowy Fear in the dark all around me, while Mr. Menefee stood and looked at us and waited for his words to sink in.

"We're all going to have to help," he said finally. "I hate to take you away from your fun. You're entitled to it on Hallowe'en. But this is a time when everybody has to pitch in. Are you willing to help?"

That gave us our tongues, like a chorus of dogs after a porcupine. "Sure," we said. "Sure, Mr. Menefee!"

He lined it up for us. We were to go to the drugstore and get bundles of flu masks and bottles of eucalyptus oil, which we were to distribute to every house in town, warning people not to come out without their masks, and not to come out at all except when they had to. The town was going to be quarantined and nobody could leave it.

It was like being Paul Revere, and in the excitement of hearing all that I forgot for a minute about Mah Jim locked in the overturned privy. Then I caught myself listening, and all at once I remembered what I was listening for. I was expecting the Chink to hammer on the door and yell to get out. But there wasn't a sound from out in back.

Mr. Menefee snapped to attention the way he did when we were having fire drill in school. "All right, men! What are we standing around for?"

The crowd shuffled their feet, and I knew most of them were thinking, just as I was, of the privy out behind with the Chink in it.

"Mr. Menefee," I said, and stopped.

"What?" I could see him bend over and stare around at us sharply. "You haven't started anything already, have you?" he said.

The silence came down again. Every one of us was ashamed of what we'd just done, I imagine, except Tad McGovern. But none of us dared admit we'd done anything. It would have been a kind of treason. We were soldiers in the army, helping protect the town against the plague. We couldn't just stand there and admit we'd done something pretty raw, something we shouldn't have dared do to a white man. It made us look small and mean and vicious, and we wanted to look heroic.

Tad McGovern was right at my elbow. "Naw," he said. "We were just getting ready to start."

Mr. Menefee snapped to attention again. "Good!" he said. "All right, on the jump now. Divide up into squads, half of you into each end of town. And remember to put on your own masks and keep them on."

Some of the boys jumped and ran, and in a second we were all running for the drugstore. All the time I wanted to turn around and go back and say, "Mr. Menefee, we pushed over the Chinks' privy and Mah Jim's in there." But I kept on running, and got my bundle of masks in the drugstore, and my package of eucalyptus oil bottles, and opened one and soused a mask with it and put it on, and gathered with the others outside, where we split.

The eucalyptus oil smelled so bad, and came so strong into my mouth and nose through the mask, that I almost gagged, and that made me think about myself for a while. But while we were running from door to door up in the Poverty Lane end of town I got thinking more and more about how the Chinks didn't ever wear very heavy clothes, and how Mah Jim might be freezing out there, catching the flu, and how he'd be too big to crawl out through the hole. I mentioned it to the boy I was with, but he said he was sure a grown man could kick that nail loose with one kick. The Chink was already out, he said. He'd be sitting by his fire right now, cussing us in Chinese.

Still I wasn't satisfied. Suppose he was hurt? Everything had been dark when we pushed the privy over. That meant that if Mah Li had gone to bed in his laundry room he wouldn't know Mah Jim was still out. And if Mah Jim was hurt he'd lie there all night.

It gnawed at me until, after we had raised Orullian's house, I was ready to quit the army and go back to see if the Chink was all right. The excitement had worn off completely. I was cold, my nose was running into my mask, the stink of the oil made my stomach roll every time I took a breath. And so the first chance I got I stuck the remaining masks and bottles into my mackinaw pocket and cut out across the irrigation ditch toward town.

Everything was quiet when I slipped into the black back yard. Probably everything's all right, I thought. Probably he did kick the door out and get loose. But when I felt for the door and tried to open it, it was still nailed down.

"Mah Jim!" I said. I knocked on the boards and listened. Not a sound. I could feel sweat start out all over me, and my hands shook as I groped around in the dark for a stone. What if he was dead? What if we'd killed him?

With the rock I hammered and pulped the edge of the board where the nail was, until I could spring the door past. And when I scratched a match and looked down inside, into the overturned privy that looked like a big coffin, I saw not Mah Jim, but Mah Li, and he was sprawled back against the downward wall with his legs across the seat, absolutely quiet, and his pigtail hanging across the bend of his arm.

It took me five minutes to rouse Mah Jim. I could hear him moving inside, and I yelled and cried that Mah Li was hurt, but he didn't open the door for a long time, and then only a crack. I suppose he thought it was another trick. My flu mask had slipped down over my chin, and I was crying. "Help me get him out," I said. "He's back here. He's hurt. Come on."

Finally he came, and we got Mah Li out and carried him into the kitchen. He lay perfectly still, his face like a mask, every line smoothed out of it and his eyes shut. His breathing sounded too loud in the bare room. I couldn't take my eyes off his face, and while Mah Jim was squatting and feeling over his body I thought of the butterflies that used to crawl on Mah Li's face when he was resting. This was a different kind of stillness, and it scared me.

For five minutes Mah Jim squatted there, his pigtail hanging, and didn't say a word. I could feel the silence in the kitchen swell up around me; the only audible sound was the slow loud breathing of Mah Li, each breath coming with a hard finality, as if it were the last one he'd ever breathe. My nose kept running, and I'd lost my handkerchief, so that I had to sniffle every minute or so. I hated it, because it sounded as if I were crying, and I didn't want to seem to cry.

I kept thinking how I could have done something when the privy went over and I heard the yell from inside, how I'd had the chance to tell Mr. Menefee and get Mah Li out, but hadn't taken it. And I stood there thinking, What if I'd hauled off and socked Tad McGovern when he first jumped on that door to hold it down? I had just come up, not knowing anything about the privy-tipping, and I said loudly, What's going on here? and then I hit Tad and he fell down and I felt the jar in my wrist from the blow, and then three or four others jumped me, and I tossed them off and punched them in the nose until they all stood around me in an amazed ring, and I stood there with my fists up and said, "Come on, you cowards! You're so brave, picking on a poor harmless old Chink. Come on and get a taste of knuckles, any three of you at a time!"

But all the time while I was doing that in my mind I heard that rough slow breathing, and saw Mah Jim in the lamplight squatting by Mah Li's body, and I was sick with shame, and sniffled, and hated the smell of eucalyptus hanging under my nose.

"Is he hurt bad?" I said. "Can you tell what's the matter?"

I almost whispered it, afraid to talk right out loud. Mah Jim rose, and his eyes glittered. His face, like a slotted mask the color of dry lemon peel, made me swallow. I began to remember all the stories I'd heard about Chinks—how if they ever got it in for you, or if you did them an injustice, they'd slice your eyeballs and cut off your ears and split your nostrils and pierce your eardrums and pull out your toenails by the roots. Staring into his glittering slit eyes, I thought sure he was going for me, and my knees went weak. A kind of black fog came up in front of me; I lost Mah Jim's face, the room rocked, I could feel myself falling. Then the fog cleared again, and I was still on my feet, Mah Jim was staring at me, Mah Li was unconscious on the floor.

My shame was greater than my fear, and I didn't run, but I couldn't meet Mah Jim's eyes. I looked away to where the magpie was sitting on a chair back, with his white wing feathers almost hidden and his eyes as black and glittering as Mah Jim's.

"I better get the doctor," I said, and swallowed. The moment I said it I wondered why I hadn't done it already. I was starting for the door, full of relief at being able to do something, glad to get away, when I took a last look at Mah Jim, hoping he'd look kinder, hoping perhaps that he'd give me a word that would make me feel better about my own shame. And I stood there, half turned, staring at him. He hadn't moved, hadn't raised a hand, hadn't spoken, but I knew exactly what he meant. He meant no. He didn't want the doctor, even to save Mah Li's life. He didn't want any white man around, didn't want anything to do with us any more. There was bitterness, and anger, and a strange unreachable patience in his look that stopped me cold in the doorway.

And after a minute, in the face of Mah Jim's bitter dignity, I mumbled that I hoped Mah Li would be all right, that I'd come to see him tomorrow, and sneaked out. As I shut the door and stood shivering on the step I heard the magpie croaking and jawing inside. "Nice!" it said. "Nice, O-Fi'!"

Later, when I lay in bed at home with my head under the covers, shivering between the cold sheets and breathing hard with my mouth open to warm the bed, I resolved that next morning I would take the doctor down, Mah Jim or no Mah Jim. "You can't just lock the doors when somebody's sick or hurt," I'd tell him. "You have to have help, and I'm the one that's going to see you get it."

But I never did wake up to do what I planned. My sleep was haunted by wild dreams, flashes, streamers of insane color that went like northern lights across my nightmares. Once I woke up and discovered that I had been vomiting in my bed, but before I could do more than gag and gasp for somebody to come I was out again. I remember a hand on my head, and a face over me, and once a feeling of floating. I opened my eyes then, to see the stair rails writhing by me like snakes, and I shut my eyes again to keep from dying. When I woke up it was a week later; I was in bed with my mother in the sixth-grade room of the schoolhouse, and my nose was bleeding.

They kept us in the schoolhouse ten more days. After I was home, lying in bed in the dining room where it was warm, I felt good, full of the tired quietness that comes after sickness, and sleepy all the time, and pleased that I was getting well. Once or twice a day I got up in a bathrobe and tottered a few steps on crazy knees so that everybody laughed at me as if I were a child just taking his first steps.

On the fourth morning at home I felt perfectly well. When I woke up the sun was shining in the dining-room windows, and outside I could see the clean snow and the tracked path that led up past Shawn's house. Then I realized that something had awakened me, and listened. There was a mild, light tapping on the kitchen door. For a minute I forgot I was still weak, and jumped out of bed so fast that I sprawled on hands and knees, but laughing at myself, still feeling well and full of life. I got up and found my slippers and tottered into the kitchen, hanging to walls and doorjambs. On the back step Mah Jim was standing, with a basket on his arm.

"Nice day, O-Fi'," he said, just the way Mah Li used to say it when he brought the vegetables. All in a rush the memory of that Hallowe'en night came back to me. I'd forgotten it completely during my sickness. I pulled Mah Jim inside and shut the door. "How's Mah Li?" I said.

His face perfectly blank, Mah Jim passed me the basket, covered with a clean dish towel. I lifted the cover and there was the magpie, looking ruffled and mad. I didn't understand. "You mean he's giving me the magpie?" I said.

Mah Jim nodded.

"Is he all right now?"

Like a wooden man, full of ancient and inscrutable patience, Mah Jim stood with his hands in the sleeves of his blouse. "All lightee now," he said.

The magpie shook its feathers, snapped its long tail, opened its beak, and its harsh squawk cut in. "O-Fi'! O-Fi'! Nice, O-Fi'!" I put out a finger to stroke its head the way Mah Li did, and it pecked me a sharp dig on the hand. I was so relieved about Mah Li, and so bursting with the feeling of being well, that I laughed out loud.

"That's swell," I said. "Tell him thanks very much. Tell him I sure appreciate having it, Mah Jim. And tell him I'm glad he's well again."

He stood silently, and I began to remember how sinister he'd looked in the kitchen that night, and how he'd scared me then. To keep the silence from getting too thick I kept on talking. "I've been sick myself," I said. "I got sick that same night, or I'd have been over to see him." The sunlight flashed on the windshield of a car turning around in the road, and the light was so bright and gay that I wanted to yell for just feeling good. I bragged. "They thought I was going to die. I had a fever of a hundred and five, and was unconscious for a week, and my nose bled like anything."

I stopped. Mah Jim had not moved; his face was yellow parchment with the slit eyes bright and still in it. "So you tell Mah Li I'll be down to see him soon as I get on my feet," I said.

Something in the way he looked stopped me. Why did Mah Li send him with the magpie? I wondered. Why didn't he come himself? Mah Jim took his hands out of his sleeves and made a short, stiff little bow.

"Mah Li dead," he said. "We go back China. Bye, O-Fi'. Nice day."

He opened the door and shuffled out, and I sat still in the kitchen chair too shocked to feel anything really, except just the things around me. I felt the cold draft on my bare ankles, and I felt the sun warm on my arm and shoulder, but I couldn't feel anything about Mah Li. I didn't really feel anything yet when I started to cry. The tears just came up slowly the way a spring fills, and hung, and brimmed over, and the first ones ran down my face and splashed warm on the back of my hand.

CHIP
OFF THE
OLD BLOCK

■ ■ ■

Sitting alone looking at the red eyes of the parlor heater, Chet thought how fast things happened. One day the flu hit. Two days after that his father left for Montana to get a load of whiskey to sell for medicine. The next night he got back in the midst of a blizzard with his hands and feet frozen, bringing a sick homesteader he had picked up on the road; and now this morning all of them, the homesteader, his father, his mother, his brother, Bruce, were loaded in a sled and hauled to the schoolhouse-hospital. It was scary how fast they all got it, even his father, who seldom got anything and was tougher than boiled owl. Everybody, he thought with some pride, but him. His mother's words as she left were a solemn burden on his mind. "You'll have to hold the fort, Chet. You'll have to be the man of the house." And his father, sweat on his face even in the cold, his frozen hands held tenderly in his lap, saying, "Better let the whiskey alone. Put it away somewhere till we get back."

So he was holding the fort. He accepted the duty soberly. In the two hours since his family had left he had swept the floors, milked old Red and thrown down hay for her, brought in scuttles of lignite. And sitting now in the parlor, he knew he was scared. He heard the walls tick and the floors creak. Every thirty seconds he looked up from his book, and finally he yawned, stretched, laid the book down, and took a stroll through the whole house, cellar to upstairs, as if for exercise. But his eyes were sharp, and he stepped back a little as he threw open the doors of bedrooms and closets. He whistled a little between his teeth and looked at the calendar in the hall to see what day it was. November 4, 1918.

A knock on the back door sent him running. It was the young man named Vickers who had taken his family away. He was after beds and blankets for the schoolhouse. Chet helped him knock the beds down and load them on the sled. He would sleep on the couch in the parlor; it was warmer there, anyway; no cold floors to worry about.

In the kitchen, making a list of things he had taken, Vickers saw the keg, the sacked cases of bottles, the pile of whiskey-soaked straw sheaths from the bottles that had been broken on the trip. "Your dad doesn't want to sell any of that, does he?" he said.

Chet thought briefly of his father's injunction to put the stuff away. But gee, the old man had frozen his hands and feet and caught the flu getting it, and now when people came around asking . . . "Sure," he said. "That's what he bought it for, flu medicine."

"What've you got?"

"Rye and bourbon," Chet said. "There's some Irish, but I think he brought that special for somebody." He rummaged among the sacks. "Four dollars a bottle, I think it is," he said, and looked at Vickers to see if that was too much. Vickers didn't blink. "Or is it four-fifty?" Chet said.

Vickers's face was expressionless. "Sure it isn't five? I wouldn't want to cheat you." He took out his wallet, and under his eyes Chet retreated. "I'll go look," he said. "I think there's a list."

He stood in the front hall for a minute or two before he came back. "Four-fifty," he said casually. "I thought probably it was."

Vickers counted out twenty-seven dollars. "Give me six rye," he said. With the sack in his hand he stood in the back door and looked at Chet and laughed. "What are you going to do with that extra three dollars?"

Chet felt his heart stop while he might have counted ten. His face began to burn. "What three dollars?"

"Never mind," Vickers said. "I was just ragging you. Got all you need to eat here?"

"I got crocks of milk," Chet said. He grinned at Vickers in relief, and Vickers grinned back. "There's bread Ma baked the other day, and spuds. If I need any meat I can go shoot a rabbit."

"Oh." Vickers's eyebrows went up. "You're a hunter, eh?"

"I shot rabbits all last fall for Mrs. Rieger," Chet said. "She's 'nemic and has to eat rabbits and prairie chickens and stuff. She lent me the shotgun and bought the shells."

"Mmm," Vickers said. "I guess you can take care of yourself. How old are you?"

"Twelve."

"That's old enough," said Vickers. "That's pretty old, in fact. Well, Mervin, if you need anything you call the school and I'll see that you get it."

"My name isn't Mervin," Chet said. "It's Chet."

"Okay," Vickers said. "Don't get careless with the fires."

"What do you think I am?" Chet said in scorn. He raised his hand stiffly as Vickers went out. A little tongue of triumph licked up in him. That three bucks would look all right, all right. Next time he'd know better than to change the price, too. He took the bills out of his pocket and counted them. Twenty-seven dollars was a lot of dough. He'd show Ma and Pa whether he could hold the fort or not.

But holding the fort was tiresome. By two o'clock he was bored stiff, and the floors were creaking again in the silence. Then he remembered suddenly that he was the boss of the place. He could go or come as he pleased, as long as the cow was milked and the house kept warm. He thought of the two traps he had set in muskrat holes under the river bank. The blizzard and the flu had made him forget to see to them. And he might take Pa's gun and do a little hunting.

"Well," he said in the middle of the parlor rug, "I guess I will."

For an hour and a half he prowled the river brush. Over on the path toward Heathcliff's he shot a snowshoe rabbit, and the second of his traps yielded a stiffly frozen muskrat. The weight of his game was a solid satisfaction as he came up the dugway swinging the rabbit by its feet, the muskrat by its plated tail.

Coming up past the barn, he looked over towards Van Dam's, then the other way, toward Chapman's, half hoping that someone might be out, and see him. He whistled loudly, sang a little into the cold afternoon air, but the desertion of the whole street, the unbroken fields of snow where ordinarily there would have been dozens of sled tracks and fox-and-goose paths, let a chill in upon his pride. He came up the back steps soberly and opened the door.

The muskrat's slippery tail slid out of his mitten and the frozen body thumped on the floor. Chet opened his mouth, shut it again, speechless with surprise and shock. Two men were in the kitchen. His eyes jumped from the one by the whiskey keg to the other, sitting at the table drinking whiskey from a cup. The one drinking he didn't know. The other was Louis Treat, a halfbreed who hung out down at the stable and sometimes worked a little for the Half-Diamond Bar. All Chet knew about him was that he could braid horsehair ropes and sing a lot of dirty songs.

"Aha!" said Louis Treat. He smiled at Chet and made a rubbing motion with his hands. "We 'ave to stop to get warm. You 'ave been hunting?"

"Yuh," Chet said automatically. He stood where he was, his eyes swinging between the two men. The man at the table raised his eyebrows at Louis Treat.

"Ees nice rabbit there," Louis said. His bright black button eyes went over the boy. Chet lifted the rabbit and looked at the frozen beads of blood on the white fur. "Yuh," he said. He was thinking about what his father always said. You could trust an Indian, if he was your friend, and you could trust a white man sometimes, if money wasn't involved, and you could trust a Chink more than either, but you couldn't trust a halfbreed.

Louis's voice went on, caressingly. "You 'ave mushrat too, eh? You lak me to 'elp you peel thees mushrat?" His hand, dipping under the sheepskin and into his pants pocket, produced a long-bladed knife that jumped open with the pressure of his thumb on a button.

Chet dropped the rabbit and took off his mitts. "No thanks," he said. "I can peel him."

Shrugging, Louis put the knife away. He turned to thump the bung hard into the keg, and nodded at the other man, who rose. "Ees tam we go," Louis said. "We 'ave been told to breeng thees wiskey to the 'ospital."

"Who told you?" Chet's insides grew tight, and his mind was setting like plaster of Paris. If Pa was here he'd scatter these thieves all the way to Chapman's. But Pa wasn't here. He watched Louis Treat. You could never trust a halfbreed.

"The doctor, O'Malley," Louis said. Keeping his eye on Chet, he jerked his head at the other man. " 'Ere, you tak' the other end."

His companion, pulling up his sheepskin collar, stooped and took hold of the keg. Chet, with no blood in his face and no breath in his lungs, hesitated a split second and then jumped. Around the table, in the dining-room door, he was out of their reach, and the shotgun was pointed straight at their chests. With his thumb he cocked both barrels, click, click.

Louis Treat swore. "Put down that gun!"

"No, sir!" Chet said. "I won't put it down till you drop that keg and get out of here!"

The two men looked at each other. Louis set his end gently back on the chair, and the other did the same. "We 'ave been sent," Louis said. "You do not understan' w'at I mean."

"I understand all right," Chet said. "If Doctor O'Malley had wanted that, he'd've sent Mr. Vickers for it this morning."

The second man ran his tongue over his teeth and spat on the floor. "Think he knows how to shoot that thing?"

Chet's chest expanded. The gun trembled so that he braced it against the frame of the door. "I shot that rabbit, didn't I?" he said.

The halfbreed's teeth were bared in a bitter grin. "You are a fool," he said.

"And you're a thief!" Chet said. He covered the two carefully as they backed out, and when they were down the steps he slammed and bolted the door. Then he raced for the front hall, made sure that door was locked, and peeked out the front window. The two were walking side by side up the irrigation ditch toward town, pulling an empty box sled. Louis was talking furiously with his hands.

Slowly and carefully Chet uncocked the gun. Ordinarily he would have unloaded, but not now, not with thieves like those around. He put the gun above the mantel, looked in the door of the stove, threw in a half-scuttle of lignite, went to the window again to see if he could still see the two men. Then he looked at his hands. They were shaking. So were his knees. He sat down suddenly on the couch, unable to stand.

* * *

For days the only people he saw were those who came to buy whiskey. They generally sat awhile in the kitchen and talked about the flu and the war, but they weren't much company. Once Miss Landis, his school-teacher, came apologetically and furtively with a two-quart fruit jar under her coat, and he charged her four dollars a quart for bulk rye out of the keg. His secret hoard of money mounted to eighty-five dollars, to a hundred and eight.

When there was none of that business (he had even forgotten by now that his father had told him not to meddle with it), he moped around the house, milked the cow, telephoned to the hospital to see how his folks were. One day his dad was pretty sick. Two days later he was better, but his mother had had a relapse because they were so short of beds they had had to put Brucie in with her. The milk crocks piled up in the cellarway, staying miraculously sweet, until he told the schoolhouse nurse over the phone about all the milk he had, and then Doctor O'Malley sent down old Gundar Moe to pick it up for the sick people.

Sometimes he stood on the porch on sunny, cold mornings and watched Lars Poulsen's sled go out along the road on the way to the graveyard, and the thought that maybe Mom or Bruce or Pa might die and be buried out there on the knoll by the sandhills made him swallow and go back inside where he couldn't see how deserted the street looked, and where he couldn't see the sled and the steaming gray horses move out toward the south bend of the river. He resolved to be a son his parents could be proud of, and sat down at the piano determined to learn a piece letter-perfect. But the dry silence of the house weighed on him; before long he would be lying with his forehead on the keyboard, his finger picking on one monotonous note. That way he could con-centrate on how different it sounded with his head down, and forget to be afraid.

And at night, when he lay on the couch and stared into the sleepy red eyes of the heater, he heard noises that walked the house, and there were crosses in the lamp chimneys when he lighted them, and he knew that someone would die.

On the fifth day he sat down at the dining-room table determined to write a book. In an old atlas he hunted up a promising locale. He found a tributary of the Amazon called the Tapajós, and firmly, his lips together in concentration, he wrote his title across the top of a school tablet: "The Curse of the Tapajós." All that afternoon he wrote enthusiastically. He created a tall, handsome young explorer and a halfbreed guide very like Louis Treat. He plowed through steaming jungles, he wrestled pythons and other giant serpents which he spelled "boy constructors." All this time he was looking for the Lost City of Gold. And when the snakes got too thick even for his taste, and when he was beginning to wonder himself why the explorer didn't shoot the guide, who was constantly trying to poison the flour or stab his employer in his tent at midnight, he let the party come out on a broad pampa and see in the distance, crowning a golden hill, the lost city for which they searched. And then suddenly the explorer reeled and fell, mysteriously stricken, and the halfbreed guide, smiling with sinister satisfaction, disappeared quietly into the jungle. The curse of the Tapajós, which struck everyone who found that lost city, had struck again. But the young hero was not dead. . . .

Chet gnawed his pencil and stared across the room. It was going to be hard to figure out how his hero escaped. Maybe he was just stunned, not killed. Maybe a girl could find him there, and nurse him back to health. . . .

He rose, thinking, and wandered over to the window. A sled came across the irrigation ditch and pulled on over to Chance's house. Out of it got Mr. Chance and Mrs. Chance and Ed and Harvey Chance. They were well, then. People were starting to come home cured. He rushed to the telephone and called the hospital. No, the nurse said, his family weren't well yet; they wouldn't be home for three or four days at least. But they were all better. How was he doing? Did he need anything?

No, Chet said, he didn't need anything.

But at least he wasn't the only person on the street any more. That night after milking he took a syrup pail of milk to the Chances. They were all weak, all smiling. Mrs. Chance cried every time she spoke, and they were awfully grateful for the milk. He promised them, over their protests, that he would bring them some every day, and chop wood and haul water for them until they got really strong. Mr. Chance, who had the nickname of Dictionary because he strung off such jaw-breaking words, told him he was a benefactor and a Samaritan, and called upon his own sons to witness this neighborly kindness and be edified and enlarged. Chet went home in the dark, wondering if it might not be a good idea, later in his book somewhere, to have his explorer find a bunch of people, or maybe just a beautiful and ragged girl, kept in durance vile by some tribe of pigmies or spider men or something, and have him rescue them and confound their captors.

On the afternoon of the eighth day Chet sat in the kitchen at Chance's. His own house had got heavier and heavier to bear, and there wasn't much to eat there but milk and potatoes, and both stores were closed because of the flu. So he went a good deal to Chance's, doing their chores and talking about the hospital, and listening to Mr. Chance tell about the Death Ward where they put people who weren't going to get well. The Death Ward was the eighth-grade room, his own room, and he and Ed Chance speculated on what it would be like to go back to that room where so many people had died—Mrs. Rieger, and old Gypsy Davy from Poverty Flat, and John Chapman, and a lot of people. Mrs. Chance sat by the stove and when anyone looked at her or spoke to her she shook her head and smiled and the tears ran down. She didn't seem unhappy about anything; she just couldn't help crying.

Mr. Chance said over and over that there were certainly going to be a multitude of familiar faces missing after this thing was over. The town would never be the same. He wouldn't be surprised if the destitute and friendless were found in every home in town, adopted and cared for by friends. They might have to build an institution to house the derelict and the bereaved.

He pulled his sagging cheeks and said to Chet, "Mark my words, son, you are one of the fortunate. In that hospital I said to myself a dozen times, 'Those poor Mason boys are going to lose their father.' I lay there—myself in pain, mind you—and the first thing I'd hear some old and valued friend would be moved into the Death Ward. I thought your father was a goner when they moved him in."

Chet's throat was suddenly dry as dust. "Pa isn't in there!"

"Ira," said Mrs. Chance, and shook her head and smiled and wiped the tears away. "Now you've got the child all worked up."

"He isn't in there now," said Mr. Chance. "By the grace of the Almighty"—he bent his head and his lips moved—"he came out again. He's a hard man to kill. Hands and feet frozen, double pneumonia, and still he came out."

"Is he all right now?" Chet said.

"Convalescing," Mr. Chance said. "Convalescing beautifully." He raised a finger under Chet's nose. "Some people are just hard to kill. But on the other hand, you take a person like that George Valet. I hesitate to say before the young what went on in that ward. Shameful, even though the man was sick." His tongue ticked against his teeth, and his eyebrows raised at Chet. "They cleaned his bed six times a day," he said, and pressed his lips together. "It makes a man wonder about God's wisdom," he said. "A man like that, his morals are as loose as his bowels."

"Ira!" Mrs. Chance said.

"I would offer you a wager," Mr. Chance said. "I wager that a man as loose and discombobulated as that doesn't live through this epidemic."

"I wouldn't bet on a person's life that way," she said.

"Ma," Harvey called from the next room, where he was lying down. "What's all the noise about?"

They stopped talking and listened. The church bell was ringing madly. In a minute the bell in the firehouse joined it. The heavy bellow of a shotgun, both barrels, rolled over the snowflats between their street and the main part of town. A six-shooter went off, bang-bang-bang-bang-bang-bang, and there was the sound of distant yelling.

"Fire?" Mr. Chance said, stooping to the window.

"Here comes somebody," Ed said. The figure of a boy was streaking across the flat. Mr. Chance opened the door and shouted at him. The boy ran closer, yelling something unintelligible. It was Spot Orullian.

"What?" Mr. Chance yelled.

Spot cupped his hands to his mouth, standing in the road in front of Chet's as if unwilling to waste a moment's time. "War's over!" he shouted, and wheeled and was gone up the street toward Van Dam's.

Mr. Chance closed the door slowly. Mrs. Chance looked at him, and her lips jutted and trembled, her weak eyes ran over with tears, and she fell into his arms. The three boys, not quite sure how one acted when a war ended, but knowing it called for celebration, stood around uneasily. They shot furtive grins at one another, looked with furrowed brows at Mrs. Chance's shaking back.

"Now Uncle Joe can come home," Ed said. "That's what she's bawling about."

Chet bolted out the door, raced over to his own house, pulled the loaded shotgun from the mantel, and burst out into the yard again. He blew the lid off the silence in their end of town, and followed the shooting with a wild yell. Ed and Harvey, leaning out their windows, answered him, and the heavy boom-boom of a shotgun came from the downtown district.

Carrying the gun, Chet went back to Chance's. He felt grown-up, a householder. The end of the war had to be celebrated; neighbors had to get together and raise cain. He watched Mrs. Chance, still incoherent, rush to the calendar and put a circle around the date, November 11. "I don't ever want to forget what day it happened on," she said.

"Everyone in the world will remember this day," said Mr. Chance, solemnly, like a preacher. Chet looked at him, his mind clicking.

"Mr. Chance," he said, "would you like a drink, to celebrate?"

Mr. Chance looked startled. "What?"

"Pa's got some whiskey. He'd throw a big party if he was home."

"I don't think we should," said Mrs. Chance dubiously. "Your father might . . ."

"Oh, Mama," Mr. Chance said, and laid his arm across her back like a log. "One bumper to honor the day. One leetle stirrup-cup to those boys of the Allies. Chester here is carrying on his father's tradition like a man." He bowed and shook Chet's hand formally. "We'd be delighted, sir," he said, and they all laughed.

Somehow, nobody knew just how, the party achieved proportions. Mr. Chance suggested, after one drink, that it would be pleasant to have a neighbor or two, snatched from the terrors of the plague, come and join in the thanksgiving; and Chet, full of hospitality, said sure, that would be a keen idea. So Mr. Chance called Jewel King, and when Jewel came he brought Chubby Klein with him, and a few minutes later three more came, knocked, looked in to see the gathering with cups in their hands, and came in with alacrity when Chet held the door wide. Within an hour there were eight men, three women, and the two Chance boys, besides Chet. Mr. Chance wouldn't let the boys have any whiskey, but Chet, playing bartender, sneaked a cup into the dining room and all sipped it and smacked their lips.

"Hey, look, I'm drunk," Harvey said. He staggered, hiccoughed, caught himself, bowed low and apologized, staggered again. "Hic," he said. "I had a drop too much." The three laughed together secretly while loud voices went up in the kitchen.

"Gentlemen," Mr. Chance was saying, "I give you those heroic laddies in khaki who looked undaunted into the eyes of death and saved this ga-lorious empire from the rapacious Huns."

"Yay!" the others said, banging cups on the table. "Give her the other barrel, Dictionary."

"I crave your indulgence for a moment," Mr. Chance said. "For one leetle moment, while I imbibe a few swallows of this delectable amber fluid."

The noise went up and up. Chet went among them stiff with pride at having done all this, at being accepted here as host, at having men pat him on the back and shake his hand and tell him, 'You're all right, kid, you're a chip off the old block. What's the word from the folks?" He guggled liquor out of the sloshing cask into a milk crock, and the men dipped largely and frequently. About four o'clock, two more families arrived and were welcomed with roars. People bulged the big kitchen; their laughter rattled the window frames. Occasionally Dictionary Chance rose to propose a toast to "those gems of purest ray serene, those unfailing companions on life's bitter pilgrimage, the ladies, God bless 'em!" Every so often he suggested that it might be an idea worth serious consideration that some liquid refreshments be decanted from the aperture in the receptacle.

The more liquid refreshments Chet decanted from the aperture in the receptacle, the louder and more eloquent Mr. Chance became. He dominated the kitchen like an evangelist. He swung and swayed and stamped, he led a rendition of "God Save the King," he thundered denunciations of the Beast of Berlin, he thrust a large fist into the lapels of new arrivals and demanded detailed news of the war's end. Nobody knew more than that it was over.

But Dictionary didn't forget to be grateful, either. At least five times during the afternoon he caught Chet up in a long arm and publicly blessed him. Once he rose and cleared his throat for silence. Chubby Klein and Jewel King booed and hissed, but he bore their insults with dignity. "Siddown!" they said. "Speech!" said others. Mr. Chance waved his hands abroad, begging for quiet. Finally they gave it to him, snickering.

"Ladies and gen'lemen," he said, "we have come together on this auspicious occasion . . ."

"What's suspicious about it?" Jewel King said.

". . . on this auspicious occasion, to do honor to our boys in Flanders Field, to celebrate the passing of the dread incubus of Spanish Influenza . . ."

"Siddown!" said Chubby Klein.

". . . and last, but not least, we are gathered here to honor our friendship with the owners of this good and hospitable house, Bo Mason and Sis, may their lives be long and strewn with flowers, and this noble scion of a noble stock, this tender youth who kept the home fires burning through shock and shell and who opened his house and his keg to us as his father would have done. Ladies and gen'lemen, the Right Honorable Chester Mason, may he live to bung many a barrel."

Embarrassed and squirming and unsure of what to do with so many faces laughing at him, so many mouths cheering him, Chet crowded into the dining-room door and tried to act casual, tried to pretend he didn't feel proud and excited and a man among men. And while he stood there with the noise beating at him in raucous approbation, the back door opened and the utterly flabbergasted face of his father looked in.

There was a moment of complete silence. Voices dropped away to nothing, cups hung at lips. Then in a concerted rush they were helping Bo Mason in. He limped heavily on bandaged and slippered feet, his hands wrapped in gauze, his face drawn and hollow-eyed and noticeably thinner than it had been ten days ago. After him came Chet's mother, half carrying Bruce, and staggering under his weight. Hands took Bruce away from her, sat him on the open oven door, and led her to a chair. All three of them, hospital-pale, rested and looked around the room. And Chet's father did not look pleased.

"What the devil is this?" he said.

From his station in the doorway Chet squeaked, "The war's over!"

"I know the war's over, but what's this?" He jerked a bandaged hand at the uncomfortable ring of people. Chet swallowed and looked at Dictionary Chance.

Dictionary's suspended talents came back to him. He strode to lay a friendly hand on his host's back; he swung and shook his hostess's hand; he twinkled at the white-faced, big-eyed Bruce on the oven door.

"This, sir," he boomed, "is a welcoming committee of your friends and neighbors, met here to rejoice over your escape from the dread sickness which has swept to untimely death so many of our good friends, God rest their souls! On the invitation of your manly young son here we have been celebrating not only that emancipation, but the emancipation of the entire world from the dread plague of war." With the cup in his hand he bent and twinkled at Bo Mason. "How's it feel to get back, old hoss?"

Bo grunted. He looked across at his wife and laughed a short, choppy laugh. The way his eyes came around and rested on Chet made Chet stop breathing. But his father's voice was hearty enough when it came. "You got a snootful," he said. "Looks like you've all got a snootful."

"Sir," said Dictionary Chance, "I haven't had such a delightful snootful since the misguided government of this province suspended the God-given right of its free people to purchase and imbibe and ingest intoxicating beverages."

He drained his cup and set it on the table. "And now," he said, "it is clear that our hosts are not completely recovered in their strength. I suggest that we do whatever small tasks our ingenuity and gratitude can suggest, and silently steal away."

"Yeah," the others said. "Sure. Sure thing." They brought in the one bed from the sled and set it up, swooped together blankets and mattresses and turned them over to the women. Before the beds were made people began to leave. Dictionary Chance, voluble to the last, stopped to praise the excellent medicinal waters he had imbibed, and to say a word for Chet, before Mrs. Chance, with a quick pleading smile, led him away. The door had not even closed before Chet felt his father's cold eye on him.

"All right," his father said. "Will you please tell me why in the name of Christ you invited that God-damned windbag and all the rest of those sponges over here to drink up my whiskey?"

Chet stood sullenly in the door, boiling with sulky resentment. He had held the fort, milked the cow, kept the house, sold all that whiskey for all it was worth, run Louis Treat and the other man out with a gun. Everybody else praised him, but you could depend on Pa to think more of that whiskey the neighbors had drunk than of anything else. He wasn't going to explain or defend himself. If the old man was going to be that stingy, he could take a flying leap in the river.

"The war was over," he said. "I asked them over to celebrate."

His father's head wagged. He looked incredulous and at his wits' end. "You asked them over!" he said. "You said, 'Come right on over and drink up all the whiskey my dad almost killed himself bringing in.'" He stuck his bandaged hands out. "Do you think I got these and damned near died in that hospital just to let a bunch of blotters . . . Why, God damn you," he said. "Leave the house for ten days, tell you exactly what to do, and by Jesus everything goes wrong. How long have they been here?"

"Since about two."

"How much did they drink?"

"I don't know. Three crocks full, I guess."

His father's head weaved back and forth; he looked at his wife and then at the ceiling. . . . "Three crocks. At least a gallon, twelve dollars' worth. Oh Jesus Christ, if you had the sense of a pissant . . ."

Laboriously, swearing with the pain, he hobbled to the keg. When he put his hand down to shake it, his whole body stiffened.

"It's half empty!" he said. He swung on Chet, and Chet met his furious look. Now! his mind said. Now let him say I didn't hold the fort.

"I sold some," he said, and held his father's eyes for a minute before he marched out stiff-backed into the living room, dug the wad of bills from the vase on the mantel, and came back. He laid the money in his father's hand. "I sold a hundred and twenty-four dollars' worth," he said.

The muscles in his father's jaw moved. He glanced at Chet's mother, let the breath out hard through his nose. "So you've been selling whiskey," he said. "I thought I told you to leave that alone?"

"People wanted it for medicine," Chet said. "Should I've let them die with the flu? They came here wanting to buy it and I sold it. I thought that was what it was for."

The triumph that had been growing in him ever since he went for the money was hot in his blood now. He saw the uncertainty in his father's face, and he almost beat down his father's eyes.

"I suppose," his father said finally, "you sold it for a dollar a bottle, or something."

"I sold it for plenty," Chet said. "Four-fifty for bottles and four for quarts out of the keg. That's more than you were going to get, because I heard you tell Ma."

His father sat down on the chair and fingered the bills, looking at him. "You didn't have any business selling anything," he said. "And then you overcharge people."

"Yeah!" Chet said, defying him now. "If it hadn't been for me there wouldn't've been any to sell. Louis Treat and another man came and tried to steal that whole keg, and I run 'em out with the shotgun."

"What?" his mother said.

"I did!" Chet said. "I made 'em put it down and get out."

Standing in the doorway still facing his father, he felt the tears hot in his eyes and was furious at himself for crying. He hoped his father would try thrashing him. He just hoped he would. He wouldn't make a sound; he'd grit his teeth and show him whether he was man enough to stand it. . . . He looked at his father's gray expressionless face and shouted, "I wish I'd let them take it! I just wish I had!"

And suddenly his father was laughing. He reared back in the chair and threw back his head and roared, his bandaged hands held tenderly before him like helpless paws. He stopped, caught his breath, looked at Chet again, and shook with a deep internal rumbling. "Okay," he said. "Okay, kid. You're a man. I wouldn't take it away from you."

"Well, there's no need to laugh," Chet said. "I don't see anything to laugh about."

He watched his father twist in his chair and look at his mother. "Look at him," his father said. "By God, he'd eat me if I made a pass at him."

"Well, don't laugh!" Chet said. He turned and went into the living room, where he sat on the couch and looked at his hands the way he had when Louis Treat and the other man were walking up the ditch. His hands were trembling, the same way. But there was no need to laugh, any more than there was need to get sore over a little whiskey given to the neighbors.

His mother came in and sat down beside him, laid a hand on his head. "Don't be mad at Pa," she said. "He didn't understand. He's proud of you. We all are."

"Yeah?" said Chet. "Why doesn't *he* come and tell me that?"

His mother's smile was gentle and a little amused. "Because he's ashamed of himself for losing his temper, I suppose," she said. "He never did know how to admit he was wrong."

Chet set his jaw and looked at the shotgun above the mantel. He guessed he had looked pretty tough himself when he had the drop on Louis Treat and his thieving friend. He stiffened his shoulders under his mother's arm. "Just let him start anything," he said. "Just let him try to get hard."

His mother's smile broadened, but he glowered at her. "And there's no need to laugh!" he said.

THE
SWEETNESS
OF THE
TWISTED
APPLES

For a while the road was graded, with the marks of a scraper blade gouged into the banks on both sides. Then the graded road swung right, and a painted sign on a stake said "Harrow." Harrow was where they had come from. But straight ahead a barely traveled road led on between high banks like hedgerows. From the brief clearing at the fork they saw the wild wooded side of South Maid Hill, the maples stained with autumn, and far up, one scarlet tree like an incredible flower.

Ross slowed down—his foot on the clutch. "Which?"

"Oh, straight on!" Margaret said. "That other one circles right back to the highway."

"Chance of getting stuck."

"There are tracks."

"Not many."

"Enough to show it's passable."

"You're crazy," he said. "Vermont-autumn crazy."

He eased the car into the trail, and Margaret leaned back in the open car and watched the sky pour over her in one blue rounding cascade, carrying with it branches of trees and little cream-puff clouds.

She said, "Who wouldn't be? Days like these. There's such a wonderful resigned tranquillity about everything."

She got a sour-fragrant whiff of his pipe and rolled her head back against the seat to look at him—a shaggy man with a kind face, a painter, inexplicably her husband. It was so fine for him to be there, smoking, his square hairy hands on the wheel, and so wonderful that the day was such a day as it was, that she shivered with an almost unbearable sense of life and well-being.

In the quick sun-and-shadow of the woods, white trunks of birches flashed. The car wallowed through a low spot where a spring muddied the road, and she got the scent of mint, clean and cold. On the other side of the swale they met a stone wall that within a few feet bent off to the right and was swallowed in impenetrable brush.

Margaret turned and stared back, but the wall did not appear again. It was lost in the woods, still carefully enclosing some obliterated and overgrown meadow, and all the labor that had built it was gone for the greater comfort of woodchucks and foxes. "It doesn't seem as if anything in America could be this old," she said.

The trail climbed steeply, rocky as the bed of a brook, and gravel chattered under the tires. Someone had chopped away limbs that over-hung the road. At one place a log had been laid across the ruts and half buried, to act as a dam against washouts. Then, at the top of the rise, a fence of split cedar rails jutted out of the trees, and a weathered house with staggering sheds and a sag-backed barn. A foxhound charged out, heavy-voiced, and a man working in one of the sheds straightened up and stared silently. When they were almost past, Margaret saw a woman in the doorway of the house.

The bay of meadow slipped behind; the woods came close again, beeches and maples leaning inward, black spruces edging into the narrow way. A dead-windowed house stared at them suddenly from a clearing; across the road a barn had collapsed in a spiral of timbers and twisted roof.

They nosed on across the almost-wiped-out opening and into more woods, where hazel scrub scraped the sides of the car and poplars made yellow intervals like sunlight. The road went steadily up, gullied by rains. It bore only wagon tracks now; the automobile tracks had stopped with the first barn they had passed.

On the left a barbed-wire fence came out of the brush and paralleled the road. Through the thinning woods something glittered in the direct sun, and as they pulled out into another farmyard Margaret saw that there were tin patches on the barn's roof like bright metal teeth in a mouth, and that the gray side of the barn was streaked with new yellow boards. The slanting gable window of the house was stuffed with burlap bags, but there were signs of busyness around the yard: a homemade saw rig with an old car hooked on for power, and under the loft window of the barn a new homemade hay wagon with automobile wheels and two flat tires.

Ross stopped. A woman and a child were already on their way out to the road. The woman wore burst and run-over shoes, and her hair needed combing, but she had a rather sweet, serene face. The child was wizened, sharp-featured; she hugged her skinny elbows as she walked along beside her mother.

For an instant Margaret had an almost shamefaced image of how she and Ross must appear to these isolated farm people—the expensive glitter and shine of the car, the hand-blocked yellow scarf around her own hair, the silver watch band on Ross's wrist.

"Hello," she said, and smiled.

The woman smiled back. "Guess you folks are lost."

"Not exactly," Margaret said. "We were driving around and found this road and decided to see where it went."

"*Used* to go on over to Island Pond."

"Doesn't it any more?"

"Runs smack into the woods and stops!" the child said.

The words came in a burst and ended in a startled hiccup of laughter. Looking closer, Margaret saw that the girl was not a child at all. She couldn't have been five feet tall or weighed more than eighty pounds, but her face, when you looked at all closely, was not a child's face. It would have been impossible to say how old she was. But the thing that burned behind the pinched features and the shy eyes was no child's spirit. It was sharp and tart, medicinal as woods' herbs.

"What's happened on this road?" Ross said. "People all move away?"

The woman bent forward, her arms folded conversationally "Seem's if they did. We ain't been here but three years ourselves. We lost our other place, over by Willoughby—it was three years, wa'n't it, Sary? Your last year in high school, and while you was goin' out. Yes, three years. Seem's if we hardly moved in. The road was closed long before we come. Used to be a carriage road run from the four corners, where you folks turned off, clean into Island Pond. We're the only folks on it on this side any more. Us and Will Canby's boy, back down a piece."

"How far on can we get?" Margaret asked.

"Maybe a half-mile. Up to the schoolhouse anyway."

"Past that," the girl said. "Up to the orchard."

"You sure, Sary? In a car?"

An expression that was almost disdain crossed Sary's face. "I *know*, Mumma. We used to go up there when I was goin' out."

"That was a year," her mother said doubtfully.

" 'Tisn't changed," Sary said.

The mother regarded her daughter briefly with an expression that seemed to Margaret at once anxious and complacent. "Sary had a disappointment," she said mildly. "For over a year she was a-goin' out . . ."

"Oh, *Mumma*!" Sary said, and swung half around. There was a pause.

"I'm sorry my mister's not home to meet you folks," the woman said. "He went in to see if he could get some kind of a gear for his car. He's had it all over the shed for two weeks—ain't been able to get together all the parts."

"Maybe we'll have another chance," Margaret said. "We're staying through the winter. My husband's a painter, and we'll be driving all over after pictures."

"Well, now," the woman said.

She stepped back as Ross shifted gears, and she and her daughter stood together looking after the car. Margaret waved, and they both lifted their hands. Then a lane of ancient maples, lopsided and burly and with leaves that stained the sun into puddles of red and gold, cut them off.

"I gather we're going on to the head of navigation," Ross said.

"Just to see," she said. "Doesn't it give you a funny feeling to think that twenty or thirty years ago this was a carriage road with farms all along it, and now it's just a dead-end ghost road in the wilderness?"

"Ghosts are only interesting up to a point," Ross said. "I'd rather paint people than ghosts."

"Even funny little people like those women?"

He gave her a straight, surprised look. "What was funny about them?"

"I don't know," she said, feeling obscurely rebuked. "Maybe they weren't."

In the dooryard of another abandoned farm, just above the boarded-up shell of a one-room school, a tall elm had split and blocked the road. Below the house they looked down a gentle slope through gnarled apple trees to a multiple fold of the hills.

Against the crawling edge of woods and the eyeless emptiness of the farmhouse, against the whole irrational patternlessness of decay, the orchard kept its design. Though the tops were unpruned and overgrown, the trunks marched where a farmer's hands had set them to march, and among the thinning leaves hung an unbelievably heavy crop of runty apples, reddening for no harvest.

Ross sat still a moment, looking, and then with a grunt reached into the back seat for the easel and water colors.

While he painted she took a walk up past the split elm, up the road which had once been the street of a little village of a half-dozen houses. There was a church, as blind-windowed as the schoolhouse down the road, one corner of its steeple collapsed so that the squat spire tilted drunkenly forward. There were four houses scattered up the road for a quarter of a mile, all of them gutted, their shingles overgrown with moss, their sheds sagging open. In an old sugarhouse she found, stacked carefully on a landing above the rusty pan and arch, several dozen old-fashioned wooden sap buckets, handmade, hooped with twisted pliable wood rather than with iron. They seemed as ancient as artifacts out of a buried city; she took a pair of them along for flowerpots.

At the head of the village she came through a broken rail fence into the burying ground. A half-dozen graves had pretentious monuments above them; most had only rounded headboards of stone or wood. There were dates as early as 1778, but the latest date she found was on the grave of a child who had died in 1914.

In the open sunlight she sat on a gravestone and thought how it might have been to be the last family left on such a road, and to bury your child among the dead who had been gathering for a hundred and fifty years, and then to move away and leave the road empty behind you. She imagined how it might have seemed to some old grandmother who had lived in the village for eighty years, watching the hill farms go dead like lights going out, watching the decay spread inward from the remote farms to the near ones, to the place next door.

There would have been attempts to bring farms back; the banks would have found renters. But after a while the renters would be gone too. There would be auctions and then empty barns, empty houses. There would be a day when you would come to your door and see nothing alive, hear no human sound, in your whole village.

She stood up uneasily. A hawk was methodically coursing the meadow beyond the graveyard. It was very still. She felt oppressed by the wide silent sky and afraid of the somehow threatening edge where meadow met woods, where not a leaf stirred but where something watched. The thought of Ross painting down in the orchard, abstracted, his pipe in his teeth, was like the thought of home on a cold night. She went back down the blighted road carrying her archaic sap buckets. On every house and building she passed, failure and death were posted like contagion warnings.

The moment she got where she could see him at his easel down in the orchard everything was safe again. She turned off and came through the old trees, running her fingers over the welted scars of prunings, picking a runty apple and rubbing it on the sleeve of her flannel shirt. It took a lovely waxy shine, for all its warped shape, and she experimentally bit into it, half expecting the woody bitter pucker of a wild apple.

Instead, the flesh of the apple cracked firmly, and juice spurted out onto her chin—sweet, golden, with a strange wild tang.

"Ross," she called. "For heaven's sake, you know what?"

She gathered some of the apples and took them over to him, talking as she came, eating her apple and waving it. The whole performance was a gabble.

Ross laughed at her. "Somewhere I've read about this," he said. "An excited woman with an apple."

"But just taste one!" she said. "They're *wonderful*!"

"That's what the other woman said."

"Oh, get excited for once," she said, and threw an apple at him. He made a gagging face and bit into it.

"Isn't that delicious?" she said.

His munching paused, and he leered. "Suddenly," he said, "I perceive that you are naked. Go find a fig tree."

"Oh, hush! You know what I *am* going to do? I'm going to fill the whole back end of the car with these, and we're going to take them down and have Robidoux make them into cider."

Ross threw the gnawed core away and wiped his fingers on his jeans. "Okay. Make that your project for the afternoon."

"You're about as sensitive as an oak burl," she said. "Who ever told you you should be an artist?"

"It was my father's dying wish," he said.

She took her two sap buckets and went to picking, staggering the full buckets up to dump them into the turtleback and then going into the orchard for more. The sun was mellow through the gnarled trees, the air was winy with apples. She entirely forgot her ominous sense of being watched, and in the orchard's ripe warmth she did not remember that she was still on the road of failure and decay—not until she looked up from pouring a bucketful of apples into the car and saw with a jarring shock the thin girl from down the road. In the moment of irritation that followed the shock it seemed to her that the girl had a face like a jackal—something that sniffed around dead campfires and rocked-over graves.

"Look's if you was takin' home some apples," the girl said.

"I hope nobody minds. We took it for granted nobody picked them any more."

"Nobody minds," the girl said. "They just fall off and rot, mostly."

Margaret picked up her buckets and started back. The girl came along. They started picking from a tree behind Ross, and the girl looked curiously at the picture growing on the easel. With her starved collarbones and peaked face, she herself was part of the general decay, and Margaret asked a question that might have been unfortunate.

"How do you like living up here? Isn't it sort of haunted, living near a dead village?"

The girl's eyes flashed up, quick and shy. " 'Tisn't haunted. I used to come up here considerable with my young man when I was goin' out."

"Really? You mean you had dates up here, in this place?"

"Went out for near a year," the girl said, and her look touched Margaret again, an odd look of importance or pride—the look a little girl might wear when showing off her dolls. "He was real interested. Mumma says she never saw a young man more interested."

Down at the easel Ross turned half around to listen. For some reason Margaret felt that she should move slowly and speak quietly, as she would around a nervous horse. "Don't you go out with him any more?"

The girl's thin lips closed down; her eyes were on Margaret's face as if watching the effect of her words.

"I had a disappointment," she said flatly.

"Oh, I'm sorry," Margaret said.

The girl went on busily gathering apples. "Went and got married."

"He did? To someone else?"

"That's what."

"Where has he gone to now?"

"Hasn't gone nowhere. Lives right down below us there."

"And he's still your only neighbor?" Margaret said. "That must be terribly hard."

The girl's glance was direct, a little puzzled. "We still neighbor," she said. "Won't for long, though. He's aimin' to get another place."

"And then you'll be the only family on the road."

"E-yeah," the girl said.

Margaret went on picking, watching the girl sidelong. Like a little brown bird hopping in a garden after all the other birds have gone south, she went around under the gnarled trees—reaching, stretching, tiptoeing for apples free from worms—and for a moment she seemed the saddest thing on the whole sad road.

The leaf-stained sunlight tranced Margaret's eyes, and she saw the orchard and the old buildings on a summer night, a chilly Vermont summer night after chores—the dim flare of northern lights in the sky and the blackboard darkness at the edge of the woods scratched with chalk lines of light by the fireflies.

She saw this girl and her young man under the old orchard trees, the only young things in a place of age and death. Especially, and with pitiless clarity, she saw this girl, too frail for love, too childish or too prematurely old, too skimped and bony-chested, lying in his arms with her peaked face upturned for kisses and her scrawny little body quiet under the farm boy's big hard hands.

The single chance that her lifetime would offer her, the one moment when pollen might blow from stamen to pistil, when the accident of fertility might cheat a sterile heritage. And something had gone wrong. She wondered what. Any trivial thing might have done it. Probably the girl herself didn't know. Perhaps it was only that she herself wasn't adequate, that skin and bones and an eagerness for love were not enough.

Ross's picture was finished, and as he stepped back Margaret saw that he had moved the house down into the orchard for dramatic contrast, to get the sagging corner, the broken window, the gaunt decay of the entrance, into the same composition with the fruited orchard retreating in perfect order to the edge of the folded hills. The girl came close to look.

"It's real like," she said. "A body'd know it in a minute."

With difficulty Margaret shook herself out of the mood.

"I wonder how long," she said, "how many years an orchard like this will go on living and bearing?"

"Years and years," the girl said. "It's wonderful how apple trees hang on sometimes."

Wiping a brush, Ross turned his easy warm smile on her. "How is it in the spring? Pretty?"

It was surprising how responsive her wry little face was. "Oh, land, just like a posy bed! It don't have very big apples any more, but it's a sight in the spring."

She stood with folded arms, as her mother had stood by the side of the car in the farmyard. Margaret, for all her watching, could find no trace of bitterness or frustration or anger in the girl. Starved as it was, the gnomish face was serene.

"Springtime, we used to come up here most every night, when I was goin' out," she said.

THE
BLUE-WINGED
TEAL

till in waders, with the string of ducks across his shoulder, he
stood hesitating on the sidewalk in the cold November wind. His
knees were stiff from being cramped up all day in the blind, and
his feet were cold. Today, all day, he had been alive; now he was back
ready to be dead again.

Lights were on all up and down the street, and there was a rush of
traffic and a hurrying of people past and around him, yet the town was
not his town, the people passing were strangers, the sounds of evening
in this place were no sounds that carried warmth or familiarity. Though
he had spent most of his twenty years in the town, knew hundreds of
its people, could draw maps of its streets from memory, he wanted to
admit familiarity with none of it.

Then what was he doing here, in front of this poolhall loaded down
with nine dead ducks? What had possessed him in the first place to
borrow gun and waders and car from his father and go hunting? If he
had wanted to breathe freely for a change, why hadn't he kept right
on going? What was there in this place to draw him back? A hunter

had to have a lodge to bring his meat to and people who would be glad of his skill. He had this poolhall and his father, John Lederer, Prop.

He stepped out of a woman's path and leaned against the door. Downstairs, in addition to his father, he would find old Max Schmeckebier, who ran a cheap blackjack game in the room under the sidewalk. He would find Giuseppe Sciutti, the Sicilian barber, closing his shop or tidying up the rack of *Artists and Models* and *The Nudist*. He would probably find Billy Hammond, the night clerk from the Windsor Hotel, having his sandwich and beer and pie, or moving alone around a pool table, whistling abstractedly, practicing shots. If the afternoon blackjack game had broken up, there would be Navy Edwards, dealer and bouncer for Schmeckebier. At this time of evening there might be a few counter customers and a cop collecting his tribute of a beer or that other tribute that Schmeckebier paid to keep the cardroom open.

And he would find, sour contrast with the bright sky and the wind of the tule marshes, the cavelike room with its back corners in darkness, would smell that smell compounded of steam heat and cue-chalk dust, of sodden butts in cuspidors, of coffee and meat and beer smells from the counter, of cigarette smoke so unaired that it darkened the walls. From anywhere back of the middle tables there would be the pervasive reek of toilet disinfectant. Back of the counter his father would be presiding, throwing the poolhall light switch to save a few cents when the place was empty, flipping it on to give an air of brilliant and successful use when feet came down the stairs past Sciutti's shop.

The hunter moved his shoulder under the weight of the ducks, his mind full for a moment with the image of his father's face, darkly pale, fallen in on its bones, and the pouched, restless, suspicious eyes that seemed always looking for someone. Over the image came the face of his mother, dead now and six weeks buried. His teeth clicked at the thought of how she had held the old man up for thirty years, kept him at a respectable job, kept him from slipping back into the poolroom-Johnny he had been when she married him. Within ten days of her death he had hunted up this old failure of a poolhall.

In anger the hunter turned, thinking of the hotel room he shared with his father. But he had to eat. Broke as he was, a student yanked from his studies, he had no choice but to eat on the old man. Besides, there were the ducks. He felt somehow that the thing would be incomplete unless he brought his game back for his father to see.

His knees unwilling in the stiff waders, he went down the steps, descending into the light shining through Joe Sciutti's door, and into the momentary layer of clean bay rum smell, talcum smell, hair tonic smell, that rose past the still-revolving barber pole in the angle of the stairs.

Joe Sciutti was sweeping wads of hair from his tile floor, and hunched over the counter beyond, their backs to the door, were Schmeckebier, Navy Edwards, Billy Hammond, and an unknown customer. John Lederer was behind the counter, mopping alertly with a rag. The poolroom lights were up bright, but when Lederer saw who was coming he flipped the switch and dropped the big room back into dusk.

As the hunter came to the end of the counter their heads turned towards him. "Well, I'm a son of a bee," Navy Edwards said, and scrambled off his stool. Next to him Billy Hammond half stood up so that his pale yellow hair took a halo from the backbar lights. "Say!" Max Schmeckebier said. "Say, dot's goot, dot's pooty goot, Henry!"

But Henry was watching his father so intently he did not turn to them. He slid the string of ducks off his shoulder and swung them up on to the wide walnut bar. They landed solidly—offering or tribute or ransom or whatever they were. For a moment it was as if this little act were private between the two of them. He felt queerly moved, his stomach tightened in suspense or triumph. Then the old man's pouchy eyes slipped from his and the old man came quickly forward along the counter and laid hands on the ducks.

He handled them as if he were petting kittens, his big white hands stringing the heads one by one from the wire.

"Two spoonbill," he said, more to himself than to others crowding around. "Shovelducks. Don't see many of those any more. And two, no three, hen mallards and one drake. Those make good eating."

Schmeckebier jutted his enormous lower lip. Knowing him for a stingy, crooked, suspicious little man, Henry almost laughed at the air he could put on, the air of a man of probity about to make an honest judgment in a dispute between neighbors. "I take a budderball," he said thickly. "A liddle budderball, dot is vot eats goot."

An arm fell across Henry's shoulders, and he turned his head to see the hand with red hairs rising from its pores, the wristband of a gray silk shirt with four pearl buttons. Navy Edwards' red face was close to his. "Come clean now," Navy said. "You shot 'em all sitting, didn't you, Henry?"

"I just waited till they stuck their heads out of their holes and let them have it," Henry said.

Navy walloped him on the back and convulsed himself laughing. Then his face got serious again, and he bore down on Henry's shoulder. "By God, you could've fooled me," he said. "If I'd been makin' book on what you'd bring in I'd've lost my shirt."

"Such a pretty shirt, too," Billy Hammond said.

Across the counter John Lederer cradled a little drab duck in his hand. Its neck, stretched from the carrier, hung far down, but its body was neat and plump and its feet were waxy. Watching the sallow face of his father, Henry thought it looked oddly soft.

"Ain't that a beauty, though?" the old man said. "There ain't a prettier duck made than a blue-wing teal. You can have all your wood ducks and redheads, all the flashy ones." He spread a wing until the hidden band of bright blue showed. "Pretty?" he said, and shook his head and laughed suddenly, as if he had not expected to. When he laid the duck down beside the others his eyes were bright with sentimental moisture.

So now, Henry thought, you're right in your element. You always did want to be one of the boys from the poolroom pouring out to see the elk on somebody's running board, or leaning on a bar with a schooner of beer talking baseball or telling the boys about the big German Brown somebody brought in in a cake of ice. We haven't any elk or German Browns right now, but we've got some nice ducks, a fine display along five feet of counter. And who brought them in? The student, the alien son. It must gravel you.

He drew himself a beer. Several other men had come in, and he saw three more stooping to look in the door beyond Sciutti's. Then they too came in. Three tables were going; his father had started to hustle, filling orders. After a few minutes Schmeckebier and Navy went into the cardroom with four men. The poolroom lights were up bright again, there was an ivory click of balls, a rumble of talk. The smoke-filled air was full of movement.

Still more people dropped in, kids in high school athletic sweaters and bums from the fringes of skid road. They all stopped to look at the ducks, and Henry saw glances at his waders, heard questions and answers. John Lederer's boy. Some of them spoke to him, deriving importance from contact with him. A fellowship was promoted by the ducks strung out along the counter. Henry felt it himself. He was so mellowed by the way they spoke to him that when the players at the first table thumped with their cues, he got off his stool to rack them up and collect their nickels. It occurred to him that he ought to go to the room and get into a bath, but he didn't want to leave yet. Instead he came back to the counter and slid the nickels towards his father and drew himself another beer.

"Pretty good night tonight," he said. The old man nodded and slapped his rag on the counter, his eyes already past Henry and fixed on two youths coming in, his mouth fixing itself for the greeting and the "Well, boys, what'll it be?"

Billy Hammond wandered by, stopped beside Henry a moment. "Well, time for my nightly wrestle with temptation," he said.

"I was just going to challenge you to a game of call-shot."

"Maybe tomorrow," Billy said, and let himself out carefully as if afraid a noise would disturb someone—a mild, gentle, golden-haired boy who looked as if he ought to be in some prep school learning to say "Sir" to grown-ups instead of clerking in a girlie hotel. He was the only one of the poolroom crowd that Henry half liked. He thought he understood Billy Hammond a little.

He turned back to the counter to hear his father talking with Max Schmeckebier. "I don't see how we could on this rig. That's the hell of it, we need a regular oven."

"In my room in back," Schmeckebier said. "Dot old electric range."

"Does it work?"

"Sure. Vy not? I t'ink so."

"By God," John Lederer said. "Nine ducks, that ought to give us a real old-fashioned feed." He mopped the counter, refilled a coffee cup, came back to the end and pinched the breast of a duck, pulled out a wing and looked at the band of blue hidden among the drab feathers. "Just like old times, for a change," he said, and his eyes touched Henry's in a look that might have meant anything from a challenge to an apology.

Henry had no desire to ease the strain that had been between them for months. He did not forgive his father the poolhall, or forget the way the old man had sprung back into the old pattern, as if his wife had been a jailer and he was now released. He neither forgot nor forgave the red-haired woman who sometimes came to the poolhall late at night and waited on a bar stool while the old man closed up. Yet now when his father remarked that the ducks ought to be drawn and plucked right away, Henry got to his feet.

"I could do ten while you were doing one," his father said.

The blood spread hotter in Henry's face, but he bit off what he might have said. "All right," he said. "You do them and I'll take over the counter for you."

So here he was, in the poolhall he had passionately sworn he would never do a lick of work in, dispensing Mrs. Morrison's meat pies and tamales smothered in chile, clumping behind the counter in the waders which had been the sign of his temporary freedom. Leaning back between orders, watching the Saturday night activity of the place, he half understood why he had gone hunting, and why it had seemed to him essential that he bring his trophies back here.

That somewhat disconcerted understanding was still troubling him when his father came back. The old man had put on a clean apron and brushed his hair. His pouched eyes, brighter and less houndlike than usual, darted along the bar, counting, and darted across the bright tables, counting again. His eyes met Henry's, and both smiled. Both of them, Henry thought, were a little astonished.

Later, propped in bed in the hotel room, he put down the magazine he had been reading and stared at the drawn blinds, the sleazy drapes, and asked himself why he was here. The story he had told others, and himself, that his mother's death had interrupted his school term and he was waiting for the new term before going back, he knew to be an evasion. He was staying because he couldn't get away, or wouldn't. He hated his father, hated the poolhall, hated the people he was thrown with. He made no move to hobnob with them, or hadn't until tonight, and yet he deliberately avoided seeing any of the people who had been his friends for years. Why?

He could force his mind to the barrier, but not across it. Within a half minute he found himself reading again, diving deep, and when he made himself look up from the page he stared for a long time at his father's bed, his father's shoes under the bed, his father's soiled shirts hanging in the open closet. All the home he had any more was this little room. He could not pretend that as long as he stayed here the fragments of his home and family were held together. He couldn't fool himself that he had any function in his father's life any more, or his father in his, unless his own hatred and his father's uneasy suspicion were functions. He ought to get out and get a job until he could go back to school. But he didn't.

Thinking made him sleepy, and he knew what that was, too. Sleep was another evasion, like the torpor and monotony of his life. But he let drowsiness drift over him, and drowsily he thought of his father behind the counter tonight, vigorous and jovial, Mine Host, and he saw that the usual fretful petulance had gone from his face.

He snapped off the bed light and dropped the magazine on the floor. Then he heard the rain, the swish and hiss of traffic in the wet street. He felt sad and alone, and he disliked the coldness of his own isolation. Again he thought of his father, of the failing body that had once been tireless and bull-strong, of the face before it had sagged and grown dewlaps of flesh on the square jaws. He thought of the many failures, the jobs that never quite worked out, the schemes that never quite paid off, and of the eyes that could not quite meet, not quite hold, the eyes of his cold son.

Thinking of this, and remembering when they had been a family and when his mother had been alive to hold them together, he felt pity, and he cried.

His father's entrance awakened him. He heard the fumbling at the door, the creak, the quiet click, the footsteps that groped in darkness, the body that bumped into something and halted, getting its bearings. He heard the sighing weight of his father's body on the bed, his father's sighing breath as he bent to untie his shoes. Feigning sleep, he lay unmoving, breathing deeply and steadily, but an anguish of fury had leaped in him as sharp and sudden as a sudden fear, for he smelled the smells his father brought with him: wet wool, stale tobacco, liquor; and above all, more penetrating than any, spreading through the room and polluting everything there, the echo of cheap musky perfume.

The control Henry imposed upon his body was like an ecstasy. He raged at himself for the weak sympathy that had troubled him all evening. One good night, he said to himself now, staring furiously upward. One lively Saturday night in the joint and he can't contain himself, he has to go top off the evening with his girl friend. And how? A drink in her room? A walk over to some illegal after-hours bar on Rum Alley? Maybe just a trip to bed, blunt and immediate?

His jaws ached from the tight clamping of his teeth, but his orderly breathing went in and out, in and out, while the old man sighed into bed and creaked a little, rolling over, and lay still. The taint of perfume seemed even stronger now. The sow must slop it on by the cupful. And so cuddly. Such a sugar baby. How's my old sweetie tonight? It's been too long since you came to see your baby. I should be real mad at you.

The cheek against the lapel, the unreal hair against the collar, the perfume like some gaseous poison tainting the clothes it touched.

The picture of his mother's bureau drawers came to him, the careless simple collection of handkerchiefs and gloves and lace collars and cuffs, and he saw the dusty blue sachet packets and smelled the faint fragrance. That was all the scent she had ever used.

My God, he said, how can he stand himself?

After a time his father began to breathe heavily, then to snore. In the little prison of the room his breathing was obscene—loose and bubbling, undisciplined, animal. Henry with an effort relaxed his tense arms and legs, let himself sink. He tried to concentrate on his own breathing, but the other dominated him, burst out and died and whiffled and sighed again. By now he had resolution in him like an iron bar. Tomorrow, for sure, for good, he would break out of his self-imposed isolation and see Frank, see Welby. They would lend him enough to get to the coast. Not another day in this hateful relationship. Not another night in this room.

He yawned. It must be late, two or three o'clock. He ought to get to sleep. But he lay uneasily, his mind tainted with hatred as the room was tainted with perfume. He tried cunningly to elude his mind, to get to sleep before it could notice, but no matter how he composed himself for blankness and shut his eyes and breathed deeply, his mind was out again in a half minute, bright-eyed, lively as a weasel, and he was helplessly hunted again from hiding place to hiding place.

Eventually he fell back upon his old device.

He went into a big dark room in his mind, a room shadowy with great half-seen tables. He groped and found a string above him and pulled, and light fell suddenly in a bright cone from the darker cone of the shade. Below the light lay an expanse of dark green cloth, and this was the only lighted thing in all that darkness. Carefully he gathered bright balls into a wooden triangle, pushing them forward until the apex lay over a round spot on the cloth. Quietly and thoroughly he chalked a cue: the inlaid handle and the smooth taper of the shaft were very real to his eyes and hands. He lined up the cue ball, aimed, drew the cue back and forth in smooth motions over the bridge of his left hand. He saw the balls run from the spinning shock of the break, and carom, and come to rest, and he hunted up the yellow 1-ball and got a shot at it between two others. He had to cut it very fine, but he saw the shot go true, the 1 angle off cleanly into the side pocket. He saw the cue ball rebound and kiss and stop, and he shot the 2 in a straight shot for the left corner pocket, putting drawers on the cue ball to get shape for the 3.

Yellow and blue and red, spotted and striped, he shot pool balls into pockets as deep and black and silent as the cellars of his consciousness. He was not now quarry that his mind chased, but an actor, a willer, a doer, a man in command. By an act of will or of flight he focused his whole awareness on the game he played. His mind undertook it with intent concentration. He took pride in little two-cushion banks, little triumphs of accuracy, small successes of foresight. When he had finished one game and the green cloth was bare he dug the balls from the bin under the end of the table and racked them and began another.

Eventually, he knew, nothing would remain in his mind but the clean green cloth traced with running color and bounded by simple problems, and sometime in the middle of an intricately planned combination shot he would pale off into sleep.

At noon, after the rain, the sun seemed very bright. It poured down from a clearing sky, glittered on wet roofs, gleamed in reflection from pavements and sidewalks. On the peaks beyond the city there was a purity of snow.

Coming down the hill, Henry noticed the excessive brightness and could not tell whether it was really as it seemed, or whether his plunge out of the dark and isolated hole of his life had restored a lost capacity to see. A slavery, or a paralysis, was ended; he had been for three hours in the company of a friend; he had been eyed with concern; he had been warmed by solicitude and generosity. In his pocket he had fifty dollars, enough to get him to the coast and let him renew his life. It seemed to him incredible that he had alternated between dismal hotel and dismal poolroom so long. He could not understand why he had not before this moved his legs in the direction of the hill. He perceived that he had been sullen and morbid, and he concluded with some surprise that even Schmeckebier and Edwards and the rest might have found him a difficult companion.

His father too. The fury of the night before had passed, but he knew he would not bend again towards companionship. That antipathy was too deep. He would never think of his father again without getting the whiff of that perfume. Let him have it; it was what he wanted, let him have it. They could part without an open quarrel, maybe, but they would part without love. They could part right now, within an hour.

Two grimy stairways led down into the cellar from the alley he turned into. One went to the furnace room, the other to the poolhall. The iron rail was blockaded with filled ash cans. Descent into Avernus, he said to himself, and went down the left-hand stair.

The door was locked. He knocked, and after some time knocked again. Finally someone pulled on the door from inside. It stuck, and was yanked irritably inward. His father stood there in his shirt sleeves, a cigar in his mouth.

"Oh," he said. "I was wondering what had become of you."

The basement air was foul and heavy, dense with the reek from the toilets. Henry saw as he stepped inside that at the far end only the night light behind the bar was on, but that light was coming from Schmeckebier's door at this end too, the two weak illuminations diffusing in the shadowy poolroom, leaving the middle in almost absolute dark. It was the appropriate time, the appropriate place, the stink of his prison appropriately concentrated. He drew his lungs full of it with a kind of passion, and he said, "I just came down to—"

"Who is dot?" Schmeckebier called out. He came to his door, wrapped to the armpits in a bar apron, with a spoon in his hand, and he bent, peering out into the dusk like a disturbed dwarf in an underhill cave. "John? Who? Oh, Henry. Shust in time, shust in time. It is not long now." His lower lip waggled, and he pulled it up, apparently with an effort.

Henry said, "What's not long?"

"Vot?" Schmeckebier said, and thrust his big head far out. "You forgot about it?"

"I must have," Henry said.

"The duck feed," his father said impatiently.

They stood staring at one another in the dusk. The right moment was gone. With a little twitch of the shoulder Henry let it go. He would wait a while, pick his time. When Schmeckebier went back to his cooking, Henry saw through the doorway the lumpy bed, the big chair with a blanket folded over it, the roll-top desk littered with pots and pans, the green and white enamel of the range. A rich smell of roasting came out and mingled oddly with the chemical stink of toilet disinfectant.

"Are we going to eat in there?" he asked.

His father snorted. "How could we eat in there? Old Maxie lived in the ghetto too damn long. By God, I never saw such a boar's nest."

"Vot's duh matter? Vot's duh matter?" Schmeckebier said. His big lip thrust out, he stooped to look into the oven, and John Lederer went shaking his head up between the tables to the counter. Henry followed him, intending to make the break when he got the old man alone. But he saw the three plates set up on the bar, the three glasses of tomato juice, the platter of olives and celery, and he hesitated. His father reached with a salt shaker and shook a little salt into each glass of tomato juice.

"All the fixings," he said. "Soon as Max gets those birds out of the oven we can take her on."

Now it was easy to say, "As soon as the feed's over I'll be shoving off." Henry opened his mouth to say it, but was interrupted this time by a light tapping at the glass door beyond Sciutti's shop. He swung around angrily and saw duskily beyond the glass the smooth blond hair, the even smile.

"It's Billy," he said. "Shall I let him in?"

"Sure," the old man said. "Tell him to come in and have a duck with us."

But Billy Hammond shook his head when Henry asked him. He was shaking his head almost as he came through the door. "No, thanks, I just ate. I'm full of chow mein. This is a family dinner anyway. You go on ahead."

"Got plenty," John Lederer said, and made a motion as if to set a fourth place at the counter.

"Who is dot?" Schmeckebier bawled from the back. "Who come in? Is dot Billy Hammond? Set him up a blate."

"By God, his nose sticks as far into things as his lip," Lederer said. Still holding the plate, he roared back, "Catch up with the parade, for Christ sake, or else tend to your cooking." He looked at Henry and Billy and chuckled.

Schmeckebier had disappeared, but now his squat figure blotted the lighted doorway again. "Vot? Vot you say?"

"Vot?" John Lederer said. "Vot, vot, vot? Vot does it matter vot I said? Get the hell back to your kitchen."

He was, Henry saw, in a high humor. The effect of last night was still with him. He was still playing Mine Host. He looked at the two of them and laughed so naturally that Henry almost joined him. "I think old Maxie's head is full of duck dressing," he said, and leaned on the counter. "I ever tell you about the time we came back from Reno together? We stopped off in the desert to look at a mine, and got lost on a little dirt road so we had to camp. I was trying to figure out where we were, and started looking for stars, but it was clouded over, hard to locate anything. So I ask old Maxie if he can see the Big Dipper anywhere. He thinks about that maybe ten minutes with his lip stuck out and then he says, 'I t'ink it's in duh water bucket.' ''

He did the grating gutturals of Schmeckebier's speech so accurately that Henry smiled in spite of himself. His old man made another motion with the plate at Billy Hammond. "Better let me set you up a place."

"Thanks," Billy said. His voice was as polite and soft as his face, and his eyes had the ingenuous liquid softness of a girl's. "Thanks, I really just ate. You go on, I'll shoot a little pool if it's all right."

Now came Schmeckebier with a big platter held in both hands. He bore it smoking through the gloom of the poolhall and up the steps to the counter, and John Lederer took it from him there and with a flourish speared one after another three tight-skinned brown ducks and slid them on to the plates set side by side for the feast. The one frugal light from the backbar shone on them as they sat down. Henry looked over his shoulder to see Billy Hammond pull the cord and flood a table with a sharp-edged cone of brilliance. Deliberately, already absorbed, he chalked a cue. His lips pursed, and he whistled, and, whistling, bent to take aim.

Lined up in a row, they were not placed for conversation, but John Lederer kept attempting it, leaning forward over his plate to see Schmeckebier or Henry. He filled his mouth with duck and dressing and chewed, shaking his head with pleasure, and snapped off a bite of celery with a crack like a breaking stick. When his mouth was clear he leaned and said to Schmeckebier, "Ah, *das schmeckt gut*, hey, Maxie?"

"*Ja*," Schmeckebier said, and sucked grease off his lip and only then turned in surprise. "Say, you speak German?"

"Sure, I speak German," Lederer said. "I worked three weeks once with an old squarehead brickmason that taught me the whole language. He taught me about *sehr gut* and *nicht wahr* and *besser I bleiben* right *hier*, and he always had his *Frau* make me up a lunch full of *kalter Aufschnitt* and *gemixte pickeln*. I know all about German."

Schmeckebier stared a moment, grunted, and went back to his eating. He had already stripped the meat from the bones and was gnawing the carcass.

"Anyway," John Lederer said, "*es schmeckt* God damn good." He got up and went around the counter and drew a mug of coffee from the urn. "Coffee?" he said to Henry.

"Please."

His father drew another mug and set it before him. "Maxie?"

Schmeckebier shook his head, his mouth too full for talk. For a minute, after he had set out two little jugs of cream, Lederer stood as if thinking. He was watching Billy Hammond move quietly around the one lighted table, whistling. "Look at that sucker," Lederer said. "I bet he doesn't even know where he is."

By the time he got around to his stool he was back at the German. "*Schmeckebier*," he said. "What's that mean?"

"Uh?"

"What's your name mean? Tastes beer? Likes beer?"

Schmeckebier rolled his shoulders. The sounds he made eating were like sounds from a sty. Henry was half sickened, sitting next to him, and he wished the old man would let the conversation drop. But apparently it had to be a feast, and a feast called for chatter.

"That's a hell of a name, you know it?" Lederer said, and already he was up again and around the end of the counter. "You couldn't get into any church with a name like that." His eyes fastened on the big drooping greasy lip, and he grinned.

"Schmeckeduck, that ought to be your name," he said. "What's German for duck? *Vogel?* Old Man Schmeckevogel. How about number two?"

Schmeckebier pushed his plate forward and Lederer forked a duck out of the steam table. Henry did not take a second.

"You ought to have one," his father told him. "You don't get grub like this every day."

"One's my limit," Henry said.

For a while they worked at their plates. Back of him Henry heard the clack of balls hitting, and a moment later the rumble as a ball rolled down the chute from a pocket. The thin, abstracted whistling of Billy Hammond broke off, became words:

> *Annie doesn't live here any more.*
> *You must be the one she waited for.*
> *She said I would know you by the blue in your eye—*

"Talk about one being your limit," his father said. "When we lived in Nebraska we used to put on some feeds. You remember anything about Nebraska at all?"

"A little," Henry said. He was irritated at being dragged into reminiscences, and he did not want to hear how many ducks the town hog could eat at a sitting.

"We'd go out, a whole bunch of us," John Lederer said. "The sloughs were black with ducks in those days. We'd come back with a buggyful, and the womenfolks'd really put us on a feed. Fifteen, twenty, thirty people. Take a hundred ducks to fill 'em up." He was silent a moment, staring across the counter, chewing. Henry noticed that he had tacked two wings of a teal up on the frame of the backbar mirror, small, strong bows with a band of bright blue half hidden in them. The old man's eyes slanted over, caught Henry's looking at the wings.

"Doesn't seem as if we'd had a duck feed since we left there," he said. His forehead wrinkled; he rubbed his neck, leaning forward over his plate, and his eyes met Henry's in the backbar mirror. He spoke to the mirror, ignoring the gobbling image of Schmeckebier between his own reflection and Henry's.

"You remember that set of china your mother used to have? The one she painted herself? Just the plain white china with the one design on each plate?"

Henry sat stiffly, angry that his mother's name should even be mentioned between them in this murky hole, and after what had passed. Gabble, gabble, gabble, he said to himself. If you can't think of anything else to gabble about, gabble about your dead wife. Drag her through the poolroom too. Aloud he said, "No, I guess I don't."

"Blue-wing teal," his father said, and nodded at the wings tacked to the mirror frame. "Just the wings, like that. Awful pretty. She thought a teal was about the prettiest little duck there was."

His vaguely rubbing hand came around from the back of his neck and rubbed along the cheek, pulling the slack flesh and distorting the mouth. Henry said nothing, watching the pouched hound eyes in the mirror.

It was a cold, skin-tightening shock to realize that the hound eyes were cloudy with tears. The rubbing hand went over them, shaded them like a hatbrim, but the mouth below remained distorted. With a plunging movement his father was off the stool.

"Oh, God damn!" he said in a strangling voice, and went past Henry on hard, heavy feet, down the steps and past Billy Hammond, who neither looked up nor broke the sad thin whistling.

Schmeckebier had swung around. "Vot's duh matter? Now vot's duh matter?"

With a short shake of the head, Henry turned away from him, staring after his father down the dark poolhall. He felt as if orderly things were breaking and flying apart in his mind; he had a moment of white blind terror that this whole scene upon whose reality he counted was really only a dream, something conjured up out of the bottom of his consciousness where he was accustomed to comfort himself into total sleep. His mind was still full of the anguished look his father had hurled at the mirror before he ran.

The hell with you, the look had said. The hell with you, Schmeckebier, and you, my son Henry. The hell with your ignorance, whether you're stupid or whether you just don't know all you think you know. You don't know enough to kick dirt down a hole. You know nothing at all, you know less than nothing because you know things wrong.

He heard Billy's soft whistling, saw him move around his one lighted table—a well-brought-up boy from some suburban town, a polite soft gentle boy lost and wandering among pimps and prostitutes, burying himself for some reason among people who never even touched his surface. Did he shoot pool in his bed at night, tempting sleep, as Henry did? Did his mind run carefully to angles and banks and englishes, making a reflecting mirror of them to keep from looking through them at other things?

Almost in terror he looked out across the sullen cave, past where the light came down in an intense isolated cone above Billy's table, and heard the lugubrious whistling that went on without intention of audience, a recurrent and deadening and only half-conscious sound. He looked toward the back, where his father had disappeared in the gloom, and wondered if in his bed before sleeping the old man worked through a routine of little jobs: cleaning the steam table, ordering a hundred pounds of coffee, jacking up the janitor about the mess in the hall. He wondered if it was possible to wash yourself to sleep with restaurant crockery, work yourself to sleep with chores, add yourself to sleep with columns of figures, as you could play yourself to sleep with a pool cue and a green table and fifteen colored balls. For a moment, in the sad old light with the wreckage of the duck feast at his elbow, he wondered if there was anything more to his life, or his father's life, or Billy

Hammond's life, or anyone's life, than playing the careful games that deadened you into sleep.

Schmeckebier, beside him, was still groping in the fog of his mind for an explanation of what had happened. "Vere'd he go?" he said, and nudged Henry fiercely. "Vot's duh matter?"

Henry shook him off irritably, watching Billy Hammond's oblivious bent head under the light. He heard Schmeckebier's big lip flop and heard him sucking his teeth.

"I tell you," the guttural voice said. "I got somet'ing dot fixes him if he feels bum."

He too went down the stairs past the lighted table and into the gloom at the back. The light went on in his room, and after a minute or two his voice was shouting, "John! Say, come here, uh? Say, John!"

Eventually John Lederer came out of the toilet and they walked together between the tables. In his fist Schmeckebier was clutching a square bottle. He waved it in front of Henry's face as they passed, but Henry was watching his father. He saw the crumpled face, oddly rigid, like the face of a man in the grip of a barely controlled rage, but his father avoided his eyes.

"Kümmel," Schmeckebier said. He set four ice-cream dishes on the counter and poured three about a third full of clear liquor. His squinted eyes lifted and peered towards Billy Hammond, but Henry said, on an impulse, "Let him alone. He's walking in his sleep."

So there were only the three. They stood together a moment and raised their glasses. "Happy days," John Lederer said automatically. They drank.

Schmeckebier smacked his lips, looked at them one after another, shook his head in admiration of the quality of his kümmel, and waddled back towards his room with the bottle. John Lederer was already drawing hot water to wash the dishes.

In the core of quiet which was not broken even by the clatter of crockery and the whistling of Billy Hammond, Henry said what he had to say. "I'll be leaving," he said. "Probably tonight."

But he did not say it in anger, or with the cold command of himself that he had imagined in advance. He said it like a cry, and with the feeling he might have had on letting go the hand of a friend too weak and too exhausted to cling any longer to their inadequate shared driftwood in a wide cold sea.

POP
GOES THE
ALLEY CAT

■   ■   ■

Getting up to answer the door, Prescott looked into the face of a Negro boy of about eighteen. Rain pebbled his greased, straightened hair; the leather yoke of his blazer and the knees of his green gabardine pants were soaked. The big smile of greeting that had begun on his face passed over as a meaningless movement of the lips. "I was lookin'," he said, and then with finality, "I thought maybe Miss Vaughn."

"She's just on her way out."

The boy did not move. "I like to see her," he said, and gave Prescott a pair of small, opaque, expressionless eyes to look into. Eventually Prescott motioned him in. He made a show of getting the water off himself, squee-geeing his hair with a flat palm, shaking his limber hands, lifting the wet knees of his pants with thumb and finger as he sat down. He was not a prepossessing specimen: on the scrawny side, the clothes too flashy but not too clean, the mouth loose and always moving, the eyes the kind that shifted everywhere when you tried to hold them but were on you intently the moment you looked away.

But he made himself at home. And why not, Prescott asked himself, in this apartment banked and stacked and overflowing with reports on delinquency, disease, crime, discrimination; littered with sociological studies and affidavits on police brutality and the mimeographed communications of a dozen betterment organizations? The whole place was a temple to the juvenile delinquent, and here was the god himself in the flesh, Los Angeles Bronzeville model.

Well, he said, I am not hired to comment, but only to make pictures.

Carol came into the hall from her bedroom, and Prescott saw with surprise that she was glad to see this boy. "Johnny!" she said. "Where did you drop from?"

Over the boy had come an elaborate self-conscious casualness. He walked his daddylonglegs fingers along the couch back and lounged to his feet, rolling the collar of the blazer smooth across the back of his neck. Prescott was reminded of the slickers of his high school days, with their pinch-waisted bell-bottomed suits and their habit of walking a little hollow-chested to make their shoulders look wider. The boy weaved and leaned, pitching his voice high for kidding, moving his shoulders, his mouth, his pink-palmed hands. "Start to *rain* on me," he said in the high complaining humorous voice. "*Water* start comin' down on me I think I have to drop *in*."

"How come you're not working?"

"That job!" the boy said, and batted it away with both hands. "That wasn't much of a job, no kiddin'."

"Wasn't?"

"*You* know. Them old flour bags *heavy*, you get tired. Minute you stop to rest, here come that old foreman with the *gooseroo*. Hurry up there, boy! Get along there, boy! They don't ride white boys like that."

Carol gave Prescott the merest drawing down of the lips. "That's the third job in a month," she said, and added, "Johnny's one of my boys. Johnny Bane. This is Charlie Prescott, Johnny."

"Pleased to meet you," Johnny said without looking. Prescott nodded and withdrew himself, staring out into the dripping garden court.

"You know a fact?" Johnny said. "That old strawboss keep eyeballin' me and givin' me that old hurry-up, hurry-up, that gets *old*. I get to carryin' my knife up the sleeve of my sweatshirt, and he comes after me once *more*, I'm goin' *cut* him. So I quit before I get in bad trouble out there."

Carol laughed, shaking her head. "At least that's ingenious. What'll you do now?"

"Well, I don't *know*." He wagged his busy hands. "No future pushin' a truck around or cuttin' *lemons* off a tree. I like me a job with some *class*, you know, something where I could *learn* something."

"I can imagine how ambition eats away at you."

"No kiddin'!" the burbling voice said. "I get real industrious if I had me the right *kind* of a job. Over on Second Street there's this Chinaman, he's on call out at Paramount. Everytime they need a Chinaman for a mob scene, out he goes and runs around for a couple of hours and they hand him all this *lettuce*, man. You know anybody out at MGM, Paramount, anywhere?"

"No," she said. "Do you, Charlie?"

"Nobody that needs any Chinamen." Prescott showed her the face of his watch. Johnny Bane was taking in, apparently for the first time, the camera bag, the tripod, the canvas sack of flash bulbs beside Prescott's chair.

"Hey, man, you a photographer?"

"Charlie and I are doing a picture study of your part of town for the Russell Foundation," Carol said.

"Take a long time to be a photographer?" Johnny's mouth still worked over his words, but now that his attention was fixed his eyes were as unblinking as an alligator's.

"Three or four years."

"Man, that's a rough *sentence*! Take a long time, uh? Down by the station there's this place, mug you for a quarter. Sailors and their chicks always goin' in. One chick I was watchin' other night, she had her picture five times. Lots of cats and chicks, every night. *Money* in that, man."

She shook her head, saying, "Johnny, when are you going to learn to hold a job? You make it tough for me, after I talk you into a place."

"I get me in trouble, I stay over there," he said. "I know you don't want me gettin' into trouble." Lounging, crossing his feet, he said, "I like to learn me some trade. Like this photography. I bet I surprise you. That ain't like pushin' a truck with some *foreman* givin' you the eyeballs all the time."

Prescott lifted the camera bag to the chair. "If we're going to get anything today we'll have to be moving."

"Just a minute," Carol said. To Johnny she said, "Do you know many people over on your hill?"

"Sure, man. *Multitudes.*"

"Mexicans too?"

"They're mostly Mexicans over there. My chick's Mexican." He staggered with his eyes dreamily shut. "Solid, solid!" he said.

"He might help us get in some places," Carol said. "What do you think, Charlie?"

Prescott shrugged.

"He could hold reflectors and learn a little about photography."

Prescott shrugged again.

"Do you mind, Charlie?"

"You're the doctor." He handed the sack of flash bulbs and the tripod to Johnny and picked up the camera bag. "Lesson number one," he said. "A photographer is half packhorse."

The *barrio* was a double row of shacks tipping from a hilltop down a steep road clayily shining and deserted in the rain, every shack half buried under climbing roses, geraniums, big drooping seedheads of sunflowers, pepper and banana trees, and palms: a rural slum of the better kind, the poverty overlaid deceptively with flowers. Across the staggering row of mailboxes Prescott could see far away, over two misty hilltops and an obscured sweep of city, the Los Angeles Civic Center shining a moment in a watery gleam of sun.

Johnny hustled around, pulling things from the car. As Prescott took the camera bag, the black face mugged and contorted itself with laughter. "You want me and my chick? How about me and my chick cuttin' a little *jive*, real mean? Colored and Mexican hobnobbin'. That okay?"

"First some less sizzling shots," Carol said dryly. "Privies in the rain, ten kids in a dirt-floored shack. How about Dago Aguirre's? That's pretty bad, isn't it?"

"Dago's? Man, that's a real *dump*. You want dumps, uh? Okay, we try Dago's."

He went ahead of them, looking back at the bag Prescott carried. "Must cost a lot of lettuce, man, all those *cameras*."

Prescott shook the bag at him. "That's a thousand dollars in my hand," he said. "That's why I carry it myself."

Rain had melted the adobe into an impossible stickiness; after ten steps their feet were balls of mud. Johnny took them along the flat hilltop to a gateless fence under a sugar palm, and as they scraped the mud from their shoes against a broken piece of concrete a Mexican boy in Air Force dungarees opened the door of the shack and leaned there.

"*Ese, Dago*," Johnny said.

"*Hórale, cholo.*" Dago looked down without expression as Johnny shifted the tripod and made a mock-threatening motion with his fist.

"We came to see if we could take some pictures," Carol said. "Is your mother home, Dago?"

Dago oozed aside and made room for a peering woman with a child against her shoulder. She came forward uncertainly, a sweet-faced woman made stiff by mistrust. Carol talked to her in Spanish for five minutes before she would open her house to them.

Keeping his mouth shut and working fast as he had learned to on this job, Prescott got the baby crawling on the dirt floor between pans set to catch the drip from the roof. He got the woman and Dago and the baby and two smaller children eating around the table whose one leg was a propped box. By backing into the lean-to, between two old iron bedsteads, and having Carol, Johnny, and Dago hold flashes in separate corners, he got the whole place, an orthodox FSA shot, Standard Poverty. That was what the Foundation expected. As always, the children cried when the flashes went off; as always, he mollified them with the blown bulbs, little Easter eggs of shellacked glass. It was a dump, but nothing out of the ordinary, and he got no picture that excited him until he caught the woman nursing her baby on a box in the corner. The whole story was there in the protective stoop of her figure and the drained resignation of her face. She looked anciently tired; the baby's chubby hand was clenched in the flesh of her breast.

Johnny Bane, eager beaver, brisk student, had been officious about keeping extension cords untangled and posing with the reflector. By the time Prescott had the camera and tripod packed Johnny had everything else dismantled. "How you get all them *lights* to go off at *once?*" he said.

Prescott dropped a reflector and they both stooped for it, bumping heads. The boy's skull felt as hard as cement; for a moment Prescott was unreasonably angry. But he caught Carol's eye across the room, and straightening up without a word, he showed Johnny and Dago how the flashes were synchronized, he let them look into the screen of the Rolleiflex, he explained shutter and lens, he gave them a two-minute lecture on optics. "Okay?" he said to Carol in half-humorous challenge.

She smiled. "Okay."

The Aguirre family watched them to the door and out into the drizzle. Johnny Bane, full of importance, a hep cat, a photographer's assistant, punched the shoulder of the lounging Dago. "*Ay te wacho,*" he said. Dago lifted a languid hand.

"Now what?" Prescott asked.

"More of the same," Carol said. "Unfortunately, there's plenty."

"Overcrowding, malnutrition, lack of sanitation," he said. "Four days of gloom. Can't we shoot something pretty?"

"There's always Johnny's chick."

"Maybe she comes under the head of lack of sanitation."

They were all huddled under the sugar palm. "What about my chick?" Johnny demanded. "You want my chick now?"

Carol stood tying a scarf over her fair hair. In raincoat and saddle shoes, she looked like a college sophomore. "Does your chick's family approve of you?" she said. "Most Mexican families aren't too happy to see boy friends hanging around."

Tickled almost to idiocy, he cackled and flapped his hands. "Man, they think I'm *rat* poison, no kiddin'. They think *any* cat's rat poison. They got this old Mexican jive about keepin' chicks at *home*. But I come there with *you*, they got to let me *in*, don't they?"

"So who's helping whom?" Prescott said.

That made him giggle and mug all the way down the slippery hill. "Hey, man," he said once, "you know these Mexicans believe in this Evil Eye, this *ojo*. When I hold up that old reflector I'm sayin' the Lord's *Prayer* backwards and puttin' the eyeballs on him, and when here comes that big flash, man, her old man really think he got the *curse* on him. I tell him I don't take it off till he let Lupe go out any time she want. Down to that *beach*, man. She look real mean down there on that sand gettin' the eyeballs from all the cats. *Reety!*"

"Spare us the details," Carol said, and turned her face from the rain, hanging to a broken fence and slipping, laughing, coming up hard against a light pole. Prescott slithered after her until before a shack more pretentious than most, almost a cottage, Johnny kicked the mud from his shoes and silently mugged at them, with a glassy, scared look in his odd little eyes, before he knocked on the home-made door.

It was like coming into a quiet opening in the woods and startling all the little animals. They were watched by a dozen pairs of eyes. Prescott looked past the undershirted Mexican who had opened the door and saw three men with cards and glasses and a jug before them

on a round table. A very pregnant woman stood startled in the middle
of the floor. On a bed against the far wall a boy had lowered his comic
book to stare. There was a flash of children disappearing into corners
and behind the stove. The undershirted man welcomed them with an
enveloping winy breath, but his smile was only for Carol and Prescott;
his recognition of Johnny was a brief, sidelong lapse from politeness.
Somewhere behind the door a phonograph was playing "*Linda Mujer*";
now it stopped with a squawk.

Once, during the rapid Spanish that went on between Carol and the
Mexican, Prescott glanced at Johnny, but the boy's face, with an unreal
smile pasted on it, blinked and peered past the undershirted man as if
looking for someone. His forehead was puckered in tense knots. Then
the undershirted man said something over his shoulder, the men at the
table laughed, and one lifted the jug in invitation. The host brought it
and offered it to Carol, who grinned and tipped and drank while they
applauded. Then Prescott, mentally tasting the garlic and chile from the
lips that had drunk before him, coldly contemplating typhoid, diphtheria,
polio, drank politely and put the jug back in the man's hands with
thanks and watched him return it to the table without offering it to
Johnny Bane. They were pulled into the room, the door closed, and he
saw that the old hand-cranked Victrola had been played by a Mexican
youth in drape pants and a pretty girl, short-skirted and pompadoured.
The girl should be Lupe, Johnny's chick. He looked for the glance of
understanding between them and saw only the look on Johnny's face
as if he had an unbearable belly-ache.

This was a merry shackful. The men were all a little drunk, and posed
magnificently and badly, their eyes magnetized by the camera. The boy
was lured from his comic book. Lupe and the youth, who turned out
to be her cousin Chuey, leaned back and watched and whispered with
a flash of white teeth. As for Johnny, he held reflectors where Prescott
told him to, but he was no longer an eager beaver. His mouth hung
sullenly, his eyes kept straying to the two on the couch.

Dutifully Prescott went on with his job, documenting poverty for
humanitarianism's sake and humanizing it as he could for the sake of
art. He got a fair shot of the boy reading his comic book under a hanging
image of the Virgin, another of two little girls peeking into a steaming
kettle of frijoles while the mother modestly hid her pregnancy behind
the stove. He shot the card players from a low angle, with low side-
lighting, and when an old grandmother came in the back door with a

pail of water he got her there, stooping to the weight in the open door, against the background of the rain.

Finally he said into Carol's ear, with deliberate malice, "Now do we get that red-hot shot of Johnny jiving with his chick?"

"You're a mean man, Charlie," she said, but she smiled, and looking across to where Johnny stood sullen and alone, she said, "Johnny, you want to come over here?"

He came stiff as a stick, ugly with venom and vanity. When Carol seated him close to Lupe the girl rolled her eyes and bit her lip, ready to laugh. The noise in the room had quieted; it was as if a dipperful of cold water had been thrown into a boiling kettle. Carol moved Chuey in close and laid some records in Lupe's lap. Prescott could see the caption coming up: *Even in shacktown, young people need amusement. Lack of adequate entertainment facilities one of greatest needs. Older generation generally disapproves of jive, jive talk, jive clothes.*

The girl was pretty, even with her ridiculous pompadour. Her eyes were soft, liquid, very dark, her cheekbones high, and her cheeks planed. With a *rebozo* over her head she might have posed for Murillo's Madonna. She did not stare into the camera as her elders did, but at Prescott's word became absorbed in studying the record labels. Chuey laid his head close to hers, and on urging, Johnny sullenly did the same. The moment the flash went off Johnny stood up.

Prescott shifted the Victrola so the crank handle showed more, placed Chuey beside it with a record in his hands. "All right, Lupe, you and Johnny show us a little rug-cutting."

He watched the girl glance from the corners of her eyes at her parents, then come into Johnny's arm. He held her as if she smelled bad, his head back and away, but she turned her face dreamily upward and sighed like an actress in a love drama and laid her face against his rain-wet chest. "*Qúe chicloso!*" she said, and could not hold back her laughter.

"*Surote!*" Johnny pushed her away so hard she almost fell. His face was contorted, his eyes glared. Spittle sprayed from his heavy lips. "*Bofa!*" he said to Lupe, and suddenly Prescott found himself protecting the camera in the middle of what threatened to become a brawl. Chuey surged forward, the undershirted father crowded in from the other side, the girl was spitting like a cat. With a wrench Johnny broke away and got his back to the wall, and there he stood with his hand plunged into the pocket of his blazer and his loose mouth working.

"Please!" Carol was shouting, "Chuey! Lupe! Please!" She held back the angry father and got a reluctant, broken quiet. Over her shoulder she said, "Johnny, go wait for us in the car."

For a moment he hung, then reached a long thin hand for the latch and slid out. The·room was instantly full of noise again, indignation, threats. Prescott got his things safely outside the door away from their feet, and by that time politeness and diplomacy had triumphed. Carol said something to Lupe, who showed her teeth in a little white smile; to Chuey, who shrugged; to the father, who bowed over her hand and talked close to her face. There was handshaking around, Carol promised them prints of the pictures, Prescott gave the children each a quarter. Eventually they were out in the blessed rain.

"What in hell did he call her?" Prescott said as they clawed their way up the hill.

"Pachuco talk. Approximately a chippy."

"Count on him for the right touch."

"Don't say anything, Charlie," she said. "Let me handle him."

"He's probably gone off somewhere to nurse his wounded ego."

But as he helped her over the clay brink on to the cinder road he looked towards the car and saw the round dark head in the back seat. "I must say you pick some dillies," he said.

Walking with her face sideward away from the rain, she said seriously, "I don't pick them, Charlie. They come because they don't have anybody else."

"It's no wonder this one hasn't got anybody else," he said, and then they were at the car and he was opening the door to put the equipment inside. Johnny Bane made no motion to get his muddy feet out of the way.

"Lunch?" Carol said as she climbed under the wheel. Prescott nodded, but Johnny said nothing. In the enclosed car Prescott could smell his hair oil. Carol twisted around to smile at him.

"Listen!" she said. "Why take it so hard? It's just that Chuey's her cousin, he's family, he can crash the gate."

"Agh!"

"Laugh it off."

He let his somber gaze fall on her. "That punk!" he said. "I get him good. Her too. I kill that mean little bitch. You wait. I kill her sometime."

For a moment she watched him steadily; then she sighed. "If it helps to take it out on me, go ahead," she said. "I'll worry about you, if that's what you want."

A few minutes later she stopped at a diner on Figueroa, but when she and Prescott climbed out, Johnny sat still. "Coming?" she said.

"I ain't hungry."

"Oh, Johnny, come off it! Don't sulk all day."

The long look he gave her was so deliberately insolent that Prescott wanted to reach through the window and slap his loose mouth. Then the boy looked away, picked a thread indifferently from his sleeve, stared moodily as if tasting some overripe self-pity or some rich revenge. Prescott took Carol's arm and pulled her into the diner.

"Quite a young man," he said.

Her look was sober. "Don't be too hard on him."

"Why not?"

"Because everybody always has been."

He passed her the menu. "Mother loved me, but she died."

"Stop it, Charlie!"

He was astonished. "All right," he said at last. "Forget it."

While they were eating dessert she ordered two hamburgers to go, and when she passed them through the car window Johnny Bane took them without a word. "What do you want to do?" she said. "Come along, or have us drop you somewhere?"

"Okay if I go along?"

"Sure."

"Okay."

In a street to which she drove, a peddler pushed a cart full of peppers and small Mexican bananas through the mud between dingy frame buildings. No one else was on the street, but two children were climbing through the windows of a half-burned house. The rain angled across, fine as mist.

"What's here?" Prescott said.

"This is a family I've known ever since I worked for Welfare," Carol said. "Grandmother with asthma, father with dropsy, half a dozen little rickety kids. This is to prove that bad luck has no sense of proportion."

Fishing for a cigarette, Prescott found the package empty. He tried the pockets of coat and raincoat without success. Carol opened her purse; she too was out. Johnny Bane had been smoking hers all morning.

"We can find a store," she said, and had turned the ignition key to start when Johnny said, "I can go get some for you."

"Oh, say, would you, Johnny? That would be wonderful."

Prescott felt dourly that he was getting an education in social workers. One rule was that the moment your delinquent showed the slightest sign of decency, passed you a cigarette or picked up something you had dropped, you fell on his neck as if he had rescued you from drowning. As a matter of fact, he had felt his own insides twitch with surprised pleasure at Johnny's offer. But then what? he asked himself. After you've convinced him that every little decency of his deserves a hundred times its weight in thanks, then what?

"No stores around here," Johnny said. "Probably the nearest over on Figueroa."

"Oh," she said, disappointed. "Then I guess we'd better drive down. That's too far to walk."

"You go ahead, do your business here," Johnny said. He leaned forward with his hands on the back of the front seat. "I take the car and go get some weeds, how's that?"

Prescott waited to hear what she would say, but he really knew. After a pause her quiet voice said, "Have you got a driver's license?"

"Sure, man, right here."

"All right," she said, and stepped out. "Don't be long. Charlie dies by inches without smokes."

While Prescott unloaded, Johnny slid under the wheel. He was as jumpy as a greyhound. His fingers wrapped around the wheel with love.

"Wait," Carol said. "I didn't give you any money."

With an exclamation Prescott fished a dollar bill from his pocket and threw it into the seat, and Johnny Bane let off the emergency and rolled away.

"What was that?" Prescott said. "Practical sociology?"

"Don't be so indignant," she said. "You trust people, and maybe that teaches them to trust you."

"Why should anybody but a hooligan have to be *taught* to trust you? Are you so unreliable?"

But she only shook her head at him, smiling and denying his premises, as they went up the rotted steps.

This house was more than the others. It was not merely poor, it was dirty, and it was not merely dirty, but sick. Prescott looked it over for picture possibilities while Carol talked with a thin Mexican woman, worn to the bleak collarbones with arms like sticks. In the kitchen the sink was stopped with a greasy rag, and dishes swam in water the color of burlap. On the table were three bowls with brown juice dried in them. There was a hole clear through the kitchen wall. In the front room, on an old taupe overstuffed sofa, the head of the house lay in a blanket bathrobe, his thickened legs exposed, his eyes mere slits in the swollen flesh of his face. By the window in the third room an old woman sat in an armchair, and everywhere, in every corner and behind every broken piece of furniture, were staring broad-faced children, incredibly dirty and as shy as mice. In a momentary pause in Carol's talk he heard the native sounds of this house: the shuffle of children's bare feet and the old woman's harsh breathing.

He felt awkward, and an intruder. Imprisoned by the rain, quelled by the presence of the Welfare lady and the strange man, the children crept soft as lizards around the walls. Wanting a cigarette worse than ever, Prescott glanced impatiently at his watch. Probably Johnny would stop for a malt or drive around showing off the car and come in after an hour expecting showers of thanks.

"What do you think, Charlie?" Carol's voice had dropped; the bare walls echoed to any noise, the creeping children and the silent invalids demanded hushed voices and soft feet. "Portrait shots?" she whispered. "All this hopeless sickness?"

"They'll be heartbreakers."

"That's what they ought to be."

Even when he moved her chair so that gray daylight fell across her face, the old woman paid no attention to him beyond a first piercing look. Her head was held stiffly, her face as still as wood, but at every breath the cords in her neck moved slightly with the effort. He got three time exposures of that half-raised weathered mask; flash would have destroyed what the gray light revealed.

Straightening up from the third one, he looked through the doorway into the inhuman swollen face of the son. It was impossible to tell whether the Chinese slits of eyes were looking at him or not. He was startled with the thought that they might be, and wished again, irritably, for a cigarette.

"Our friend is taking his time," he said to Carol, and held up his watch.

"Maybe he couldn't find a store."

Prescott grunted, staring at the dropsical man. If he shot across the swollen feet and legs, foreshortening them, and into the swollen face, he might get something monstrous and sickening, a picture to make people wince.

"Can he be propped up a little?" he asked.

Carol asked the thin, hovering wife, who said he could. The three of them lifted and slid the man up until his shoulders were against the wall. It troubled Prescott to see Carol's hands touch the repulsive flesh. The man's slits watched them; the lips moved, mumbling something.

"What's he say?"

"He says you must be a lover of beauty," Carol said.

For a moment her eyes held his, demanding of him something that he hated to give. Once, on his only trip to Mexico, he had gone hunting with his host in Michoacán, and he remembered how he had fired at a noise in a tree and brought something crashing down, and how they had run up to see a little monkey lying on the bloodied leaves. It was still alive; as they came up its eyes followed them, and at a certain moment it put up its arms over its head to ward off the expected death blow. To hear this monster make a joke was like seeing that monkey put up its arms in an utterly human gesture. It sickened him so that he took refuge behind the impersonality of the camera, and when he had taken his pictures he said something that he had not said to a subject all day. "Thanks," he said. *"Gracias, señor."*

Somehow he had to counteract that horrible portrait with something sweet. He posed the thin mother and one of the children in a sentimental Madonna and Child pose, pure poster art suitable for a fund-raising campaign. While he was rechecking for the second exposure he heard the noise, like a branch being dragged across gravel. It came from the grandmother. She sat in the same position by the window of the other room, but she seemed straighter and more rigid, and he had an odd impression that she had grown in size.

The thin woman was glancing uneasily from Prescott to Carol. The moment he stepped back she was out of her chair and into the other room.

The grandmother had definitely grown in size. Prescott watched her with a wild feeling that anyone in this house might suddenly blow up with the obscene swelling disease. Under the shawl the old woman's chest rose in jerky breaths, but it didn't go down between inhalations. Her gray face shone with sudden sweat; her mouth was open, her head held stiffly to one side.

"Hadn't I better try to get a doctor?" Prescott said.

Bending over the old woman, Carol turned only enough to nod.

Prescott went quickly to the door. The peddler had disappeared, the children who had been climbing in the burned house were gone, the street lay empty in the rain. Johnny Bane had been gone for over an hour; if this woman died he could take the credit. In a district like this there might not be a telephone for blocks. Prescott would have to run foolishly like someone shouting fire.

A girl of ten or so, sucking her thumb, slid along the wall, watching him. He trapped her. "Where's there a telephone?"

She stared, round-eyed and scared.

"*Teléfono?* You *sabe teléfono?*"

He saw comprehension grow in her face, slapped a half-dollar into her hand, motioned her to start leading him. She went down the steps and along the broken sidewalk at a trot.

It took four calls from the little neighborhood grocery before he located a doctor who could come. Then, the worst cause for haste removed, he paused to buy cigarettes for himself and a bag of suckers for the children. His guide put a sucker in her mouth and a hand in his, and they walked back that way through the drizzle.

The street before the house was still empty, and he cursed Johnny Bane. Inside, the grandmother was resting after her paroxysm, but her head was still stiffly tilted, and a minute after he entered she fell into a fit of coughing that pebbled her lips with mucus and brought her halfway to her feet, straining and struggling for air. Carol and the thin woman held her, eased her back.

"Did you get someone?" Carol said.

"He's on his way."

"Did he tell you anything to do?"

"There's nothing to do except inject atropine or something. We have to wait for him."

"Hasn't Johnny come back?"

"Did you really expect him to?"

Her eyes and mouth were strained. She no longer looked like a college sophomore; a film from the day's poverty and sickness had rubbed off on her. Without a word she turned away, went into the kitchen, and started clearing out the sink.

As Prescott started to pack up it occurred to him that a picture of an old woman choking to death would add to the sociological impact of Carol's series, but he was damned if he would take it. He'd had enough for one day. The dropsical man turned his appalling swollen mask, and on an impulse Prescott stood up and gestured with the packet of cigarettes. The monster nodded, so Prescott inserted a cigarette between the lips and lighted it. Sight of the man smoking fascinated him.

The Rolleiflex was just going into the bag when it struck him that he had not seen the Contax. He rummaged, turned things out on to the floor. The camera was gone. Squatting on his heels, he considered how he should approach the mother of the house, or Carol, to get it back from whichever child had taken it. And then he began to wonder if it had been there when he unpacked for this job. He had used it at the Aguirre house for one picture, but not since. The bag had been in the car all the time he and Carol had been eating lunch. So had Johnny Bane.

Carefully refusing to have any feeling at all about the matter, he took his equipment out on the porch. Four or five children, each with a sucker in its mouth, came out and shyly watched him as he smoked and waited for the doctor.

The doctor was a short man with an air of unhurried haste. He examined the grandmother for perhaps a minute and got out a needle. The woman's eyes followed his hands with terror as he swabbed with an alcohol-soaked pad, jabbed, pushed with his thumb, withdrew, dropped needle and syringe into his case. It was like an act of deadpan voodoo. Within minutes the old woman was breathing almost normally, as if the needle had punctured her swelling and let her subside. For a minute more the doctor talked with Carol; he scribbled on a pad. Then his eyes darted into the next room to where the swollen son lay watching from his slits.

"What's the matter in here?"

"Dropsy," Carol said. "He's been bedridden for months."

"Dropsy's a symptom, not a disease," the doctor said, and went over.

In ten more minutes they were all out on the porch again. "I'll expect you to call me then," the doctor said.

"I will," Carol said. "You bet I will."

"Are you on foot? Can I take you anywhere?"

"No thanks. We're just waiting for my car."

It was then four-thirty. Incredulously Prescott watched her sit down on the steps to wait some more. The late sun, scattering the mist, touched her fair hair and deepened the lines around her mouth. Behind her the children moved softly. Above her head the old porch pillar was carved with initials and monikers: GJG, Mingo, Lola, Chavo, Pina, Juanito. A generation of lost kids had defaced even the little they had, as they might deface and abuse anyone who tried to help them in ways too unselfish for them to understand.

"How long do you expect to sit here?" he said finally.

"Give him another half hour."

"He could have gone to Riverside for cigarettes and been back by now."

"I know."

"You know he isn't going to come back until he's brought."

"He was upset about his girl," she said. "He felt he'd been kicked in the face. Maybe he went up there."

"To do what? Cut her throat?"

"It isn't impossible," she said, and turned her eyes up to his with so much anxiety in them that he hesitated a moment before he told her the rest.

"Maybe it isn't," he said then, "but I imagine he went first of all to a pawnshop to get rid of the camera."

"Camera?"

"He swiped the Contax while we were having lunch."

"How do you know?"

"Either that or one of the kids here took it."

Her head remained bent down; she pulled a sliver from the step. "It couldn't have been here. I was here all the time. None of the children went near your stuff."

She knew so surely what Johnny Bane was capable of, and yet she let it trouble her so, that he was abruptly furious with her. Social betterment, sure, opportunities, yes, a helping hand, naturally. But to lie down and let a goon like that walk all over you, abuse your confidence, lie and cheat and steal and take advantage of every unselfish gesture!

"Listen," he said. "Let me give you a life history. We turn him in and he comes back in handcuffs. Okay. That's six months in forestry camp, unless he's been there before."

"Once," she said, still looking down. "He was with a bunch that swiped a truck."

"Preston then," Prescott said. "In half a year he comes back from Preston and imposes on you some more, and you waste yourself keeping him out of trouble until he gets involved in something in spite of you, something worse, and gets put away for a stretch in San Quentin. By the time they let him out of there he'll be ripe for really big-time stuff, and after he's sponged on you for a while longer he'll shoot somebody in a hold-up or knife somebody in a whorehouse brawl, and they'll lead him off to the gas chamber. And nothing you can do will keep one like him from going all the way."

"It doesn't have to happen that way. There's a chance it won't."

"It's a hell of a slim chance."

"I know it," she said, and looked up again, her face not tearful or sentimental as he had thought it would be, but simply thoughtful. "Slim or not, we have to give it to him."

"You've already given him ten chances."

"Even then," she said. "He's everything you say—he's mean, vicious, dishonest, boastful, vain, maybe dangerous. I don't like him any better than you do, any better than he likes himself. But he's told me things I don't think he ever told anyone else."

"He never had such a soft touch," he said.

"He grew up in a slum, Harlem. Routine case. His father disappeared before he was born, his mother worked, whatever she could find. He took care of himself."

"I understand that," Prescott said. "He's a victim. He isn't to blame for what his life made him. But he's still unfit to live with other people. He isn't safe. Nine out of ten, maybe, you can help, but not his kind. It's too bad, but he's past helping."

"He wasn't a gang kid," she said. "He's unattractive, don't you see, and mean. People don't like him, and never did. He tries to run with the neighborhood Mexican gang here, but you saw how Chuey and Dago and Lupe just tolerate him. He doesn't belong. He never did. So he prowled the alleys and dreamed up fancy revenges for people he hated, and played with stray cats."

Prescott moved impatiently, and the children slid promptly further along the wall. Carol was watching him as steadily as the children were.

"He told me how he ran errands to earn money for liver and fish to feed them. He wanted them to come to him and be *his* cats."

Prescott waited, knowing how the script ran but surprised that Carol, a hardened case worker, should have fallen for it.

"But they were all alley cats, as outcast as he was," she said. "He'd feed a cat for a week, but when he didn't have anything for it, it would shy away, or he'd grab it and get clawed. So he used to try to tie cats up when he caught them."

Prescott said nothing.

"But when a cat wouldn't let itself be petted, or when it fought the rope—and it always did—he'd swing it by the rope and break its neck," Carol said.

She stirred the litter in the step corner and a sow bug rolled into its ball and bounced down into the dirt. " 'I give them every chance, Miss Vaughn,' that's what he told me. 'I give them every chance and if they won't come and be my friend I pop their neck.' "

Cautiously Prescott moved the camera bag backwards with his foot. He looked at the afternoon's grime in the creases of his hands. "That's a sad story," he said at last. "I mean it, it really is. But it only proves what I said, that he's too warped to run loose. He might try that neck-popping on some human being who wouldn't play his way—Lupe, for instance."

"Would you pop a cat's neck if it wouldn't come to you?" Carol said softly.

"Don't be silly."

"But you'd pop Johnny's."

They stared at each other in the rainy late afternoon.

Prescott told himself irrelevantly that he had not fallen in love with her on this job. Anyone who fell in love with her would have to share her with every stray in Greater Los Angeles. But he liked her and respected her and admired her; she was a fine human being. Only she carried it too far.

And yet he had no answer for her. "Good God," he said, "do you know what you're asking?"

"Yes," she said. "I know exactly. But I know you can't come with liver and fish heads six days a week and on the seventh come with a hangman's rope. You can't say, 'I gave him every chance,' unless you really did."

The brief sun had disappeared again in the mist and smog. The street was muddy and gray before them. Behind them the thin woman came to the door and opened it, shooing the children in with an unexpected harsh snarl in her voice. Prescott felt disturbed and alien, out of his proper setting and out of his depth. But he still could find no answer for her. You could not come with liver and fish heads six days a week and with a hangman's knot on the seventh. You could not put limits on love—if love was what you chose to live by.

"All right," he said. "We don't call the cops, is that it?"

She smiled a crooked smile. "Let's try to get along without the police as long as we can."

The thin woman stood in the doorway and said good-bye and watched them down the steps, and the children pressing around her flanks watched too. Prescott waved, and the woman smiled and nodded in reply. But none of the children, solemnly staring, raised a hand. After a moment he was angry with himself for having expected them to.

MAIDEN
IN A
TOWER

The highway entering Salt Lake City from the west curves around the southern end of Great Salt Lake past Black Rock and its ratty beaches, swings north away from the spouting smoke of the smelter towns, veers toward the onion-shaped domes of the Saltair Pavilion, and straightens out eastward again on the speedway. Ahead, across the white flats, the city and its mountains are a mirage, or a mural: metropolitan towers, then houses and trees and channeled streets, and then the mountain wall.

Driving into that, Kimball Harris began to feel like the newsreel diver whom the reversed projector sucks feet first out of his splash. Perhaps fatigue from the hard day and a half across the desert explained both the miragelike look of the city and his own sense that he was being run backward toward the beginning of the reel. But the feeling grew as he bored townward along the straight road, the same road out which, as a high school boy, he had driven much too fast in a stripped-down Ford bug with screaming companions in the rumble seat. They must have driven back, too, but he remembered only the going out. To see the city head-on, like this, was strange to him.

Middle-aged, rather tired, but alert with the odd notion that he was returning both through distance and through time, he passed the airport and the fair grounds and slowed for the first streets of the city.

Twenty-five years had made little difference. The city had spread some, and he was surprised, after the desert, by the green luxuriance of the trees, but the streets were still a half-mile wide, and water still ran in the gutters. It was really a good town, clean, with a freshness about it that revived him. Circling the Brigham Young monument, he nodded gravely to the figure with the outstretched hand, and like a native returning, he went through the light and turned around the button in the middle of the block and came back to park before the Utah Hotel, careful to park well out from the curb so as not to block the flowing gutter. They gave you a ticket for that. It tickled him that he had remembered.

The doorman collared his bag; a bellhop climbed in to take the car around to the garage. Still running pleasantly backward into the reel, he went into the unchanged lobby and registered, and was carried up the unchanged elevators to the kind of room he remembered, such a room as they used to take when they held fraternity parties in the hotel, back in Prohibition times. During those years he had been on a diet for ulcers, and couldn't drink, but he had retired religiously with the boys, gargled raw Green River redeye, and spat it out again in the washbowl, only for the pleasure of lawbreaking and of carrying a distinguished breath back to the ballroom and the girls.

He shook his head, touched for a moment with his giddy and forgotten youth.

Later, fresh from the shower, with a towel around him, he picked up the telephone book, so dinky and provincial-seeming after the ponderous San Francisco directory that he caught himself feeling protective about it. But when he found the Merrill Funeral Parlors in the yellow pages he sat thinking, struck by the address: 363 East South Temple. On the Avenues side, just below Fourth East. He tried to visualize that once familiar street but it was all gone except for a general picture of tall stone and brick houses with high porches and lawns overtaken by plantain weeds. One, the one Holly had lived in, had a three-story stone tower.

That tower! With all the Jazz Age Bohemians crawling in and out.

Havelock Ellis, Freud, Mencken, *The Memoirs of Fanny Hill, Love's Coming of Age, The Well of Loneliness*, Harry Kemp, Frank Harris. My Lord.

He was flooded with delighted recollection, they were all before him: reed-necked aesthetes, provincial cognoscenti, sad sexy yokels, lovers burning with a hard gemlike flame, a homosexual or two trying to look blasted and corroded by inward sin. Painters of bile-green landscapes, cubist photographers, poets and iconoclasts, scorners of the bourgeoisie, makers of cherished prose, dream-tellers, correspondence-school psychoanalysts, they had swarmed through Holly's apartment and eddied around her queenly shape with noises like breaking china. He remembered her in her gold gown, a Proserpine or a Circe. For an instant she was slim and tall in his mind and he saw her laughing in the midst of the excitement she created, and how her hair was smooth black and her eyes very dark blue and how she wore massive gold hoops in her ears.

He wrote the number down and tucked it in the pocket of the suit laid out on the bed. But when he had dressed and gone down and was walking up South Temple past Beehive House, Lion House, Eagle Gate, the old and new apartment buildings, he began to look at numbers with a feeling that approached suspense, and he searched not so much for the Merrill Funeral Parlors as for the house with the round stone tower. Finally he saw it, lifting across the roof of a mansion gone to seed, and in another thirty paces he could see the sign and the new brass numbers on the riser of the top porch step. It was the very house.

Quickly he looked around for landmarks to restore and brace his memory. Some of the old maples and hickories he remembered along the sidewalk were gone, the terrace rolled down with an unfamiliar smooth nap of grass. The porch no longer carried its sagging swing, and porch and steps had been renewed and painted. The door was as he remembered it, with lozenges of colored glass above it, and the doorknob's massive handful was an almost startling familiarity. But inside all was changed. Partitions had been gutted out. The stairs now mounted, or levitated, a spiral of white spokes and mahogany rails, from an expanse of plum-colored carpet. Instead of the cupping old parquetry his feet found softness, hushedness. The smells were of paint and flowers.

He was eyeing the stairs when a young man came out of an office on the left and bent his head a little leftward and said softly and pleasantly, "Yes, sir. Can I help?"

Harris brought himself dryly back to what he had driven eight hundred miles to do. He said, "I'm Kimball Harris. My aunt, Mrs. George Webb, died day before yesterday at the Julia Hicks Home. They telephoned me she would be here."

"We've been expecting you," the young man said, and put out his hand. "My name is McBride." A brief handshake, a moment when the young man regarded Harris with his head tilted. "Did you fly in?" he asked.

"Drove."

"All the way from San Francisco?"

"I slept a few hours in Elko."

"It wasn't so bad, then."

"Oh, no," Harris said. "Not bad at all."

In his mind was a faint amusement: this young man might have been left over from one of Holly's parties. He looked better equipped to write fragile verses than deal with corpses.

"She's in the parlor just back here," McBride said. "Would you like to see her? She looks very nice."

That would be young McBride's function, of course. He would be the one who made them look nice. "Maybe later," Harris said. "I expect there are some details we ought to settle."

"Of course," McBride said. "If you'll just step in here. We can look at caskets after a minute. You have a family cemetery plot, I believe? It will only take a minute for this. The details you can leave to us." He held the door wide, standing gracefully and deferentially back, and ushered Harris through.

A very few minutes seemed to settle the details. They rose, facing each other across the desk coolly glimmering in muted afternoon light. "Now would you like to see her?" McBride said.

Why, he takes pride, Harris thought. He probably stands back estimating his effects like a window dresser. Mister McBride, the Mortuary Max Factor. "All right," he said, "though it's not as if I had any tears to shed. I haven't seen her for twenty-five years, and she's been senile for ten."

McBride guided him around the unfamiliar stairs to where the plum carpet flowed smoothly into what had evidently once been a dining-room. "She does look nice," he said. "Very sweet and peaceful."

Which is more than she did alive, Harris thought, and went forward to the table with the basket of chrysanthemums at its foot. To remind himself that this was his mother's sister, his last near relative, made him feel nothing. Not even a deliberate attempt to squeeze sentimental recollections out of the past and remember suppers at Aunt Margaret's, Christmas visits at Aunt Margaret's, times when Aunt Margaret had unexpectedly given him a quarter, made the wax figure any dearer or realer. His indifference was so marked that he separated it and noticed it, wondering with a tinge of shame if he was callous. He supposed that if he had been attached to the dead woman he might think her peaceful, touching, even terrible. All he could think as he looked at her was that she looked well-embalmed—but then she had probably been close to mummified before she died.

Old Aunt Margaret, never very lovable, never dear to him in his childhood, and in his maturity only a duty and an expense, thrust her sharp nose, sharp cheekbones, withered lips, up through the rouge and lipstick and was, if she was not a total stranger, only old Aunt Margaret, mercifully dead at eighty-three. Harris did not even feel the conventional disgust with young McBride, who tampered with the dead. Considering what he had had to work with, McBride had done reasonably well.

Back in the hall again, he stood looking up the spiral stairs, apparently as unsupported as the Beanstalk, and remembered a time when Holly and three room-mates—which three didn't matter, they changed so fast—came down the shabby old steps arguing about the proportions of the perfect female figure, and he met them on the second landing, and like a chorus line they raised their skirts and thrust out their right legs before him, clamoring to know which was the most shapely. An undergraduate Paris and four demanding goddesses. He had picked Holly; why would he not?

McBride was in the office doorway. "We've just redone the whole place," he said. "It was the home of a Park City silver king originally, but it was all run-down."

Harris was still looking up the stairs. McBride's words were no more important than the decorative changes, but upstairs there was something that *was* important, that pulled at him like an upward draft.

"I used to know this house twenty-five years ago," he said, "Some people I knew had an apartment on the third floor."

"Really? The front one or the back?"

"Front. The one with the round tower window."

"Oh, yes," said McBride. "We haven't done much to that yet—just painted it."

"I wonder," Harris said, and made a little shrugging deprecatory motion and felt irritably ashamed, like a middle-aged man recalling last night's revels and his own unseemly capers and his pawing of the host's wife. It was fatuous to want to go up there, yet he did.

"Go on up if you want," McBride said. "The only thing, there's a woman laid out there."

"Well, then . . ."

"That wouldn't matter, if you don't mind. She's . . . presentable."

For a moment Harris hung on the word, and on the thought that McBride's professional vanity was one of the odder kinds, and on a little fit of irritability that a corpse should intrude upon a sentimental but perfectly legitimate impulse. Then he put his hand on the mahogany rail. "Maybe I will."

The second-floor hall, at whose doors he had knocked or entered, was as much changed as the ground floor, but up the second flight of stairs he mounted into a growing familiarity. And he climbed against the pressure of a crowd of ghosts. The carpet ended at the stairhead; he put his feet down softly and held back his breath with the wild notion that he heard voices from the door of Holly's old apartment. Up these stairs, a hundred, two hundred, three hundred times, through how long? a year? two years? he had come with books or bottles or manuscripts in his hands and (it seemed to him now) an incomparable capacity for enthusiasm in his heart. From the high burlap-hung windows of the apartment inside they had let their liquid ridicule fall on the streets of the bourgeois city. He half expected, as he moved into the doorway, to see their faces look up inquiringly from chair and couch and floor.

But in the room there was only the dead woman, and she was not looking at him.

She lay on a wheeled table, with beside her one stiff chair and a tabouret bearing a bowl of flowers, all of it composed as if for a macabre still life. Looking toward the window across the woman's body, he saw how the gray light of afternoon blurred in her carefully waved hair.

For a minute or two, perhaps, he stood in the doorway, stopped partly by the body and partly by the feeling of an obscure threat. He must summon and gather and re-create his recollections of this room; he was walking in a strange neighborhood and needed his own gang around him.

In Holly's time the tower bay had held an old upright piano, its backside exposed to the room like the hanging seat of a child's sleepers.

Afternoons, evenings, Sunday and holiday mornings, there had been loud four-hand renderings of "Twelfth Street Rag," "St. Louis Blues," "Mood Indigo." On at least one Christmas morning they had even sung carols around it, syncopating them wickedly. That was the morning when he brought Holly the facsimile copy of *The Marriage of Heaven and Hell*—a mutinous book full of mottoes for their personalities and their times.

But what he remembered now, hanging in the doorway, was how in some lull in the bedlam that always went on there they had found themselves smiling foolishly at each other by the piano and she had put up her hands to his face and kissed him sweet and soft, a kiss like a happy child's. He realized now that he had recalled that kiss before, waking or sleeping, and that the memory of it had acquired a kind of caption, a fragment of the world's wisdom contributed to his adolescent store by a returned Mormon missionary: "*Das ewig Weibliche zieht uns hinan*," that remembered moment said.

How they had flocked and gathered there, debated, kissed, lied, shocked and astonished and delighted each other, there in the tower with Holly at their center, there by the vanished piano: poets and athletes, Renaissance heroes, fearless Stoics and impassioned Epicureans and abandoned Hedonists, girls with the bloom on their loveliness, goddesses with Perfect Proportions, artists and iconoclasts, as delighted with their own wickedness as if it had meant something.

He felt the stairs in his legs, the years in his mind, as he went in softly past the woman who lay so quietly on her back, and when he had passed her he turned and searched her face, almost as if he might surprise in it some expression meaningful to this wry and confusing return.

She was a plain woman, perhaps fifty. McBride had not yet made her look nice with rouge and lipstick. She lay in a simple black dress, but she had a Navajo squash-blossom necklace around her throat. It struck him as a remarkable piece of realism—perhaps something she had especially liked and had stubbornly worn even past the age when costume jewelry became her. It gave her a touching, naïvely rakish air.

Yet she shed a chill around her, and her silence spread to fill the room. Hardly a sound came through the stone walls. In the old days there had always been the piano banging, the phonograph going, two or six or sixteen voices making cosmic conversation. And he never remembered daylight in the apartment. Holly had affected a romantic gloom; the windows were always shrouded by the artistically frayed burlap, and the light was from lamps, most of them low on the floor and some of them at least with red globes in them. And always the smell of sandalwood.

Like a Chinese whorehouse. He shook his head, pitying and entranced, and sat down on the window seat overlooking the reach of South Temple. Directly across was a Five Minute Car Wash with a big apron of concrete and a spick dazzle of white paint and red tiles. In the times he remembered, that lot had held a Peewee Golf Course where men in shirt sleeves, women in summer dresses, young couples loud with laughter, putted little white balls along precise green alleys and across precise circles of green artificial grass and over gentle and predictable bridges and causeways into numbered holes.

"Look at them," Holly said to him once as they sat in the tower looking down at the after-dinner golfers moving under the bright floodlights. "*Toujours gai*, my God. Some day I'm going to build a miniature golf course with fairways six inches wide and rough all over the place. I'll fill the water holes with full-sized crocodiles and sow the sandtraps with sidewinders. How would it be to hide a black widow spider in every hole so that holing out and picking up your ball would earn you some excitement? What if you sawed the supports of all the little bridges nearly in two?"

Live it dangerously. It was strange to recall how essential that had seemed. Go boom, take chances. He touched the casement windows, thinking that this was the pose, sitting right here and looking out, that Holly had assumed when Tom Stead painted her in her gold velvet gown.

Probably that portrait wasn't anything special. It couldn't have been. The chances were that Tom Stead was painting signs somewhere now, if he hadn't drunk himself to death. But then, in this room, in the presence of its subject whose life overflowed upon them all, that slim golden shape with the velvet highlights was Lilith, Helen, Guenevere, *das ewig Weibliche*. And it was hardly a day before other girls, less fortunately endowed or graced, had begun dropping comments on how *warm* that Stead-Holly romance was getting, and hinting that there was hidden away somewhere a companion portrait—a nude.

Well, well, what a bunch of Bohemian puritans. Harris did not believe in any nude, or in its importance if there had been one, though at the time it had bothered him, and he had been malely offended, surprised that she would *lower* herself, you know?

Now, sitting bemused in the window, he reflected that what had truly shone out of that golden portrait, as out of Holly herself, was not so much glamour as innocence. Under the sheath she was positively virginal; if you cracked the enamel of her sophistication you found a delighted little girl playing Life.

Again he remembered the soft, childlike kiss by the piano on a Christmas morning, and he stood up so sharply that he startled himself with the sight of the dead woman. It *was* innocence. She could put away the predatory paws of college boys, twist laughing from the casual kiss, pass among the hot young Freudians as untouched as a nun, shed like water the propositions that were thrown at her seven to the week. There she sat in her gold gown by her window opening on the foam: a maiden in a tower.

He crossed the room and tried the bedroom door, wanting to look in on her intimately. In this room, now completely bare, aseptically painted, he had sat dozens of times when she was ill or when on Sunday mornings she made it a charming point of her sophistication to entertain in bed. While she lay propped with pillows he had read to her, talked to her, kissed her, had his hands fended away. The empty room was still charged with the vividness with which she invested everything. There was one night very late, two or three o'clock, when he had sat on one side of the bed and a mournful and lovesick jazz trumpeter had sat on the other, neither willing to leave the other alone there, and all that night he had read aloud into the smell of sandalwood the life story of a mad woman from Butte, Montana. *I, Mary MacLean*, that one was called.

What an occasion she made of it, laid up by flu, hemmed in by rival young men, covered to the chin in an absurd, high-necked, old-fashioned nightgown, taking aspirin with sips of ginger beer, laughing at them alternately or together with that face as vivid on the pillow as a flower laid against the linen. It was innocence. In that crackpot Bohemian pre-crash wonderful time, it was innocence.

How he and the trumpeter broke the deadlock, what had ever happened to the Tom Stead flurry, what had happened to any of Holly's string of admirers—all gone. She sent them away, or they quarreled at her over their bruised egos, or they grew huffy at finding her always in a crowd. Plenty of self-appointed humming-bird catchers, but no captures.

And yet, maybe . . .

* * *

Summer and winter, day and night were telescoped in his memory. How old would he have been? Twenty? Twenty-one? It must have been near the end of Holly's reign in this apartment, before everything went sour and the delayed wave of the crash reached them and he left school to go to work and Holly herself went away. There was neither beginning nor end nor definite location in time to what he most vividly remembered. What they were doing, whether there had been a party there or whether they had been out on a date, whether she had room-mates then or was living alone, none of that came back. But they were alone in a way they had seldom been.

They must have been talking, something must have led up to it, for there she was with the clarity of something floodlighted in his mind, Holly pressing against him and crying with her face against his chest, clinging and crying and saying—he heard only the refrain, not the garble against his chest—"Kim, Kim, get me out of here! I want to get out of this. This is all no good, I've got to, Kim, please!"

Both the tears and the way she clung excited him. But the game had been played so long by other rules that he went on in the old way, laughing, burlesquing gestures of consolation, patting the crow-wing hair, saying, "There, there, little girl." Inanities, idiocies . . . She wore an evening dress cut very low in the back, and he played his fingers up and down her spine. He slid his hand in against her skin, slid it further, expecting the competent twist and shrug and fending and the laugh that would mean the emotional fit was over. But his hand went on around, clear around, and with a shock like an internal explosion he found it cupping the frantic softness of her breast.

Even in recollection, all his sensations were shocking to him. He remembered how smoothly the curve of her side swelled upward, how astonishingly *consecutive* her body seemed. Also, also, and almost with revulsion, how rigid and demanding the nipple of her breast. Innocence—he had never touched a girl there, never imagined, or rather had imagined wrong. Stupefied by the sudden admission to her flesh, made uneasy by the way she crowded and clung, he stood wrapping her awkwardly, and kissed her and tasted her tears, and thought with alarm and conviction of Tom Stead and the rumored nude, and was anguished with eagerness to escape.

He could remember not a scrap, not a detail, of how he got away. She offered herself passionately in his memory, and that was all. The

Peewee Golfer putting his little white ball up the little green alley of his youth came suddenly upon the sidewinder in the sandtrap, the crocodile in the artificial lake.

Harris closed the door on the ridiculous and humiliating memory. It had begun to occur to him that he had been an extraordinary young man, and very little of what had been extraordinary about himself pleased him. Innocence? Well, maybe, though there were more contemptuous names for it. He had been a fraud, a gargler of whiskey he would obediently not drink. A great yapper with the crowd, but when the cat stopped running, what a frantic sliding to a stop, what digging not to catch what he was after.

Weakly he tried to prop up the slack thing he had been. He told himself that it was a pose with all of them, the life that revolved around Holly was an absurd and perhaps touching and certainly unimportant part of growing up. Or was it? What might he be at this moment, would he have more or less to regret, if he had taken Holly at her passionate word, married her, lived it, as she was determined to live it in her innocence, dangerously?

The last time he saw Holly she was boarding a train for Seattle, on her way to Shanghai and a job they all publicly envied but would probably not have risked taking themselves. Her life, whatever happened to her, would not have been dull. And yet it might have been more thoroughly wasted than at that moment he thought his own had been.

He had played it the other way, not so much from choice as from yielding to pressures, and he had done the best he could with it. How would he look to Holly now, at this very minute? How had he looked then?

Like a bubble of gas from something submerged and decaying in deep water, there rose to the surface of his mind one of Blake's "Proverbs of Hell" that they had admired together that long-gone Christmas morning. It burst, and it said, "Prudence is a rich ugly old maid courted by Incapacity."

It shamed him to remember, though he half repudiated it. From the life of prudence he had got a wife he loved and respected, children he adored, a job he could do with interest and almost with content. He regretted none of them. But he stood here remembering that moment when Holly stopped playing make-believe, and it seemed to him that his failure to take her when she offered herself was one of the saddest failures of his life. The fact that he might make all the same crucial choices the same way if he had them to make again helped not at all; it did him no good to remind himself that no one could turn in any direction without turning his back on something. The past had trapped him, and it held him like pain.

Angrily he looked at his watch. Past five. Starting for the door, he passed the dead woman's table and saw her calm pale face, the skin delicately wrinkled like the skin of a winter-kept apple, but soft-looking, as if it would be not unpleasant to touch. What was her name, what had she died of, what had she looked like when she wore expression? Who mourned her, who had loved her, what things in her life did they regret or had she regretted? Would they think it disagreeable that a total stranger had been alone with her here, staring into her dead face? And in that face what was it that the caution of death enclosed and hid?

The barbaric silver necklace seemed somehow to define her. What it said of frivolity, girlishness, love of ornament and of gaiety and of life made him like her; the way it lay on the sober black crepe breast preached the saddest lesson he had ever learned.

He thought of how she had been transported and tampered with by McBride, and how further touches of disguise would complete her transformation from something real and terrible and lost to something serene, removed, bearable. Alone with her here, before the arrival of others, before she went away, he felt almost an anguish for this woman he had never known, and a strange gratitude that he had been permitted to see her.

Gratitude, or something near it. And yet as he started for the door he threw a sick, apologetic glance around the room as quiet and empty as a chapel, and at the woman who lay so quietly at its center. He meant to tiptoe out, but he heard, almost with panic, the four quick raps his heels made on the bare floor before they found the consoling softness of the stairs.

IMPASSE

By the time they dropped down off the heights, the reluctant sun, which had hung interminably on the Col de Vence and forced Louis to dodge and shield his eyes as he cramped the Citroën around the curves, had finally been dragged below the rim, and the glare of the day was taken off them. Along the grateful gray edge of evening they bounced through the streets of Nice and on to the highway returning back up the coast.

Out on the water it was still full afternoon. Sails passed like gulls; close in, the bay was creased with the water-bug tracks of paddle boats. But where they drove, the day had quieted, and in the confined car the bickering seemed to have quieted, too. Straightening out with the traffic toward Monte Carlo, a drink, dinner, Louis appraised the lengthening silence and grew halfway hopeful.

But he said nothing; the quiet was too pleasant. Only in the sloping windshield he saw the reflection of his wife's face, the mouth drawn down ruefully, and he dropped his hand from the wheel to cover hers. That got him a wan, surprised smile.

Pretending to stretch, he focused his daughter's face in the rearview mirror. No smile there, wan or otherwise. Margaret sat like a captive barbarian queen. Her hair stood up from her forehead in an abrupt black mane. Her eyebrows were heavy, level, finely outlined. Photographs always showed her handsomer than she was, perhaps because photographs, like his shadowed view of her in the mirror, obscured the coarse and roughened skin. But no photograph ever hid what he could not miss now—the arrogant curl of her mouth, the way her eyes looked flatly out in insolence and challenge.

Not a pretty girl. That, of course, was a good part of the trouble. In the windshield he surprised on his own face the rueful, puzzled expression he had seen on his wife's. He heard their friends saying, "How I envy you your three months in France. And how nice you could arrange to take Margaret. How wonderful for all of you, especially for her."

The mildness of evening drifted down off the hills, the first faint, perfumed stirring of the land breeze. Through trees and across gray headlands he saw villas clinging like balconies on the mountain, and turning to see what view they would have, he found Cap Ferrat flood-lighted, sharp and cleanly colored, its white villas and red roofs, gray shore and blue encircling sea drenched in light. It seemed to have emerged that minute from the water, wet and fresh. Stuck behind the stinking exhaust of a bus, he watched the promontory, and forgetting that they were silent and at odds, he said, "Somerset Maugham has a villa out there somewhere."

Jean looked, interested. She had read everything Somerset Maugham ever wrote. But from the back seat, Louis heard what he knew he should have anticipated—the contemptuous noise and the voice. "What are we supposed to do about *that?* Make a pilgrimage?"

Patience, he told himself. Aloud he said lightly, "Nothing as strenuous as that, I guess."

"Everybody's got a villa around here someplace, the King of Sweden and the Aga Khan and the Duke of Windsor and King Farouk— everybody you ever heard of. Why go into a tizzy about an old hack like Maugham?"

"Did I go into a tizzy?" Louis said.

"Anyway, how did we get so superior to a great writer all of a sudden?" Jean said, turning half around. "If we're taking that tone, what's so fascinating about King Farouk?"

"I didn't say he was fascinating."

"You implied he was a whole lot more fascinating than Maugham."

"That wouldn't be hard," Margaret said, and turned from the discussion, leaning out the window and raising her indifferent eyes to the hanging houses of Èze Village high on their crag. Louis opened and closed his hands on the wheel and pulled around the bus.

Curving through Villefranche, they looked across the harbor and saw the slim shapes of three destroyers—beautiful, precise toys. The waterfront was dotted with the white figures of sailors.

"Why, they're American," Jean said.

"The Mediterranean Fleet's visiting for a few days. I saw it in the paper." He waited for some contradiction from Margaret, thinking, If she doesn't say something contentious, it'll be the first time since we came here.

But she was silent, and they climbed, circling a hill, and left that harbor and came above another, and there, too, were ships—two more destroyers, a cruiser, and a tanker. The ragged stone of the mountains pitched down to the man-smoothed cirque of the town and its sea fortress, and on a sudden impulse Louis cramped the steering wheel and turned down a steep, narrow street into Beaulieu.

"Where are you going?" Jean said.

"I thought we might have a drink and maybe dinner here. Is there any reason we have to go back to the hotel?"

She glanced at him curiously, but said nothing. He had a feeling that she was thinking exactly what he was—that anything was better than going back to their suite and being alone with their child.

And what a melancholy pass that was, he thought, as he parked and held open the door. Margaret had always been too much for them. It was as if she were dedicated to revenging herself on them for something, as if her rebellious spirit, which turned on everybody in blind, competitive rage, turned most of all on them.

Looking at her now, her dress wrinkled across her too-heavy hips, her face too strong for a girl's, her hair too blue-black, her skin too rough, Louis felt a sad emptiness, a consciousness of failure and loss. Am I to blame? he asked her or himself or the world. Is it my fault you were born unattractive? How much blame shall parents take for begetting and rearing a child? Is that the matter? Do you resent being born? Or have we compounded failure for eighteen years in your bringing-up?

Touched by pity and love, he took an arm of each of his women to escort them across the street; but Margaret pulled her elbow free and walked alone into the open street along the quay, looking into the doors of cafés and cabarets, from which the noise of American jazz erupted. The street was full of sailors, most of them young, hurrying toward something they were very eager about. Their laughter and loudness insulated them, as if behind a layer of glass; they poured by, unseeing; not one so much as looked at the slouching girl who moved along the wall, and she paid no attention to them.

As Jean and Louis turned on to the quay between awninged cafés and shops on one side and the oily harbor water on the other, Jean said, "She'll just make everybody miserable till she gets her way. She's already spoiled the trip for me. I almost wish we could go home."

"Would it be any better there?" he said. He steered her toward the beckoning finger of a waiter in the last café on the quay, and as he seated her, he saw her biting her lip, close to tears. "What would you like to drink?" he said.

"I don't care. Anything."

"Vermouth cassis?"

"All right."

"Two," he told the waiter, and sat down.

For a while, it was as if they were calm. Across the cobbled street a moored barge rocked and thumped softly against the stone. A half-dozen shrill, bare-legged boys played tag from barge to shore and back again. Down by the corner at which they had entered the waterfront, a Navy launch was unloading sailors. A pair of shore patrol sauntered and watched. The waiter brought their drinks and turned over two saucers. Margaret had wandered past all the cheap shops and was now wandering back again.

"Is she even going to come and sit down with us?" Jean said.

Louis moved his shoulders. "She has to punish us, I expect."

"I wish I knew what for."

"You know what for."

Her eyes, suddenly full again of weak tears, sought his across the table. "How could we fail so badly?" she said. "She's rude, isn't she? She's insolent and rude, and she hates people and lets them know it. Why? You're not that way, and I don't think I am. Where did she learn it?"

Shrugging his shoulders down over his drink, Louis brooded without answering. He remembered how, when Margaret was a child, he had imagined her grown up, imagined them dining out, the attractive girl fresh and interested and warm, clear-colored and with candid eyes, and he protective, gravely courteous, the two of them watched by people because of the obvious trust and gentleness between them. He saw himself standing to help his tall daughter into her wrap, moving with her among the crowded tables of such a sidewalk café as this, in some fashionable international place that would delight her. With his elbows on the table, his hands around the cool glass, he looked up and saw his lumpish, arrogant daughter standing above him with her discontent like alum in her mouth.

He rose, pulled out the chair next to him, and said to her gently, "Sit down, Margaret."

"I'd rather stand."

Jean put in, "Please, you must be tired, dear," and got only an overbearing stare.

Quietly Louis sat down again. A bell clinked rapidly, and the launch started with a roar and swung in a speeding arc toward the cruiser.

After a few seconds its wake spread under the barge and set it to knocking hollowly on the stone. The little French boys squealed and leaped aboard. Sometime before the barge stopped pitching, Margaret abruptly sat down. "I'd like a drink."

Wordlessly Louis signaled the waiter, and when he came, waited wordlessly for his daughter to order. He would not have risked asking her what she wanted.

She kept the waiter standing for thirty seconds and then tossed him the order without looking at him. "Martini, very dry."

The waiter had a dark, smooth face with a prominent widow's peak that looked and might have been the prow of a wig. Stumblingly, not knowing whether or not you said s'il vous plaît to waiters, but determined to say it anyway in penance for Margaret, Louis said in his careful school French, "If you please, two more vermouth cassis and the dinner menu." He couldn't tell whether the waiter was grateful or contemptuous or wore impassiveness like his apron, to keep him from being soiled.

The light was withdrawing; the paved curve of quay and fortifications and the town lost their clean outline in smoky dusk. The ships in the harbor had been prematurely lighted for fifteen minutes; now street lights popped on palely, and one after another the shops glowed. A new load of sailors pulled up to the dock, unloaded, stood in line before the money-changing booth under the eyes of the shore patrol. From a half dozen unseen streets music and talk and laughter emptied on to the dock. The new arrivals seized their handfuls of francs and took off. Their white hats were over their eyes; their walks were shore-leave swaggers.

Louis watched them half in amusement, half in distaste. The irrepressible young heading for a binge, they went past in threes and sixes, and talk poured from them. Of an almost comic variety, little ones and big ones, heavy and light, dark and fair, snake hips and fat hips, they moved with one mind and one compulsion. What are they after? he thought. What do they hope to find? The ancient, waiting town took them in as it had taken sailors from the ships of two thousand years. They would not be different from others; their money and their seed would flow in the same abundance, and the town's ancient professions, ancient beds, ancient stones would accept these, too. The dusk that was rising from buildings and streets and thickening the air along the quay hummed faintly with the revels of antique ghosts.

Jean stirred with a forlorn attempt at comfort and relaxation. She loved coziness; the slightest intrusion of peace into their domestic circle could delude her into gratification. "This is nice," she said. "This was a nice idea, Papa."

He nodded, not to tempt Providence with talk. With Margaret along, conversation was too dangerous. She terrorized them; she was like a rodeo cowboy waiting at the gate, ready to burst out on any bewildered steer of opinion that showed in the arena. If you said anything, affirmed anything, denied anything, liked or disliked anything, you grew horns for her to throw you with.

But she astonished him by saying, "It's at least got it over that phony ritziness at Monte Carlo."

Incautious pleasure was in the look Jean threw Louis. "It has, hasn't it?" she said. "You know, maybe we should move here, if we don't like it there."

"I'm willing."

"All right, let's! It isn't so full of tourists, either."

"Plenty of tourists in sailor suits," Louis said.

"They'll be gone. They don't count. Let's come tomorrow!" Her warm eyes rested on Margaret, slouching in her chair, and something sly moved the corners of her mouth. "Isn't it cool all of a sudden?" she said. "You'll have to grant that the Riviera has *something* nice about it, after all."

"It's all right," Margaret said.

"Maybe it's even as nice as Paris."

Without moving from her slouch, Margaret abandoned docility. Louis could see it happen. "You couldn't resist, could you?" she said. "You had to work in that I-told-you-so. Mother *did* know best, didn't she? Look at the pretty ships, see the handsome sailors. Paris was only a passing fancy, after all, wasn't it?" Like an irritated wild animal—maybe a buffalo, Louis thought, hypnotically watching her—she heaved erect to say loudly, "Paris was *not* a passing fancy! This place is *not* as good as Paris! I can put up with it, but don't feed me that Mother-knows-best stuff!"

"Well, for the love of heaven," Jean said, "what brought on that outburst?"

Margaret gave her a venomous look. "That was no outburst. That was a statement of fact. This place is *not* as good as Paris. I couldn't be less interested in this place. I'm still going to study in Paris next year if it's the last thing I do." Like a truck driver on a narrow road, she crowded Jean into the ditch.

"It's impossible to talk to you," Jean said shakily. "It gives you pleasure to be rude and headstrong. I think you like to hurt us. As for Paris, that's the maddest kind of foolishness."

"Good God, please!" Louis said. The waiter came with the menus, and he ordered dinner for all of them without asking what they wanted. They could eat what they got, *escalopes de veau*, or whatever else. At least they could avoid argument on that.

It was all but dark now; darkness rose from the water to meet the dusk seeping down from the hills; between the two darks the harbor moved in steely glints and darts of red and green. Its sound was a companionable mutter against the quay. On the outer rim of their now dark-enclosed world the ships hung like Christmas decorations, the path that encircled the fort was a half circle of lemon-yellow globes. The mild and misty air took and diffused the light of their water-edged street; from the darker side streets he heard the tom-toms and the squeals. The very thought of all that hopped-up gaiety made him tired. He felt middle-aged and cornered.

With ironic wonder he reflected that some parents, from their children's happy infancy to their successful maturity, had only experiences that inspired affection and pride. Some bright children had no personality problems; they actually liked school, instead of having vomiting spells at six, breaking windows at eight, stealing supplies at ten, defying the teachers at twelve. Some parents had yet to be visited by advisers and child psychologists, who talked of unused capacities and maladjustment and lack of motivation, and who snooped for conflicts in the child's home life and advised more warmth and companionship, the creation of security.

Security! Her parents had created so much security that she could defy them and everything in the world. The very look on her mouth now told him she was coming at him like a fullback.

"How about it?" she demanded.

"How about what?"

"Paris."

"But, Margaret darling, be sensible," Jean said. "What would you do in Paris?"

"Study art," Margaret said, her unblinking eyes on her father.

"Look, Maggie," he said, "has any art teacher in any of your schools told you you had talent?"

"None of them would have known enough to recognize it."

"But you recognize it in yourself."

"Not recognize it, no. I never really *tried* to paint."

"That's what's so foolish!" Jean cried. "I never heard of anything so——"

"Did I ever try anything I didn't do?" she said, still watching Louis. Her nostrils tightened, her lips thrust out in a thin, fierce line. "Maybe I haven't tried very many things, really. Maybe I never gave a damn. But when I set out to beat that snotty Gerhard kid on the rifle team, I did it, didn't I? The only girl that ever made the rifle team. And when I wanted to be editor of the paper, I got to be, didn't I, over the dead bodies of all the snobs in that journalism class?"

"Those weren't exactly major triumphs," he permitted himself to say, thinking that no accomplishment had ever given her pleasure. The only thing that gave her pleasure was to win out over someone she scorned. And she scorned everybody; she walked on prostrate necks. At any minute the ego that steamed inside her could boil over and scald somebody. "Determination is one thing; talent is another," he said quietly.

"*Opportunity* is what I'm talking about," she said. "Do those stupids with the beards have talent? All those phonies we saw sitting around the Flor or imitating Burl Ives in the Lapin Agile?"

"Do you want to be a stupid with a beard?"

"You know what I mean. If they've got a right there, I sure have. How do I know whether I've got talent unless I try? I'll make talent. I can do anything I make up my mind to."

"Maybe so, maybe so."

"You could try back home," Jean said. "There are art teachers at home. Paris is just not a place for a young girl alone. And you've still got three years more of college."

"Oh, young girl alone!" Margaret said. "College! Good heavens! This is the twentieth century. Grow up and wipe off your chin."

Jean jerked back and pinched her trembling lips together. "Margaret, you're insufferably rude! I can't even talk to you."

"Why try, then?" Margaret said, her hard, intractable eyes fixed on Louis. She had not glanced at her mother since making her demand.

He started to slap his hand on the table, caught himself in time, and laid it down softly. She was where she had always loved best to be, backed into a corner with the dogs at her. Her spirits rose to that sort of thing. With his hand pressing the cool marble, he said, "You *are* insufferable. Now be quiet, before you make a scene."

Perhaps because he said it quietly, she sagged back and indifferently shook and contemplated the olive in her glass. At a certain point she raised the glass and tossed the olive into her mouth. The waiter came with hors d'oeuvres.

The French word that covered so many things nudged itself into Louis' mind as he watched her sulk—*formidable*, maybe even *magnifique*, if you cared for the type. Medea might have been one of these, or Clytemnestra, or Lady Macbeth—all the murderer-queens. But what was he thinking? His child.

Their eyes met, and she said, "I'm sorry, Father."

Instantly he was touched. "Of course," he said. "We all are. But it's your mother you should speak to."

"I'm sorry, Mother," Margaret said.

Jean patted her hand; tears were beaded on her lashes.

So the food that had gone down the throat in ragged, insoluble lumps began to taste better. Louis ordered a bottle of Beaujolais. They remarked on the trick by which the wake of the incoming launch caught all the lights of town and ships and poured them down its rolling trough. They were pleasantly uncrowded; only half a dozen tables in the quayside cafés were occupied. The quay lay open and empty, like a stage.

Into the opening between the *escalopes de veau* and the salad, Louis inserted what he thought of as a simple act of justice and a chance for everybody to close off the bitterness of the recent conversation. Margaret knew she had gone too far; in her more quelled mood she could be talked to reasonably.

"You know we wouldn't deny you anything in reason, if we thought it was good for you, Maggie. But you've never had the slightest interest in art. You have to admit it looks like a whim, because you were excited by Paris."

"It's no whim."

"You've got brains and determination, maybe even talent. But you're only eighteen. Wait till you finish college. Besides, it would cost a lot of money we don't have."

"I could live cheap in Paris."

"Not any more."

"I could work, then."

"At what?"

"I'd find something."

"And if you worked, when would you study art?"

"At night, or after work, or before work. There'd be some time free, for heaven's sake."

He shook his head. "There's a limit to human energy."

"Not to mine."

On the empty stage of the quay a character appeared—a bit player, a walk-on. He came out of the muted revelry of a side street all by himself, a slim young sailor walking the exact middle of the street. His head was down, his white hat was pushed back to expose dark, clustered curls. Concentrating with a seriousness that showed in every move of his body, he came on; his legs buckled him forward, jerked him upright, wobbled him to the left, kinked him back to equilibrium, buckled him forward again. He seemed to have four-way hinges in his knees; his hands hung like things carried in paper bags. As he passed the money-changing booth, the shore patrol moved out alertly. When they took his elbows, he collapsed as if they had kicked his feet from under him. Carefully, more like nurses than police, they dragged him to the wall and propped him on a bench. He leaned and fell off, and they propped him up again.

After two minutes, three more sailors came into the lighted space, the two on the outside supporting the middle one like football players assisting a hurt team-mate off the field. They turned him over to the shore patrol, talked for half a minute, and with their hats over their eyes headed at a fast walk back where they had come from. There was still revelry in them; they were still after something. Only the two casualties and a doleful warrant officer with packages beside him and his nose in a comic book inhabited the disciplined area of the dock.

"Thank heavens, you're not a boy and have to go into the service," Jean said. "I should think their officers could control them better. Those boys can't have been ashore two hours."

"It doesn't take long if you work at it," Louis said.

"It's pretty disgraceful all the same," she said. "Do you think we ought to go before they all come back like that?"

"Oh, Mother, relax," Margaret said. "They're making a liberty, for heaven's sake. They've probably been stuck aboard ship for two or three months. This is like in *Mister Roberts*. They're free, for a change."

"Free to make an awful spectacle of themselves. I wonder what the French think."

"Oh, hell!" Margaret said. Her eyes burned oddly, her dark, twisted face thrust forward from the shadows where she sat.

An uncertain silence fell upon them.

At last Jean stood up. "I think I'll hunt up a bathroom," she said abruptly. "Margaret?"

"No," Margaret said. Her eyes were absently fixed across the mistily lighted street. For several minutes she and her father sat in silence.

"I guess we're your prison, aren't we, Maggie?" Louis said at last.

Her hawklike face, handsome in the dusk, snapped around. "What?"

"Paris doesn't really mean art; it means freedom. Isn't that it?"

"Maybe," she said. "It's meant that for a lot of people."

"Stupids with beards?"

"More than those."

"Yes," he said, "I suppose it has." For a while there seemed nothing to say. In spite of her hostility, this was his daughter; he loved her, she anguished him, she broke his heart. He wanted to help her. Finally he said, "Your mother would be heartbroken to think the home she's tried to make for you has been a prison."

Margaret made a deprecatory motion with her hand.

"I could sympathize more with your wish for liberty if I knew what you expected liberty to do for you."

"How do I know till I try?"

"I'm surprised that it's Paris," he said. "Paris is such a stereotype. I shouldn't have thought you'd be taken in by it."

"Stereotype or not," she said.

"Lord, Lord," he said wearily. "Well, we'll see. Your mother will take a good deal of convincing."

So, to his astonishment, he had given in, weakly and behind Jean's back. He looked at his single-minded daughter almost with horror. Yet how could they not give in? How could they hold her? She would slip the collar or chew the leash and be gone in spite of them.

When Jean returned, they were deep in a silence that on his part was sheepish and guilty. She looked at them sharply, perhaps to see if they had been quarreling, and sat down with a sigh. No sooner had she seated herself than two new shore patrol came on to the stone-floored stage, escorting three sailors, one with a smeared blouse and a bloody nose, and all with the signs of belligerence upon them. The patient guardians of the dock accepted these, too, adding them to the casualties on the bench.

"I should think——" Jean started.

Louis, looking to see what had stopped her, saw a tanned, grinning face, a bristly white crew cut, white eyebrows, a rakish hat, a pair of square red hands knuckled on the table top.

"Hi," the sailor said. "I mistaken, or you folks Americans?"

"Are we as obvious as all that?" Jean said, smiling up at him glassily.

"Heard you talkin'," the sailor said. "It sounded good. Where you folks from?"

"Illinois," Jean said. "Aurora."

"That over by Chicago someplace?"

"Very near."

"Well, well," he said. "I'm from Pennsylvania myself—Wilkins-burg—practically part of Pittsburgh."

"My," Jean said with her glassy smile, "we're all a long way from home."

"You ain't kiddin'," the sailor said. "Been here long?"

"Two days. We're staying at Monte Carlo."

"Ha!" He ducked his head, leaning his weight heavily on the table, and looked around at them carefully. "If I'd of had time, I'd of gone. Lots of boys did. They all want to be the guy that busts the bank at Monte Carlo."

"They don't have to go there," Margaret said. "There are casinos in all these towns." She was sitting back in the shadow of the awning, but Louis could see the proud head, the strong profile.

The sailor was giving her his full attention. "Don't I know it," he said. "These French crap games are brutal."

Struck by something in Margaret's voice, even in the way she sat, Louis said impulsively. "Buy you a drink?"

The sailor straightened up easily, loose-shouldered, and Margaret bent forward into the flaky light to turn an empty chair.

The sailor looked at her with his half-shut eyes, grinning amiably. "No, thanks," he said. "I got to go see if I can get me one of these tortoise-shell cigarette cases for my girl friend. They got 'em here for three hundred francs, come from Capri or somewhere." He raised a polite hand to each of them in turn. "Take it easy, now," he said, and passed on with only a slight roll and an excessive dignity to show the load of alcohol he carried.

Jean laughed in relief. "Pleasant enough boy," she said. "I expect anything from the United States looks good to him."

In pity Louis watched Margaret. She had leaned back again into obscurity, but he knew the sailor's casual rejection burned her like thrown lye. She would be savage and untouchable the rest of the evening.

And what had happened so undramatically was forever beyond talk. He could never say to her, "I saw you invite him, and I saw him take one good look and pass." Could you say to your daughter, "Accept your looks for what they are?" Could you tell her, "You were born struck out, and it won't help to stand in the batter's box demanding that the pitcher throw you a fourth strike?"

In anguish he watched her armor herself with scorn; but what dismayed him was not the scorn but what had for a moment been revealed. Somewhere, back in secret daydreams unknown to anyone, most of all hidden from the parents who were her prison, she had lounged in cafés and joints with long-haired, irresponsible, reckless companions; she had walked with a lover on the Île St. Louis, and watched the lazy river and lazier fishermen from the Pont Neuf; she had heard the whisper of passion in dark doorways; she had mounted dark stairs with an arm around her and kisses hot upon her lips.

My God, she has *hope*, he said to himself. Everybody young has hope.

It seemed a pathetic and tremendous thing. At that moment he would have given anything if he could have hired someone to make love to his daughter and bring to pass every denouement her mother feared.

Yet he knew that the Margaret she would find in Paris would be the same Margaret she had hated and had tried to flee at home.

He could say none of it. He could only, watching from the sad reductions of middle age, let her go, and expect almost with anger that the prison she would flee would sometime become a refuge and a sanctuary.

The launch was coming in, its powerful, water-muffled roar rising against the piled stone of the town. The barge lifted and knocked against the quay. Somehow, while he wasn't watching, the street had filled with sailors, and now they crowded aboard, subdued. The shore patrol herded in the intractables and lifted in the casualties. One gave the launch's bow a hard shove with his foot. The bell clinked, and the motor opened from an idling chuckle to the full-throttle roar as the launch swung out swiftly toward the lighted outlines of the ships pinned against the dark.

"Shall we be getting along?" Louis said.

THE
VOLUNTEER

■　　　■　　　■

When my Latin teacher said she had always wanted a scale model of a Roman *castra* so that pupils reading about the campaigns against the Helvetians could see exactly how the legions built their defenses, of course I volunteered. I was always volunteering. The year must have been 1922. I was thirteen years old, two years behind myself in physical growth, two years ahead of myself in school. Around the high school I drew two kinds of attention, one kind from teachers and another from boys, especially big boys and most especially stupid ones. These last I ignored, or tried to, and I cultivated the praise of the teachers, which was easy to win. Nevertheless, I suppose I would have given considerable to be big and stupid so that I too could sneer at my little peaked face focused on the teacher ready to cry answers, and my little skinny arm flapping at every call to special duty.

A *castra*? I'll make one! I said. I know a slough where there's good clay. I'll get some tonight after school.

Now that, David, said Miss Van der Fleet, is the spirit I like to see.

I lived at the south-east edge of town, where the streets faded out into truck gardens and lucerne fields. The slough was at the south-west, a long two miles added to my walk home. A month before, I had made another volunteering expedition out there to get hydras and paramecia and amoebas for my zoology teacher, but this trip, in late November, was not quite the sunny autumn holiday the other had been. By the time I was laying my books on dry ground at the edge of the slough the afternoon was already late and blue. The wind went dryly through tules and yellow grass, and the sky over the mountains was the color of iron.

It was too cold to take off my shoes and wade. I had to hop from hummock to hummock until I found a place wet enough to dig in. The clay lay under the sod like blue icy grease; it numbed me to the wrists as I filled my lunch pail. I saw a mouse dart through the reeds, and the sad cry of a marsh hawk coasting over made me feel little and alone, and wish that I had brought someone along. I had to remind myself that though it was less fun to do things alone, there was more distinction in it that way. And anyway, who would have come?

The slimy clay stuck like paint on my hands, and it was impossible to get to open water where I could wash. I wiped them as well as I could on the grass, but I had a hard time, working with wrists and elbows and the very tips of my fingers, trying to get my books tucked down inside my belt without smearing them and my clothes with mud.

My way home led across fields and down country roads with few houses. As I came down off the slope the day grew bluer and colder, the wind cut my face, my hand carrying the heavy lunch pail stiffened into an iron hook. Every time I shifted the pail from hand to hand I had to stick out my stomach hard to keep the books from sliding down inside my corduroy knickers. If they had slipped I wouldn't have dared, with those hands, to get them out.

The heroic and indispensable feeling I had started with, the spirit Miss Van der Fleet liked to see, had leaked away. I was not really a hero. I was thin and pale, weak, stick-armed, a cry baby. And no matter how I hawked and snuffled, no matter how many times I tried to clear my nose through my mouth, a clammy and elastic gob began to droop lower and lower on my upper lip.

My muddy frozen claws couldn't have handled a handkerchief if I had owned one; they couldn't even have got it out of my pocket. Working my face against the sting and stiffness of the wind, holding my stomach pouted out against books and belt, miserably snuffling and spitting, I went crabwise homeward down a road, across a field, past a yard where a dog leaped out roaring. At last I came to the big cabbage field, still unharvested, that covered many acres just west of us, and passed it with my face sideward to the wind so that the cabbages made changing ranks and then diagonals and then new ranks down the gray field; and finally, my shoulder blades aching and my arms dead and my hands numb and bloodless under the mud, I made it through our sagging picket fence and up on to our gingerbread-framed porch.

There was a car in our drive; there often was; I was too far gone to pay it any attention. The books were held only by one slipping corner, the clot sagged frantically under my nose. It was like a nightmare in which you have to get to some special safe place before whatever is behind you makes its grab. This time I made it to the door, fell against the jamb, and braced the books there. Some rule would be violated, something would happen bad, if I set the pail of mud down until I was clear inside. I hung on to it, braced against the jamb and jamming my frozen thumb at the bell.

Down each side of our door, relic of some time when this had been a fairly pretentious country house, went a panel made up of leaded panes of glass of many colors. Through a violet one just level with my eyes was a neat bullet hole. Nobody knew how it had come there. It hinted of old crimes, feuds, jealous lovers, better days. Sometimes, inside the hall, you could feel through it a thin cold secret draft like the stream of air a dentist squirts into a cavity just before he fills it. Now I put my tongue to the bullet hole, but there was no draft, only cold glass. I remembered that the doorbell hadn't worked since last week, and raised my dirty fist and pounded. Instantly such pain went through my frozen knuckles that I moaned in fury and kicked on the door.

The books slid down inside my pants leg. The clot drooped a dangerous eighth of an inch. Then my father opened the door.

He was very annoyed. "Have you lost the use of your hands?" he said.

Desolately snuffling, tilted into agonies by the contrary strains of the heavy pail in my hand, the heavy books in my pants, I whined, "I was all muddy."

For a second he looked me over in silence; his look was like a hand in the scruff of my neck. Then he said, "What's the matter with your handkerchief?"

He was extraordinarily fussy about things like that. A snuffly nose or somebody who smacked at the table or the sight of someone's dirty fingernails could drive him half wild. And I *had* gone off to school again without a handkerchief. I said once more, "I'm all *mud!*"

Somehow I sidled past him into the hall, wonderfully warm with the dry breath from the register. But I didn't dare set down the pail or relax, so long as he was looking at me that way. "Jesus Christ," he said finally. "Thirteen years old and running around with a lamb's leg under your nose making mud pies."

That stung. I whirled around and howled, "I was not! I'm supposed to make a *castra!*"

"Oh, are you," he said. But he was stopped for the moment. I knew he hadn't the slightest idea what a *castra* was, and he wasn't going to ask me and expose his ignorance. I knew things that he hadn't even heard of; that was a sweet fierce pleasure. In the parlor somebody had started to play my new Victrola record, a piece called "Nobody Lied," with a big slaptongue baritone sax solo embedded in it. The clot drooped again and I dragged wetly at it, my nose stuffed shut with the sudden warmth of the hall. My father's lips turned inside out. He gave me a push on the shoulder. "Go get yourself cleaned up, and stay out of the front room. There's company."

He didn't need to tell me. Company meant there were people in there buying drinks. That's what we were, a speakeasy. About the time I was born my father was running the same sort of thing in Dakota, but there it had been called a blind pig. I had no desire to go into his crummy parlor, but I said to myself that I wished his damn company would quit wearing out my new record. I started for the kitchen, spraddling because of the books in my pants, and my father said after me, "For God's sake, have you messed your pants too?"

That really made me bawl. I started yelling, "No! My books slipped down, I was just . . ." But he shut me up with one furious motion of his hand. The kitchen door opened and my mother, with an instant cry, stooped to help me: I had finally made it home. Behind me I heard my father saying something humorous to the company.

"Great day," my mother said, "you've got yourself tied hand and foot. What on earth . . ."

She wiped my nose. She pried the pail out of my frozen fingers. She slid my belt buckle open and reached down and got the books. Then she stood me at the sink and ran warm water on my hands until they stung and tingled and grew clean and red while I snarled and complained.

Last she rubbed lotion into the bleeding cracks in the backs of my hands and put me at the kitchen table and made me a cup of cocoa.

All I would tell her when she asked what I had been doing and why my lunch pail was full of mud was that my Latin teacher wanted me to make a *castra*. What was a *castra*? she asked, and I flew out at her bitterly. It was a thing for school, a thing the legions built, what did she suppose? Finally she found out that it was something I was going to build with clay on some sort of board base, and she gave me her extra breadboard to build it on. Before supper I spent an intent hour, sitting stocking-footed soaking up the pouring heat from the kitchen register, drawing a *castra* to scale on the clean bleached wood.

Life in our house was full of tensions. For one thing, we were always afraid of the law, and for that reason moved often, even though every move meant losing customers who would never find us again. For another, my mother was the wrong woman to be the wife of a speakeasy owner. She had been brought up in a decent Presbyterian family in Nebraska, and though she wasn't religious she had a full, even a yearning belief in honesty, law, fairness, the respectabilities of family life. When company came she most often stayed in the kitchen; if the party in the parlor grew loud she sat wincing as if she had cramps, and threw looks at me, with little grimaces and jerky movements of hands and shoulders. She was a worn, humble, and decent woman married to the wrong man. Unless my memory is all wrong, I never saw a sadder, more resigned face.

My father was a perfectionist, of a kind; he aspired to run a classy and genteel joint. Even in the ratty old tin-wainscoted, Congoleum-floored places we rented he went around with a towel on his arm, always flicking and dusting things, cranking the Victrola, tidying up, making conversation, setting up a free one for good spenders. When, as sometimes happened, he needed help, he expected my mother or me to hop; nothing was more important than the customer's desires. He could fly into a fury over a two-minute delay.

Still, I escaped him all day by going to school, and at home I found it convenient to have loads of homework. At home I was not a volunteer. My mother, having no such escapes, sat next to what she hated and hoped it would not make demands on her or me; for we were, though we never talked openly about it, in mutinous league against our life.

That night new customers came in after five. My father took his plate into the dining-room, which could be shut off by sliding doors from the parlor but from which he could hear them if they wanted anything. My mother and I ate in the kitchen. Once, coming in for hot water to make a toddy, he stood in the doorway talking for a moment. He parted his hair in the middle and slicked it down on both sides like an old-fashioned bartender. I honestly think he had a sense of vocation. As he stood flicking his towel I saw his eyes drift over to the table where my breadboard lay with its walls and ditch half molded and its wad of blue clay in the middle. His glance came back across mine like saw teeth across a nail. Through the register, sounding plain but far away, there was the dark, remote throbbing, the last beats of the slaptongue sax, and the voice started chanting, with what seemed inappropriate vivacity.

> *Nobody lied when they said I cried over you.*
> *Nobody lied when they said that I most died over you.*
> *Got so blue I scarce know what to do. . . .*

"Don't you want some pie?" my mother said.

"Later," he said, and left.

After supper I went straight back to the *castra*. I wanted to take it to school with me in the morning and dazzle Miss Van der Fleet with the speed of my accomplishment, and force reluctant admiration from the big and stupid, and set the girls a-twitter. One girl in that class thought I had a roguish face; somebody had told me. That word was like a secret twenty-dollar bill in a deep inner pocket that no one knew of. Carefully I went on smoothing the greasy clay into walls, gates, rows of little tents. I would make such a *castra* as Caesar and all his legions had never thrown up in all the plains and mountains of Gaul—roguish I, that brilliant boy, with the spirit the teachers liked to see.

Behind me my mother tipped the coal scuttle into the stove. From the sound I knew there was nothing in it but coal dust and papers, but I did not rise and get her a new bucket of coal. I bent my head and worked on, and I worked in great absorption while she went past me and the door let a cold draft across my neck and closed again, while the returning scuttle knocked against the jamb and then went solidly down on the asbestos stove mat. Later there was a noise of dishes in a pan, a smell of soap and steam; nothing disturbed me. Eventually she stood behind me and I heard the dry rubbing of a towel on china. "Oh," she said, pleased, "it's a kind of little fort!"

"It's a *castra*," I said in scorn. "A Roman camp."

*   *   *

"Have your pie now, I've kept it warm," my mother said about seven o'clock. He took the slab in his clean, round-nailed hand. "Who's in there?" she said.

"Just Lew McReady and his lady friend, now."

"His lady friend. One week he's here with his wife, and the next with his lady friend. Which one, that nurse?"

"Yeah."

"I wonder if she knows he's got children seventeen years old."

"Oh, Lew's all right," he said. "He just likes a change."

He was trying to kid her, but she wouldn't be kidded. She gave him a queer, mixed, unbelieving look. "What a life we lead!" she said. "What friends we have!"

"If you can't tell the difference between a friend and a customer," said my father, "you don't know which side your bread's buttered on."

"Maybe that's the trouble. Maybe all we have is customers."

"If we're starting that again," he said, "I'm going back to the dining-room and read the *Post*."

With a push of the shoulder he was gone from the doorway, and my mother looked at me and smiled bleakly. I made no response except to go on smoothing with the back of a paring knife the triangular bits of clay that served as tents. Their wrangling was not a concern of mine. I did not live at that house. I lived at school, where teachers lighted up when I came around and girls thought I had a roguish face. In this country of the enemy inhabited by hostile barbarians I erected my defenses and mounted guard.

"It's beginning to look real good," my mother said after five minutes of clock-ticking, stove-ticking, tap-dripping silence. "You do a nice neat job of things."

Praise made me more businesslike. "I wish I had a little eagle," I said.

"A what?"

"An eagle. Legion standards had eagles on them. In camp they planted the standard in front of the commander's tent."

"I guess . . . I don't quite know what a standard is?" she said. I did not even bother to answer her.

For a while she read a magazine at the other kitchen table. I had not heard any noise, either from my father in the dining-room or from the company in the parlor, for some time. The radiator puffed its warm breath against my legs, the dust-puppies fluttered in its grill, the tin pipes sighed and popped. "I've got a pin shaped like a bird," my mother said. "Would that help you? Maybe you could fasten it on to this . . . standard . . . some way."

She bothered me, always trying to horn in on this thing she didn't even understand. On the other hand, maybe I could use the pin. I leaned back. "Let's see it."

"We'll have to wait till they go, in there. It's in my sewing basket."

"I think they're gone."

"I haven't heard the door."

"They're gone," I said. "I'd hear them through the register."

"Well, but . . ." I was already up, skating in stocking feet across the slick linoleum. "Well, all right," she said. "I'll have to find it for you. You'd never know where."

Down the darkish hall, lighted only by a high dim bulb that brought a dull shine out of the newel post and tangled the shadows of the coat-rack, I stroked with skating strides, made a detour to pass my hand across the cold stream of air at the bullet hole, and slid up to the open parlor door.

I was there just a split second before the tap of my mother's heels startled them. Lew McReady was bent far over his girl on the sofa, whispering in her ear or kissing her, I couldn't see. But I could see, in the spread of light that the table lamp shed, the white satin softness of the lady friend's blouse, and Lew McReady's hand working like a cat's claws in it.

Then they heard. McReady snapped around and spread his arm in a big elaborate gesture along the sofa back, and yawned as if he had just been roused from a nap. The girl made a sound like a laugh. Behind me my mother said in a tight, strained voice (had she seen?), "I'm sorry, David needed something for a thing he's making for school. Excuse me . . . just a second . . . he's making something . . ."

McReady crossed his legs and made a sour mouth. I knew his son at high school, one of the big stupid ones, a football player who was supposed to star if he ever got eligible. But I couldn't stay looking at McReady; I had to stare at the nurse, who smiled back at me. She seemed extraordinarily pretty. I could not understand how she could be so pretty and let old McReady paw her. She had a laughing sort of face, and she was lost and damned.

She said, "What is it you're making?"

"A *castra*—a Roman camp."

"For Latin?"

"Yes."

My mother was rummaging through the sewing basket; I wished she would bring the whole thing so we could escape from there, and yet I was glad for every extra second she took. McReady lighted a cigarette, still spread-eagled elegantly over the couch. He had a red face with large pores and the hair on top of his head was very thin, about twelve hairs carefully spread to cover as much skull as possible. When he took the cigarette from his lips and looked at the tip and saw lipstick there he put the back of his hand to his mouth and looked across it and saw me watching him. So he separated himself from us and interested himself in a long wheezing coughing spell; his eyes glared out of his purpling face with a kind of dull patience, waiting for things to die down. The nurse smiled at me, and, loathing her, I smiled back. She said, "I took Latin once. 'Gallia est omnis divisa in partes tres.'"

"My Go-guho-guhod!" McReady said through his coughing, his bulging eyes staring at her glassily. "An unexpec-uhec-uhected talent!"

My mother was surprised too. I saw both her surprise and her pleasure that something from the world of my school meant something to somebody, even though she herself couldn't share it and even though the one who could was this lady friend of McReady's. Maybe she was as mixed about this girl as I was, and I was truly mixed. I could still see that hand in her breast, and the softness under the satin was like the voluptuous softnesses that coiled around me in bed some nights until I lay panting and glaring into the dark, feeling my ninety-pound body as hot and explosive as if my flesh had been nitroglycerin packed on my bones. This girl looked at me with clear eyes, she had several wholesome freckles, she laughed with a dimple. Above all she quoted Caesar (and what if it was only the first line, it was *correct*: most dopes said *omnia* instead of *omnis*). I could hardly have been more shaken if I had run into Miss Van der Fleet having a snort of Sunnybrook Farm in our parlor. Actually that would have shaken me less, for Miss Van der Fleet would never crawl naked and voluptuous through my dreams, and this one would, oh, this one would!

I said sullenly and stupidly, "*Quarum unum incolunt Belgae.*"

"Lucy," Lew McReady said, "we are dealing with a pair of real scholars." His face, mocking me, was exactly the face of any number of the big and stupid at school. I hated him. I hated his whiskey breath and his red mocking face and the memory of his hand in this lost girl's breast. I hated the way he called my mother by her first name, as if she were some friend of his. I hated everything about him and he knew it.

"Ma," I said passionately, "I got to . . ."

"Yes," she said, coming along but hesitating, out of politeness, for a few more words. "You'd think the world depended on it," she said to the nurse. "He's fixing this *castra* and he needed a bird for the standard. That's what we came in to get. School is awful important to him," she said with an abrupt, unexpected laugh. "If I didn't chase him out to play he'd study all the time. . . ."

The dining-room door slid back and my father came in. His eyes were heavy on my mother and then me, but just for an instant. He said heartily, "Well, well, old home week. Everything O.K.?"

"Just getting ready to beat it," McReady said.

My father flicked his towel across his hand. "One for the road?"

"Naw, we got to go," McReady said. He wadded out his cigarette, looking down with smoke still puffing from his mouth and nose and drifting up into his eyes, and the elk's tooth on his watch chain jiggled with his almost noiseless wheezing.

The nurse rose. "I bet he's bright in school," she said. (And what did her smiling mean as she looked from my mother to me? Did she find my face roguish?)

My mother said, "We hadn't been here a month till they moved him ahead another grade. He's only thirteen. He won't be quite sixteen when he graduates."

I could have killed her, talking about me in front of everybody with that proud proprietary air. Their eyes were all on me like sash weights: my mother's full of pride, the nurse's smiling, with a question of some kind in them, my father's speculative, McReady's just dull and steady and streaked. Then McReady picked up a book from the end table by the sofa and knocked it on his knuckles. "This something you read for school?" he said.

The book was mine, all right. They must have been looking at it earlier, and seen my name in it. It was by Edgar Rice Burroughs, and it was called *At the Earth's Core*. It was about a man who invented an underground digger in which he broke through the crust of the earth and into the hollow inside, where there was another world all upside down and concave instead of convex, and full of tyrannosauri and pterodactyls and long-tailed people covered with fine black fur. So McReady cracked it open and of course it opened to the page I had most consulted, a picture of the tailed furry girl who fell in love with the hero. She didn't have anything on.

He showed it around, and he and my father laughed and the nurse smiled and shook her head and my mother smiled too, but not as if she felt like it. "You better stick to Latin, kiddo," McReady said, and dropped the book back on the table.

All my insides were pulled into a knot under my wishbone. I think I must have shivered like a dog. If asked, I suppose I could have given a very logical explanation of why McReady chose to humiliate a runty thirteen-year-old: I was too much smarter than his own dumb son, I had walked in on his necking party, I might talk. On the last he might have saved his worry. About things that happened in my non-school life I never said anything, not a word. But though I could have explained McReady's act, I didn't survive it. It paralyzed me, it reduced me to a speck in front of them all, especially that girl. I left them laughing— some of them were laughing, anyway—and vanished. By the time they left I was back at the *castra* in the kitchen.

Almost at once I heard my parents. Their voices came plainly through the kitchen register.

"What went on in here?" my father said. "Something drove him away. He was good for all night."

"He was good for all night if we provided a bed for him and his lady friend," said my mother's strange, squeaky, trembling voice. It burst out in a furious loud whisper. "What a thing for him to see in his own parlor! Oh, Buck, I could . . . if we don't . . ."

"What are you talking about? Talk sense. What went on here? What do you mean?"

"I mean," she said, "Lew and that girl. We came in to get something from my sewing basket, and they were so—they didn't even hear us coming. His hands were all over her. David couldn't help seeing, because *I* saw, and I was behind him."

The register sighed with the empty rush of air. Then he said, "Well, God Almighty, I've told you a hundred times to keep him out of there. How the hell do you suppose people like to have kids peeking around the corners at them when they're out partying? Kids who know your own kids, for God's sake! Do you think you'd ever come back? Not on your life. Kiss him good-bye . . . and he was good for ten or fifteen dollars a week every week. Oh, God *damn*, if either of you had the sense of a . . ."

My hands were shaking so that I could hardly stick the match stem down into the clay before the commander's tent. When I pressed the pin down into the end of the wood I split it clumsily, and snatched it and threw it furiously away. My mother was saying out of the register's warm rush, "Will you tell me why—just tell me why—a boy should have to stay out of part of his own home, and hang out in the kitchen like the hired girl, for fear of what he'll see if he doesn't? Is that the way a home should be? How can he grow up right, or have any self-respect, or even know what's right and wrong, when all he sees at home is people like Lew McReady?"

The sigh and steady rush of air. My father said, "This is a place of business, too, remember? This is how we make a living. We stop this we don't eat."

"Sometimes I think I'd rather not eat," she said. "So help me God, I'd rather starve!" In the tin insides of the register something boomed like a drum. My mother said, "I wonder how we'll feel if he turns out bad? What if we make him into a thief, or something worse? Do you want him to be like . . ."

"Like me?" he said, in a voice so soft and ugly that I held my breath.

"I'm as guilty as you are," she said, and the register boomed so that with all my straining I heard only a mumble for a second, and then words again, ". . . fifteen years to pretend it was only bad times, something temporary, you'd get into something decent. But, Buck . . . I'm . . . there's a limit."

"Yes," he said heavily, "I guess there is."

I sat with my eyes squeezed half shut and my ears trying to repudiate the quarreling voices, frozen in some frantic, desolated rejection of everything that surrounded and threatened me. The humiliation of a few minutes before was still sour as bile in my throat, and now this new outburst of an old quarrel, the threat of separation and break-up. What would happen to me, did they ever think of that? I would be pulled out of school, everything I lived for would be yanked away from me. It wasn't fair. Quite suddenly the *castra* with its *vallum* and its ditch and its rows of tents swam distorted and watery. I ground my teeth in shame and rage. It wasn't fair. The register was silent. I could imagine them in there, speechless.

Blindly I kicked my feet into my shoes under the table, bent on getting out, but a noise at the hall door made me whirl around. My mother came quietly in. In the one wild glance I threw I saw only her still, white face. She smiled, and her voice was low, almost matter of fact. "Does it work all right?" she said.

It took me a moment to understand that she was talking about the pin. "No," I said then. "It's too big. It splits the match." Accusingly I glared at her where she wavered in the big lens of tears.

"Why, Davey!" she said. "You're crying! Oh, poor little kid!"

She started for me, but I yanked my sweater from the hook and tore open the outside door. Down the steps I lurched and recovered and ran and stopped in the shadow where the old pear tree tangled its branches with the overgrown lilac hedge. My mother's silhouette was back there in the lighted rectangle of the door. "Davey!" her high voice said. After that one cry she stood very still, not calling, seeming to listen. Then with her head bowed she turned back in, and the rectangle of light and the glimpse of lighted kitchen like a Dutch painting narrowed and were gone.

Under the pear tree's darkness it was still and cold; when I went out through the hole in the hedge I saw my breath white against the light from the corner. I stood there with my fists clenched and my teeth clenched and my mind clenched against the sobs that rattled and shook me, and it was some time before I stopped crying. Then as I raised my head I heard the faint distant rush and hum of traffic from uptown, but immediately around me there was not a sound. It was as if we lived not merely at the edge of town but outside the boundaries of all human warmth, all love and companionship and neighborliness, all light and noise and activity, all law.

I had never been able to bring a friend home from school. Once, when a good-natured bigger boy rode me home on his handlebars, I gave him the wrong address and stood at a strange gate until he disappeared. The very sight of that dark house, divided within itself, but enclosing its total secret behind thick hedges, closed doors, drawn blinds, shook me with desolation and self-pity. I set off up the sidewalk, which after half a block became a dirt path, and as I walked I cursed aloud in a methodical filthy stream.

I cursed my father and Lew McReady and the wicked girl who had started all this; she was as repulsive to me as if I had seen her copulating with animals. I shed tears for my mother and for myself, forced to live in a way we hated. After a while, exhausted with tears and cursing, under trees that rattled stiffly in a little night wind, I stood imagining revenges, triumphs, ways of growing rich. I magnified myself in years, strength, wealth, confidence, nerve. I whipped my father with my tongue and mind till he cried and begged my pardon for all he had ever done against me and all the impatience and contempt he had ever had for my weakness. At one point I made him stand at one side while I broke all his bottles of homemade Sunnybrook until the cellar swam with whiskey and he was knee-deep in broken glass. I switched away from that to destroy Lew McReady, going on along the dark path stumbling and erratic, my mind full of carnage. I saw McReady in a dozen postures of defeat, collapse, unconsciousness, cowardly begging. I saw the girl, too; she came up to me soft and beguiling, and my image of her was totally obscured for a moment by the picture of my own scornful eyes and the twist on my mouth as I repudiated her. Would I touch anything that McReady had touched? But within seconds after that magnificent rejection I was thinking how it *would* be to touch her, and I was beside her in some very private place with a grate fire when I came to myself and fell to cursing again. When I thought of how close I had come to admitting that nurse, or letting her lure me, into those dreams of voluptuousness and concupiscence, I shook with self-loathing. Passing a tree, I smashed my fist against it and howled with instant fury at the pain.

There was a moon like a chip of ice; the air smelled of smoke and frost. I was the loneliest creature alive. With my hands tucked under my sweater armpits, my eyes glaring bleakly into the dark, shaken occasionally with a long shuddering diminishing sob, I went on. Now I was at the edge of the big cabbage field I had passed that afternoon. Out of pitch-black shadow the heads lifted their even rows, touched by the moon with greenish light.

Reminded of the *castra* with its even rows of tents, I yearned for that job I had begun. I wanted to be back there safe above the warm register, removed, intent, and inviolate. I saw the warm lighted kitchen then as a sanctuary; though I had fled from it, I had had enough already of loneliness and cold and dark. And anyway what I had really fled from was in the parlor. In the kitchen-sanctuary were not only the light and warmth but the true thing that made it sanctuary: my mother, sitting with her magazine, glancing across from her isolation to mine, making tentative, humble suggestions that might for a moment gain her admittance to the other world I escaped to.

It seems to me that understanding and shame dawned on me together, coming on gradually like the rheostat-controlled light in a darkened theater. I had had all the contempt I wanted, that day, and yet I began then to heap more on myself, and not only to accept it but almost to relish it. With my chin on a fencepost I stared out across the glimmering cabbage field and gnawed my chapped knuckles, thinking, admitting, condemning myself. There was this one person in the entire world who loved me wholly, only this one that I could wholly trust. And if I thought myself lonely, desolate, friendless, abused, what should I think of her? I had my escape, and I was almost as used to praise as to contempt. Outside my hateful house I had been able to gather praise with both hands, and bring it back to her and have it doubled. But who praised her? Who helped her? What did she have?

My father said, *How else would we eat? Did you ever hear of money?*

It would be better to starve, my mother said. *So help me God, I'd rather.*

I won't let us starve, I said. *I'll get a job. I'll quit school if I have to. I'll . . .*

Roguish I, the ninety-pound volunteer.

In the thin moonlight the cabbages went row on row like the crosses in the poem; their ranks swam and melted and re-formed greenishly, shadowily, a great store of food left carelessly unplucked, while in our house we ran a speakeasy because it was the only thing my father knew how to do, and my mother submitted because she must—perhaps because of me. In my nostrils, shrunken by the cold, lay the sourish smell of the field. I dived under the fence and in a moment was wrestling with an enormous cabbage, trying to unscrew its deep root from the ground. Before I defeated it I was crying again with anger and exhaustion, but there it lay at last, a great cold vegetable rose. Stripping off the outer leaves, I rolled it under the fence, crept through after it, gathered it in my arms, and went staggering toward home.

I heard the phonograph the moment I opened the door; my mother was sitting alone in the kitchen. Her life was right where I had left it. As I stuck my head and half my body into the light and warmth she jerked to her feet, and her eyes went from my face to the front of my sweater where dirt from the cabbage root had rubbed off on me, and from that to my hand, still out of sight holding the cabbage behind the door jamb.

"Where did you go?" she said. "Are you all right?"

Already my confidence in what I had done was leaking away; the last block of the way home, the cabbage had weighed like solid lead. It seemed to me that all that day I had been carrying weights too heavy for my arms up to that house I hated and took refuge in. Now by its root I dragged the upended head around the door, and searching her face for her response, I said, "I brought you something."

She was standing straight by her chair. Her head did not move as she glanced at the cabbage; only her eyes flicked down and then back. She said nothing—not "Oh, how nice!" or even "Where did you get it?" Nothing.

Panic began to rise in me, for here in the kitchen I couldn't pretend that the cabbage was anything but ridiculous, a contribution to our household that would have made my father snort in incredulous contempt. Moreover—and this was worse because it concerned her, not him—it had been stolen. She knew at once it was a theft I offered her. I remembered her angry whisper coming with the rush of air through the register: *I wonder how we'll feel if he turns out bad? What if we make him into a thief, or worse? How will he ever be able to tell right from wrong?*

"Ma . . ." I said.

It was more than I could do to support her still look. Still clutching the cabbage, I let my eyes wander away until they settled upon the *castra*. There lay reassurance: the daubed walls were tight and neat, the tents lay in mathematically precise rows. Like a dog on a track, my mind ducked to one side, and I found myself repeating other words like *castra* that had a different meaning in singular and plural—words like *gratia-gratiae*, and *auxilium-auxilia*, and *impedimentum-impedimenta*, and *copia-copiae*—and even going over some of the words that customarily took *in* with the accusative: names of towns, small islands, *domus, rus*.

Out of the register came the squawk of a record ending, a big burst of laughter, a woman's squeal, shouts whose words I resolutely would not hear, then the music again: good old "Nobody Lied," my own contribution to the parlor fun. I brought my eyes around again to her, opening my mouth to say, "I . . ." She was still looking at me intently; her hands hung awkwardly before her as if she had forgotten them there. Her mouth twitched—smile, or grimace such as she made when the parlor got rowdy?

Perhaps the true climax of that rueful day and that rueful period of our lives is this tableau in which I after a fashion present and she in some sort accepts the grotesque vegetable I have stolen to compensate her for the wrongs and uncertainties and deprivations of her life. I bring her this gift, this proof of myself, and we stare at each other with emotions mixed and uneasy. What shall we say there in that kitchen? What another family might greet with great belly laughs we cannot meet so easily. We have no margin for laughter.

The slaptongue sax is pounding and throbbing through the pipes. I want to say to her, I am awful, I have filthy thoughts, I steal, I would even cheat if I couldn't get A any other way. I'm a cry baby and people laugh at me and I'm sorry I . . .

I say none of it. She says, with her eyes glittering full, "Ah, poor Davey," and puts up her arms and I creep into them, and I suspect that, hugging each other in the sanctuary kitchen, we are both about half comforted.

A FIELD GUIDE
TO THE
WESTERN
BIRDS

■ ■ ■

I must say that I never felt better. I don't feel sixty-six, I have no gerontological worries; if I am on the shelf, as we literally are in this place on the prow of a California hill, retirement is not the hangdog misery that I half expected it to be. When I stepped out of the office, we sold our place in Yorktown Heights because even Yorktown Heights might be too close to Madison Avenue for comfort. The New Haven would still run trains; a man might still see the old companions. I didn't want to have to avoid the Algonquin at noon or the Ritz bar after five. If there is anything limper than an ex-literary agent it is an ex-literary agent hanging around where his old business still goes on. We told people that we were leaving because I wanted to get clear away and get perspective for my memoirs. Ha! That was to scare some of them, a little. *What I Have Done for Ten Percent*. I know some literary figures who wish I had stayed in New York where they could watch me.

But here I sit on this terrace in a golden afternoon, finishing off an early, indolent highball, my shanks in saddle-stitched slacks and my feet in brown suede; a Pebble Beach pasha, a Los Gatos geikwar. What I have done for ten percent was never like this.

Down the terrace a brown bird alights—some kind of towhee, I think, but I can't find him in the bird book. Whatever he is, he is a champion for pugnacity. Maybe he is living up to some dim notion of how to be a proper husband and father, maybe he just hates himself, for about ten times a day I see him alight on the terrace and challenge his reflection in the plate glass. He springs at himself like a fighting cock, beats his wings, pecks, falls back, springs again, slides and thumps against the glass, falls down, flies up, falls down, until he wears himself out and squats on the bricks, panting and glaring at his hated image. For about ten days now he has been struggling with himself like Jacob with his angel, Hercules with his Hydra, Christian with his conscience, old retired Joe Allston with his memoirs.

I drop a hand and grope up the drained highball glass, tip the ice cubes into my palm, and scoot them down the terrace. "Beat it, you fool." The towhee, or whatever he is, springs into the air and flies away. End of problem.

Down the hill that plunges steeply from the terrace, somewhere down among the toyon and oak, a tom quail is hammering his ca-*whack*-a, ca-*whack*-a, ca-*whack*-a. From the horse pasture of our neighbor Shields, on the other side of the house, a meadowlark whistles sharp and pure. The meadowlarks are new to me. They do not grow in Yorktown Heights, and the quail there, I am told, say Bob White instead of ca-*whack*-a.

This terrace is a good place just to lie and listen. Lots of bird business, every minute of the day. All around the house I can hear the clatter of house finches that have nested in the vines, the drainspouts, the rafters of the carport. The liveoaks level with my eyes flick with little colored movements: I see a red-headed woodpecker working spirally around a trunk, a nuthatch walking upside down along a limb, a pair of warblers hanging like limes among the leaves.

It is a thing to be confessed that in spite of living in Yorktown Heights among the birdwatchers for twenty-four years I never got into my gaiters and slung on my binoculars and put a peanut butter sandwich and an apple in my pocket and set off lightheartedly through the woods. I have seen them come straggling by on a Sunday afternoon, looking like a cross between the end of a Y.W.C.A. picnic and Hare and Hounds at Rugby, but it was always a little too tweedy and muscular to stir me, and until we came here I couldn't have told a Wilson thrush from a turkey. The memoirs are what made a birdwatcher out of Joseph Allston; I have labored at identification as much as reminiscence through the mornings when Ruth has thought I've been gleaning the busy years.

When we built this house I very craftily built a separate study down the hill a hundred feet or so, the theory being that I did not want to be disturbed by telephone calls. Actually I did not want to be disturbed by Ruth, who sometimes begins to feel that she is the Whip of Conscience, and who worries that if I do not keep busy I will start to deteriorate. I had a little of that feeling myself: I was going to get all the benefits of privacy and quiet, and I even put a blank wall on the study on the view side. But I made the whole north wall of glass, for light, and that was where I got caught. The wall of glass looks into a deep green shade coiling with the python limbs of a liveoak, and the oak is always full of birds.

Worse than that for my concentration, there are two casement windows on the south that open on to a pasture and a stripe of sky. Even with my back to them, I can see them reflected dimly in the plate glass in front of me, and the pasture and the sky are also full of birds. I wrote a little thumbnail description of this effect, thinking it might go into the memoirs somewhere. It is something I learned how to do while managing the affairs of writers: "Faintly, hypnotically, like an hallucination, the reflected sky superimposed on the umbrageous cave of the tree is traced by the linear geometry of hawks, the vortical returnings of buzzards. On the three fenceposts that show between sky and pasture, bluejays plunge to a halt to challenge the world, and across the stripe of sky lines of Brewer's blackbirds are pinned to the loops of telephone wire like a ragged black wash." I have seen (and sold) a lot worse.

I am beginning to understand the temptation to be literary and indulge the senses. It is a full-time job just watching and listening here. I watch the light change across the ridges to the west, and the ridges are the fresh gold of wild oats just turned, the oaks are round and green with oval shadows, the hollows have a tinge of blue. The last crest of the Coast Range is furry with sunstruck spikes of fir and redwood. Off to the east I can hear the roar, hardly more than a hum from here, as San Francisco pours its commuter trains down the valley, jams El Camino from Potrero to San Jose with the honk and stink of cars, rushes its daytime prisoners in murderous columns down the Bayshore. Not for me, not any more. Hardly any of that afternoon row penetrates up here. This is for the retired, for the no-longer-commuting, for contemplative ex-literary agents, for the birds.

Ruth comes out of the French doors of the bedroom and hands me the pernicious silver necklace that my client Murthi once sent her in gratitude from Hyderabad. The bird who made it was the same kind of jeweler that Murthi is a writer; why in *hell* should anyone hand-make a little set screw for a fastener, and then thread the screw backward?

I comment aloud on the idiocy of the Hyderabad silversmith while I strain up on one elbow and try to fasten the thing around her neck, but Ruth does not pay attention. I believe she thinks complaints are a self-indulgence. Sometimes she irritates me close to uxoricide. I do not see how people can stay healthy unless they express their feelings. If I had that idiot Murthi here now I would tell him exactly what I think of his smug Oxonian paragraphs and his superior sniffing about American materialism. If I hadn't sold his foolish book for him he would never have sent this token of gratitude, and all the comfortable assumptions of my sixty-six years would be intact. I drop the screw on the bricks; *invariably* I try to screw it the wrong way. Cultural opposites; never the twain shall meet. Political understanding more impossible than Murthi thinks it is, because the Indians insist on making and doing and thinking everything backward.

"No fog," Ruth says, stooping. At Bryn Mawr they taught her that a lady modulates her speaking voice, and as a result she never says anything except conspiratorially. A writer who wrote with so little regard for his audience wouldn't sell a line. On occasion she has started talking to me while her head was deep inside some cupboard or closet so that nothing came out but this inaudible thrilling murmur, and I have been so exasperated that I have deliberately walked out of the room. Five minutes later I have come back and found her still talking, still with her head among the coats and suits and dresses. "*What?*" I am inclined to say then. The intent is to make her feel chagrined and ridiculous to have been murmuring away to herself. It never does. A Bryn Mawr lady is as unruffled as her voice.

"*What?*" I say now, though this time I have heard her well enough. It just seems to me that out on the terrace, in the open air, she might speak above a whisper.

"No fog," she says in exactly the same tone. "Sue was afraid the fog would come in and chase everybody indoors."

I get the necklace screwed together at last and sink back exhausted. I am too used up even to protest when she rubs her hand around on my bald spot—a thing that usually drives me wild.

"Are you ready?" she says.

"That depends. Is this thing black tie or hula shirt?"

"Oh, informal."

"Slacks and jacket all right?"

"Sure."

"Then I'm ready."

For a minute she stands vaguely stirring her finger around in my fringe. It is very quiet; the peace seeps in upon the terrace from every side. "I suppose it isn't moral," I say.

"What isn't?"

"This."

"The house? What?"

"All of it."

I rear up on my elbow, not because I am sore about anything but because I really have an extraordinary sense of well-being, and when I feel anything that strongly I like a reaction, not a polite murmur. But then I see that she is staring at me and that her face, fixed for the party, is gently and softly astonished. It is as definite a reaction as they taught her, poor dear. I reach out and tweak her nose.

"I ought to invest in a hair shirt," I say. "What have I done to deserve so well-preserved and imperturbable a helpmeet?"

"Maybe it's something you did for ten percent," she whispers, and that tickles me. I was the poor one when we were married. Her father's money kept us going for the first five or six years.

She laughs and rubs her cheek against mine, and her cheek is soft and smells of powder. For the merest instant it feels *old*—too soft, limp and used and without tension and resilience, and I think what it means to be all through. But Ruth is looking across at the violet valleys and the sunstruck ridges, and she says in her whispery voice, "Isn't it beautiful? Isn't it really perfectly beautiful!"

So it is; that ought to be enough. If it weren't I would not be an incipient birdwatcher; I would be defensively killing myself writing those memoirs, trying to stay alive just by stirring around. But I don't need to stay alive by stirring around. I am a bee at the heart of a sleepy flower; the things I used to do for a living and the people I did them among are as remote as things and people I knew in prep school.

"I am oppressed with birdsong," I say. "I am confounded by peace. I don't want to move. Do we have to go over to Bill Casement's and drink highballs and listen to Sue's refugee genius punish the piano?"

"Of course. You were an agent. You know everybody in New York. You own or control Town Hall. You're supposed to help start this boy on his career."

I grunt, and she goes inside. The sun, very low, begins to reach in under the oak and blind me with bright flashes. Down at the foot of our hill two tall eucalyptuses rise high above the oak and toyon, and the limber oval leaves of their tips, not too far below me, flick and glitter like tinsel fish. From the undergrowth the quail cackles again. A swallow cuts across the terrace and swerves after an insect and is gone.

It is when I am trying to see where the swallow darted to that I notice the little hawk hovering above the tips of the eucalyptus trees. It holds itself in one spot like a helicopter pulling somebody out of the surf. The sparrow hawk or kestrel, according to the bird book, is the only small hawk, maybe the only one of any kind, that can do that.

From its hover, the kestrel stoops like a falling stone straight into the tip of the eucalyptus and then shoots up again from among the glitter of the leaves. It disappears into the sun, but just when I think it has gone it appears in another dive. Another miss: I can tell from its angry *kreeeeee!* as it swerves up. All the other birds are quiet; for a second the evening is like something under a belljar. I watch the kestrel stop and hover, and down it comes a third time, and up it goes screeching. As I stand up to see what it can be striking at, it apparently sees me; it is gone with a swift bowed wingbeat into the sun.

And now what? Out of the eucalyptus, seconds after the kestrel has gone, comes a little buzzing thing about the size of a bumblebee. A hummingbird, too far to see what kind. It sits in the air above the tree just as the kestrel did; it looks as if it couldn't hold all the indignation it feels; I think of a thimble-sized Colonel Blimp with a red face and asthmatic wheezings and exclamations. Then it too is gone as if shot out of a slingshot.

I am tickled by its tiny wrath and by the sense it has shown in staying down among the leaves where the hawk couldn't hit it. But I have hardly watched the little buzzing dot disappear before I am rubbing my eyes like a man seeing ghosts, for out of this same eucalyptus top, in a kind of Keystone Kop routine where fifty people pour out of one old Model T, lumbers up a great owl. He looks as clumsy as a buffalo after the speed and delicacy of the hawk and the hummingbird, and like a lumpish halfwit hurrying home before the neighborhood gang can catch and torment him, he flaps off heavily into the woods.

This is too much for Joseph Allston, oppressed with birdsong. I am cackling to myself like a maniac when Ruth comes out on to the terrace with her coat on. "Ruthie," I tell her, "you just missed seeing Oliver Owl black-balled from the Treetop Country Club."

"*What?*"

"Just as Big Round Red Mr. Sun was setting over the California hills."

"Have you gone balmy, poor lamb," Ruth whispers, "or have you been nibbling highballs?"

"Madame, I am passionately at peace."

"Well, contain your faunish humor tonight," Ruth says. "Sue really wants to do something for this boy. Don't you go spoiling anything with your capers."

Ruth believes that I go out of my way to stir up the animals. Once our terrier Grumpy—now dead, but more dog for his pounds than ever lived—started through the fence in Yorktown Heights with a stick in his mouth. He didn't allow for the stick and the pickets, and he was coming fast—he never came any other way. The stick caught solidly on both sides and pretty near took his head off. That, Ruth told me in her confidential whisper, was the way I had approached every situation in my whole life. In her inaudible way, she is capable of a good deal of hyperbole. I have no desire to foul up Sue's artistic philanthropies. I can't do her boy any good, but I'll sip a drink and listen, and that's more help than he will get from any of the twelve people who will be there when he finally plays in Town Hall.

II

In California, as elsewhere, alcohol dulls the auricular nerves and leads people to raise their voices. The noise of cocktail parties is the same whether you are honoring the Sitwells in a suite at the Savoy Plaza, or whether you are showing off a refugee pianist on a Los Gatos patio. It sounds very familiar as we park among the Cadillacs and Jaguars and one incredible sleek red Ferrari and the routine Plymouth suburbans and Hillman Minxes of the neighbors. The sound is the same, only the setting is different. But that difference is considerable.

Dazed visitors from the lower, envious fringes of exurbia—and those include the Allstons, or did at first—are likely to come into the Casement cabaña and walk through it as if they have had a solid thump on the head. This cabaña has a complete barbecue kitchen with electrically operated grills thirty feet long. It has a bar nearly that size, a big television screen and a hi-fi layout, a lounge that is sage and gray and tangerine or lobster, I am not decorator enough to tell. It is chaste and hypnotically comfortable and faintly oppressive with money, like an ad for one of the places where you will find *Newsweek* or see men of distinction.

The whole glass side of the cabaña slides back and the cabaña becomes continuous with a patio that spreads to the edge of the pool, which is the color of one of the glass jars that used to sit in the windows of drugstores in Marshalltown, Iowa, when I was a boy. Across the pool, strung for a long distance along the retaining wall that holds the artificial flat top on to this hill, are the playing fields of Eton. I think I have never toured them all, but I have seen a croquet ground; a putting green; a tennis court and a half-sized paddle-tennis court; a Ping-Pong table; a shuffle-board court of smooth concrete; and out beyond, a football field, full-sized and fully grassed, that was built especially for young Jim Casement and his friends and so far as I have observed is never used. Beyond the retaining wall the hill falls away steeply, so that you look out across it and across the ventilators of the stables below the wall, and into the dusk where lights are beginning to bloom in beds and borders down the enormous garden of the Santa Clara Valley.

A neighborhood couple of modest means—and there are some—contemplate gratefully their admission to these splendors. A standing invitation amounts to a guest card at an exclusive club, and the Casements are generous with invitations. At some stage of their first tour through the layout any neighbor couple is sure to be found standing with their heads together, their eyes gauging and weighing and estimating, and you can hear the IBM machinery working in their heads. Hundred thousand? More than that, a lot more. Hundred and fifty? God knows what's in the house itself, in which the Casements do not entertain but only live. Couldn't touch the whole thing for under two hundred thousand, probably. A pool that size wouldn't have come at less than ten thousand; the cabaña alone would have cost more than our whole house. . . .

I have been around this neighborhood for more than six months, and in six months the Casements can make you feel like a lifelong friend.

And I have not been exactly unfamiliar in my lifetime with conspicuous consumption and the swindle sheet. But I still feel like whistling every time I push open the gate in the fence that is a design by Mondrian in egg crates and plastic screen, and look in upon the pool and the cabaña and the patio. The taste has been purchased, but it is taste. The Casement Club just misses being extravagantly beautiful; all it needs is something broken or incomplete, the way a Persian rug weaver will leave a flaw in his pattern to show that Allah alone is perfect and there is no God but God. This is all muted colors, plain lines, calculated simplicities. As I hold open the gate for Ruth, with the noise of the party already loud in the air, I feel as if I were going aboard a brand new and competitively designed cruise ship, or entering the latest Las Vegas motel.

We have not more than poked our heads in, and seen that the crowd is pretty thick already, before Sue spots us and starts over. She has a high-colored face and a smile that asks to be smiled back at, a very warm good-natured face. You think, the minute you lay eyes on her, What a nice woman. And across clusters of guests I see Bill Casement, just as good-natured, waving an arm, and with the same motion savagely beckoning a white-coated Japanese to intercept us with a tray. It is one of Bill's beliefs that guests at a Casement party spring into the splendid patio with bent elbows and glasses in their hands. He does not like awkward preliminaries; he perpetuates a fiction that nobody is ahead of anybody else.

"Ah," Sue says, "it's wonderful of you to come!" The funny thing is, you can't look at that wide and delighted smile and think otherwise. You are doing her an enormous favor just to *be*; to be at her party is to put her forever in your debt.

I scuff my ankles. "It is nothing," I say. "Where are the people who wanted to meet me?"

Sue giggles, perfectly delighted. "Lined up all around the pool. Including the next-most-important guest. You haven't met Arnold, have you?"

"I don't think he has met me," I say with dignity.

She has us by the elbows, starting us in. I twist and catch up two glasses off the tray that has appeared beside me, and I exchange a face of fellowship with the Japanese. Then the stage set swallows us. Mr. and Mrs. Allston, Ruth and Joe, the Allstons, neighbors, we are repeated every minute or two to polite inattentive people, and we get people thrown at us in turn. Names mean less than nothing, they break like bubbles on the surface of the party's sound. We are two more walk-ons with glasses in our hands; our voices go up and are lost in the clatter that reminds my bird-conscious ears of a hundred blackbirds in a tree.

Groups open and let us in and hold us a minute and pass us on. My recording apparatus makes note of Mr. Thing, a white-haired and astonishingly benevolent-looking music critic from San Francisco; and of Mr. and Mrs. How-d'ye-do, whose family has supported music in the city since Adah Menken was singing "Sweet Betsy from Pike" to packed houses at the Mechanics' Hall. We shake the damp glass-chilled hand of Mr. Monsieur, whom we have seen on platforms as the accompanist of a celebrated Negro soprano, and Ruth has her hand kissed by a gentleman whom I distinguish as Mr. Budapest, a gentleman who makes harps, or harpsichords, and who wears a brown velvet jacket and sandals.

Glimpses of Distinguished Guests, *filets* of conversation *au vin, verschiedener kalter Aufschnitt* of the neighborhood:

Sam Shields, he of the robust cement mixer and the acres of home-made walks and patios and barbecue pits and incinerators, close neighbor to the Joseph Allstons; home-builder who erected by hand his own house, daring heaven and isostasy, on the lip of the San Andreas fault. With a Navy captain and a Pan Am pilot, both of the neighborhood (the pilot owns the Ferrari) he passes slowly, skinny-smiling, blue-bearded, with warts, ugly as Lincoln, saying: *I do not kid you. A zebra. I rise up from fixing that flat tire and I am face to face with a zebra. I am lucky it wasn't a leopard. Hearst stocked that whole damn duchy with African animals, including giraffes. It wouldn't surprise me if pygmies hunt warthogs through those hills with blowguns.* . . . And as he passes, the raised glass, the *salud*: Ah there, Joe!

Four Unknowns, two male and two female, obviously not related by marriage because too animated, but all decorous, one lady with cashmere sweater draped shawl-like over her shoulders, the other winking of diamonds as she lifts her glass; the gentlemen deferential, gray, brushed, double-breasted, bent heads listening: *Bumper to bumper, all the way across, and some idiot out of gas on the bridge* . . .

Mrs. Williamson, beagle-breeder extraordinary, Knight of the AKC, leather-faced, hoarse-voiced (*Howdy, Neighbor!*) last seen on a Sunday morning across the canyon from the Allstons' house, striding corduroy-skirted under the oaks, blowing her thin whistle, crying in the bar-room voice to a pack of wag-tailed long-coupled hounds, *Pfweeeet! Here Esther!*

come Esther! Here we go a-beagling. Wrists like a horsewoman, maybe from holding thirty couple of questing hounds on leash. Now, from quite a distance, rounding the words on the mouth, with a white smile, brown face, tweed shoulders, healthy-horsy-country woman, confidential across forty feet of lawn: *How are the memoirs?*

More Unknowns, not of the local race. City or Upper Peninsula, maybe Berkeley, two ladies and a gentleman, dazzled a little by the Casement Club, watchful. Relax and pass, friends. It is no movie set, it was made for hospitality. The animals who come to drink at this jungle ford are not what they seem. No leopards they, nor even zebras. Yon beagle-breeding Amazon is a wheelhorse of the League of Women Voters, those two by the dressing-room doors at the end of the pool spend much of their time and all of their surplus income promoting Civil Liberties and World Government. Half the people here do not work for a living, for one reason or other, but they cannot be called idlers. They all do something, sometimes even good. And you do not need, as on Martha's Vineyard, to distinguish between East Chop and West Chop. Here we live in a mulligan world, though it is made of prime sirloin. . . . *Ah, how do you do? Yes, isn't it? Lovely* . . .

Bill Casement, with his golfer's hide, one eye on the gate for new arrivals—shake of the head, *Quite a struggle, boy*, stoops abstractedly to listen to a short woman with a floury face. Somebody comes in. *Excuse me, please.* Short woman looks around for another anchorage—turn away, quick.

And what of the arts? Ah there, again, in a group: Mr. Thing, Mr. Budapest, Mr. and Mrs. How-d'ye-do, surnamed Ackerman, a tight enclave of the cognoscenti, on their fringes an eager young woman, not pretty, perhaps a piano teacher somewhere; this her big moment, prob-ably, thrilled to be asked here, voice shaking and a little too loud as she wedges something into the conversation, *But Honegger isn't really— do you think? He seems to me* . . . And to me, thou poor child. You have not gone to heaven, you do not have to prove angelhood, you are still in the presence of mortals. Listen and you shall hear.

And what of the Great Man? He is coming closer. There is a kind of progress here, though constantly interrupted, like walking the dog around Beekman Place and up to 51st and back down First Avenue. Magnetic fields, iron filings, kaleidoscopic bits of colored glass that snap into pattern and break again.

On around the diving board, on to the lawn, softer and quieter and with a nap like a marvelous thick rug. Something underfoot—whoop! what the hell? Croquet wicket. Half a good drink gone—on Ruth's dress? No. To the rescue another Japanese, out of the lawn like a mushroom. Thank you, thank you. Big tooth-gleaming grin, impossible to tell what they think. Contempt? Boozing Americans? But what then of all the good nature, the hospitality, the generosity? What of that, my toothy alert impeccable friend? Would you prefer us to be French aristocrats out of Henry James? Absurd. Probably has no such thoughts at all, good waiter, well trained.

"Ah," Sue says, "there he is!"

It is in her face like a sentence or a theorem: Here is this terrific musician, the best young pianist in the world. And here is this ex-literary agent, knows everybody in New York, owns Town Hall, lunches with S. Hurok twice a week. And here I have brought them together, carbide and water, and what will happen? Something will—there will be an explosion, litmus paper will change color, gases will boil and fume, fire will appear, a gleaming little nugget of gold or radium will form in the crucible.

Mr. Kaminski, Mr. and Mrs. Allston. Arnold, Joe and Ruth.

Now hold your breath.

III

My first impression, in the flick of an eye, is *What in hell can Sue be thinking of?* My second, all but simultaneous with the first, is *Bill Casement had better look out.*

Taking inventory during the minute or two of introductions and Ruth's far inland murmur and Sue's explanations of who we all are, I can't pick out any obvious reason why Kaminski should instantly bring my hackles up. His appearance is plus-minus. His skin is bad, not pitted by smallpox or chickenpox but roughened and lumpy, the way a face may be left by a bad childhood staphylococcus infection. His head is big for his body, which is both short and slight, and his crew-cut hair, with that skin, makes him look like a second in a curtain-raiser at some third-rate boxing arena: his name somehow ought to be Moishe, pronounced Mushy. But he has an elegant air too, and he has dressed for the occasion in a white dinner jacket. His eyes are large and brown and slightly bulging; some women would probably call them "fine." They compensate for his mouth, a little purse-slit like the mouth of a Florida rock fish.

The proper caption for the picture in its entirety is "Glandular Genius." I suppose if you are sentimental about artistic sensibility, or fascinated by the neurotic personality, you might look at a face like Kaminski's with attention, respect, perhaps sympathy and a shared anguish. He has all the stigmata of the type, and it is a type some people respond to. But if you are old Joe Allston, who has had to deal in his time with a good many petulant G.G.'s, you look upon this face with suspicion if not distaste.

It makes, of course, no difference to me what he is. Nevertheless, Bill Casement had better look out. This pianist is pretty expressionless, but such expression as he permits himself is so far a little shadowy sneer, a kind of controlled disdain. Bill might note not only that expression, but the air of almost contemptuous ownership with which Kaminski wears Sue's hand on his white sleeve. And it does not seem to me that even Sue can look as delighted and proud as she looks now out of simple good nature. It is true that she is as grateful for a friendly telephone call as if it had cost you fifty dollars to make it, and true that if you notice her and speak to her and joke with her a little she is constitutionally unable to look upon you as less than wonderful. It is a kind of idiotic and appealing humility in her; she is as happy for a smile as Sweet Alice, Ben Bolt. But right now she looks at Kaminski in a way that can only be called radiant; no woman of fifty should look at any young man that way, even if he *can* play the piano. If she knew how she looks, she would disguise her expression. The whole tableau embarrasses me, because I like Sue and automatically dislike the cool smirk on Kaminski's face, and I am sorry for Sue's sake that no chemical wonder is going to take place at our meeting. As for Kaminski, he is not stupid. Within three seconds he is giving me back my dislike as fast as I send it.

Sue stands outside the closed circuit of our hostility like a careless person gossiping over an electric fence.

"People who have as much to give as you two ought to know each other. Though what the rest of us do to deserve you both is more than I know. It's so *good* of you to be here! And shall I tell you something, Joe? Do you mind being *used*? Isn't that an awful question! But you see, Arnold, Joe was a literary agent for years and years in New York—the best, weren't you, Joe? For who? Hemingway? John Marquand? Oh,

James Hilton and James M. Cain and all sorts of people. And we know he couldn't be what he was without having a lot of influence in the other arts too. So we're going to use you, unscrupulously. Or *I* am. Because it's so difficult to make a career as a concert pianist. It's as if there were a conspiracy. . . ."

She is holding a glass, but does not seem to have drunk from it. Her hand is on Kaminski's arm, and her face shines with such goodness that I am ready to grind my teeth.

It is Ruth's belief that I take instant and senseless dislikes to people and that when I do I go out of my way to pick quarrels. Nothing, in fact, could be more unjust. Right now I am aching to harpoon this Kaminski and take the smirk off his face, or at least make him say something dishonestly modest, but what do I say? I say, "I'm afraid you're wrong about my having any influence where it would count. But we're looking forward to hearing you play." I could not have bespoke him more fair. He drops his arrogant head a little to acknowledge that I live.

"It's a wonder you haven't heard him clear over on your hill," Sue says. "All he does all day and night is sit down in the cottage and practice and practice and practice—terribly difficult things. He doesn't even remember meals half the time; I have to send them down on a tray." She gives his arm a slap—you naughty boy. "And he's got such power," she cries. "Look at his hands!"

She turns over his hand, which is the hand of a man half again as big as he is, a big thick meaty paw like a butcher's. The little contemptuous shadow of his expression turns towards her. "If I make too much noise?" he says. These are the first actual words we have heard him say.

I am not a Glandular Genius. I am not even an Artist, and hence I am not Sensitive. But I can recognize a challenge when I hear one, especially when there is an edge of insult in it. Poor Sue takes his remarks, apparently, as some sort of apology.

"Too much noise nothing! If the neighbors hear you, that's their good luck. And when you break down and play Chopin—which is never often enough—then they're double lucky. You know what we did the other night, Ruth—Joe? We heard Arnold playing Chopin down below, to relax after all the terribly difficult things, and we all just pulled up chairs on the patio and had a marvelous concert for over an hour. Even

Jimmy, and if you can make *him* listen! Really, *nobody* plays Chopin the way Arnold does."

Arnold's expression says that he concurs in this opinion, though generally opinions from this source are uninformed.

He stands there aloofly, not contaminating his art by brushing too close to Conspicuous Consumption. I am reminded irritably of my ex-client Murthi, who would have been astonished by nothing in this whole evening; he would have recognized it as the American Way from old Bob Montgomery movies. He would have recognized Kaminski too: the Artist (imported, of course—the technological jungle could only borrow, not create) captive to the purse and whim of the Nizam-rich, the self-indulgent plutocracy. Murthi would have welcomed in Kaminski a fellow devotee of the Spirit.

Nothing gives me a quicker pain than that sort of arrogance, whether it is Asian, European, or homegrown. I suppose I am guilty of impatience. Our neighbor Mrs. Shields, who does a good deal of promoting of International Understanding among foreign and native students at Stanford, ropes us in now and then for receptions and such. Generally we stand around making polite international noises at one another, but sometimes we really get a good conversation going. It seems to me that invariably, when I get into the middle of a bunch of thoroughly sensible Indians and Siamese and West Germans and Italians and Japanese and Guamanians, and we begin to get very interested in what the other one thinks, there is sure to come up someone in the crowd with a seed in his teeth about American materialism. This sets my spirituality on edge, and we're off.

It will not do for me to be too close to Kaminski tonight. He has hardly said a word, but I can see the Spirit sticking out all over him.

The Japanese passes with a tray. "Arnold?" Sue says. He makes a gesture of rejection with his meaty hand. He is above a drink. But I am pleased to see that when Ruth engages him in one of her conspiratorial conversations he is as vulnerable as other mortals. He listens with his head bent and a pucker between his eyes, not hearing one damned word, but forced to listen.

Well out of it, I stand back and watch, and remember nights when my ten percent involvement in artists didn't permit me to stand back, such a night as the Book-of-the-Month party when the Time-Life boy got high and insulted his publisher's wife, and punches flew, and in the melee someone—I swear it was a *Herald Tribune* reviewer—bit a chunk out of the lady's arm. She got blood poisoning and nearly died. A critic's bite is as deadly as a camel's, apparently. None of that for me, ever again. Let Art pursue its unquiet way, be content to be a birdwatcher of Los Gatos.

I hear Sue say lightly, "You're so dressed *up*, Arnold. You're the dressiest person at your party."

And wouldn't that be true, too; wouldn't Caliban, in this crowd where nothing is conventional except the thinking, just have to be correct as a haberdasher's clerk? Oh, a beauty. I bury my nose in a third highball, feeling ready and alert and full of conversational sass, but not wanting to get involved with Kaminski, and having no one else handy. Sue and her pianist are listening intently to Ruth's whisper. Teetering on my toes, I catch fragments of talk from people passing by, and think of Sam Shields and his zebra, and of Murthi again, and of how zebras roaming the California hills would not surprise Murthi at all. He would have seen them in some movie. Spiritually empty Americans are always importing zebras or leopards or crocodiles for pets. Part of the acquisitive and sensational itch. Roman decadence.

The whole subject irritates me. How in hell do zebras get into an intelligent conversation?

Some god, somewhere, says Let there be light, and a radiance like moonlight dawns over the patio and the clusters of guests. A blue underwater beam awakes in the pool; the water smokes like a hot spring. Sue's eyes are on the velvet-coated man, who is describing something with gestures to the music-patronizing Ackermans. One of the neighbors, in a loud plaid tweed, stands aside watching the musicians as he would watch little animals digging a hole. I have a feeling that I have failed Sue; Kaminski and I have already practically dropped one another's acquaintance. Her eyes wander around to me. She looks slightly puzzled, a little tired. She rounds her eyes to indicate how pleasantly difficult all this is, and bursts into laughter.

"Everybody here?" I ask.

"Almost, I think. At least the ice seems to be getting broken. Honestly, I don't know half the people here myself. Isn't that a giveaway? This is the first stock I ever bought in musical society."

"Very pretty party," I say. It is. From across the pool it is strikingly staged: light and shade, composition of heads and shoulders, moving faces, glints of glass and bright cloth. For a moment it has the swirl and flash of a Degas ballet, and I say so to Sue. I hear Bill Casement's big laugh; white coats dart around; the Mondrian gate opens to spill four late arrivals into the patio.

"Excuse me," Sue says. "I must go greet somebody. But I particularly wanted Arnold to meet the Ackermans, so I'm going to steal him now. Arnold, will you come . . ."

He stands with his fish mouth flattened; he breathes through his nose; he does not trouble to keep his voice down. He says, "For God's sake, how long is this going to go on?"

Sue's eyes jump to his; her lips waver in an imbecilic smile. Her glance swerves secretly to me, then to Ruth, and back to Kaminski. "Well, you know how people are," she says. "They don't warm up without a . . ."

"Good God!" says Kaminski, in a sudden, improbable rage, gobbling as if his throat were full of phlegm. "I am supposed to play for pigs who swill drinks and drinks and drinks until they are falling-down drunk and then will stuff themselves and sleep in their chairs? These are not people to listen to music. I can't play for such people. They are the wrong people. It is the wrong kind of party, nothing but drinks."

Ruth is already trying to pull me away, and I am pretending to go with her while at the same time holding back for dear life; I wouldn't for a fat fee miss hearing what this monster will say next. Sue swings him lightly around, steers him away from us, and I hear her: "Oh, please, Arnold! There's no harm done. We talked about it, remember? We thought, break the ice a little first. Never mind. I'm sorry if it's wrong. We can serve any time now, they'll be ready to listen as soon as . . ."

I am dragged out of earshot, and wind up beside Ruth, over against the dressing rooms under a cascade of clematis. Ruth looks like someone who has just put salt in her coffee by mistake. With her white hair and black eyebrows, she has a lot of lady-comedian expressions, but she doesn't seem to know which one to use this time. Our backs against the dressing-room wall, we sneak a cautious look back where we have just casually drifted from. Sue's Roman-striped cotton and Kaminski's white coat are still posed there at the far edge of the illumination. Then he jerks his arm free and walks off.

Ruth and I look at each other and make a glum mouth. There goes the attempt of a good-natured indiscreet well-meaning culture-craving woman to mother an artistic lush. Horrible social bust, tiptoes, hush-

hush among her friends. Painful but inevitable. She looks forlorn at the edge of the artificial moonlight of her patio. A performance is going on, but not the one she planned. The audience is there, but it will have no recital to attend, and will not see the real show, which is already over.

Now don't be stupid and go after him, I say to Sue in my mind, but I have hardly had the thought before she does just that. What an utter fool.

That is the moment when the white coats line up in front of the cabaña, and one steps out ahead of the others. He raises his hands with the dramatics of an assistant tympani player whose moment comes only once, and knocks a golden note from a dinner gong.

An arm falls across my shoulders, another sweeps Ruth in. "Come on," says Bill Casement's gun-club golf-course dressing-room voice. "Haven't had a word with you all night. By God, it's a pleasure to see a familiar face. How's it going? O.K.? Good, let's get us some food."

IV

Assembly line along a reach of stainless steel; the noisy, dutiful, expectant shuffling of feet, the lift of faces sniffing, turning to comment or laugh, craning to look ahead. *Mnnnnnnnnn!* Trenchers as big as cafeteria trays, each hand-turned from a different exotic wood. Behind the counter white coats, alert eyes, ready tongs, spoons, spatulas. A state fair exhibit of salads—red lettuce crinkly-edged, endive, romaine, tomatoes like flowers, hearts of artichokes *marinée*, little green scallions, *caveat emptor*. Aspic rings all in a row. A marvelous molded crab with pimento eyes afloat in a tidepool of mayonnaise. Some of that . . . that . . . that.

Refugees from Manhattan. Load these folks up, they haven't had a square meal since 1929.

A landslide, an avalanche: slabs of breast from barbecued turkeys, gobs of oyster dressing, candied yams dripping like honeycomb. A man with a knife as long as a sword and as limber as a razorblade whips off paper-thin slices from a ham, leafs them on to trenchers. Another releases by some sleight of hand one after another of a slowly revolving line of spits from a Rube Goldberg grill. Shishkebab. Tray already dangerous, but still pickles, olives, celery frizzled in crushed ice, a smörgasbord of smoked salmon, smoked eel, smoked herring, cheeses. Ovens in the opulent barbecue yield corn fingers, garlic bread.

No more, not another inch of room—but as we turn away we eye three dessert carts burdened with ice-cream confections shaped like apples, pears, pineapples, all fuming in dry ice. Also pastries, petits fours, napoleons, éclairs. Also batteries of coffee flasks streaming bright bubbles. Also two great bowls in which cherries and fat black berries and chunks of pineapple founder in wine-colored juice. Among the smokes of broiling, freshness of scallions, stink of camembert, roquefort, liederkranz, opulence of garlic butter, vinegar-bite of dressings, sniff that bouquet of cointreau and kirsch in which the fruits are soaked. Lucullus, Trimalchio, *adsum*.

But hardly Trimalchio. Instead, this Bill Casement, tall and brown, a maker and a spender loaded with money from lumber mills in the redwood country; no sybarite, but only a man with an urgent will to be hospitable and an indulgent attitude towards his wife's whims. He herds us to a table, looks around. "Where the hell's Sue?" A man behind the counter flashes him some signal. "Excuse me, back in a second. Any of these musical characters tries to sit down here, say it's saved, uh?" Down-mouthed, with his head ducked, he tiptoes away laughing to show that this party is none of his doing, he only works here.

The lawn where Sue and Kaminski have been standing until just a few minutes ago stretches empty and faultless in the dusk. No hostess, no guest of honor. "Quite an evening," I say.

Ruth smiles in a way she has. "Still oppressed with birdsong?"

"Why don't you save that tongue to slice ham with?" I reply crossly. "I'm oppressed all right. Aren't you?"

"If she weren't so nice it would be almost funny."

"But she *is* so nice."

"Yes," she says. "Poor Sue."

As I circle my nose above the heaped and delectable trencher, the thought of Kaminski's bald scorn of food and drink boils over in my insides. Is he opposed to nourishment? "A pituitary monster," I say, "straight out of Dostoevsky."

"Your distaste was a little obvious."

"I can't help it. He curdled my adrenal glands."

"You make everything so endocrine," she says. "He wasn't that bad. In fact, he had a point. It *is* a little alcoholic for a musicale."

"It's the only kind of party they know how to give."

"But it still isn't quite the best way to show off a pianist."

"All right," I say. "Suppose you're right. Is it his proper place to act as if he'd been captured and dragged here? He's the beneficiary, after all."

"I expect he has to humiliate her," Ruth says.

Sometimes she can surprise me. I remark that without an M.D. she is not entitled to practice psychiatry. So maybe he does have to humiliate her. That is exactly one of the seven thousand two hundred and fourteen things in him that irritate the hell out of me.

"But it'll be ghastly," says Ruth in her whisper, "if she can't manage to get him to play."

I address myself to the trencher. "This is getting cold. Do we have to wait for Bill?" When I fill my mouth with turkey and garlic bread, my dyspeptic stomach purrs and lies down. But Ruth's remark of a minute before continues to go around in me like an auger, and I burst out again: "Humiliate her, uh? How to achieve power. How to recover from a depressing sense of obligation. How to stand out in every gathering though a son of a bitch. Did it ever strike you how much attention a difficult cross-grained bastard gets, just by being difficult?"

"It strikes me all the time," Ruth murmurs. "Hasn't it ever struck you before?"

"You suppose she's infatuated with him?"

"No."

"Then why would she put up with being humiliated?"

Her face with its black brows and white hair is as clever as a raccoon's. But as I watch it for an answer I see it flatten out into the pleasant look of social intercourse, and here is Bill, his hand whacking me lightly on the back. "Haven't been waiting for me, have you? Fall to, fall to! We're supposed to be cleared away by nine-thirty. I got my orders."

Our talk is of barbecuing. Do we know there are eighteen different electric motors in that grill? Cook anything on it. The boys got it down to a science now. Some mix-ups at first, though. Right after we got it, tried a suckling pig, really a shambles. Everybody standing around watching Jerry and me get this thing on the spit, and somebody bound to say how much he looks like a little pink scrubbed baby. Does, too. Round he goes, round and round over the coals with an apple in his mouth and his dimples showing, and as his skin begins to shrink and get crisp, damn if his eyes don't open. By God! First a little slit, then wide open. Every time he comes round he gives us a sad look with these baby blue eyes, and the grease fries out of him and sizzles in the fire like tears. If you'd squeezed him he'd've said mama. He really clears the premises, believe me. Two or three women are really *sick*. . . .

Big Bill Casement, happy with food and bourbon, looks upon us in friendship and laughs his big laugh. "Pigs and all, barbecuing is more in my line than this music business. About the most musical I ever get is listening to Cottonseed Clark on the radio, and Sue rides me off the ranch every time she catches me." He rears back and looks around, his forehead wrinkles clear into his bristly widow's peak. "Where d'you suppose she went to, anyway?"

Ruth gives him one of her patent murmurs. It might as well be the Lord's Prayer for all he hears of it, but it comforts him anyway. Sue and Kaminski are nowhere to be seen—having a long confab somewhere. Thinking of what is probably being said at that meeting, I blurt out, "What about the performer? Who is he? Where'd Sue find him?"

"Well," Bill says, "he's a Pole. Polish Jew," he adds apologetically, as if the word were forbidden. "Grew up in Egypt, went back to Poland before the war, just in time to get grabbed by the Polish army and then by the Nazis. His mother went into an incinerator, I guess. He never knew for sure. I get all this from Sue."

His animation is gone. I am damned if he doesn't peek sideways and bat his eyes in a sheepish way around the patio pretending to be very disinterested and casual. He seems set to start back to attention at any slightest word with "What? Who? Me?"

"Very bright guy," he says with about the heartiness of a postscript sending love to the family. "Speaks half a dozen languages—German, Polish, French, Italian, Arabic, God knows what. Sue found him down here in this artist's colony, What's-its-name. He was having a hell of a time. The rest of the artists were about ready to lynch him—they didn't get along with him at all for some reason. Sue's been on the board of this place, that's how she was down there. She can see he's this terrific prospect, and not much luck so far except a little concert here and there, schools and so on. So she offers him the use of the cottage, and he's been here three weeks."

I watch his hand rubbing on the creased brown skin of cheek and jaw. The hand is manicured. I can imagine him kidding the manicurist in his favorite barbershop. He is a man the barbers all know and snap out their cloths for. He brings a big grin to the shoeshine boy. The manicurist, working on his big clean paw, has wistful furtive dreams.

"You met him yet?" Bill asks.

"We talked for a little while."

"Very talented," Bill says. "I *guess*. Make a piano talk. You'd know better than I would—artists are more in your line. I'm just a big damn lumberjack out of the tall timber."

In that, at least, he speaks with authority and conviction. Right now he would be a lot more at home up to his neck in a leaky barrel in some duck marsh than where he is.

Now I see Sue coming down along the fence from the projecting wing of the main house. She is alone. She stops at a table, and in the artificial moonlight I can see her rosy hostess's smile. "Here comes your lady now," I say.

Bill looks. "About time. I was beginning to . . . Say, I wonder if that means I should be . . . Where's Kaminski? Seen *him*?"

"Over across the pool," Ruth whispers, and sure enough there he is, walking pensively among the croquet wickets with his hands behind his white back. The Artist gathering his powers. I cock my ear to the sounds of the party, but all is decorous. All's well, then.

"Maybe I better push the chow line along, I guess," Bill says. He raises an arm and a white coat springs from beside the cabaña wall. In a minute we are confronted by a pastry cart full of all those éclairs and petits fours and napoleons and creampuffs. An arm reaches down and whisks my plate away, slides another in. Right behind the pastry cart comes another with a bowl of kirsch-and-cointreau-flooded fruit and a tray of fruity ice-cream molds. Forty thousand calories stare me in the face; my esophagus produces a small protesting conscientious *pwwk!* From the pastry man with his poised tongs and poised smile Ruth cringes away as if he were Satan with a fountain pen.

"Pick something," I tell her. "Golden apples of the sun, silver apples of the moon. You have a duty."

"Ha, yeah, don't let that bother you," Bill says, like a man who gets a nudge without letting it distract him from what he is looking at. Sue has stopped at a nearby table to talk to the Ackermans and the white-haired critic and the harpsichord man. The little music teacher, type-cast for the homely sister of a Jane Austen novel, has managed to squeeze into the musical company. It is all out of some bird book, how the species cling together, and the juncoes and the linnets and the seed-eaters hop around in one place, and the robins raid the toyon berries *en masse*, and the jaybirds yak away together in the almond trees. The party has split into its elements, neighbors and unknown visitors and the little cluster of musicians. And now Sue, bending across them, beckons Kaminski, and he comes around the diving board, the hatchings of some cuckoo egg whose natural and unchangeable use it is to thrust his bottomless gullet up from the nest and gobble everything a foolish foster mother brings.

The rather dour accompanist moves to make place for him. Sue will not sit down; she stands there animated, all smiles. And Kaminski has changed his front. His politeness is as noticeable as perfume. He talks. He shows his teeth in smiles. The little music teacher leans forward, intent to hear.

With a tremendous flourish the waiter serves Ruth a bowl of fruit. "You do that like Alfredo serving noodles," I say, but Ruth, who knows what I mean, does not say anything, and the waiter, who may or may not, smiles politely, and Bill, who hasn't the slightest idea, comes back beaming into the conversation as if glad of any innocent conversational remark. With a bite of éclair in my mouth I wag my head at him, how delicious. I force down a few spoonfuls of ambrosial fruit. I succeed in forestalling ice-cream. The carts go away. Jerry comes around with a coffee flask. I dig out a couple of cigars.

I am facing the musical table, but I have lost my interest in how they all act. Full of highballs, food, smoke, coffee, my insides coil around heavily like an overfed boa constrictor. The only reason I don't slide down in my chair and get really comfortable is that Kaminski is sitting where he can see *me*, and I will not give him the satisfaction of seeing me contented and well nourished. For his performance I shall make it a point to be as wide-awake as a lie detector, and though I shall listen with an open mind, I shall not be his most forgiving critic.

But there is a clash between comfort and will, and a little balloony pressure in my midsection. Damn Kaminski. Damn his Asiatic spirituality and his coddled Art and his ghetto defensiveness and his refugee ar-rogance. My esophagus comes again with a richly flavored *brwwp!* Just an echo, hoo hoo.

"Say," says Bill, "how would a brandy go? Or calvados? I got some damn good calvados. You never had any till you taste this."

The impetuous arm goes up, but Sue, who must have had her eye sharp on him, is there before the waiter. "Bill, do me a favor?"

"Surest thing you know. What?"

"Have Jerry close the bar. Don't serve any more now till afterward."

"I was just going to get Joe a snifter of calvados to go with his cigar."

"Please," she said. "Joe won't mind postponing it."

I have not been asked, but I do not mind.

"O.K.," Bill says. "You know what you're doing, I guess. Did you get anything to eat? I kept looking around for you."

"I'll get something later. As soon as people seem to be through, Jerry can start arranging the chairs. I went over it with him this afternoon."

"Check," says Bill. A smile, puzzled, protective, and fond, follows her back to the musician's table. "Bothers her," Bill says. "She's got her heart set on something great. Old Arnold had better be good."

We are silent, stuffed. I commune with my cigar, looking sleepily around this movie set where the standard of everything is excess. Somewhere down deep in my surfeited interior I conduct a little private argument with my client and conscience, Murthi. He is bitter. He thinks it is immoral to fill your stomach. In India, he tells me, the only well-fed people are money-changers and landlords, grinders of the faces of the poor. But these people, I try to tell him, grind no poor. They are not money-changers or landlords. They are the rich, or semi-rich, of a rich country, not the rich of a poor one. Their duty to society is not by any means ignored; they do not salve their own consciences with a temple stuck with pieces of colored glass. They give to causes they respect, and many of them give a great deal. And they don't put on a feast like this because they want to show off, or even because they are themselves gluttonous. They do it because they think their guests will enjoy it; they do it to introduce a struggling young artist. And anyway, why should good eating be immoral?

You pay nothing for it, Murthi says. It is too easy. It does not come after hard times and starvation, but after plenty. It is nothing but self-indulgence. It smothers the spiritual life. In the midst of plenty, that is the time to fast.

I am too full to argue with him. I feel as if I might lift into the air and float away, and the whole unreal patio with me, bearing its umbrella of artificial moonlight and its tables and people and glass-fronted cabaña, its piano and its Artist, high above the crass valley. It is like a *New Yorker* cartoon, and me with my turned-up Muslim slippers and baggy pants, one of the Peninsula pashas on a magic carpet of the latest model, complete with indirect lighting, swimming pool, Muzak, and all modern conveniences.

All? Nothing forgotten? My feet insist on my notice. I stoop on the sly and feel the cement. Sure enough, the magic carpet has radiant heating too.

V

Kaminski is booted and spurred and ready to ride. The audience is braced between the cabaña and the pool. The moonlight is turned off. The air is cool and damp, but the pavement underfoot radiates its faint expensive warmth. Inside, one light above the piano shines on Kaminski's white jacket as he sits fiddling with the knobs, adjusting the bench. The shadow of the piano's open wing falls across his head. The Degas has become a Rembrandt.

On a lounge sofa between Sue and Ruth, old Joe Allston, very much overfed, is borne up like a fly on meringue. Bill has creaked away somewhere. A partition has slid across the barbecue, and from behind it, during pauses in the hum of talk, comes the sound of a busy electric dishwasher.

"Are people too comfortable, do you think?" Sue asks. "Would it have been better to put out undertaker's chairs?"

I assure her that she has the gratitude of every over-burdened pelvis in the house. "There is no such thing as *too* comfortable," I say, "any more than there is such a thing as a large drink of whiskey."

Her hands pick at things on her dress and are held still. Her laugh fades away in a giggle.

I say, "What's he going to play?" and quite loudly she bursts out, "I don't know! He wouldn't tell me!" One or two shadowy heads turn. Kaminski stares out into the dusk from his bench, and the shadow wipes all the features off his face.

We are sitting well back, close to the edge of the pool. "How did you manage to get him to play after all?" Ruth murmurs.

It is as improbable to see the sneering curl of Sue's lip as it would be to see an ugly scowl on her face. "I *crawled!*" she says.

The cushions sigh as Ruth eases back into them. But I am sitting where I can watch Sue's face, and I am not so easily satisfied. "Why?" I ask.

"Because he's a great artist."

"Oh." After a moment I let myself back among the cushions with Ruth. "I hope he is," I say, and at least for the moment I mean it.

The eyeless mask of Kaminski's face turns again. Even when he speaks he does not seem to have lips. "For my first number I play three Chopin Nocturnes. I play these as suitable to the occasion, and especially for Mrs. Casement."

Beside me I can feel Sue shrink. I have a feeling, though it is too dark to see, that she has flushed red. While the murmur rising from the audience says How nice, handsome gesture, what a nice compliment, she looks at her hands.

At the piano, Kaminski kneads his knuckles, staring at the empty music rack. When he has held his pose of communing with his *Geist* long enough for the silence to spread to the far edges of the audience, but not long enough so that any barbarian starts talking again, he drops into the music with a little skip and a trill. It is well timed and well executed. Without knowing it, probably, Sue takes hold of my hand. She is like a high school girl who shuts her eyes while the hero plunges from the two-yard line. Did he make it? Oh, did he go over?

The cabaña acts like a shell; the slightest pianissimo comes out feathery but clear, and Kaminski's meaty hands are very deft. Behind us the faint gurgle and suck of the pool's filter system is a watery night sound under the Chopin.

God spare me from ever being called a critic or even a judge of music—even a listener. Like most people, I think I can tell a dub from a competent hand, and it is plain at once that Kaminski is competent. The shades of competence are another thing. They are where the Soul comes in, and I look with suspicion on those who wear their souls outside. I am not capable in any case of judging Kaminski's soul. Maybe it is such a soul as swoons into the world only once in a hundred years. Maybe, again, it is such a G.G. soul as I have seen on Madison Avenue and elsewhere in my time.

But I think I can smell a rat, even in music, if it is dead enough, and as Kaminski finishes one nocturne and chills into abashed silence those who have mistakenly started to applaud too soon, and pounds into the second with big chords, I think I begin to smell a rat here. Do I imagine it, or is he burlesquing these nocturnes? Is he contemptuous of them because they are sentimental, because they are nineteenth century, because they don't strain his keyboard technique enough, or because he knows Sue adores them? And is he clever enough and dirty enough to dedicate them to her as an insult?

It is hard to say. By the third one it is even harder, because he has played them all with great precision even while he gives them a lot of bravura. I wish I could ask Ruth what she thinks, because her ear for music and her nose for rats are both better than mine. But there is no chance, and so I am still nursing the private impression that Kaminski is hoaxing the philistines when I am called on to join in the applause, which is loud, long, and sincere. If the philistines have been hoaxed, they are not aware of the fact. Beside me, Sue wears her hands out; she is radiant. "Oh, didn't he play them *beautifully?* They loved it, didn't they? I told you, *nobody* can play Chopin the way Arnold can."

In the second row of lounge chairs the musical crowd, satisfactorily applauding, bend heads each to other. Mr. Ackerman's big droopy face lifts solemnly against the light. Kaminski, after his bow, has seated himself again and waits while the clapping splatters away and the talk dies down again and a plane, winking its red and white wing lights, drones on down and blinks out among the stars over Black Mountain. Finally he says, "I play next the Bach Chaconne, transcribed for piano by Busoni."

"What is it?" Sue says. "Should I know it?"

Over Sue's head Ruth gives me one of her raccoon looks. I am delighted; I rouse myself. This time my lie detector is going to be a little more searching, because I have heard a dozen great pianists play the Chaconne, and I own every recording ever made, probably. Every time I catch a competent amateur at a piano I beg it out of him. In my opinion, which I have already disparaged, it is only the greatest piece of music ever written, a great big massive controlled piece of mind. If Kaminski can play the Chaconne and play it well, I will forgive him and his bad manners and his tantrums and the Polish soul he put into Chopin. It takes more than Polish soul to play the Chaconne. It takes everything a good man has, and a lot of good men don't have enough.

Maybe Kaminski does have enough. He states those big sober themes, as they say in music-appreciation circles, with, as they also say, authority. The great chords begin to pile up. Imagine anyone writing that thing in the first place for the violin. As usual, it begins to destroy me. Kaminski is great, he's tremendous, he is tearing into this and bringing it out by the double handful. A success, a triumph. Listen to it roll and pour, and not one trace, not a whisker, of Polish soul. This is the language you might use in justifying your life to God.

As when, in the San Francisco Cow Palace, loudspeakers announce the draft horse competition, and sixteen great Percherons trot with high action and ponderous foot into the arena, brass-harnessed, plume-bridled, swelling with power, drawing the rumbling brewery wagon

lightly, Regal Pale; ton-heavy but light-footed they come, the thud of
their hoofs in the tanbark like the marching of platoons, and above them
the driver spider-braced, intent, transmits through the fan of lines his
slightest command; lightly he guides them, powerfully and surely they
bring their proud necks, their plumed heads, their round and dappled
haunches, the blue and gold wagon Regal Pale—sixteen prides guided
by one will, sixteen great strengths respondent and united: so the great
chords of Bach roll forth from under the hands of Arnold Kaminski.

And as, half-trained or self-willed, the near leader may break, turn
counter to his driver's command, and in an instant all that proud
unanimity is a snarl of tangled traces and fouled lines and broken step
and cross purposes and desperate remedies, so at a crucial instant fails
the cunning of Kaminski. A butch, a fat, naked, staring discord.

To do him credit, he retrieves it instantly, it is past and perhaps not
even noticed by many. But he has lost me, and when I have recovered
from the momentary disappointment I am cynically amused. The boy
took on something too big for him. A little later he almost gets me
back, in that brief lyrical passage that is like a spring in a country of
cliffs, but he never does quite recover the command he started with,
and I know now how to take him.

When he finishes there is impressed silence, followed by loud admiration. This has been, after all—Allston *dicens*—the most magnificent
piece of music ever written, and it ought to be applauded. But it has
licked Kaminski in a spot or two, and he can't help knowing it and
knowing that the musicians present know it. As he stands up to take
a bow, his face, thrust up into the light, acquires features, a mask of
slashes and slots and knobs, greenish and shadowed. He looks like a
rather bruised corpse, and he bows as if greeting his worst enemy. In
the quiet as the applause finally dies out I hear the gurgle of the pool's
drain and catch a thin aseptic whiff of chlorine, a counterwhiff of cigar
smoke and perfume.

Says Sue in my ear, tensely. "What did I tell you?"

"For my last number," Kaminski's thick voice is saying, "I play the
Piano Pieces of Arnold Schoenberg, Opus Nineteen."

I have had Schoenberg and his followers explained to me, even urged
upon me, several times, generally by arty people who catch me with
my flank exposed at a cocktail party. They tell me that these noises are
supposed, among other things, to produce *tension*. Tension is a great
word among the tone-row musicians. God bless them, they are good at

it. It astonishes me anew, as Kaminski begins, that sounds like these can come out of a piano. They can only be recovered from through bed rest and steam baths, maybe shock therapy.

For no amount of argument can convince me that this music does not hurt the ears. And though I am prepared to admit that by long listening a man might accustom himself to it, I do not think this proves much. Human beings can adjust to anything, practically; it is a resilient race. We can put up with the rule of kings, presidents, priests, dictators, generals, communes, and committees; we learn to tolerate diets of raw fish, octopus, snails, unborn ducklings, clay, the bleeding hearts of enemies, our own dung; we learn to listen without screaming to the sounds of samisens, Korean harps, veenas, steam whistles, gongs, and Calypso singers; we adjust bravely to whole-tone, half-tone, or quarter-tone scales, to long skirts and short skirts, crew cuts and perukes, mutton-chops and dundrearies and Van Dykes and naked chins, castles and paper houses and *barastis* and bomb shelters. The survival of the race depends upon its infinite adaptability. We can get used to anything in time, and even perhaps develop a perverted taste for it. But *why*? The day has not come when I choose to try adapting to Schoenberg. Schoenberg hurts my ears.

He hurts some other ears, too. The audience that has swooned at the Chopin and been respectful before the Bach is systematically cut to ribbons by the saw edges of the Piano Pieces. I begin to wonder all over again if Kaminski may have planned this program with perverse cunning: throw the philistines the Chopin, giving it all the *Schmalz* it will stand; then stun them with the Bach (only the Bach was too much for him); then trample them contemptuously underfoot with the Schoenberg, trusting that their ignorance will be impressed by this wrenched and tortured din even while they writhe under it. A good joke. But then what is he after? It is his own career that is at stake, he is the one who stands to benefit if the musicians' corner is impressed. Does he mean to say the hell with it on these terms, or am I reading into a not-quite-good-enough pianist a lot of ambiguities that don't exist in him?

It slowly dawns on me, while I grit my teeth to keep from howling like a dog, that Kaminski *means* this Schoenberg. He gives it the full treatment; he visibly wrestles with the Ineffable. Impossible to tell whether he hits the right notes or the wrong ones—probably Schoenberg himself couldn't tell. Wrong ones better, maybe—more tension. But Kaminski is concentrating as if the music ties him into bundles of raw nerves. For perhaps a second there is a blessed relief, a little thread of something almost a melody, and then the catfight again. Language of expressionism, tension and space, yes. Put yourself in the thumbscrew and any sort of release is blessed. Suite for nutmeg grater, cactus, and strings. A garland of loose ends.

He is putting himself into it devotionally; he *is* Schoenberg. I recall a picture of the composer on some record envelope—intense staring eyes, bald crown, temples with a cameo of raised veins, cheeks bitten in, mouth grim and bitter, unbearable pain. Arnold Schoenberg, Destroyer and Preserver. Mouthful of fire and can neither swallow nor spit.

In the cone of light under which Kaminski tortures himself and us, I see a bright quick drop fall from the end of his nose. Sweat or hay fever? Soul or allergy? Whatever it is, no one can say he isn't trying.

The piano stops with a noise like a hiccup or a death rattle. Three or four people laugh. Kaminski sits still. The audience waits, not to be caught offside. This might be merely space, there might be some more tension coming. But Kaminski is definitely through. Applause begins, with the over-enthusiastic sound of duty in it, and it dies quickly except in the musical row, where the accompanist is clapping persistently.

Sue is clapping her hands in intense slow strokes under her chin. "Isn't that something?" she says. "That's one thing he's been working on a lot. I just don't see how anybody plays it at all—all those minor ninths and major sevenths, and no key signature at all."

"Or *why* anybody plays it," I am compelled to say. But when her hands start another flurry I join in. Kaminski sits, spiritually exhausted, bending his head. Encore, encore. For Sue's sake, try. My arms begin to grow tired, and still he sits there. A full minute after my impertinent question, her hands still going, Sue says, "I admit *I* don't understand that kind of music, but because I'm ignorant is no reason to throw it away."

So I am rebuked. She is a noble and innocent woman, and will stoop to beg Kaminski and leave a door open for Schoenberg, all for the disinterested love of art. Well, God bless her. It's almost over, and she can probably feel that it was a success. Maybe she can even think of it as a triumph. Later, when nothing has come of all her effort and expense, she can console herself with a belief that there is a conspiracy among established musicians to pound the fingers of drowning genius off the gunwale.

"Well, anyway, *he's* terrific," I say like a forktongued liar. "Marvelous." Rewarded by all the gratitude she puts into her smile, I sit back for the encore that is finally forthcoming. And what does Kaminski play? Some number of Charles Ives, almost as mad as the Schoenberg.

Probably there might have been enough politeness among us to urge a second encore, but Kaminski cuts us off by leaving the piano. Matches flare, smoke drifts upward, the moonlight dawns again, Bill Casement appears from somewhere, and a discreet white coat crosses from the barbecue end of the cabaña and opens the folding panels of the bar.

V I

It seems that quite a number of times during the evening I am condemned to have Sue at me with tense questions. She is as bad as a Princeton boy with a manuscript: *Have I got it? Is it any good? Can I be a writer?* "What do you think?" Sue says now. "Am I wrong?"

"He's a good pianist."

Her impatience is close to magnificent. For a second she is Tallulah. "Good! Good heavens, I know that. But does he have a chance? Has he got so *much* talent they can't deny him? They say only about one young pianist in a hundred . . ."

"You can't make your chances," I say. "That's mostly luck."

"I'll be his luck," she says.

The crowd is rising and drifting inside. Trapped on the lounge, I lean back and notice that over our heads, marbled by the lights, white mist has begun to boil on some unfelt wind. The air is chilly and wet; the fog has come in. Ruth stands up, shivering her shoulders to cover the significant look she is giving me. I stand up with her. So does Sue, but Sue doesn't let me go.

"If you're his luck, then he has a chance," I say, and am rewarded by one of her smiles, so confident and proud that I am stricken with remorse, and add, "But it's an awful skinny little chance. Any young pianist would probably be better off if he made up his mind straight off to be a local musician instead of trying for a concert career."

"But the concert career is what he *wants*. It's what he's been preparing for all his life."

"Sure. That's what they all want. Then they eat their hearts out because they miss, and when you look at it, what is it they've missed? A chance to ride a dreary circuit and play for the local Master Minds and Artists series and perform in the Art Barn of every jerk town in America. It might be better if they stayed home and organized chamber groups and taught the young and appeared once a year as soloist with the local little symphony."

"Joe, dear," Sue says, "can you imagine Arnold teaching grubby little unwilling kids to play little Mozart sonatas for PTA meetings?"

She could not have found a quicker way to adjust my thermostat upward. It is true that I can't imagine Kaminski doing any such thing as teaching the young, but that is a commentary on Kaminski, not on the young. Besides, I am the defender, self-appointed, of the good American middle-class small-town and suburban way of life, and I get almighty sick of Americans who enjoy all its benefits but can't find a good word to say for it. An American may be defined as a man who won't take his own side in an argument. "Is Arnold *above* Mozart?" I ask. "For that matter, is he above the PTA?"

She stares at me to see if I'm serious. "Now you're being cute," she says, and blinks her eyes like a fond idiot and rushes inside to join the group around Kaminski. I note that Kaminski now has a highball in his hand. The Artist is only mortal, after all. If we wait, we may even see him condescend to a sandwich.

"Shall we get out of this?" I ask Ruth.

"Not yet."

"Why not?"

"Manners," she says. "You wouldn't understand, lamb. But let's go inside. It's cold out here."

It is, even with the radiant-heated magic carpet. The patio is deserted already. The air above boils with white. Between the abandoned chairs and empty lawn the transparent green-blue pool fumes with underwater light as if it opened down into hell. Once inside and looking out, I have a feeling of being marooned in a space ship. Any minute now frogmen will land their saucers on the patio or rise in diving helmets and snorkels from the pool.

Inside there are no frogmen, only Kaminski, talking with his hands, putting his glass on a tray and accepting another. The white head of the critic is humorously and skeptically bent, listening. The dour accompanist, the velvet-coated Mr. Budapest, the solid Ackermans, Sue, three or four unknowns, the little piano teacher, make a close and voluble group. Kaminski pauses amid laughter; evidently these others don't find him as hard to take as I do. As if he feels my thoughts, he looks across his hearers at Ruth and me, and Ruth raises her hands beside her head and makes pretty applauding motions. Manners. I am compelled to do the same, not so prettily.

Sam Shields goes past us, winks sadly, leaving. His wife is crippled and does not go out, so that he is always among the first to leave a party. This time he has five or six others for company, filing past Bill and being handshook at the door. To us now comes Annie Williamson, robust dame, and inquires in her fight-announcer's voice why we don't join the Hunt. They have fourteen members now, and enough permissions so that they can put hurdles on fences and get a run of almost fourteen miles. Of course we're not too old. Come on . . . Herman Dyer will still take a three-bar gate, and he's five years older than God. Or maybe we'd like the job of riding ahead dragging a scent or a dead rabbit. Make me Master of the Hunt, any office I want. Only come.

"Annie," I tell her sadly, "I am an old, infirm, pathetic figure. I have retired to these hills only to complete my memoirs, and riding a horse might cut them untimely short. Even art, such as tonight, can hardly make me leave my own humble hearth any more."

"What's the matter?" she says. "Didn't you like it? I thought it was swell. The last one was kind of yowly, but he played it fine."

"Sure I liked it," I say. "I thought it was real artistic."

"You're a philistine," Annie says. "An old cynical philistine. I'd hate to read your memoirs."

"You couldn't finish them," I say. "There isn't a horse or a beagle in them anywhere."

"A terribly limited old man," she says, and squeezes Ruth's arm and goes off shaking her head and chuckling. She circles the Kaminski crowd, interrupts something he is saying. I see her mouth going: Thank you, enjoyed it very much, blah blah. She first, and now a dozen others, neighbors and unknowns . . . so much . . . envy Sue the chance to hear you every day . . . luck to you . . . great treat. Some more effusive than others, but all respectful. Kaminski can sneer at his overfed alcoholic audience, but it has listened dutifully, and has applauded louder than it sometimes felt like doing, and has stilled its laughter in embarrassment when it didn't understand. If he had played nothing but Chopin they would have enjoyed him more, but he would have to be even more arrogant and superior and cross-grained than he is to alienate their good will and sour their wonderful good nature. Luck to you . . . And mean it. Would buy tickets, if necessary.

"Madame," I say to my noiseless wife, "art is troublesome and life is long. Can't we go home?"

For answer she steers me by the arm into the musical circle. Except for four people talking over something confidential in a corner, and the white coats moving around hopefully with unclaimed highballs on their trays, the musical circle now includes the whole company. Kaminski, we find, is still doing most of the talking. His subject is—guess what? The Artist. Specifically, the Artist in America.

I claim one of the spare highballs in self-defense. I know the substance of this lecture in advance, much of it from Murthi. And if Kaminski quotes Baudelaire about the great gaslighted Barbarity that killed Poe, I will disembowel him.

The lecture does not pursue its expected course more than a few minutes, and it is done with more grace and humor than I would have thought Kaminski had in him. A couple of highballs have humanized his soul. Mainly he talks, and without too obvious self-pity, about the difficulties of a musical career: twenty years or so of nothing but practice, practice, practice; the teachers in Boston and New York and Rome; the tyranny of the piano (I can't be away from a piano a single day without losing ground. On the train, and even in an automobile, I carry around a practice keyboard to run exercises on). It is (with a rueful mouth) a rough profession to get established in. He wonders sometimes why one doesn't instead take the Civil Service examinations. (Laughter.) But it is understandable, Kaminski says, why the trapdoor should be closed over the heads of young musicians. Established performers, and recording companies and agencies clinging to what they know is profitable, are naturally either jealous of competition or afraid to risk anything on new music or new men. (That charming little Ives that I used for an encore, for instance, has practically never been played, though it was composed almost fifty years ago.)

The case of Kaminski is (with a shrug) nothing unique. The critic and the Ackermans know how it goes. And of course, there is the problem of finding audiences. Whom shall one play for? Good audiences so few and so small, in spite of all the talk about the educational effect of radio and recordings. People who really know and love good music available only in the large cities or—with a flick of his dark eyes at Sue—in a few places such as this. Oh, he is full of charm. The little music teacher bridles. But generally, Kaminski says, there is only the sham audience with sham values, and the whole concert stage which is the only certain way of reaching audiences one can respect is dominated by two or three agencies interested only in dollars.

"Shyme, shyme," says old Joe Allston from the edge of the circle, and draws a startled half-smile from his neighbors and a second's ironic stare from Kaminski.

"What, a defender of agents in the crowd?" the critic says, turning his white head.

"Literary only," I say. "And ex, not current. But a bona fide paid-up member of the Agents' Protective Association, the only bulwark between the Artist and the poor farm."

"Are agents so *necessary*?" Sue says. "Isn't it possible to break in somehow without putting yourself in the clutches of one of them?"

"Clutches!" I say. "Consider my feelings."

Ruth gives me an absolutely expressionless, pleasant look in which I read some future unpleasantness, but what the hell, shall a man keep quiet while his lifework is trampled on?

"Would you admit," says Kaminski with his tight dogfish smile, "that an agent without an artist is a vine without an oak?"

The little music teacher brings her hands together. Her eyes are snapping and her little pointed chin, pebbled like the Pope's Nose of a plucked turkey, quivers. Oh, if she were defending the cause of music and art against such commercial attacks, she would . . . She is listening, comprehending, participating, right in the midst of things. Kaminski turns to her and actually winks. As a tray passes behind him he reaches back and takes a third highball. Joe Allston collars one too. The benevolent critic pokes his finger at old Joe and says encouragingly, "How about it, Agents' Protective Association? Can you stand alone?"

"I don't like the figure," I say. "I don't feel like a vine without an oak. I feel like a Seeing Eye dog without a blind man."

This brings on a shower of protests and laughter, and Sue says, "Joe, if you're going to stick up for agents you'll have to tell us how to beat the game. How could an agent help Arnold, say, get a hearing and get started?"

"Any good agency will get him an audition, any time."

"Yes, along with a thousand others."

"No, by himself."

"And having had it, what does he get out of it?" murmurs Mr. Ackerman. He has winesap cheeks and white, white hair, but his expression is not benevolent like the critic's, mainly because his whole face has come loose, and sags—big loose lips, big drooping nose, a forehead that hangs in folds over his eyebrows. He reminds me of a worried little science-fiction writer I used to know who developed what his doctor called "lack of muscle tone," so that his nose wouldn't even hold up his glasses. It was as if he had been half disintegrated by one of his ray guns. Mr. Ackerman's voice sags like his face; he looks at me with reddish eyes above hound-dog lower lids.

They all obviously enjoy yapping at me. Here is the Enemy, the Commercial Evil Genius that destroys Art. This kind of thing exhilarates me, I'm afraid.

"That's not the agent's fault," I say. "It's a simple matter of supply and demand. A hundred good young pianists come to New York every year all pumped full of hope. They are courteously greeted and auditioned by the agents, who take on anyone they can. Agents arrange concerts, including Town Hall and Carnegie Hall concerts, for some of them, and they paper the hall and invite and inveigle the critics and clip the reviews, and if the miracle happens and some young man gets noticed in some special way, they book him on a circuit. But if ninety-nine of those young pianists slink out of New York with a few pallid clippings and no rave notices and no bookings, that isn't the agents' fault."

"Then whose fault is it?" cries Sue. "There are millions of people who would be thrilled to hear someone like Arnold play. Why can't they? There seems to be a stone wall between."

"Overproduction," murmurs old Devil's-Advocate Allston, and sips his insolent bourbon.

Mr. Ackerman's face lifts with a visible effort its sagging folds; the critic looks ironical and skeptical; Kaminski watches me over his glass with big shining liquid eyes. His pitted skin is no longer pale, but has acquired a dark, purplish flush. He seems to nurse some secret amusing knowledge. The music teacher at his elbow twists her mouth, very incensed and impatient at old commercial Allston. Her mouth opens for impetuous words, closes again. Her pebbled chin quivers.

"Overproduction, sure," I say again. "If it happened in the automobile industry you'd blame it on the management, or the government, or on classical capitalist economics, or creeping socialism. But it's in music, and so you want to blame it on the poor agent. An agent is only a dealer. He isn't to blame if the factory makes too many cars. All he can do is sell the ones he can."

"I'm afraid Mr. Allston is pulling our leg," the critic says. "Art isn't quite a matter of production lines. Genius can't be predicted and machined like a Chevrolet, do you think, Mr. Casement?"

He catches Bill by surprise. Evidently he is one of those who like to direct and control conversations, pulling in the hangers-on. But his question is no kindness to Bill, who strangles and waves an arm. "Don't ask me! I don't know a thing about it." Even after the spotlight has left him, he stands pulling his lower lip, looking around over his hand, and chuckling meaninglessly when he catches anyone's eye.

"So you don't think a New York concert does any good," Sue says—pushing, pushing. After all, she held this clambake to bring us all together and now she has what she wanted—patrons and critics and agents in a cluster—and she is going to find out everything. "If they don't do any good, why bother?"

"Why indeed?" I say, and then I see that I have carried it too far, for Sue's face puckers unhappily, and she insists, "But Joe . . ."

The critic observes, "They may not do much good, but nothing can be done *without* one."

"So for the exceptional ones they *do* do some good."

"For the occasional exception they may do everything," the critic says. "Someone like William Kapell, who was killed in a plane crash just a few miles from here. But Kapell was a *very* notable exception."

I cannot read Kaminski—it is being made increasingly clear to me that one of my causes of irritation at him is precisely that I don't know what goes on inside him—but I can read Sue Casement without bifocals, and the look she throws at Kaminski says two things: One is that here, just five feet from her, is another Notable Exception as notable as Kapell. The other is that since Kapell has been killed on the brink of a brilliant career, he has obviously left a vacancy.

"A lot of young pianists can't afford it, I expect," she says—hopefully, I think.

The critic spreads his hands. "Town Hall about fifteen hundred, Carnegie two thousand. Still, a lot of them find it somewhere. It's a lot of money to put on the turn of a card."

Determination and resolve, or muscular contractions that I interpret in these terms, harden in Sue's rosy face. "Is it hard to arrange?"

I can't resist. "Any good agent will take care of it for you," I say. She throws me a smile: you old devil, you.

"But no one can count on one single thing's coming from it," the critic says, and he looks kindly upon both Sue and her protégé. I respect this benevolent old creature in spite of his profession. He is trying to warn them.

Not being one of these socially clairvoyant people, I would not feel extraordinarily at home in a Virginia Woolf novel. But I get a glimpse, for the most fragmentary moment, of an extreme complexity pressing in upon us. There is of course Ruth emanating silent disapproval of her husband's big argumentative mouth, and there is Sue, radiant and res-olute, smiling promises at Kaminski. There is Kaminski with his deer eyes wide and innocent, his mouth indifferently half smiling—a pure enigma to me, unidentifiable. And there are the critic, ruminating kindly and perhaps with friendly sorrow his own private doubts, and Ackerman incognito behind the heavy folds of his face, and Mrs. Ackerman, who looks as if she would like nothing better than to get off her aching feet and start home, and the music teacher bristling with excitement and stimulation, saying to Kaminski, "But *imagine* getting up on the stage at Carnegie Hall with Virgil Thomson and Olin Downes and everybody there. . . ." Also there is Bill Casement with his long creased face that looks as overworked as Gary Cooper trying to register an emotion. What emotion? Maybe he is kissing two thousand dollars good-bye and won-dering if he is glad to see it go. Maybe he is proud of his wife, who has the initiative and the culture to do all this of this evening. Maybe he is contemplating the people in his cabaña and thinking what funny things can happen to a man's home.

So only one thing is clear. Sue will stake Kaminski to a New York concert. I don't know why that depresses me. It has been clear all along that that is exactly what she has wanted to do. My depression may come from Kaminski's indifference. I would like to see the stinker get his chance and goof it good.

An improbable opening appears low down in the droops and folds of Mr. Ackerman's face, and he yawns. "Darling," his wife says at once, "we have a long drive back to the city."

In a moment the circle has begun to melt and disintegrate. Sue is accosted with gratitude from three sides. The accompanist and the velvet-coated Mr. Budapest stay with Kaminski to say earnest friendly things: I want you to come up and meet . . . He will be interested that you have appeared with . . . of course they will have heard of you . . . I should think something of Hovhaness' . . . yes . . . excellent. Why not?

Since the discussion took his career out of his hands, Kaminski has said nothing. He bows, he smiles, but his face has gone remote; the half-sneer of repose has come back into it. He is a Hyperborean, beyond everybody. All this nonsense about careers bores him. Why do the heathen rage furiously together? Beyond question, he is one of the greatest bargains I have ever seen bought.

Also, as he turns and shakes hands with Mr. Budapest and recalls himself for the tiresomeness of good nights, I observe that perhaps what I took for snootiness is paralysis. He does not believe in alcohol, which is drunk only by pigs, but I have seen him take four highballs in twenty minutes, and Bill Casement's bartenders have been taught not to spare the Old Granddad.

V I I

While the other ladies are absent getting their coats, Kaminski holds collapse off at arm's length and plays games of solemn jocularity with the homely little music teacher. He leans carefully and whispers in her ear something that makes her flush and laugh and shake her head, protesting. "Eh?" he cries. "Isn't it so?" With his feet crossed he leans close, rocking his ankles. Out of the corner of the music teacher's eye goes an astonishingly cool flickering look, alert to see if anyone is watching her here, tête-à-tête with the maestro. All she sees is old Joe Allston, the commercial fellow. Her neck stiffens, her eyes are abruptly glazed, her face is carefree and without guile as she turns indifferently back. Old Allston is about as popular as limburger on the newlyweds' exhaust manifold. He hates us Youth. The Anti-Christ.

"You can joke," she says to Kaminski, "but I'm serious, really I am. We know we aren't very wonderful, but we aren't so bad, either, so there. We've got a very original name: The Chamber Society. And if you don't watch out, I will sign you up to play with us sometime. So don't say anything you don't mean!"

"I never say anything I don't mean," Kaminski grins. "I'd love to play with you. All ladies, are you?"

"All except the cello. He's a math teacher at the high school."

"Repulsive," Kaminski murmurs. The teacher giggles, swings sideways, sees me still there, nails me to the wall with a venomous look. Snoop! Why don't I move? But I am much too interested to move.

"Three ladies and one gentleman," Kaminski says, smiling broadly and leaning over her so far he overbalances and staggers. "A Mormon. Are the other ladies all like you?"

Because I know that none of this will sound credible when I report it to Ruth, I strain for every word of this adolescent drooling. I see the music teacher, a little hesitant, vibrate a look at Kaminski's face and then, just a little desperately, towards the group of men by the door. Kaminski is greatly amused by something. "I tell you what you should do," he says. "You reorganize yourself into the Bed-chamber Society. Let the Mormon have the other two, and you and I will play together. Any time."

He has enunciated this unkind crudity very plainly, so plainly that at fifteen feet I cannot possibly have misheard. The little teacher does not look up from her abstract or panicky study of certain chair legs. Her incomplete little face goes slowly scarlet, her pebbled chin is stiff. That little cold venomous glance whips up to me and is taken back again. If I were not there, she would probably run for her life. As it is, she is tempted into pretending that nothing has been said. She is like Harold Lloyd in one of those old comedies, making vivacious and desperate chatter to a girl, while behind the draperies or under the tablecloth his accidentally snagged pants unravel or his seams burst or his buttons one by one give up the ghost. Sooner or later the draperies will be thrown open by the butler, or someone's belt buckle will catch the tablecloth and drag it to the floor, and there will be Harold in his hairy shanks, his Paris garters. Oh Lord. I am not quite able to take myself away from there.

Kaminski leans over her, catches himself by putting a hand on her shoulder, says something else close to her red-hot ear. That does it. She squirms sideways, shakes him off, and darts past the ladies just returning from the cloakroom. Kaminski, not so egg-eyed as I expect to see him, looks at me with a smile almost too wide for his mouth, and winks. He could not be more pleased if he had just pulled the legs off a live squirrel. But the music teacher, darting past me, has given me quite another sort of look. There is a dead-white spot in the center of each cheek, and her eyes burn into mine with pure hatred. That is what I get for being an innocent bystander and witnessing her humiliation.

For a few seconds Kaminski stands ironically smiling into thin air; he wears a tasting expression. Then he motions to one of the Japanese at the bar, and the Japanese scoops ice cubes into a glass.

It is time for us to get away from there. The elegant cabaña smells and looks like Ciro's at nine o'clock of a Sunday morning. Outside, the pool lights are off, but the air swirls and swims, dizzy with moonlighted fog. The sliding doors are part way open for departing guests. Sue comes and catches Kaminski by the arm, holding his sleeve with both hands in a too friendly, too sisterly pose. They stand in the doorway with the mist blowing beyond them.

"Now please do come and see me," Ackerman says. "One never knows. I would like to introduce you. Perhaps some evening, a little group at my home."

"Good luck," says the critic. "I shall hope before long to write pleasant comments after your name."

"Ah, *vun*derful," says Mr. Budapest, "you were *vun*derful! I have so enjoyed it. And if you should write to Signor Vitelli, my greetings. It has been many years."

"Not at all, not at all," says Bill Casement. "Happy to have you."

"It was so good of you all to come," Sue says. "You don't know how . . . or rather, you do, all of you do. You've been generous to come and help. I'm sure it will work out for him somehow, he has such great talent. And when you're as ignorant as I am . . . I hope when you're down this way you won't hesitate . . . Good-bye, good-bye, good-bye."

The women pull June fur coats around them, their figures blur in the mist and are invisible beyond the Mondrian gate. But now comes the music teacher with a bone in her teeth, poor thing, grimly polite, breathless. She looks neither to left nor right past Sue's face: Good night. A pleasant time. You have a very beautiful place. Thank you. And gone.

Her haste is startling to Sue, who likes to linger warmly on farewells, standing with arms hugged around herself in lighted doorways. Kaminski toasts the departing tweed with a silent glass. The figure hurries through the gate, one shoulder thrust ahead, the coat thrown cape-wise over her shoulders. Almost she scuttles. From beyond the gate she casts back one terrible glance, and is swallowed in the fog.

"Why, I wonder what's the matter with her?" Sue says. "Didn't she act odd?"

Bill motions us in and slides the glass door shut. With his back against the door Kaminski studies the ice cubes which remain from his fifth highball. All of a sudden he is as gloomy as a raincloud. "I'm the matter with her," he says. "I insulted her."

"You *what?*"

"Insulted her. I made indecent propositions."

"Oh, Arnold!" Sue says with a laugh. "Come on!"

"It's true," Arnold says. "Ask the agent, there. I whispered four-letter words in her ear."

She stares at him steadily. "And if you did," she says, "in heaven's name *why* did you?"

"Akh!" Kaminski says. "Such a dried-up little old maid as that, so full of ignorance and enthusiasm. How could I avoid insulting her? She is the sort of person who invites indecent exposure." There is a moment of quiet in which we hear the sound of a car pulling out of the drive. "How could I help insulting her?" Kaminski shouts. "If I didn't insult people like that I couldn't keep my self-respect." Nobody replies to this. "That is why nobody likes me," he says, and looks around for a white coat but the white coats are all gone. Automatically Sue takes his empty glass from him.

Ruth says, quite loudly for her, "Sue, we must go. It was a lovely party. And Mr. Kaminski, I thought you played beautifully."

His flat stare challenges her. "I was terrible," he says. "Ackerman and those others will tell you. They are saying right now in their car how bad it was. The way I played, they will think I am fit for high school assemblies or Miss Spinster's chamber society. I am all finished around here. Nothing will come of any of this. I have muffed it again."

"Finished?" Sue cries. "Arnold, you've just begun."

"Finished," he says. "All done."

"Oh, what if you did insult Miss What's-her-name," Sue says. "You can go and apologize tomorrow. It's your playing that's important, and you played so beautifully. . . ."

Bill Casement, by the door jamb, rubs one cheek, pulling his mouth down and then up again. He gives me a significant look; I half expect him to twirl a finger beside his head. "Well, good night," I say. "I'm tired, and I imagine you all are."

Bill slides the door open a couple of feet, but Sue pays no attention to me. She is staring angrily at Kaminski. "How can you *talk* that way? You did beautifully—ask anybody who heard you. This is only the first step, and you got by it just—just wonderfully! I told you I'd back you, and I will."

I have never observed anyone chewing his tongue, but that is what

Kaminski is doing now, munching away, and his purple cheeks working. His face has begun to degenerate above the black and white formality of jacket and pleated shirt and rigid black tie. "You're incurably kind," he says thickly—whether in irony or not I can't tell. He spits out his tongue and says more plainly, "You like me, I know that. You're the only one. Nobody else. Nobody ever did. This is the way it was in Hollywood too. Did you know I was in Hollywood a while? I had a job playing for the soundtrack of a Charles Boyer movie. So what did I do? I quarreled with the director and he got somebody else."

With a resolute move, Ruth and I get out of the door. Pinpricks of fog are in our faces. From inside, Sue says efficiently, "Arnold, you've had one too many. It was a great success, really it was."

"Every time, I fail," wails Kaminski. His Mephisto airs have been melted and dissolved away; he is just a sloppy drunk with a crying jag on. His eyes beg pity and his mouth is slack and his hands paw at Sue. She holds him off by one thick wrist. "Every time," he says, and his eyes are on her now with a sudden drunken alertness. "Every time. You know why? I *want* to fail. I work like a dog for twenty years so I'll have the supreme pleasure of failing. Never knew anybody like that, did you? I'm very cunning. I plan it in advance. I fool myself right up to the last minute, and then the time comes and I know how cunningly I've been planning it all the time. I've been a failure all my life."

I am inclined to agree with him, but I am old and tired and fed up. I would also bet that he is well on his way to being an alcoholic, this anti-food-and-drink Artist. He has the proper self-pity. If you don't feel sorry for yourself in something like this you can't justify the bottle that cures and damns you. This Kaminski is one of those who drink for the hangover; he sins for the sweet torture of self-blame and confession. A crying jag is as good a way of holding the stage as playing the piano or bad manners.

Now he is angry again. "Why should a man have to scramble and crawl for a chance to play the soundtrack in a Boyer picture? That is how the artist is appreciated in this country. He plays offstage while a ham actor fakes for the camera. Why should I put up with that? If I'm an artist, I'm an artist. I would rather play the organ in some neon cocktail bar than do this behind-the-scenes faking."

"Of course," Sue says. "And tomorrow we can talk about how you're going to go ahead and be the artist you want to be. You can have the career you want, if you're willing to work hard—oh, so hard! But you have to have *faith* in yourself, Arnold! You have to have confidence that nothing on earth can stop you, and then it can't."

"Faith," says Kaminski. "Confidence!" He weaves on his feet, and his head rolls, and for a second I hope he has passed out so we can tote him off to bed. But he gets himself straightened up and under control again, showing a degree of co-ordination that makes me wonder all anew whether he is really as drunk as he seems or if he is putting on some fantastic act.

And then I find him looking out of the open door with his mouth set in a mean little line. "*You* don't like me," he says. "You disliked me the minute you met me, and you've been watching me all night. You want to know why?"

"Not particularly," I say. "You'd better get to bed, and in the morning we can all be friends again."

"You're no friend of mine," says Kaminski, and Sue exclaims, "Arnold!" but Kaminski wags his head and repeats, "No frien' of mine, and I'll tell you why. You saw I was a fake. Looked right through me, didn' you? Smart man, can't be fooled just because somebody can play the piano. When did you decide I wasn't a Pole, eh? Tell me tha'."

I lift my shoulders. But it is true, now that I have had my attention called to it, that the slight unplaceable accent that was present earlier in the evening is gone. Now, even drunk and chewing his tongue, he talks a good deal like . . .

"Well, what is the accent?" I ask. "South Boston?"

"See, wha' I tell you?" he cries, and swings on Sue so that she has to turn with him and brace herself to hold him up. Her face puckers with effort, or possibly disgust, and now for the first time she is looking at Bill as a wife looks towards her husband when she needs to be got out of trouble. "See?" Kaminski shouts. "Wasn't fooled. You all were, but he wasn'. Regnize Blue Hill Avenue in a minute."

Again he drags himself up straight, holding his meaty hand close below his nose and studying it. "I'm a Pole from Egypt," he says. "Suffered a lot, been through Hell, made me diff'cult and queer. Eh?" He swings his eye around us, this preposterous scene-stealer; he holds us with his glittering eye. "Le' me tell you. Never been near Egypt, don't even know where Poland is on the map. My mother was not made into soap; she runs a copper and brass shop down by the North Station. So you wonner why people detes' me. Know why? I'm a fake, isn't an hones' thing about me. You jus' le' me go to Hell my own way, I'm good at it. I can lie my way in, and if I want I can lie my way out again. And what do you think of that?"

Bill Casement is the most good-natured of men, soft with his wife and over-generous with his friends and more tolerant of all sorts of difference, even Kaminski's sort, than you would expect. But I watch him now, while Kaminski is falling all over Sue, and Sue is making half-disgusted efforts to prop him up, and I realize that Bill did not make his money scuffing his feet and pulling his cheek in embarrassment at soirées. Underneath the good-natured husband is a man of force, and in about one more minute he is due to light on Kaminski like the hammer of God.

Even while I think it, Bill reaches over and yanks him up and holds him by one arm. "All right," he says. "Now you've spilled it all. Let's go to bed."

"You too," Kaminski says. "You all hate me. You'll all wash your hands of me now. Well, why not? That Carnegie Hall promise, that won't hold when you know what kin' of person I am, eh? You'll all turn into enemies now."

"Is that what you *want*, Arnold?" Sue says bitterly. She looks ready to burst into tears.

"Tol' you I wanted to fail," he says—and even now, so help me, even out of his sodden and doughy wreckage, there looks that bright, mean, calculating little gleam of intelligence.

Bill says, "The only enemy you've got around here is your own mouth."

"My God!" Kaminski cries loudly. Either the fog has condensed on his face or he is sweating. I remember the bright drop from his nose while he struggled with the Piano Pieces. "My God," he says again, almost wearily. He hangs, surprisingly frail, from Bill's clutch; it is easy to forget, looking at his too-big head and his meaty hands, that he is really scrawny. "I'll tell you something else," he says. "You don't know right now whether what I've tol' you is true or if it isn'. Not even the smart one there. You don't know but what I've been telling you all this for some crazy reason of my own. Why would I? Does it make sense?" He drops his voice and peers around, grinning. "Maybe he's crazy. *C'est dérangé.*"

"Come on," Bill says. He lifts Kaminski and starts him along, but Kaminski kicks loose and staggers and almost falls among the chairs in the foggy patio, and now what has been impossible becomes outrageous, becomes a vulgar burlesque—and I use the word vulgar deliberately, knowing who it is that speaks.

"Don't you worry about me!" Kaminski shouts, and kicks a chair over. "Don't you worry about a starving kike pianist from Blue Hill Avenue. Maybe I grew up in Egypt and maybe I didn't, but I can still play the piano. I can play the God damn keys off a piano."

He comes back closer, facing Sue with a chairback in his hands, bracing himself on it. "Don't worry," he says. "I can see you worrying, but don't worry. I'll be out of your damned little gardener's cottage in the morning, and thank you very much for nothing. Will that satisfy you?" With a jerk he throws the chair aside and it falls and clatters.

Bill Casement takes one step in Kaminski's direction, and the outrageous turns instantly into slapstick. The pianist squeaks like a mouse, turns and runs for his life. Behind a remoter chair he stops to show his teeth, but when Bill starts for him again he turns once more and runs. For a moment he hangs in mid-air, his legs going like a cat's held over water, and then he is in the pool. The splash comes up ghostly into the moonlight and the fog, and falls back again.

Maybe he can't swim. Maybe in his squeaking terror of what he has stirred up he has forgotten that the pool is there. Maybe he is so far gone that he doesn't even know he has fallen in. And maybe, on the other hand, he literally intends to drown himself.

If he does, he successfully fails in that too. By the time Bill has run to flip on the underwater lights the white coat is down under, and Kaminski is not struggling at all. While the women scream, Bill jumps into the water, and here he comes wading towards the shallow end dragging Kaminski under his arm. He hauls him up the corner steps and dangles him, shaking the water out of him, and Kaminski's arms drag on the tile and his feet hang limp.

"Oh my God," Sue whispers, "is he dead?"

Bill looks disgusted. After all, Kaminski couldn't have been in the pool more than a minute altogether. As Bill lowers him on to the warm pavement and straightens him out with his face turned sideways on his arm, Kaminski shudders and coughs. His hands make tense, meaty grabs at the concrete. The majordomo, Jerry, pops out of the kitchen end of the cabaña in his undershirt, takes one look, and pops back in again. In a moment he comes running with a blanket.

Kaminski is not seriously in need of a blanket. For the first time that evening, he is not seriously in need of an audience, either. We stay only long enough to see that Bill and Jerry have everything under control, and then we get away. Sue walks us to the gate, but it is impossible to say anything to her. She looks at us once so hurt and humiliated and ashamed that I feel like going back and strangling Kaminski for keeps where he lies gagging on the patio floor, and then we are alone in the surrealist fog-swept spaces of the parking area. In the car we sit for a minute or two letting the motor warm, while the windshield wipers make half-circles of clarity on the glass.

"I wonder what . . ." Ruth begins, but I put my hand over her mouth.

"Please. I am an old tired philistine who has had all he can stand. Don't even speculate on what's biting him, or why he acts the way he does. I've already given him more attention than I can justify."

As soon as I take my hand away, Ruth says softly, "The horrible part is, he played awfully well."

We are moving now out the fog-shrouded drive between curving rows of young pines. "What?" I say. "Did you think so?"

"Oh yes. Didn't you?"

"He hit a big blooper in the Chaconne."

"That could happen to anybody, especially somebody young and nervous. But the interpretation—didn't you hear how he put himself into first the one and then the other, and how the whole quality changed, and how really authoritative he was in all of them? Some pianists can only play Mozart, or Beethoven, or Brahms. He can play anybody, and play him well. That's what Mr. Arpad said, too."

"Who's Mr. Arpad?"

"The one that accompanies singers."

"He thought he was good?"

"He told me he had come down expecting only another pianist, but he thought Kaminski had a real chance."

Tall eucalyptus trees are suddenly ghostly upreaching, the lights shine on their naked white trunks, the rails of a fence. I ease around a turn in second gear. "Well, all right," I say in intense irritation. "All right, he was good. But then why in the hell would he . . ."

And there we are back on it. Why would he? What made him? Was he lying at first, lying later, or lying all the time? And what is more important to me just then, where in God's name does he belong? What can the Sue Casements do for the Arnold Kaminskis, and where do the Bills come in, and what function, if any, is served by the contented, beagle-running, rabbit-chasing, patio-building, barbecuing exurbanites on their hundred hills? How shall a nest of robins deal with a cuckoo chick? And how should a cuckoo chick, which has no natural home except the one he usurps, behave himself in a robin's nest? And what if the cuckoo is sensitive, or Spiritual, or insecure? Christ.

Lights come at us, at first dim and then furry and enormous, the car behind them vaguely half seen, glimpsed and gone, and then the seethe of white again. I never saw the fog thicker; the whole cloudy blanket of the Pacific has poured over the Coast Range and blotted us out. I creep at ten miles an hour, peering for the proper turn-off on these unmarked country lanes.

The bridge planks rumble under us as I grope into our own lane. Half a mile more. Up there, the house will be staring blindly into cottonwool; my study below the terrace will be swallowed in fog; the oak tree where I do my birdwatching will have no limbs, no shade, no birds. Leaning to see beyond the switching wiper blades, I start up the last steep pitch, past the glaring-white gate, and on, tilting steeply, with the brown bank just off one fender and the gully's treetops fingering the fog like seaweed on the left. All blind, all difficult and blind. I taste the stale bourbon in my mouth and know myself for a frivolous old man.

In the morning, probably, the unidentifiable bird, towhee or whatever he is, will come around for another bout against the plate glass, hypnotized by the insane hostility of his double. I tell myself that if he wakes me again at dawn tomorrow with his flapping and pecking I will borrow a shotgun and scatter his feathers over my whole six acres.

Of course I will not. I know what I will do. I will watch the fool thing as long as I can stand it, and ruminate on the insanities of men and birds, and try to convince myself that as a local idiocy, an individual aberration, this behavior is not significant. And then when I cannot put up with the sight of this towhee any longer I will retire to my study and sit looking out of the window into the quiet shade of the oak, where nuthatches are brownly and pertly content with the bugs in their home bark. But even down there I may sometimes hear the banging and thrashing of this dismal towhee trying to fight his way past himself into the living-room of the main house.

We coast into the garage, come to a cushioned stop, look at each other.

"Tired?" Ruth whispers.

Her pet coon face glimmers in the dim light of the dash. Her eyes seem to be searching mine with a kind of anxiety. I notice that tired lines are showing around her mouth and eyes, and I am filled with gratitude for the forty years during which she has stood between me and myself.

"I don't know," I say, and kiss her and lean back. "I don't know whether I'm tired, or sad, or confused. Or maybe just irritated that they don't give you enough time in a single life to figure anything out."

SOMETHING SPURIOUS FROM THE MINDANAO DEEP

A half-hour before noon, Burns had the bar to himself. Warm air blew in gusts through the room; outside, awnings and pool and umbrellas and lounges blazed under the vertical sun. Beyond the breakwater and the bordering palms, Manila Bay was congealed lead, with three rusty hulks jutting above the surface, not quite melted down. It was all as lurid as a surrealist painting; it half fused in his mind with a picture he had in his study at home—a painting by the Mexican Meza, a desert water hole and a shrouded Indian with feet like bird claws or like roots. He was as metamorphosed as that Indian; his own feet might be claws or roots, the emaciated face reflected back at him from a dusky glass door might be a caricature of his real face, or again it might be face of beast or bird.

In the sharp lime taste of his gimlet was concentrated a memory of all the places where in the last seven months he had braced himself with that characteristic drink of the Empire. Cairo, Alexandria, Karachi, Bombay, Bangalore, Hyderabad, Madras, Calcutta, Singapore, Bangkok— in all of them there had been residual fortresses like this one where

Europeans and Americans kept themselves aloof. They had drawn his criticism, those segregated compounds.

As a cultural ambassador, representing a foundation dedicated to the unity of mankind, he was eager to show himself the very opposite of a snob. Unfortunately, he had found that there were other reasons than snobbery for the compounds. By mingling democratically with all levels of life around the globe, snooping in *suqs* and bazaars, eating and drinking everything that hospitality and good will put before him, Burns had managed to contract most of the diseases that snobbery might have saved him from. He reflected with gloomy irony that it was in payment for an excess of democracy that he now dragged on doctor's orders over to the Army and Navy Club every morning to build himself up with regular, gentle exercise. Nearing the end of his tour of duty, he was also nearing the rueful admission that East was East and West was West. All men were human but their humanity took very different forms; and to insist on overlooking the differences was to come finally to massive doses of vitamin C and a reliance on the gimlet to get you from breakfast to lunch, from lunch to dinner, and from dinner to bed.

It was near the time of his appointment with the editor, Avellanos. Burns signaled the waiter, signed his chit, and got out. Outside, the sun was pale and intense, the air milky. The promontories that enclosed the bay reached out and faded distantly in veils of heat. MacArthur Boulevard poured with the converted jeep taxis they called jeepneys; a squad of constabulary had stacked arms and was resting in the shade of Rizal's statue. Walking slowly, not to heat or exert himself, Burns had made it halfway across the lawn that stretched to the Manila Hotel when he saw the pearl peddler coming. The transparent sport shirt with its tails blowing, the bony grinning Malay face, made him feel tired. If he had had a hearing aid he would have tuned it out.

From twenty feet away the peddler hailed him. "Hey, Joe, how about those pearls today? You think it over? Real Mindanao pearls, my brother just come back with them. Real bargain, four for eighty pesos."

Burns waved him away. Quite apart from his professional determination to be friendly to everyone, he could not dislike this cheerful crook, but he had heard the spiel every day for five days. He said, smiling fiercely, "Go sell your phony pearls to someone else!"

"Phony pearls? Now hey, Joe, you just look. My brother dives, he got these himself. . . ."

"Right out of the Mindanao Deep," Burns said, still walking.

"You guessed it, Joe." The peddler hopped backward, untying a knotted bandanna. His grin, Burns thought, was part of a considered practice of scoundrelship; it said that of course you were as crooked as he was, you came into the racket as a sort of guest. "Look! Pearls, they're small, go in your shoe, anywhere. Customs never look. You sell these in the States a hundred dollars apiece. You don't get these big oysters, with these big pearls, anywhere but Mindanao, down in that Deep like you say."

Burns walked through him. "Away, away!"

"You got a girl," said the peddler, skipping at his side. "Maybe wife. Man like you. Nice present for a lady. Just take a look. I make them seventy-five."

Finally he succeeded in blocking Burns off and shoving the opened bandanna before his eyes. The pearls were the size of flattened marbles, rather pretty, opalescent, with a look like moonstones. Someone had evidently ground them out of an abalone shell on an emery wheel.

"Very pretty," Burns said. "But no. I don't need any pearls. Find some other sucker."

The pearl man was not upset. He did not affect the injured dignity that an Egyptian or Indian sharper would have assumed if his integrity had been doubted. "You come out again soon?"

"Not if I see you waiting."

"I be around," the pearl man said with great friendliness. "I wait for you."

Shaking his head, Burns went into the hotel and looked in the bar for Avellanos. The editor was not yet there. He sat down and ordered a gimlet.

Within ten minutes Avellanos came in, a short man, compact, full of energy. Being patriot and politician as well as editor, he wore a pineapple cloth shirt. He carried an important briefcase, he smoked cigars like torpedoes, he had a cocky air that reminded Burns a little of the pearl peddler. And he had a change of plans to suggest.

It was his assignment and his pleasure to open up Manila to Mr. Burns for three weeks. Very well. But instead of going this afternoon to three universities, at each of which Burns would probably be asked to make a speech on English as a world language, how about going to a party? With a smile that was boyish and sly he took a newspaper from his briefcase and pointed out a small box advertisement at the foot of page one. It said:

> Pacita Delgado, feeling that it is much too long since the old crowd of writers met, is taking this means of inviting them all for roast pig and plenty tuba at her house on January 10. For old times' sake, come.

Politely but positively Burns shook his head. "It would be charming, I know. But I've been sick, and I have to be careful."

"Of roast pig? That's delicious, a feast. That won't hurt you."

"In the last six months," Burns said, "I have had hepatitis, a strep throat, mononucleosis, and two bouts of what is affectionately called Delhi Belly. All I need is a case of amoebic to set me right up. No, I'm sorry, I'd love to come otherwise. But I just don't have any resistance to strange bugs."

"Don't eat, then. Just drink."

"Is it important to you? Is there some special reason?"

Avellanos wagged his head. "It's a literary crowd. You'd meet most of Manila's writers."

Watching his brown face, the face of a tough good-natured boy, Burns said, "It seems an odd way to issue an invitation."

The editor rocked back on the hind legs of his chair and guffawed so that people lunching under the windows looked up. "All right, I'll confess," he said, and the chair legs came down with a clack as he hunched close. "This advertisement is aimed at me, you see? In my own paper. How she ever got that front-page space is interesting, too. I would like to know. This Pacita is my mistress—my ex-mistress, you understand? I haven't been to see her for three months."

Beginning to feel like the captive audience of a tale by Conrad or Somerset Maugham, Burns licked the taste of Rose's lime juice off his lips. He was not eager to share this Avellanos' overlively private life. But out of politeness he said, "You haven't? Why not?"

"Naturally a man has other things to think of. She was becoming possessive. Also, as a politician I have to be careful." His cheeks crumpled in the wide delighted grin that seemed his most natural expression. "Besides, there are so many women, all charming. And I dislike scoldings."

"Why do you think she advertised this barbecue?"

Avellanos cocked thumb and finger, winked his eye. "Maybe she plans to shoot me."

"You're kidding, of course."

"She's a reckless woman."

"Maybe she's just sentimental."

"Sentimental too. I admit. I'm curious to know what this girl has in her head. She is never dull, and she is also very good-looking."

"Well, let's go, then," Burns said. "It must be marvelous to be so sought after."

The smile that Avellanos threw at the ceiling was ecstatic; his brown throat worked with laughter. "My friend," he said, "you have no idea!"

There was no chance for a rest after lunch. Already tired, Burns waited for Avellanos at the hat-check stand under the sign, "Check all firearms here." After five days in Manila he was used to giving cultural speeches while a guard with a carbine patrolled the hall, and he had dined in gardens where a watchman, also with a carbine, moved steadily up and down. But he thought the hat-check sign absurd and melodramatic. Filipinos lived for drama; if the Huks had not existed they would have had to be invented. Burns said so, in effect, and Avellanos, giving the girl his check, accepted with a broad smile the automatic she handed him. He slipped it into the briefcase and hooked his arm in that of Burns.

"There are all sorts of possibilities," he said.

On the way to Pacita Delgado's house, which seemed to be far out, Burns leaned back and closed his eyes, opening them once when the car stopped at a roadblock and brown faces of constabulary looked in, and again when they parked in an unpaved street of banana trees and small fenced houses on stilts. Avellanos had slammed the door and started up the path when Burns, noticing, said, "You're forgetting your briefcase." The editor tossed his fingers in the air with a laugh.

"Did you think I carried it for Pacita? No, if she shoots me, she shoots me."

This house was built not on stilts but on the ground, with a garden that went around behind. Inside the bamboo fence they met whiffs of richly flavored smoke and cascades of brittle talk. That was another thing about Filipinos: they spoke English as if it were another language, they reduced it to its particles and made it a language not of words but of syllables. Burns braced himself for the party chatter, the amenities of thoroughly decent people whom he would never see again and who were marked in his mind as unalterably different from himself. His long, idealistic, exhausting tour came down in the end to a reiteration of banalities, a constant assertion of good will as empty as a Presidential handshake. Avellanos knocked on the door.

The young woman who appeared in the doorway had to be Pacita Delgado from the way she looked at Burns' companion—nothing so vulgar as spite or fury, but a look watchful, intimate, composed, smiling. Avellanos took her hand and held it. "Pacita."

"Ramón. It's nice of you to come to my party."

"I couldn't have stayed away," he said, watching her. "Also I brought a guest, Mr. Robert Burns, the greatest American novelist, editor, and critic."

"At least," Burns said. When her dark eyes lifted with a sweep of lashes, he was jolted. The delinquent lover was right: she was very good-looking—small, well-made, with soft dark hair parted in the middle, and a golden skin. Her clothes looked so starched and cool that he thought of her as something caramel flavored in a crisp, crinkled cone.

"I know all about Mr. Burns," Pacita said. "I have heard him speak." Burns bowed politely.

"If I had known you were there I would have spoken better."

Her eyes played an amused game with his. Avellanos lifted his blunt chin, chortling meaninglessly; he replaced the girl's hand at her side as if leaning a gun against a wall. "Pacita is one of our best writers, you know. She has won prizes for stories."

"Ah?" Burns said. "I must get them and read them."

"They wouldn't be worth your time. But come and meet my friends." She was impeccable and composed. Behind her back Avellanos winked at Burns, to Burns' irritation. The editor was a fool, both for letting so charming a girl go and for flattering himself she was breaking her heart over him. Burns found himself wishing he could touch her skin, which should feel as cool and smooth as old ivory; and the thought of old ivory recalled the little figurine of the goddess Lakshmi that he had bought in Darjeeling, the one he had been stung on. Straight out of a Tibetan temple, stained brown with temple incense through hundreds of years, yah! Soaked in soy sauce to age it, more likely, or buried in a manure pile. Now what had made him think of that thing, and the taint of the spurious that clung to it? This girl was not spurious—but then neither was the goddess Lakshmi. Only the image was spurious; and anyway, spurious or not, he liked that figurine as well as anything he had collected on his travels.

A thin man with a Chinese face put a gin and tonic in his hand. Shouting over the noise, Pacita introduced him to three short story writers, a pair of poets, the widow of a hero of the resistance, a man who worked at the American Embassy, a girl who had been to the States on a YWCA fellowship. The standard literary crowd: he had met them in India, Burma, Thailand, except that here they were less likely to be Communists. They all looked absurdly young; they were ardent, perhaps talented; they flattered him by being eager to meet him. So he would answer questions, arouse awe by admitting that he had met Caldwell and Steinbeck and Faulkner, say earnestly and with complete conviction that there ought to be the freest kind of cultural exchange between their two countries. And he would remain a fatigued stranger in a crowd not his own.

It was jammed and steaming in the small rooms. In the back yard he saw men working over the pit where a pig on a pole hissed fat into the embers. As Burns watched through the open window they slid the brown carcass onto a board and a vehement little man started sharpening a knife the size of a machete. There were cheers, much laughter. Temporarily relieved of social demands, Burns sat in a rattan chair and sipped his second drink, and it was there that Pacita Delgado, hunting through the house with a plate of food, found him.

Because she gave him a brilliant dark glance and a smile of a certain warmth, he took the plate when she offered it. It contained only fragments of roast pig and something like French beans—those seemed safe. Gingerly, while her smile encouraged him, he tasted. The pig was crisp and melting at the same time, the beans tender and salty.

"Delicious," he said.

Abruptly she sat down by him; the rest of the party was out in the yard. Feeling absurd, wearied with his own routines, he asked her what she was writing now, and she replied that she was not writing: she had to be happy to write.

"You're not happy?"

Her lips pursed; her eyes glowed at him as if tears had momentarily brightened them; she shook her head with a quick, sober smile.

"Oh, come on!" Burns said. "If the young, beautiful, and talented can't be happy, what chance do the rest of us have?"

Instead of answering, she laid her hand on his wrist; he expected her touch to be cool, but it was warm. "I'm grateful to you for making Ramón come."

"I? It was he who brought me."

"He wouldn't have come without you for an excuse. This way he could tell himself he was introducing you to Manila writers. Without you he would have seemed to be coming to see *me*."

"And he wouldn't want to give that impression?"

Her mouth twitched. "No."

"I can't understand why not."

"Of course you can." She brushed aside his implied admiration as of no consequence. "We were lovers. He told you, didn't he?"

Burns was embarrassed. He filled his mouth with food and made a wordless, deprecating face.

"It isn't my doing that we aren't now," Pacita said in her low intense voice. Her eyes followed Avellanos, who had just come in the back door, joking with two other men. He did not look toward her, but her eyes stayed on him somberly. "He is the best man in the Philippines." The way she said it, pronouncing it "Pilippines," made Burns smile, but Pacita did not smile. "He is. The very best. He did incredible things during the occupation; he was a real hero, he is full of talents. Next election, Magsaysay is going in and Ramón is going in with him, into something big. He is going to help end this *jefe* government of grafters and landlords and put down the Huks. He is going to be one of the fathers of his country."

"I hope so," Burns said, embarrassed by the obscure demands she seemed to make on him. "Well, I'm sorry," he mumbled, and then, to make a diversion, slid his emptied plate onto a table and said, "The pig was marvelous, and so were the beans."

"Beans?"

"The vegetables. Weren't they beans?"

For a moment her face was blank. "Oh. Those aren't vegetables. Those are something from the pig's insides."

At the pit of his stomach Burns felt something deadly uncoil itself— tapeworms, trichina worms, liver flukes, my God. Pig's insides! Pacita was saying intensely, "I wanted him here. I wanted him to know I don't hate him because he doesn't come any more. Do you think he has got that idea?"

Burns hesitated before he said it. "Maybe he thinks you held the party to try to get him back."

The flattening or hardening of her eyes told him he had struck something sensitive, but he was only half attending to her. His mind kept returning to the alimentary indiscretion he had committed. There was nothing to do except to drown the things, whatever they were, in alcohol, but his glass was empty.

"Of course that's what he would think," Pacita said. "I was depending on it that he would sniff a danger, and therefore come. He is not one of these cautious or cowardly or cry-baby people. Ramón is a rare kind. He is not afraid of anything, even me."

More people were crowding in; the room was insufferably hot. Burns stood up to be introduced to someone, and when the someone had passed by he shook the ice in his sweating glass and met Pacita's wide and rather stary eyes. She bothered him; he felt something false or hysterical in her manner or her words, and so he coughed in bright awkwardness and said, "Well, probably it will work out right after all," and tipped his empty glass to his lips. Eventually she caught on and took it from him; the hostess look came back to her face. "Another drink?"

"Please," Burns said. "It's very warm."

Later he was at the door when Pacita and Avellanos said good-bye, but he could detect in the girl's face no chagrin at having failed. So far as Burns had seen, Avellanos had not said a word to her except in arriving and departing. Now he picked up her hand again and said, "Well, Pacita, it was a wonderful party. I'll see you around."

"I hope so." She took her hand from Avellanos and gave it to Burns.

"Did I mislead you?" the editor said on the way back. "She's good-looking, eh? Like an essence of woman. Today you heard her purr. Sometime you should hear the tiger roar. Oh, oh!" He fended off imaginary claws. "Well, what time shall I come tomorrow?"

So there went little Pacita's chances, as casually as that. They turned off the boulevard into the hotel drive. The palms hung without stir in the red evening, the hulks were black on the molten water, the promontory of Bataan was a dark low silhouette against a salmon-colored sky.

"How's nine o'clock?" Burns said. "I should be over at the club around eleven." Privately, he wondered if what he had eaten would let him rise at all in the morning.

But it was not he who called off the date next day. At a quarter of nine Avellanos telephoned in great agitation. Pacita, he said, had seen the last of her guests home, cleaned the house, washed the dishes, and swallowed a half bottle of sleeping pills.

"My God!" Burns said. "Is she dead?"

"Not dead," said the crackling voice. "A neighbor found her. But I can't meet you—you understand. What a fierce little . . . well. I am at the hospital now."

"Don't have me on your mind for a minute," Burns said. "There's nothing special till Monday anyway. But I'd like to hear how she is, if you get a minute to call."

He found he was genuinely upset. The embarrassment he had felt at her party, the feeling of falseness she had communicated to him, had its explanation in this news, and it gave him gooseflesh. Not falseness, but a more passionate reality than he had been prepared for, had looked out at him from the girl's hostess face. She had advertised all her friends into her house and carried her death around among them like canapés on a tray.

That day he did not go to the club at all, but lay in pajamas with the doors open to the breezy galleries, and wrote letters and brought his journal up to date and read a collection of Filipino poets. Through the late afternoon, nursing a succession of gin-and-tonics, he watched the hours pass over hotel and palms to quench themselves in another volcanic burst in Manila Bay. He had no bad effects from the pig's insides; there was no word from Avellanos; he felt lonely and abandoned and somehow abused.

In sleep that night he returned home, and struggling back toward consciousness as through a traumatic birth, he woke wringing wet, and looked mournfully, and saw the foreign sky, the galleried balconies, the palms, the leaden bay, and in the room the portable typewriter, the notebooks, the suitcases of exile. Home was still a month and a half away. Meanwhile, on Monday afternoon he had a talk to give at the USIS.

After breakfast he sat in bed making notes, saying that the peaceful co-existence of peoples depended not on arms or alliances but on knowledge, sympathy, the freest exchange of ideas and attitudes and the value systems by which each people conducted its life. Exchange of people, ideas, books, more important than sale of copra or iceboxes, and not just a few books, but whole sciences, whole literatures. Must apologize for fact that despite long friendly relations etc. with Ph., he and his countrymen knew so little of Ph. cultural life. Except for Rizal's

Noli Me Tangere, no knowledge Ph. literature. Since coming to Manila, eyes opened: every sign of young, lively, vigorous lit. both prose and poetry, both English and Tagalog. Dismiss Tagalog—incomp. to comment. But in English, a new, a real variety, fresh intentions, new names: González, Santos, Joaquín, others. Delgado? Well enough known? Get her stuff, read. . . .

The telephone rang.

It was Avellanos, jubilant. "Listen! Everything is all right! She is being let out of the hospital. It's a weight off a man's soul. What are you doing?"

"Oh, say, that's wonderful!" Burns said. "I've been worried . . . Doing? Why?"

"Because you are coming to a cockfight. Nobody knows the Philippines till he has gone to a cockfight when he should have been in church."

The very thought was exhausting to Burns. He said cautiously, "You know, I wonder if I should. I'd like to, but I'm not feeling so stout, and there's this speech on Monday. Also I shouldn't miss my exercise session. Anyway, isn't it illegal?"

"Illegal?" Avellanos roared into the telephone. "You are not in Stockton, California!" Burns held the receiver away, and it bellowed at him from arm's length, "By God, man, I'm relieved. I want to celebrate. Come along."

Burns hesitated only a moment, held firm. "Really, I hadn't better. Some other time, maybe, when I'm back on my feet."

"All right, all right!" the editor roared. "I won't press you. But I want to see you anyway. I'll be by the hotel in twenty minutes."

It seemed as good an excuse as any for Burns to get dressed. Waiting in the lobby—he somehow did not want Avellanos invading the private clutter of his room—he found himself thinking of Pacita Delgado's melodramatics as an illustration of the peculiar ardency of the Filipino temperament. People elsewhere might die for love, or pretend to, but where else would you encounter a gesture like that party? She was already an anecdote in his mind, and so he was surprised when, as the government car pulled in, he saw in the front seat beside Avellanos the glimmer of a sheer *camisa* and the flash of a woman's face. She was on his side of the car; her golden skin was paler, her eyes were shadowed, but the smile she turned toward him as he crossed the drive was utterly natural, slightly amused, as if they shared a joke. Well, perhaps they did.

"Hello, hello!" he said, and bent to the window, took her small cool hand. "This is a very pleasant surprise. I heard you were ill."

"You heard worse than that," said Avellanos. "You heard she was so stupid she tried to kill herself. What you didn't hear yet is that I have talked her out of all that. We are going to get married. What do you think of that?"

Moved to excessive and awkward congratulation, Burns said it was the best conclusion to a dramatic story he could think of. It seemed to him that Pacita's upturned face was astonishingly demure. Studying the blunt angle of Avellanos' jaw and the look of cocky satisfaction on that smiling face, Burns thought, though he did not say, that no bridegroom had ever looked less trapped. And yet he had been very neatly trapped indeed.

"Let me persuade you about this cockfight," Avellanos said. "You want to see the Philippines; this is where you see us best. You don't know Filipinos until you have seen some little fellow who has trained a chicken for months put it into the ring against another's rooster. He bets everything he owns on it, steals his wife's savings, sells his children's shirts to raise a peso. If he wins, glorious; if in one pass his rooster gets its throat cut, then you will see how a philosopher takes disaster. His first act after losing everything will be to beat his wife to shut her mouth, which he thinks opens only to say no and raise objections. His next will be to go hunting for a new rooster. You should come along and meet this philosopher."

"I'm afraid I hadn't better."

"Would you send away a visitor to the States before he had seen a baseball game?"

Burns still shook his head, smiling. The editor regarded him for a second in a friendly, appraising way. Then he gave up, slapped his shirt pocket, and sprang out of the car. "Well, I'm sorry we'll have to celebrate alone. Excuse me a minute. I am out of cigars and I have to make a phone call." Ahead of his energetic rush the door man opened just in time; otherwise, Burns was sure, the editor would have bolted right through the glass.

From the car Pacita smiled up enigmatically, and taking a chance, curious to hear her say what he knew was true, Burns slid in beside her. "I congratulate you," he said.

"Thank you. I am very lucky."

He studied her. She was extraordinarily attractive, and she feigned well the weakness of recent illness. He said, "You did me the honor of being frank with me at your party. Will you be frank with me again?"

"Of course."

"I'm afraid you may be offended."

"No, please. Why?"

He plunged. "Does Ramón think this suicide attempt was really serious?"

Smiling, with a forming wrinkle between her brows, she said, "I don't suppose he thinks it was a joke."

"But he believes you swallowed the pills."

The wrinkle between her brows became a knot; hard lines and planes appeared under the softness of her face; her eyes flickered at him. "You don't?"

He would have retreated, but he was in too deep. "It occurred to me to doubt," he said. "According to Freud, anyone who wants to kill himself succeeds."

Literary curiosity, as he now saw, had led him into an inexcusable gaffe; her eyes were hard to meet. "So I win him back by a trick," she said, or spat. "I am full of weak despair and cunning. I bribe some intern to pump my stomach and give me something to make me look sick. I pretend I am dying so he comes to the hospital, and pity restores him to me. Let me tell you, that would be the way to drive him away forever."

"Then why . . ." he said. "I'm sorry, I've offended you, and I truly didn't mean to. It just seemed to me you have so much to live for, I couldn't believe you seriously meant to die."

"I didn't mean to die."

"You said you swallowed the pills."

"Thirty of them." She threw a hand in the air in a gesture exactly like one of Avellanos'. "A neighbor came over around midnight. I had asked her to come."

"Telling her why?"

"No, of course not."

"But to take such a risk!" Burns burst out. "Good heavens, suppose she hadn't come?"

"Then I would have lost," Pacita said, and turned her stiff, unfriendly face to look across the bayside lawns dotted with strollers. Burns felt that erratic winds were plucking at his feelings as the gusts plucked at the dresses of women out there. After a thoughtful moment he opened the door and stepped out, just as Avellanos burst from the entrance with an enormous cigar at an angle in his mouth. When he removed the cigar to smile at them he took it in his whole fist, the way he might have held a cold chisel. "Changed your mind?"

Surer than ever now, Burns said, "I'm afraid I'd better not."

Avellanos climbed in and slammed the door. "Well, you will miss something. Pacita knows, she is a gambler like these chicken people. Eh?" He laid a hand on her knee, filling the car with laughter. "Pacita knows all about these dramatic gestures," he said. "Well, I'll see you tomorrow and you will make a speech." He raised his fist in farewell and stamped on the starter. Pacita's head turned, and her eyes touched those of Burns. She smiled slightly.

He stood with his hand raised and watched them shoot off in an explosion of small gravel toward the boulevard.

It was nearly eleven. Gloomily, upset by his own gaucherie and ruffled by the girl's show of temper, however justified, Burns went across to the club and worked dutifully on the weights a little and tried a few push-ups that instantly drained him of strength. He swam two lengths of the pool, struggling to keep his fleshless bones from sinking like lead. At eleven-thirty he gave up and went into the bar.

There was one other person there, the sort of Army-wife, foreign-colony woman he had seen plenty of times: a little ravaged, the figure better than the face, the hair blonded. As Burns entered, she was just sitting down from having put a record on the player, and now the music began to throb through the room with a deep sad booming of the double bass. A lugubrious contralto mourned that she was dancing with her sweetheart to the Tennessee Waltz when an old friend she happened to see. A little later her friend stole her sweetheart from her. She remembered the night and the Tennessee Waltz.

Burns sat consulting his drink. The record ended and the woman rose and started it over. Across the space of thirty feet her eyes brushed his, with what expression? Indifference? Dislike? Petulance? Apathy? Hatred? Self-pity? While the homesick music mourned, she brooded, holding her cigarette like a conductor's baton, and her forefinger tapped, and tapped, and tapped, shaking off ashes that were not there. Her mouth was fixed on bitterness. With quick impatience she tinkled her rings against the glass to summon the steward. She seemed to Burns the epitome of every weak nostalgia, every self-pitying and spiteful yearning, every failure of contact. She offended him with her half-obscured resemblances to himself, and though he knew that the comparison was unfair, he rose abruptly and called for his chit. It occurred to him that those who feared getting wet should not walk in the rain.

As he crossed the lawn toward the hotel he saw the pearl man coming in his transparent shirt. The worst thing about him was that he made Burns feel so much like a tourist, a boob whom persistence would sooner or later fetch. Before he could speak, Burns leveled a finger at him. "Now look. I don't want your pearls. I wouldn't want them even if they were real. But I do want to be left alone. I'll give you five pesos to disappear."

The mouthful of white uneven teeth gleamed, incredulous. "You want buy eighty peso pearls for five pesos?"

"No pearls. Just to be left alone."

A gust struck them. Burns staggered; the flimsy shirt was plastered against the pearl man's chest so that his ribs, his hard pectoral muscles, his rigid nipples, stood out through it. Along shore the palms clashed with a noise like surf, the water was heavily uneasy. The edge of a typhoon, according to the papers, was due to strike Luzon in the next few hours. For a second they stood braced and squinting. Then the peddler shrugged. "Okay."

Smiling broadly, seeming to search Burns' face for some corroboration, he took the five pesos. The wind flapped his shirt tails. "Well, what the hell," he said, and emptied into Burns' palm the four polished bits of shell. Moving away, he threw his open hand into the air in cheerful, perhaps mocking, salute.

Burns walked on, rubbing between his fingers the satiny pebbles: something spurious from the Mindanao Deep, something to put with the ivory image of Lakshmi, goddess of wealth, aged in soy sauce. He rather liked having the pearls; they were a commitment, of a sort. And yet it seemed to him that the mementos of his mission, like his relations with the people he met, too often turned out to be spurious or ambiguous, or forced upon him. The real thing eluded him, or he evaded it. But why, when he took this journey seriously, believed in one world and (on the hardest sort of practical ground) in the brotherhood of men and nations? Why, when what he tried hardest for was sympathetic contact? Too much sickness? Timidity? Not enough vitality? A real temperamental revulsion against life itself, that betrayed him when he least expected betrayal? Or simply good sense, a habit of forethought and sanity, a perception that it was better to be a live ambassador than a difficult foreign corpse?

Nevertheless he wished he had gone to the cockfight, however hot and uncomfortable and swarming with xenophobic germs. He would have liked to find a way of telling Pacita Delgado that he admired her spirit, the way she risked everything on a throw and posted a life for a forfeit.

Walking through the noon crowd in the lobby, he wondered what they did when a cock would not fight. Step in and wring its neck like a yard chicken's, probably. Among plungers, combatants, the vital and the reckless, the reaction to weakness or fear could only be contempt or shame. It was a sort of rebellious, wistful shame, as he discovered without surprise, that he had been feeling for the past hour. Even if you didn't approve—and he didn't—of recklessness, even if you could cite the ten thousand ills that living dangerously brought into human affairs, even though you had always been on the side of those who lived by reason against those who lived by passion, with what a glitter the reckless ones recommended themselves, how that kind of temperament strutted high-toed around the chicken yard among the drab feathers and the submissive envy of the chickens dedicated to eggs and *arroz con pollo*! It was not a pleasant thought that that pair of gamblers, if they were thinking of him at all, which was improbable, were thinking of him only to feel sorry for him.

For the way he was feeling now there was a solution, rational but temporary. At the hat-check stand he looked up at the sign suggesting that firearms be checked at the door. Phony? Maybe. But as Avellanos said, there were all sorts of possibilities. He ordered a gimlet and sat at a table by a window. Ironically he reflected that if there were a jukebox he could put on the "Tennessee Waltz." When the gimlet was on the table before him and its penetrating lime odor was rising to his nostrils as clean as the sniff of Benzedrine from an inhaler, he fished from his shirt pocket the envelope he carried there, and out of its assortment of pills and capsules selected an iron pill, a multi-vitamin capsule, and a concentrated capsule of vitamin C.

GENESIS

■   ■   ■

The summer of 1906 was very wet. It seemed to rain for weeks and the coulees ran knee deep and the Frenchman River was as high as a spring flood. The dirt roofs of the log houses of that day became so sodden that water dripped from them whether it rained or not. It stayed so wet that we had difficulty getting the hay in. The winter started early with a light snow on the 5th of November, followed by a terrific three-day blizzard that started on the 11th. From then till Christmas was a succession of bad storms. The range cattle were dying in December.

CORKY JONES AS AN OLD MAN

It seemed to the young Englishman that if anyone had been watching from the bench he would have seen them like a print of Life on the Western Plains, or like a medieval procession. The sun was just rising, its dazzle not yet quite clear of the horizon, and flooding down the river valley whitened with the dust of snow, it gilded the yellow leaves that still clung to the willows, stretched the shadow of every bush and post, glazed the eastern faces of the log ranch buildings whose other side was braced with long blue shadows. And moving now, starting to roll, the outfit was strung out along the Mounted Police patrol trail. He was enclosed in it, moving with it, but in his excitement he saw it as it would look from outside and above, and it made him want to stand up in his stirrups and yell.

Leading the lithograph procession went the five hounds—the four Russian wolfhounds and the thing its owner called a staghound, a dog as big as a calf and with a head like a lioness. Across the bottoms in the morning cold they cut loose and ran for the love of running; within seconds they were out of sight among the willows by the ford. Behind them rode Schulz, the wolfer, as new to the outfit as the Englishman himself; and after him his fifteen-year-old son driving a packhorse; and after them old Jesse in the wagon pulled by a team of hairy-footed Clydesdale stallions. Then the horse herd, seventy or eighty saddle horses in a flow of dark tossing motion across the flat, and then the riders, two and two.

They carried no lances or pennons, the sun found no armor from which to strike light, but in the incandescence of being nineteen, and full of health, and assaulted in all his senses by the realization of everything splendid he had ever imagined, the English boy knew that no more romantic procession had ever set forth. The Crusades could not have thrilled him more. Though they went, and he with them, like an illumination in an old manuscript, they had their own authentic color. Among the bays and blacks and browns and buckskins and roans of the horse herd was one bright piebald; in substitution for slashed doublets and shining silks they offered two pairs of woolly goatskin chaps and Ed Spurlock's red mackinaw.

Only a week in that country, the Englishman with practically no urging would have started running with the dogs. It rattled the brains in his head like seeds in a pod to think where he was—here, in Saskatchewan, not merely on the way to the great lone land, or on its edge, but in it, and going deeper. He had lived a dream in which everything went right. Within an hour of the time he stepped off the train in Maple Creek, hesitant and a little scared, he had learned that all the big cattle outfits using the open range east of the Cypress Hills were shorthanded. Within two hours, he had found a ride with Joe Renaud, the mail driver. Within twelve, he was sleeping in the T-Down bunkhouse, an authentic cowboy. Within a week here he went, part of a company bound for adventure, on the late fall roundup to gather and bring in to feeding stations the calves that could not be expected to winter on the range.

He was face to shining face with everything new. Names he had heard here knocked and clanged in his mind—places where anything could happen, and from the sound of them, *had* happened—Jumbo's Butte, Fifty-Mile, Pinto Horse Butte, Horse Camp Coulee, the War Holes. He blew his exultant breath out between his pony's ears, and when he breathed in again he felt the cold at the root of every bared tooth. He noticed that the horses felt as he did: though they had been on the roundup and then on the long drive to Montana and then on the long drive back, and had been worked steadily since May, they were full of run; they joined him in snorting smoke.

The column turned down toward the river, and looking back, the Englishman saw Molly Henry, the foreman's wife, hugging her elbows by the ranch-house door. He waved; her hand lifted. He and Ed Spurlock were the last in the line, and he saw how they would look to her, his new sheepskin and Spurlock's red mackinaw just disappearing into the willows. He thought it a lonesome piece of luck for a girl married only three weeks to be left now, with no help except a crippled handy man and no company except the Mountie on his weekly patrol from Eastend, and no woman nearer than twenty-five miles. To Spurlock, jogging beside him with his mittened hands stacked on the horn, he said with feeling, "I'm certainly glad it's not *me* being left behind!"

Spurlock glanced sideward with restless brown eyes; he said nothing; his expression did not change.

The Englishman grew aware, under Spurlock's glance, that he was posting to his pony's jogtrot. As if stretching muscles he pushed down hard into the unfamiliarly long stirrups, shoved back against the cantle, leaned a little, and stacked his hands casually on the horn in imitation of Spurlock's. As soon as he had them there he felt that he seemed to be hanging on to ease the jolt of sitting the trot, and he took his hands away again. With a complex sense of being green, young, red-headed, and British—all potentially shameful—but at the same time strong, bold, high-spirited, and ready for anything, he appraised Spurlock's taciturnity and adjusted his seat in the big strange saddle and threw at random into the air a look that was cocky, self-conscious, and ingratiating all at once.

The wagon had crushed through the thin ice at the ford, and the horses waded into the broken wake and stood knee deep, bobbing away ice-pans with their noses, plunging their muzzles to suck strongly. Here and there one pulled its nose out and stood with a thoughtful, puckered, tasting expression at the corners of its dripping lips; they looked as if the water had made their teeth ache.

Then Slippers and Little Horn and Ray Henry rode in and hazed them across, and Buck and Panguingue and Spurlock and the Englishman picked up the stragglers. The cold sound of splashing became a drumming and thudding on the bank. Above and ahead, the wagon was just tilting out of sight over the dugway edge. They took the herd up after it in a rush, and burst out onto the great glittering plain.

It was tremendous, it was like a plunge over a cliff. The sun looked them straight in the eyes, the earth dazzled them. Over and under and around, above, below, behind, before, the Englishman felt the unfamiliar element, a cleanness like the blade of a knife, a distance without limits, a horizon that did not bound the world but only suggested endless space beyond. Shading his eyes with his hand while his pony rocked into a lope, he saw all ahead of him the disk of the white and yellow world, the bowl of the colorless sky unbearable with light. Squatting on the horizon right under the searchlight sun were a pair of low mounds, one far off, one nearer. The closer one must be Jumbo's Butte, the far one Stonepile. They were the only breaks he saw in the plains except when, twisting backward, he found the Cypress Hills arched across the west, showing in coulees and ravines the faded white and gold of aspen, the black of jackpines. By the time they had ridden five minutes the river valley out of which they had risen was almost invisible, sunk below the level of sight.

The wolfer and his son were already far ahead, the dogs only running specks out on the shining plain. Jesse and the pilot wagon were leading the rest of them on a beeline toward Jumbo's Butte, and as the Englishman settled down and breathed out his excitement and relaxed to the shuffle of his pony he watched the broad wheels drop and jolt into holes and burnouts and old Jesse lurch and sway on the high seat, and he let his back ache with sympathy. Then he saw Jesse's teeth flash in his face as he turned to shout something at Ray Henry riding beside the wagon, and he decided that sympathy was wasted. Jesse had been a bullwhacker with supply trains between Fort Benton and the Montana mining camps in the early days, he had known these plains when the buffalo were still shaking them, he had been jolting his kidneys loose across country like this for thirty years. If he had wanted another kind of job he could have had it. The Englishman admired him as a man who did well what he was hired to do. He believed old Jesse to be skilled, resourceful, humorous, close-mouthed, a character. Briefly he contemplated growing a mustache and trying to train it like Jesse's into a silky oxbow.

The saddle horses followed along smartly after the pilot wagon, and there was hardly any need to herd them, but the boys were fanned out in a wide semicircle, riding, as if by preference, each by himself. And among them—this was the wonder, this was what made him want to raise his face and ki-yi in pure happiness—rode Lionel Cullen, by now known as Rusty, the least of eight (as he admitted without real humility) but willing, and never more pleased with himself. That morning in early November, 1906, he would not have traded places with Sir Wilfrid Laurier.

He wanted to see everything, miss nothing, forget nothing. To make sure that he would not forget what happened to him and what he saw, he had begun a journal on the train coming west from Montreal, and every evening since then he had written in it seriously with posterity looking over his shoulder. He watched every minute of every day for the vivid and the wonderful, and he kept an alert eye on himself for the changes that were certain to occur. He had the feeling that there would be a test of some sort, that he would enter manhood—or cowboyhood, manhood in Saskatchewan terms—as one would enter a house. For the moment he was a tenderfoot, a greenhorn, on probation, under scrutiny. But at some moment there would be a door to open, or to force, and inside would be the self-assurance that he respected and envied in Jesse, Slippers, or Little Horn, the calm confidence of a top hand.

As they moved like the scattered shadow of a cloud across the face of the plain he knew practically nothing except how to sit a horse, and even that he knew in a fashion to get him laughed at. But he was prepared to serve an apprenticeship, he would prove himself as and when he must. And in the pocket of his flannel shirt he had a notebook and two pencils, ready for anything.

At noon, a little to the east of Jumbo's Butte, they stopped to boil coffee and heat a kettle of beans. The thin snow did not cover the grass; the crust that had blazed in their eyes all morning was thawing in drops that clung to the curly prairie wool. On a tarpaulin spread by the wagon they sprawled and ate the beans that Jesse might just as well not have heated, for the cold tin plates congealed them again within seconds. But the coffee burned their mouths, and the tin cups were so hot to hold that they drank with their mittens on. The steam of their coffee-heated breath was a satisfaction; Rusty tried to blow rings with it.

When he finished he lay on the tarp next to Panguingue. There was always, it seemed, room next to Panguingue; it was said of him that he took a bath every spring whether he needed it or not. In the cold, and so long as Panguingue wore a sheepskin and overshoes, Rusty did not mind. And anyway, since arriving he had seen no one take a bath, not even Buck, who was fastidious; certainly he had taken none himself. So he relaxed by Panguingue and felt the ground satisfyingly hard under the tarp, and let Panguingue thump him monotonously between the shoulder blades and dust cigarette ashes through his hair. Through half-closed eyes he heard the horses working on the curly grass all around; he saw a snowbird come boldly to pick at a scrap of salt pork by the edge of the tarp; his ears heard the sounds of ease, the scratchings, the crackle of a match; his nose smelled sour pipe, smelled Bull Durham, smelled Ray Henry's sybaritic cigar. He loved every minute, every sensation, and when, just as they were rising to tighten cinches and move on, they heard the hysterical yapping of hounds, and saw Schulz's pack, two miles away, pursue and run down a coyote, he climbed on the wagon and watched as eager as a spectator at a horse race. He thought of Schulz as belonging somehow with Jesse, the two of them survivors of an earlier stage of Plains life; he rather envied Schulz's boy, brought up to lonely cabins, skimpy cowchip campfires on the prairies, familiarity with wild animals, the knack and habit of casual killing. From high on the wagon seat, bracing himself on Jesse's shoulder, he watched Schulz ride in and scatter the hounds and dismount, while the boy gathered up the loose packhorse. He expected that the wolfers would come in and get something to eat, but he saw Schulz mount again and the three horses and the five dogs move out eastward. Even more than the cowboys, these were the wild ones; they had gone as far as it was possible to go back toward savagery. He regretted not seeing them ride in with the scalp of the coyote, the hounds bloody-muzzled from the kill. He hoped to get a chance to course a coyote or a wolf across such a marvelous plain as this on such a glorious day, when you could see for twenty miles. It was tremendous, every bit of it.

During the afternoon the country roughened, broke into coulees that opened down toward the river. They rode, it seemed, endlessly, without a break and with little talk. Rusty stiffened in the saddle, he rode lounging, stood in the stirrups, hung his feet free while under him the shaggy little horse shuffled on. The sun went down the sky toward the Cypress Hills, now no more than a faint clean lifting of the horizon. They felt the thin warmth on their necks if their collars were down; their faces felt the cold.

When they arrived at Stonepile the sun was already down. The sky back over the hills was red, the snow ahead of them lay rosy across the flats. Until they reached the coulee's rim they would not have known it was there; as for the river, it was sunk among indistinguishable rough coulees to the north, but no more than a mile away. As they dipped downward toward the Stonepile buildings, once a Mounted Police patrol post, the valley was already full of violet shadow. Rusty creaked and eased himself, letting the horse pick his way. He was stiff and chilled, his face felt like sheet metal, his eyes watered and smarted from the day's glare.

They were not talkative as they unsaddled and turned the horses loose, or during the time while they lugged bedrolls and food into the old barracks. Two or three men would be stationed here later to feed to the calves the three hundred and fifty tons of wild hay stacked in the coulee; they had brought flour, rice, oatmeal, sugar, matches and prunes, tinned corn and syrup and jam and peas, dried apples and peaches, to stock the place. There was a good deal of tracking in and out from the cold blue dusk. Jesse had stuck two tallow dips in china holders that said Peerless Hotel. They were all in each other's way in the narrow bunkhouse, and all in the way of Jesse, trying to get supper going. They bumped shoulders, growled. Rusty, who had thrown his bedroll forehandedly into one of the upper bunks, came in with a load later and found that Ed Spurlock had thrown it out and put his own in its place. There were only six bunks for the ten of them. In the end, Rusty spread his bed beside Panguingue's on the floor, and the wolfers, coming in a half hour after them, looked in the door briefly and decided to sleep in the stable with the Clydes, the night horses, and the dogs.

"Be careful them studs," Jesse told Schulz. "It wouldn't do if them and your lion got to mixing it."

The wolfer was a man, Rusty thought, to be noticed, perhaps to be watchful of. He still wore, in the warming barracks, a muskrat cap with earlaps. Under it his eyes were gray as agates, as sudden as an elbow in the solar plexus. His face was red, his mustache sandy. Between his eyes, even when he smiled, which was not often, he wore a deep vertical wrinkle. He had what Rusty thought of as a passionate taciturnity. He looked watchful and besieged, he would be quick to strike back, he was not a man you could make a joke with. In a low growling voice he said that he valued his hound too highly to let any forty-dollar horse kick him in the head.

Jesse looked at him, holding a stove lid half off the smoking fire, and his silky mustaches moved as if a small animal had crawled under the thatch. He said, "If one of the Clydes hit him, that wouldn't be no forty-dollar kick. That would be a genuine gold-plated eight-hundred-dollar kick guaranteed to last."

Schulz grunted and went out; Rusty told himself that he had been right in guessing him as a man with whom you did not joke. The boy, sullen-looking, with a drooping lip and eyes that looked always out their corners, went silently after him. They came back in for supper, cleaned their plates, and went out again for good.

"What's the matter with him?" Spurlock asked. "Don't he like our company?"

"Likes his dogs better," Buck said. He reared his red turkey neck up and glared out into the jammed corridor between the bunks. From the end, where he sat braced against the wall fooling with the harmonica, Rusty saw the disgust on his skinned-looking face. "What about somebody that would sleep with a God damn dog?" Buck said.

From the lower, talking around the dead cigar that poked upward from his face, Little Horn said gently, "We ain't got any right to criticize. We all been sleepin' with Panguingue for a year."

"B.S.," Panguingue said. "My feet don't smell no worse'n yours."

"Well, for the love of God," Jesse said, hanging the dishpan on the wall, "let's not have any contests. There ain't a man here would survive it."

Rusty took the slick metal of the harmonica from his mouth and ventured; his feelers, tentative always to estimate his own position as one of them, told him that now, while they were criticizing the unsociable wolfer, his own position was more solid; and yet he admired the wildness and the obvious competence of the wolfer, too. The very fact that he rode in moccasins and thick German socks gave him a distinction over the rest of them in their overshoes. Rusty said, "Do you suppose it's only that he's used to living out alone, don't you know . . . that he's almost like a wild animal himself? He seems that way to me . . . or is that only fancy?"

They hooted at him, and he felt his ears grow red. "Aow, it's only fawncy, p'raps," they told each other for the next minute or two. "Deah!" they said. "Rilly?" Rusty blew into the mouth organ. He heard Little Horn saying, "It's natural enough. Yell at a dog, he minds. Yell at one of you sonsofbitches, what does he do? I don't blame the guy. There's no satisfaction in a cowpuncher's company like there is in a dog's."

Spurlock said, "Can his kid talk? I never heard him say a word yet."

"Probably all he knows is 'bow-wow,' " Buck said.

Jesse pawed his yellow-white silky mustache and said with the look of foolery in his faded blue eyes, "Schulz don't look to me like he's got a steady conscience. I'd say mebbe he was a windigo."

Rusty waited, hoping someone else would take the bait, but resigning himself when no one spoke. And anyway, he was interested. "What's a windigo?"

"What the Crees used to call an Injun that had made use of man-meat," Jesse said. "Most generally seemed to sort of drive a man wild, he wasn't right afterwards. I recall hearing Bert Willoughby tell about one the Mounties had to go get up on the Swift Current, back in the early days. His tribe got suspicious, he come out of a starvin' winter lookin' so fat and slick. Also his fambly was missin'. So they collared this buck and he took 'em up to his winter camp on Bigstick Lake, and here was all these bones and skulls around, and he'd kick 'em and laugh, and say, 'This one my wife, hee hee hee,' and 'That one my mother-in-law, ho ho,' and 'This one here my father, ha ha.' He'd et the whole damn bunch, one after the other."

"Well," Little Horn said. "I wonder if somebody is settin' oncomfortable on old Schulzie's stomach?"

"Maybe we could get him to eat Panguingue before he gets too God damn high," Spurlock said.

Little Horn said regretfully, "I doubt if even a windigo would take a chance on Panguingue."

"B.S.," Panguingue said.

From the white cloud of cigar smoke that filled the enclosed space above his bunk, Ray Henry whispered, "You can all take it easy. Schulz and his boy will be stayin' here or at Bates Camp all winter, while you boys is up to your ass in dried apple pies back at the ranch."

"Good," Buck said.

"Sure, Ray," said Jesse, "I know that was the arrangement. But is it safe?"

"Safe, how?"

Jesse kicked the stove leg. "This-here my boy," he said. "Hee hee hee."

They left Schulz and his silent boy behind them at the Stonepile camp and made a hard drive eastward to the Fifty-Mile Crossing of the

Whitemud, on the eastern boundary of the range that, by mutual consent among all the outfits, was called the T-Down's. Already, within a day, Rusty felt how circumstances had hardened, how what had been an adventure revealed itself as a job. He rose from his bed on the floor so stiff he hobbled like a rheumatic dog, and when he stumbled out of the foul barracks and took a breath of the morning air it was as if he had had an icicle rammed clear to his wishbone. Another cold day— colder than the one before by a good deal—and an even harder ride ahead. And leaving the Schulzes affected him unpleasantly: these two were being separated off to carry on a specific and essential duty, but no one was sorry to see them go. The outfit that he had thought of as ten was really only eight. If the others chose to find him as disagreeable as they found Schulz, it was only seven. He hung at their fringes, hoping to earn a place among them. He was painfully alert, trying to anticipate what was expected of him. What was expected was that he should climb in the saddle, on a new pony this morning—one with a trot like a springless wagon over cobblestones—and ride, and ride, and ride, straight into the blinding glare of the sun.

The night before, he had entered in his journal information on how the open range from Wood Mountain on the east to Medicine Lodge Coulee on the west was run. From the Whitemud north to the Canadian Pacific tracks the Circle Diamond and the 76, both very large outfits, divided it. South of the river there were several. Between Wood Mountain and Fifty-Mile was the Turkey Track, running about twenty-five thousand head. Then their own outfit, the T-Down Bar, running ten thousand. Between the T-Down ranch house and the Cypress Hills the Z-X ran about two thousand purebred shorthorns and whitefaces, and through the Cypress Hills to Medicine Lodge Coulee an association of small ranchers called the Whitemud Pool ran their herds together. It seemed reasonable; it even seemed neat; but it seemed terribly large when you had to ride across it at the wagon's pace.

By noon the sky had hazed over. They blessed it because of their eyes and cursed it because the wind developed a sting. Then away out on the flats in the middle of a bleak afternoon they met the wagon and four riders from the Turkey Track, bound for a camp they had on the big coulee called the War Holes. They were on the same errand as the T-Down boys: combing parts of the range missed in the spring roundup, and separating out the calves and bulls to be wintered on hay in the sheltered bottoms. Their greeting was taciturn and numb. The T-Down boys looked to them exactly as they looked to the T-Down, probably: frostbitten, with swollen watery eyes, their backs humped to the cold wind, their ponies' tails blowing between their legs as they waited out the fifteen minutes of meeting.

It had not been made clear to Rusty Cullen, until then, that they were on a belated and half-desperate job. A green hand did not inquire too closely for fear of asking foolish questions; an experienced hand volunteered nothing. And so he was surprised by the gloominess of the Turkey Track boys and their predictions of heavy losses on the range. They quoted signs and omens. They ran mittened hands against the grain of their ponies' winter hair, to show how much heavier it was than normal. They had seen muskrat houses built six feet high in the sloughs—and when the rats built high you could depend on a hard winter. Mounted Police freighters reported a steady drift of antelope from the north across the CPR tracks.

The chinook winds, he gathered, should keep the range clear enough for the stronger animals to get feed, but calves didn't winter well. Fortunately all the stock was fat; the summer range had been good. If they could get the calves in where there was feed, maybe there wouldn't be too much loss. Having exchanged omens, predictions, reassurances, and invitations to Christmas blowouts, they raised their mitts to each other and ducked each his own way into or away from the wind, and the tracks that had briefly met crawled apart again across the snow.

Somehow the brief, chilled, laconic encounter in the emptiness and cold of the flats left Rusty depressed. By the time they dragged in to camp in the willows of the river bottom at Fifty-Mile his eyes were swollen almost shut, and burned and smarted as if every little capillary and nerve in them had been twisted and tied in knots; he knew how streaked and bloodshot they were by looking at the eyes of the others. He was tired, stiff, cold; there was no immediate comfort in camp, but only more cold hard work, and the snow that was only a thin scum on the prairie was three inches deep down here. They shoveled off a space and got the tent set up in the blue dusk, and he looked it over and felt that their situation was gloomily naked and exposed. When he chopped through the river's inch of ice and watched the water well up and overflow the hole it seemed like some dark force from the ancient heart of the earth that could at any time rise around them silently and obliterate their little human noises and tracks and restore the plain to its emptiness again.

The wind dropped after sundown, the night came on clear and cold. Before turning in, Rusty stepped outside and looked around. The other boys were all in their bedrolls, and the light in the tent had been blown out so that even the pale human efflorescence was gone; the tent was a misty pyramid, the wagon a shadow. Tied to the wheels, the blanketed night horses and the Clydes moved their feet uncomfortably and rustled for a last grain of oats in the seams of their nosebags.

The earth showed him nothing; it lay pallid, the willows bare sticks, the snow touched with bluish luminescence. A horn of moon was declining toward the western horizon. But in the north the lights were beginning, casting out a pale band that trembled and stretched and fell back and stretched out again until it went from horizon to horizon. Out of it streaks and flares and streamers began to reach up toward the zenith and pale the stars there as if smoke were being blown across them.

He had never felt so small, so lost, so inconsequential; his impulse was to sneak away. If anyone had asked his name and his business, inquiring what he was doing in the middle of that empty plain, he would have mumbled some foolish and embarrassed answer. In his mind's eye he saw the Turkey Track camp ten or fifteen or twenty miles out in the emptiness, the only other thing like themselves, a little lonesome spark that would soon go out and leave only the smudge of the wagon, the blur of the tent, under the cold flare of the Northern Lights. It was easy to doubt their very existence; it was easy to doubt his own.

A night horse moved again, a halter ring clinked, a sound tiny and lost. He shuddered his shoulders, worked his stiffened face, stirred up his numbed brains, and shook the swimming from his eyes. When the tent flap dropped behind him and he stooped to fumble the ties shut the shiver that went through him was exultant, as if he had just been brushed by a great danger and had escaped. The warmth and the rank human odors of the tent were mystically rich with life. He made such a loud, happy, unnecessary row about the smell of Panguingue's feet when he crawled into his bedroll in their cramped head-to-foot sleeping space that three or four sleepy voices cursed him viciously and Panguingue kicked him a few good hard ones through his blankets and kicked the vapors out of him.

Sometime during that roundup they may have had a day of decent weather, but it seemed to Rusty it was a procession of trials: icy nights, days when a bitter wind lashed and stung the face with a dry sand of snow, mornings when the crust flashed up a glare so blinding that they rode with eyes closed to slits and looked at the world through their eyelashes. There was one afternoon when the whole world was overwhelmed under a white freezing fog, when horses, cattle, clothes, wagon grew a fur of hoar frost and the herd they had gathered had to be held together in spooky white darkness mainly by ear.

On bright days they were all nearly blind, in spite of painting their cheekbones with charcoal and riding with hats pulled clear down; if they could see to work at all, they worked with tears leaking through swollen and smarting lids. Their faces grew black with sun and glare, their skin and lips cracked as crisp as the skin of a fried fish, and yet they froze. Every night the thermometer dropped near zero, and there was an almost continuous snake-tongue of wind licking out of the north or west.

The river bottom and the big rough coulees entering from the south held many cattle, and they soon collected a large herd. They were hard to move; if he had had a gun Rusty would have been tempted more than once to make immediate beef of them. The Canadian cattle, whiteface or whiteface-and-shorthorn cross, were impenetrably stupid and slow; their whole unswerving intention was to break past a rider and get back into the bottoms. The longhorns, most of which carried the Turkey Track or Circle Diamond brand and which had to be cut away from their own, were exactly the opposite: fast, agile, wicked, and smart. They could lead a man a wild chase, always in a direction he didn't want to go; they hid among other cattle and couldn't be cut out; they milled and stampeded the T-Down herd at every chance; all the boys had spills, chasing longhorns through rough country and across the icy flats; and they wore the horses, already weak and thin, to the bone.

On the third day out from Fifty-Mile, Slip, Panguingue, and Rusty were cutting out a bunch of ten or fifteen Circle Diamond longhorns from a dozen T-Down whitefaces. They wanted the whitefaces up on the bench where they could turn them into the herd; the longhorns were welcome to the coulee. Of course the whitefaces hung on to the coulee and the longhorns stampeded up onto the flats. It was astonishing how fast those cattle could move and how much noise they made. Their horns cracked; their hooves cracked; their joints cracked; it seemed as if even their tails snapped like bullwhips. In a wild clamor they went up the coulee bank, agile as goats, with Rusty after them.

He came out onto the rim in a sting of snow and wind. The longhorns were well ahead of him, racing with their bag-of-bones clatter toward the wagon and the herd that Jesse and Spurlock were holding there. Rusty ducked his head and squinted back at Slip; he was waving and shouting: Rusty understood that he was to head the longhorns before they got too close to the herd.

The cattle, very fast for a short distance, began to slack off. His dogged little horse came up on a roan haunch, then on a brindle, then past a set of wild horns, and finally up on the leader, so close the boy could have kicked his laboring shoulder or reached out and grabbed his thirty-inch horn. He lashed him with the rope across the face; still going hard, the steer ducked and began to turn.

The next he knew, Rusty was over the pony's head like a rock shot from a slingshot. It happened so fast he knew nothing about it until he was flying through the air, frantically clawing at nothing, and lit sliding, and rolled. His wind and wits went out of him together; he sat up groggily, spitting blood and snow.

And oh, how beautiful a thing it is to work with men who know their job! He sat up into a drama of danger and rescue. The steer had turned and was coming for him; Slip was riding in hard from the side to head him off. But he was too far back; Rusty saw it with the hardest sort of clarity, and he was up on hands and knees, into a crouch, his eyes estimating distances, watching the wide horns and the red eyes of the steer, noting even how the stiff ice-encased hairs sprayed back from his nostrils. While he crouched there laboring to get wind back into his lungs, Rusty saw Slip's bay in the air with all four legs stiff, coming down to a braced landing. The wide loop came snaking in the air, Slip's left hand was making a lightning dally around the horn. The timing was so close that the rope did not even sag before the steer's rush took up the slack. It simply whistled out straight and was snapped tight and humming as the pony came down stiff-legged in the snow. The steer was yanked off his feet, the horse slipped, went nearly down, recovered, the air was full of hooves and horns, and the longhorn crashed as if he had fallen from the sky. Liquid dung rolled from under his tail; Rusty thought he had broken his neck.

Shakily he went toward the steer to unhook Slip's rope for him, but Slip warned him sharply away. His horse stepped nervously, keeping the rope tight when the steer tried to rise. A little way off, Panguingue was reaching from his saddle to catch the trailing reins of Rusty's pony. "Bust anythin'?" Slip said.

"No," Rusty said. He had sense enough to swallow his gratitude. With his cracked and blackened face, Slip looked like a dwarfish Negro jockey on that big strong horse. He was watching the herd, and Rusty turned to look too, just as Panguingue rode up and handed him his reins. All three stood a moment looking toward the wagon and listening to the uproar of shouts and curses that came from Spurlock and Jesse.

"God damn!" Panguingue said.

The longhorns, bursting into the compact herd of whitefaces, were stirring them like a great spoon. Even as they watched, the milling movement spread, the edges scattered, the whole herd was on the run back toward the coulee. Slip shook off his rope and he and Panguingue started off at a lope without a glance at Rusty. The steer rose and stood spraddling, watching him with red eyes. Limping, cursing the treacherous icy hole-pocked prairie, sorry for himself in his unregarded pain, Rusty reached his numb left arm up and took hold of the horn and mounted. Gritting his teeth, he spurred the pony into a trot, but that so agonized his arm and shoulder that in a moment he slowed to a walk. Then he swore and kicked him into a canter. He would show them. He would ride it out the whole mortal day, and they would never know until that night, after he had done without a complaint all the duty demanded of him, that he was really a stretcher case with a broken shoulder or collarbone or something. He knew he was going to be laid up, but he would stay in the saddle till he dropped. A grim campaigner, a man with the right stuff in him, he crippled along after Slip and Panguingue and the accursed cows.

He managed to get through the rest of the day, but when he was unsaddling that night at the wagon, his face skinned, his left hand helpless and his right fumbling and clumsy, no one came around with help or sympathy. One or two of them gave him bleary glances and went on past as he picked at the latigo with one freezing unmittened hand. Perhaps he dropped a tear or two of rage and weakness and pain into the snow. When he finally got the saddle off and turned the pony loose, he stumbled into the tent and lay down and turned his back to them. He heard Jesse's cooking noises, he smelled the smoke of frying meat, he felt the heat of the stove filling the canvas space. The boys talked a little, growling and monosyllabic. The wind puffed on the tent wall near his face; he cradled his aching arm the best he could and concentrated on stoicism.

Panguingue came in, crawled into his bed to warm up, and kicked Rusty companionably to get his attention. The jar shook such pain through the boy that he rose up with gritted teeth. Panguingue's astonished grin glimmered through his beard, and he said to the tent at large, "You should of seen old Rusty get piled today. How'd that feel, Rusty? You was up in the air long enough to grow feathers."

"It felt like hell, if you want to know. I think I broke my shoulder."

"Oh, well," Panguingue said. "Long as it wasn't your neck."

His callousness absolutely enraged Rusty, but Spurlock enraged him more when he remarked from the other corner of the tent, "You sure chose a hell of a time to get piled, I'll say that. You fall off and we lose the whole God damn herd."

"Fall off?" Rusty said shrilly. "*Fall* off? What do *you* do when your pony steps in a hole?"

"Not what you did," Spurlock said. In the light of the two candles Jesse had stuck onto his grub box, his bloodshot eyes moved restlessly, here, there, first on Rusty, then on one of the others, never still. There was a drooping, provocative smile on his face. Rusty pulled his anger in and stayed silent.

Slippers said into the air from where he lay on his back next to Panguingue, "Rusty was doin' all right. He was headin' 'em."

"When he see his horse was too slow, he took off and flew," Panguingue said.

In imbecile good nature his rough hand jarred out, half blow and half push, and Rusty fell awkwardly on the bad shoulder. "Look out, you silly bastard!" he screamed, so much like a hysterical schoolboy that he turned again, ashamed, and gave his back to them. He knew they were watching, speculatively and with expressions of calculated neutrality. Judgment was going on in their minds, and he hated what they were thinking.

In a few minutes Ray Henry came in, the last but one into camp.

"Somebody'll have to spell Buck in an hour," he said. "After that we can take it in two-hour shifts. Little Horn, you take it first, then Panguingue, then Slip." His inflamed eyes came around to Rusty, blinked at him across the stove and candles. "Rusty, you healthy? Was that you took a spill today?"

"That was me."

"Hurt yourself?"

"I don't know. I can't move my left arm."

The foreman picked his way between the bedrolls and squatted. "Roll over and let's see." Obediently, justified and finally vindicated, Rusty helped unbutton sheepskin and both flannel shirts he wore, and the thick hands probed and squeezed and punched around his shoulder and collarbone and down the arm. Rusty flattered himself that he did not wince.

For a second or two Ray stayed squatting there, dark-faced, burly as a boulder, expressionless. "I don't think she's bust," he said. "It don't wiggle anywhere. I'll take your shift tonight, and you better lay up with the wagon tomorrow and see how it goes."

"No," Rusty said. "I can work."

"Excelsior," said Spurlock from his corner.

"What?" Ray said.

Nobody said anything.

That was always a bad time, those few minutes before supper, when they came in and lay around the tent waiting for food with their bones melting away with tiredness. But it didn't last. They were cheerful enough afterward, lying in bed, smoking, and Spurlock even went to the length of rolling Rusty a cigarette and passing it across in silence. "Oh, I say," Rusty said. "Thanks very much!" Spurlock threw his muzzle in the air and gave himself up to silent laughter, or to communion with his ironic gods, and shook his head in amused despair, but the edge was out of him, out of all of them.

Buck came in, cold and morose, and fussily hunted up a pan and heated water in it and washed himself before he ate the supper Jesse had kept warm. Little Horn, groaning, hunched into his sheepskin and went out. They could hear him asking the sympathy of the horse as he saddled up.

One by one the other boys made their way outside and in a few seconds came chattering in again. When it came Rusty's turn he ducked out with his arm hugged against his chest. The cold froze his teeth clear to the roots at the first breath; he shuddered and shook. It is awkward enough for a man to button and unbutton his pants with his right hand at any time, but in that freezing circumstance he might as well have tried to do it with tongs. The big pale earth was around him, the big mottled sky arched over with a slice of very white moon shining on icy-looking clouds. It was so quiet he heard his own heart thudding. For a moment he stood taking it in, and then he opened his mouth and let out a very loud yell, simply to announce himself and to crack the silence. When he went back in, hissing and shaking, he found them all staring at him.

"What in hell was that?" Buck said.

"That was me," Rusty said. "It was too quiet to suit me."

Jesse was paring a sliver of tobacco off a plug, working at it slowly and carefully as he might have peeled an apple. His faded eyes glinted up, his oxbow mustaches parted briefly. "You hadn't ought to do a thing like that, son," he said. "I reckon you don't know, though."

"Know what?"

"When it's this cold," Jesse said, "man has to be careful how loud he talks."

"What?" Rusty said. "Get too cold air into your lungs, you mean? Freeze your windpipe?"

"Tell you," Jesse said. "I used to know this feller name Dan Shields."

Rusty crept into his blankets, not willing to give any of them, even Jesse, a handle. "Anybody feel like a game of stud?" Spurlock said.

"Too damn cold," Panguingue said. "You'd freeze your hands."

"Down by where I used to work," Jesse said, in his soft insisting voice, "down there by Sheridan, there's this guy Dan Shields. He's tellin' me one time about some cold weather *he* seen. Said him and another guy was up on the mountain workin' a gold mine one winter, and it chilled off considerable. Man walk along outside, he'd steam like a laundry. Wood froze so hard it'd last all night in the stove—they never had a bit of fuel trouble. Go to spit, you'd have to break yourself free before you could walk away. They figured seventy-five, eighty below. Couldn't tell, the thermometer froze solid at sixty-five."

"I hope they had a steam-heated backhouse," Panguingue said. "I had to break myself free out there just now."

"Better look close, Pan," said Spurlock. "Man could make a serious mistake breakin' too careless."

"B.S.," Panguingue said. "Even broke off short I'll match you."

"Said they had them a nice warm cabin and they made out fine," Jesse said, "except the grub began to run low. One mornin' they're talkin' about what they should do, and they step outside to sort of look at the weather. They're standin' there talkin', and it seems to Dan this other guy's voice is sort of failin' him. He gets squeakier and squeakier, and finally he pinches out. The fella looks surprised and clears his throat, and spits, and breaks himself loose, and tries again. Not a whisper.

" 'Is your tonsils froze, or what?' Dan says to him—and you know, *he* don't break the silence any, either. He tries his lips, and they're workin', and he wags his tongue, and *it* ain't bogged down, and he takes a big breath and tries to rip off a cussword, and nothin' happens at all.

"His partner is lookin' at him very queer. He says somethin' that Dan don't get. 'By God,' says Dan at the top of his voice, 'there's somethin' almighty damn funny here!' and all he hears is nothin', just nothin'. They turn their heads and listen, and there ain't a sound.

"Dan cusses some more, thinkin' he may jar somethin' loose the way you'd kick a jammed endgate. He can't make a peep. Said he was beginnin' to get scared. Said he looks across at his partner and the sweat was up on the guy's forehead size of buckshot. The drops froze as fast as they popped out, and they roll off his face and hit the snow. You'd think they'd patter—sort of human hailstones. Not a speck, Dan says. They roll off his partner's brow and hit the ground and he can see them bounce and they don't make no more noise than feathers.

"The partner begins to get excited. His mouth is goin' like a stampmill, and yet it's just as quiet as three o'clock in the mornin'. His eyes bug out, and he makes these yellin' motions, and all of a sudden he busts inside the cabin and throws his stuff together and takes off down the mountain."

"And never was seen again," Spurlock said. "The end."

"Well, that relieves the grub situation, and after Dan has gone inside and warmed up he tries out his voice again and it works, so he stays on. The weather never lets up, though, not till way 'long in the spring. Then one mornin' the sun comes up bright and first thing Dan notices the thermometer has thawed out and begun to slide down, and she's only sixty below, and then a little later she's fifty. She's gettin' so mild he sits down on the doorstep after breakfast and smokes a pipe. While he's sitting there he hears his partner, somewhere a good ways away, but comin' closer, sayin' somethin' like, 'figger we could get down and back in three-four days if on'y it wasn't so God damn cold.'

"Said it cheered him like anythin' to hear a human voice again, and he raises up on the doorstep and looks down the trail, but ain't a sign of anybody. He's lookin' all around when his partner says, quite close, 'I don't mind bein' out of sugar, but I sure as hell don't aim to stay long where they ain't any Climax Plug.'

" 'I see what you mean,' Dan says conversationally. 'I expect you get the bulk of your nourishment thataway,' and then he looks very fast behind him and all around that front yard, because it ain't him that's said it, he ain't moved his mouth or had any intention of sayin' anything. It ain't him but it's his voice.

" 'My notion is we ought to go on down,' the partner says, very clear and close, and then there is a good deal of hackin' and spittin' and clearin' of the throat and the partner says, 'What in the God damn hell is happenin' to me?' and Dan hears his own voice say, 'Is your tonsils froze, or what?' and then there is a very considerable duet of cussin' and yellin', and more throat clearin' and more yellin' and a sound like a hailstorm patterin' all around, and out of this big uproar the partner says, 'By God, I'm gettin' out of here!' Well that's just what Dan does. He ducks inside that cabin and leans against the door till all the fuss dies down outside, and when she's quiet he gathers together his plunder and he hightails her off the mountain too.

"He had it figured out by then, easy enough. It was so cold out there while they was talkin' that their words froze right there in the air, froze up plumb solid and silent. Then when that quick thaw comes on they broke up all at once and come down on old Dan's head like icicles off a roof. But Dan said he didn't want to stay up there even after he figured it out. Said it made him uncomfortable to think that any time somebody might yell right in his ear three months ago. Said he never did learn to care for cold-storage conversation as well as the fresh article."

"Now ain't it funny?" Buck said. "That ain't my taste at all. I'd just as soon have everything you just said all froze up nice and solid so the coyotes could listen to it next spring and I could just lay here now with no noise going on and get some sleep."

"That's the biggest pile of cold-storage bullshit I ever heard," Spurlock said. "Jesse, you could chop that up and use it for cowchips for a month."

"I guess," Jesse said mildly. "But I tell you, kid, don't you go yellin' so loud outside there no more. This is one of those winters when you might deefen somebody in 1907."

With his arm hanging in a sling made of a flour sack and a horse-blanket pin, and the loose sleeve of his sheepskin flapping, Rusty managed to go on riding. The weather was clear and bitter, full of signs that the boys said meant change—sundogs by day, Northern Lights by night. Even the noontime thermometer never climbed much above twenty. Flushing the stubborn cattle out of coulees and draws, they left behind them a good many cold-storage curses to startle the badgers and coyotes in the first thaw.

Day by day they worked their herd a few miles closer to Horse Camp Coulee; night by night they took turns riding around and around them, beating their arms to keep warm, and after interminable star-struck icy hours stumbled into the sighs and snores and faint warmth of the tent and shook the shoulder of the victim and benefactor who would relieve them. Some days one or another couldn't see to work, and when that happened they all suffered, for Jesse rode with the hands, instead of making camp, and in the icy evening they all had to fall to and shovel off a patch of prairie and set up the tent and fit the sooty lengths of stovepipe through the roof thimble, and anchor themselves to the earth with iron picket pins, the only thing they could drive into the frozen ground.

After an hour or two the stove would soften up the ground close around it, but near the edges and under their beds it never thawed more than just enough to moisten the tarps and freeze the beds fast, so that they pulled them up in the morning with great ripping sounds. The tent walls that they banked with snow to keep out the wind had to be chopped free every morning, and wore their clots and sheets of ice from one day to the next.

That cloth house stamped itself into Rusty's mind and memory. It spoke so plainly of the frailty and impermanence of their intrusion. And yet that frailty, and the implication of danger behind it, was what most nettled and dared and challenged him. Difficult as this job was, it was still only a job, and one done in collaboration with seven others. It called only for endurance; it had very little of the quality of the heroic that he had imagined Saskatchewan enforced upon the men who took its dare. Sometime, somehow, after he had gone through this apprenticeship in the skills of survival, he would challenge the country alone—some journey, some feat, some action that would demand of him every ounce of what he knew he had to give. There would be a real testing, and a real proof, and the certainty ever afterward of what one was. The expectation had no shape in his mind, but he thought of it in the same way he might have thought of sailing a small boat singlehanded across the Atlantic, or making a one-man expedition to climb Everest. It would be something big and it would crack every muscle and nerve and he would have to stand up to it alone, as Henry Kelsey had, wandering two years alone among unheard-of tribes in country not even rumored, or as young Alexander Mackenzie did when he took off from Fort Chipewyan to open the mysterious Northwest and track down the river that would carry his name. There were even times when he thought of the wolfer Schulz with near envy. Like him or not, he didn't run in pack, he was of an older and tougher breed, he knew precisely what he was made of and what he could do, and he was the sort from whom one might learn something.

Meantime he was the greenhorn, the outcast tenderfoot of the outfit, and he would remain so until he personally turned a stampeding herd, or rode seventy-five miles and back in twenty-four hours to bring a doctor for someone critically hurt, or plucked somebody from under the horns of a crazy longhorn steer. He nursed his sore shoulder, evidence of his so-far failure to perform heroically, like a grudge that must sometime be settled, or a humiliation that must be wiped out.

The first night, when he had come out and confronted a sinking moon and a rising banner of Northern Lights, and the other one, after his fall, when he had been tempted into a yell of defiance, had several counterparts. Sometimes, riding around the dark mass of the herd, numbly aware of the click of hoofs, the sigh of a cow heaving to her feet, the flurry of movement from a scared or lost calf, the muted tramplings and mooings and lowings, he seemed to guard all life inside his round, and heard its confusion and discomfort and dismay, and witnessed its unsleeping vigilance against the dangers that might come at it from outside the ritual circle his pony trod. The fact of living, more even than the fact of a job or a duty or the personal need to prove himself fit to call himself a man in this country's own terms, bound him to the cattle. The steam that hung above them was relative to the breath that plumed before his own face. It seemed to him a fact of tremendous significance that a cow never closed its eyes in sleep in all its life. These calves were on watch against the world from the time their mothers licked away the membrane from their wet faces until the axe fell between their eyes in Kansas City or Chicago. He felt that nothing living could afford *not* to be on guard, and that the warm blood of men and cattle was in league against the forces of cold and death. Like theirs, his mortality mooed and bellowed, keeping up its courage with its voice or complaining of its discomfort. He sang to the herd, or to himself, and sometimes played them tunes on the harmonica.

They had to be content with a limited repertoire—the mouth organ had been his study for no more than ten days, on the boat coming over—so that he found himself running through a few songs many times. Sometimes, for variety, he rendered, talking aloud to himself, the pony, and the cattle, like a fool or a hermit, certain poems, especially one he had memorized in his first enthusiasm for Canada—a ballad of *coureurs de bois* and of a stranger that walked beside them and left no footprints in the snow. When he had succeeded in scaring himself with ghosts and shadows he might fall back upon a jigging Canuck tune,

> *Rouli roulant, ma boule roulant,*
> *Rouli roulant ma boule.*

But everything he said or played or sang during his hours on the night herd was meant seriously, even soberly, even ritually, for he felt in every deceptive snow-shadow and every pulse of the Northern Lights and every movement of the night wind the presence of something ancient and terrible, to which the brief stir and warmth of life were totally alien, and which must be met head on.

On those miraculously beautiful and murderously cold nights glittering with the green and blue darts from a sky like polished dark metal, when the moon was dark, leaving the hollow heavens to the stars and the overflowing cold light of the Aurora, he thought he had moments of the clearest vision and saw himself plain in a universe simple, callous, and magnificent. In every direction from their pallid soapbubble of shelter the snow spread; here and there the implacable plain glinted back a spark—the beam of a cold star reflected in a crystal of ice.

He was young and susceptible, but he was probably not far wrong in his feeling that there never was a lonelier land, and one in which men lived more uneasily on sufferance. And he thought he knew the answer to the challenge Saskatchewan tossed him: to be invincibly strong, indefinitely enduring, uncompromisingly self-reliant, to depend on no one, to contain within himself every strength and every skill. There were evenings when he sorted through the outfit, examining models, trying on for fit Ray Henry's iron, Slip's whalebone, Little Horn's leather. Though he had ambitions beyond any of them, he admitted that there was not a man in the outfit who could not teach him something, unless it was Spurlock. And Spurlock, he perceived, was the one on whom he might have to prove himself. The others would tease him, Little Horn and Jesse would pull his leg, Panguingue would thump him in brainless good humor, but Spurlock would push his nasty little nagging persecution until he might have to be smashed. It even occurred to Rusty once or twice that that was exactly what Spurlock wanted: a test of strength. Well, so be it. Riding narrow-eyed, he compared their physical equipment. Spurlock probably had some weight on him, and Rusty had a picture in his mind of big hands, thick wrists. On the other hand, Spurlock must be at least thirty-five, and it was said that for five years he had dealt in a Butte gambling joint, an occupation to soften and weaken a man. Let him come; he might not be half as tough as he sounded or acted; and in any case, let him come.

And then, with singing stopped, and talking stopped, and harmonica stopped, riding slowly, thinking of challenges and anticipating crises and bracing himself against whatever might come, he might have word from his night companions of the prairie, and hear the *yap-yap-yap* and the shivering howl of coyotes, or the faint dark monotone of the wolves. Far more than the cattle or their protectors, they were the proper possessors of the wilderness, and their yelling was a sound more appropriate there than human curses or growls or songs, or the wheezy chords of the mouth organ, and certainly than the half-scared screech of defiance he had let off that one night. The wolves' hunting noises were always far off, back north in the river bottoms. In the eerie clarity of the white nights they seemed to cry from inexpressible distances, faint and musical and clear, and he might have been tempted to think of them as something not earthly at all, as creatures immune to cold and hunger and pain, hunting only for the wolfish joy of running and perhaps not even visible to human eyes, if he had not one afternoon ridden through a coulee where they had bloodied half an acre with a calf.

By day the labor and the cold and the stiffness of many hours in the saddle, the bawling of calves, the crackle and crunch of hooves and wheels, the reluctant herded movement of two or three hundred cows and calves and six dozen horses, all of whom stopped at every patch of grass blown bare and had to be whacked into moving again. By night the patient circling ride around the herd, the exposure to stars and space and the eloquent speech of the wolves, and finally the crowded sleep.

Nothing between them and the stars, nothing between them and the North Pole, nothing between them and the wolves, except a twelve by sixteen house of cloth so thin that every wind moved it and light showed through it and the shadows of men hulked angling along its slope, its roof so peppered with spark holes that lying in their beds they caught squinting glimpses of the stars. The silence gulped their little disturbances, their little tinklings and snorings and sighs and the muffled noises of discomfort and weariness. The earth and the sky gaped for them like opened jaws; they lay there like lozenges on a tongue, ready to be swallowed.

In spite of his dream of a test hoped-for, met, and passed, the tenderfoot pitied himself, rather. The pain of his arm as he lay on the frozen ground kept him turning sleeplessly. Some nights his fingers throbbed as if he had smashed them with a maul, and his feet ached all night with chilblains. To be compelled to bear these discomforts and these crippling but unvaliant pains he considered privately an outrage.

They told each other that it couldn't last—and yet they half prayed it would, because cold as it was, it was working weather: they could collect and move their herd in it. Nevertheless the boys spoke of change, and said that this early in November, weather like this shouldn't last more than a few days, and that the sundogs meant something for sure. Not at all fond of what they had, they feared what might replace it.

At the end of the eighth day, with a herd of nearly four hundred cows and calves and two dozen bulls, they camped within ten miles of Horse Camp Coulee. The streaked sky of sunset hazed out in dusk. Before Jesse had supper hot the wind was whistling in the tent ropes and leaning on the roof in strange erratic patches, as if animals were jumping on the canvas. In an hour more they were outside trying to keep the tent from blowing away, half a dozen of them hauling the wagon by hand around on the windward side and anchoring the tent to it. The darkness was full of snow pebbles hard and stinging as shot, whether falling or only drifting they couldn't tell, that beat their eyes shut and melted in their beards and froze again. While they were fighting with the tent, Slip came in from the cattle herd and talked with Ray. He did not go back; it would have been risking a man's life to try to keep him riding. They did not discuss what was likely to happen to the cattle, though even Rusty could guess; they crawled into their beds to keep warm, let the fire go out to save fuel, gave at least modified thanks for the fact that they would not have to ride night herd, and because they could do nothing else, they slept.

They slept most of the time for the next two days. When the wind eased off and they dug their way out, the wagon and the tent were surrounded by a horned dune of snow. Snow lay out across the plains in the gray, overcast afternoon, long rippled drifts like an ocean petrified in mid-swell, a dull, expressionless, unlit, and unshadowed sea. There was not a sign of the herd; the only horses in sight were the four they had kept miserably tied to the wagon—Jesse's Clydes and two night saddle ponies.

Slip and Little Horn hunted up the horses, far downwind, before dark. They reported bunches of cattle scattered through all the coulees in that direction for a dozen miles. They also found that range steers had drifted in among them during the storm, which meant that all of that separation of whiteface and longhorn and steer and cow and calf had to be gone through again.

The prospect appalled Rusty Cullen; he waited for them to say it couldn't be done, that they would give it up and head for the ranch. It apparently never even occurred to Ray that they might quit. They simply chased and swore and floundered through the drifts, and wore out horses and changed to others, and worked till they couldn't see, and fell into their beds after dark with about a hundred head reassembled. Next day they swung around in a big half circle to the south and east and brought together about a hundred and fifty more.

Sweeping up a few strays as they went, they moved on the third day toward the corrals at Horse Camp Coulee and made half of the ten miles they had to cover. The hard part was about over. They spoke at supper of Molly Henry's dried apple pies, disparaging Jesse's beefsteak and beans. That night, sometime between midnight and dawn, the wind reached down out of the iron north and brought them a new blizzard.

Into a night unfamiliarly black, whirling with snow, a chaos of dark and cold and the howl of a wind that sometimes all but lifted them from their feet, they struggled out stiff and clumsy with sleep, voiceless with outrage, and again anchored themselves to that unspeakable plain. While they fought and groped with ropes in their hands, ducking from the lash of wind and snow, apparitions appeared right among them, stumbled over a guy rope and almost tore the tent down, snorted and bolted blindly into the smother: range horses drifting before the storm. The cowboys cursed them and repaired their damage and got themselves as secure as they could and crawled back into their blankets, knowing sullenly what the drifting horses meant. When they dug out of this one they would have lost their herd again.

Jesse had started the fire as soon as it seemed clear that the tent would not go down. When Rusty had got back into his bed next to Buck, with Panguingue's feet jammed for a headboard against his skull, he could see the glow through the draft door and feel his stung face loosening in the warmth. The canvas roof bucked and strained, slacked off, stiffened in a blast. The wind came through in needles of cold. It was close to morning; he could make out the faint shapes inside the tent. He waited for Ray to say something—something to console them, perhaps, for their failure and their bad luck—but no one spoke at all. They lay appraising the turmoil half seen and half heard on the straining roof. Finally, after several minutes, Jesse said, "Anybody feel like a cup of coffee?"

Only then did Ray speak. His hoarse, ironic whisper croaked across the tent, "Looks like you boys could have the day off. Sleep in, if you want."

"Sleep!" Ed Spurlock said. "How could anybody sleep when he thinks where them God damn cows are going?"

"Just the same you better sleep," Ray whispered. "You'll need your rest, boy."

"You going to try rounding them up again?"

Ray said, "We're in this business to raise calves, not fertilize some prairie with their carcasses."

"*Jesus!*" Spurlock said. He rocked his head back and forth on his rolled mackinaw, glaring at the tent roof with eyes that shone oilily in the glimmer from the firebox. The wind took hold of the tent and shook it, testing every rope; they waited till the blast let go again. "You can't drive cows in this kind of weather, Ray," Spurlock said.

"I know it," Ray whispered. "That's why you get the day off."

"I bet you we end up by leaving the whole herd to scatter."

"We do, we'll lose ever' damn calf," Ray said. His face turned and craned toward Spurlock, above and across from him. His indomitable croak said, "I don't aim to lose any, if work'll save 'em."

"No, I can see," Spurlock said. "You might lose a few of us, though."

Ray laughed through his nose. "Why, Ed," he said, "you sound like you thought you was more valuable than a calf."

"I'd kind of like some coffee, myself," old Jesse said. "Don't anybody else feel thataway?"

"Shut up!" said Buck's voice from under the blankets. He had a capacity for always sounding furious, even when he was talking through four layers of wool. "Shut up and let a guy get some sleep."

Panguingue produced a few exaggerated snores.

There was a brief silence. The wind gripped the tent, fell away, pounced once more; they could hear it whining and ricocheting off the guy ropes. "Good God," Ed Spurlock said restlessly, "listen to the God damn wind blow."

"I think I'll just put the pot on anyhow, long as we got that fire," Jesse's soft voice said. Rusty heard the stiff creak of his bedroll tarp and the fumbling sounds as he got on his boots. There was a grunt, and Spurlock said savagely, "God damn it to hell, Jesse, watch out where you put your feet!"

"Don't leave your face hanging out, then," Jesse said. "How can I see your face in this dark? I been huntin' for ten minutes with both hands, and I just now found my ass."

"Step on me once more and you'll find it in a sling," Spurlock said. "Why can't you stay in bed? There's nothing to get up for."

"Yes, there is," Jesse said. "Coffee."

His shape reared up against the graying canvas; when he opened the lid the glow from the stove illuminated his intent face with the white bristles on cheeks and chin, and the mustache drooping in a smooth oxbow. This, Rusty thought, was all familiar to Jesse. He must have done this same thing, camped in the same brutal kind of weather, a hundred times, with Indians, with *métis hivernants*, with hide hunters, with wagon trains hauling supplies into the Montana camps, with cattle outfits like this one. His relation to the country was almost as simple as that of the wolves; no matter how fast the province changed, it remained to Jesse merely a few known forms of hardship, a known violence of weather, one or two simple but irreplaceable skills. He had the air, standing ruminatively above his stove, of a man who could conceive of no evil that a cup of hot coffee or a beefsteak fried in flour would not cure.

*   *   *

Daylight came as dusk and stayed that way. They dozed, and when the fire was up high for cooking they took advantage of the warmth to play poker or blackjack. When anyone had to go outside he took a look at the horses, which they had picketed to give them a little more chance to move around and keep warm, but which crowded close up against the wagon for the little shelter it gave them. Morning and evening someone hung on their noses a nosebag of their limited oat supply.

Their wood was running low too; they had been depending on getting fuel from the willows in Horse Camp Coulee. After meals they had to let the fire die, and then if they played cards they passed around a lighted candle to warm their hands by. When even that got too cold they dug down under their blankets to sleep or think. Talk flared up like matches and went out again; they cocked their ears to the howl of the wind, remoter as the tent snowed in. Once or twice one of them went out and carefully cleared the worst of the snow off the roof while the rest, inside, watched with concern the sausage-tight canvas which a careless shovel might easily slit, leaving them exposed to the storm like an out-turned nest of mice. Every hour or so Ray Henry, taciturn and expressionless, took a look outside.

When he had got his hands well warmed under the blankets, Rusty played the harmonica. There were more requests than he could gratify, with a heavy favoritism for old Red River tunes which they tried to teach him by whistling or humming. If he quit, with his hands too numb to feel the fingers and his chapped lips sore from the sliding of the little honeycomb back and forth across them, they urged him for a while, and then cursed him languidly and gave up. The afternoon waned; they yawned; they lay resting.

Once the notebook in his shirt pocket crunched as Rusty turned over, and he took it out and amused himself for a while reading the journal entries he had made. There was nothing since his catalog of information about the Stonepile Camp, but before that there was a very windy and prize-essay series of notations. He had put them down in the first place as colorful items to be incorporated into letters home; they expected him not to write very often, and he would oblige them; but they expected him, when he did write, to fill pages with cowboys and Indians and wild game and the adventures and observations of a well-educated young gentleman in the North American wilderness. In this too he had set out to oblige them. He read what he had had to say about the ranch, and the thumbnail sketches he had made of some of the cowboys, and the lyrical flights he had gone into during the days of perfect Indian Summer hay-making weather that preceded the first storm—only the night before they had set out on this belated roundup. He could imagine the family all around his mother as she read, and he cocked an inner ear to the sound of his own prose describing the apelike Panguingue with his good nature and his total disregard for cleanliness, and wry little birdy Slippers with his sore feet, as if he had walked all the way from Texas; even on roundup he wore no boots like the rest of them but elastic-sided slippers under his overshoes. Rusty told them Slip was the best bronc rider in Saskatchewan, which may have been going it a bit strong, and about how Buck kept a row of tobacco tins on the two-by-four above his bunk, with all his smaller private effects filed away in them in neat and labeled order. He described, with the proper tone of sober appraisal and respect, Ray Henry and his new wife, whom he had brought from Malta, Montana, in a buckboard, a hundred and twenty miles across country, for a wedding trip. Rusty had loaded that part of the journal with data on the country, much of it, as he saw now, in error. It was the sort of stuff which, written as a letter, would surely set his younger brother to itching, and produce another emigration from the family, but it seemed false and shrilly enthusiastic and very, very young when he read it over in the tent, while a frozen guy rope outside, within three feet of his ear, hummed like a great struck cable.

"What you got there, Rusty?" Little Horn said. "Something to read?"

"No," he said. "Oh no, just an old notebook."

"Notebook?" Spurlock said.

"Just . . . notes, don't you know," Rusty said. He was frantic with the notion that they would sit on him and take it away from him and read in it what he had said about them. If they tried it he would die fighting. He put it in his shirt pocket and buttoned it down. "Things I wanted to remember to put in letters home," he said.

"All about the cow country and the cattle business, uh?" Little Horn said.

"More or less."

"She's a real good business," Little Horn said. "You ought to think about her, Rusty." Staring at the roof, his red nose one of a half dozen projecting toward the lashed and laboring canvas, he plucked a thread from the frayed edge of his blanket and drew it dreamily between his front teeth. "Young fella from the old country could do a lot worse," he said. "There's this Englishman over on Medicine Lodge Coulee, kind of a remittance-man colony they got over there, he was tellin' me about cattle ranchin' one time. He said there was millions in it. All you do, you just get some cows and a few bulls, and you turn 'em out on the range. Say you start with a hundred cows. You get a hundred calves the first year, and fifty of them are cows and fifty you make into steers. Next year you got a hundred and fifty cows and they give you a hundred and fifty calves, and you make seventy-five steers and keep the seventy-five cows, and that builds your breeding herd to two hundred and twenty-five. That year you get two hundred and twenty-five calves, and by now you're sellin' your two-year-old and three-year-old steers, and your herd keeps growin' and you keep sellin' the bull calves, and that's all they is to her. He had it all mapped out. You ought to talk to him, Rusty."

"I'll look into it the first chance I get," Rusty said. "I've been inquiring around for a good opportunity."

"You do that," Little Horn said. "If I didn't have me this job here with Ray, I'd do somethin' about it myself. There ain't a thing to her. Once you get your herd and start them cows to calfin', all you do is set back and count the dollars rollin' in.

"They'll tell you: mange. Hell, they ain't nothin' to mange. All you got to do about that, you dip 'em twice a year. You get yourself one of them steam boilers and a tank, and you lay in some sulphur and so on. And you dig yourself a big hole in the ground, maybe a hundred feet long, say, and thirty wide, and at one end you build a couple corrals, one big one to hold maybe a couple hundred head and the other a little one to take a dozen or so. From this little one you build a chute that leads down into the hole. At the other end of the hole you make a slatted slope out of planks for the cows to climb out on, and a couple drippin' pens where the ones that has been dipped can stand, and under those pens you dig a ditch so the dip that runs off them can run back into the vat. It ain't anything, hardly. If you got ten or fifteen hands around it'll only take you a couple-three weeks' hard work altogether to build this rig.

"Then you bring your stock into the big corral, see, and feed 'em out a few at a time into the little corral and on into the chute, and on both sides of the vat you put guys with long poles with a yoke onto them, and they get the yoke over these cattle as they come down the chute and duck 'em clear under. Then you prod 'em on through the vat and up the slope and into the drippin' pens and you're done with that bunch.

"They'll tell you it's lots of work. Shucks. You got, say, ten thousand head to dip, like we would on the T-Down, and you got maybe twelve men in the outfit. You can do a dozen ever' twenty minutes, thirty-six an hour, three hundred and sixty in a ten-hour day, thirty-six hundred in ten days. You can get the whole herd through in three or four weeks, if you can get the inspector there when you want him. They'll tell you it's hell to catch the inspector, and hard to keep the herd together that long, and hard to keep the sulphur mixture strong enough and the right temperature, and a lot like that, but it ain't nothing to bother a man. Some people would talk down anything.

"Or they'll tell you it's dangerous. Shoot! Suppose one of them steers does get on the peck when he's pushed under and gets his eyes full of sulphur, what can he do? He can thrash around in the vat, maybe, and drowned himself or some other steer, or maybe he climbs out and chases you up onto the barn, or he scrambles back into the corral and gets them to millin' there till they break something down, but that ain't only a little delay. Even if some old ringy longhorn catches you before you can climb out of the corral, what can he do to you? His horns is so wide he just rams you against the fence with his forehead and holds you there till somebody twists his tail or spits Bull Durham in his eye and pulls him off, and there you are good as ever, maybe bruised up some is all.

"No, sir," Little Horn said, pulling his thread back and forth, "it's a mistake to listen to these calamity howlers about what a tough business the cow business is. Mange, that's only a sample of how they exaggerate. They'll tell you: wolves. Wolves! They won't pick off more'n one calf in ten or twenty all winter long. Sure three or four of them will pull down a cow sometimes, get her by the hind leg and a flank and pull her over and pile on, but mostly it's just calves. Say you start with two thousand head in the fall, you still got eighteen hundred in the spring. And if you want to, you can hire somebody like this Schulz to wolf your range."

"Schulz!" Buck said from down under. "I wonder if he's et his boy yet?"

"Only cost you ten dollars a scalp," Little Horn said. "If he puts out poison baits, course you might lose a few dogs. Sure a wolf is hard to poison and he's too smart to step in a trap or come within gunshot very often, but that don't have to bother you. There's other ways of handlin' wolves. You just lay around and keep an eye open and when you catch one out on the flats you can run him down on a horse. I did it once myself. I had me a little old pony that could run, and I come right up on that old white wolf and run over him. I missed him that first time, somehow, and had to come over him again, and I missed him again, but I kep' tryin'. This wolf can't get away—he's down there under the pony's feet somewhere duckin' and snarlin'. I'd of had him sure if the pony hadn't of stepped in a hole. The wolf run off then and I couldn't chase him. I was out quite a few miles, and after I shot the horse I had me quite a walk carryin' the saddle, but that experience taught me quite a bit about runnin' down wolves, and I know how it's done. I'll show you sometime, if you want."

"Oh, I say, thanks," Rusty said.

"Old Rusty, I bet he figures just like your other Englishman," Spurlock said. "Ain't it the fact, Rusty? You come out here thinking you'd get yourself a few thousand acres and a herd of cows and be a lord of the manor like Dan Tenaille, uh?"

"That's right," Rusty said. "Just now, I'm out here learning the business first hand from the experts."

"Or did you *have* to come out?" Spurlock said. "You're a remittance man too, ain't you? Tell us the story of how you happened to leave England. I bet it'd be interesting. Help pass the time, don't you know."

"I'm afraid you'd find it a bit dull."

"A bit dull?" Spurlock said heartily. "Not at all, lad, not at all. Come on, give us your reasons for trailing out to the cow country."

They were not a talking bunch, and so far as he knew they had not discussed him. He was too common a phenomenon. Unless he took pains to prove himself otherwise, any young Englishman in that country was assumed to be the second son, third son, scapegrace son, of a baronet, a KCB, a shooting partner of Edward VII. Or he was a cashiered guardsman or disgraced country vicar. Rusty was none of those, but it seemed unnecessary to insist. He said only, "I'm afraid my reasons wouldn't be as colorful as yours."

He put into his voice just the quantity of sneer that would make Spurlock rise up without realizing precisely where he was stung. Or perhaps the sneer did not do it at all, perhaps Spurlock was only bored, uncomfortable, irritable, ready to pluck any little thread that would ravel, quarrelsome out of no motive except tedium. If that was it, fine;

let him come. And there he came, rearing up on one elbow and throwing across the tent a literary badman look as if he thought he was wearing black gloves and black guns like a villain in *The Virginian*. "What do you mean by that, exactly?"

From the side, Ray Henry's whisper said, "The kid's not crowding you any, Ed."

"I can tell when I'm crowded," Spurlock said.

"Pull in your elbows," Ray whispered, amused. "Then you'll have more room."

Spurlock lay down again. "Little English punks," he said. "Coming out pretending to be cowhands."

Rusty looked at Ray, but Ray only smiled. The boy said, fairly hotly, "The cows can't tell the difference."

"No," Spurlock said, "no, but a man sure can."

"I haven't heard any *men* discussing it."

Once more he reared up on his elbow. "Is its little arm sore?" he said. "Got piled, did it?"

"How are its little sore eyes?" Rusty said. Out of nothing, out of nowhere, as random and unprepared for as an August whirlwind kicking up a dust, Spurlock had produced the quarrel he evidently wanted. Rusty was angry enough to take him on, arm or no arm. He pretended to himself that he was annoyed with Ray when the foreman whispered equably, "In about a second I'm kickin' both you quarrelsome bastards out in the snow."

Rusty lay ready, smoldering, waiting for Spurlock to say something else that could not be borne, or to rise and stalk outside where it would be necessary to go out and fight him. But Spurlock did not move or speak; he only breathed through his nose in so eloquent and contemptuous a way that Rusty had to hold himself back from springing over and smashing him. The wind slammed against their canvas roof in a furious gust. Against some rope or edge or corner it howled like a wolf, and then trailed off to the steady whisper and rush again.

"They'll tell you," Little Horn said dreamily, "they'll say to you it's terrible hard work. Why, God damn, now, you just can't pay attention to that. How long we been on this-here roundup? Since first of May, more or less? And it's only November now. And they'll tell you it gets cold, but where would you find a nicer, more comfortable little tent than this one, if we only had some wood?"

Jesse crawled out and stood stretching in the narrow space among the mussed beds. Rusty noticed that he was careful to stay clear of Ed Spurlock's blankets. "Well," he said, "time for a little grub?"

Ray went past Jesse and pulled the flap aside and looked out. Beyond him the horizontal blast streaked with snow dipped and swirled; flakes settled and whirled away again; there was a curved drift building up at the tent corner. Ray's back looked bulky and solid; he was a powerful man, single-minded and devoted. A little hollow in the solar plexus from the nearness of a fight, Rusty had a wry feeling that if Spurlock and he had started something, and the foreman wanted to interfere, he could have thrashed them both. But what his hunched back and his bent head reminded Rusty of really was the burden he bore. He was foreman, he wore responsibility for both men and cattle, and he had left his bride of less than a month at the ranch house with only a crippled handy man for company. Rusty did not envy Ray, but he respected him a great deal. He wanted to do well for him; he was ashamed of having had to be reprimanded along with Spurlock. The foreman dropped the flap and came back and sat down.

"They'll tell you," Little Horn said, endless and ironic and contemplative, "they'll say, all that ridin' and brandin' and weanin' and nuttin' and chasin' cows up and down the hills and dales. How else would you want a cowpuncher to spend his time? He don't have any work to do, he just gets himself into trouble playin' cyards and fightin' and chasin' women. Lots better for him to be out in a nice tent like this, camped out comfortable in some blizzard."

Sometime before the gray afternoon howled itself out, Ray Henry shouldered into his sheepskin and went outside. The rest lay in their blankets, which they had inhabited too long for their blankets' good or their own, in their postures that were like the postures of men fallen in war. Panguingue sprawled with his drawn-up knees wide, his whiskered face glimmering a vacant grin straight upward. Little Horn and Buck were unexpected angles of arms and legs, Slip lay curled as if around a mortal body wound. Spurlock had locked his hands under the back of his head and crossed his knees under the covers. They listened to the undiminished wind. After what may have been ten minutes Jesse rose and said he guessed he'd take a look at the Clydes. He followed his jet of white breath outside, and they lay on.

Their cloth house shook, and gave way, and shuddered stiff and tight again. They heard the whistle and scream go flying through and away, and in a lull Buck said, "This one's the worst one yet." They lay considering this for quite a long time. At last Rusty heard the sound of feet, and with a relief that astonished him he cried, "Here they are!"

But no one entered. The wind pounded through and over and past. It had a curving sound; it dipped to the ear like telegraph wires to the eye. Everyone in the tent was listening for the steps Rusty had announced. At last Spurlock grumbled, "Just fawncy." Panguingue blurted a laugh.

"Christ A'mighty!" Slip said abruptly, and snapped nimble as a monkey out of his bed. He was stepping in his slippers across Ray Henry's tarp when the flap opened and Ray and Jesse stooped in on a flurry of snow. Slippers sat quietly down again on his blankets. His leathery, deeply lined, big-nosed face said nothing. Neither did any of the other smudged and whiskered faces around the tent. But they were all sitting up or half propped on their elbows; the concern that had moved Slip had been a fear in all of them. In silence they watched Ray throw down beside the cold stove three or four round cake-like chunks of ice. Rusty reached across and picked up a frozen cowchip.

"Are we burning ice now?"

With a wipe of a bare hand around on his wet, beef-red face, the foreman said, "We may be lucky to have that to burn, it's drifting pretty deep all over."

"Still from the northwest?" Buck asked.

"Oh, dear," said Little Horn. "All those poor little calves and their mamas. They'll be clear the hell and gone down to Wood Mountain."

"Or else they'll be piled up in some draw," Ray said.

"You think it's pretty bad, then," Rusty said—a small, inconsequent, intrusive voice of ignorance and greenness that he himself heard with shame and dismay.

"Yes, kid," Ray said. "I think it's pretty bad."

They ebbed away into silence. With only a few sticks of wood left Jesse gave them no more for supper than warm gravy poured over frozen biscuits; not even coffee. Part of the stove, while the gravy was warming, held two of the cowchips that Ray had kicked up from under the snow, and the smell of wetted and baking manure flavored their supper. But at least the cakes dried out enough so that Jesse could use them for the breakfast fire.

The single candle gave a blotted light. When they were all still Rusty saw the humps of bedrolls fuming like a geyser basin with their eight breaths, until Little Horn said, "Well, nighty-night, kids," and blew out the candle. The wind seemed to come down on their sudden darkness with such violence that in the cold tent they lay tensely, afraid something would give. Both Slip and Little Horn had pulled their goatskin chaps over their beds for extra cover. Rusty's icy hands were folded into his armpits; he wore all his clothes except sheepskin and boots. He blew his breath into the air, moved his sore shoulder experimentally, smelled his own stale nest, thinking Holy Mother, if my people could see me now! There was a brief, vivid picture of rescuers in the spring reverently uncovering eight huddled figures, identifying each one, folding the tarp back over the frozen face. His head was full of vague heroisms related to Commodore Peary and the North Pole.

Once the thought popped whole and astonishing into his head: I might, except for one or two decisions made in excitement and stuck to through tears and argument, be sleeping in my old room right now, and if I opened my eyes I would see the model of the *Kraken* hanging from the ceiling like a ship of thanksgiving in a Danish church. Except for the excitement that his father thought wild whimsy and his mother thought heartlessness, he might be getting his exercise these days pushing a punt up and down the Cher, disturbing the swans (Swans! From here they sounded fabulous as gryphons), or drinking too much port with sporty undergraduates from his college, or sitting on some cricket pitch, or (assuming he *hadn't* chosen Oxford and the family's program) he might be guiding the tiller of the yawl with his backside while he shouted questions, jeers, comments, or other conversation at sailors leaning over the stern rails of old rustpots anchored in the stream off Spithead.

The fact that he was here in a tent on the freezing Saskatchewan plains, that one decision rashly made and stubbornly stuck to had taken him not only out of the university, out of home, out of England, but out of a whole life and culture that had been assumed for him, left him dazed. A good job he didn't have much chance to think, or he might funk it yet, and run straight home with his tail tucked. He was appalled at the effectiveness of his own will.

A numbness like freezing to death stole through him gradually, Panguingue restored him to wakefulness with a kick in the head, and he cursed Panguingue with a freedom he would not have adopted toward anyone else in the outfit. Sometime during or just after the flurry of profane protest he fell asleep.

* * *

Solitary flutes, songs from the Vienna woods, chirpings and twitterings so that he opened his eyes thinking *Birds?* and heard the awakening sounds of the outfit, and old Jesse whistling with loose lips while he stood over the stove. He lifted a can and tipped it in a quick gesture; the tent filled with the smell of kerosene. Jesse hobbled about in his boots like an old crone. His right knee crooked upward, there was a swoop and a snap, and a match popped into flame across his tight seat. The stove *whoofed* out a puff of smoke. The lids clanged on. Fire gleamed through the cracks in the ash door and Jesse shoved the coffee pot against the stovepipe. Looking, Rusty saw that Ray, Slip, and Buck were missing.

He sat up. "I say! The wind's died!"

"You say, hey?" Jesse said.

Rusty hustled to the door and looked out. Deep tracks went through the drift that curved all around them; the sky was palest blue, absolutely clear. Ray was trotting the Clydes up and down a fifty-foot trampled space, getting them warm. Their breasts and rumps and legs were completely coated in ice. Buck and Slip already had saddles on the night ponies. Whatever had been brown in the landscape had disappeared. There were no scraggly patches of bare grass in the snow waves, but packed, rippled white ran off into the southeast where the sun was just rising. He could almost see the plain move as if a current ran strongly toward where the sun squatted on the rim and sent its dazzle skipping across the million little wave crests into his eyes. Spurlock, looking over his shoulder, swore foully. "Here goes for some more God damn snow-blindness." He stepped past Rusty and blew his nose with his fingers, first one nostril, then the other.

Rusty shouted over to Ray, "Working weather!"

"Yeah." He laughed his dry laugh through his nose. "Come here and curry some of the ice out of these studs."

"Uh-huh!" Spurlock said behind Rusty, with I-told-you-so emphasis. The boy stared at him. "Working weather!" Spurlock said. "Jesus Christ! I guess."

His guess was right. Within minutes of the time Rusty woke he was working; they paused only long enough to bolt a steak and gulp scalding coffee and warm their hands over the fire; their last wood and all the cowchips had gone into it. Before they had more than spread their palms to the beautiful heat, Slip and Buck came in with the horse herd.

"Jesse," Ray said, "you better tear down here and get loaded and beat it on a beeline for Horse Camp. If we ain't there when you get there, which we won't be, you can improve your time and warm your blood gettin' in wood, and there ain't any such thing as too much. The rest of you is goin' to round up every cow within fifteen miles downwind, and we're going to put them all in the corrals at Horse Camp before we sleep any more. So pick you a pony with some bottom."

They looked at the shaggy, scrawny, long-maned and long-tailed herd picking at the wisps of a few forkfuls of hay that the boys had thrown out. There was not a pony among them whose ribs did not show plainly under the rough winter hair. Here and there one stood spraddled, head hanging, done in, ready to fall.

"Boneracks," Little Horn said. "Some of them ponies ain't goin' to make it, Boss."

"Then we got to leave them," Ray said. "They can maybe make out, poor as they are, but unless we get a chinook this is starvin' time for cattle."

They saddled and rode out, Ray, Slip, Panguingue, and Rusty to the southeast, straight into the sun, Spurlock and Buck and Little Horn to the northeast. They would pinch everything in to the middle and then swing and bring them back. The tent was already coming down as they rode off.

They rode a long way before they raised any cattle. When they did, down in a draw, they were humped in the deep snow, making no effort to get out. They stood and bellowed; they moved as if their blood had frozen thick, and they had among them range steers, including a few longhorns, which the boys did not want at all but had no time to cut out. They threw them all into a bunch, and attended by an intensely black and unlikely looking crow, rode on into the diamond glitter, gradually swinging eastward so that they could get some relief by ducking their heads and pulling their hats clear down on the sun side. Ray kept them pushing hard through the difficult going, knee high sometimes, hock high the next moment, crusted just enough to hold the horse's weight for a split second before he broke down through. It was hard enough in the saddle; it must have been a good deal worse under it.

"Got to hustle," Ray said. "For some reason I'm gettin' so I don't trust the damn weather." They fanned out, riding wide. Far north, across a spread of flats and one or two shallow coulees whose depressions could hardly be seen in the even glare, the black dots that were Spurlock and Little Horn and Buck were strung out across a mile or so of snow.

They headed in toward the center of their loop every sad whiteface whose red hide showed. The cattle bellowed, blinking white eyelashes, and they moved reluctantly, but they moved. The crow flapped over, following companionably, flying off on some investigation of his own and returning after a few minutes to coast over and cock his wise eye down and caw with laughter to hear them talk.

About noon, far to the south and east of where they had camped, they came to the river, angling down from the northwest in its shallow valley. The willows along the banks looked thin as a Chinaman's whiskers, hardly more than weeds, but they held a surprising number of cattle, which the outfit flushed out by the dozens and scores and hazed, plunging and ducking and blindly swinging back until a horse blocked them or a rope cut across their noses, up onto the flats. They had everything in that herd: whiteface, shorthorn, longhorn, all sorts of crosses; steers, cows, bulls, calves; T-Down, Circle Diamond, Turkey Track. Ray pointed some out to Rusty when they rested their ponies for a minute on the flat and let Slip chase a half-dozen whiteface yearlings back into the bottoms. "The Seventy-Six," he said. "Their range is way up by Gull Lake, on the CPR. They've drifted twenty-five miles."

Whatever they were, whoever they belonged to, if they could not be easily cut out the riders swept them in and drove them westward, pushing them without a pause toward Horse Camp. The afternoon changed from blue-white to lavender. The crow had left them—disgusted, Rusty thought, that they never stopped to eat and threw away no scraps. The trampled waste of snow bloomed for a minute or two a pure untroubled rose, and the sun was gone as if it had stepped in a hole. Gray-blue dusk, grateful to their seared eyes, lay in every slightest hollow; the snowplain was broken with unexpected irregularities. The "drag" of cows and calves slowed, poked along, stopped, and had to be cursed and flogged into starting. Their ponies, poor boneracks, plodded gamely, and if a cow tried to break away or swing back they had to gather themselves like a tired swimmer taking one last stroke. Their breath was frozen all over them, stirrups and overshoes were enameled in ice; Rusty could hear his pony wheezing in his pipes, and his skinny ewe neck was down. He stumbled in the trodden snow.

It grew dark, and they went on, following Jesse's track, or whatever track it was that Ray kept, or no track at all, but only his wild animal's sense of direction. The faint eruption of color in the west was gone; and then as the sky darkened, the stars were there, big and frosty and glittering, bright as lamps, and Rusty found the Dipper and Cassiopeia and the Pole Star, his total astronomy. He moved in his saddle, lame and numb, his face stiff, his shoulder aching clear down across his collarbone into his chest. Ahead of him, a moving blur on the snow, the herd stumbled and clicked and mooed, the joints of their random longhorns cracked, the traveling steam went up. Off to his right he heard Buck trying to sing—a sound so strange, revelatory, and forlorn that he had to laugh, and startled himself with the voiceless croak he produced.

How much farther? Up above, the sky was pure; the Northern Lights were beginning to flare and stretch. He heard his old friend the wolf hunting down the river valleys and coulees of his ordained home and speaking his wolfish mind to the indifferent stars. Lord God, how much longer? They had been in the saddle since six, had eaten nothing since then. Neither horse nor rider could take much more of this. But nobody said, We can stop now. Nobody said, We'll camp here. They couldn't, obviously. Jesse had taken their bubble of shelter God knew how many more empty miles to Horse Camp. He thought to himself, with a qualm of panic, My God, this is *desperate*. What if we don't find him? What if a horse should give clear out?

He gave his pony clumsy mittened pats; he enlisted its loyalty with words; it plodded and stumbled on.

Eventually there was a soft orange bloom of light, and shouts cut through the luminous murk, and as he stopped, confused, Ray Henry came riding from his left and they crowded the cattle into a tighter mass. Over their moving backs and the sounds of their distress and irritation he heard poles rattle; someone ki-yi-ed. Ray pushed his horse against the rear cattle and in his almost-gone whisper drove and urged them on. They moved, they broke aside, they were turned back; the mass crawled ahead, tedious, interminable, a toss and seethe of heads and horns, until suddenly it had shrunk and dwindled and was gone, and Panguingue was down in the snow, ramming gate poles home. The whole world smelled of cow.

They sat there all together, stupid with cold and fatigue; they dismounted like skeletons tied together with wire. Ray croaked, "Let's see if Jesse ain't got a spare oat or two for these ponies," and they walked toward the wagon and the bloom of the tent. The air, which had been bright at sunset and in the first hour of dark, was blurred as if a fog were rising from the snow; beyond the tent the faint shadow of the coulee fell away, but the other side was misted out. Rusty's eyes were so longingly on Jesse's shadow as he hopped around the stove, obviously cooking, that he fell over the pile of willows stacked by the wagon: Jesse had not wasted his time; there was cooking wood for a week.

"Dad," Ray called, "you got any oats? These ponies are about done." The white head appeared in the flap, a hand with a fork in it held the canvas back, the soft old voice said, "I got a couple-three bushel left, I guess. That has to hold the Clydes and the night horses till we get back to the ranch."

"They'll have to get along," Ray said. "I'm afraid we're going to lose some ponies anyway. They just don't have the flesh for this kind of a job."

Rusty stood with the reins in his hand, letting Jesse and Ray heave the oat bag out of the wagon. The tent with its bloom of light and its smell of frying was a paradise he yearned for as he had never yearned for anything, but he had to stand there and care for the horse first, and he hated the poor beast for its dependence. It was no tireder than he was. Nevertheless Ray's was an inescapable example. He unsaddled and threw the saddle into the wagon; he tramped a little hollow in the snow. and poured out a quart or two of oats and pulled his pony's bridle and let him drop his head to them. One after the other the outfit did the same. After what seemed an hour Rusty found the tent flap and crept in. The little stove was red hot; the air was full of smoke. Jesse had unrolled their beds for them. Rusty stepped over Buck and fell full length and shut his eyes. What little strength he had left flowed out of him and was soaked up; his bones and veins and skin held nothing but tiredness and pain.

Jesse hopped around, juggling pans, going on cheerfully. He had thought by God they were never going to get in. Chopped wood till he like to bust his back. (Yeah, said somebody, *you* did a day's work!) Horse herd come all the way with him, right along behind the pilot. Those few scraps of hay the other day made tame ponies of the whole bunch. Looks like you guys got a pretty good herd of calves, considering. Anybody like a cup of coffee now?

"By God," he said after a short silence, "you fellers look *beat*."

And after another little silence in which nobody spoke, but somebody groaned or grunted, Jesse said, "Here, I don't reckon coffee has got enough nourishment for the occasion."

Beside Rusty, Buck rolled over. Rusty opened his eyes. Slip and Little

Horn had rolled over too. Ray was sitting on his bed, holding a quart of whiskey, shaking his head. "Jesse," he said, "by God, remind me to raise your wages."

Their common emotion while Ray worked on the cork was reverence. They sat or lay around in a ring, as bleary a crew as ever ate with its fingers or blew its nose with the same all-purpose tool, and they watched each motion of his thick wrist and big dirty hand. None of them had shaved for more than two weeks; they had all, except possibly Buck, lost any right to browbeat Panguingue about his filthiness. They felt— or at least Rusty did—that they had endured much and labored incredibly. He wondered, as the greenest hand there, how well he had done, and hoped he had done at least passably, and knew with unaccustomed humility that he could not have done more. Considering everything, the three hundred-odd cattle they had finally brought to the Horse Camp corrals were an achievement. The work still to be done, the separating and weaning, and the driving of calves and bulls to the home ranch, could only be trifling after what they had been through.

The stove's heat beat on their bearded red faces, the candles gleamed in their bloodshot eyes. They watched Ray Henry's thick hands, and when the cork slipped out of the neck with a soft *pok* some of them smiled involuntarily, and Panguingue giggled, a high, falsetto sound that set off another round of smiles and made Jesse say, "Listen at old Pan, he sounds like a jack after a mare."

Ray held the bottle to the light and looked through it; he shook it and watched the bead rise. He was like a priest before an altar. He would not hurry this. "Well," he said at last, "here's looking at you, boys," and tipped the bottle to his blackened mouth. They watched the contents gurgle around the spark of candle that lived inside the amber bottle. He let the bottle down. "Whah!" he said. "Kee-rist!" and wiped the neck politely with the heel of his palm and passed it to Slip, whose bed lay beside his next to the wall. The smell of whiskey cut through the smoke of the tent; they sat like Indians in the medicine lodge and passed the ceremonial vessel around, and each, as he finished, wiped the neck carefully with his palm. Slip to Jesse, Jesse to Little Horn, Little Horn to Spurlock, Spurlock to Panguingue. Panguingue drank and shook his head and wiped the neck once and started to pass the bottle and then, as if not satisfied, wiped it again. Rusty loved him for it, he loved them all; he felt that he had never known so mannerly a group of men. Buck took the bottle from Panguingue, and from Buck it came to the greenhorn, its neck flavored with all their seven mouths and hands. He raised it to his mouth and let its fire wash down his throat and felt it sting in his cracked lips. His eyes watered. He lowered the bottle and choked down a cough, and as he passed the bottle back to Ray and talk broke out all at once, he took advantage of the noise and cleared his throat and so was not shamed.

"Well, Jesse," Ray said, "what do you think? Want to save that little-bitty dab?"

"Why, I can't see it'd be much good from now on," Jesse said.

They passed it around again, and their tongues were loosened. They told each other how cold it had been and how hard they had worked. Jesse had made up a raisin-and-rice pudding, practically a pailful. It was pure ambrosia; they ate it all and scraped the kettle, and for a few minutes after supper Rusty even roused up enough strength to get out the harmonica. There was not the slightest remnant left of the irritability they had felt with one another in the snowed-in time; the boy could feel how they had been welded and riveted into a society of friends and brothers. Little Horn sang some filthy verses of "The Old Chisholm Trail." Spurlock supplied some even filthier ones from "Johnny Mc-Graw." The whole bunch joined in a couple of songs.

Then all at once they were done in again. The talk dropped away, Rusty put the harmonica in his pocket. They went outside and walked a few steps from the tent and stood in a row and made water, lifting their faces into the night air that was mistier than ever, and warmer than any night since they had left the ranch.

"I don't know," Ray said, sniffing for wind. "I don't quite like the looks of the sky."

"Oh but hell," they said. "Feel how warm it is."

He gave in doubtfully to their optimism. The mild air might mean snow, but it also might mean a chinook coming in, and that was the best luck they could hope for. There was not enough grass bare, even out on the flats, to give the cattle a chance to feed. Rusty had never seen or felt a chinook, but he was so positive this was the birth of one that he offered to bet Little Horn and Panguingue a dollar each that it was a chinook coming. They refused, saying they did not want to hoodoo the weather. Ray remarked that such weather as they had had couldn't be hoodooed any worse. They kicked the snow around, smelling the night air soft in their faces; it smelled like a thaw, though the snow underfoot was still as dry and granular as salt. Every minute or so a hungry calf bawled over in the corral.

"Well," Ray said, "maybe this is our break."

Rusty hardly heard him. His eyes were knotted, the nerves and veins snarled together, the lids heavy with sleep. Back inside the tent there was a brief flurry of movement as they crawled in. Somebody cursed somebody else feebly for throwing his chaps across him. He heard the fire settle in the stove; after a minute or two he was not sure whether it was the stove or the first whiffling of some sleeper. Then he was asleep too, one of the first.

But not even his dead tiredness could lift from him the habits of the last ten days. In his dreams he struggled against winds, he felt the bite of cold, he heard the clamor of men and animals and he knew that he had a duty to perform, he had somehow to shout "Here!" as one did at a roll call, but he was far down under something, struggling in the dark to come up and to break his voice free. His own nightmared sounds told him he was dreaming, and moaning in his sleep, and still he could not break free into wakefulness and shove the dream aside. Things were falling on him from above; he sheltered his head with his arms, rolled, and with a wrench broke loose from tormented sleep and sat up.

Panguingue was kicking him in the head through his blankets. He was freezing cold, with all his blankets wound around his neck and shoulders like shawls. By the light of a candle stuck on the cold stove lid he saw the rest all in the same state of confused, unbelieving awakening. There was a wild sound of wind; while he sat leaning away from Panguingue's feet, stupidly groping for his wits, a screeching blast hit the tent so hard that old Jesse, standing by the flap, grabbed the pole and held it until the shuddering strain gave way a little and the screech died to a howl.

Rusty saw the look of disbelief and outrage on every face; Panguingue's grin was a wolfish baring of teeth, his ordinary dull-witted good nature shocked clear out of him. "What is it?" Rusty asked idiotically. "Is it a chinook?"

"Chinook!" Buck said furiously.

He yanked his stiff chaps on over his pants and groped chattering for his boots. They were all dressing as fast as their dazed minds and numbed fingers would let them. Jesse let go the tent pole to break some willow twigs in his hands and shove them into the stove. At that moment the wind swooped on them again and the tent came down.

Half dressed, minus mittens, boots, mackinaws, hats, they struggled under the obliterating canvas. Somebody was swearing in an uninterrupted stream. Rusty stumbled over the fallen stovepipe and his nostrils were filled with soot. Then the smothering canvas lifted a couple of feet and somebody struck a match to expose them like bugs under a kicked log, dismayed and scuttling, glaring around for whatever article they needed. He saw Jesse and Ray bracing the front pole, and as the match died he jumped to the rear one; it was like holding a fishing rod with a thousand pound fish on: the whole sail-like mass of canvas flapped and caved and wanted to fly. One or two ropes on the windward side had broken loose and the wall plastered itself against his legs, and wind and snow poured like ice water across his stockinged feet. "Somebody get outside and tie us down," Ray's grating whisper said. Little Horn scrambled past, then Spurlock. Panguingue crawled toward the front flap on hands and knees, Slip and Buck followed him. Braced against the pole, old Jesse was laughing; he lit a match on his pants and got a candle going and stuck it in its own drip on the stove. The stovepipe lay in sooty sections across the beds.

Ropes outside jerked; the wall came away from Rusty's legs, the tent rose to nearly its proper position, the strain on the pole eased. Eventually it reached a wobbly equilibrium so that he could let go and locate his boots in the mess of his bed. The five outsiders came in gasping, beating their numbed hands. In the gray light of storm and morning, they all looked like old men; the blizzard had sown white age in their beards.

"*God* A'mighty!" Slip said, and wiped away an icicle from under his nose.

"Cold, uh?" Ray whispered.

"Must be thirty below."

"Will the tent hold?"

"I dunno," Slip said. "Corner ropes is onto the wheels, but one of the middle ones is pulled plumb out."

They stood a second or two, estimating the strain on the ropes, and as if to oblige their curiosity the wind lit on them and heeled them halfway over again. The whole middle of the windward wall bellied inward; the wind got under the side and for an instant they were a balloon; Rusty thought for certain they would go up in the air. He shut his eyes and hung on, and when he looked again three of the boys had grappled the uplifting skirt of the cloth and pinned it down.

"We got to get in off these flats," Jesse said.

"I guess," Ray said. "The question is how. It's three-four miles to the river."

"We could keep the wind on our left and drift a little with it. That'd bring us in somewhere below Bates Camp."

"Well," Ray said, and looked at the rest of them, holding the tent down, "we haven't got much choice. Slip, you reckon we could find any horses in this?"

"I reckon we could try."

"No," Ray said. "It'd be too risky. We couldn't drive them against this wind if we found them."

"What about the cattle?" Buck said.

"Yeah," said Little Horn. "What about them?"

"D'you suppose," Ray whispered, and a spasm like silent mirth moved his iron face, "after we get things ready to go, you boys could pull about three poles out of the corral gate?"

"You mean turn 'em loose?"

"I mean turn 'em loose."

Ed Spurlock said, "So after all this, we wind up without a single God damn calf?" and Ray said, "You rather have a corral full of dead ones?"

Rusty leaned against the swaying pole while the furious wind whined and howled down out of the Arctic, and he listened to them with a bitterness that was personal and aggrieved. It seemed to him atrocious, a wrong against every principle and every expectation, that the devoted and herculean labors of eight good men should be thwarted by a blind force of nature, a meteorological freak, a mere condition of wind and cold.

Now on with the boots over feet bruised and numb from walking stocking-footed on the frozen ground, and on with the overshoes, and stamp to get life going. Now button the sheepskin collar close and pull the fur cap down, earlaps and forehead piece, leaving exposed only the eyes, the chattering jaw, the agonized spuming of the breath, *huh-huh-huh, huh-huh-huh-huh*. Clumsy with clothing, beat mittened hands in armpits, stoop with the others to get the stovepipe together, the grub box packed, the beds rolled. "Keep out a blanket apiece," Ray Henry says.

The tent tugs and strains, wanting to be off. In the gray light, snow sifts dry as sand down through the open stovepipe thimble and onto the stove—a stove so useless that if anyone touched it with a bare hand he would freeze fast.

As in a nightmare where everything is full of shock and terror and nothing is ever explained, Rusty looks around their numb huddle and sees only a glare of living eyes, and among them Panguingue's eyes that roll whitely toward the tent roof to ask a question.

"We'll leave it up till we get set," Ray says. "It ain't a hell of a lot, but it's something."

They duck outside, and shielding faces behind shoulders and collars, drive into the wind. The paralyzing wind hammers drift against eyelids, nose, and lips, and their breath comes in gasps and sobs as they throw things into the wagon. Jesse and Ray are harnessing the Clydes over their yellow blankets, Slip pounds ice off the blanket of the night pony getting ready to throw the saddle on. From their feet plumes of drift streak away southward. Beyond the figures in the squirming dusk the whole visible world moves—no sky, no horizon, no earth, no air, only this gray-white streaming, with a sound like a rush of water, across and through it other sounds like howling and shouting far off, high for a moment and lost again in the whistle and rush.

The cheek Rusty has exposed feels scorched as if by flame. Back in the icy, half-cleared tent, the hollow of quiet amid the wind seems a most extravagant sanctuary, and he heaves a great breath as if he has been running. He does not need to be told that what moves them now is not caution, not good judgment, not anything over which they have any control, but desperation. The tent will not stand much more, and no tent means no fire. With no horses left but the Clydes and one night pony, they will have to walk, and to reach either of the possible shelters, either Stonepile or Bates Camp, they will have to go north and west, bucking the wind that just now, in the space of a dozen breaths, has seared his face like a blowtorch. He has a feeling outraged and self-pitying and yet remotely contemplating a deserved punishment, a pre-dicted retribution, the sort of feeling that he used to have in childhood when something tempted him beyond all caution and all warnings and he brought himself to a caning in the iodine- and carbolic-smelling office where his father, the doctor, used to look him down into shame before laying the yardstick around his legs. They have got what they deserved for daring Authority; the country has warned them three separate times. Now the punishment.

Into the wagon, jumbled any old way, goes everything the tent holds— grub box, saddles, stove, stovepipe, kerosene can—and again they gather in the still, icy hollow, strangely empty without the stove. Ray Henry has two lariats in his hands, Buck an axe, and Jesse a lighted lantern. The foreman wipes his nose on the back of his mitt and squints at old Jesse. "Dad, you sure you want to drive? It'll be colder up there than walkin'."

The old-timer shakes the lantern, and his eyes gleam and his square teeth gleam. "Lantern between m'feet, buffler robe over the top," he says, "I don't care how cold I get upstairs if I'm warm from the tail down."

"Long as you don't set yourself afire," Ray says. "How about somebody ridin' up there with you?"

"Dee-lighted!" Jesse says, flashing his teeth like Teddy Roosevelt, and they laugh as if they were all short of wind. The foreman's gray thinking eyes go over them. When his look pauses on Rusty Cullen, the boy's breath is held for a moment in sneaking hope, for he has never been so miserable or so cold; the thought of going out there and fighting across six miles of snowflats in the terrible wind has paralyzed his nerve. Also, he tells himself, he is the injured one; his arm still hurts him. The possibility pictures itself seductively before him: to ride, bundled under the buffalo robe and with the lantern's warmth. Like a child pretending sleep when a night emergency arises and the rain beats in an open window or the wind has blown something loose, to sit snug beside old Jesse, relieved of responsibility, while the grownups take care of it . . . He cannot read the foreman's gray eyes; he feels his own wavering down. A crawl of shame moves in his guts, and he thinks, If he picks me it will be because I'm the weakest as well as the greenest.

The thinking eye moves on. "Slip," Ray says, "you ain't got the feet for walkin'. You can spell Dad with the lines. It'll be bad on the hands."

To cover his relief Rusty is beating his hands rhythmically in his armpits and jiggling on nerveless feet. He watches Ray pass the lariats to Little Horn. "If you're tied together, we won't lose nobody."

"Where'll you be?"

"I'll be ridin' pilot."

They are all moving constantly, clumsily. Spurlock has wrapped a woolen muffler around his mouth so that only his restless eyes show. Buck and Panguingue already have hung blankets over their heads and shoulders. Little Horn pulls off a mitt to pat the chimney of Jesse's lantern with a bare hand. "Well," Ray says, "I guess it's time she came down."

They lurch outside. Rusty, unsure of what to do, astonished at their instant obedience, finds himself standing stupidly while Buck with the butt of the axe knocks out one picket pin, then another, and chops off the ropes that tie the tent to the wheels. Jesse and Panguingue, at the ends, reach inside the flaps and lift and yank at the poles, and down it comes in a puddle of frozen canvas that they fall upon and grapple together and heave into the wagon. They curse and fight the wind, pushing and folding the tent down, throwing the poles and two saddles on it to hold it, hauling and lashing the wagon cover tight. Rusty looks back at where their shelter has been and his insides are pinched by cold panic. Drift is already streaking across the patch of thawed and refrozen grass; the little space their living warmth has thawed there in the midst of the waste looks as passionately and finally abandoned as the fresh earth of a grave.

Little Horn is tying them together, using the rope to snug and hold the blankets they have wrapped around themselves, when out of the tattered edge of storm cattle appear, longhorns that swerve away at a stumbling half-trot. After them and among them, a streaming miserable horde, come the whitefaces and shorthorns, cows and calves, some steers, a few bulls, with no noise except an occasional desperate blat from a calf, and the clicking of longhorn hooves and joints carried headlong southward by the wind. Well fleshed and round-bellied no more than a week ago, they stream and flinch past, gaunt ghosts of themselves, and Rusty thinks sullenly, while Little Horn ties the rope tight around him and their four hands tuck the blanket under, that it has been human foolishness that has brought the cattle to this condition. Driven all day by cowboys, and every other night by blizzards, they have eaten hardly anything for days. Left alone, yarding up in the coulees and river bottoms, they could at least have gnawed willows.

He is furious at their violent futile effort, and at Ray Henry for insisting upon it. Inhuman labor, desperate chances, the risk of death itself, for what? For a bunch of cattle who would be better off where their instinct told them to go, drifting with the storm until they found shelter. For owners off in Aberdeen or Toronto or Calgary or Butte who would never come out themselves and risk what they demanded of any cowboy for twenty dollars a month and found.

The tip of his mitt is caught under the rope; he tears it loose, and for a moment Little Horn's barely exposed eyes glint sideways, surprised. Out of the storm behind the last straggling cattle rides Ray Henry, already plastered white. He waves, somebody shouts, the wind tears the sound away and flings it across the prairie, the Clydes jerk sideways, the frozen wheels of the wagon crackle loose and crush through a crested foot-deep drift. The five walkers bunch up to get the protection of the wagon for their faces and upper bodies; the wind under the box and through the spokes tears at their legs as they swing half around and jolt off angling across the storm—northeast, Rusty judges, if the wind is northwest—following the stooped figure of the foreman on the horse. As they pass the corrals, Rusty sees the stained ground humped with carcasses already whitening under the blast of snow and wind.

He huddles his blanket across his chest, clenching and unclenching his numb hands; he crowds close to the others, eager to conform; he plants his feet carefully, clumsily, in the exact footprints of Ed Spurlock, and he tries to keep the rope between them just slack enough so that it does not drag and trip him. His face, unless he carelessly falls behind, is out of the worst lash of the wind; with walking, he has begun to feel his feet again. It seems possible after all—they can walk under these conditions the necessary five or six miles to shelter. He is given confidence by the feel of the rope around his waist, and the occasional tug when Spurlock or someone else up ahead stumbles or lurches, or when he feels Little Horn coming behind. Beside his cheek the wheel pours dry snow, and every turning spoke is a few inches gained toward safety.

Once, as they bounced across the flats, Slippers leaned out and shouted something down to Buck, leading the single-file walkers. An unintelligible word came down the line, the wheels beside them rolled faster, and they were forced into a trot to keep up. Rusty staggered sideways in the broken snow, kept himself from falling under the wheel by a wild shove against the wagon box, lurched and was yanked forward into step so roughly that it kinked his neck. The line of them jogged, grunting in cadence, trotting awkwardly armless, wrapped in their blankets, beside the ponderous wagon. Eventually Buck shouted up at the seat, and they slowed to a walk, but the run had done them good. The blood was out at their edges and extremities again. Rusty felt it sharp and stinging in his cheeks.

Up ahead, revealed and half covered, and revealed and nearly obscured, moving steadily through the lateral whip and crawl of the storm, went the whitened horse, the humped white figure of Ray Henry. Once when Rusty looked he was down, walking and leading the pony. A few minutes later he was up again. The plain stretched on, interminable.

Rusty dropped his head turtle-fashion, wiped an edge of the blanket across his leaking and freezing nose, concentrated on putting his feet precisely into the tracks of Ed Spurlock. Dreamlike and hypnotic, body moved, brain moved, but both sluggishly, barely awake. Life was no more than movement, than dull rhythm. Eyes were aware only of the drooping rope, the alternating feet ahead, and once in a while the glimpse of Ray Henry moving through the blizzard out at the edge of visibility. Walking or riding, he went with the inevitability of a cloud driving across the sky; to look up and find him not there would have been a shock and a dismay. And yet he went ambiguously too, something recognized or remembered from an old charade or pantomime or tableau, Leader or Betrayer, urgent, compulsive, vaguely ominous, so that one hurried to keep him in sight and cursed him for the way he led on, and on.

In the thudding hollows of the skull, deep under the layered blanket, the breath-skimmed sheepskin, inside the stinging whiskered face and the bony globe that rode jolting on the end of the spine, deep in there as secret as the organs at the heart of a flower or a nut inside shell and husk, the brain plodded remotely at a heart's pace or a walking pace, saying words that had been found salutary for men or cattle on a brittle and lonesome night, words that not so much expressed as engendered what the mind felt: sullenness, fear, doubt.

Up ahead the foreman moved steadily, dusky stranger, silent companion, and if he did not "bend upon the snowshoe with a long and limber stride," he had a look as tireless and unstoppable as if he had in fact been that Spirit Hunter, that Walker of the Snow, one of the shapes with which the country deluded frightened men.

The wind had changed, and instead of driving at their legs under the box between the spokes was coming much more from behind them. Rusty felt Little Horn's hand on his back, but when he turned to see what was wanted, Little Horn shook his head at him from under the blanket hood: only a stumble, or the wind hustling him along too fast. The pour of dry snow from the wheel blew on forward instead of sideward into their faces. Except for his hands and his impossible leaky nose, he was not cold. They must have come more than half of the three miles that would bring them to the river, where there would be protection among the willows and under the cutbanks, and where they might even choose to make some sort of shelter of the wagon and the tent—build a big wood fire and thaw out and wait for the storm to blow by. He hoped they would; he did not relish the thought of turning into the wind, even in the more sheltered river valley.

He saw the Walker coming back, bent double, his face turned aside. When he reached them his pony turned tail to wind and Jesse cramped the Clydes around and they stood for a brief conference. It seemed that the wind had not changed. The horses simply wouldn't head across it, and kept swinging. That meant they would hit the river lower down, and have a longer upwind pull to Bates.

Only Ray's eyes showed through the mask-like slot of a felt cap that came clear down around his throat. To Jesse and Slip he whisper-shouted something that Rusty could not hear, and mounted and rode off again. The wagon crunched after him, the segmented ten-footed worm beside it took up its lockstep. Deafened by fur and wool, anesthetized by cold and the monotony of walking, the next-to-last segment, joined to the segments before and behind by a waist of half-inch hard-twist rope, plodded on, thinking its own dim thoughts, which were concerned with cosmic injustice and the ways of God to man.

Why couldn't there be, just at this moment, the lucky loom of an unknown or unexpected cowcamp, the whiff of lignite smoke on the wind? Why, just once, could not rescue come from Heaven, instead of having to be earned foot by foot? He dreamed of how warmth would feel in the face, the lovely stink of four or five shut-in cowboys in a hot shack, and he sucked and sniffed at the drooling of his mouth and nose, a hateful, inescapable oozing that turned to ice in his beard and on his lips.

Head down, he plodded on, one step and then another. Once as he put his foot in the print that Spurlock's foot had just left, he caught the heel of Spurlock's overshoe with his toe, and saw Spurlock fling an irritable snarl over the shoulder. Oh, the hell, he thought. Can't you be decent even when we're like this? The rope tugged tight around him, he hopped to get in step again, walking carefully, left, right, left, right, wiping his leaking nose against the blanket's edge and feeling slick ice there.

Sancta Maria, speed us!
The sun is falling low;
Before us lies the valley
Of the Walker of the Snow!

Later—hours or days, for time whipped and snaked past in unceasing movement like the wind and the trails of drift, and all its proportions were lost—Rusty bumped into Spurlock and an instant later felt Little Horn bump into him in turn. The wagon had stopped, and Ray was back, leading his pony by the bridle. His visor of felt was iron-stiff with ice, so that he pulled it down and craned his neck and lifted his chin to shout over it to Jesse, perched on the high seat beside Slip with the buffalo robe folded up around him under the armpits. Rusty, squinting to see what they were looking at, felt the sticky drag of ice on his lashes as if his eyes were fringed with crickets' legs, and saw that ahead of them the land fell away beyond an edge where the grass was blown bare. Ahead or below, the ground-hugging trails of drift were gone, leaving only air murky as dusk, with fitful swirls and streaks of dark at its bottom which he realized were brush. He dragged at his wet nose. The river.

But the brief, gratified expectation he had that this would be an easier stage lasted no more than two minutes. The hills dipping down to the floodplain were gullied and washed, and drifted deep. Even with Ray riding ahead to try the going, the wheels dropped into holes and hollows, rose over knobs; the wagon canted at perilous angles, groaning and jolting its way slanting, with the wind almost dead behind it. Pulling out wide from the rocking wagon, the men were caught in the open wind and blown along. Rusty saw the Clydes braced back in the breeching, their hairy fetlocks coming up out of the snow rattling with balls of ice, and their muscular haunches bunching under the blankets, and then here came Slip digging out from under the buffalo robe to throw his weight on the brake. Ice against ice, shoe slid on tire and held nothing; the wagon rolled heavily down upon the Clydes, who braced lower, slipping. The walkers jumped aside and then, as the wagon lumbered past them, jumped to the endgate to try to hold it back. Its ponderous weight yanked them along, their dug heels plowed up snow. They could feel it under their hands getting away, they knew it without Jesse's yell that snapped off on the wind above their heads. Jesse rose half to his feet, braced between seat and box. The wagon jackknifed sharply as he swung the Clydes along the sidehill to slow them. The left side dropped down, the right heaved up, and with a neat final motion like the end of a crack-the-whip the wagon tipped over and cast off Slip in a spidery leap down the hillside. Jesse, hanging to the tilted seat to the end, slid off it to land on his feet with the reins in one hand and the lantern in the other. By the time Ray discovered what had happened and rode back, he had unhooked the Clydes and got them quiet. The wagon lay with its load bulging out of the lashed cover, the busy wind already starting to cover it with snow.

Rusty would not have believed that in that wind and cold it was possible to work up a sweat, but he did. It was a blind and furious attack they launched on the tipped wagon, unloading almost everything and carrying it down to more level ground where the abrupt hill aproned off, stacking it there while they floundered back to dig and pry at the jackknifed wheels. Ray hitched on with his saddle horse, they heaved while their held breath burst out of them in grunts and straining curses, until they righted it, and straightened the wheels, and a spoke at a time got them turning; three of them carrying the tongue and the others ready to push or hold back, they angled it down onto leveler and smoother ground.

There they wasted not a second, but hitched up and loaded as if they raced against time. When the muffled-up figure of Spurlock started to heave a saddle up, and slipped and fell flat on its back with the saddle on its chest, Rusty coughed out one abrupt bark of laughter, but no one else laughed. Panguingue and Buck picked the saddle off Spurlock's chest and tossed it aboard, and before Spurlock was back on his feet Little Horn and Buck were starting to tie together the worm of walkers. Up where Jesse and Slip were fussily folding the buffalo robe around and under them it looked bitterly cold, but down where Rusty stood it was better. He could feel his hands all the way, his feet all but the tips of the toes. Where the fur cap covered it, his forehead was damp, and under the ponderous layers of clothing and blanket his body itched a little with warmth. He was winded, and dead tired, and his shoulder ached as if the fierce haul and heave of the unloading and loading had pulled it from its socket, but the dismay of the accident was worked off. They were all right, they would make it yet.

He twisted to help Little Horn tuck the blanket ends under the rope, and at that moment Spurlock, moving awkwardly in front, put his foot down crooked, reeled against him, landed on his foot and anchored him there, and bore him helplessly over in the drift. If it had been anyone else, Rusty might have laughed, reassured and warmed by work as he was; but since it was Spurlock he rose to one knee anticipating trouble. He was not wrong; the hand he put on Spurlock's arm was knocked

off angrily, and through the layers of the muffler the words were savage:
". . . the Christ you're doing!"

The boy's anger blew up instant and hot, and he bounded to his
feet, freeing his elbows from the blanket. They faced each other, tied
together by four feet of rope like gladiators coupled to fight to the
death, and then the shadow above them made itself felt and Rusty
looked up to see Ray Henry sitting hands-on-horn and looking down
on them.

"What's trouble?" the foreman said.

The unintelligible growl that came out of Spurlock's muffled mouth
could have told him nothing, but Rusty pulled the collar away from his
chin and said passionately, "Look, put me somewhere else in this line!
I'm not going to stand for . . ."

"What's trouble?" Ray said again.

"He keeps stumbling around and falling down and then blaming
me. . . ."

"If he falls down, help him up," Ray croaked, and kneed his frosted
pony around and rode off in front. The wheels jerked, the icy axles
shrieked, their feet automatically hopped to get in step, and they were
walking again. Rusty pulled his chin back inside the collar and went
sullenly, furious at the injustice of the rebuke, and alert to make the
most of any slightest slip or stumble ahead of him.

Down in the bottoms among the willows the wind was less, and they
could bring the horses to turn halfway into it, feeling for the river. But
if the wind was less, the snow was deeper; the Clydes floundered belly
deep and the wagon box scraped up a great drift that piled up over the
doubletree and against the stallions' rumps and finally stopped them
dead. They shoveled it away and cleared the Clydes' feet, never quite
sure whether or not they would have their brains kicked out. Then they
fell into two lines out in front and tramped a way for the horses and
the wagon wheels down through smothered rosebushes and between
clumps of willow whose bark gleamed red under the hood of snow.
Ten feet of it was enough to wind a man; they panted their way ahead,
turned to tramp backward and deepen the track, stopped every twenty
yards to dig away the snow that the wagon box scooped up. They
worked like people fighting a fire, exhausted themselves and stood
panting a minute and fell to it again, frenzied for the easy going on the
river ice.

The wagon eased over the edge of a bushy bank, the Clydes plunged as Jesse took them over straight on. The front wheels went down, pushing the stallions out onto the ice. Just as Rusty saw them lunging to pull the wagon through, a jerk from behind dragged him over in the drift and the whole line of walkers came down. When they got to their feet there was the wagon on the river.

Getting up watchfully, Rusty thought he felt Spurlock yanking at the rope, and he yanked back harshly. Sunk between the muskrat cap and the muffler, and blindered on both sides by the wings of the mackinaw collar, Spurlock's eyes peered out like the eyes of a fierce animal peering from a crack in the rock, but he turned away without a word, giving Rusty at least the smoldering satisfaction of having yanked last, of having finished something that the other had started.

The cutbank partially shielded them from the wind. Upriver was a straight reach with an irregular streak of clear, blown ice down its center, grading up to shelving drifts against both banks. Drift skated and blew down it like dust down an alley. The last lap of the road to shelter lay before them as smooth as a paved highway.

Ray Henry, leading his pony down the broken bank, stopped by them a moment where they hung panting on the wagon. "Everybody all right?"

They looked at him from among their wrappings.

"Ed?" Ray said.

It seemed to Rusty terribly unjust that particular attention should have been paid to Spurlock rather than to himself. It meant that the foreman still looked upon Spurlock as in the right, himself in the wrong. It meant that he had no concern for the one of his men who was hurt, and might be in trouble. He saw Ray's eyes within the visor that was like the helmet of a hero, and his unhappiness that he had lost prestige and respect drove words to his lips, impulsive and too eager, anything to be recognized and accepted again. He did not care about Spurlock, actually; he was already ashamed of that quarrel. But he wanted Ray Henry to notice him, and so he said, "What do we do now, Ray? Camp here till it's over?"

"Not hardly," Ray said. "The Clydes have had all the fresh air they need."

"How much farther?"

"Three miles, maybe four."

"Do we ride from here?"

The gray, thinking eye examined him from within the helmet of ice-hardened felt. The foreman said, "You reckon you're any more petered than them studs?"

He went stooping and slipping out in front to confer with Jesse and Slip, and Rusty, avoiding Little Horn's eyes and with his back to Spurlock and the others, watched the smothered rosebushes on the bank quiver in a gust. The slow warmth under all his wrappings might have come from the heavy work of getting the wagon through the brush and the drifts, but it might just as well have been shame, and he hated them all for never giving a man a chance, for taking things wrong, for assuming what should not be assumed. He hadn't been wanting to quit, he had asked only for information. Sullenly he waited, resolved to keep his mouth shut and plod it out. Once they got back to the ranch, he could simply leave the job; he was under no obligation to stay at it any longer than he pleased to. Neither Ray nor anyone else could compel a man to stick it through months of this kind of thing, no matter how short-handed the T-Down was. There was sure to be a great change as soon as he announced he was leaving. He could see Ray Henry's face—all their faces. Every man who left, left more for the remaining ones to do. Too late, chaps. Sorry. Ta-ta, gentlemen. Enjoy the winter.

In the river bottom the wind was louder, though he felt it less. The bare willows and the rosebushes, bent like croquet wickets into the drifts, whistled with it, the cutbank boomed it back in hollow eddies, every corner and edge and groove of the valley gave it another tongue. More than out on the flats, even, it echoed with hallucinatory voices, shouts, screams, whistles, moans, jeers. Rusty concentrated on it. He had only been asking a perfectly reasonable question, considering that they were running for their lives and still had an unknown distance to go. Would it be so terrible to climb up and let those big strong horses pull them for a little while along the level ice? Would it, for that matter, be entirely unheard of to sacrifice the Clydes, if necessary, to save eight lives? He asked himself what about a leader who thought more of his horses than of his men.

The blood in his veins was sluggish with cold, his mind was clogged with sullen hatred. Ray, shouting up to Jesse and Slip, and Spurlock, weaving bearlike from one foot to the other, were both part of a nightmare which he loathed and wanted to escape, but the numbness held him and he stood spraddling, squinting from behind the wagon box, hearing the shouts of those ahead torn from their lips and flung streaming down the ice to become part of the headlong illusory wailing that blew and moaned around the river's bends. His mind, groping among images, was as clumsy as his mittened unfeeling hands would have been, trying to pick up a coin from the snow. He thought of old Jesse's friend down by Sheridan, with his frozen conversation, and of how others had explained, not so humorously, the voices that haunted the wind in this country.

> For I saw by the sickly moonlight
> As I followed, bending low,
> That the walking of the stranger
> Left no footmarks on the snow.

The voices of all the lost, all the Indians, métis, hunters, Mounted Police, wolfers, cowboys, all the bundled bodies that the spring uncovered and the warming sun released into the stink of final decay; all the starving, freezing, gaunt, and haunted men who had challenged this country and failed; all the ghosts from smallpox-stilled Indian camps, the wandering spirits of warriors killed in their sleep on the borders of the deadly hills, all the skeleton women and children of the starving winters, all the cackling, maddened cannibals, every terrified, lonely, crazed, and pitiful outcry that these plains had ever wrung from human lips, went wailing and moaning over him, mingled with the living shouts of the foreman and the old-timer, and he said, perhaps aloud, remembering the legend of the Crying River, and the voices that rode the wind there as here, Qu'appelle? Qu'appelle?

Heartless and inhuman, older than earth and totally alien, as savage and outcast as the windigo, the cannibal spirit, the wind dipped and swept upon them down the river channel, tightening the lightly sweating inner skin with cold and the heart with fear. Rusty watched Ray hump his back and shake off the worst of the blast, saw the arm wave. The wagon rolled again. Ed Spurlock, unready, was pulled sideways a stumbling step or two by the tightening of the rope, and Rusty got one clear look into the brown, puckered eyes. Out of his fear and misery and anger he sneered, "Learn to walk!" But if Spurlock heard he made no sign. In a moment he was only the hooded, blanketed, moving stoop, not human, not anything, that Rusty imitated movement for movement, step for step, plodding up the river after the wagon.

Exhaustion and cold are a kind of idiocy, the mind moves as numbly as the body, the momentary alertness that a breathing spell brings is like the sweat that can be raised under many clothes even in the bitterest weather; when the breathing spell is over and the hard work past, mind and body are all the worse for the brief awakening. The sweaty skin chills, the images that temporary alertness has caught scrape and rasp in the mind like edged ice and cannot be dislodged or thought away or emptied out, but slowly coagulate there.

For Rusty they were the images of fear. No matter how much he tried to tie his mind to the plod-plod-plod of foot after foot, he heard the spirit of that bitter country crying for cold and pain. Under his moving feet the ice passed, now clear, with coin-like bubbles in it, now coated with a pelt of dry smooth snow, now thinly drifted. The world swung slowly, the dry snow under their feet blew straight sideward, then quartered backward; his quickly lifted eyes saw that the right bank had dropped to a bar and the left curved up in a cutbank. The wind lashed his face so that he hunched and huddled the blanket closer, leaving only the slightest hole, and still the wind got in, filled the blanket, threatened to blow it off his back. His eyes were full of water and he wiped them free, terrified that they would freeze shut. With his head bowed clear over, almost to the rope, he stumbled on. Through the slits of sight remaining to him he saw that the drift now was blowing straight backward from Spurlock's feet. The river had swung them directly into the wind. The line of walkers huddled to the left until they were walking bunched behind the feeble protection of the wagon.

The wagon stopped, the line of walkers bumped raggedly to a halt. Rusty had forgotten them; he was surprised to find them there, glaring from the frozen crevices of their clothes. From out in front Ray Henry came looming, a huge indomitable bulk, leading the pony whose bony face was covered with a shell of ice, the hairy ears pounded full of snow, the breast of the blanket sheathed. He unlooped the halter rope and tied it to the endgate, pulled the bridle and hung it on the saddle horn. For a minute he rubbed and worked at the pony's face, turned grunting, and said from inside his visor, "They just can't buck it. We're gonna have to lead 'em." He helped Little Horn pull open the loose, frozen knot in the rope and free himself from the others. "Rusty," he said, "see if you can find a blanket up in the load somewhere."

Rusty found the blanket, the foreman and Little Horn flapped off with it, the walkers huddled back to the wagon, eyeing the miserable pony which now took half their shelter. After a minute or two the yell came back, they turned, they stirred their stiffened legs and moved their wooden feet. The wind shrieked around the wagon, between the spokes, along the axles and the snow-clogged reach, and Rusty, colder now than at any time since he had awakened half frozen in his blankets, heard the blizzardy bottoms wild with voices. *Qu'appelle? . . . Qu'appelle? . . . Qu'appelle?*

In an hour, or four hours, or ten minutes, the river blessedly bent rightward, and the wind went screaming and flying above them but touched them only in swoops and gusts. There was a stretch where the inshore drifts let them go close up under the bank, and for a brief time the air was almost still, the snow settling almost gently as on any winter's day, a day to put roses in the cheeks.

Sancta Maria, speed us!

During that brief, numbed lull Spurlock tangled his feet and fell again, pulling over Panguingue ahead of him. Rusty, hopping awkwardly to keep from getting entangled with the sliding, swiveling figures, saw Buck squat and grab the rope to maintain his balance against the drag of the fallen ones. There went the three of them, helplessly dragged along on back or feet, and here came Rusty, a lead-footed dancer, prancing and shouting in their wake until those up ahead heard and they stopped.

Ray was back again. Panguingue and Buck stood up and cleared the rope, but Spurlock sat on the ice with his head down, pawing at his face and heaving his shoulders under the blanket. Rusty stayed back in scorn and contempt, sure that the blame would somehow be pinned on him. He was the proper scapegoat; everything that happened was caused by his awkwardness.

Ray was stooping, shaking Spurlock's shoulder. His hand worked at the muffler around Spurlock's face. Then he straightened up fierce and ready and with so much power left that Rusty moved a step back, astonished. "The lantern!" Ray shouted, and lunged around the line of walkers to reach and take the lantern from Jesse's hand. Back at Spurlock, stooping to hold the lantern directly against the muffler, he said over his shoulder, "Rusty, unhitch yourself and rustle some wood. We're gonna have to stop and thaw out."

The knot was stiff with ice, his fingers like sticks, but he got loose and stumped around in the deep snow breaking dead stalks out of willow clumps. Slip appeared to help him, and Rusty said, pausing a second in his fumbling, "What's the matter with Spurlock?"

"Smotherin'," Slip said. "God damn muffler froze to his whiskers."

"Are we going to camp here?"

"Why?" said Slip in surprise. "Do you *want* to?"

Rusty floundered down the bank with his handful of twigs, watched Panguingue cone them on the ice and souse them with kerosene. The smell cut his nostrils, and he sniffed back the wetness and spat in the snow. It was that drooling that had got Spurlock in trouble. Drool and freeze fast. Dully curious, he watched Ray moving the lantern glass around on the frozen wool, while Buck pulled on the unfrozen ends. Spurlock's head was pulled out of his collar; he looked like a fish on a hook. Then Panguingue found a match and reached across Buck to scratch it on the dry bottom of the lantern. The little cone of sticks exploded in bright flame.

"More," Panguingue said thickly.

Little Horn, who had led the Clydes around in a half circle, was already up over the endgate, unlashing the wagon cover. Stupidly Rusty watched as he loosened it all across the windward side and dropped it in the lee, and then, comprehending, he helped tie it to the spokes to make a windbreak. The fire had burned out its splash of kerosene, and was smoldering in the snow until Panguingue swished it again and it blazed up. "More!" he said. "We need wood."

"In the wagon," Jesse said. "What do you think I chopped all that wood for yesterday?"

He climbed the wheel to burrow into the uncovered load, and his face with its bowed mustaches emerged from under the tangled tent like a walrus at a waterhole and he winked in Rusty's face, handing him out wood two and three sticks at a time. His manner was incredible to the boy. He acted as if they were out on a picnic or a berry picking and were stopping for lunch. Buck and Ray were holding Spurlock's face close to the little fire and working away at the muffler. The wind, here, was only a noise; they squatted in their bivouac with the fire growing and sputtering in the water of its melting, and they gathered close around it, venturing their faces a little out of their coverings.

Spurlock cursed clearly for the first time, the muffler came loose in

Buck's hands. Ray set the lantern aside while Spurlock breathed deeply and passed his hands around on his face.

"Stick her right in," Jesse said. "That's the quickest way to thaw her. Set those weeds on fire."

They sat knee to knee, they put their mittens on sticks of wood in the snow and held stiff red hands in the very flames, they opened collars and exposed smarting faces. Life returned as pain; far down his legs Rusty felt a deep, passionate ache beginning in his feet. He knew from the burn of his cheeks and the chilblain feel of his fingers that he would have some frostbite to doctor. But he loved the snug out-of-the-wind shelter, the fire, even the pain that was beginning now and would get worse. For no matter how they came out, or whether they camped here to wait out the storm or went on after a rest to Bates, which couldn't be more than another mile or two, he would go with a knowledge that warmed him like Jesse's lantern under the robe: it hadn't been *he* that cracked. And what a beautiful and righteous and just thing it was that the one who did crack should be Spurlock! In triumph and justification he looked across the fire at the sagging figure, but he couldn't make the restless reddened eyes hold still. Spurlock hadn't said a word since they released him from the smothering scarf.

A half hour later, when Ray said they must go on, Rusty received the words like a knife in his guts. He had been sitting and secretly willing that they should stay. But he glanced again across the fire and this time caught Ed Spurlock's moving eyes, and the eyes ducked like mice. He told himself that if he was unwilling, Spurlock was scared to death. When they lashed the wagon cover back on and tied themselves together again and hooded the Clydes in the red Hudson's Bay blanket and Little Horn and Ray swung them by the bits and the forlorn night pony stretched his neck and came unwillingly, Rusty had a feeling that the moving line literally tore Spurlock from the side of the fire, now sunk into the crust and sizzling out blackly at the edges in steam and smoke.

The river swung, and the wind got at them. It swung wider, and they were plucked and shoved and blinded so that they walked sideward with their backs to the bar and their faces turned to the fantastic pagoda-roof of snow along the cutbank. In fury and anguish they felt how the river turned them. Like things with an identical electrical charge, their faces bent and flinched away, but in the end there was no evading it.

The wagon stopped and started, stopped and started. The feet that by the fire had felt renewed life began to go dead again, the hands were going back to wood, the faces, chafed and chapped and sore, were pulled deep into the wool and fur. Gasping, smelling wet sheepskin and the tallowy smell of muskrat fur, feeling the ice at their very beards and the wind hunting for their throats, they hunched and struggled on.

Rusty, bent like a bow, with every muscle strained to the mindless plod, plod, plod of one foot after the other, and his eyes focused through the blanket's crack on Spurlock's heels, saw the feet turn sideward, the legs go out of sight. Apparently Spurlock had simply sat down, but the rope, tightening on him, pulled him over. Sliding on the ice, hauled after the backward-walking, braced, and shouting Panguingue, he was trying to untie the rope around his waist with his mittened hands.

Again their yells were torn away downwind, voices to blend with the blizzard's crying, or thaw out to haunt hunters or cowboys in some soft spring. They dragged Spurlock a hundred feet before those up in front heard. Then Rusty stood furiously over him and cursed him for his clumsiness and cried for him to get up, but Spurlock, straightening to sit with his arms hung over his knees, neither looked up nor stood up. He mumbled something with his head down.

"Lone," he mumbled, "rest minute."

Rusty's leg twitched; he all but kicked the miserable bundle. Slip and Jesse or both were shouting from the wagon seat, Ray Henry was coming back—for the how many'th time? They were utterly exposed, the wind whistled and the drift blinded them. He dropped his mouth again to Spurlock's ear, shouted again. Panguingue was hauling at Spurlock's armpits. "Can't sit down," he said. "Got to keep him movin'."

Not until then did the understanding grow into Rusty's mind, a slow ache of meaning like the remote feeling in his feet. Spurlock was done. It wasn't just awkwardness, he wasn't just quitting, he was exhausted. The danger they had been running from, a possibility in which Rusty had never thoroughly believed, was right among them. This was how a man died.

His hands found an arm under blanket and coat, and he and Panguingue helped Spurlock's feeble scrambling until they had him on his feet. They held him there, dragged down by his reluctant weight, while Ray peered grimly into his face. "He's played out," Panguingue said, and Rusty said, "Couldn't we put him in the wagon? He can't walk any farther."

Ray said, "Put him in the wagon he'd be froze stiff in twenty minutes." His hands went out to Spurlock's shoulders and he shook him roughly. "Ed! You hear? You got to keep movin'. It's only another mile. Just keep comin'."

" 'mall right," Spurlock said. "Just rest minute."

"Not a damn minute," Ray said. "You rest a minute and you're dead."

Spurlock hung between Rusty and Panguingue until they were holding almost his whole weight. "You hear, Ed?" Ray said, glaring from his visor like a hairy animal. "You stop to rest, you're dead. Come on now, stand up and walk."

Somehow he bullied strength into the legs and a glitter of life into the eyes. Then he drove back against the wind to take the bridle of the off horse, and the halting, laborious crawl moved on. But now Rusty and Panguingue had hitched their ropes around and walked one on each side of Ed Spurlock, each with a hand under the rope around his waist to haul him along, and to support him if he started to go down. He came wobbling, and he murmured through the blanket they had wrapped over his whole head, but he came.

Rusty's shoulder ached—he ached all over, in fact, whenever he had any feeling at all—and the strain of half supporting Spurlock twisted his body until he had a stabbing stitch in his side. The hand he kept in Spurlock's waist rope was as unfeeling as an iron hook.

A mile more, Ray said. But the river led them a long time around an exposed loop. He had all he could do to force himself into the blast of snow and wind that faded and luffed only to howl in their faces again more bitterly than ever. When Spurlock, stumbling like a sleepwalker, hung back or sagged, trying to sit down, Rusty felt Panguingue's strength and heard Panguingue's stout cursing. His own face was so stiff that he felt he could not have spoken, even to curse, if he tried; he had lost all feeling in his lips and chin. His inhuman hook dragged at Spurlock's waist rope, he threw his shoulder across to meet Panguingue's when the weight surged too far forward, and he put foot after foot, not merely imbecilic now with cold and exhaustion, but nearly mindless, watching not the feet ahead, for there were none now, with three of them abreast and Buck trailing them behind, but the roll of the broad iron tire with the snow spume hissing from it.

He watched it hypnotically, revolving slowly like the white waste of his mind where a spark of awareness as dim as the consciousness of an angleworm glimmered. His body lived only in its pain and weariness.

The white waste on which the wheel moved broke into dark angles, was overspread by blackness that somehow rose and grew, strangely fluid and engulfing, and the air was full of voices wild and desolate and terrible as the sound of hunting wolves. The led pony reared and broke its halter rope and vanished somewhere. Then Rusty felt himself yanked sideward, falling into Spurlock and Panguingue in an encumbered tangle, seeing even as he fell, shocked from his stupor, that the endgate was clear down, the hub drowned in black water that spread across the snow. Kicking crabwise, he fled it on his back, helped by someone hauling on the rope behind, until they stood at the edge of the little shallow rapid and saw Jesse and Slip in the tilted wagon ready to jump, and the round wet heads of stones among the broken ice, and the Clydes struggling, one half down and then up again, Little Horn hanging from the bits, hauled clear of the ice as they plunged. There was a crack like a tree coming down, the stallions plunged and steadied, and then Ray was working back along the broken tongue to get at the singletrees and unhook the tugs and free them.

Ray was standing on the broken tongue and calming the stallions with a hand on each back while he yelled downwind. Rusty pulled at his cap, exposed one brittle ear, and heard the foreman shouting, "Get him on up to the cabin . . . two or three hundred yards . . . right after you."

So with hardly a pause longer than the pause of their falling sideward away from the crunch of ice and the upwelling of water from the broken shell of the rapid, he and Panguingue were walking again, cast free from the rope and supporting Spurlock each with one arm around his shoulders, the other hands locked in front of him. He drooped and wobbled, mumbling and murmuring about rest. He tricked them with sudden lurches to left or right; when he staggered against them his weight was as hard to hold as a falling wall. Twice he toppled them to the ice. Compelled to watch where he walked, Rusty had to let the blanket blow from head and face, and without its protection he flinched and gasped, blinded, and felt the ice forming stickily along his eyelashes, and peered and squinted for the sight of the dugway that would lead them out of the channel and up the cutbank and across a little flat to the final security, so close now and so much more desperately hard to reach with every step.

The river bent, they dragged their burden along, they yielded to his murmurings and to their own exhaustion and let him sag a minute onto the ice, and then hauled and dragged him onto his feet and staggered on. The right bank was low and brushy; the wind came across it so that they leaned and fought across its whipping edge. Rusty freed his left hand and scoured the wrist of the mitten across his eyes and looked into the blast for the slant of the dugway, and saw nothing but the very throat of the blizzard. It was more than muscle and will could endure; panic was alive in his insides again. Even a hundred yards was too much; they could fall and die before the others could overtake them, right here within a few rods of safety. He gasped and sucked at his drooling lip, lost his hold on Panguingue's hand, felt with anguish how Spurlock slid away and went down.

Somehow they got him up again; somehow they struggled another hundred feet along the ice, and now a cutbank curving into a left-hand bend cut off some of the wind, and Rusty heard Panguingue grunt and felt the veer and stagger as he turned in toward the bank. Rusty still could not see it, but starting up, slipping, he put a hand down to stay himself and felt the dugway. Strengthless, they leaned into the bank; Spurlock tried to lie back; they held him with difficulty, and lifting the blanket to look into his face, Rusty saw his eyes frozen wholly shut with teardrops of ice on the lashes. Above the dark beard the cheekbones were dead white.

When they tried to move him again, he sagged back against the bank and gave them his limp arms to haul at, and their combined strength was not enough to get him onto his feet, much less to start him up the steep dugway. They tried to drag him and stopped exhausted after six feet. The glare of uncertainty, fear, helplessness, was in Panguingue's glimmer of eyes and teeth. Rusty understood him well enough. Leave him? The others would soon come along. But if they didn't come in a few minutes he would be dead. Again they lifted and hauled at Spurlock, got him halfway, and felt him slip and go comfortably down again. Panguingue let go. "We better try to get up to the cabin. Schulz might be there."

"Suppose he isn't?"

He heard the forlorn, hopeless sound of Panguingue's snuffling. The face looked at him, bearded clear to the eyes.

"You go," Rusty said. "I'll wait here with him."

A snuffle, a momentary look, and Panguingue ducked away, scrambling with hands and feet, to disappear over the dugway edge.

For a while Rusty lay beside Spurlock on the slope, his blanket huddled over to cover both their faces, and simply waited, without mind or thought, no longer afraid, not hopeful, not even aware or sentient, but simply waiting while the gasp of breath and hammer of heart labored toward some slowing point. He could not feel his feet at all; his hands were clubs of wood. Driven inward from its frontiers, his life concentrated itself in his chest where heart and lungs struggled.

A little later there was a stage in which his consciousness hung above him, like the consciousness in a dream where one is both actor and observer, and saw him lying there, numb already nearly to the knees, nearly to the elbows, nose and lips and forehead and the tender sockets of the eyes gone feelingless, ears as impersonal as paper ears pinned to his head. What he saw was essentially a corpse huddling over another corpse. He recognized the fact without surprise or alarm. This was the way it ended, this was the way they would be found.

Under the blanket's hood were a darkness and stillness. He felt how absurd it was, really. Absurd for men to chase around an arctic prairie wearing themselves and their cattle to death. Absurd. Take a rest, now, and . . .

Coming? Who? *Qu'appelle?* Old wolf, old walker of the snow, old windigo, *qu'appelle?* He smiled. It was a joke between them.

He heard now neither the wind nor the dry rustle of his mind. Inside the blanket the air was still, red-dusky, not cold. But as he moved to make his legs more comfortable the hillside toppled, a dull anguish of unwilling sensation spread in his throat, and he struggled back up, straightening the elbow that had given way and let him fall across Spurlock's up-jutting face. A powder flash of terror lighted up his whole head. The imprint of Spurlock's chin, unyielding as stone, ached in his Adam's apple. The face of a corpse—his too? But it was not his own pain so much as the appalling rigidity of Spurlock's jaw that shocked him. The man was dying, if not dead. Something had to be done, he couldn't just wait for help from Panguingue or the others.

His hands clutched and shook the stiffening bundle, the unfeeling hooks tried to close, to lift. "Ed! Ed, come on! We're almost there, man! Get up, you can't lie here. Only a little way farther. Ed! *Ed!* You hear? God damn it, Ed, get up! Come on, move!"

His eyes were full of catastrophic tears; he dashed them away with a fold of the blanket and threw a look up the dugway and gulped a burning throatful of the wind. He heard the voices wail and howl around the eaves of the riverbank, and he bent and slapped and pounded and tugged, screaming at the clownish, bearded, ice-eyed, and white-cheek-boned face that turned and whimpered under his attack.

Gasping, he stopped a moment, threw another look upward. The top of the bank was less than thirty feet above him. Beyond that, within two hundred feet, should be the cabin. Five minutes, no more than ten even on hands and knees. He looked in anguish for the outfit, possibly coming up the river ice, and saw only trails of drift vanishing around the bend. The boys rendering their fantastic duty to the horses could not possibly come in time. And Panguingue must have found the shack deserted or he would have been back by now. Was he stopping to build a fire, or was he too exhausted to come back? Or was he lying in the snow himself, somewhere between the cutbank and the cabin?

"Ed! Wake up! Get up and walk! It's only a little way!"

Hopeless; inert and hopeless. He could not help the tears, though he knew they would be his blindness and his death. "Please, Ed! Please, come on!"

In a clumsy frenzy he hauled and yanked and dragged; his frantic strength skidded Spurlock a yard or two up the dugway, and when Spurlock began mumblingly to resist with arms and legs, Rusty attacked him with three times more fury and by slaps and kicks and blows reinforced his resistance until, miraculously, Spurlock was on his feet. With hooks and shoulder Rusty helped him, braced him, shoved him upward, moved him a step, and another; and crying encouragement, panting, winded and dead-armed and dead-legged, forced the man foot by foot up the dugway path until he felt the ground level off and the wind fling itself full against them.

They toppled and almost fell. Spurlock sagged and started to sit down and Rusty barely managed to hold him. He could not see more than a bleared half-light—no objects at all. His tears were already ice, his lashes stitched together, and he could make no move to clear his sight without letting Spurlock slip away, probably for the last time. Savagely he rasped his face across the snow-slick wool of Spurlock's blanketed shoulder; with what little vision he could gain he glared straight into the wind for the dark wall or icicled eaves that would be the cabin. The wind drove down his throat; his shouting was strangled and obliterated; it was like trying to look and shout up a waterfall. The wilderness howled at him in all its voices. He was brought to a full stop, sightless, breathless, deafened, and with no strength to move and barely enough to stand, not enough—frantically not enough—to hold the weight of Ed Spurlock that despite every effort he could make slid away and down.

With a groan Rusty let him go. Both hands rose to rub the wristlets of his mittens across his sealed eyes. Pain stabbed through his eyeballs as if he had run across them with sandpaper, but he broke the threads of ice that stitched him shut, and looked again into the gray and howling wind, saw a square darkness, a loom of shadow in the murk, and thought in wonder, My God, we've been right against the shack all the time, and then the darkness moved and the wind's voice fell from whine and howl to a doglike barking, and Panguingue was there shouting in his face.

Relief was such pure bliss to him that he was rendered imbecilic by it, and stood mouth open and cheeks stretched to force open his eyes, watching Panguingue try to pull Spurlock erect. He loved Panguingue, the stoutest and decentest and bravest and most dependable man alive. Merely his presence brought not only hope but assurance. It would be no trouble now. And even while he was bending to help he heard the unmistakable dig and clump of the Clydes behind him, and turned to see them clear the dugway with tennis balls of ice rattling in their fetlocks and Jesse hanging to the lines behind them, and then the others—one, then another, then another, leading the pony.

What had been impossible was suddenly easy, was nothing. Among them they hoisted Spurlock to his feet. Rusty felt an arm around him, the urge of someone else's undiminished strength helping him along through a thigh-deep drift that gave way abruptly to clear ground. His head sounded with hollow kickings and poundings and with one last defeated howl of wind, and he saw icicles under the shack's eaves like yard-long teeth, and the wind stopped, the noises fell, the light through his sticky eyelids darkened, his nostrils filled with smells of mice, kerosene, sheepskins, ham rind, sardines, and a delirious tropical odor of cinnamon and cloves like his mother's spice cupboard, and someone steered him and turned him and pushed on his shoulders, and Ray Henry's whisper said, "O.K., kid, take a load off your feet." He felt safety with his very buttocks as he eased himself down on the rustly hay-stuffed tick of a bunk.

Later he sat with his aching feet in a dishpan of snow and water, and when the pain in his hands swelled until it seemed the fingers would split like sausages, he stooped and numbed the ache into bearability in the same dishpan. His eyes were inflamed and sore; in each cheek a spot throbbed with such violence that he thought the pulse must be visible in the skin like a twitching nerve. His ears were swollen red-hot fungi, his nose that had run and drooled incontinently all the way through the blizzard was now so stuffed and swollen that he gurgled for air. He knew how he looked by looking at Little Horn, who had got wet to the knees when the Clydes went through the rapid, and who sat now on an apple box with first one foot and then the other in a bucket of snow. Little Horn's skin showed like a flaming sunburn through his reddish beard. He had innocent blue eyes like Jesse's, and the same blunt chin. When he was twenty years older he would look a good deal like Jesse—they were members of the same tribe. Now he lifted one tallowy foot from the deep snowprint in the pail and set it tenderly on the floor and lifted the other into its place, and looked across at Rusty with his mild ironic eye and shook his head in acknowledgment of something.

Ray and Jesse were squatting by the bunk against the side wall where Spurlock lay. Each had a blotched foot in his hands, each was massaging it and sousing it with snow. At the head of the bunk Buck worked on Spurlock's hands. Spurlock's fiery face looked straight upward; his teeth were set; he said nothing. Back by the door Slip and Panguingue had just finished washing each other's faces with snow. All of them, emerged from their cumbersome wrappings, looked disheveled as corpses dredged from a river. Rusty marveled at their bony hairless feet, their red hands, their vulnerable throats. They were making a good deal of talkative noise, their skins were full of the happiness of rescue, and not yet quite full of pain.

Little Horn looked at Panguingue's wet face. He said to Rusty, "Ain't that the way it goes? Of all the people that might of froze their feet and got a good wash out of it, who is the one God damn boy in the outfit without even a frozen toe but old Pan?"

Jesse said from the end of Spurlock's bunk, "Cold couldn't get through that crust."

"B.S.," Panguingue said. "I'm just tougher than you. And besides, I froze my face damn good."

"Snow washed some of the protective layer off," Little Horn said. "No, more I think of it, more I think you shouldn't make any mistake and wash them feet till spring, Pan. We'll need somebody around to do the chores while we get well."

"Hey, by God," Panguingue said. "How about my face?"

"Just leave it go. A little proud flesh would improve it."

"B.S.," said Slip, in imitation of Panguingue's growl, and he and Panguingue threatened each other with pans of snow. From the other bunk Ray Henry said, "Feelin' 'em yet?"

"You're damn right," Ed Spurlock said through his teeth.

"Better let 'em set in the water for a while," Ray said. "The slower they come back the better." He stood up, looking at Rusty. "Rusty, you needin' that dishpan for a while?"

"No, take it." He moved his feet carefully out onto the dirty board floor, and the foreman shoved the pan under Spurlock's dangling feet. Standing over Rusty, burly, matted-haired, grave-eyed, totally enigmatic to the boy but restored to his position of authority and respect, he said, "How you doin'? Feelin' yours?"

"Enough," Rusty said. He raised his head a little. "What's the cure for frostbite?"

"Whiskey," Jesse said from beside Spurlock.

"Fine," said Little Horn. "Just what we ain't got."

"If we had some rocks we could have some rock and rye," Slip said. "If we had some rye."

"No particular cure," Ray said to Rusty. "Thaw it out slow, keep away from heat, little arnica if you get sores, cut it out if you get gangrene. And wait."

"How long?"

"Depends how bad you are. You and Little Horn, maybe a week, ten days. Ed maybe two-three weeks. It's the hands and feet that lay you up."

"What do we do, stay here till we're well?"

"I expect we'll cobble up that tongue and beat it for the ranch soon as it clears off."

"Vacation with pay," Little Horn said. "Peach pies. Whiskey every hour, while Panguingue does the chores. I tell you, Rusty, there's no life like a cowboy's."

But Rusty was thinking of the two weeks they had just gone through, and of the cattle that had gone streaming miserably downwind from the Horse Camp corrals, the gaunt exhausted horses that had hung around the tent and wagon until the wind literally blew them away. "What about the calves?" he asked. "And what about the horses?"

"Horses we'll have to round up, some of them anyway. They'll winter out all right, but we need work ponies."

"You mean—ride out there and hunt through all that country and drive them on back to the ranch?"

"Uh-huh."

"I tell you," Little Horn said, and lifted his left foot out of the bucket and raised his right tenderly in, "there's no business like the cow business to make a man healthy and active. There's hardly a job you can work at that'll keep you more in the open air."

Rusty smelled the coffee that Jesse had put on the fire as soon as he got it going. He saw the flaw of moisture the spout cast on the stovepipe, and he moved his pain-distended hands cautiously, cradling them in his lap. The shack's growing warmth burned in his cheeks. Over on the other side of the stove Slippers' face, purple in the bare patches, black where the beard grew, brooded with its eyes on the floor. This was the leathery little man who would ride out to bring the ponies back across sixty miles of rough country. And maybe one or two others— maybe himself—with him. The very notion, at that moment, moved the boy to something like awe.

"What about the calves?" he said.

For the first time expression—disgust? anger? ironic resignation?— flickered across Ray's chapped, bearded mouth. "The calves. Well, the ones that ain't dead by the time this one blows out may find some willows to gnaw in a coulee, and if we get a chinook they'll have feed and come through all right. If we don't get a chinook the wolves are gonna be very fat by spring."

"But we aren't going to try rounding them up again."

Ray turned away with the flicker widening momentarily on his mouth. "I wouldn't worry about it," he said.

"Don't be impatient," Little Horn said, and hissed sharply as he moved his foot and bumped the pail. He set the heel on the floor and looked at the swollen toes, looked at his sausage-like fingers, shook his head. On the bunk Spurlock raised one foot from the dishpan. "Wait a minute," Jesse said. "Got enough of that footbath for a while?"

He helped the legs with their rolled-up pants to straighten out in the bunk. In the silence that came down as the pain of returning blood preoccupied them Rusty heard the undiminished wind shriek along the icicled eaves of the shack and swoop away. Smoke puffed out around the rings of the stove lids, lay there for a minute like fat white circular worms, and was sucked in again. Shaggy as cavemen, weather-beaten and battered, they huddled back against the walls and away from the stove and contemplated each in his own way the discomforts of the outraged flesh. Each retired within his skinful of pain and weariness, and among them Rusty Cullen, as weary as any, as full of pain as any— pain enough to fill him to the chin and make him lock his jaw for fear of whimpering. He made note that none whimpered, not even Spurlock; the worst was an occasional querulous growl when one moved too fast. Jesse, the old-timer, the knowing one, Nestor and patriarch, unfrozen except for a touch on the fingers and ears, moved between them in stockinged feet and flipped the coffeepot lid with the edge of his palm, saving his tender fingertips, and looked in. The mystic smells of brotherhood were strong in the shack. The stove lids puffed out worms of smoke once more, and once more sucked them inward. The wind went over and around them, the ancient implacable wind, and tore away balked and shrill.

The Rusty Cullen who sat among them was a different boy, outside and inside, from the one who had set out with them two weeks before. He thought that he knew enough not to want to distinguish himself by heroic deeds: singlehanded walks to the North Pole, incredible journeys, rescues, what not. Given his way, he did not think that he would ever want to do anything alone again, not in this country. Even a trip to the privy was something a man might want to take in company.

The notion insinuated itself into his head, not for the first time, that his sticking with Spurlock after Panguingue left was an act of special excellence, that the others must look upon him with a new respect because of it. But the tempting thought did not stand up under the examination he gave it. Special excellence? Why hadn't anyone praised him for it, then? He knew why: because it was what any of them would have done. To have done less would have been cowardice and disgrace. It was probably a step in the making of a cowhand when he learned that what would pass for heroics in a softer world was only chores around here.

Around him he heard the hiss of air drawn between clenched teeth, he saw the careful, excruciating slowness of hands and feet being moved in search of more comfortable positions, he saw and smelled and felt how he was indistinguishable from the other seven. His greenness did not show, was perhaps not quite so green as it had been. And he did not take it ill, but understood it as a muffled acceptance or acknowledgement, when Spurlock sniffed thickly and said to the sagging springs above his nose, "Is that coffee I smell, Jesse, or is it only fawncy?"

THE
WOLFER

Yes, I saw a good deal of it, and I knew them all. It was my
business to, and in those days it wasn't hard to know nearly
every man between Willow Bunch and Fort Walsh, even the
drifters; the women you could count on your two thumbs. One was
Molly Henry at the T-Down Bar, the other was Amy Schulz, living with
a reformed whiskey trader named Frost up on Oxarart Creek. I knew
Schulz, too, and his miserable boy. At least I had seen him a good many
times, and stopped with him a half-dozen times at one or another shack
when I was out on patrol, and at least that many times had come within
an ace of being eaten by his hound. Probably I knew him better than
most people did, actually. Friends—that's another matter. He was about
as easy to be friendly with as a wolverine.

Summers, he camped around in the Cypress Hills, hunting, but in
winter he used the shacks that the cattle outfits maintained out along
the Whitemud, on the patrol trail between the Hills and Wood Mountain. Two of them, at Stonepile and Pinto Horse Butte, were abandoned
Mounted Police patrol posts—abandoned in the sense that no constables

were stationed there, though we kept the barracks stocked with emergency supplies and always cut and stacked a few tons of prairie wool there in the fall. Both Schulz and I used the barracks now and then, for he as a wolfer and I as a Mountie covered pretty much the same territory. If the truth were known, I kept pretty close tab on him in my patrol book, because I was never entirely sure, after Amy left him, that he wouldn't go back up on Oxarart Creek and shoot Frost.

Probably I wronged him. I think he was glad to get rid of Amy; it freed him to be as wild as the wolves he hunted, with his snuffling adenoidal boy for a slave and daily killing for occupation and his staghound for friend and confidant. They were a pair; each was the only living thing that liked the other, I guess, and it was a question which had the edge in savagery. Yet love, too, of a kind. I have heard him croon and mutter to that thing, baby talk, in a way to give you the creeps.

Whenever I found Schulz at Stonepile or Pinto Horse I picked an upper bunk; if the hound got drooling for my blood in the night I wanted to be where he'd at least have to climb to get at me. There was no making up to him—he was Schulz's, body and soul. He looked at every other human being with yellow eyes as steady as a snake's, the hackles lifting between his shoulders and a rumble going away down in his chest. I'd hear him moving in the dark shack, soft and heavy, with his nails clicking on the boards. He wore a fighting collar studded with brass spikes, he stood as high as a doorknob at the shoulder, and he weighed a hundred and forty pounds. Schulz bragged that he had killed wolves single-handed. The rest of the pack, Russian wolfhounds and Russian-greyhound crosses, slept in the stable and were just dogs, but this staghound thing, which Schulz called Puma, was the physical shape of his own savagery: hostile, suspicious, deadly, unwinking. I have seen him stand with a foolish, passive smile on his face while that monster put his paws up on his shoulders and lapped mouth and chin and eyes with a tongue the size of a coal shovel.

He was a savage, a wild man. He hated civilization—which meant maybe two hundred cowpunchers and Mounties scattered over ten thousand square miles of prairie—but it was not civilization that did him in. It was the wild, the very savagery he trusted and thought he controlled. I know about that too, because I followed the last tracks he and his hound made in this country.

My patrol books would show the date. As I remember, it was toward the end of March 1907. The patrol was routine—Eastend, Bates Camp, Stonepile, the Warholes, Pinto Horse Butte, Wood Mountain, and return—but nothing else was routine that winter. With a month still to go, it was already a disaster.

Since November there had been nothing but blizzards, freezing fogs, and cold snaps down to forty below. One chinook—and that lasted only long enough to melt everything to mush, whereupon another cold snap came on and locked the country in a four-inch shell of ice. A lot of cattle that lay down that night never got up: froze in and starved there.

That time, just about Christmas, I passed the Warholes on a patrol and found a *métis* named Big Antoine and twenty of his Indian relatives trapped and half-starved. They had made a run for it from Wood Mountain toward Big Stick Lake when the chinook blew up, and got caught out. When I found them they hadn't eaten anything in two weeks except skin-and-bone beef that had died in the snow; they were seasoning it with fat from coyotes, the only thing besides the wolves that throve.

A police freighter got them out before I came back on my next trip. But the cowpunchers out in the range shacks were by that time just about as bad off. For weeks they had been out every day roping steers frozen into the drifts, and dragging them free; or they had been floundering around chasing cattle out of the deep snow of the bottoms and out onto the benches where the wind kept a little feed bare. They had got them up there several times, but they hadn't kept them there. The wind came across those flats loaded with buckshot, and the cattle turned their tails to it and came right back down to starve. At one point the two Turkey Track boys stationed at Pinto Horse had even tried to make a drag of poles, and drag bare a patch of hillside for the cattle to feed on. All they did was kill off their ponies. When I came by in March they had given up and were conducting a non-stop blackjack game in the barracks, and laying bets whether the winter would last till August, or whether it would go right on through and start over.

We had a little poker game that night. Whenever the talk died we could hear, through the logs and sod of the shack, the heavy hunting song of wolves drawn down from the hills for the big barbecue. It was a gloomy thing to hear. Say what you want about cowpunchers, they don't like failing at a job any better than other people. And they were sure failing.

In November there had been close to seventy thousand head of cattle on that Whitemud range. At a conservative guess, half of them were dead already. If we didn't get a chinook in the next week, there wouldn't be a cow alive come spring.

I quit the game early to get some sleep, and for a joke pushed the deck over toward Curly Withers for a cut. "Cut a chinook," I said. He turned over the jack of diamonds. Then we went to the door for a look-see, and everything was wooled up in freezing fog, what nowadays they call a whiteout. You could have cut sheep out of the air with tin shears. "Some chinook," Curly said.

In the morning there was still no wind, but the air was clear. As I turned Dude down the trail and looked back to wave at the Turkey Track boys I had the feeling they were only six inches high, like carved figures in a German toy scene. The shack was braced from eaves to ground with icicles; the sky behind the quiver of heat from the stovepipe jiggled like melting glass. Away down in the southeast, low and heatless, the sun was only a small painted dazzle.

It seemed mean and cowardly to leave those boys out there. Or maybe it was just that I hated to start another day of hard cold riding through all that death, with nobody to talk to. You can feel mighty small and lonesome riding through that country in winter, after a light snowfall that muffles noises. I was leading a packhorse, and ordinarily there is a good deal of jingle and creak and sound of company with two ponies, but that morning it didn't seem my noises carried ten feet.

Down in the river trough everything was still and white. Mainly the channel had a fur of frozen snow on it, but here and there were patches of black slick ice full of air bubbles like quarters and silver dollars. Depending on how the bends swung, drifts sloped up to the cutbanks or up to bars overgrown with snow-smothered rose bushes and willows. I crossed the tracks of three wolves angling upriver, side by side and bunched in clusters of four: galloping. They must have been running just for the hell of it, or else they had sighted an antelope or deer. They didn't have to gallop to eat beef.

Without wind, it wasn't bad riding, though when I breathed through my mouth the aching of my teeth reminded me that under the Christmas frosting the world was made of ice and iron. Now a dead steer among the rose bushes, untouched by wolves or coyotes. I cut a notch in a tally stick, curious about how many I would pass between Pinto Horse and Eastend. Farther on, a bunch of whitefaces lying and standing so close together they had breathed frost all over one another. If they hadn't been such skeletons they would have looked like farmyard beasts in a crèche. They weren't trapped or frozen in, but they were making no move to get out—only bawled at me hopelessly as I passed. Two were dead and half drifted over. I cut two more notches.

In three hours I cut a good many more, one of them at a big wallow and scramble near the mouth of Snake Creek where wolves had pulled down a steer since the last snowfall. The blood frozen into the snow was bright as paint, as if it had been spilled only minutes before. Parts of the carcass had been dragged in every direction.

Those wolves rubbed it in, pulling down a beef within a half mile of where Schulz and his boy were camped at Stonepile. I wondered if he had had any luck yet—he hadn't had any at all last time I saw him— and I debated whether to stop with him or go on to Bates and heat up a cold shack. The decision was for Bates. It was no big blowout to spend a night with the Schulzes, who were a long way from being the company the T-Down and Turkey Track boys were, and who besides were dirtier than Indians. Also I thought I would sleep better at Bates than I would at Stonepile, in an upper bunk with my hand on a gun while that hound prowled around in the dark and rumbled every time I rolled over. Sure Schulz had it trained, but all he had hold of it with was his voice; I would have liked a chain better.

Just to make a check on Stonepile for the patrol book, I turned up Snake Creek, and a little after noon I came up the pitch from the bottoms and surprised the Schulz boy standing bare-armed before the barracks door with a dishpan hanging from his hand. The dishpan steamed, his arm steamed, the sunken snow where he had flung the dishwater steamed. I was quite pleased with him, just then; I hadn't known he and his old man ever washed their dishes. He stood looking at me with his sullen, droop-lipped watchful face, one finger absentmindedly up his nose. Down in the stable the wolfhounds began to bark and whine and howl. I saw nothing of Schulz or the big hound.

"Howdy, Bud," I said. "How's tricks?"

He was sure no chocolate-box picture. His gray flannel shirt was shiny with grease, his face was pimply, long black hair hung from under the muskrat cap that I had never seen off his head. I think he slept in it, and I'll guarantee it was crawling. He never could meet a man's eyes. He took his finger out of his nose and said, looking past me, "Hello, constable."

I creaked down. Dude pushed me from behind, rubbing the icicles off his nose. "Pa not around?" I said.

Something flickered in his eyes, a wet gray gleam. One eye socket and temple, I saw, were puffy and discolored—about a three-day-old black eye. He touched one cracked red wrist to his chapped mouth and burst out, "Pa went out yesterday and ain't come back!" With a long drag he blew his nose through his mouth and spit sideways into the snow. His eyes hunted mine and ducked away instantly. "And Puma got out!" he said—wailed, almost.

At that moment I wouldn't have trusted him a rope length out of my sight. He looked sneakily guilty, he had that black eye which could only be a souvenir from Daddy, he had fifteen years of good reasons for hating his old man. If Schulz and his hound were really missing, I had the conviction that I would find them dry-gulched and stuffed through the ice somewhere. Not that I could have blamed young Schulz too much. In the best seasons his old man must have been a bearcat to live with. In this one, when he had hunted and trapped all winter and never got a single wolf, he was a crazy man. The wolves walked around his traps laughing—they fed much too well to be tempted. They sat just out of rifle shot and watched him waste ammunition. And though he had the best pack of dogs in that country, he hadn't been able to run them for months because of the weather and the deep snow. Out on the flats the dogs could have run, but there were no wolves there; they were all down in the bottoms hobnobbing with the cattle. The last time I had passed through, Schulz had talked to me half the night like a man half-crazed with rage: red-faced, jerky-voiced, glassy-eyed. To make his troubles worse, he had headaches, he said; "bunches" on his head. A horse had fallen on him once.

So in a winter of complete hard luck, who made a better whipping boy than that sullen son of his? And who more likely, nursing his black eye and his grievance, to lie behind the cabin or stable and pot his father as he came up the trail?

It was a fine theory. Pity it wasn't sound. I told young Schulz to hold it while I turned the horses into the police haystack, and while I was down there I got a look around the stable and corrals. No bodies, no blood, no signs of a fight. Then up in the barracks, in the hot, close, tallowy-mousy room with muskrat and marten pelts on bows of red willow hanging from the ceiling and coyote and lynx hides tacked on the wall, and three spirals of last year's flypaper, black with last year's flies, moving in the hot air above the stove, I began asking him questions and undid all my nice imaginary murder.

I even began to doubt that anything would turn out to be wrong with Schulz or his hound, for it became clear at once that if Schulz was in trouble he was in trouble through some accident, and I didn't believe that the Schulzes had accidents. They might get killed, but they didn't have accidents. It was about as likely that he would freeze, or get lost, or fall through a rapid, or hurt himself with a gun, as it was that a wolf would slip and sprain his ankle. And if you bring up those bunches on his head, and the horse that he said fell on him, I'll bet you one thing. I'll bet you the horse got hurt worse than Schulz did.

Still, he was missing, and in that country and that weather it could be serious. He had left the barracks the morning before, on foot but carrying snowshoes, to check on some carcasses he had poisoned down by Bates Camp. Usually he didn't use poison because of the dogs. Now he would have baited traps with his mother, or staked out his snuffling boy, if he could have got wolves that way. He shut the wolfhounds in the stable and the staghound in the barracks and told the boy to keep them locked up. The staghound especially had to be watched. He was used to going everywhere with Schulz, and he might follow him if he were let out.

That was exactly what he did do. Young Schulz kept him in the barracks—it would have been like being caged with a lion—until nearly dark, when he went down to the stable to throw some frozen beef to the other dogs. He slid out and slammed the door ahead of the staghound's rush. But when he came back he wasn't so lucky. The dog was waiting with his nose to the crack, and when it opened he threw his hundred and forty pounds against the door and was gone. No one but Schulz would have blamed the boy—ever try to stop a bronc from coming through a corral gate, when you're there on foot and he's scared and ringy and wants to come? You get out of the way or you get trompled. That hound would have trompled you the same way. But Schulz wouldn't think of that. The boy was scared sick of what his father would do to him if and when he came back.

I thought that since the hound had *not* come back, he obviously must have found Schulz. If he had found him alive and unhurt, they would be back together before long. If he had found him hurt, he would stay with him, and with any luck I could find them simply by following their tracks. I asked the boy if he was afraid to stay alone two or three days, if necessary. He wasn't—it was exactly the opposite he was scared of. Also I told him to stay put, and not get in a panic and take off across a hundred miles of open country for Malta or somewhere; I would see to it that his old man laid off the horsewhip. Somebody—his old man, or me, or somebody—would be back within three days at the latest.

He stood in the doorway with his arms still bare, a tough kid actually, a sort of wild animal himself, though of an unattractive kind, and watched me with those wet little gleaming eyes as I rode off down Snake Creek.

I couldn't have had better trailing. The light snow two nights before had put a nice firm rippled coating over every old track. When I hit the river the channel was perfectly clean except for Schulz's moccasin tracks, and braided in among them the tracks of the hound. A wolf makes a big track, especially with his front feet—I've seen them nearly six inches each way—but that staghound had feet the size of a plate, and he was so heavy that in deep snow, even a packed drift, he sank way down. So there they went, the companionable tracks of a man and his dog out hunting. If I hadn't known otherwise I would have assumed that they had gone upriver together, instead of six hours apart.

The day had got almost warm. Under the north bank the sun had thawed an occasional rooty dark spot. I kneed Dude into a shuffle, the packhorse dragged hard and then came along. I could have followed that trail at a lope.

It led me four miles up the river's meanders before I even had to slow down, though I cut four more notches in the tally stick and saw two thin does and a buck flounder away from the ford below Sucker Creek, and took a snapshot with the carbine at a coyote, fatter than I ever saw a coyote, that stood watching me from a cutbank. My bullet kicked snow at the cutbank's lip and he was gone like smoke. Then a mile above Sucker Creek I found where Schulz had put on his snowshoes and cut across the neck of a bend. The hound had wallowed after him, leaving a trail like a horse.

The drifts were hard-crusted under the powder, but not hard-crusted enough, and the horses were in to their bellies half the time. They stood heaving while I got off to look at a little tent-like shelter with fresh snow shoveled over it. The hound had messed things up some, sniffing around, but he had not disturbed the set. Looking in, I found a marten in a No. 2 coyote trap, caught around the neck and one front leg. He wasn't warm, but he wasn't quite frozen either. I stuffed marten and trap into a saddlebag and went on.

The trail led out of the river valley and up a side coulee where among thin red willows a spring came warm enough from the ground to stay unfrozen for several feet. The wolfer had made another marten set there, and then had mushed up onto the bench and northwest to a slough where tules whiskered up through the ice and a half-dozen very high muskrat houses rose out of the clear ice farther out.

At the edge of the slough I got off and followed where man and hound had gone out on the ice. Where the ice was clear I could see the paths the rats make along the bottom. For some reason this slough wasn't frozen nearly as deep as the river, maybe because there were springs, or because of organic matter rotting in the water. The Royal Society will have to settle that sometime. All I settled was that Schulz had chopped through the ice in two places and set coyote traps in the paths, and had broken through the tops of three houses to make sets inside. He had a rat in one of the house sets. Since I seemed to be running his trapline for him, I put it in the other saddlebag.

Nothing, surely, had happened to Schulz up to here. The hound had been at every set, sniffing out the trail. That would have been pretty late, well after dark, when the fog had already shut off the half moon. It occurred to me as I got back on Dude and felt the icy saddle under my pants again that I would not have liked to be out there on that bare plain to see a wild animal like that hound go by in the mist, with his nose to his master's track.

From the slough the trail cut back to the river; in fifteen minutes I looked down onto the snowed-over cabin and buried corrals of Bates Camp. There had been nobody stationed in it since the T-Down fed its last hay almost two months before. No smoke from the stovepipe, no sign of life. My hope that I would find the wolfer holed up there, so that I could get out of the saddle and brew a pot of tea and eat fifty pounds or so of supper, went glimmering. Something had drawn him away from here. He would have reached Bates about the same time of day I reached it—between two and three in the afternoon—for though he was a tremendous walker he could not have covered eight miles, some of it on snowshoes, and set seven traps, in less than about four hours. I had then been on his trail more than two hours, and pushing it hard.

I found that he hadn't gone near the shack at all, but had turned down toward the corrals, buried so deep that only the top pole showed. Wading along leading the horses, I followed the web tracks to the carcass of a yearling shorthorn half dug out of the snow.

There were confusing tracks all around—snowshoes, dog, wolf. The shorthorn had died with his tongue out, and a wolf had torn it from his head. The carcass was chewed up some, but not scattered. Schulz had circled it about six feet away, and at one place deep web tracks showed where he had squatted down close. I stood in the tracks and squatted too, and in front of me, half obscured by the dog's prints, I saw where something had rolled in the snow. Snagged in the crust was a long gray-black hair.

A wolf, then. This was one of the poisoned carcasses, and a wolf that rolled might be sick. Squatting in the quenched afternoon, Schulz would have come to his feet with a fierce grunt, darting his eyes around the deceptive shapes of snow and dusk, and he would not have waited a second to track the wolf to his dying place. The coyotes he ran or shot, and the marten and muskrat he trapped when nothing better offered, were nothing to him: it was wolves that made his wild blood go, and they had cheated him all winter.

For just a minute I let myself yearn for the cabin and a fire and a hot meal. But I still had an hour and a half of light good enough for trailing— about what Schulz himself had had—and after that maybe another half-hour of deceptive shadows, ghostly moonlight, phosphorescent snow, and gathering mist and dark. If he had got hurt somehow chasing the wolf, he might have survived one night: he couldn't possibly survive two. So I paused only long enough to put the packhorse in the stable and give him a bait of oats, and to light a fire to take a little of the chill out of the icy shack. Then I set the damper and took out on the trail again.

It was like a pursuit game played too long and complicated too far, to the point of the ridiculous—like one of those cartoons of a big fish swallowing a smaller fish swallowing a smaller fish swallowing a small fish. There went the sick wolf running from the heat of the strychnine in his guts, and after him the wolfer, implacable in the blue-white cold, and after him the great hound running silently, hours behind but gaining, loping hard down the river ice or sniffing out the first marten set. There went wildness pursued by hate pursued by love, and after the lot of them me, everybody's rescuer, everybody's nursemaid, the law on a tired horse.

Schulz never did catch up with that wolf. Probably it had never been sick at all, but had rolled in the snow in sassy contempt, the way a dog will kick dirt back over his scats. Up on the bench its tracks broke into the staggered pairs that showed it was trotting, and after a half mile or so another set of wolf tracks came in from the west, and the two went off together in the one-two-one of an easy lope.

Schulz quit, either because he saw it was hopeless or because the light gave out on him. I could imagine his state of mind. Just possibly, too, he had begun to worry. With darkness and fog and the night cold coming on, that open flat bare of even a scrap of sagebrush was no place to be. In an hour the freak windlessness could give way to a blizzard; a wind right straight off the North Pole, and temperatures to match, could light on him with hardly a warning, and then even a Schulz could be in trouble.

Above me, as I studied his tracks where he broke off the chase, a chip of moon was pale and blurry against a greenish sky; the sun over the Cypress Hills was low and strengthless. It would go out before it went down. And I was puzzled by Schulz. He must have been lost; he must have looked up from his furious pursuit and his furious reading of failure, and seen only misty dusk, without landmarks, moon, stars, anything, for instead of heading back for the river and the cabin he started straight eastward across the plain. So did I, because I had to.

It took him about a mile to realize his mistake, and it was easy to read his mind from his footprints, for there out in the middle of the empty snowflats they milled around a little and made an eloquent right angle toward the south. Probably he had felt out his direction from the drifts, which ran like shallow sea waves toward the southeast. I turned after him thankfully. But he hadn't gone back to Bates, and he hadn't gone back downriver to Stonepile. So where in hell *had* he gone? I worked the cold out of my stiff cheeks, and flapped my arms to warm my hands, and kicked old Dude into a tired trot across the packed flats.

In twenty minutes I was plowing down into the river valley again. The sun was blurring out, the bottoms were full of shadows the color of a gunbarrel, the snow was scratched with black willows. I judged that I was not more than a mile upriver from Bates. The plowing web tracks and the wallowing trail of the hound went ahead of me through deep drifts and across the bar onto the river ice, and coming after them, I saw under the opposite cutbank the black of a dead fire.

I stopped. There was no sign of life, though the snow, I could see, was much tracked. I shouted: "Schulz?" and the sound went out in that white desolation like a match dropped in the snow. This looked like the end of the trail, and because it began to look serious, and I didn't want to track things up until I got a chance to study them, I tied the horse in the willows and circled to come into the bend from below. When I parted the rose bushes to slide down onto the ice, I looked straight down on the body of Schulz's hound.

Dead, he looked absolutely enormous. He lay on his side with his spiked collar up around his ears. I saw that he had been dragged by it from the direction of the fire. He had bled a great deal from the mouth, and had been bleeding as he was dragged, for the snow along the drag mark had a filigree of red. On the back of his head, almost at his neck, was a frozen bloody patch. And along the trough where the body had been dragged came a line of tracks, the unmistakable tracks of Schulz's moccasins. Another set went back. That was all. It was as clear as printing on a page. Schulz had dragged the dead dog to the edge of the bank, under the overhanging bushes, and left him there, and not come back.

I tell you, I was spooked. My hair stood on end. I believe, and I know I looked quickly all around, in a fright that I might be under somebody's eyes or gun. On the frozen river there was not a sound. As I slid down beside the hound I looked both ways in the channel, half expecting to see Schulz's body too, or somebody else's. Nothing. Clean snow.

The hound's body was frozen rock hard. His mouth was full of frozen blood, and the crusted patch on the back of his neck turned out to be a bullet hole, a big one. He had been shot in the mouth, apparently by a soft-nosed bullet that had torn the back of his head off. And no tracks, there or anywhere, except those of Schulz himself. I knew that Schulz never used any gun but a .22, in which he shot long rifle cartridges notched so they would mushroom and tear a big internal hole and stop without making a second puncture in the hide. If he had shot the hound—and that was totally incredible, but who else could have?—a .22 bullet like that would not have gone clear through brain and skull and blown a big hole out the other side unless it had been fired at close range, so close that even in fog or half-dark the wolfer must have known what he was shooting at.

But I refused to believe what my eyes told me must be true. I could conceive of Schulz shooting his son, and I had already that day suspected his son of shooting *him*. But I could not believe that he would ever, unless by accident, shoot that dog. Since it didn't seem he could have shot it accidentally, someone else must have shot it.

It took me ten minutes to prove to myself that there were no tracks around there except the wolfer's. I found those, in fact, leading on upriver, and since I had looked at every footprint he made from Stonepile on, I knew these must be the ones he made going out. Instead of going home, he went on. Why?

Under the cutbank, in front of the fire, I found a hard path beaten in the snow where Schulz had walked up and down many times. The fire itself had never been large, but it had burned a long time; the coals were sunk deeply into the snow and frozen in their own melt. Schulz had evidently stayed many hours, perhaps all night, keeping the little fire going and walking up and down to keep from freezing. But why hadn't he walked a mile downriver and slept warm at Bates?

I might have followed to try to find out, but the light was beginning to go, and I was too cold and tired to think of riding any more of that crooked river that night. Still, just thinking about it gave me an idea. In any mile, the Whitemud ran toward every point of the compass, swinging and returning on itself. If Schulz had hit it after the fog closed in thick, he would have known that Bates lay downriver, but how would he know which way was downriver? There were no rapids in that stretch. There would have been no landmarks but bends and bars endlessly repeating, changing places, now on the right and now on the left. Some of the bends were bowknots that completely reversed their direction.

That might answer one question, but only one. I put myself in the path he had made, and walked up and down trying to see everything just as he had. I found the mark where he had stuck his rifle butt-down in the snow, probably to leave his arms free for swinging against the cold. There were hound tracks on the path and alongside it, as if the dog had walked up and down with him. At two places it had lain down in the snow off to the side.

That answered another question, or corroborated what I had guessed before: Schulz couldn't have shot the hound not knowing what it was; it had been there with him for some time.

Standing by the fire, I looked back at the deep tracks where Schulz, and after him the hound, had broken down off the bar onto the ice. The hound's tracks led directly to the fire and the path. I walked the path again, searching every foot of it. I found only one thing more: just where the path went along a streak of clear ice, where ice and snow joined in a thin crust, there were the deep parallel gouges of claws, two sets of them, close together. Would a heavy hound, rearing to put its front paws on a man's shoulders and its happy tongue in a man's face, dig that way, deeply, with its hind claws? I thought it would.

I stood at the spot where I thought Schulz and the hound might have met, and again studied the tracks and the places where the hound had lain down. In front of one of them was a light scoop, just the rippled surface taken off the new snow. Made by a tongue lapping? Maybe. By pure intensity of imagining I tried to reconstruct what might have happened. Suppose it went this way:

Suppose he fumbled down to the river with the visibility no more than fifty or a hundred feet, and could not tell which way it ran. The fact that he had lost himself up on the bench made that not merely possible, but probable. A fire, then, until daylight let him see. Willows yielded a little thin fuel, the tiny heat along leg or backside or on the turned stiff hands made the night bearable. But caution would have told anyone as experienced as Schulz that the night was long and fuel short—and at Pinto Horse the night before the thermometer had stood at fifteen below. He would have had to keep moving, the rifle stuck in a drift and his arms flailing and the felt cap he wore pulled down to expose only his eyes and mouth—a figure as savage and forlorn as something caught out of its cave at the race's dim beginning.

The sound of hunting wolves would have kept him company as it had kept us company in our social poker game, and it would have been a sound that for many reasons he liked less than we did. Except for that dark monotone howling there would have been no sound in the shrouded bend except the creak of his moccasins and the hiss of the fire threatening always to melt itself out—no other sound unless maybe the grating of anger in his own aching head, an anger lonely, venomous, and incurable, always there like the pressure of those "bunches" on his skull. I could imagine it well enough: too well. For the first time, that day or ever, I felt sorry for Schulz.

Endless walking through frozen hours; endless thinking; endless anger and frustration. And then—maybe?—the noise of something coming, a harsh and terrifying noise smashing in on his aloneness, as something big and fast plowed through the snowy brush and came scraping and sliding down the bank. Schulz would have reached the gun in one leap (I looked, but could find no sign to prove he had). Assuming he did: while he crouched there, a wild man with his finger on the trigger and his nerves humming with panic, here came materializing out of the white darkness a great bony shape whining love.

And been shot as it rushed up to greet Schulz, shot in the moment of fright when the oncoming thing could have been wolf or worse? It would have been plausible if it hadn't been for those hound tracks that went up and down along the path on the ice, and that place where the toenails had dug in as if the hound had reared to put its paws on the wolfer's shoulders. If there was ever a time when Schulz would have welcomed the hound, greeted it, talked to it in his mixture of baby talk, questions, and grunts of endearment, this would have been the time. The coming of the dog should have made the night thirty degrees warmer and hours shorter.

Surely the hound, having pursued him for ten miles or so, would have stuck close, kept him company in his pacing, stood with him whenever he built up the fire a little and warmed his feet and hands. But it had walked up and down the path only two or three times. Twice it had lain down. Once, perhaps, it had lapped up snow.

And this hound, following Schulz's tracks with blind love—and unfed all day, since it had escaped before the Schulz boy could feed it—had passed, sniffed around, perhaps eaten of, the carcass of the yearling at Bates Camp.

Suppose Schulz had looked up from his stiff pacing and seen the hound rolling, or feverishly gulping snow. Suppose that in the murk, out of the corner of his eye, he had seen it stagger to its feet. Suppose, in the flicker of the fire, its great jaws had been opening and closing and that foam had dripped from its chops. Suppose a tight moment of alarm and disbelief, a tableau of freezing man and crazed hound, the deadliest creature and his deadly pet. Suppose it started toward him. Suppose the wolfer spoke to it, and it came on; yelled his peremptory command of "Charge!" which usually dropped the dog as if it had been poleaxed—and the hound still came on. Suppose he yelled a cracking yell, and the hound lumbered into a gallop, charging him. The spring for the gun, the mitt snatched off between the teeth, the stiffened finger pulling the trigger, a snapshot from the waist: Schulz was a good shot, or a lucky one; he had had to be.

Suppose. I supposed it, I tell you, in a way to give myself gooseflesh. By the vividness of imagination or the freakishness of the fading light, the hound's tracks arranged themselves so that only those decisive, final ones were clear. They led directly from one of the places where it had lain down to the bloody scramble where it had died, and if I read them right they came at a scattering gallop. Standing in the path, Schulz would have fired with the hound no more than thirty feet away. Its momentum had carried it in a rolling plunge twenty feet closer. I stepped it off. When Schulz, with what paralysis in his guts and shaking in his muscles, lowered his gun and went up to the dead pet that his own poison had turned into an enemy, he had only three steps to go.

I went over to the hound and took off his collar, evidence, maybe, or a sort of souvenir. Dude was drooping in the willows with his head down to his knees. It was growing dark, but the fog that had threatened was evidently not going to come on; the moon's shape was in the sky.

What Schulz had done after the shooting of the hound was up for guesses. He had had to stay through the night until he knew which way was which. But then he had made those tracks upriver—whether heading for the T-Down for some reason, or wandering out of his head, or simply, in disgust and despair, starting on foot out of the country.

I would find out tomorrow. Right now it was time I got back to camp. When I led Dude down onto the ice and climbed on, the moon had swum clear, with a big ring around it. There was no aurora; the sky behind the thin remaining mist was blue-black and polished. Just for a second, when I took off a mitt and reached back to unbuckle the saddlebag and put the hound's collar inside, I laid my hand on the marten, stiff-frozen under soft fur. It gave me an unpleasant shock, somehow. I pulled my hand away as if the marten might have bitten me.

Riding up the channel, I heard the wind beginning to whine under the eaves of the cutbanks, and a flurry of snow came down on me, and a trail of drift blew eastward ahead of me down the middle of the ice. The moon sat up above me like a polished brass cuspidor in a high-class saloon, but that could be deceptive; within minutes the wrack of another storm could be blowing it under.

Then I rode out into an open reach, and something touched my face, brushed it and was gone, then back again. The willows shuddered in a gust. Dude's head came up, and so did mine, because that wind blew out of hundreds of miles of snowy waste as if it wafted across orange groves straight from Florida: instantly, in its first breath, there was a promise of incredible spring. I have felt the beginnings of many a chinook; I never felt one that I liked better than that one.

Before I reached Bates I was riding with my earlaps up and my collar open. I had heard a willow or two shed its load of snow and snap upright. The going under Dude's feet was no longer the squeaky dryness of hard cold, but had gone mushy.

By morning the coulees and draws would be full of the sound of water running under the sagged and heavied drifts; the rims of the river valley and patches of watery prairie might be worn bare and brown. There might be cattle on their feet again, learning again to bawl, maybe even working up toward the benches, because this was a wind they could face, and the prairie wool that had been only inches below their feet all winter would be prickling up into sight. Something—not much but something—might yet be saved out of that winter.

That night I went to bed full of the sense of rescue, happy as a boy scenting spring, eased of a long strain, and I never thought until morning, when I looked out with the chinook still blowing strong and saw the channel of the Whitemud running ten inches of water on top of the ice, that now I wouldn't be able to follow to their end the single line of tracks, by that time pursuing nothing and unpursued, that led upriver into ambiguity. By the time I woke up, Schulz's last tracks were on their way toward the Milk and the Missouri in the spring breakup; and so was his last fire; and so, probably was the body of his great hound; and so, for all I or anyone else ever found out, was he.

CARRION
SPRING

∎   ∎   ∎

The moment she came to the door she could smell it, not really rotten and not coming from any particular direction, but sweet-ish, faintly sickening, sourceless, filling the whole air the way a river's water can taste of weeds—the carrion smell of a whole country breathing out in the first warmth across hundreds of square miles.

Three days of chinook had uncovered everything that had been under snow since November. The yard lay discolored and ugly, gray ashpile, rusted cans, spilled lignite, bones. The clinkers that had given them winter footing to privy and stable lay in raised gray wavers across the mud; the strung lariats they had used for lifelines in blizzardy weather had dried out and sagged to the ground. Muck was knee deep down in the corrals by the sod-roofed stable; the whitewashed logs were yellowed at the corners from dogs lifting their legs against them. Sunken drifts around the hay yard were a reminder of how many times the boys had had to shovel out there to keep the calves from walking into the stacks across the top of them. Across the wan and disheveled yard the willows were bare, and beyond them the floodplain hill was brown. The sky was roiled with gray cloud.

Matted, filthy, lifeless, littered, the place of her winter imprisonment was exposed, ugly enough to put gooseflesh up her backbone, and with the carrion smell over all of it. It was like a bad and disgusting wound, infected wire cut or proud flesh or the gangrene of frostbite, with the bandage off. With her packed trunk and her telescope bag and two loaded grain sacks behind her, she stood in the door waiting for Ray to come with the buckboard, and she was sick to be gone.

Yet when he did come, with the boys all slopping through the mud behind him, and they threw her trunk and telescope and bags into the buckboard and tied the tarp down and there was nothing left to do but go, she faced them with a sudden, desolating desire to cry. She laughed, and caught her lower lip under her teeth and bit down hard on it, and went around to shake one hooflike hand after the other, staring into each face in turn and seeing in each something that made it all the harder to say something easy: Goodbye. Red-bearded, black-bearded, gray-bristled, clean-shaven (for her?), two of them with puckered sunken scars on the cheekbones, all of them seedy, matted-haired, weathered and cracked as old lumber left out for years, they looked sheepish, or sober, or cheerful, and said things like, "Well, Molly, have you a nice trip, now," or "See you in Malta maybe." They had been her family. She had looked after them, fed them, patched their clothes, unraveled old socks to knit them new ones, cut their hair, lanced their boils, tended their wounds. Now it was like the gathered-in family parting at the graveside after someone's funeral.

She had begun quite openly to cry. She pulled her cheeks down, opened her mouth, dabbed at her eyes with her knuckles, laughed. "Now you all take care," she said. "And come see us, you hear? Jesse? Rusty? Slip? Buck, when you come I'll fix you a better patch on your pants than that one. Goodbye, Panguingue, you were the best man I had on the coal scuttle. Don't you forget me. Little Horn, I'm *sorry* we ran out of pie fixings. When you come to Malta I'll make you a peach pie a yard across."

She could not have helped speaking their names, as if to name them were to insure their permanence. But she knew that though she might see them, or most of them, when Ray brought the drive in to Malta in July, these were friends who would soon be lost for good. They had already got the word: sweep the range and sell everything—steers, bulls, calves, cows—for whatever it would bring. Put a For Sale sign on the ranch, or simply abandon it. The country had rubbed its lesson in. Like half the outfits between the Milk and the CPR, the T-Down was quitting. As for her, she was quitting first.

She saw Ray slumping, glooming down from the buckboard seat with the reins wrapped around one gloved hand. Dude and Dinger were hipshot in the harness. As Rusty and Little Horn gave Molly a hand up to climb the wheel, Dude raised his tail and dropped an oaty bundle of dung on the singletree, but she did not even bother to make a face or say something provoked and joking. She was watching Ray, looking right into his gray eyes and his somber dark face and seeing all at once what the winter of disaster had done to him. His cheek, like Ed's and Rusty's, was puckered with frost scars; frost had nibbled at the lobes of his ears; she could see the strain of bone-cracking labor, the bitterness of failure, in the lines from his nose to the corners of his mouth. Making room for her, he did not smile. With her back momentarily to the others, speaking only for him, she said through her tight teeth, "Let's git!"

Promptly—he was always prompt and ready—he plucked whip from whipsocket. The tip snapped on Dinger's haunch, the lurch of the buggy threw her so that she could cling and not have to turn to reveal her face. "Goodbye!" she cried, more into the collar of her mackinaw than to them, throwing the words over her shoulder like a flower or a coin, and tossed her left hand in the air and shook it. The single burst of their voices chopped off into silence. She heard only the grate of the tires in gravel; beside her the wheel poured yellow drip. She concentrated on it, fighting her lips that wanted to blubber.

"This could be bad for a minute," Ray said. She looked up. Obediently she clamped thumb and finger over her nose. To their right, filling half of Frying Pan Flat, was the boneyard, two acres of carcasses scattered where the boys had dragged them after skinning them out when they found them dead in the brush. It did not seem that off there they could smell, for the chinook was blowing out in light airs from the west. But when she let go her nose she smelled it rich and rotten, as if it rolled upwind the way water runs upstream in an eddy.

Beside her Ray was silent. The horses were trotting now in the soft sand of the patrol trail. On both sides the willows were gnawed down to stubs, broken and mouthed and gummed off by starving cattle. There was floodwater in the low spots, and the sound of running water under the drifts of every side coulee.

Once Ray said, "Harry Willis says a railroad survey's coming right up the Whitemud valley this summer. S'pose that'll mean homesteaders in here, maybe a town."

"I s'pose."

"Make it a little easier when you run out of prunes, if there was a store at Whitemud."

"Well," she said, "we won't be here to run out," and then immediately, as she caught a whiff that gagged her, "Pee-you! Hurry up!"

Ray did not touch up the team. "What for?" he said. "To get to the next one quicker?"

She appraised the surliness of his voice, and judged that some of it was general disgust and some of it was aimed at her. But what did he want? Every time she made a suggestion of some outfit around Malta or Chinook where he might get a job he humped his back and looked impenetrable. What *did* he want? To come back here and take another licking? When there wasn't even a cattle outfit left, except maybe the little ones like the Z-X and the Lazy-S? And where one winter could kill you, as it had just killed the T-Down? She felt like yelling at him, "Look at your face. Look at your hands—you can't open them even halfway, for calluses. For what? Maybe three thousand cattle left out of ten thousand, and them skin and bone. Why wouldn't I be glad to get out? Who *cares* if there's a store at Whitemud? You're just like an old bulldog with his teeth clinched in somebody's behind, and it'll take a pry-bar to make you unclinch!" She said nothing; she forced herself to breathe evenly the tainted air.

Floodwater forced them out of the bottoms and up onto the second floodplain. Below them Molly saw the river astonishingly wide, pushing across willow bars and pressing deep into the cutbank bends. She could hear it, when the wheels went quietly—a hushed roar like wind. Cattle were balloonily afloat in the brush where they had died. She saw a brindle longhorn waltz around the deep water of a bend with his legs in the air, and farther on a whiteface that stranded momentarily among flooded rosebushes, and rotated free, and stranded again.

Their bench was cut by a side coulee, and they tipped and rocked down, the rumps of the horses back against the dashboard, Ray's hand on the brake, the shoes screeching mud from the tires. There was brush in the bottom, and stained drifts still unmelted. Their wheels sank in slush, she hung to the seat rail, they righted, the lines cracked across the muscling rumps as the team dug in and lifted them out of the cold, snowbank breath of the draw. Then abruptly, in a hollow on the right, dead eyeballs stared at her from between spraddled legs, horns and tails and legs were tangled in a starved mass of bone and hide not yet, in that cold bottom, puffing with the gases of decay. They must have been three deep—piled on one another, she supposed, while drifting before some one of the winter's blizzards.

A little later, accosted by a stench so overpowering that she breathed it in deeply as if to sample the worst, she looked to the left and saw a longhorn, its belly blown up ready to pop, hanging by neck and horns from a tight clump of alder and black birch where the snow had left him. She saw the wind make catspaws in the heavy winter hair.

"Jesus," Ray said, "when you find 'em in *trees!*"

His boots, worn and whitened by many wettings, were braced against the dash. From the corner of her eye Molly could see his glove, its wrist-lace open. His wrist looked as wide as a doubletree, the sleeve of his Levi jacket was tight with forearm. The very sight of his strength made her hate the tone of defeat and outrage in his voice. Yet she appraised the tone cunningly, for she did not want him somehow butting his bullheaded way back into it. There were better things they could do than break their backs and hearts in a hopeless country a hundred miles from anywhere.

With narrowed eyes, caught in an instant vision, she saw the lilac bushes by the front porch of her father's house, heard the screen door bang behind her brother Charley (screen doors!), saw people passing, women in dresses, maybe all going to a picnic or a ballgame down in the park by the river. She passed the front of McCabe's General Store and through the window saw the counters and shelves: dried apples, dried peaches, prunes, tapioca, Karo syrup, everything they had done without for six weeks; and new white-stitched overalls, yellow horsehide gloves, varnished axe handles, barrels of flour and bags of sugar, shiny boots and workshoes, counters full of calico and flowered voile and crepe de chine and curtain net, whole stacks of flypaper stuck sheet to sheet, jars of peppermints and striped candy and horehound. . . . She giggled.

"What?" Ray's neck and shoulders were so stiff with muscle that he all but creaked when he turned his head.

"I was just thinking. Remember the night I used our last sugar to make that batch of divinity, and dragged all the boys in after bedtime to eat it?"

"Kind of saved the day," Ray said. "Took the edge off ever'body."

"Kind of left us starving for sugar, too. I can still see them picking up those little bitty dabs of fluff with their fingers like tongs, and stuffing them in among their whiskers and making faces, *yum yum*, and wondering what on earth had got into me."

"Nothing got into you. You was just fed up. We all was."

"Remember when Slip picked up that pincushion I was tatting a cover for, and I got sort of hysterical and asked him if he knew what it was? Remember what he said? 'It a doll piller, ain't it, Molly?' I thought I'd die."

She shook her head angrily. Ray was looking sideward at her in alarm. She turned her face away and stared down across the water that spread nearly a half-mile wide in the bottoms. Dirty foam and brush circled in the eddies. She saw a slab cave from an almost drowned cutbank and sink bubbling. From where they drove, between the water and the outer slope that rolled up to the high prairie, the Cypress Hills made a snow-patched, tree-darkened dome across the west. The wind came off them mild as milk. Poisoned! she told herself, and dragged it deep into her lungs.

She was aware again of Ray's gray eye. "Hard on you," he said. For some reason he made her mad, as if he were accusing her of bellyaching. She felt how all the time they bumped and rolled along the shoulder of the river valley they had this antagonism between them like a snarl of barbed wire. You couldn't reach out anywhere without running into it. Did he blame her for going home, or what? What did he expect her to do, come along with a whole bunch of men on that roundup, spend six or eight weeks in pants out among the carcasses? And then what?

A high, sharp whicker came downwind. The team chuckled and surged into their collars. Looking ahead, she saw a horse—picketed or hobbled—and a man who leaned on something—rifle?—watching them. "Young Schulz," Ray said, and then here came the dogs, four big bony hounds. The team began to dance. Ray held them in tight and whistled the buggywhip in the air when the hounds got too close.

Young Schulz, Molly saw as they got closer, was leaning on a shovel, not a rifle. He had dug a trench two or three feet deep and ten or twelve long. He dragged a bare forearm across his forehead under a muskrat cap: a sullen-faced boy with eyes like dirty ice. She supposed he had been living all alone since his father had disappeared. Somehow he made her want to turn her lips inside out. A wild man, worse than an Indian. She had not liked his father and she did not like him.

The hounds below her were sniffing at the wheels and testing the air up in her direction, wagging slow tails. "What've you got, wolves?" Ray asked.

"Coyotes."

"Old ones down there?"

"One, anyway. Chased her in."

"Find any escape holes?"

"One. Plugged it."

"You get 'em the hard way," Ray said. "How've you been doing on wolves?"

The boy said a hard four-letter word, slanted his eyes sideward at Molly in something less than apology—acknowledgment, maybe. "The dogs ain't worth a damn without Puma to kill for 'em. Since he got killed they just catch up with a wolf and run alongside him. I dug out a couple dens."

With his thumb and finger he worked at a pimple under his jaw. The soft wind blew over them, the taint of carrion only a suspicion, perhaps imaginary. The roily sky had begun to break up in patches of blue. Beside her Molly felt the solid bump of Ray's shoulder as he twisted to cast a weather eye upward. "Going to be a real spring day," he said. To young Schulz he said, "How far in that burrow go, d'you s'pose?"

"Wouldn't ordinarily go more'n twenty feet or so."

"Need any help diggin'?"

The Schulz boy spat. "Never turn it down."

"Ray . . ." Molly said. But she stopped when she saw his face.

"Been a long time since I helped dig out a coyote," he said. He watched her as if waiting for a reaction. "Been a long time since I did anything for *fun*."

"Oh, go ahead!" she said. "Long as we don't miss that train."

"I guess we can make Maple Creek by noon tomorrow. And you ain't in such a hurry you have to be there sooner, are you?"

She had never heard so much edge in his voice. He looked at her as if he hated her. She turned so as to keep the Schulz boy from seeing her face, and for just a second she and Ray were all alone up there, eye to eye. She laid a hand on his knee. "I don't know what it is," she said. "Honestly I don't. But you better work it off."

Young Schulz went back to his digging while Ray unhitched and looped the tugs and tied the horses to the wheels. Then Ray took the shovel and began to fill the air with clods. He moved more dirt than the Fresno scrapers she had seen grading the railroad back home; he worked as if exercising his muscles after a long layoff, as if spring had fired him up and set him to running. The soil was sandy and came out in clean brown shovelfuls. The hounds lay back out of range and watched. Ray did not look toward Molly, or say anything to Schulz. He just moved dirt as if dirt was his worst enemy. After a few minutes Molly pulled the buffalo robe out of the buckboard and spread it on the drying prairie. By that time it was getting close to noon. The sun was full out; she felt it warm on her face and hands.

The coyote hole ran along about three feet underground. From where she sat she could look right up the trench, and see the black opening at the bottom when the shovel broke into it. She could imagine the coyotes crammed back at the end of their burrow, hearing the noises and seeing the growing light as their death dug toward them, and no way out, nothing to do but wait.

Young Schulz took the shovel and Ray stood out of the trench, blowing. The violent work seemed to have made him more cheerful. He said to Schulz, when the boy stopped and reached a gloved hand up the hole, "She comes out of there in a hurry she'll run right up your sleeve."

Schulz grunted and resumed his digging. The untroubled sun went over, hanging almost overhead, and an untroubled wind stirred the old grass. Over where the last terrace of the floodplain rolled up to the prairie the first gopher of the season sat up and looked them over. A dog moved, and he disappeared with a flirt of his tail. Ray was rolling up his sleeves, whistling loosely between his teeth. His forearms were white, his hands blackened and cracked as the charred ends of sticks. His eyes touched her—speculatively, she thought. She smiled, making a forgiving, kissing motion of her mouth, but all he did in reply was work his eyebrows, and she could not tell what he was thinking.

Young Schulz was poking up the hole with the shovel handle. Crouching in the trench in his muskrat cap, he looked like some digging animal;

she half expected him to put his nose into the hole and sniff and then start throwing dirt out between his hind legs.

Then in a single convulsion of movement Schulz rolled sideward. A naked-gummed thing of teeth and gray fur shot into sight, scrambled at the edge, and disappeared in a pinwheel of dogs. Molly leaped to the heads of the horses, rearing and wall-eyed and yanking the light buck-board sideways, and with a hand in each bridle steadied them down. Schulz, she saw, was circling the dogs with the shotgun, but the dogs had already done it for him. The roaring and snapping tailed off. Schulz kicked the dogs away and with one quick flash and circle and rip tore the scalp and ears off the coyote. It lay there wet, mauled, bloody, with its pink skull bare—a little dog brutally murdered. One of the hounds came up, sniffed with its neck stretched out, sank its teeth in the coyote's shoulder, dragged it a foot or two.

"Ray . . ." Molly said.

He did not hear her; he was blocking the burrow with the shovel blade while Schulz went over to his horse. The boy came back with a red willow stick seven or eight feet long, forked like a small slingshot at the end. Ray pulled away the shovel and Schulz twisted in the hole with the forked end of the stick. A hard grunt came out of him, and he backed up, pulling the stick from the hole. At the last moment he yanked hard, and a squirm of gray broke free and rolled and was pounced on by the hounds.

This time Ray kicked them aside. He picked up the pup by the tail, and it hung down and kicked its hind legs a little. Schulz was down again, probing the burrow, twisting, probing again, twisting hard.

Again he backed up, working the entangled pup out carefully until it was in the open, and then landing it over his head like a sucker from the river. The pup landed within three feet of the buckboard wheel, and floundered, stunned. In an instant Molly dropped down and smoth-ered it in clothes, hands, arms. There was snarling in her very ear, she was bumped hard, she heard Ray yelling, and then he had her on her feet. From his face, she thought he was going to hit her. Against her middle, held by the scruff and grappled with the other arm, the pup snapped and slavered with needle teeth. She felt the sting of bites on her hands and wrists. The dogs ringed her, ready to jump, kept off by Ray's kicking boot.

"God A'mighty," Ray said, "you want to get yourself killed?"

"I didn't want the dogs to get him."

"No. What are you going to do with him? We'll just have to knock him in the head."

"I'm going to keep him."

"In Malta?"

"Why not?"

He let go his clutch on her arm. "He'll be a cute pup for a month and then he'll be a chicken thief and then somebody'll shoot him."

"At least he'll have a little bit of a life. Get *away*, you dirty, murdering . . . !" She cradled the thudding little body along one arm under her mackinaw, keeping her hold in the scruff with her right hand, and turned herself away from the crowding hounds. "I'm going to tame him," she said. "I don't care what you say."

"Scalp's worth three dollars," Schulz said from the edge of the ditch.

Ray kicked the dogs back. His eyes, ordinarily so cool and gray, looked hot. The digging and the excitement did not seem to have taken the edge off whatever was eating him. He said, "Look, maybe you have to go back home to your folks, but you don't have to take a menagerie along. What are you going to do with him on the train?"

But now it was out. He did blame her. "You think I'm running out on you," she said.

"I just said you can't take a menagerie back to town."

"You said *maybe* I had to go home. Where else would I go? You're going to be on roundup till July. The ranch is going to be sold. Where on earth *would* I go but home?"

"You don't have to stay. You don't have to make me go back to ridin' for some outfit for twenty a month and found."

His dark, battered, scarred face told her to be quiet. Dipping far down in the tight pocket of his Levi's he brought up his snap purse and took from it three silver dollars. Young Schulz, who had been probing the den to see if anything else was there, climbed out of the ditch and took the money in his dirty chapped hand. He gave Molly one cool look with his dirty-ice eyes, scalped the dead pup, picked up shotgun and twisting-stick and shovel, tied them behind the saddle, mounted, whistled at the dogs, and with barely a nod rode off toward the northeastern flank of the Hills. The hounds fanned out ahead of him, running loose and easy. In the silence their departure left behind, a clod broke and rolled into the ditch. A gopher piped somewhere. The wind moved quiet as breathing in the grass.

Molly drew a breath that caught a little—a sigh for their quarreling, for whatever bothered him so deeply that he gloomed and grumped and asked something impossible of her—but when she spoke she spoke around it. "No thanks for your digging."

"He don't know much about living with people."

"He's like everything else in this country, wild and dirty and thankless."

In a minute she would really start feeling sorry for herself. But why not? Did it ever occur to him that since November, when they came across the prairie on their honeymoon in this same buckboard, she had seen exactly one woman, for one day and a night? Did he have any idea how she had felt, a bride of three weeks, when he went out with the boys on late fall roundup and was gone two weeks, through three different blizzards, while she stayed home and didn't know whether he was dead or alive?

"If you mean me," Ray said, "I may be wild and I'm probably dirty, but I ain't thankless, honey." Shamed, she opened her mouth to reply, but he was already turning away to rummage up a strap and a piece of whang leather to make a collar and leash for her pup.

"Are you hungry?" she said to his shoulders.

"Any time."

"I put up some sandwiches."

"O.K."

"Oh, Ray," she said, "let's not crab at each other! Sure I'm glad we're getting out. Is that so awful? I hate to see you killing yourself bucking this *hopeless* country. But does that mean we have to fight? I thought maybe we could have a picnic like we had coming in, back on that slough where the ducks kept coming in and landing on the ice and skidding end over end. I don't know, it don't hardly seem we've laughed since."

"Well," he said, "it ain't been much of a laughing winter, for a fact." He had cut down a cheekstrap and tied a rawhide thong to it. Carefully she brought out the pup and he buckled the collar around its neck, but when she set it on the ground it backed up to the end of the thong, cringing and showing its naked gums, so that she picked it up again and let it dig along her arm, hunting darkness under her mackinaw.

"Shall we eat here?" Ray said. "Kind of a lot of chewed-up coyote around."

"Let's go up on the bench."

"Want to tie the pup in the buckboard?"

"I'll take him. I want to get him used to me."

"O.K.," he said. "You go on. I'll tie a nosebag on these nags and bring the robe and the lunchbox."

She walked slowly, not to scare the pup, until she was up the little bench and onto the prairie. From up there she could see not only the Cypress Hills across the west, but the valley of the Whitemud breaking out of them, and a big slough, spread by floodwater, and watercourses going both ways out of it, marked by thin willows. Just where the Whitemud emerged from the hills were three white dots—the Mountie post, probably, or the Lazy-S, or both. The sun was surprisingly warm, until she counted up and found that it was May 8. It ought to be warm.

Ray brought the buffalo robe and spread it, and she sat down. One-handed because she had the thong of the leash wrapped around her palm, she doled out sandwiches and hard-boiled eggs. Ray popped a whole egg in his mouth and chewing, pointed. "There goes the South Fork of the Swift Current, out of the slough. The one this side, that little scraggle of willows you can see, empties into the Whitemud. That slough sits right on the divide and runs both ways. You don't see that very often."

She appraised his tone. He was feeling better. For that matter, so was she. It had turned out a beautiful day, with big fair-weather clouds coasting over. She saw the flooded river bottoms below them, on the left, darken to winter and then sweep bright back to spring again while she could have counted no more than ten. As she moved, the coyote pup clawed and scrambled against her side, and she said, wrinkling her nose in her freckleface smile, "If he started eating me, I wonder if I could keep from yelling? Did you ever read that story about the boy that hid the fox under his clothes and the fox started eating a hole in him and the boy never batted an eye, just let himself be chewed?"

"No, I never heard that one," Ray said. "Don't seem very likely, does it?" He lay back and turned his face, shut-eyed, into the sun. Now and then his hand rose to feed bites of sandwich into his mouth.

"The pup's quieter," Molly said. "I bet he'll tame. I wonder if he'd eat a piece of sandwich?"

"Leave him be for a while, I would."

"I guess."

His hand reached over blindly and she put another sandwich into its pincer claws. Chewing, he came up on an elbow; his eyes opened, he stared a long time down into the flooded bottoms and then across toward the slough and the hills. "Soon as the sun comes out, she don't look like the same country, does she?"

Molly said nothing. She watched his nostrils fan in and out as he sniffed. "No smell up here, do you think?" he said. But she heard the direction he was groping in, the regret that could lead, if they did not watch out, to some renewed and futile hope, and she said tartly, "I can smell it, all right."

He sighed. He lay back and closed his eyes. After about three minutes he said, "Boy, what a day, though. I won't get through on the patrol trail goin' back. The ice'll be breakin' up before tonight, at this rate. Did you hear it crackin' and poppin' a minute ago?"

"I didn't hear it."

"Listen."

They were still. She heard the soft wind move in the prairie wool, and beyond it, filling the background, the hushed and hollow noise of the floodwater, sigh of drowned willows, suck of whirlpools, splash and guggle as cutbanks caved, and the steady push and swash and ripple of moving water. Into the soft rush of sound came a muffled report like a tree cracking, or a shot a long way off. "Is that it?" she said. "Is that the ice letting loose?"

"Stick around till tomorrow and you'll see that whole channel full of ice."

Another shadow from one of the big flat-bottomed clouds chilled across them and passed. Ray said into the air, "Harry Willis said this railroad survey will go right through to Medicine Hat. Open up this whole country."

Now she sat very still, stroking the soft bulge of the pup through the cloth.

"Probably mean a town at Whitemud."

"You told me."

"With a store that close we couldn't get quite so snowed in as we did this winter."

Molly said nothing, because she dared not. They were a couple that, like the slough spread out northwest of them, flowed two ways, he to this wild range, she back to town and friends and family. And yet in the thaw of one bright day, their last together up here north of the Line, she teetered. She feared the softening that could start her draining toward his side.

"Molly," Ray said, and made her look at him. She saw him as the country and the winter had left him, weathered and scarred. His eyes were gray and steady, marksman's eyes.

She made a wordless sound that sounded in her own ears almost a groan. "You want awful bad to stay," she said.

His tong fingers plucked a strand of grass, he bit it between his teeth, his head went slowly up and down.

"But how?" she said. "Do you want to strike the Z-X for a job, or the Lazy-S, or somebody? Do you want to open a store in Whitemud for when the railroad comes through, or what?"

"Haven't you figured that out yet?" he said. "Kept waitin' for you to see it. I want to buy the T-Down."

"You *what?*"

"I want us to buy the T-Down and make her go."

She felt that she went all to pieces. She laughed. She threw her hands around so that the pup scrambled and clawed at her side. "Ray Henry," she said, "you're crazy as a bedbug. Even if it made any sense, which it doesn't, where'd we get the money?"

"Borrow it."

"Go in debt to stay up *here?*"

"Molly," he said, and she heard the slow gather of determination in his voice, "when else could we pick up cattle for twenty dollars a head with sucking calves thrown in? When else could we get a whole ranch layout for a few hundred bucks? That Goodnight herd we were running was the best herd in Canada, maybe anywhere. This spring roundup we could take our pick of what's left, including bulls, and put our brand on 'em and turn 'em into summer range and drive everything else to Malta. We wouldn't want more than three-four hundred head. We can swing that much, and we can cut enough hay to bring that many through even a winter like this last one."

She watched him; her eyes groped and slipped. He said, "We're never goin' to have another chance like this as long as we live. This country's goin' to change; there'll be homesteaders in here soon as the railroad comes. Towns, stores, what you've been missin'. Women folks. And we can sit out here on the Whitemud with good hay land and good range and just make this God darned country holler uncle."

"How long?" she said. "How long have you been thinking this way?"

"Since we got John's letter."

"You never said anything."

"I kept waitin' for you to get the idea yourself. But you were hell bent to get out."

She escaped his eyes, looked down, shifted carefully to accommodate the wild thing snuggled in darkness at her waist, and as she moved, her foot scuffed up the scalloped felt edge of the buffalo robe. By her toe was a half-crushed crocus, palely lavender, a thing so tender and un- believable in the waste of brown grass under the great pour of sky that she cried out, "Why, good land, look at that!"—taking advantage of it both as discovery and as diversion.

"Crocus?" Ray said, bending. "Don't take long, once the snow goes."

It lay in her palm, a thing lucky as a four-leaf clover, and as if it had had some effect in clearing her sight, Molly looked down the south- facing slope and saw it tinged with faintest green. She put the crocus to her nose, but smelled only a mild freshness, an odor no more showy than that of grass. But maybe enough to cover the scent of carrion.

Her eyes came up and found Ray's watching her steadily. "You think we could do it," she said.

"I know we could."

"It's a funny time to start talking that way, when I'm on my way out."

"You don't have to stay out."

Sniffing the crocus, she put her right hand under the mackinaw until her fingers touched fur. The pup stiffened but did not turn or snap. She moved her fingers softly along his back, willing him tame. For some reason she felt as if she might burst out crying.

"Haven't you got any ambition to be the first white woman in five hundred miles?" Ray said.

Past and below him, three or four miles off, she saw the great slough darken under a driving cloud shadow and then brighten to a blue that danced with little wind-whipped waves. She wondered what happened to the ice in a slough like that, whether it went on down the little flooded creeks to add to the jams in the Whitemud and Swift Current, or whether it just rose to the surface and gradually melted there. She didn't suppose it would be spectacular like the break-up in the river.

"Mumma and Dad would think we'd lost our minds," she said. "How much would we have to borrow?"

"Maybe six or eight thousand."

"Oh, Lord!" She contemplated the sum, a burden of debt heavy enough to pin them down for life. She remembered the winter, six months of unremitting slavery and imprisonment. She lifted the crocus and laid it against Ray's dark scarred cheek.

"You should never wear lavender," she said, and giggled at the very idea, and let her eyes come up to his and stared at him, sick and scared. "All right," she said. "If it's what you want."

HE WHO SPITS AT THE SKY

I had some pictures to take of the opening of a neighborhood house down by Exposition Park, and it was nearly ten before I got back to Hollywood. I had never been to Mazur's house. The address Carol had given me was on a cross street just off Franklin. As I parked and walked in, away from the snarl and slash of traffic, the quiet of a dark pocketed neighborhood closed around me. The air was damp and soft, as if it should smell of flowers, but I had such a thick head cold I could hardly breathe, much less smell the scented evening air of the city of the angels. If you want to know how I was feeling, press your face down into a tub of modeling clay and inhale.

The Mazur house turned out to be a sort of Frank Lloyd Wright prairie-style bungalow with Bauhaus extras. The picture window in front, showing fluted drapes glowing from the light inside, was obviously part of a remodeling job. So was the dim glass room that reached out along the side and threw the shadows of big cut-leaf philodendrons onto the lawn. A spotlight burned from under the low eaves into a flaming eucalyptus tree.

I heard voices through the door—pretty loud voices—but if it occurred to me that it was bad tactics to bring the Red Car kids straight out of San Quentin into a binge, I would have thought it Mazur's lookout, or the committee's. I was a spectator; I only took the pictures. It was 1946; I was just out of the army; I was a photographer for the Russell Foundation only while I waited for something better to turn up. If I had already stayed longer than I had expected to, that was Carol's doing—don't get the idea that I was either dedicated or involved. Juvenile delinquents, Mexican or otherwise, never appealed to me that much as a way of life. I was a professional photographer, Mr. Cool from up the coulee, in perfect health except for an infected frontal sinus, and my principal feeling as I stood on the Mazur doorstep was a hope that things would break up early and let me get home to bed. I found the Benzedrine inhaler in my pocket and dragged at it four or five times, until on the last drag the top of my head chilled suddenly as air came through. Then I replaced the cap and pushed my thumb against the doorbell. Nothing happened. I pushed it again.

This time steps—high heels—the bump of somebody running into something, an exclamation, the smash of breaking glass. I waited. After quite a pause the door opened, and I looked down on the platinum head of Debbie Mazur. She had reached up to open the door while she squatted by the puddle of her spilled drink. Some of her hair had come loose across her forehead. "Goddamn," she said, brooding over the starlike puddle on the hardwood. She dabbed at her dress, pulled herself up by the doorknob and leaned against the door's edge and laughed in a soft four-highball sort of way.

"Hi," she said. "I know you."

It was true, she did. She inspected me. "You're Charlie Prescott, and we've been waiting for you. In a pig's eye. Come in."

She did not get out of the way but leaned in the opening, looking at me. "Oh, Carol!" she called without turning around. Her blue eyes were wide and innocent and by no means so dumb as they sometimes tried to look. She giggled. "I'm the girl that licked all the envelopes," she said. "They're giving me a Carnegie medal. Oh, Carol!"

She moved perhaps four inches and opened the door perhaps six. Her eyes took in my camera bag. "What've you been doing? Working? This late? You look like a goddamn doctor come to deliver the twins." Disdainfully she kicked a fragment of glass across the hall. "Well, come in, come in, get a drink and shake the collective hand. This is a celebration. Virtue has triumphed, and sin is crushed to earth."

She still didn't move back, but I squeezed through and stepped across the puddle of glass and whiskey. It wasn't quite clear to me whether she was keeping the door half closed because of noise and the neighbors or because she wanted me to rub up against her. This last I couldn't help. I got a blast of bourbon and perfume, the glance of an amused blue eye, and a satisfactory glimpse of a plunging neckline where Mrs. Mazur's obvious talents surged up under a froth of lace. Down below somewhere she must have been propped up like an overburdened fruit tree.

"I see," I said (which was true).

Carol came out of the smoke and noise of the living room, and Debbie Mazur shut the door. Twiddling her fingers in farewell, intensely energetic, dressed for a calendar picture, she departed, saying, "Make yourself at home. I got to get a rag, I guess." I put the camera bag behind the door.

"Ah, Charlie," Carol said. "I ought to be kicked for letting you do that job alone. How's your poor cold?"

"Just like id souds." The inhaler had given me ninety seconds of relief; I was as thick again as a sock full of sand.

She reached up and pecked my cheek with a kiss. "Look oudt!" I said. "You'll *get* it, for hell's sake."

Just at that moment Debbie Mazur appeared at the far end of the hall. "Ah, ah!" she said, and vanished again, flapping a tea towel.

"What was that?" I said. "Edvy?"

"Edvy," Carol said. "Cub od id."

Several partitions of the old bungalow must have been knocked out to make the big room we entered. From one side of it, steps went down into the glass solarium; at the far end, double doors opened into a book-lined study. The lights were spots and floods mounted on the walls to throw melodramatic blobs and ovals of brightness against the ceiling. Everybody was in a circle like Boy Scouts at a camporee.

We swam upstream against the voices until they paused and Guy Mazur stood up to reach across chairs and heads to shake hands. You have seen his type often enough, but hardly ever so perfect. He had the tanned skin and light-metal hair of the gracefully middle-aged Southern California demigod. I could imagine him in his earlier years, taking perfect back dives at the Coral Casino, or (for a gag, without losing his dignity) doing handstands and human pyramids with the acrobats and weight lifters on Muscle Beach. Maybe he was that *mens sana in corpore sano* you hear about. Certainly the single word that most described him was "confidence"; he had the air of being utterly at ease while others watched. His voice was a bassoon that played the scales of conviction; it wooed and reconciled and persuaded and reassured. His handshake told you that he was your friend, truly your friend, and that he would always be there when you needed him, but would not push himself forward with a lot of insincere protestations. He was a lawyer associated, in some way I never quite understood, with one of the studios, but he must have given half his time to betterment committees. The campaign that freed the Red Car boys was his initiative from beginning to end; he was much in the papers; his name appeared on the letterheads of two dozen good causes.

"Charlie, my friend!" he said with crinkling eyes. "Glad you got here. This is a great day. We doed it, boy, we doed it."

"Thanks to you," I said.

"Thanks to a hell of a good committee. They can all take a deep, deep bow, no kidding. You know everybody?"

I didn't, but it was easier to pretend I did. I shook some hands, waved at some people. Some I recognized: Jean Gauss, a radio sob sister, homely, freckled like a thrush; Pete Welling, a scriptwriter from MGM; a lawyer named Nemerov; a couple of church do-gooders; a graduate student from UCLA; some old-time radicals who looked as if they had done time with Debs. There were about a dozen of them, densely circled and deeply talkative, with glasses in their hands, and among them, oil trying its best to mix with water, looking grateful and trapped, were the Red Car boys and their chicks. The girls were as expected—little still-faced *pachucas* in tight skirts and high pompadours, wearing adjustable smiles. But the boys were changed from the last time I had seen them. San Quentin had sent them home without their drapes and their ducktails, and they looked like anybody's teenagers, not the baby gangsters, tea pushers, and knife-wielding zoot-suiters that the newspapers used to foam about.

Guy Mazur let himself back into the sofa with a comradely hand on the shoulder of Dago Aguirre, while Dago, angel-faced and deer-eyed, saluted me with a raised can of beer. Then he half stood up and stretched a long way to shake hands. "*Ese*, Señor Pictures." I waved at Chuey

Bernal, out of reach on the other side. Chuey snapped to his feet, bowed stiffly three times. "Greetings, sir," he said. "*Hórale, jefe, hórale.* Good evening. Hello." He collapsed. From his cousin Lupe I got a sidelong smile *provocativo*; she was one of the prettiest, one I had photographed a good deal on the theory that if you are photographing Mexican poverty and social disruption, you may as well photograph it in a shape you would like to take to the movies. Away across the circle, outside of it really, Pepe Garcia was hunched confidentially close to a *pachuca* in a fringed skirt. From him I had what was his closest approach to a greeting—a backward jerk of the head, a thin smile, a glitter as black and expressionless as light flaking off a pair of obsidian chips. He had a high Aztec nose, a bladed face, and he was built long and limber, with a flexed look, a whiplike tension. I have seen a few boxers like that, middleweights at six feet one, with long arms and fast hands.

"I don't think you know all the girls," Carol was saying. "With Dago, that's Luz Esposito. Lupe you know. And with Pepe, that's Angelina Flores." Nods, smiles, salutes. Luz gave me an open, friendly stare, and Lupe wrinkled her nose with laughter; we had a game going that she was my chick. And from Angelina I had exactly the opposite of Pepe's cold glitter—a glance so hot and challenging that my hair prickled. God help the foolish and feeble; this one was a fiery furnace.

I dislike coming to parties late. There is a period during which all that you doused by your entrance has to come to a boil again, and in this case I couldn't miss the perception that the committee and their rescued lambs were having difficulty finding grounds for conversation. Eventually I found myself behind the sofa where Dago and Luz sat, and they twisted around to talk to me.

"It's good to see you out, Dago," I said. "You ought to feel good. How's your mother?"

It came out "bother," but he was too polite to smile. He said that his mother was well and very happy, and his sisters also. I said that Carol and I had looked in now and then, when we could, and he shot me a look from under extravagantly long, curved eyelashes. He had eyes to melt girls down like candles in a heat wave. "You helped her live," he said. "Much thanks."

"It was Carol's idea. And anyway we didn't do much. Anybody would have done as much."

"Nobody did," Dago said. Beside him, Luz burst out that Miss Vaughn was terrific, terrific. She was one you could trust, she had this fairness and this big heart. Whenever she came into a room, something great happened, everything got happy like parades and flags. We looked across to where Carol was talking with Jean Gauss, and she worked her eyebrows at us questioningly. We all laughed. Luz said, looking sidelong, "You two go together, is that it?" I replied that I was working hard to get her to barry be, which set her off in screams. "Man," she said sympathetically, "you got a real cold there. I mean, you're really *plugged*."

"What do you do now?" I asked Dago. "Got a job?"

"I might go up to Idaho. One of my uncles runs a potato farm for a guy. Sort of a *mayordomo*. Where my father was working when he got killed. It's a year-round job. I could take my mother and sisters."

"Coyote," Luz said. "Me too!" I moved my hand to let Guy Mazur lean back in the sofa.

"You?" Dago said. "I guess you could be left behind all right."

She beat on his chest. "You take me, *cholo*, you hear? Left behind, hey? I want to see Idaho, too. *Surote*, I'll show you. I'll chase you up there on a white horse. I'll make you into a doll and stick you full of pins."

Dago cringed away and reached his can of beer from between his feet. From beyond him on the sofa Guy Mazur said, turning, "Did I hear you say you've got a job?"

"Idaho!" Luz said. "Potatoes! Without me, he says. *Jijole!*"

"We can get you a job here," Mazur said.

"Sure," Dago said. "I guess so. I don't know, though; this Idaho looks better for the mother and sisters." His shoulder lifted delicately, and he shadowboxed a moment with the air. "I kind of like to get out of here. You spend a year in that *quinta*, too many people know you, the law is always around digging up some old bone. My dad liked Idaho, till that potato digger ran over him."

Debbie Mazur came with a tray of highballs and wet cans of beer and bent her full armament two feet from Dago's deer eyes. They never flickered. He took a can of beer and thanked her with his even, white-toothed smile, and Guy Mazur, with his arms spread along the sofa back, watched his young wife. His face was smooth, agreeable, half smiling, fond, possibly a bit insistent. When she held the tray toward him, he shook his head. The tray wobbled, and the drinks slopped. Debbie leaned (*O shield her, shield sweet Christabel!*) and sipped some from each glass, watching Guy all the time. His eyes seemed to indulge her, as if he were saying, Well, all right, if you must. Then the momentary untranslatable passage of eyes was broken off and Mazur was saying, "It isn't entirely a matter of what any individual would like, right now. Maybe you could do more good staying."

"More good?"

Mazur laughed and bent forward to straighten his trouser cuff and came up again. "Did you think we got you sprung so you could spend your time on the beach? Boy, you're part of something now that's bigger than you are. You're going to help make the world safe for democracy."

While Dago took a polite and attentive sip of beer, Debbie lingered with her tray. She said, "I should think if they could all get away, it'd be——"

"Action," Mazur was saying to Dago. "Action, education, education, action. All the time. Never letting up." His voice rode over Debbie's and wiped it out, and if my eyes told me anything just then, they told me she could have slapped him. He never even noticed he had cut her off.

"We've got to learn to think of ourselves as part of something bigger. Sure it was important you should get out of jail. But it's even more important we should make sure no such atmosphere of prejudice and race hatred ever gets created again. This town will never learn until the Mexican-Americans stand up and take the rights they're entitled to, fight for 'em, put the bigots and the fascists down. We've got to organize the Mexican community and mold its weakness into strength, and you three are our strongest cards. If you run out, you weaken our hand."

"The Red Car Committee isn't disbanding, then?" I said, and got an incredulous look.

"Disband? Just when we've got them by the short hairs? When you've got them running, that's when you turn loose the cavalry on them."

He had the whole circle listening and nodding. In the middle of it, Debbie suddenly hoisted her tray up on one hand, and standing like the Statue of Liberty, she recited in a nasal, uninflected voice, "We are not disbanding until every racist is down his hole and every discriminatory ordinance is off the books and every sadist is fired from the police force. We are continuing our fight until every roller rink and swimming pool and movie house opens its doors to all alike. We shall not be content until school opportunities and job opportunities are as free to Mexican and colored and Japanese and Chinese and Filipino as to others. . . ."

Guy Mazur ironically applauded while the rest of us stared. It was like hearing a strip queen quote Spinoza. Words like those should come out of peaked immigrant faces, from throats encased in gray utility-weight sweaters. The words didn't match the neckline here, or for that matter the complexion, which I was now convinced was her own, and which was like a Dutch barmaid's. And neither the words nor the looks matched the tone, which was like the edge of a broken bottle.

Staring hotly at her husband, she said, "It seems to me these kids have had their share. If they want to drop it and go live a normal life somewhere, why not? You can't *stuff* them and trot them out as examples of police discrimination all their lives. They're *people*, for God's sake!"

With a little grimace she passed her free hand across the faces of Luz and Dago. "I didn't mean to talk about you behind your back."

Neckline, calendar-cutie dress, platinum hair, and all, she was one of the few there who knew how it might feel to be a zoot-suiter just released from San Quentin and stuck in a room with a bunch of strangers to whom you owed too much. If you demetaled the hair and changed the dress and took the props out from under the figure, you might have quite a woman there.

We were all still, waiting for something. Carol had come around to the end of the sofa near me. From the other end Guy said lightly, "Sweetheart, you were always a great one for the sentimental approach. I'll leave that to you, you do it so well, and you leave the strategy to me. These kids are too important to be private citizens."

Debbie dropped her head sideward in dubious thought, looking at him across the lowered tray of glasses and cans. Her reflection in a beer can diverted her attention; she squinted and dropped her jaw in amazement; she put out her tongue and crossed her eyes. "Is this the face that licked a thousand envelopes?" she cried tragically, and like a relay runner passing the baton, she slapped a drink into the hand of the nearest committee member and lunged away. A brief uneasy silence swirled where she had been.

"The point is," Guy said, "you *are* too important to duck out now. Of course, you can do what you like, but I hope you'll see it the way we do." His smooth gray head lifted, and he called, "Pepe, maybe you ought to hear this." From the outer fringe of the circle Pepe lounged over and sat on the floor. His chick stood behind him, and he rolled his head back against her thighs.

"Now look," Guy said. "We can't get at the Mexican community through the politicians until we get rid of old Coyote on Horseback and the others. They'd sell out their own people any day. We'll get them come election time. But first we have to work through the unions. We've got to break the logjam and organize the pickers, and we've got to work on every other union with any Mexican membership. We want every local in Greater Los Angeles to hear you kids talk. Here you are, guilty of nothing but being Mexican and wearing drapes and maybe having a rumble now and then with kids from some other neighborhood. A kid is found dead in the road one morning, and bang, because you'd been in a fight with his crowd, you're in San Quentin for life. If it weren't for this committee, you'd still be there. I'm not asking for gratitude. All I'm saying is that you owe something to your own people and this democracy we're all trying to create. Ask yourselves if it wouldn't be better to stick right here, take the jobs we'll find you, and tell your story at a lot of meetings."

The pale head lifted again; the smooth face was still, the eyes almost closed. He could have been a UCLA halfback praying in the huddle, a stern, handsome hero headed, after graduation, for a job in public relations or the movies, a hero whose head was full of muscle and the assurance that God was with him in everything, whether he was blocking for the fullback or making a better deal with his sponsor about his athletic scholarship. In some surprise I asked myself when I had started being so mistrustful of him. On the record, he was a dedicated spirit. I was as convinced as he was that the Red Car boys were innocent, had been railroaded on purely circumstantial evidence. And it was no crime, at fifty, to look as if you were still good for five sets of singles or to wear a jacket that some tailor had worked on with love.

"That's all we're asking," Guy said. "Also, in the jobs we find you, you won't have to worry about the record following you. If it does, so much the better. And don't think the committee will be sitting on its duff while you work. Just let me tell you a few things. We're putting out a little book, for instance—the whole history of this case from the dragnet arrests until the final reversal. People all over the country are going to read that Supreme Court decision in thirty-six-point capitals and know the kind of conspiracy that put you behind bars. Now! Jean here has scheduled another radio series on the Mexican-American community. She'll want all three of you one of these days for an interview. Next week? Next week. Then there's the big long-range study Carol and Charlie have been working on. That'll be terrif, simply terrif, and I hear it'll be ready for the press in another couple of months. That reminds me, Charlie, can we beg some photographs to illustrate our booklet? Pete'll see you about it. Finally—don't let this out yet because we haven't got it absolutely in the cage—I think I've got Len Fowler talked into doing a full-length documentary on the *pachucos*, and if he does it, you know how it'll be done. The most, absolutely the most." Cocking a humorous eye at Dago, he added, "How'd you like to star in a picture called *The Kid from Happy Valley*?"

That was a joke. Happy Valley was the barrio these kids from La Loma had always feuded with. They groaned. Chuey Bernal looked all around with an Emmett Kelly crying face, put his hands up in a fighting pose as if someone had pushed him, nodded, half convinced by inner voices, and then shook his head hard. You could almost hear it rattle. "Happy Valley! Those guys are from Gonesville."

"Well, it sounds better than *The Kid from Fifty-eighth Street* or *The Kid from Watts*. And there's a nice irony in Happy Valley. Happy Valley with dirt floors and typhoid wells."

Pepe Garcia, rubbing his head slowly against his girl's thighs, said in a soft voice, "Tell him to work in a beef and we'll go over there and clean the place out for the camera. A real fight scene, man."

Mazur was laughing. "The solidarity of the Mexican-American community," he said. "And you talk about disbanding." It was neatly done; he had got them to make his point for him.

"Listen," said Nemerov, slight, nervous, dark, hopelessly typecast for a conspirator, with a tic in his left eyelid. "Listen. Here's another idea. What if we got together all the great unjust trials—you know, Lawrence Strike and Sacco-Vanzetti and Joe Hill and the Scottsboro Boys and the rest. Red Car too, naturally. Get them all into one set of covers. What an indictment of capitalist justice, eh? What a book that would make. Wouldn't it? Pete, couldn't you take that on? There's bound to be transcripts of all those cases. What do you think, Guy?"

I caught Carol's eye, wordlessly asking her if we had to stick around all night while the cell plotted strategy. The circle had broken out in contributions from several sides. The Red Car boys and their chicks watched and listened. Then Debbie Mazur came in again from somewhere with a bottle of bourbon in her hand and started tipping it into glasses that would hold still. In the kitchen she may have had a quick one to cool her irritation; her eyes as well as her complexion showed it now. "What I think," she said rather loudly, "is that there's a time and place for everything. For God's sake, I gave the maid the night off so we could dance and make whoopee and have a good time. So let's adjourn the meeting and dance."

When she nudged me with the bottle, I turned away and covered my glass with my hand. "Don't you think we ought to dance?" she asked.

I said with a mucous leer, "You bead you ad be?"

"You and me," she said. "The others are all right, but you're the cutest." She flung her arms around my neck and fastened a suckerfish kiss on me. The bottle dangling from her hand banged me between the shoulder blades. I couldn't breathe, and besides that, I was a regular Typhoid Mary, a Great Dismal Swamp where germs throve. Struggling, I broke loose for air and found myself looking right into Guy Mazur's eyes. Something passed off his face like breath off a mirror—or I thought it did. On the other hand, he may have been looking all the time the way he looked when I had got my breath and could see: tolerantly amused.

Debbie's arms were still around my neck. Past her ear I saw the smile on Dago Aguirre's face and Luz's rolling eyes. "Mmmmmmmm-mmmmmmmm-*mmm*!" Debbie said, and plunged off on some other errand. Voices tentatively picked up the talk again, but if she had meant to break up the meeting and force Guy off his planned course, she had done it. We were no longer a captive audience.

Taking my arm, Carol walked me over to the top of the steps looking down into the greenish dusk of the solarium. "You watch it," she said.

I went for the inhaler. "I can't take my eyes off it."

"Don't be a slob, Charlie. I mean really—watch it."

"For God's sake!" I said.

From the study at the far end of the room we heard the scrape of a needle across a record, and then Kid Ory or somebody took off on "Muskrat Ramble."

Raising her voice over the music, Carol said, "I do mean really. Guy and Debbie have had a beef going all evening. If she starts using you to get even with him, you could get hurt. And don't think you could play it cool. She's got too many hormones, and she's too damned smart."

I said, "I'm touched that you should worry, but relax. Otorhinolaryn-
gology is working on your side."

The band, whatever it was, had a real beat. I saw Dago and Luz rise
and excuse themselves from among the feet along the sofa. Chuey was
already up, snapping his fingers and jerking his head with a gone spastic
look while he waited for Lupe to fix her belt. Then Pepe uncoiled from
the floor, folded his chick in his arm, and moved her off with jerky,
light movements. Angelina made even jitterbugging, which is about as
personal as pole vaulting, look sexy. Her face was wiped clean of all
expression; the fringes on her skirt snapped.

As cleanly as a good axman splits a straight-grained block, the music
had split the party in two. A couple of the nameless do-gooders rose
and said good-bye all around. The double doorway of the study was
full of prancing, jerking, twirling shapes. "Muskrat Ramble" rambled
itself out; Chuey Bernal yelped and clapped and staggered with exhaustion; the phonograph squawked a horrible amplified squawk as
somebody scraped the needle again.

"Darling," Guy Mazur called from a deep conversation with Nemerov
and Welling, "can you turn it down a little? We hardly want the
neighbors protesting."

Debbie appeared promptly in the study door. "In the words of Papa
Hemingway, obscenity the neighbors."

"Not a bad idea," Mazur called good-naturedly. "But the committee
might like to hear themselves think."

"Obscenity the committee, too," Debbie said. She disappeared, and
in a moment Louis Armstrong came on in "Gut Bucket Blues," loud
and dirty.

I said to Carol, "What are we? Planners or jivers? Saviors or delinquents?"

"The delinquents seem to be having more fun."

So we danced across the living room and into the study. It was a
good thing to do; they welcomed us. When the record ended, we were
all in a big collapse of laughing and clapping.

"You dance too mean," Chuey told his cousin Lupe. "I can't stand
it."

"Angelina, she's who dances mean," Lupe said. "*Jijole!* Pepe, you
better watch out."

Pepe smiled. Angelina's expressionlessness took on a shading of disdain. Then Debbie, who was minding the phonograph, put on a new

record, set down her drink, and slid her feet in an exaggerated stalk across the floor. "Whose idea was this? I get up a dance and everybody's dancing except me. This is ladies' tag night. Tag!" She slapped Dago's arm, and Luz moved away, giggling. The loudspeaker hidden among the bookshelves was hammering out "Lady Be Good." Chuey tagged Carol, and I leaned against the desk between Luz and Lupe and dragged on the inhaler.

"Poor Señor Pictures," Lupe said. "You're smooched, too." She touched my mouth with a paper napkin and it came off red.

"It's a privilege," I said.

"She's beautiful," Luz said.

"You think so?"

"Oh, yes. Like a movie star."

"Keep your eye on your boyfriend."

"Don't you worry."

"He's already limping. She's wearing him down."

"Oh, limping. That's not her; that's his ankle."

"What's the matter with his ankle?"

"He broke it boxing, up in that jail. In the first round. But he finished the last two rounds with it broken, and still won."

We watched Dago hand off Debbie and turn and pick her up smoothly. She wasn't as smooth as he was, but she was giving her all. They were like a couple of old silent stars restored in their prime, Valentino and La Marr, personal appearance tonight only. And I could imagine Dago in that ring with his broken ankle. Not to quit, not even to grimace: His whole morality and the morality of his kind would have been involved. And however limited that morality was, it was neither small nor weak. "Quite a boy, your Dago," I said.

She smiled at me sidelong with her Indian eyes half closed. "I believe it," she said.

"You want to go to Idaho?"

"What do you think?"

"You'd get to dance squaw dances on some reservation," Lupe said. "What's so good with Idaho?"

"I don't know," Luz said. "I just don't want Dago in no more trouble. He goes out with the guys and they do something, steal a car or beat somebody up, and he won't tell on them and then he's in it, too. Maybe in Idaho there isn't this trouble all the time."

"Maybe in Idaho there isn't anything," Lupe said. "I bet they have last year's movies once a week. John Wayne in *The Fighting Seabees. Que suave!*"

The dance ended, and Debbie planted an enthusiastic kiss on Dago. Lupe cheered; Luz groaned. From the living room the sob sister and the graduate student in need of a haircut came to replenish their drinks. The sob sister smiled upon us, an indulgent auntie. "I wish I could do that. It looks like fun." It was not clear whether she meant the jitter-bugging or the smooching, and her companion did not offer to teach her either one. He said only, "Soda or water?" and after a minute they drifted back to join the planning commission.

Chuey put on a slow, sullen blues, returned Carol to me, and picked up Lupe. Luz with a finger rubbed at the lipstick smear on Dago's mouth, and Pepe, in his controlled slouch, stood with a little smile before Debbie. Angelina twitched her fringed skirt out of the way and leaned with her hands behind her against the bookcases. Her indifference was considerable: She read titles on books; she opened an atlas on the desk. I wondered if I should go over and ask her to dance, but then her eyes wandered back from following Pepe in his graceful, dangerous, foot-placing, foot-withdrawing, spinning-and-releasing, handing-off and taking-back movements with Debbie, and she caught me looking. She so obviously hated me for watching her watch them that I stayed where I was.

We danced for a half hour or so, and before long Debbie had us all smeared with lipstick. She was everybody's big loving sister. She told Dago to go on up to Idaho and not let himself get captured by Guy's medicine show. She leaned back to look into the living room and laugh at the shrunken group there. "The planners," she said. "The thinkers. My God, they think the first thing you do to have fun is elect a chairman pro tem." Touching glasses again with Dago, she gave him an impulsive smooch. The girls laughed, but not very hard.

"Tell you a secret," Debbie said. "Mazur thinks he made you all out of tin and wound you up. Tell you another secret. He thinks he made me out of tin and wound me up, too." Silent and gleeful, she shrank her shoulders together with mirth and at once stiffened and marched around in a marvelously precise imitation of a mechanical toy. When she stopped, she found Pepe Garcia in front of her, wanting to dance again. Chuey put on another record.

Poor Angelina. I have a friend who practices a science he calls kinesics, the language of the body. From Angelina he would have got a plain statement. She had only three kinetic expressions. She could switch her tail, she could be as stiff as a wooden image, and she could shrivel like a wronged vampire. She was at the wronged-vampire stage as she moved in on Dago and led him off in a dance, and if she had danced mean before, she was pure poison now.

Pepe did not notice. Dancing with Debbie, he was a graceful scorpion carrying his stinger ready over his back, and when at the end of the record Debbie as usual flung her arms around him for the kiss, he was ready for her. Their bodies tightened together; their mouths made one mouth. The laughter and the talk died away in the study. I noticed that the kissers were right in the double doors, in plain sight from the living-room plotters. The sudden quiet from the study would make them look up if anything would.

Carol took my hand and led me, walking loud on her heels, to the still-spinning record player. As she turned it off, she hissed at me, "This is getting out of hand!"

"Well, you can't expect them to push her away."

Voices had begun again behind us; apparently Carol's movement had broken up the big clutch in the doorway. "It's all wrong," Carol said. "The kids are getting the idea that anything goes."

"Apparently it does."

"I wish to hell people wouldn't involve other people in their squabbles," she said, and for a second she looked as mean as Angelina. "If anything happens, it's the kids who'll suffer. They're vulnerable."

"Think we should go?"

She did not answer. Somebody was calling for more music. She put something on without looking. "Muskrat Ramble" again. When we turned around, Angelina and Dago were dancing by. She was throwing her little tail around and wearing the smile that the Gorgon made fashionable. Pepe was still dancing with Debbie, who looked about ready to pop out of her cocoon.

"We'd better stay," Carol said. "Somebody's got to keep the peace."

"Shall I hide the liquor? Pull a wire on the record player?"

She shook her head irritably.

"Why don't you talk to her?"

"She's past talking to."

"What if I went around shooting some pictures? Would that help?"

"Ah, Charlie," she said. "You're an angel, you're a darling."

So I went around snapping flashbulbs in people's faces, but the principal effect was to bring on a clamor from Debbie that I shoot her and Pepe jiving. She said she would blow it up into a photomural and paper the wall with it. I did my best to disperse things by posting people in corners with reflectors, but I did not capture Angelina. She and Dago were jiving on their own, and by now she was pure provocation. While I focused, I was aware of her out of the corner of my eye, her feet in an intricate pattern of yield and go, her tail wagging, her fringes snapping, her arms and shoulders suggesting embracings and entwinings and her face like cold stone. A deadly one, what the kids called a *bruja*. I hardly paid attention to the immortalizing of Debbie and Pepe, I was so interested in the other two.

So was Luz interested. I heard her mutter to Carol, "That Angie is mean, man. *Qué relajo!* If she tries anything with Dago, I'll scratch her eyes out."

"Dago's all right," Carol said. He did seem to be, at that. He was not contributing much to Angelina's show but looked amused and a little high. Debbie and Pepe, once I was through shooting them, were back practicing steps. Debbie missed a move, cried out with laughter, threw her arms around Pepe, stepped back, tried it again. She looked blowsy and hypnotized, purple-cheeked, moist as the captain of a Danish ladies' gymnastic team.

"Maybe it's time we all went home," Carol said finally, brightly, to Luz. "You kids have to be careful. You realize that, don't you?"

"*Se siente aviador*," Luz said, still with her eyes on Angelina. "She's high as a pilot. What does she think she's doing?"

Chuey, exhausted, had fallen into a chair and pulled Lupe on top of him and was emitting wolf cries, and Carol was turning her head in anger and bafflement from Debbie to Angelina and back when three of the ancient anarchs paused in the door to say good night. That gave Carol an opening. She shut off the record player. "We've got to go, too. Debbie, can I see you a minute?"

The look Debbie gave her was brighter and bluer than it had any right to be if she was as tight as she had been acting. "*One* minute," she said. "I'm just getting the hang of this."

They went out and off down the hall. By inspiration, a leader much in hope that he had followers, I looked into the living room, saying, "I wonder what they've got settled in there?," and walked in. When I got there, I found that everybody was with me except Pepe and Angelina.

Well, they could stay in the study and weave their hooded necks at one another. The others could be handled.

The planning commission, what was left of it, regarded us with tolerance and some curiosity. "Finally wear yourselves out?" Mazur said. After all the tensions I had been aware of, I was surprised by the big confident boom of his voice. So far as he was concerned, some of us had just been in dancing. And he went straight back to where he had been when Debbie led the kids away. "How would a warehouse job suit you?" he said.

Chuey and Dago looked doubtfully at each other. Both were smeared with Debbie's lipstick. Dago good-naturedly let his head roll as Luz, behind him, yanked at his hair. "Work?" Chuey said. "You get out of that old *calabozo*, you don't feel like diving right into some *job*."

"Out here they don't serve those nice free jailhouse meals," Mazur said.

Chuey fainted halfway to the floor. "Did you ever eat one of those nice free jailhouse meals?"

"Come on," Mazur said. "We can put one of you in a warehouse job at one ninety an hour. Who wants it?"

"Hey," Chuey said. "One ninety? That ain't birdseed."

"ILWU," Mazur said. "A strong union and a great hiring hall." He was looking steadily at Dago.

"I don't know," Dago said softly. "My mother's sort of thinking Idaho."

"You won't get pay like that in the potatoes."

Dago nodded and lifted his shoulders dubiously. Nemerov, looking irritated, put a cigarette between his lips and took out a matchbook and said, with the matchbook in his fingers and the cigarette wobbling from his lips, "You've got a responsibility in this fight, too. Don't you think the rest of us have got families to think about? What do you think we're out here on the barricades for, fun? Nobody's persecuting *us*, or sending *us* to San Quentin." The tic winked in his eyelid; he broke a match trying to light it and tore off another. When he had lighted his cigarette, he shook out the match and dropped it on the floor and looked at Dago hard through the smoke. "We can't have just a few working and the rest getting the benefits. Everybody's got to work."

Dago sat silent, smiling and thinking, with his head a little on one side. Welling broke in in his light, eager voice, running all his words together. He was one of the hardest people to understand I ever listened to. I gathered that Dago would feel pretty crummy if he let others carry the whole load.

"Hey," Chuey said, "if Dago don't want that buck ninety, how about me?"

"I thought you didn't want to work," Nemerov said, still staring at Dago.

"Well, jeez," Chuey said, "I thought the idea was we all had to."

Dago sat still, with the dubious, demurring half-smile on his face and Luz's hand still in his hair. Then all at once Guy Mazur reached his arms along the sofa back in a long stretch. He yawned, and laughed at his own uninhibited noise. "Let's let it ride for now," he said. "You kids are O.K. You'll be in there, I know you will. A few days' vacation won't hurt you any. Let's call the meeting adjourned. How about one for the road?"

His hand slapped Chuey's knee, and as he rose, slapped again on Dago's back. He went over and mended the drinks of Nemerov and Welling and himself.

"Well," I said to Dago, "you've got lots of opportunities for public service."

"Sure. I guess I ought to, when you think about it. It's just . . . I don't know. I kind of think Idaho could be better."

"But you feel grateful to Guy and the committee."

"Why not?" Dago said. "We'd still be in there if it hadn't been for them." He shrugged, a handsome, almost a beautiful boy, and a thoughtful one, with feelings. His laugh was troubled. "Who do you say no to?" he said, and, twisting toward Luz, said something in Spanish or *pachucana*.

"No secrets," I said.

"It's just a saying. *El que al cielo escupe a la cara le cae.*"

"You know I don't speak Spanish."

"You spit at the sky, you get it back in the face," Luz said.

I was very thick in the head, and dry from breathing through my mouth. Cautiously, feeling that I had missed something, I said, "Who's been spitting at the sky?"

"Who hasn't?" Dago said. "Who wouldn't be?" As he pinched out his cigarette and dropped it in his cuff, here came Pepe and Angelina. She was three steps ahead of his easy slouch. They did not look like reconciled lovers; they looked like fighters going to their corners at the bell.

The sight of them curdled me. It was one thing to talk to a pair of nice youngsters like Dago and Luz, and another to deal with that pair. I felt what a mating theirs would be, corrupt seedbed and poisoned seed and a hatch of snakes and dragons, and I was suddenly irritated at Dago and Luz for even associating with such obvious bad ones. I was struggling for air like an asthmatic, and in no mood for Spanish riddles. I didn't care whether Dago himself or Mazur or Pepe or Angelina or Debbie or the whole bunch of them had been spitting at the sky. It was possible even Carol had been. It was more than possible that she ought to change her profession. My head ached, I needed air, and I had already hit the inhaler so many times that I could expect not to sleep.

Debbie and Carol came in from the hall. Debbie had combed her hair and tucked herself in, but she looked sulky. She carried a tray of cheese and crackers; Carol had a percolator that she plugged into a floor plug by the coffee table.

"Well," I said sourly as we walked aside. "What cheer?"

"Tears," Carol said. "Furies. He treats her like a child or a plaything. She's a muff dog who wants to retrieve ducks or trail bears. Nothing new for her, it just blew up tonight. She says he won't let her be a person."

"Is being a person such a delight?"

"Poor Charlie. Do you feel awful?"

"Yes."

"Could you stand it just a few more minutes? I'd like to get some coffee into the kids before they take off. Wouldn't you like some?"

"My head's too stuffed."

"Just five minutes," she said. "How has it been in here?"

"All right. Pressure on Dago to take their warehouse job and be an exhibit."

"Is he going to?"

"I don't know."

"I hope not. Debbie's absolutely right about that part of it."

"They want him here," I said. "Obviously he's the one they could make the most use of. Chuey's a featherbrain, and Pepe is a bad one on sight."

Silent, lips pursed, she stood looking back at them all. It struck me how complex a roomful of people could get, some manipulating others, some feeling responsibility to others, or to causes, or programs, or ideas, or the gang, or the party line, or something else. It was like a ship's deck full of lines and rigging all entangling your feet, and I wanted out. I said, "You start everybody to laughing merrily, and bring the party to a climax, and get some coffee down your kids. I'm going outside for some oxygen."

The night air was marvelously cool and damp, and I opened my mouth and took it in by the lungful. On both sides, down toward Franklin and up toward Los Feliz, went the hum and hush and whisper of traffic. Searchlights scissored around overhead, racing across the belly of the overcast. It seemed very peaceful; nobody was mad at anybody, or using anybody, or getting even with anybody. But my nose was still impenetrably shut, and a sharp pain stabbed me between the eyes as I stepped down onto the lawn.

The spotlight glared into the eucalyptus tree, the only color or decoration in the yard. There were no flower beds. The brilliant tree was posed there in a sweep of grass, its bloodred blossoms bedded in leaves lighted almost white against black holes of shadow. A true, calculated Mazur effect. I walked toward the corner of the solarium, not lighted itself but glowing with diffused light from the living room and shadowy with the hothouse jungle inside. Dew showered up from my toes, and looking back, I saw my own dark tracks. Wet feet would be fine for my cold. But the air was so pleasant and the lawn so soft underfoot that I went on. I was near the corner of the solarium when I saw the movement inside.

I didn't think; I simply stepped into the angle between house and glass porch, where it was darkest. As if a tube had been pushed through my head, I got a sudden, merciful draft of air. In the same instant I recognized the shadows inside. They were dancing—no, wrestling. She was pushing and beating at him as he bent her backward. Their heads darted and feinted like the heads of snakes. He was trying to kiss her.

She twisted sideways and wrenched away from him. They were no more than ten feet from me, and through the glass I heard him laugh. "You jealous bitch," he said, and brought his face close again. Her fingers flew at his face, but he caught one wrist, then the other, and got them into one hand and held them behind her while he hunted down her mouth again. Flattened back against the wall, my cleared head now sour with smog, I felt ugly spying on them, but I did not dare move now and reveal myself. Through the glass I heard her grunt as she tried to free her hands. Then one hand flashed up, and he jerked his head aside with an exclamation. They wrestled again; again he captured her wrists. He forced his face down to hers. Beyond them I saw Dago Aguirre's silhouette move into the doorway from the living room, at the head of the steps, and pause, looking down, with a coffee cup half raised to its lips.

He couldn't have missed seeing what I saw. Pepe, still with Angelina's wrists locked in his left hand, straightened backward and sideward from his conquering kiss, and as he did so, he knocked the girl down with one quick hooking blow.

I ran tiptoe across the wet grass to the door. There I waited a few breaths, wiping my wet shoes up the backs of my trousers and listening. A frantic uproar was going on inside. With everyone's attention focused on that, I turned the knob and slipped in.

Carol ran past down the hall without even seeing me. From the solarium Angelina's screaming came in raw bursts as mindless as a fire siren. When I stepped into the living room, there was a confused, vehement cluster at the top of the solarium steps. Debbie and Welling each held one of Angelina's arms; without them she would have fallen on her face. The floor all around her was splashed with blood, there was blood on her clothes and on the clothes of those who held her. Borne on by Angelina's weight, Debbie slipped in blood and nearly went down. The girl was bleeding incredibly, as if her throat had been cut.

Then Carol came running with towels in her hands, and Mazur and Nemerov moved in to help hold Angelina while Carol and Debbie worked with towels on her face, blotting the steady screaming and letting it burst out again and then blotting it once more. When they straightened her under the light, trying to see where she was hurt, I had a glimpse of the foolish, disarranged pompadour, the artificial little *pachuca* face smeared with blood and tears, and the quick, welling gash. Pepe had split her lips from her nose to the point of her chin.

Debbie was crying, "Stand up, Angelina, we can't . . . Don't cry, honey, you'll make it worse. Guy, call a doctor, we can't stop it, it just keeps coming!"

They led Angelina to the couch and got her lying down. Debbie and Carol were kneeling with their towels at her head. Mazur stood back, gnawing his lip, thinking.

"Guy," Debbie screamed at him, "do something, for God's sake! Call Schwartz!"

"No," Mazur said. "No doctor. Not here. We'll take her to the clinic. But we've got another problem."

"Oh, how can you talk about other problems? She's *bleeding* to death!"

"Not from a cut lip," Mazur said. He looked around at the room, spattered with blood—blood on Debbie and Carol, blood on the couch, blood all over Angelina, and pressed his lips together. "What happened?" he said. "Who saw it?"

But nobody had anything to say. The Mexican kids, all but Pepe, were in a tight, still group. Pepe stood against the wall, a red scratch across his cheekbone, his hands behind him. For a couple of seconds he stood the weight of all the eyes on him; then he shrugged the faintest, iciest little shrug. "She fell down."

Angelina sat up, tearing at the towels pressed against her face. In an instant her chin was wet with blood, she spattered blood as she screamed, "He hit me! Pepe hit me!"

Carol and Debbie fought her back down and muffled her in towels. We were all still watching Pepe, who hung there still as a gun on a wall. One shoulder moved. "*Anda pedo*," he said. "She's crazy drunk. She don't know what she's doing. She fell down and hit her face on the steps."

Carol said, bitterly for her, "It doesn't upset you much that your girl's hurt."

"I didn't make her fall down," Pepe said.

"But you saw her fall?" Mazur said.

"I didn't say that. I'm coming up the steps ahead of her, and I hear her stumble, and look back, and there she is on the steps."

Unexpectedly, not knowing I was going to get into it until the words were out of my mouth, I said, "What's that scratch on your cheek?"

His hand started up—his right—and then he switched and brought out the left. His fingers touched the scratch, and they knew exactly where to find it. He put his hand back behind him and shrugged.

"Let's see your right hand."

He made no move to show it. His eyes said that he would have killed me as casually as he would have wrung a chicken's neck.

"Are you scared to?"

"What are you getting at?" Mazur said. "What makes you think he's lying? It was dark, the girl was high. She could have tripped."

"Could have, but didn't. I still want to see his hand."

"What would that show you?"

"Maybe the marks of her teeth."

"You think he did hit her."

"I know damned well he hit her. I saw him."

Now I was the one they were all looking at. "How?" Guy said. "From where?"

"Through the window. I was outside."

Mazur thought that over, with all its implications, while Angelina sobbed and hiccuped and moaned and was blotted with towels. "We've got to think about this," Mazur said.

"You can't!" Debbie cried, across Angelina's bloody length. "We've got to get this girl to a doctor!"

"In a minute," Mazur said. To me he said, "Suppose you're right."

"Suppose Angelina and I are right."

"Yes. But it's still your word against his."

"Thanks for your confidence," I said. I went into the hall and dug the Rolleiflex out of the bag and without flash, without anything but the oval blobs of Mazur's theatrical houselights, I went bang, bang, bang: the still Mexican kids; Pepe with his back to the wall; the committee leaning and crouched over Angelina, portraits of complicity.

"Nah, nah, nah!" Nemerov was saying. The tic jumped like a trapped insect in his eyelid.

Mazur said, "What was that for, Charlie?"

"Evidence, maybe."

"You want to turn Pepe in?"

"I don't want him to get away with it."

"What good would it do?" Mazur said. "What evidence have you got? Your word and Angelina's against his. Maybe that's enough to put him back in jail. Then what? Then what happens to our program, and the cause of justice, and all the rest? What happens to those kids over there?"

Those kids over there had turned to stone. Innocent as they were, they could not have been picked out in a lineup, by the best psychologist in America, as the innocent ones. They wore the same expressionlessness as Pepe wore. I looked for some acknowledgment or help in Dago's face and found nothing. His eyes were as flat as dry stones.

"We haven't got a lot of time," Mazur said. "We've got to get Angie to the clinic. It wouldn't do to bring a doctor here; he'd look around and deduce a massacre; he'd *have* to report to the cops. Let's think long-range. We're trying to right social injustice. We're all instruments in a cause. Think what else you'll do if you try to put Pepe back in jail."

I looked at Carol, crouched by the sofa with bloody towels in her hands. I listened to Angelina's diminishing moans and sobs. I looked at Pepe, tight-wound and ready to spring from his nonchalance against the wall. I looked at Chuey, foolish and stony, and at Lupe, beautiful and stony, and at Luz, dark and Indian and stony, and at Dago, the best of this whole bunch, stony.

"What if there's other evidence?" I said. "When I was outside there, I saw someone else through the window, someone at the head of the stairs. He saw it as plain as I did."

"Who?" Mazur said.

"I couldn't quite tell."

He gave a harsh bark of justified skepticism.

"Let's give whoever it was a chance to say."

I looked straight at Dago, and he looked straight back at me. We had an extraordinary exchange that included his past and present and future, his commitments, his hopes, most of all his solidarity with whatever had always been his enemy.

"I was there," he said. "I saw it. She fell down."

For another instant our eyes held. I could imagine what Carol was seeing and thinking, for she was the one truly committed to these kids, but I could not look at her. I looked only at Dago, the deer-eyed one, the one with a mother and sisters, the one whose father had been run over by a potato digger, the one who except for the Red Car Committee might still be in San Quentin and who except for the Red Car Committee might still have a chance at Idaho and a life. I could read his future now without tarot cards: Sometime some of his crowd would stick up a truckload of cigarettes or rob a liquor store; he would be involved, or an accomplice, or innocent; everybody would go back to San Quentin; sometime—a year, two years, three—we would hear on the radio that a prisoner had knifed a guard or another prisoner, and we would hear the name, Pepe Garcia, and hear the name of Dago Aguirre, a friend of the accused, who refused to talk. He would be blotted out as Angelina was blotted out, but not by compassionate helpers.

"O.K., that settles it," I said. "Let's get Angie to the clinic. Let's clean up after ourselves."

I opened the Rollei and took out the exposed film and found a wastebasket for it. Carol's big, troubled eyes met mine briefly as she and Debbie eased Angelina up off the sofa. But what I was most interested in, what held me, was Dago's face, still in a tight protective group with his friends. He pursed his lips; his stoniness dissolved into an ironic, fatalistic, rueful half-smile. He tipped his head back and made a motion of spitting upward.

THE CITY
OF THE
LIVING

■　　　　■　　　　■

At a certain moment he looked around him and was overcome by a feeling almost like terror at how strange this all was.

Not even the international familiarity of washbowl and water closet, not even the familiar labels of pill bottles on his table or the familiar carbolic reek of disinfectant, could make him quite accept the fact that this was happening to him and his son, and in this place. The darkened room next door was real to him, and this bathroom with its iron shutters open to night and the mosquitoes, but their reality was an imprecise reality of nightmare. It was hard to keep from believing that under the ghostly mosquito net in the next room lay not his son but someone with a strange face, or no face at all; and that in this tiled cell sat not himself but some alien enduring an ordeal by light and silence.

Outside the window, across the tops of the palms whose occasional dry clashing was the only sound he heard, were the unseen minaret from which the muezzin had cried the hour of prayer at the oncoming of dark, the unseen mud houses of Moslems and Copts, the fluted lotus columns, the secret shine of the Nile, the mud flats spreading towards the rims that guarded the Valley of the Kings. Against his windows the ancient dark of Egypt sucked like the vacuum created by wind under a lee wall. It made him conscious of the beating of his heart.

Turning from the outside dark and the soft clash of palms, he listened at the bedroom door, opened it and slipped in. He could not see the face but only the vague shape under the net. Yet he thought he felt the fever through sheet and net and three feet of air, and when he slipped his hand under to touch the boy's forehead he felt how tentative and fearful a gesture that was.

The luminous hands of his watch showed only one thirty-five. More Chloromycetin at two. He was tempted to get the thermometer and see if the heavy dosages since noon had brought the fever down at all. But it wouldn't be fair to wake the boy. He needed the sleep—if it *was* sleep.

Back in the bathroom with his eye to the narrowing crack of the door he watched the sickroom gather its darkness. The netted bed retreated, the shiny bathroom was restored to him, with the vacuum of night at its windows. He stepped out onto the narrow iron balcony, and as he did so something crashed and scrambled in the top of a palm on a level with the rail, almost in his face. Fright, and the thought that whatever it was had been crouched there looking in at him, froze him rigid; and he heard first the pound of his heart, then a small rustling, then silence, then the mosquitoes gathering with a thin whine around his head. Whatever had been among the palm fronds, rat or monkey or bird, was quiet. And there was no sound from the town either, not even the bark of a dog.

Above him the sky was the rich blue-black he had seen in fine Persian rugs, with the Milky Way a pale cloud across it and many brilliant dry stars. He thought of shepherds watching their flocks by night and Arab astronomers among the cumbersome stone instruments of their observatories, and he looked for lights but saw only a mysterious red glow like a cigar end in the blackness beyond the Nile, where the City of the Dead had extended in the time of ancient Thebes. He had no idea what it might be. It hung there as enigmatic and watchful as himself on the balcony or his stealthy neighbor in the palm top. After a time it faded. Though he looked hard he saw not a glint, not a reflected glimmer of a star, from the river sweeping the town's flank.

A fumbling from behind him sent his hand instantly to the light chain above the washbowl, and as he turned the boy came in, blinking and stumbling, holding up his pajamas with one hand, and groped numbly past and dropped on the toilet and was racked with explosive diarrhea. With a groan he put his elbows on his knees and held his head in his hands; to his father's scared eyes he looked fatally skinny, his arms pipestems too weak for the big man's hands. His face when he lifted it was puffed at the eyes with fever and sleep but wasted to skeleton thinness along the jaws.

The father held his hand against the boy's forehead to help the weak neck. The forehead was very hot, the lips glazed like agate. "Better now?"

The boy bent his head but sat still. In a moment he was racked again. His stench was almost unbearable. Holding his breath against the smell, the father shook down the thermometer and put it to the agate lips. They opened obediently, even in the midst of a spasm—how touchingly obedient he was in his sickness—and the two sat on, the boy absorbed with his inward war, the father unwilling to say anything that might demand his son's strength for an answer. Sitting on the tub's edge, he removed the thermometer and read it. A hundred and two and a half, exactly what it had been since the night before.

He saw the boy's foot and skinny leg, the Achilles' tendon standing out from the heel, the long body jack-knifed in an agony of cramps, and the feeling that came over him was like the slipping of a knot or the fraying of a rope that had held something secure until then. He looked with horror at the way the disease had wasted his son in barely more than a day, and he drew into his lungs the inhuman, poisonous stench of the sickness. That was the moment when it first occurred to him that the boy could die.

The thermometer rattled in the glass of germicide as he put it back. With an arm around the skinny shoulders he helped the boy back to bed, where he fed Chloromycetin capsules one by one into the obedient mouth and after each one offered the water glass to the enameled lips. He smoothed the sheet and turned the pillow. "Now back to sleep," he said.

For a moment he continued to stare fascinated at the wasted face, the closed eyes. He was talking to a nothing, to a silence. The boy had folded back into the bed with a little groan and had moved nothing but his lips since. The act of drawing the sheet up to his chin was so intimately associated in the father's mind with the last act of a deathbed that he ground his teeth. In one fierce grab he caught a mosquito that had got in under the net. Then he tucked in the edges and tiptoed out. Looking back from the door, he felt guilt in him like a knife for all the things he might have done and had failed to do. There was a darkness in his mind where this only child had been. Already the memory of him was all but unbearable.

In the harsh light of the bathroom he felt trapped like an animal in a flashlight beam. The sight of his own trapped eyes glittering was an intense, dreamlike plausibility until he realized that he was looking into a mirror. Darkness would have been a relief, but not the darkness outside. He had a fantasy that the light and the unreal solidity of brass and porcelain, himself and the stench of his son's sickness might all be sucked out into the night and lost. It was better to cling to this, to his separateness and identity, for somehow, at some totally unbearable crisis in his dream of personal pain and loss, he had a faith that he might waken and be saved.

In the end he found occupation in the routines of a sickbed vigil. He scrubbed the toilet and dumped disinfectant in it, washed his hands a long time in germicidal water, drove the mosquitoes out of the room with the DDT bomb. But those jobs, treat them as carefully as he might, lasted him no more than twenty minutes. Then he was back again, caught between the light and the darkness, the only wakeful thing in all the dark city of Thebes except for the animal in the palm top and whoever was responsible for the red glow across the river. The thought of the light raised sudden goose flesh on him, as if grave robbers or vampires prowled there.

After a while he got out his briefcase and set about bringing his correspondence up to date. That morning he had filled his pen at the hotel desk. At the same time, as if with foresight, he had picked up a new supply of hotel stationery. He had Egyptian stamps folded into a slip of waxed paper in the briefcase. He comforted himself with his own efficient work habits, and he cleaned up several things:

A note to the American Express in Rome returning some unused railroad tickets for refund. A letter of recommendation for a junior colleague trying for a Government job. A word to his secretary saying briefly that illness had changed their plans so that it didn't look as if any mail should be sent to Athens at all. Send anything up to December first to Rome.

The three stamped and addressed envelopes gave him such satisfaction that he wished he had fifty to do. He addressed the two picture postcards he found and wished there were more. But if no more cards and no more details to clear up, then a personal letter or two. With a sheet of stationery before him and his full pen in his hand, his eyes a little scratchy from sleeplessness, he considered whom he should write to. Not instantly, but over a period of seconds or minutes, it occurred to him that there was no one.

Not for the kind of letter he wanted and feared to write. He had no family closer than cousins, strangers he had not seen for years. His wife was worse than a stranger—an enemy—and though he owed her reports on their son's health and a monthly alimony check he owed her no more than that, and from her he could expect nothing at all. Friends? To what golf companion or bridge companion or house-party acquaintance or business associate could he write a letter beginning, as it must, "My son is in the next room very sick, perhaps dying, with typhoid . . ."?

He put his hands palms down on the desk and held them there a moment before he crumpled the sheet on which he had written the date and a confident "Dear . . ." *Dear who? I am sitting in the bathroom of a hotel in Luxor, Egypt, at nearly three in the morning, and I am just beginning to realize that here or anywhere else I am almost completely alone. I have spent my life avoiding entanglements. I breathed a sigh of relief when Ruth left. The only person I have cared about is this boy in the next room, and he is half a stranger. You should hear the machinery creak when we try to talk to each other. And I have to go and bring him into this rotten country where everybody is stuffed to the eyes with germs. . . .*

On a new sheet of paper he wrote, lifting his face while he tried to remember the figures, certain statistics on Egyptian public health he had read somewhere.

Trachoma	97 percent
Bilharziasis	96 percent
Syphilis	20 percent
Tuberculosis	? percent
Cholera?	
Typhoid?	

It seemed important to have them down. He wished he had clipped the newspaper or World Health report or whatever he had seen them in. For a moment's flash of memory he remembered Giles at the Mahdi Club in Cairo saying to him quietly as they waited for the boy to wipe off their bowls and hand them back, "Wash your hands in carbolic water after we go in. This kid's got a beautiful case of pink-eye." He saw himself quoting Egyptian health statistics to head-wagging men who dropped in to the office, or to people who listened to him around grate fires. It's no joke, he heard himself say. Practically every Egyptian you see is one-eyed, and they've all got bilharzia worms. All the filth diseases, of course—cholera and typhoid are endemic. It was typhoid that nearly got Dan, you know, in Luxor.

He listened, hypnotized by the even, world-traveled voice, and raised a hand to brush away a mosquito and smelled the germicide, and said to himself that if the hotel doctor and the manager hadn't been decent Dan might be in a fever hospital right now instead of quarantined in this wing. He went back over his remarks, polishing them, and came to the word "nearly" and stopped.

The thing that he wanted to think about or write about as an adventure of the trip, successfully passed, rose up before him suddenly and blanked his whole mind with fear. Controlling himself, forcing the discipline, he picked up papers and one by one put them away in the briefcase, refolding the stamps into their waxed paper. Under some odds and ends of folders he found the return envelope of an insurance company. A premium due. With relief, escaping, he opened the checkbook and unscrewed the pen and wrote the check neatly and tore it out. It lay in his hand, a yellow slip like thousands he had written, a bond with the order and security of home. A checkbook wasn't any good here, of course, but in any good international bank on proper identification and after a reasonable delay, it would . . . they had to know who you were, that was all. Just a little of the machinery of security, a passport, letter of credit, the usual identifications, maybe filling out a form or two . . .

Robert Chapman, age forty-two; nationality, American; place of birth, Sacramento, California; residence, San Francisco; education, B.A. University of California, 1931. Married? Divorced. Children? One son, Daniel. Member Bohemian Club of San Francisco, Mill Valley Club, Kiwanis. Property: one-twelfth of a co-operative apartment house on Green Street, week-end cottage Carmel, certain bonds, Oldsmobile hard-top convertible. Income around eighteen thousand annually. Contributions: the usual good causes, Community Fund, Red Cross, Civil Liberties

Union, the Sierra Club's conservation program. Insurance program the usual—forty thousand straight life plus annuity plan.

I believe in insurance, he told the smooth-faced, gray-haired man across the desk. Always have. My parents bought my first policy for me when I was ten, and I've added to it according to a careful plan from time to time. I've known too many people who were wiped out for lack of it. I carry a hundred thousand—fifty thousand on my car, plus all the rest except the freak stuff. Personal injury, property damage, collision, fire, theft—they all pay, even if you never have to collect on them. Real property too. My place at Carmel has comprehensive coverage, practically every sort of damage or accident—window breakage, hail, wind, fire, earthquake, falling airplanes. I carry a twenty-five-dollar deductible personal-property floater. It's indispensable, when you're traveling especially. Protects you wherever you are. Same with my health-plan membership. Anywhere in the world I'm protected on my medical and hospital bills.

For that matter, he said, smiling, my physician gave me some good advice before this last trip. He prescribed me a little kit of pills—penicillin tablets, Empirin, sulfaguanidine, Dramamine against travel sickness, Chloromycetin and Aureomycin in case we got sick anywhere out of reach of medical care and had a real emergency. I can tell you we were glad of that doctor's advice when we got way up the Nile, in Luxor, and my son, Dan, in spite of inoculations and everything, came down with typhoid. . . .

Neatly he folded the check and folded a sheet of stationery around it and the premium notice and put them in the return envelope, half irritated that they made it so easy. A man didn't mind addressing an envelope.

His face was greasy with sweat. Restlessly he rose and washed in cool water, looked at his shadowed eyes in the mirror, turned away, slipped into the bedroom and eased into the chair by the bedside. The breathings and the spasmodic small twitchings made the boy under the net seem utterly vulnerable somehow. In the dark, his eyes tiredly closed, he sat for an indefinite time seeing red shapes flow and change in the pocket of his lids. Among them, abruptly, coned with light like an operating table, appeared his son, dead, openmouthed, horribly wasted, and he awoke with a shudder and found his shirt clammy and his lungs laboring at the close air. His watch read twenty minutes to four.

To wait until four was impossible. He opened the bathroom door wide to let in light, and brought the capsules and a glass of water. The boy awoke at a touch, his dry lips working, his eyelids struggling open, and lifted his head weakly to swallow the medicine.

"How do you feel now? Better?"

"Hot," the stiff lips said.

"Would you like a damp towel on your eyes?"

"Yes."

The father slipped the thermometer into the boy's mouth and went into the bathroom. The disease-and-disinfectant smell was newly obnoxious to him as he wrung out the towel. When he returned, the boy had turned his head and the thermometer had slipped half out of his parted lips. With a swift searching of the emaciated face the father took it and held it to the light. At first the hairline of mercury would not reveal itself, and helpless anger shook him at people who would make an instrument nobody could read. Then he caught the glittering line, twisted carefully. Its end lay at 102°.

Down half a degree? Suspiciously he felt the forehead, but it was wet from the towel. The dry, slippery hands were still hot. But less hot than they had been? Or had the thermometer slipped out long enough to make the reading inaccurate?

Starting to take the temperature again, he stopped, and then he deliberately pulled down and tucked in the net. He did this, he knew, not out of reassured hope but out of cowardice. His heart had leaped so at that half degree of hope that he did not want to find he had been wrong. In a minute or two he was back in the bathroom, sitting at the table before his worthless and undemanding briefcase and the little pile of cards and envelopes. He felt exposed to all the eyes of Luxor; once, after the Long Beach earthquake in 1933, he had seen a man shaving in such a bathroom as this, with the whole outside wall peeled away, and he stood there before the mirror at ten o'clock on a Sunday morning, with his suspenders down and the world looking in. It was a ridiculous image. But he did not get up and pull down the shutters and close himself in.

His eyes were full of the pattern of square tile three feet before his eyes. He found that by squinting or widening his eyes he could make the squares begin to dissolve and spin in a vortex of glittering planes and reflections. When he wanted to he took hold again and forced the spinning to stop and the tiles to settle back to order. Then he narrowed his eyes again and watched the spinning recommence.

Some level of mind apart from his intense concentration told him, without heat, that he could hypnotize himself that way, and some other layer still deeper and more cunning smiled at that warning. He held the squares firmly in focus for a minute, stretched them, let them spin, brought them back under the discipline of will and eye, relaxed again and let them spin, enjoying the control he had of them and of himself. It was as if the whole back of his head was a hollow full of bees.

He was facing the blank wall and his neck was stiff. His head ached dully and his eyes were scratchy in the tired light of the bathroom. The muezzin was crying prayer again across the housetops of Thebes, the open shutters gave not on darkness but on gray twilight, and at the end of his reach of vision, against a sky palely lavender, he saw the minaret and the jutting balcony high up, and on the balcony the small black movement. He could distinguish no words in the rise and fall of the muezzin's cry; it was as empty of meaning as a yodel.

Stiffly he stretched and rolled his stiff neck. His left arm was sore from yesterday's reinoculation; the memory of his night's watch was like a memory of delirium. He felt pleased that it had passed, and looked at his watch. Five-thirty. His mind groped. And then the pretense of awakening to sane reality fell away, and he stood in the pale, overtaken electric light sick with shame at the trick he had played upon his own anxiety and responsibility. What if he had missed a time for the pills?

His flesh lay like putty on his bones. In the membranes of his mouth he tasted all the night's odors—the smell of sickness that was like no human or animal odor but virulent, deadly, and obscene; the smells of the things one relied on to stay alive, the disinfectant smell and the DDT spray. His arm was a swollen, throbbing ache. He belched and tasted bile, and bent to hold cool water in cupped handfuls against his eyes. When he took a drink from the carafe the chlorine bite of the halazone tablets gagged him. The effort, the steady, unrelieved, incessant effort that it took in this place to stay alive! He looked at his haggard, smudged face in the mirror and he hated Egypt with a kind of ecstasy. Finally, unwillingly, he went through the bedroom door.

Daybreak had not come here. The room was the vaguest gloom, yet when he turned on the light it had somehow the look that closed rooms have in daylight, a dissipated air like that of a room where a drunkard sleeps through the day. Shaking down the thermometer as he stepped across the rug, holding his breath to hear anything from the bed, the father approached and bent across the net. He bent his head lower, listening. "Dan?" he said. Then in a convulsive panic he tore away the net, knowing his son was dead.

The boy slept peacefully, lightly, his breathing even and soft. His forehead was cool to his father's shaking hand. There was no need for the thermometer: the fever was not merely down but gone. In his jubilation the father picked up the little vulture-headed image he had bought for the boy the first day and tossed it to the ceiling and caught it. He moved around the room, retrieved a horsehair fly whisk from the floor and hung it on the dresser post, eased the shutter up a little way for air. The boy slept on.

Outside in the hall he heard soft sounds, and going quickly to the door, he surprised the hall boy depositing his shined shoes. The white eyes flashed upward in the face of the crouching figure, the bare feet moved respectfully backwards a step, the long, belted robe swung like a dancer's.

"*Saeeda*," the soft voice whispered.

"*Saeeda*. Can I have tea?"

"Only tea?"

"Fruit, maybe. Oranges or plantains."

"Yes. How is your son?"

"Better," the father said, and knew that this was why he had opened the door, just for the chance of telling someone. "Much better. The fever is gone."

The floor boy seemed genuinely pleased. After all, Chapman thought, he probably hadn't liked the business of being quarantined and inoculated any better than anybody else. To an Egyptian typhoid normally meant, if not death, several weeks in a fever hospital and a long, feeble convalescence. This one now was smiling and delighted as he went away on his sliding black feet. He should have a good tip when they left— a pound note at least.

The muezzin was still calling. It seemed an hour since he had begun. Returning to the bathroom, Chapman stood in the French doors looking out at the town. In the gray light the palm tops lay as quiet as something under glass. The yellow paths of the back garden were quiet geometry below him, and he smelled the authentic, wet-mud smell of Egypt.

Across wall and roofs was a yellow reach of river, with a narrow mud island lying against the far shore, then a strip of taffy-colored water, then the shore itself and the far lines of palms indicating villages or canals, and clear beyond, binding the edge of the pure sky, the long desert rim that divided habitable Egypt from the wastes.

Over there was the City of the Dead, where the light had been last night and where he had half imagined ghouls and vampires, jackal-headed men with square shoulders, obscene prowling things. It was innocent and clean now, and the river that when they first came had seemed to him a dirty, mud-banked sewer looked different too. It came down grandly, one of the really mighty rivers, pouring not so much out of the heart of the continent as out of all backward time, and in its yellow water it carried the rich silt for delta cotton fields, the bilharzia worms to infect the sweating fellahin at the ditch heads, the sewage and the waste, the fecundity, the feculence. The river was literally Egypt. Lotus and papyrus, ibis and crocodile, there it came. Incomprehensibly, tears jumped to his eyes. He went into the bedroom and got the binoculars and returned to watch.

The blurry yellow haze sharpened into precise lines as he turned the knob. Beyond the mud margins he saw a line of people coming, leading donkeys and camels loaded with something, perhaps produce for the market. He saw them carry burdens from beast to boat. Farther down, a family was bathing in the river, a woman and four children, who ran and splashed each other and launched themselves like sleds on the water. The thought of swimming in that open drain appalled him—and yet why not? Probably it never occurred to them that the river was polluted. And it was a touching and private thing, somehow, to see the brown-skinned family playing and see them so close and unaware and yet not hear their shouting and laughter.

The far bank was fully alive now. Two feluccas were slanting out across the current of the river, and the river seemed not so much to divide as to unite its two shores. Birds flew over it, camels and donkeys and people clustered at the landing places, the feluccas moved, leaning farther in a riffle of wind. All the Nile's creatures, as inexhaustible as the creatures of the sea, began to creep and crawl and fly. Safe, relieved of anxiety, reassured, rescued, Chapman watched them from his little cell of sanitary plumbing, and on his hands as he held the binoculars to his eyes he smelled the persistent odor of antiseptic.

It was ridiculous, but they made him feel alone and timid. He wished his son would awake so they could talk. He could read aloud to him during the time he was getting stronger; the thought occurred to him as an opportunity he must not miss.

"What a damned country!" he said.

Watching the river, he had not noticed the movement at the far corner of the garden below him, but now as he swung the glasses down he saw there one of the ragged, black-robed boys who raked and sprinkled the paths every day. He had taken off his turban and was kneeling, folding it back and forth until it made a little mat beside one of the garden water taps. On this he knelt, and with a reaching haul pulled the robe over his head. He wore nothing else. His ribs were like the ribs of a basket, his shoulder blades moved as he turned on the tap.

Steadying the glasses against the jamb, Chapman watched the brown boy's face, very serious and composed, and as it turned momentarily he thought he saw one milky blind eye. Face, neck, shoulders, arms, chest and belly, and carefully the loins and rectum, the boy washed himself with cupped handfuls of water. He washed his feet one after the other; he bent and let the tap run a moment over his head. On the yellow ground a dark spot of wet grew.

He stood up, and Chapman stepped back, not to be caught watching, but the boy only pulled on his robe again. Then he knelt once more on the rug of his turban and bowed himself in prayer towards the east.

Chapman kept the glasses steadily on him. The intense concentration and stillness of the bent figure bothered him obscurely. He remembered himself staring at the tiled wall and did not like the memory. Moreover, the shame of that evasion was mixed with an irritated, unwilling perception that the boy kneeling in the garden was humble, touching, even dignified.

Dignified? A skinny, one-eyed boy with a horizon no wider than the garden he worked in, with one dirty robe to his back, and for home a mud hut where the pigeons nested in the living-room and the buffalo owned the inner, safest, most desirable room? The image of Egyptian workmen he had seen picking up the dirt-caked hems of their robes and holding them in their teeth for greater freedom of action stood in his mind like stiff sculpture.

And yet the praying boy was not pathetic or repulsive or ridiculous. His every move was assured, completely natural. His touching of the earth with his forehead made Chapman want somehow to lay a hand on his bent back.

They have more death than we do, Chapman thought. Whatever he is praying to has more death in it than anything we know.

Maybe it had more life too. Suppose he had sent up a prayer of thanksgiving a little while ago when he found his son out of danger? He had been doing something like praying all night, praying to modern medicine, propitiating science, purifying himself with germicides, placating the germ theory of disease. But suppose he had prayed in thanksgiving, where would he have directed his prayer? Not to God, not to Allah, not to the Nile or any of its creature-gods or the deities of light. To some laboratory technician in a white coat. To the Antibiotic God. For the first time it occurred to him what the word "antibiotic" really meant.

The distant rim was light-struck now. The first of the morning buzzards came from somewhere and planed across the motionless palm tops. It teetered and banked close so that Chapman saw the curve of its head like the vulture-headed image on the boy's bed table: the vulture head of Mut, the Lady of Thebes, the Mother of the World. They eyed each other with a kind of recognition as it passed. It had a look like patience, and its shadow, passing and returning over the garden, brushing the ragged boy and the palms and the balcony where Chapman stood, might have seemed a threat but might also have been a kind of patrolling, almost a reassurance.

One of America's most distinguished writers, WALLACE STEGNER was born in 1909 in Lake Mills, Iowa, and grew up in North Dakota, Montana, Utah, Nevada, and western Canada. He received his B.A. from the University of Utah and his M.A. and Ph.D. from the State University of Iowa. In 1933 he began an esteemed career as a teacher of English and writing at such universities as Utah, Wisconsin, Harvard, and Stanford, where he was head of the creative writing center.

He published his first novel in 1937 and has consistently earned critical acclaim for his compelling renderings of the American landscape and its people. In 1972 he won the Pulitzer Prize for *Angle of Repose*, and in 1976 *The Spectator Bird* received the National Book Award.

Dr. Stegner has contributed articles and stories to many publications, including *Harper's* magazine, *The Atlantic, The New Yorker, Saturday Review, Mademoiselle, Yale Review*, and *Virginia Quarterly*, and has served as an editor-at-large of *Saturday Review*.